WHALE IN THE WAVES

As Mandy and James watched, Nordica rose up out of the waves and looked at them. They were so close that they could see the gleaming whiteness of her enormous mouth and they could see the series of springy whalebone plates that Minke whales have instead of teeth.

Her massive tail flipped and came down on the water with a loud smack, sending a huge wave surging towards them. It broke over the ledge, showering them with spray. It almost seemed as if Nordica was playing a game with them, although Mandy knew the whale was too lost and upset to be in the mood for play.

Nordica stared at her for a moment, and to Mandy, it seemed an understanding passed between them. A promise that Mandy would do everything in her power to help.

Animal Ark series

LUCY DANIELS

Whale
—— *in the* ——
Waves

Illustrations by Jenny Gregory

Hodder
Children's
Books

a division of Hodder Headline plc

Special thanks to Sue Welford
Thanks also to C. J. Hall, B.Vet.Med., M.R.C.V.S., for reviewing
the veterinary material contained in this book.

Text copyright © 1998 Ben M. Baglio
Created by Ben M. Baglio, London W12 7QY
Illustrations copyright © 1998 Jenny Gregory

First published in Great Britain in 1998
by Hodder Children's Books

A Catalogue record for this book is available from the British Library

ISBN 0 340 69954 X

Typeset by Avon Dataset Ltd, Bidford-on-Avon, Warks

Printed and bound in Great Britain by
Clays Ltd, St Ives plc

Hodder Children's Books
a division of Hodder Headline plc
338 Euston Road
London NW1 3BH

One

'Look, Mandy, there's Abersyn!' Mandy Hope's best friend, James Hunter, pointed excitedly. His dad's car had just driven over the crest of a hill and the Welsh fishing village where James and Mandy were to stay for the half-term week's holiday came into view.

'Ooh, it looks brilliant!' Mandy exclaimed. She felt a tight knot of expectation in her stomach. The village *did* look brilliant . . . white cottages gleaming in the sun, the sea bordering a curving stretch of golden sand.

Moored in the harbour the other side of the

breakwater was a fleet of brightly-painted fishing boats. Against the blue sky, they looked like something out of a picture postcard.

Beside her, James craned his neck. Then he pointed again. 'Hey, look! You can just see my cousin's house!'

James's cousin, Jenny, lived with her parents in a white fisherman's cottage set just back from the road that ran parallel with the sea wall. When James's uncle and aunt had invited him to spend a week's holiday there, they had asked if Mandy would like to come too. Mandy, James and Mr Hunter had left the Yorkshire village of Welford early that morning. James's dad had taken a day off to drive them there. He was staying for lunch, then returning home that afternoon.

'What a lovely place to live,' Mandy breathed. She loved Welford, but to live so close to the sea must be wonderful too. Mandy's parents, Adam and Emily Hope, were Welford's vets and ran a busy surgery called Animal Ark. Mandy loved all animals and wanted to be a vet herself one day. She just couldn't wait to meet Jenny and her mongrel dog, Muffin. James had already told her Muffin was full of mischief, like his dog, Blackie, who was back home in Welford.

As they drove down the hill, James pointed out one of the fishing boats in the harbour. 'That blue one could be Ivor's,' he said. 'Jenny told me he'd given it a new coat of blue paint.'

'Who's Ivor?' Mr Hunter asked from the driver's seat.

'You remember, Dad,' James answered. 'Uncle Thomas's friend, Ivor Evans.' James's uncle was his dad's brother. 'We met him when we came here before. He took me and Jenny out for a trip in his boat.'

Mr Hunter shifted around in his seat, stiff from the long journey from Yorkshire. 'Oh, yes. Tall chap with red hair. He was only a teenager then. I remember thinking he was a bit young to have a fishing boat all of his own.'

James grinned. 'He told me he'd had a boat since he was ten.'

'Lucky thing,' Mandy said. Her feeling of excitement grew and grew as the car headed down towards the village. The village was set in a natural harbour shaped like a horseshoe. On its northern curve was the village. The southern side was steeper with rocks running down to the sea.

A small terrace of houses, a little cafe, a village store and a fish and chip shop flanked the seafront road.

On either side of the harbour, waves surged against rugged outcrops of rock. Seagulls circled, and beyond, the Atlantic Ocean stretched, blue and shimmering, out to the horizon. Mandy could hardly tear her eyes away.

Then suddenly she spotted something that made her gasp with surprise. She clutched James's sleeve. 'Hey, James, look!'

'What?'

'There!' As Mandy spoke, a silvery spray of water jetted from the surface of the sea. A huge humped back broke through the waves, then another . . . then a smaller one close behind.

Mandy could hardly believe her eyes. Three whales were swimming out in the deep water! It was almost as if they had come to welcome her.

Beside her, James drew in his breath. 'Wow! Whales!'

'Don't be silly,' Mr Hunter said from the

front seat. 'You're imagining things.'

'No, we're not, honestly,' Mandy said quickly. 'Look.'

But when Mr Hunter pulled in to the side of the road and looked, the water was smooth and flat again. The whales had disappeared beneath the surface.

'They *were* there, Dad,' James insisted. 'I saw them too.'

Mr Hunter grinned and shook his head. 'Wishful thinking, you two,' he said. 'You'll have to be content with Welsh sheep and Welsh ponies this holiday. There's bound to be plenty of both.'

Mandy's heart pounded. It didn't matter what Mr Hunter said. There *were* whales out there. She and James had definitely seen them.

All the way down the hill she kept her eye on the sea. But now there was only a fishing vessel chugging out from the harbour. Maybe the whales had just been swimming by and she would never see them again.

By now they had reached the bottom of the hill and James was waving madly at a dark-haired girl with a ponytail who was standing at the top of a flight of stone steps. She had a round face and dark, sparkling eyes, and was holding a small, scruffy, honey-coloured dog on a lead. She was gazing anxiously up the road.

'There's Jenny!' James wound down the window and yelled. 'Hey, Jenny, we're here!'

A grin spread across Jenny's face as she waved back. She picked up the little dog and waggled his paw at them. Mandy laughed and waved too. James had told her the dog's name – Muffin – was short for 'Ragamuffin', and now she could see why he had been called that.

Jenny put the dog down and began running along the top of the wall. She jumped down just as the car stopped outside the house. She opened the door and put her head inside. 'Hi! We thought you'd never get here.'

Jenny spoke with a soft Welsh accent. Muffin was jumping up and barking excitedly. 'Meet Muffin,' she said, grinning. 'He's heard all about you.'

Later, when Mandy had been introduced to Jenny's mum – James's Auntie Gwyn – and they'd all had lunch, Jenny took them upstairs to unpack their things. Jenny's dad, Thomas, was a coast

warden and was out on patrol. He would be back
later.

Mandy was going to share Jenny's bedroom. It
was a sunny room that overlooked the sea. *How lovely
it will be to lie in bed and listen to the sound of the waves
breaking on the shore*, Mandy thought.

'So what sort of things do you like to do in
Welford?' Jenny asked Mandy, as they unpacked her
rucksack and put her things away.

'Well, I spend as much time as I can with animals,'
Mandy replied. 'My mum and dad are both vets,
and I want to be one too.' They had finished putting
her things away now and she sat on the bed cuddling
Muffin.

Jenny laughed. 'That's lucky, then.'

'Yes.' Mandy laughed too.

'My dad gets to deal with quite a lot of animals,'
Jenny said. 'Wild ones, that is . . . and seabirds,
they're his favourite thing.'

Mandy was just about to ask her exactly what a
coast warden did when James came in. He was going
to sleep in a tiny room right up under the eaves of
the cottage and had been upstairs unpacking his
rucksack.

'Come on, you two,' he said. 'I'm dying to get down to the beach.'

Downstairs, James's dad was just off.

'Give Blackie a hug for me, please,' James asked him as they said farewell.

'I will,' Mr Hunter said. 'And behave yourselves, you two.'

'We will,' James promised.

After waving goodbye to Mr Hunter, Mandy, James and Jenny told Auntie Gwyn they were going down to the beach. Muffin was barking excitedly at the prospect of going for a walk.

'It's his favourite thing,' Jenny explained as they crossed the road and went down the beach steps. 'He's mad about hunting in the rock pools.'

James laughed. 'What does he hunt for?'

'Anything that moves,' Jenny said. 'Shrimp, crabs, tiny fish . . . but he never catches any of them. They're too quick for him.'

They saw exactly what she meant as they ran along the beach and round the corner of the cliff to the rock pools. Mandy took deep breaths of fresh, sea air as the soft breeze brushed her face. It felt wonderful.

Muffin was way ahead, running to and fro sniffing each pool, his bushy tail waving like a flag. Once or twice he jumped in, splashing around until he was soaking wet. Then he leaped on to a tall rock and stood there waiting for them to catch up.

Mandy told Jenny about the whales. 'I *know* we saw them,' she said. 'Even though James's dad said we were imagining things.'

Jenny laughed. 'You definitely weren't imagining things,' she assured Mandy. 'I saw them too when I was hanging about waiting for you.'

She had clambered up on to the rock with Muffin and was gazing out to sea, her hands shielding her eyes from the glare of the sun. 'But I can't see them now,' she called.

'Maybe they were just swimming past,' Mandy said.

'Yes,' Jenny agreed. 'Maybe.' She jumped down. 'Come on, let's go and tell Ivor. Do you remember Dad's friend, Ivor, James? He'll be sorry if he missed the whales. He loves them.'

James nodded enthusiastically

Jenny called Muffin but he had scrambled down and disappeared.

'That dog!' Jenny stood with her hands on her

hips. 'He *never* comes when he's called.'

Mandy and James looked at one another then burst out laughing.

'What's up?' Jenny said, her eyes still scanning the rocks for signs of Muffin.

'He reminds us of my dog, Blackie,' James said. 'He hardly ever comes when *he*'s called either.'

They eventually found Muffin at the mouth of a cave, barking and listening to the echo of his voice as it bounced back at him. Jenny scolded him and fixed on his lead.

On the way to the harbour she said, 'I'll take you to meet Ivor's mum first if you like. She runs the cafe on the seafront. Her cat, Mickey, is Muffin's best friend.'

Muffin wasn't allowed inside so they tied him up by the door and went in. The cafe was quite small, but brimming with customers. The tables were covered with bright checked cloths and napkins to match. Behind the counter, a cook was busy frying burgers and chips. Mrs Evans was serving people with their meals. She had blonde hair, wore bright red lipstick and chatted to the customers as she trotted to and fro.

Jenny introduced her to Mandy and James.

'James!' Mrs Evans exclaimed. 'I remember you when you were a little boy. My, how you've grown.'

James went red and shuffled his feet. 'Well, it *was* five years ago,' he mumbled.

Mandy chuckled to herself. James always got embarrassed when people said things like that.

Mrs Evans laughed. 'So it was. It would be funny if you hadn't grown then, wouldn't it? I remember when you—'

'And this is Mandy,' Jenny interrupted hastily before Mrs Evans could go on about James's previous visit. 'She's James's best friend. Her mum and dad are vets.'

'Vets? How wonderful. Do you have lots of animals of your own?' Mrs Evans asked.

Mandy shook her head. 'No, but I know lots of people with pets and I help out with them sometimes. It's almost as good.'

'That's nice, then, dear.' Mrs Evans said. 'My father kept goats . . . a real nuisance they were. They ate everything they could find. Ate my mother's best Sunday hat once. She was livid.'

Mandy laughed. 'I bet.'

Mrs Evans went on, hardly stopping to take a breath. 'We've got a cat. His name's Mickey. He's long haired, black with a white patch over his eye and one white ear. We got him from the rescue centre in Rhydfellin. He just loves Jenny's dog. I've never seen a dog and cat play like they do.'

Mandy couldn't help eyeing the ice-cream cabinet.

Mrs Evans must have seen her looking because she broke off telling them about the cat and said, 'Why don't you all help yourself to an ice cream?'

'Oh, wow, can we?' Jenny said.

Mrs Evans smiled. ' 'Course you can, dear. Don't let it spoil your tea, though. And you can take one to Ivor. If you hurry, you might just get there before it melts.'

'Thanks!' Mandy said.

'Why don't you fetch Muffin and take him round the back to see Mickey first?' Mrs Evans suggested. 'I'm sure he'll be pleased to see him.'

Mickey was asleep in a little patch of sun by the window of Mrs Evans's sitting-room. When Mandy, James and Jenny arrived with Muffin, he got up, stretched and yawned, then began rubbing himself against Muffin's face.

'Ooh, he's beautiful!' Mandy tickled Mickey behind his white ear. 'And I can see he and Muffin are great friends.'

They played with the dog and cat for a while, then got their ice creams and made their way down to the harbour.

They found Ivor mending nets on his fishing boat. The boat's name was written on the side: *Seaspray*, along with a number, RX 43, her registered fishing fleet number.

Mandy thought *Seaspray* was a great name and could just imagine the boat's sharp bow cutting through the waves as she ploughed her way to the fishing grounds.

Jenny called Ivor's name from the harbour wall and he peered over the side at them. When he saw who it was, he waved and grinned and told them to climb aboard.

Ivor was tall and lean with a face brown from the sun and red hair, just as Mr Hunter had said. He wore jeans and long wellington boots and a white T-shirt. Mandy thought he looked about the same age as Simon, the nurse at Animal Ark.

He took his ice cream gratefully as Jenny introduced Mandy and James.

'James!' Ivor said. 'I remember you. You've grown
a bit.'

James raised his eyebrows. 'Yes,' he said.

When they told Ivor about the whales, his face lit
up. 'I'd hoped we'd see some this year. They're such
wonderful creatures,' he said.

'They came to welcome us to Wales,' Mandy said,
laughing.

Suddenly, Jenny had an idea. 'Oh, Ivor, I don't
suppose you could take us out so we can get a closer
look, could you?'

'What, a whale-watching trip?' Ivor said. 'That
sounds fun.'

Mandy drew in her breath. 'It would be lovely if
you could,' she said. She had read about whale-
watching trips in America and had always longed
to go on one. 'I'd really love to see them close up.'

'It's a great idea.' Ivor finished his ice cream, then
piled the net on the deck beside a coil of rope. 'But
I think you'd better ask your parents if it's OK first,
Jenny.'

'I'm sure it will be, but we'll ask anyway.' Jenny

was already halfway down the gangplank. 'Come on, you two,' she called impatiently. 'Let's go!'

Mandy felt a quick heartbeat of excitement as she and James hurried after Jenny. A real whale-watching trip! It would be absolutely fantastic.

Ivor leaned over the side. 'If your mum says it's OK, could you pop into the cafe and tell Mum I'll be late for my tea?'

Jenny waved her hand as they dashed along the quayside.

'OK,' she called. 'See you soon!'

Two

Jenny's mum was watering her pot plants in the back yard when Jenny, Mandy and James arrived. They burst through the gate and blurted out their request to go out in *Seaspray*.

'Of course you can,' she said. 'But you be careful now and do as Ivor tells you. And make sure you wear life-jackets.'

Jenny hugged her mother quickly. 'We will.' Her eyes shone. 'Thanks, Mum.'

'And look after Muffin,' her mum said. 'We don't want him falling over the side.'

'We will. Thanks, Auntie Gwyn,' James called over

his shoulder as they ran out and raced along to the cafe. They hurriedly gave Mrs Evans Ivor's message, then dashed along to the harbour.

When they ran up the gangplank Ivor was just tuning into the weather forecast on his two-way radio.

'Going to be a bit stormy this week,' he told them as they put on life-jackets. 'So this might be the only chance you get. I'm not sure you'd like it out there in heavy weather.'

Mandy stood in the bow, breathing in the fresh, salty air as *Seaspray* chugged out to sea. She didn't care *how* rough it might get; seeing whales was an opportunity she simply couldn't miss.

'Ever been on a fishing boat before?' Ivor asked her when she went into the wheelhouse to talk to him.

Mandy shook her head. 'No.'

'Take a look around then if you like,' he said.

Mandy was fascinated by the compact wheelhouse and cabin, the lockers where everything was stowed, the little stove for making hot drinks and soup when Ivor was out at sea on cold winter days.

'Do you go fishing by yourself?' Mandy asked Ivor.

He shook his head. 'I run *Seaspray* with a mate of mine,' he said. 'He's on holiday this week so I'm having to manage by myself.'

Mandy went back on deck. The fishing gear was stowed neatly along the sides and there was a winch to wind in the nets that lay in neat coils along the decks.

The wind blew a lock of Mandy's fair hair across her eyes as she gazed out to sea. Her eyes searched desperately for sight of the whales. Her heart thudded as she whispered under her breath, 'Please be here.' This would *really* be something to tell everyone when she got home. She brushed her hair back, holding her face to the breeze. The air was fresh and clear as crystal.

Jenny leaned against the rail with Muffin close to her side. She held tightly on to his lead. James had gone into wheelhouse and was examining all the dials and switches on the radio and asking Ivor details about the engine.

When they were a good distance out to sea, Ivor called out: 'Whales tend to stick to the lay of the land so we'll cruise along the coastline, see if we can spot them.'

Mandy scanned the water. Once or twice she thought she spotted something but it was only the dark greeny-blue of the waves, rising and falling in front of the bow.

Then, suddenly, Jenny gave a cry, stood up and pointed excitedly. 'There they are . . . look!'

James came out of the wheelhouse. Ivor leaned out with a pair of binoculars in his hand. He put them to his eyes. 'You're right, Jenny. It's them!'

Mandy's heart gave a great thump. She could see the whales easily without the aid of binoculars – two great, grey heads rising and falling, then another smaller one beside them.

'I think they've got a baby with them!' Jenny shouted above the noise of the engine.

'A calf,' Mandy called. 'A baby whale is called a calf.'

'Calf, then,' Jenny answered. 'I'm sure it is one. Can you see it?'

Mandy *could* see the whale calf. It was a lot smaller than the other two, only about three or four metres long. The others, at least nine metres in length, Mandy thought, swam close to it, their dark grey heads and bodies rising up and down with the swell of the ocean.

'We won't go too close,' Ivor called. 'We don't want to scare them.'

As he spoke, two great spouts of warm gas and steam jetted from the surface, then one smaller one. Mandy clutched on to the rail. Her heart was pounding. The whales had got to be the most wonderful creatures she had ever seen. They were so huge, yet so elegant in the water, it was almost unbelievable.

Beside her, James stood spellbound. He took off his glasses, rubbed the lenses on the knee of his jeans, then put them back on again, as if he couldn't really believe what he was seeing.

'Wow,' he breathed. 'Excellent!'

Ivor slowed the engine to a chug. The boat bobbed up and down like a cork. The whales were closer now, swimming then turning, their enormous fish-like tails appearing briefly above the surface before smacking the waves in a burst of white foam as they turned and headed in towards the shore.

'It's so nice here, they don't want to leave,' Mandy said.

Ivor laughed. 'I'm afraid some of the other fishermen wouldn't be very pleased about that!'

Mandy felt puzzled. Surely *everyone* thought whales were wonderful creatures. 'Why not?' she asked.

'Whales eat a lot of fish,' Ivor explained. 'They mostly feed on krill and plankton . . . you know, the really tiny sea creatures, but these smaller whales eat cod and haddock, too. And other fish – fish that we catch for our living.'

Mandy drew in her breath indignantly. 'But they're wild creatures . . . they're *entitled* to eat exactly what they like.'

'You don't have to convince *me* of that, Mandy, but you might have to convince some of the other fishermen,' Ivor said.

Mandy frowned. Surely the fishermen couldn't be so mean as to begrudge the whales a few fish!

'I will,' she said. 'Definitely. If you hear any of them complaining, just send them to me.'

Ivor laughed. 'I will, I promise.'

Ivor turned *Seaspray* in a circle, chugging back to the place where they had seen the whales. He sailed up and down for a while but it looked as if they had gone for the time being. Eventually, he turned the boat and headed back towards the harbour.

'Thanks, Ivor,' James said, as they disembarked and helped tie the mooring ropes. 'That was absolutely great.'

'No problem,' Ivor grinned.

'Come on,' Jenny said, impatient as usual. 'I'm dying to tell Mum and Dad.'

When they got back to the cottage, James's Uncle Thomas was home. His green and white van was parked at the bottom of the cottage steps. The van had COAST WARDEN written on the side and a small badge with a picture of a puffin on it.

Mandy, James and Jenny went through the back door and into the kitchen.

James's aunt took one look at their faces and guessed their trip had been successful. 'You saw them, then?' she said with a smile.

'We certainly did,' James said. 'They were fantastic, absolutely huge . . .'

'And so graceful,' Mandy said. 'I was amazed how something that size could look so elegant in the water.'

'And they've got a baby . . . a calf,' Jenny added.

Before she could say any more, Muffin suddenly barked and sat up on his hind legs.

Jenny's mum laughed. 'I'm afraid Muffin isn't at all impressed by your whale tales . . . all he can think about is his tea.'

She filled his food bowl and bent to put it beside him. She frowned. 'Pooh,' she said. 'This dog smells of fish. You'd better give him a bath after tea, love.'

Jenny pulled a face. 'Do I have to?' she said. She turned to the others. 'He loves splashing around in the sea but he hates being bathed,' she said. 'I end up getting wetter than he does.'

Mandy laughed. 'We'll help, won't we, James?'

'Certainly will,' James agreed.

Jenny's dad was sitting at the dining-room table reading the local paper and still wearing his green warden's uniform. Jenny ran in and gave him a hug. 'You'll never guess where we've been.'

'No need,' her dad said, hugging her back. 'Your mum's already told me.'

He shook hands with James and grinned at Mandy. She felt surprised. She hadn't expected him to look so much like James's dad, even though they were brothers. He had the same shock of brown hair and round face but his skin was weathered by the sun and the wind.

'Great to meet you, Mandy,' he said.

'Dad, we saw three—' Jenny began breathlessly.

Her mum interrupted. 'Tell your dad while we're having tea, love,' she said. 'Go and wash your hands, all of you.'

She set a pot of tea down in the centre of the table. There was a loaf of bread cut into thick slices, a dish of creamy butter, some cheese, scones and home-made cakes. Mandy's mouth watered. The sea air had really given her an appetite.

When they came back from washing their hands, Jenny blurted out the details of their whale-watching trip.

'They'll be Minke whales, I expect,' her dad said, after he had listened to their description.

Mandy and James looked at one another, then at Uncle Thomas.

'Minke?' Mandy repeated. 'What a lovely name. How do you spell it?'

He told her.

'It rhymes with Pinky,' she chuckled.

'Yes – and "stinky",' Auntie Gwyn said. She

frowned down at Muffin who was sitting at her feet hoping for a titbit. She pushed him gently away with her toe. 'The sooner you give this dog a bath, the better, Jenny.'

'I will, honestly,' Jenny said. She turned eagerly to her dad. 'Tell us more about the whales, Dad,' she begged.

'Well . . .' he went on. 'Minke whales are shallow water whales. That's why they sometimes come so close to the shore.'

'What are they doing here, though?' James stared at his uncle.

'They're probably on their way south to the Antarctic,' Uncle Thomas told him. 'The calves are born in the north where the water is warmer, then they come south in the spring. The youngster you saw will still be feeding on its mother's milk. You know that whales are sea mammals, of course, and that they breathe air.'

Mandy nodded. 'But I'd love to know more about them.'

'Why do they keep spouting out those jets of water?' Jenny asked.

'It's not actually water,' her dad explained. 'When

they come up to the surface to breathe, they send
out the air that's already in their lungs because
there's no oxygen left in it.'

'Through their blowholes,' James added.

'That's right,' Uncle Thomas said. 'It's like a big
nostril.' He got up from his chair. 'I've got a book
about whales that'll tell you all you want to know.'
He went into the other room and came back with a
large book with a picture of a killer whale on the
front. He flicked through it until he came to the
section on Minke whales, then handed it to Mandy.
'There you are,' he said. 'There's lots of information
in there.'

'Thanks,' Mandy said. There was a picture of a
whale family, two adults and a calf just like the ones
they had seen out in the bay.

James peered over her shoulder. 'How big does it
say they are?' he asked.

' "Mean length nine metres",' Mandy quoted,
reading from the book. ' "And an average of seven
tonnes".'

'Actually they're quite small compared to some
other whales,' Uncle Thomas said.

James blinked at him. '*Small?* That doesn't sound

very small to me. It's as long as a double decker bus!'

'They can be a lot bigger,' Uncle Thomas told them, 'And some can be smaller. *Mean* means half-way between the biggest and the smallest.'

'I hate to interrupt.' Auntie Gwyn said, 'but the tea's going cold.'

They all laughed and Mandy put the book down. The whales were so fascinating she had almost forgotten how hungry she was.

After tea, James went to help Jenny bathe Muffin

while Mandy helped Uncle Thomas clear away the tea things.

'It must be great being a coast warden,' she said to him.

Uncle Thomas smiled at her. 'It's very interesting,' he said. 'And I get to be out in the fresh air most of the time.'

'What exactly do you do?' Mandy said. 'Jenny said you see lots of animals . . .'

Uncle Thomas grinned again. 'Quite a lot,' he said. 'Part of my job is to monitor the wildlife and report injured birds or animals if I see them. We've got a good few foxes up on the heathland and the occasional badger. We've also got rabbits and squirrels, stoats and weasels, ponies and wild goats.'

'Wild goats!' Mandy exclaimed.

'Yes,' he said. 'You should see them climbing up and down the rock face. They're amazing. Oh . . .' he added, '. . . and we've got a small colony of grey seals below Hoopers Point.'

'Seals!' Mandy exclaimed. 'I love seals, especially the babies.'

'They have got some pups,' Uncle Thomas said. 'I'll try to find time to take you to see them.'

'That would be great,' Mandy said. 'What else do you do?'

'Oh, lots of things,' Uncle Thomas told her. 'I monitor the colonies of seabirds. This area has huge amounts of them and there's a small bird sanctuary just off the coast.'

'Are there puffins?' Mandy asked, remembering the badge on the side of his van.

'Yes,' he confirmed. 'And kittiwakes, fulmars, oyster-catchers . . . loads and loads. You should hear the noise they make, especially during nesting time.'

'I bet,' Mandy laughed.

'Then I keep the Nature Conservancy Council and the Royal Society for the Protection of Birds informed about any problems that arise,' Uncle Thomas went on. 'I patrol the long coastal path to check for erosion and damage by holidaymakers—'

'Check sites of rare plants, keep an eye on the footpaths and signposts, patrol the carparks, check fences, walls and hedges . . .' Auntie Gwyn interrupted, coming in for the remaining dirty dishes. 'Report any pollution to the environment agency . . .' She laughed. 'I could go on and on.'

'Wow!' Mandy said. 'You must be really busy.'

Uncle Thomas laughed. 'I am, especially in the summer when there are a lot of holidaymakers around. I'm afraid they don't always know how to treat the countryside. But it's a great job.'

Mandy suddenly realised that she had been so busy since they'd arrived that she had forgotten to phone home. She was dying to tell Mum and Dad about the whales.

'Yes, of course, go ahead,' Jenny's mum said, when she asked permission.

Mandy dialled the number and tapped her fingers impatiently on the table as she waited for someone to answer.

It was her dad. She blurted out everything about the whales before he even had a chance to say hello.

He sounded really impressed. 'So you're having a great time already, Mandy!'

'Yes, we are,' Mandy confirmed. 'How's everyone there? Is Mum OK? And Simon and Gran and Grandad?'

'Everyone's fine,' her dad assured her.

When Mandy had sent her love to everyone at home, she put the phone down and went back into the kitchen. Jenny's parents were talking about the whales.

'I knew there was a school heading down the coast,' Thomas was telling his wife. 'Some of the fishermen won't be very pleased, that's for sure.'

Mandy bit her lip. That was two people who'd said the fishermen would be annoyed about the whales. Ivor *and* Uncle Thomas.

'Oh dear,' Auntie Gwyn said. 'I hope they don't drive them away before the youngsters get a chance to see them again. Or worse . . .'

'What do you mean . . . worse?' Mandy couldn't help interrupting. 'They won't hurt them, will they?'

Uncle Thomas and Auntie Gwyn exchanged glances.

'They might try to destroy them,' Uncle Thomas said. 'That happened a few years ago. A couple of adult Minkes got separated from their school and were eating lots of fish. I'm afraid a few of the local fishermen went out and killed them.'

Mandy's heart turned over. 'They're not allowed to do that, surely?'

Uncle Thomas shrugged. 'Not officially . . . no. Of course, *hunting* whales for meat and oil has been banned, because the huge amount of whaling almost wiped them out.'

'That's what I thought,' Mandy said.

Uncle Thomas shrugged again. 'But unfortunately, no-one's going to know if a few are disposed of whether its against the law or not.'

'Surely three whales can't eat *that* many fish,' Mandy exclaimed indignantly.

'There could be more of them,' Uncle Thomas told her. 'Minkes usually migrate in quite large schools. And a large number of whales means hundreds of tons of fish being eaten.'

'Well, we only saw three,' Mandy insisted.

Auntie Gwyn patted her shoulder gently. 'It's no good worrying about it, Mandy. We'll just have to hope they carry on down the coast before the fishermen really feel threatened.'

But Mandy couldn't help worrying.

When she got to bed that night, she lay there staring at the ceiling. Muffin was snoring gently at her feet. The moon was shining through the window. She thought about the whale family, swimming out there in the ocean. She hoped they would swim away before anyone could harm them. She knew whales talked to one another. They made sounds like singing, whistling and clicking through the ocean depths. What were they saying to each other, she wondered.

And with that thought, and the sound of waves breaking on the shore outside, she gently drifted off to sleep.

Three

The following morning, Mandy was awake first. She threw back the covers and jumped out of bed. Muffin opened one eye, looked grumpy, yawned, then went back to sleep.

All Mandy could see of Jenny was a clump of dark hair sticking out at the top of the duvet. She had stayed up late with James to watch a football match on television and was still fast asleep. Mandy tiptoed to the window and drew back the curtains.

The sea was smooth and calm. The sun's reflection made a ribbon of silver from the horizon to the shore. Further out, the waves broke gently against the rocks. She opened the window and took a deep breath of sea air. It smelled fresh and sharp with a tang of salt.

Out in the harbour something caught Mandy's attention. Something large was swimming round and round, an enormous back rising and falling with the waves. Then, suddenly, a spout of steamy air jetted and a dark grey head appeared just above the surface. She gasped. One of the whales had come right into the harbour! Her heart jumped with excitement.

Then Mandy saw that far out, beyond the harbour, the other two whales were swimming up and down. But her smile turned to a frown when she suddenly remembered stories she had read about whales getting separated from their families by swimming into estuaries and harbours and not being able to find their way out. Was this what had happened here?

Heart still thudding, Mandy noticed that the whales swimming out at sea were of a different size. So one must be the calf and the other an adult whale. Her stomach suddenly turned over with fear. Supposing the whale in the harbour was the calf's mother? Supposing it *was* stranded? Jenny's father had told them that the calf would still be dependent on its mother and feeding on her milk. If they were separated, the baby could die!

By now, Jenny was awake. Mandy turned. 'Jenny, Jenny, come and look!'

Jenny threw back the duvet and ran to stand beside her. She stared for a minute, rubbed sleep from her eyes then stared again. She turned to Mandy, eyes round with disbelief. 'Wow!'

'Do you think it'll find its way out OK?' Mandy asked anxiously.

Jenny shook her head. 'I don't know.'

'Come on,' Mandy said. 'Let's tell James.'

They ran upstairs to his room.

James was already up and staring out of his little attic room window. 'I was just about to come down and tell *you*,' he said. 'I thought I was imagining things at first.' He took off his glasses and rubbed his eyes.

'Poor thing,' Mandy said, gazing out of the window. 'It found its way into the harbour but it doesn't look as if it can find its way out again.'

They ran down to tell Jenny's parents what they had seen. Her dad was just finishing his breakfast.

When he heard about the whale he drained his mug of coffee and stood up. 'Come on,' he said. 'I've got a pair of binoculars in the van; we'll take a look through those.'

Outside, they crossed the road and stood on the sea wall. Uncle Thomas put the binoculars to his eyes. 'It looks totally lost.' He sighed, and shook his head. 'Sometimes when whales get separated from their family groups they get so confused they don't know which way to turn.'

He handed the binoculars to Mandy. 'Here, take a look.'

Through them, Mandy could see the whale's grey head clearer than ever, and the white underside of its body and head as it rose above the water. She could even see its eyes. They looked scared and anxious, just as any lost animal would be. 'Do you know if it's the male or the female?' she asked.

Uncle Thomas shook his head. 'Difficult to tell,' he replied.

James was wriggling impatiently. 'Let's have a look, Mandy.'

She gave him the glasses. 'Wow!' he said, adjusting the lenses. 'Poor thing.'

Mandy turned to Uncle Thomas. 'What will happen to it?' she asked anxiously.

'Hopefully, it'll find its way back to its family,' he said. 'We'll just have to wait and see.'

'There must be something we can do,' Jenny said, as she grabbed the binoculars from James. 'It looks really frightened.'

Her father couldn't help smiling. 'I don't know how you can tell.'

'Well, I can,' Jenny said. 'And you'd be scared too if you'd lost your family.'

Her dad smiled again. He patted Jenny's shoulder. 'Sorry, love. You're right about that. But try not to worry. We'll give it a day or two before we really start getting anxious.'

Mandy didn't want to wait a day or two. She wanted to help the whale now. 'We can't just sit by and do nothing,' she said after breakfast as they took Muffin for a walk along the shore.

Jenny kicked at the little ridges of sand left by the receding tide. 'I suppose Dad knows best,' she said. 'Anyway, he'll know what to do.'

Mandy picked up a piece of driftwood and threw it for Muffin, then went on to tell Jenny about the time they had helped with some fox cubs and had rescued a baby owl that had fallen from its nest.

'And we've saved a badger,' James said.

'Yes, but foxes and owls and badgers are a bit different from whales, aren't they?' Jenny said.

Mandy and James couldn't help agreeing.

Mandy sighed. If it was the female that was stranded, how long could the calf survive without her? How long would the other two wait before they gave up hope and set off once more on their long swim to the Antarctic? A half-starved baby would never survive *that* journey.

Tears came into her eyes. She could hardly bear to think about the calf getting weaker and weaker and perhaps eventually dying of hunger.

They left the beach and walked along the harbour road towards the fishing boats. Mandy looked thoughtful as she racked her brain for ideas to help the whale. She remembered a story she had read in a wildlife magazine. A whale had got stranded in a narrow inlet on the coast of Australia. The local people had got into their small boats and herded it out, just like a sheepdog herds sheep. Maybe that's what people could do here if the whale didn't find its way out of the harbour by itself.

She told James and Jenny what she had been thinking about.

'It's really up to my dad,' Jenny repeated. 'Honestly, he'll know what to do.'

'Yes, of course,' Mandy said. 'But we could help him organise things.'

'It'll take bags of hard work so he's bound to need someone to help,' James said enthusiastically.

As they got near the quay they could see a crowd of people there. Word must have got around about the whale. Some were sitting in their cars, others were peering through binoculars. Lots had cameras.

When they reached the harbour, *Seaspray* was moored up alongside the other fishing vessels.

'Maybe Ivor will take us to see the whale in the harbour,' James said. 'It's only a few metres out. You could almost *row* a boat out there, and the water's really calm.'

But Ivor was nowhere to be seen.

'Let's hang around until he gets back,' James suggested.

'I've got a better idea,' Jenny said. 'Let's go and look in the cafe. I bet he's there.'

Stepping carefully over the ropes and shrimp pots that lined the quayside, they made their way back along the road to Mrs Evans's cafe.

It was full. A couple of fishermen were sitting at a table by the door. They were dressed in blue overalls and wore huge, chunky wellington boots. They were discussing the whales.

'Wretched nuisance, if you ask me,' the younger man said. He had a tanned face, weathered by the sun and the wind, and long hair tied back in a ponytail. 'Where there's one family there's bound to be more, you know. A whole school probably heading this way.'

'Aye,' his companion replied. 'Not sure what we can do about it, though.'

'I've got a few ideas.' The man with the ponytail leaned closer to his companion and Mandy couldn't hear any more. But there was something about the way he had lowered his voice that made her stomach turn with fear.

Jenny must have seen her worried face. 'What's up, Mandy?'

'Those men,' she said in a low voice. Jenny turned and stared at them.

'That's Bryan Jackson and his son, Will.'

'Do you know them?' Mandy asked.

Jenny shrugged. 'I was with my dad once when we met them along the harbour. They come from up the coast. What about them?'

Mandy suddenly realised they were staring at her and Jenny. She turned away and pulled Jenny's arm. 'Tell you later,' she whispered.

A young woman with short dark hair and wearing a denim jacket and jeans was sitting on one of the stools at the counter drinking coffee. A mini voice recorder sat on the bar in front of her. The cook was behind the counter busy frying bacon and eggs.

'Is Mrs Evans around, please?' Jenny asked him.

'She's out the back. Go and find her if you like,' he said.

Mrs Evans was sitting in her front room with her cat. 'Mickey's sick,' was the first thing she said as Mandy and James came through. 'I'm really worried about him.'

Jenny had gone round to untie Muffin from the front of the cafe. When she brought him in through the back door, the dog gave a little whine when he saw Mickey looking so poorly and went to lick his nose. Then he sat down quietly at Mrs Evans's feet.

Mandy crouched down in front of Mrs Evans and began to stroke Mickey softly. 'What's wrong, then?' she murmured softly.

'He doesn't seem to be able to keep anything down,' Mrs Evans told them.

'Isn't there a vet in the village?' Mandy asked anxiously. Mickey looked really ill and could hardly lift up his head.

'There is a surgery,' Jenny answered. 'But it's only open two days a week. Abersyn isn't big enough to have a vet of its own.'

'The main surgery's in Rhydfellin,' Mrs Evans told them. 'But that's ten miles away and I can't close the cafe to take Mickey there. Especially with all these visitors who've come to look at the whale. And I haven't a clue how long Ivor's going to be.'

Mandy stood up. 'Wouldn't the vet come to see Mickey at home?'

'I've already phoned,' Mrs Evans explained. 'But she's out on a call. The receptionist said she would tell her as soon as she gets back.'

'That's good,' Mandy said. 'Let's hope it's not too long.'

Mrs Evans lifted Mickey from her lap and laid him gently in his basket. 'I'd better get back to the counter,' she said. 'Chef can't do the cooking and the serving as well.'

Mandy covered the cat up with his blanket. He miaowed softly and closed his eyes. She bit her lip. She'd got a terrible feeling there was something dreadfully wrong with Mickey. It could be so many things – flu, a stomach infection, a virus of some kind. He could even have been in a fight, or been injured by a car. You couldn't always see wounds on long-haired cats. She sighed. The sooner the vet got here, the better.

Four

'So you don't know how long Ivor's going to be,'
Jenny said to Mrs Evans when they had left the cat
and gone back out into the cafe. 'He's going to be
really upset about Mickey.'

Mrs Evans shook her head. 'He went off
early,' she said. 'He's gone to the chandlers to get
something for the boat. It's on the other side of
Rhydfellin. He could be gone for ages.'

The young woman with the voice recorder was
still sitting at the counter. Mandy plonked herself
down on the stool next to her and put her chin
in her hands. 'I suppose we'll just have to wait

then, won't we,' she said unhappily.

'Cheer up,' the young woman said when she saw their glum faces.

Mandy gave a sigh. 'We're really worried about Mrs Evans's cat,' she told her. '*And* the stranded whale in the harbour. Have you seen it?'

The young woman nodded. She pointed at her camera and tape recorder. 'That's why I'm here. My name's Kim – I work for the *Abersyn Herald*. I've come to do a story about the whale.'

'Oh?' Mandy said. She told Kim what they'd found out about Minke whales. 'And the trouble is,' she went on, 'if it's the calf's mother that's stranded, they could both die.'

Kim looked at her worried face. 'Oh, dear,' she said. 'But I'm sure someone will come up with some ideas to help it.'

'My dad's the coast warden,' Jenny informed her. 'He said we've got to wait a while before there's any need to get really worried. It could still manage to find its own way out.'

'But we still *are* worried,' Mandy added. 'The calf won't survive very long without its mother's milk.'

'Do you think I could interview your dad?' Kim

asked Jenny. 'I've talked to a few locals and one or two of the fishermen but I'd like to hear your dad's point of view.'

'Point of view?' James looked puzzled.

Kim took a sip of her coffee. 'Yes, some of the fishermen aren't too pleased about the whales. I heard one of them say they could stick around for ages hoping the stranded one will get back to them. I'd like to know what your dad feels about it.'

'I'm sure he'll talk to you,' Jenny said. 'He's out on patrol at the moment, but he'll be back later.'

'Great.' Kim shut her notebook. 'Well I'm off to the quay to see what the people down here have got to say. Your whale is certainly causing a stir, that's for sure. I've never seen this place so crowded!'

'It gets pretty crowded in high summer,' came a voice from behind. 'Sometimes you can't move on the beach.'

When they looked up, it was Ivor.

Jenny jumped off her stool. 'Ivor, we've been waiting for you.'

'Waiting for me?' he said. 'Why?'

'It's Mickey,' Mandy told him. 'He's really sick.'

Ivor hurried round the back of the counter with a worried frown on his face.

'Might see you later,' Kim called as she left the cafe and headed off down to the harbour.

Mandy, James and Jenny found Ivor crouched down by Mickey's basket. Mrs Evans was there too and had told him how busy the vet was.

Ivor stroked Mickey's soft head. 'There's nothing we can do until she gets here,' he said. 'Let's hope it's soon.'

They sat with the cat for a while, then Ivor said he'd got to get back to *Seaspray*. 'I really need to fix a new rope before I go out to sea again. I'll give you a ring from the harbour, Mum, to find out if the vet's been.'

'Can we walk down with you?' Mandy enquired. 'There's something we want to ask you.'

' 'Course you can.' Ivor said.

'We wanted to ask if you could take us out to see the whale again,' Jenny explained on the way. Ivor had left Abersyn early that morning and hadn't spotted the whale in the harbour before he left.

'Oh, my goodness,' he said when they pointed it out to him. 'I hope it isn't the calf's mother.'

'So do we,' Mandy said. 'And we thought as it was so close, perhaps . . . ?'

' 'Course I will,' Ivor said. 'I just need to do a few things on board the boat, but I won't be long.'

When they reached the harbour, Jenny's dad had returned from his coast patrol and was chatting to a group of sightseers. They had been watching the whale through binoculars and one had just sailed quite close to it in his small motor-launch.

Ivor went aboard *Seaspray* with the new rope he'd bought at the chandlers.

Uncle Thomas was listening to what the man was saying. Mandy's heart turned over when she heard.

'It's definitely the female,' the man was telling Uncle Thomas. 'I've seen whales off the coast of America and learned to recognise the nursing mothers.'

Mandy frowned anxiously. It *was* the mother-whale. All their worst fears had come true.

Uncle Thomas's face was grim. He thanked the man and turned to Mandy and the others. Kim had come up to them and they introduced her to him.

'I hoped you'd be able to give me some more information for my story in the paper,' Kim said.

'Sure,' Uncle Thomas said. 'What do you want to know?'

Mandy felt sad as she turned to watch the whale swimming around in the harbour. It must seem so strange. The whale was used to open seas and the freedom of the waves . . . not houses and rocks and lots of people pointing and staring. Maybe she was thinking about the crystal waters of the Antarctic. She would be missing her calf desperately. Mandy imagined she could hear the mother whale's mournful cry, echoing beneath the waves searching for her baby.

Uncle Thomas was still talking to Kim.

'And what about a rescue?' Kim asked. 'How would you go about it?'

'Well . . .' Uncle Thomas replied, 'we need to give the whale a day or two to find her own way out. But if we *did* then need to stage a rescue, the most likely method would be to herd it back out to sea with a flotilla of boats.'

'That's what I thought,' Mandy said in a louder voice than she had intended.

Uncle Thomas and Kim both gazed at her in surprise.

Mandy felt herself go red. 'It's just that I remem-bered reading about a whale that got stranded in Australia,' she said quickly. 'That's what *they* did to rescue it.'

'It's a bit more complicated than that, though,' Uncle Thomas went on. 'We'll also need people to make as much noise as possible so the whale is scared and desperate to get away.'

'It sounds a bit cruel,' Mandy said dubiously. She hated the thought of the whale being frightened.

Uncle Thomas looked at her. 'Yes, Mandy, it does, but it's really the only thing that will work. Sometimes you have to be cruel to be kind. No one will hurt the whale. Reuniting her with her family is the most important thing.'

'What kind of a noise do you mean?' James asked.

'Anything,' Uncle Thomas told him. 'Drums, trumpets, people shouting . . .'

'We could get saucepans to bang,' Jenny began, 'And I know someone who's got a drum, and I've got that—'

Her dad held up his hand. 'OK, Jenny. Don't let your imagination run away with you. We've got to make sure we *need* to rescue the whale before we start making definite plans.'

'OK, then,' Kim said. 'Well, thanks, Mr Hunter. Is there anything else you'd like to say?'

'Only that if we should stage a rescue we'll need a lot of help from people with small boats,' Uncle Thomas added. 'But we'll wait a day or two before we decide.'

'Right.' Kim put her recorder in her bag. 'Thanks very much.'

'When will the story be in the paper?' Jenny asked eagerly.

'Tomorrow, I hope.' Kim grinned at them all. 'Let me know if there's any more news.' She took a small card out of her bag and gave it to Uncle Thomas. 'There's my number. Give me a ring.'

He put the card into his pocket. 'I will, thanks.'

'Oh,' Kim added. 'Do you know anyone who will take me out in a boat? I'd love to get a close-up picture of the whale.'

'Here's someone,' Mandy said, as Ivor turned up.

'Do you still want to get a closer look?' he asked. 'I'm not going fishing until high tide this evening so I'm free until then.'

'Oh, yes, please,' Mandy said. 'Can Kim come too?

She wants a picture for the paper.'

'Sure,' Ivor said. He looked at Uncle Thomas. 'Would you like to come too, Tom?'

Uncle Thomas glanced at his watch. 'I've got a meeting with the Nature Conservancy Council later, but if we're quick, I'd love to.'

As soon as they were all aboard *Seaspray*, Ivor cast off and chugged out into the harbour.

The whale surfaced as they drew close.

'Wow!' Kim clicked away with her camera just as a great jet of warm gas rose with a loud hiss into the air.

Mandy leaned over the deck rail. She could see the mother whale's eyes and thought they looked wide and scared. If only she would turn and head back out to sea. She was obviously lost and miserable, dizzy with swimming round and round. Mandy felt a surge of frustration. If only they could do something now!

Uncle Thomas was in the bow with Jenny, James and Kim. Jenny held Muffin in her arms so he could see the whale too.

As they came alongside the whale, Thomas called out to Ivor. 'Not too close, Ivor, whales can be dangerous, you know. If she dives, then surfaces under the keel, she'll tip us over.'

'OK,' Ivor called. He revved the engine and sailed round in a circle.

Still staring at the great creature, Mandy longed to be able to reach out and touch her, pat her and reassure her that if she needed help they would be there for her.

Out to sea, the second adult whale and the calf were still swimming up and down. Mandy could see the rise and fall of their huge backs with the swell of the ocean. Her heart went out to them.

'We'll have you back together soon,' she murmured under her breath, even though she knew they couldn't hear.

'Have you got a good picture?' Ivor called to Kim.

Kim waved her hand. 'Great, thanks. I'll give *Seaspray* a mention in the story.'

'Right.' Ivor grinned at her, then turned the wheel and headed back towards the quay. Mandy watched the whale as she rose above the surface, then dived down, disappearing in a whirlpool of white foam. She sighed, and ran to help lower the gangplank so they could all get off.

'Thanks, Ivor.' Kim shook the fisherman's hand when they were once more on the quayside. 'That should be a great picture.' She hurried off to her car.

'That was brilliant,' James said. 'Wasn't it, Uncle Thomas?'

James's uncle looked thoughtful. 'Yes,' he said. 'But to be honest I didn't like the look of that whale.'

Mandy frowned. 'What do you mean?'

'She seemed sluggish,' he said. 'Her eyes weren't very bright. I'm afraid she's suffering.'

'Perhaps she's pining for her calf,' Mandy said.

Uncle Thomas frowned. 'Yes, possibly. I think I'll have to decide soon whether to organise a rescue or not.'

'When?' Mandy asked anxiously.

'Tomorrow, I think,' Uncle Thomas said. 'I'll make the decision tomorrow.'

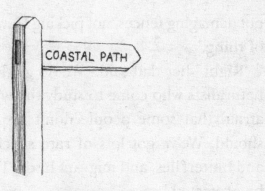

Five

Ivor went off to check how Mickey was, and Mandy, James, Jenny and Muffin walked back with Thomas to his van.

'What's your meeting with the Nature Conservancy Council about?' Mandy asked him. She hoped he wouldn't mind her being so curious.

'Well,' Uncle Thomas told her, 'part of the coast I look after is a nature reserve, and I've noticed that some damage has been done in that area.'

'Some people don't follow the country code,' Jenny piped up. 'You know, sticking to the paths, not damaging fences, not picking flowers – that kind of thing.'

'Right,' her dad said. 'We do get lots of genuine naturalists who come to study the wildlife, but I'm afraid that some people don't respect it as they should. We've got lots of rare species of flowers, and butterflies, and migrant birds. They all have to be protected.'

When Jenny's dad had gone, they decided to take Muffin for a long walk. The little dog had been jumping around and barking at everyone ever since they'd got off the boat.

'Let's take him up on to the coastal path,' Jenny suggested. 'He looks as if he's got some energy to get rid of. He's been as good as gold this morning, so he deserves a treat.'

Jenny's mum was at work in the village shop so they called in to tell her where they were going, then set off.

At the end of the High Street a stile led up a steep cliff path. They let Muffin off the lead and he scampered off, nose to the ground.

'Don't go too far,' Jenny yelled. 'He goes mad up here,' she said. 'Hunting for rabbits.'

'Does he ever catch any?' Mandy hated the thought of the little dog actually catching one.

Jenny laughed. 'Never. He's pretty fast but they're faster. They just dive down into their warren. I reckon they're just playing games with him.'

Mandy grinned. 'Thank goodness for that!'

They were at the top by now, walking a narrow path between swathes of heather and yellow gorse bushes.

Mandy lifted her face to the breeze. The air was full of the scent of the sea mingled with the dark, peaty smell of the soil and the perfume of the heather. Above, a few white cotton-wool clouds scudded across the sky. The village looked like a tiny dolls' village. The houses and the north harbour wall were shining in the sun. There was no sign of the whale in the harbour but far beyond, the other two were still swimming to and fro.

'It's great up here,' James shouted, shooting on ahead. 'A bit like our Yorkshire moors.'

He was right. If you looked inland, the landscape stretched to a horizon of dark mountains. The moorland was dotted with green and purple heather with the occasional outcrop of craggy rocks. The valley ended in a steep cliff that plunged down to the shore. The white cliff face was teeming with seabirds. Herring-gulls, cormorants, fulmars, guillemots, even a colony of puffins.

'These cliffs are called Craig-yr-Aderyn,' Jenny informed them. 'It's Welsh for *bird rock*.'

Mandy thought it was a great sounding name.

They walked on down the slope. Jenny lagged behind, waiting for Muffin to appear. 'Where can he have got to?' She called his name over and over again.

Suddenly Mandy spotted something: the reddish-brown glint of a hare. She clutched James's arm. 'Look!'

The hare was sitting in the middle of the path, long ears upright, nose twitching in the wind.

'Wow!' James breathed.

Then, suddenly, a bundle of honey-coloured fur hurtled past them. Muffin. He had appeared from nowhere.

They couldn't help laughing as the hare darted away. Its long back legs seemed to eat up the ground and Muffin didn't have a chance of catching it. But Muffin didn't seem to know that. He raced after it, disappearing into the undergrowth in no time at all.

Jenny recovered from her fit of giggles. She shook her head. 'Now he'll be gone for ever!'

'We'd better try to find him,' James said, after they had called for five minutes or more. They left the path and made their way through the clumps of thick heather until they came to some derelict stone buildings. A sign warned people to keep out.

'It's the old mine,' Jenny explained. 'The tunnels lead out under the ocean. They used to mine coal from under the sea but it's been shut for years and years.'

They were still calling Muffin when suddenly Mandy drew in her breath. 'Listen!'

They could hear barking in the distance but, strangely, the sound seemed to be coming from somewhere beneath their feet.

'Oh, no,' Jenny wailed. 'I bet he's gone down one of the shafts. Mum's going to kill me. I'm not supposed to come here.'

And, sure enough, a little further on they came across the entrance to an ancient mine shaft.

'Shh,' Jenny held her finger to her lips. Muffin's

faint bark came echoing up from below. The shaft had once been boarded up but the boards had since rotted away leaving the dangerous, gaping hole.

They lay on their stomachs and peered cautiously over the edge.

'At least he's not injured,' Mandy said. 'Or he wouldn't be making such a row.'

'Well, that's something, I suppose.' Jenny was close to tears. 'But how on earth are we going to get him up?'

'We're not,' James said matter-of-factly. 'We'll have to go and get help.'

'You two go,' Mandy said. 'I'll stay here. If I keep calling his name he'll know we haven't abandoned him.'

'OK,' Jenny said. 'We'll be as quick as we can.'

When they had gone, Mandy kept calling Muffin's name down into the shaft, listening carefully for the sound of his bark. But no sound came.

Mandy shivered in the cool breeze that had sprung up. *Please hurry, you two*, she said to herself. She wasn't sure she liked being up in this lonely spot all by herself.

There was no sight or sound of the little dog.

Once she thought she heard him but it was only the sound of the gulls squabbling on the cliff face.

Out to sea, the waves had grown bigger as the wind increased. They were breaking heavily, making white crests of foam against the rocks.

Now and then the back of the stranded Minke whale appeared in the harbour. Above, the clouds had got darker and bigger, heavy with the threat of rain. Once or twice, drops stung Mandy's face as moisture blew in on the wind.

She called into the hole again. This time, Mandy thought she heard a faint bark in reply, but she couldn't really be sure.

It seemed ages before James and Jenny got back. Ivor was with them. He had a thick coil of rope over each shoulder.

Mandy jumped up to greet them.

'Mum's still at work and Dad's out,' Jenny explained breathlessly, 'so we got Ivor. Any sign of Muffin?'

Mandy shook her head. 'I heard something but I'm really not sure it was him. The gulls are so noisy.'

'Oh . . . I do hope it was,' Jenny said.

Mandy could see she was close to tears. She put

her arm round her and gave her a hug. 'Try not to worry,' she said.

'You shouldn't have been up here in the first place, you know,' Ivor told them with a frown.

'We know,' Jenny said. 'We're sorry.'

Ivor lay on his stomach and looked over the edge of the hole. 'There's a maze of underground workings down there,' he said. 'He could be any-where.' He took a torch from his pocket. 'I'm afraid I'll never squeeze through this hole. And even if I could, you wouldn't be strong enough to pull me back up. Any volunteers?'

'I'll go,' Mandy said.

Jenny was sitting down, looking white and scared, and more upset than ever. 'I should go really because he's my dog,' she said. 'But I'm too frightened. I think I'd just go all wobbly and wouldn't be able to walk.'

'It's OK, don't worry,' James assured her. 'You stay up here and hang on to the rope with Ivor, I'll go down with Mandy.'

Jenny handed James the lead. 'Thanks, you two. I'm sorry I'm such a coward.'

Ivor gave Mandy the torch and she stuck it in the

pocket of her jeans. 'Don't go out of earshot,' he warned. 'Your parents won't thank me if we have to report *you* missing too.'

Mandy grinned, although she was feeling pretty scared. She could see by James's face that he was too.

Ivor tied the rope tightly round her waist and up underneath her arms. 'I'll lower you down slowly,' he said. 'Try not to bump against the sides.'

It seemed a long way down and Mandy let out a sigh of relief when at last her feet touched the soft ground below. She quickly undid the rope and shouted up.

'OK. Come on down, James.'

Ivor pulled up the rope and tied it round James. James was soon standing beside Mandy staring into the inky depths of the tunnel. Looking up, they saw the anxious faces of Jenny and Ivor peering over the edge.

'Remember what I said,' Ivor called. 'And be careful.'

'We will,' Mandy shouted. She clicked on the torch and shone the beam around.

'Muffin!' James called. 'Where are you?'

His voice echoed and bounced back towards them. *'Where are yoooo . . . are yooo . . . yoooo.'*

They stood holding their breath. But all they could hear was the echo of James's voice. There was no sign, or sound, of Muffin anywhere.

He had completely disappeared.

Six

Mandy and James began to make their way carefully along the dark passage. Then, suddenly, they could hear Muffin barking and whining in the distance again. But they could also hear another noise. A sound like thunder.

Mandy clutched James's arm. 'What's that?' She had a vision of a rock-fall, huge boulders tumbling down from above and trapping them.

James listened for a second or two, his head on one side. 'I think it's the sea,' he said at last.

Mandy heaved a sigh of relief. Of course, how stupid. Jenny had said they had mined coal from under the sea. James was right, it must be the ocean they could hear.

The passage seemed to stretch endlessly ahead. Just when Muffin's barks got louder they seemed to fade away again. Then, they saw daylight ahead. And something else . . . the scruffy tail of Jenny's dog, just disappearing round a corner.

They ran on, shouting his name. The passage got lighter and lighter. Then, all at once, they came out into the open air.

Mandy screwed up her eyes, blinking against the sudden brightness. James was beside her, panting.

She drew in her breath. In front of them lay the harbour, and beyond that, the village. Just above the waterline, Muffin stood on a wide overhanging ledge. The thunder they had heard was the waves breaking against the rocks.

Muffin sat down and tilted his head to one side, his ears cocked. It was as if he could see something out there but couldn't quite make out what it was.

Mandy lunged forward and grabbed him. 'Got you!' He turned in her arms and licked her face. 'You bad dog!' She tried to sound angry but was so relieved they had caught up with him at last that she just hugged and kissed him. 'Jenny will have to take you to obedience classes, won't she, James?'

But James wasn't listening. He was staring at something.

As Mandy followed his gaze she realised he was watching the Minke whale swimming only a few metres away.

'Oh, wow!' Mandy whispered.

They both held their breath as the whale came right up to the ledge, so close they could almost touch her.

Mandy gasped and her heart thudded in her chest like a drum. Muffin gave a little whine. Mandy was hugging him so tightly he could hardly breathe. 'Shh,' she managed to say. 'You'll frighten her away.'

A word from one of Thomas's books came into her mind. A word she had decided would make a brilliant name for a whale. 'Nordica,' she whispered.

'What?' James tore his eyes away and blinked at her.

Mandy explained. 'It means "comes from the north".'

'That's a good name,' James agreed.

As they watched, Nordica rose up out of the waves

and looked at them. They were so close that they could see the gleaming whiteness of her underbelly and the broad white stripe across her flippers. As she opened her enormous mouth they could see the series of springy whalebone plates that Minke whales have instead of teeth.

Her massive tail flipped and came down on the water with a loud smack. A huge wave surged towards them. It broke over the ledge, showering them with spray. It almost seemed as if Nordica was playing a game with them, although Mandy knew she was too lost and upset to be in the mood for play.

Nordica stared at her for a moment, and to Mandy, it seemed an understanding passed between them. A promise that Mandy would do everything in her power to help.

'Don't worry, Nordica,' she whispered. 'We'll help you, honestly we will.'

It seemed as if Nordica was satisfied. She whirled and dived, sending another huge wave crashing against the rocks. She swam away swiftly, then turned and came back towards them and sent a huge jet of gas up into the air. The noise was deafening.

The magical moment had passed.

Muffin began to bark.

'Muffin – shut up!' James exclaimed. He had been under Nordica's spell too.

But Muffin carried on. The sound echoed round the tunnel and seemed to be magnified ten times.

Nordica flipped her tail again then turned and sped away.

Mandy gave Muffin a gentle shake. 'You frightened her away, you monkey.'

James was still staring as the water closed over Nordica and she disappeared beneath the waves. 'Wow! Wasn't she fantastic?' he breathed.

'Absolutely,' Mandy agreed. As long as she lived she would never forget what she had seen. Nordica was so huge, yet she was so graceful in the water it seemed as if she weighed nothing at all.

At last Mandy managed to pull herself together. She knew that standing there feeling sad wouldn't do any good at all. They had to get back and ask Jenny's dad to get the rescue underway as soon as possible.

'Come on,' she said to James. 'They'll be getting worried.'

James fixed the lead to Muffin's collar and they set off back down the tunnel. Soon the daylight disappeared and Mandy clicked the torch on again.

At last they saw a shaft of daylight reaching down from above. They hurried forward and looked up to see the anxious faces of Ivor and Jenny peering down at them.

'Where on earth have you *been*?' Jenny shouted. Then she spotted Muffin. 'Oh . . . you've found him! Thank goodness! Is he OK?'

'He's fine,' Mandy shouted up. 'And we've seen Nordica.'

She saw Jenny and Ivor exchange glances.

'Seen *who*?' Jenny shouted.

'Nordica,' she answered. 'The whale. We've named her Nordica.'

It wasn't long before Ivor and Jenny had hauled all three of them up and out of the hole.

Mandy felt relieved to be out in the open air again. Breathlessly she and James told Ivor and Jenny what they had seen.

'Wow,' Jenny said, hugging Muffin. 'I wish I'd gone down after all. It would have been worth being scared.'

'I've seen that tunnel entrance when I've been on board *Seaspray*,' Ivor told them. 'I never realised it was one of the old mine workings.' He looked up at the sky. An anxious frown creased his brow. 'Come on, we'd better get back.'

By now, the clouds had gathered together and it had begun to rain. They coiled up the rope and began their trek home.

Jenny's mum had finished in the shop and was back at the cottage. Ivor went in with them to help explain what had happened.

Auntie Gwyn shook her head when they told her about their adventure. 'Jenny, you know you're not supposed to go near that place,' she scolded. 'It's really dangerous.'

'I'm sorry,' Jenny said. She had fetched a towel and was rubbing Muffin dry. 'But we couldn't just leave Muffin, could we?'

Her mum shook her head. 'No, of course not, love. But you shouldn't have been near there in the first place. You know those tunnels are dangerous. Muffin could have got lost for ever.'

'*And* they could have collapsed on top of you,' Ivor added. 'Then James and Mandy would have been lost for ever too.'

'We're really sorry,' Mandy said. 'But we're all OK and we would never have seen Nordica so close if Muffin hadn't got lost.'

'Nordica?' Auntie Gwyn said, and Mandy had to explain all over again.

'Nordica or no Nordica,' Auntie Gwyn said, shaking her head, 'you could all have got hurt.'

Then she scolded Ivor for not letting her know what was going on.

'Sorry,' he said. 'Jenny was in such a panic about Muffin I thought I'd better go with her straight away.'

Just then, the phone rang.

Jenny went into the hall to answer it. 'It's your mum, Ivor,' she said.

When Ivor came back he looked worried. 'Got to go,' he said. 'Mum's really anxious about Mickey. He's got a lot worse and the vet *still* hasn't been.'

'Can we come with you?' Mandy asked.

'Sure,' Ivor said.

When they arrived at the cafe, Mrs Evans was in her sitting-room with Mickey on her lap. His breathing sounded difficult and he was obviously in great pain. Ivor's mum was right, the cat *had* got a lot sicker since the morning.

'Why on earth hasn't the vet been?' Mandy asked.

Mrs Evans shook her head tearfully. 'I phoned again but one vet is still out on an emergency... something about a horse stuck in a bog somewhere, and the other's taking surgery. She'll be ages yet.'

Mandy looked at Ivor. He was bending down and stroking Mickey's head very gently. Mickey opened one eye to look at him then closed it again.

Ivor stood up. 'We'll have to take him to Rhydfellin. All I hope is that he can stand the journey.'

His voice cracked, and Mandy could see he was almost in tears at the thought of his beloved cat being so ill. 'Have you got a basket for him?' she asked Mrs Evans.

Ivor's mum shook her head. 'No, we've never had to take him anywhere before. He's always been such a healthy cat.'

'Never mind,' Mandy said. 'If we wrap him in a blanket I'm sure he'll be OK.'

Mandy put Nordica to the back of her mind. The most important thing at the moment was to get Mickey to the vet's before it was too late.

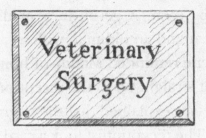

Veterinary
Surgery

Seven

Before they left, Ivor quickly phoned the vet to say they were bringing Mickey into the surgery and that it was an emergency.

Mandy held the cat on her lap, stroking his soft head gently, as the car bounced along through the rain. This seemed to soothe him but she could feel he had a high temperature and his breathing was shallow. Ivor kept glancing at him now and then and Mandy could see how worried he was. James and Jenny were sitting quietly in the back seat, hardly saying a word.

The Rhydfellin surgery was in the middle of town.

Inside, there were several people with their animals, waiting to be seen. A gerbil in a small cage, two puppies, a cat and an old man with a rabbit on his lap. The scene reminded Mandy of home.

They went straight up to the reception desk with Mickey and Ivor explained that they were expected.

'Oh, yes.' The receptionist took a card from a box beside her. 'Mickey Evans. Please take a seat, I'm sure the vet won't be long.'

Just then a woman with long blonde hair, wearing a white vet's coat, came out from the surgery. It was Gillian Orpin, one of the vets. 'Is this the emergency?' she asked when she saw Mickey cradled in Mandy's arms.

'Yes,' Ivor said. 'We'd be grateful if you'd see him straight away.' He turned to the people waiting. 'Sorry,' he said with an apologetic shrug.

A young man with a puppy on his lap waved his hand. 'You go ahead,' he said. The others all nodded in agreement.

'Thanks,' Ivor said gratefully as they followed Gillian into the examining room.

Mandy laid Mickey gently on the table. 'He seems to have got a lot worse,' she said, holding his head gently while Gillian felt his stomach. The cat gave a small yowl of pain when she touched a tender spot. Then the vet looked into his eyes and took his temperature.

She stood back looking thoughtful. 'I think it's probably a blockage of some kind in his intestine,' she said. 'I'll have to X-ray him, I'm afraid. If you'd wait in the waiting-room, it won't take long.' Her assistant was already bringing over the X-ray machine.

Back in the waiting-room Mandy walked up and down impatiently. Ivor sat staring at the wall and James and Jenny sat glancing through the magazines put out for people waiting.

It seemed ages before Gillian poked her head round the door. 'Come and see,' she said, and they all hurried into the examining room.

Mickey's X-ray was clipped up in front of a glass screen with a light behind it.

'There.' Gillian pointed to a dark mass in Mickey's intestine. 'He's either swallowed a foreign object or it's a fur ball. Either way, it's got to come out.'

'Can you do it now?' Mandy asked anxiously. She had seen this kind of X-ray at Animal Ark and knew something had to be done quickly.

'Yes,' Gillian confirmed. 'Right away.'

Ivor was looking immensely relieved. 'Thanks very much.'

The vet must have seen how worried he was. 'And don't worry,' she said. 'It's not uncommon. Cats with long fur groom themselves so much they swallow fur without realising. Sometimes they manage to cough it up but Mickey obviously hasn't been able to do that.'

'He *is* very fussy about the way he looks,' Ivor said with a grin.

'I'm sorry no one could call earlier,' the vet said. 'We've been rushed off our feet today.'

'I know what it's like,' Mandy said. 'My parents are vets and their surgery's attached to our house. They're always rushed off their feet too. I want to be a vet myself one day,' she added.

Gillian smiled as she accompanied them out to Reception. 'Would you like one of the nurses to show you round?' she asked.

'Oh, yes, please!' Mandy exclaimed. 'Can James and Jenny see too?'

'Of course,' the vet replied.

'I'll wait here for you,' Ivor said.

Gillian called Jane, one of the nurses, who took Mandy, James and Jenny out to the residential unit behind the examining rooms.

There was one rabbit, two cats, two puppies and a snake in the unit. It was just like at Animal Ark, except that the room was bigger and there were three nurses there to help instead of just Simon.

'We cover a huge area,' Jane told them. 'Lots of our work is with farm animals but we deal with pets too, and we have quite a lot of injured seabirds, with there being so many of them around here.'

Seeing the animals gave Mandy a sudden pang of homesickness. There would be so much to tell everyone when she got back.

One cage held a small monkey. Mandy was enchanted. It was black with a white, hairy front and big, wide eyes. It was huddled in a corner and clutching a fluffy blanket to its chest.

'What sort of monkey is it?' James asked. He stood beside Mandy and peered at it.

'It's a white-chested capuchin monkey,' the nurse explained. 'They live mainly in Central and South America.'

Mandy stared at it. Her heart turned over with pity. She wanted to put her finger through the bars and stroke his head but knew he would be frightened if she did. Besides, she knew monkeys can give a nasty bite.

'He comes from a little private zoo just up the coast,' Jane told them. 'And he's really missing the rest of his troop.'

'Oh,' Mandy said. She didn't like the idea of the monkeys living in cages.

Jane must have seen her face. 'Don't worry,' she assured her. 'They've got a wonderful house to live in . . . bags of space. The man who looks after them is brilliant.'

'That's good.' Mandy felt quite relieved.

'What's wrong with him?' Jenny asked, staring at the monkey.

'A nasty infection,' Jane replied. 'So he has to be isolated from the others. I'm afraid he feels a bit lonely and lost.'

Mandy suddenly thought of Nordica. She was lonely and lost too. She told Jane about the whale.

'Oh, yes, I went over to the rare breeds park with Gillian yesterday to help with delivery of a calf and someone there had been down to Abersyn to see her.'

'Rare breeds park?' Mandy's ears pricked up. She had heard about such places but never visited one.

Jane explained. 'Yes, you should go there. They've got sheep and cattle, pigs, poultry . . . oh, all sorts of old breeds that would have died out years ago if it wasn't for places like that.'

'Sounds great,' James said.

'I'll just check how your cat is,' Jane said before they left. 'I would think Gillian's finished the operation by now.'

Gillian *had* finished and she came out to confirm her diagnosis. 'A fur ball,' she said. 'Mickey's going to be fine but I'd like him to stay here for a couple of days so we can keep an eye on him. I'll give you a ring when he's well enough to go home.'

'That's fine,' Ivor said and thanked her once more. 'If I'm not there my mum will take a message.'

Outside it was still raining. Ivor held his face to the wind. 'The sea's going to be really rough,' he commented. 'There's always a big swell on when we get these westerlies.'

Mandy looked anxiously at the ocean swell as they

drove home along the coastal road. Huge breakers pounded the beach and, as they rounded the corner and headed back to Abersyn, fresh torrents of rain bounced off the windscreen. A sheet of grey mist covered the breakwater. Even the trawlers moored in the harbour were bobbing up and down like corks.

As he drew up outside Jenny's house, Ivor's face was glum. 'If that whale hasn't got out on her own yet I wouldn't hold out much hope of rescuing her in the near future,' he said. 'It'll take ages for the sea to die down, and small boats won't want to venture out. You're in for a bit of a wait, I'm afraid.'

The following morning Mandy, James and Jenny were all up early.

'The whale's still there,' James said as they went downstairs for breakfast.

Mandy had already checked. 'I know,' she said.

As they reached the bottom, the newspaper came through the door. They quickly scanned the front page. News about the local MP, a picture of the Mayor of Rhydfellin opening a new swimming pool complex, a man arrested for stealing precious birds' eggs . . . nothing about the whale.

'Oh well,' Mandy said with a sigh. 'Maybe they thought the others stories were more important, although I can't see why.'

Just then Uncle Thomas came through from the kitchen. He had been out in the rain with his binoculars, checking if Nordica was still in the harbour. Auntie Gwyn had gone off to work in the shop.

Uncle Thomas took off his jacket and boots and sat down next to Mandy. 'I think it's about time we got on with those rescue plans,' he said.

'Great!' James said.

But Uncle Thomas held up his hand. 'Now don't get too excited, James. You can see how bad the weather is. All we can do at the moment is make a list of things we need to do. The actual rescue will have to wait until the sea calms down.'

The phone rang and Jenny went to answer it. 'That was Kim,' she told them when she returned. 'She's sorry about the story. There wasn't room in the paper today. She'll try again tomorrow.'

Mandy gazed out at the rain. She could see the wind whipping crests of the waves into white foam.

Uncle Thomas had got a pad and pencil and was

writing down a few names. 'These are people I know who've got small boats and might be willing to help,' he said. 'We'll need to ring them. This evening would be best as most of them are out at work in the daytime.'

'The RSPCA have got a boat,' Jenny piped up. 'They used it to rescue a dog that got stranded on the rocks last summer.'

Her father showed her the list. 'They're already on here,' he said. He bit the end of his pen thoughtfully. 'I'll need to go and see the coastguard. He'll be able to give me an up-to-the-minute weather

forecast. Right, you three, any more suggestions?'

Jenny had one or two. A friend at school had a boat. Her teacher's husband went fishing; he might be able to help.

Mandy and James wrote down everything they could think of that would make a loud noise. Saucepans and spoons, trumpets if anyone had one, drums . . . anything people could carry.

'My football rattle,' Jenny said suddenly. 'That makes a really loud noise.'

But Mandy began to have doubts. 'Nordica is really going to be scared out of her wits,' she said.

Thomas gazed at her. 'I know, Mandy,' he said. 'I'm sorry, but we don't have any choice.'

'How will we actually do it, Uncle Thomas?' James asked. 'I mean will the boats just charge the whale so she swims away from them?'

James's uncle shook his head. 'Oh, no, it'll need a bit more organisation than that.'

He picked up his pen and drew a diagram on his note-pad: the quay wall, the rocks, then a picture of Nordica swimming in the harbour. He drew boats in a semicircle between the whale and the shore.

'There.' He showed it to James. 'If we get the boats

lined up like this, then gradually ease forward, hopefully Nordica will swim away from them, through the harbour entrance and out to sea.'

They all peered at the diagram.

'Oh, I really do hope it works,' said Jenny.

Her father put down his note-pad. 'Well, that's that. It's all we can do for now. We'll wait for a better forecast, then we can get going with those phone calls.'

'Yes,' Mandy said with a sigh. 'I just hope it won't be too long.'

'So do I,' James said gloomily.

Uncle Thomas gazed at their unhappy faces. 'Come on, you three, cheer up. It's not the end of the world.'

'It could be, for Nordica's calf, if it doesn't get back with its mother soon,' Mandy said.

'We'll just have to keep our fingers crossed,' Uncle Thomas replied. 'Look, I've got to go up to Hoopers Point. Someone's reported that part of the cliff has fallen away. Why don't you come with me? We might see those seals I was telling you about.'

Mandy's face lit up. She had been longing to go out with Jenny's dad in his van. 'Oh, yes, please.'

She turned to James and Jenny. 'Shall we?'

'You bet,' James said.

'We pass the rare breeds park on the way to Hoopers Point, don't we, Dad?' Jenny said.

'That's right,' her father confirmed. 'Why?'

Jenny explained that the vet's nurse had mentioned it.

'And we'd love to go there,' Mandy added.

Jenny's dad laughed. 'OK, if we've got time we'll call in on the way back.'

Jenny gave him a hug. 'Thanks, Dad!'

'Right.' He stood up. 'Boots and rainproof jackets, you three. And you'd better leave Muffin at home, Jenny. They don't allow dogs into the park.'

Outside, the wind was blowing a gale. It whipped their hair round their faces as they left the cottage and climbed into the van.

Uncle Thomas drove through the village and up the narrow coast road that wound steeply towards Hoopers Point. The point was a famous place for bird-watching and any rock falls might cause a hazard to ornithologists and hikers.

It took three-quarters of an hour to get there. The road wound its way past beaches, over clifftops and through small coastal villages just like Abersyn.

When they got near Hoopers Point they drew up in a carpark at the end of the clifftop road. On a notice-board there was a map with the coastal path marked, and sites where people could stop to picnic or watch the wildlife.

'We need to go on foot from here,' Uncle Thomas explained as they piled out of the van. He pointed to where a narrow path wound round the cliff edge and out of sight. The wind blew needles of rain into their faces and above, scores of seagulls wheeled and dived, squawking and squabbling in the stormy air. In places the path was very slippery. Close to the edge they could see where part of the cliff had fallen away.

'Hmm.' Uncle Thomas told them to stay on the path as he went closer, peering over at the waves pounding the foot of the cliff several hundred metres below. 'It'll need fencing off. I'll get it organised.'

They walked on up the path for fifty metres or so. In places it was very close to the cliff edge and Uncle Thomas warned them to be careful. Then they came to a place where a seat had been put for walkers to take a rest.

Uncle Thomas went closer to the edge. 'If you're careful, you three, you can see the seals from here.'

They went warily to the edge and looked over. There were a dozen or so grey seals on the beach below.

'You can only get to that beach by boat,' Uncle Thomas said. 'And it's so rocky that even then it's really dangerous.'

'That must protect the seals from being disturbed by tourists, then,' Mandy said.

'Yes,' Uncle Thomas said. 'In fact they've got no disturbances or predators at all down there, so they're a thriving colony.'

'There was a sick one once, do you remember, Dad?' Jenny said.

'I certainly do,' her father replied. 'I went round with the RSPCA chap in his boat . . . quite a dangerous operation, I can tell you.'

'What happened to the seal?' Mandy asked anxiously.

'I'm afraid it died,' Uncle Thomas said sadly. 'Some kind of virus, we thought. Luckily, none of the others seemed to get it.'

James and Jenny and her father left the cliff edge

and walked back towards the carpark. Mandy stood for a minute or two, gazing out to sea. The waves were huge, great crests of foam as far as the eye could see. There was no sign of the whales, and they were too far round the coast to get a view of Abersyn harbour to check if Nordica was still there. She sighed and turned away.

'Come on, Mandy,' Uncle Thomas called. 'Let's get under shelter before we catch pneumonia.'

'Have you got time to take us to the park?' James asked eagerly, when they had climbed back into the van.

'Oh, I should think so,' his uncle said, with a grin.

'Excellent,' James said.

The rain had stopped by now, although it was still blowing a gale and great clouds scudded across the sky. There was no sign that the weather was going to improve that day. The grey sky seemed to match Mandy's mood. She had enjoyed the trip to Hoopers Point, but she just couldn't stop worrying about Nordica and her calf.

'Have you ever been to a rare breeds park before?' Uncle Thomas asked Mandy and James when they were on their way.

They both shook their heads.

'All the animals are rare farm breeds that were threatened with extinction before the Rare Breeds Trust was set up,' Uncle Thomas explained.

'Why were they threatened?' Mandy asked.

'Oh, various reasons,' Uncle Thomas told her. 'Changes in farming methods for instance. The invention of machinery to do a lot of the work.'

Mandy leaned forward. 'You mean because people started using tractors instead of horses to plough the fields?'

'Exactly,' Uncle Thomas said. 'Several breeds of shire horse died out because of that. Then there's pigs . . .'

'Oh,' Mandy said. 'I love pigs.'

'I don't,' Jenny said. 'I'm scared of them. They're so big and I've heard they bite you if you're not careful.'

'They won't hurt you,' Mandy assured her. 'You just have to keep calm and quiet and not frighten them.'

'Frighten *them*!' Jenny exclaimed. 'They frighten *me*.'

Her father carried on telling them about the rare breeds of pig kept at the park.

'They've got some Gloucester Old Spots,' he continued. 'They used to live off windfall apples in the farmers' orchards and hardly needed any other kind of food.'

'And now farmers don't let pigs live in orchards,' James piped up.

'Exactly right,' Thomas said. 'Pigs are mostly bred in intensive units . . . so nobody wanted the Old Spot any more.'

'Poor things,' Mandy murmured.

'Ah,' Thomas said, as they turned into the narrow road that led to the park, 'but you'll see some very pampered ones today.'

They soon came to a cattle grid, then a notice announcing they had arrived. There was a white board with LLYN BRENIG RARE BREEDS PARK painted on it in red letters. Underneath it said RARE BREEDS SURVIVAL TRUST and there was a logo of a cow with enormously long horns.

'I'm going to have a chat to the manager,' Jenny's dad said when they had bought their tickets and gone through the turnstile. 'Why don't you three wander round on your own? There's a woodland farm walk you can go on when you've seen the animals in the pens.'

'The manager's a friend of Dad's,' Jenny explained as her father disappeared in the direction of the door marked 'Office'.

They turned their attention to the row of stables on the other side of the spotlessly clean yard. Mandy had visited lots of farms but this was the smartest one she had ever seen.

The first animals they found were the pigs. Middle White, Large Blacks, and the Gloucester Old Spots Uncle Thomas had told them about.

Jenny hung back.

'Come on,' Mandy insisted. 'They won't hurt you, honestly.'

Jenny followed reluctantly. A park assistant was cleaning out one of the sties. She came across to talk to them when she saw them peering over the wall at the Gloucester Old Spots. There was a huge white sow with two spots on her back snuffling around in the straw.

The assistant grinned at them and leaned on her fork. 'What do you think of her, then?'

'She's great,' Mandy said. She leaned over and scratched the pig's back. 'Feel her skin, Jenny, it's really tough – and her hairs are like bristles!'

Jenny put out a wary hand and tentatively stroked the pig's back. It gave a grunt of pleasure. Jenny laughed. 'She likes it,' she said, sounding more confident.

'Pigs always love having their backs scratched,' James told her. 'It's their favourite thing.'

Jenny laughed again and scratched the pig's back this time. The pig grunted even louder.

Then, to their delight, a dozen or so piglets suddenly scampered out from the house. They snuffled and squeaked round their mother, copying her as she rooted around.

In the sty on the other side of the yard was a red Tamworth pig. The notice on the gate said that Tamworth pigs were very like the wild boar from which all native pigs were derived. The Tamworth was a rusty red colour and had a long snout and pricked up ears. Jenny wandered off to look at her while Mandy and James stayed to watched the Gloucester Old Spot feeding her piglets.

The assistant, who had told them her name was

Sue, had finished cleaning out the sty. 'I'm just going to feed the goats,' she said. 'Want to come and watch?'

'Yes, please.' Jenny had obviously had enough of the pigs. 'Come on, you two.' She skipped on ahead.

By the time Mandy and James caught up with her, she had already offered to help feed the goats.

'Aren't they great?' Jenny's eyes were shining as she held a bucket to the mouth of a greedy honey-gold goat with long hair. 'I'm not at all scared of them. This is a Gold Guernsey.' She had already read the notice on the door. 'Her name's Hetty.'

'Right,' Sue said, when all the goats were fed. 'The Exmoor pony next. Come on you three.' She went into the feed store and came out carrying a bucket brimming with pony nuts. 'Actually,' she said, 'we've got an orphan calf in the barn. Would you like to go and see her first?'

'Yes, *please*.' Mandy said eagerly.

A nearby stable was empty although there were names above the doors.

'The Exmoor's stable is round the back,' Sue said. 'She's got a sore foot at the moment so we're keeping her in.'

'Is she the only pony you've got?' James asked as they made their way towards the barn.

Sue shook her head. 'We've got two Suffolk punches as well. They're a lot bigger, of course. They're out in the paddock at the moment. You'll see them if you go on the farm walk. Did you know there are fewer Exmoor ponies in the world than there are giant pandas?'

'Wow!' Mandy said. 'I didn't know that.'

'The Rare Breeds Survival Trust has started a programme of breeding, so their numbers are increasing,' Sue said as they reached the barn door.

She put down the bucket of pony nuts and took them inside. Housed in one of the stalls was a huge white cow with long, graceful horns that curved at the end. Her name was on the stall: 'Storm'.

They stood, wide-eyed, watching warily.

'Crikey,' James said. 'She looks fierce.'

Sue grinned. 'She is a bit difficult to handle. We've been trying to get her to accept the orphan calf . . .' She opened the door of the stall next door.

Mandy drew in her breath. Standing fetlock-deep in bright yellow straw was a beautiful calf. It was pure white with a fluffy coat and jet black ears and nose. Behind her, James and Jenny stood dumbstruck.

'What breed are they?' Mandy breathed. They were the most beautiful cattle she had ever seen.

'They're called White Park,' Sue explained. 'They used to roam in the parks of some of the great stately homes . . . that's how they got their name. They were never really handled by people and they're really quite wild.'

'I wouldn't want to get near those horns.' Jenny took a step backwards.

'Storm's OK if you speak to her gently and don't make any sudden movements,' Sue told them. 'They do spook very easily.' She went in with the calf and put her arms round its neck. 'Let's see if Storm has decided to let you feed today,' she said.

'Why can't you just feed her with a bottle?' Jenny enquired.

Sue pulled a wry face. 'She won't take to one . . . we've tried everything. She was just born awkward, I reckon.'

They stood back as Sue gently persuaded the calf to go in with Storm. Mandy held her breath as the cow's great horns swung round and she gave a low moo.

'What happened to the calf's mother? And to Storm's calf?' she asked Sue. She couldn't help thinking of another calf who was without a mother. Nordica's calf . . . swimming hungry and confused way out to sea. There wouldn't be anyone out there to try to save it from starving to death. And, anyway, you couldn't bottle-feed a whale!

The cow was pawing at the straw and mooing. She obviously wasn't keen on accepting the orphan.

'They both died,' Sue explained. 'Cows are usually good at adopting other calves . . .' She tried to heave the calf closer to the cow. 'But not this one.' She sighed. 'They're a good pair, I reckon.'

'Let me help,' Mandy said suddenly. She ran out, picked up the bucket of pony nuts and brought it inside.

'Careful,' Jenny warned.

'I'll be OK,' Mandy assured her. 'She just needs something to divert her attention.' She sidled carefully round the back of the cow and rattled the bucket softly. 'Here, Storm . . . what's this?' The cow's great head swung round. Dodging the horns Mandy shoved the bucket under her nose. 'Look,' she said. 'Dinner.'

'Hey . . .' Sue began. 'They're for the . . .' But she stopped when she saw the cow gobbling up the nuts. In fact Storm liked them so much she hardly noticed the calf beginning to suckle.

'Well . . .' Sue stood back grinning as Mandy tipped the remaining pony nuts into the trough and dodged back out. 'Who'd have thought it!'

'Some cows love pony nuts,' Mandy said. 'I went to a farm once with my dad, and there was a Jersey cow there that wouldn't eat anything else.'

'Thanks, Mandy, you've made my day,' Sue said.

'You've made the calf's day too by the look of it,' Jenny laughed.

Mandy laughed but inside she wished it could be as easy to help the young whale.

Feeling suddenly downhearted again, she turned and went outside. She looked up at the black clouds and felt the rush of cool air on her face. *Please calm down*, she said to the wind and the distant sea. *We need to rescue Nordica really soon!*

Eight

By the time they had finished the farm walk, Mandy, James and Jenny were all hungry, and ready to pay a visit to the park cafe. Mandy had already spotted a sign that said FRESHLY BAKED DOUGHNUTS and her mouth watered at the thought.

Jenny's dad was waiting for them outside the office. He was talking to someone they recognised: Gillian Orpin, the vet. She had come to look at a Soay ram with an infected foot. Soay sheep were a small breed of horned sheep originating from the Outer Hebrides.

Gillian looked pleased to see them. 'I saw the

whale earlier this morning,' she told them. 'Thomas has been telling me he's hoping to organise a rescue as soon as the weather calms down.'

'Yes,' Mandy said. 'And we really hope it's soon.'

'I've got a friend with a boat,' Gillian told them. 'Let me know when you've got things organised. I'll ask him to come along.'

'Thanks,' Mandy said. 'We're going to need all the help we can get.'

'I'm starving,' James said suddenly.

His uncle grinned. 'Let's take a look in the study centre, then we'll go to the cafe and have something to eat. Will you survive that long, James?'

'I suppose so,' James said, although he didn't look too sure.

The farm was running a special exhibition about other threatened animals. As luck would have it, part of the display was about whales.

'This is the time we see migrating whales all down the coast,' Uncle Thomas explained. 'So the manager thought it would be a good time to include them in an exhibition. Lots of school parties come here to research their nature projects.'

'See this.' James had picked up an information

sheet. 'Whales can only go short distances at speed, then they get out of breath.'

'That's what made them so easy to catch,' Uncle Thomas said. 'And that's why they were hunted almost to extinction.'

Mandy was looking at a series of photos of whaling ships. She shivered at the thought of the huge creatures being hunted so mercilessly.

'Why did they hunt them so much?' Jenny asked her dad. She was staring at a picture of a whaling ship too. The enormous carcass of a sperm whale was being winched aboard.

'Lots of reasons,' her father told her. 'Meat, blubber to make oil, the bones to boil for glue . . . hardly anything on a whale carcass was wasted.'

'Poor things,' Mandy murmured. 'Well, at least they're protected now.'

'Yes,' Uncle Thomas said. 'And their numbers are increasing, thank goodness. Although some countries still hunt them.'

James was still reading his information sheet. ' "Minke whales belong to the family of whales called rorquals," ' he quoted. ' "They were too swift for the whalers until the explosive harpoon was invented." '

Mandy shuddered. 'How horrible.'

'Come on,' Uncle Thomas said when they had finished looking at the exhibits. 'Let's get something to eat.'

After three fresh donuts and a drink each, they set off for home.

Mandy sat thoughtfully in the back of the van. Uncle Thomas had been telling people they were planning to help the stranded whale but they hadn't really done anything about it yet. Making lists and diagrams was fine, but supposing the weather calmed down all of a sudden? They hadn't phoned anyone and no one would know what they were planning or how much help they needed.

She leaned forward. 'Don't you think we should start ringing people?' she said to Jenny's dad. 'If they're going to get their boats ready to come and help us they'll need a bit of notice.'

'I know,' Uncle Thomas said. 'But really, Mandy, it's still too rough. we don't want people turning up and having to go home again. It will just be wasting their time.'

'Yes,' Mandy sat back with a sigh. 'I suppose so.'

As they drove down the road towards Abersyn,

Mandy could see the white-capped waves heaving around in the harbour. There was no sign of Nordica and it seemed that even she had taken refuge beneath the surface.

'I can't see her,' James said, craning his neck. 'Maybe she's got out by herself?'

But soon after he said that Nordica's dark head appeared. Mandy sighed again. How much longer could Nordica's baby survive without her?

They stopped off at the harbour. In spite of the bad weather there was a fresh crowd of sightseers along the quay. There was a television camera crew among them.

Then Mandy spotted the fishermen, Bryan and Will Jackson, walking on the other side of the road. They crossed over and headed towards her. They were carrying a wooden box between them. On the side it said EXPLOSIVES – HANDLE WITH CARE.

Her heart lurched. She whirled round to tell James and Jenny but they were further along, talking to some of the sightseers. The Jacksons had rounded the corner and were making their way along the quayside to where their fishing smack was moored. Their boat was called *Sea Jewel* and was painted black and white with their registered number on the side of the wheelhouse.

Mandy frowned. What on earth was in that box they were carrying? Surely it couldn't be dynamite? It would be far too dangerous to cart that through a crowd of people. But what else could it be? And more to the point, what were they going to do with it?

As Mandy took a step forward she bumped into one of the television crew.

'Sorry,' Mandy said hastily.

'That's OK,' the man said. 'What's the rush, young lady?'

Mandy didn't think she could spend time explaining. 'Oh . . . nothing,' she said.

'Have you seen the whale?' the man enquired.

'Yes, isn't she gorgeous?' Mandy said.

The television man grinned. 'Well, I don't know about gorgeous exactly, but she certainly is a magnificent creature.' He gazed down at her. He was very tall and fair-haired, and reminded Mandy of Simon.

'Are you making a film about her?' Mandy asked.

'We're from the news team,' the man explained. 'The story's creating quite a stir.'

By now, James and Jenny had arrived. 'My dad's the coast warden,' Jenny told him. 'He's planning a rescue attempt as soon as it gets a bit calmer.'

'And we're going to help,' James said. 'If you've got a boat you could come.'

'A boat?' the man laughed. 'Not likely. But it will make a good story.' He looked around. 'Is your dad here, young lady? I'd like to have a word with him.'

'He's over there.' Jenny pointed to where her dad was talking to someone.

Mandy looked thoughtful. 'Is the story really getting a lot of interest?' she asked.

'It sure is,' the TV man confirmed.

'So lots of people will be watching it on the news?'

The man nodded. 'You bet.'

'You know,' Mandy said, still looking thoughtful, 'we'll need lots of people to help with the rescue.'

'Yes,' James said. 'As many as possible.' He went on to tell the man exactly what they planned to do.

'And,' Mandy interrupted when James drew a breath, 'maybe you could mention it on the news?

Tell people we need help and ask them to contact Thomas Hunter . . .'

'Our phone number is—' Jenny began.

The man held up his hand and laughed. 'OK, OK, you're getting a bit carried away.'

'No, we're not,' Mandy said indignantly. 'It's very important. Please . . . could you?'

The man looked thoughtful. 'OK,' he said after a long pause. 'Hang on here, you three. Don't move, OK?'

He came back with his camera and a young woman with a clipboard. 'My name's Mark,' he said. 'And this is Julie, my producer. She thinks it's a good idea.'

'Great!' Mandy said. 'Thanks very much.'

'But it would be better if you explained things yourselves,' Julie said.

Mark set his camera up in front of them.

Jenny backed away. 'I'm not going on TV,' she said quickly. 'I wouldn't know what to say.'

'Neither would I,' James said. He turned to Mandy 'You do it, Mandy. You're good at that kind of thing.'

Mandy was getting cold feet. 'Don't you think we should ask Uncle Thomas first?' Talking in front of a television camera was a bit daunting to say the least.

'Ask me what?' Uncle Thomas had spotted what was going on and had come up behind them.

Mark and Julie explained. '. . . And an appeal from someone like Mandy would go down well,' Mark ended.

'That's a great idea,' Uncle Thomas said. 'And I've just been talking to the coastguard. The weather forecast is much better and with a bit of luck we might be able to attempt a rescue some time tomorrow.'

'Tomorrow!' Mandy threw her arms round Uncle Thomas and hugged him. 'That's brilliant!'

'We need an appeal right away,' Uncle Thomas said with a grin. 'So you'd better go ahead, Mandy.'

Mark had his hand poised on the button of his camera and the sound engineer was hovering round with a huge microphone covered in a kind of furry material.

James gave Mandy a little shove. 'Go *on*, Mandy!' he said impatiently. 'Before they get fed up with waiting.'

So Mandy took a deep breath, swallowed, and made her appeal. She remembered what she had learned about the millions of whales that had been hunted and killed and reminded the viewers how precious threatened wildlife is.

'The Minke whale and her family are visitors to our shores,' she said. She smiled into the camera, suddenly finding courage she didn't know she had. 'We should do everything we can to keep them safe. So if you can help with the rescue, please ring the coast warden.' She went on to give Uncle Thomas's phone number.

A little crowd had gathered round and when she had finished they all clapped. Mandy stepped back, red in the face.

Jenny gave her a hug and James gave her a huge pat on the back. 'That was brilliant, Mandy,' they both said at once.

The camera panned round to the water just as Nordica sent up a great jet of spray into the air. Everyone laughed and clapped again. *They* might have thought it was funny but Mandy felt it was Nordica's way of saying thanks.

Mandy's legs felt like jelly. Being in front of a television camera had been even more scary than she had imagined. She sat down suddenly on one of the wooden boxes piled up along the quay. Wait until she told Mum and Dad about this!

When they got back to the cottage, Uncle Thomas said he would start ringing some of the people on their list that evening.

They had just finished tea when the phone rang.

'It's your mum, Mandy,' Auntie Gwyn said. 'She sounds really excited about something.'

Mandy frowned. What on earth had happened?

'Mandy!' Mrs Hope sounded out of breath. 'We've just seen you on TV! Me, Gran and Grandad and your dad. We were all watching the news after tea and suddenly there you were! You're a star, Mandy!'

Mandy felt shocked. She had no idea Mark and Julie had come from *national* television. She'd imagined the programme would only be seen in Wales.

The phone was busy all evening. Gran and Grandad called to congratulate Mandy. Then James's mum and dad. Then, between their phone calls to people on Uncle Thomas's list, offers of help came flooding in. What time should people come? What should they bring? When would the coast warden know definitely if the rescue could go ahead or not? They took everyone's phone number and promised to ring as soon as they knew.

Mandy's heart was singing as she and Jenny climbed the stairs to bed. All those offers of help . . . all those people anxious for Nordica to be saved. She had a great feeling everything was going to be OK after all.

Before they got into their pyjamas they looked out of the window. The moon was full and bright. Its beams turned the sea to silver. The whale was swimming slowly round and round in the harbour. Further out the rest of Nordica's family was nowhere to be seen.

Mandy's happy mood suddenly seemed to evaporate. 'Supposing they've gone,' she wailed to Jenny. 'Then what will happen to the calf?'

Jenny looked glum. 'I don't know. We'll just have to keep our fingers crossed, Mandy.'

Mandy found it hard to get to sleep. Muffin was curled up at the end of the bed and Jenny had dozed off hours ago. She heard the church clock strike eleven, then twelve, then one o'clock. The wind roared round the eaves of the house. Down the street, the cafe sign squeaked to and fro and the ringing sound of the fishing boat masts clanked and tinkled across the harbour. Mandy turned over with a sigh. It was no good, the weather forecast was wrong. It wasn't calming down at all.

And then she remembered something. The Jacksons and that box they had been carrying. In the excitement of the television appearance and the phone calls she had forgotten all about them. Supposing they had already been out to sea and scared off the other whales?

Nine

Next morning, Jenny's father got up early and went out to check on the state of the sea.

When he came back indoors for breakfast his face looked glum. 'I've been to the coastguard station,' he told them. 'The weather forecast wasn't very accurate and, worse still, we've got the highest spring tide for years.'

'What does that mean?' Mandy asked anxiously. She had already seen that the sea was still rough.

'I'm afraid it means that your whale is in great danger of being washed ashore. If that happens . . .' He broke off when he saw her horrified face. 'I'm sorry . . . but it could well be the end of her.'

Mandy's hand flew to her mouth. 'But I've seen whales being rescued from the beach on the news.' She had been helping Jenny's mum lay the breakfast table but now she stopped, frozen with horror at the thought. 'They keep them alive until the tide comes up again and they're able to swim away.'

'I remember that too,' James came in from the kitchen with a plate of warm toast. 'There was a whole school of them stranded on the sand.'

'They were pilot whales,' Uncle Thomas told them. 'They're not really whales at all, more large dolphins.'

'Oh,' James said. 'But they did get rescued.'

'Yes.' Uncle Thomas sat down and helped himself to a piece of toast. 'But they only grow to about six metres in length . . . much smaller than Nordica. If she got beached, her massive bulk couldn't support her internal organs out of water.' He glanced at Mandy and Jenny. 'I'm sorry . . .'

It was all Mandy could do to stop herself bursting into tears. The thought of Nordica dying on the beach was almost too much to bear.

'Then it could be the end of her calf too,' she

said, staring mournfully out of the window.

Uncle Thomas shrugged. 'It might survive . . . it really depends upon how old it is. I'm afraid we'll probably never know.'

Mandy felt like crying. She didn't think she could bear it if Nordica came to such a terrible end.

'Try to look on the bright side,' James said to her. He turned to his uncle. 'If she doesn't get washed up, Uncle Thomas, is it likely we'll be able to rescue her today?'

Thomas shook his head. 'I'm really not sure, James. We'll just have to wait and see.'

Along the harbour road, the quay was empty. The fishing fleet had braved the weather and had sailed out to the deep Atlantic waters beyond the horizon. Mandy had spotted them earlier when she first woke up. The bright colours of their paintwork were lost in a haze of spray as they ploughed through the waves, their hulls rising and falling alarmingly.

Down on the beach, huge waves were breaking on the shore, flinging up a fountain of white spray. The surf was riding so high it raced up the sand almost to the sea wall. Nordica was swimming dangerously close to the shallow water. Once or twice she was buffeted so hard she was almost rolled right over.

Mandy hated the thought of breaking her promise . . . but at the moment there seemed absolutely nothing more she could do.

'Well at least the story's in the paper this morning.' Auntie Gwyn came in with the *Abersyn Herald* in her hand.

Jenny took it from her. Nordica's story was on the front page. Kim had obviously heard about the rescue attempt and had added an appeal for help at the bottom.

'That's great,' Mandy said. 'But it won't do any good if Nordica gets washed up on the beach before we can rescue her.'

James sighed. 'That's true.'

Mandy, James and Jenny helped clear the breakfast things, then decided they would go down to the shore. There were spots of rain in the wind and the people who had come to watch Nordica were sitting huddled in their cars. One or two had small boats on trailers but they were left firmly in place.

Halfway down the road they met Ivor.

'Why haven't you gone out fishing?' Jenny asked.

'I'm going to collect Mickey from the vet,' he explained. 'He's doing really well, and they said I can fetch him home.' He gazed at Mandy. 'I saw you on TV last night, Mandy. You're a star.'

Mandy blushed. 'Thanks. I was really nervous.'

Jenny told him about Nordica and the dangers of the high tide.

'I know,' Ivor said. 'I was afraid something like that might happen.'

They said goodbye and headed for the beach. The air was tangy with salt spray. Nordica was swimming only a few hundred metres out.

They walked along the sand, jumping back now and then to avoid the surf.

Suddenly, James stopped and pointed, his eyes wide with concern. 'Hey, look, she's being washed in!'

Horrified, they stood watching. They felt helpless as the waves brought Nordica closer and closer to the shore.

Mandy clutched Jenny's sleeve. 'She needs us to help her,' she said. 'Look at her eyes.'

Jenny was shaking her head. 'She's getting weaker. Look, she can hardly control her movements.'

It was true, the whale seemed to be rolling to one side as she fought against the waves. Nordica was having a battle with the sea. And the sea was winning.

Suddenly Mandy couldn't bear to just stand there and do nothing. She began to jump up and down and shout and wave her arms in the air. 'Go back!' she yelled. 'Go back, Nordica!'

The others joined in. Muffin too, barking louder than ever and scampering bravely up and down the edge of the waves. James ran across to the rocks and grabbed two huge pebbles. He flung them into the water. The others followed suit, yelling and running and throwing. Mandy hated frightening Nordica but she knew it was the only thing to do. The whale didn't understand the dangers of being washed up on the sand.

Then, at last, Nordica's fight with the sea turned into a victory. With a powerful flip of her tail she managed to turn and plough her way back out towards deeper water.

'Thank goodness!' James panted. He bent over with his hands on his knees to get his breath back.

They sat on the sea wall until Nordica disappeared

under the waves. They were all shivering with cold. Their trainers and the legs of their jeans were covered in soggy sand. But it had been worth it. Nordica was away from the shallows and safe for the time being.

'That's exactly the kind of noise we've got to make when we go out in the boat,' James said. 'I *know* it'll work.'

'I hope you're right,' Jenny said.

Suddenly, Mandy felt warmth on her face. She looked up to see that the clouds had cleared and blue sky was peeping out. She realised the wind had died down. She got to her feet. 'Come on, you three, let's get back.'

As they ran back along the beach Mandy suddenly felt her heart soar with hope. The weather *was* clearing up. They would be able to rescue Nordica later that day after all!

Indoors, Jenny's dad was on the phone. As they took off their wet, sand-clogged trainers in the hallway, Mandy could hear him talking.

'Yes,' he said. 'Halfpast six. It should calm down as the tide goes out. Thanks very much.'

Mandy put her head round the door. She couldn't

help her pulse racing with excitement. 'Will it really be all right by then?'

Uncle Thomas turned with a grin. 'Yes, I'm pretty sure it will. Six-thirty. Low tide and the sea should be calm. Then it'll be all systems go!'

'What can we do to help?' she asked, her stomach turning over with anticipation.

'Well,' Uncle Thomas said, 'there's a lot of people I haven't been able to contact. Lots of those people who phoned last night and left their numbers are out at work.'

'Oh dear,' Mandy said. James and Jenny had come in to listen too.

'But I've left several messages on answerphones,' Uncle Thomas told them. He glanced at his watch. 'I've got to go and have a word with the coastguard now. Maybe you three could phone a few more people and see if you have any luck.'

'Of course we will, Dad.' Jenny picked up the list of names. A dozen or so were already crossed off.

After they had all changed out of their wet jeans, they took turns in phoning.

One or two people were at home and promised

to come. Others were out so they left messages where they could.

When they got to the end of the list James sat back with a sigh. 'We'll just have to hope that they get the messages in time,' he said. 'Come on, let's go down to the harbour and see if anyone has turned up there yet.'

They put on their coats and made their way along to the harbour.

Ivor was there already, talking to a man with a small dinghy on a trailer. He had collected Mickey from the vet's and taken him home.

'Is Mickey OK?' Mandy asked, when Ivor came across to speak to them.

'He's fine,' Ivor said. 'Glad to be home, I think.'

'That's good,' Jenny said. 'We'll go and see him when we've got time.'

They told Ivor about the rescue.

His eyes lit up. 'Six-thirty! That's great,' he said. 'Hey, you three, would you like to come with me in *Seaspray*? I've already told your dad I'll help, Jenny.'

'That would be excellent,' James said. 'Thanks, Ivor.'

'You'd better make sure it's OK with your mum and dad,' Ivor said to Jenny.

'Dad will be down here soon,' Jenny told him. 'We'll ask him then.'

They went to tell the people with boats that Thomas would be along later to give instructions.

Mandy felt a heartbeat of excitement as she saw that several people had come armed with saucepans and spoons. One had a trumpet in the back of the car, another an old-fashioned brass car horn with a rubber bulb at the end. Mandy guessed it would make a loud honking noise and would be just the thing to help guide Nordica out to sea.

After that they wandered along the quay. James and Jenny had walked on ahead with Ivor, when Mandy suddenly spotted the Jacksons, stacking and sorting their boxes of fish in one of the sheds. She craned her neck upwards to look at the deck of their boat, *Sea Jewel*. She could just see the box they had been carrying stowed on deck near a great coil of ropes and fishing nets. She looked up and down. No one seemed to be looking her way. Her heart suddenly beat very loudly in her chest. Maybe she could just take a look at what was in the box . . . just

in case it *had* been explosives she'd seen.

She was halfway up the gangplank when she heard a voice behind her.

'Can I help you, young lady?'

She turned swiftly. Bryan Jackson was standing at the bottom, staring up at her with a frown on his face. She knew they realised she had overheard their conversation in the cafe. What on earth was she going to say?

Then, to make matters worse, Bryan's son, Will, noticed what was going on and came and stood beside his father, staring up at her.

Mandy hoped she didn't look too guilty. She decided there were times when you couldn't avoid telling a white lie. And this was one of them. She came running back down the gangplank. 'I'm sorry,' she said. 'We're telling people about the whale rescue and I wondered if you'd be willing to help.'

She bit her lip. These men didn't even like whales. It was hardly likely they'd want to help rescue one.

'We might,' Bryan said. 'We're not sure yet.'

'Oh . . . well,' Mandy said. 'If you can help we're going out at half past six this evening,' Mandy said.

'Right,' Will said.

She stood back as they mounted the gangplank. When they got to the top, Bryan bent and picked up the mystery box and took it into the wheelhouse.

Mandy felt annoyed. She had lost the only chance she might get to find out what was inside.

Will untied the mooring ropes and climbed aboard, *Sea Jewel's* engine gunned as he coiled them on deck. Then the boat chugged backwards away from the harbour wall, turned and carved its way through the waves and out to sea. Mandy frowned. Surely they weren't going out fishing again? They usually only went out once a day. Maybe they were going to try to scare off the other two whales.

She turned away sadly. If that's what they were up to there was really nothing she could do about it. She hated feeling so helpless.

Later, Uncle Thomas turned up with a message from Gillian Orpin, the vet from Rhydfellin.

'She's coming with a friend's boat,' he told them. 'So she said she'll see you later.'

'That's great,' James said.

'Yes,' his uncle replied. 'And we'll just have to keep our fingers crossed that lots of other people do the same.'

Mandy thought she had spent the last two days keeping her fingers crossed. But Uncle Thomas was right. That was really all they could do.

Ten

Mandy was deep in thought as they made their way along to the cafe to see Mickey. If the messages didn't get through to the volunteers in time, they could be left with only a few small boats to try to herd Nordica out. It just wouldn't be enough. In fact it might be dangerous: the whale might get confused and head the wrong way. There *had* to be a way of making sure people knew about the rescue before half past six.

They reached the cafe, tied Muffin up outside, and went in. Mrs Evans was pleased to see them.

'Have you come to see Mickey?' she asked from

behind the counter. 'Go through, he's in his basket.'

In Mrs Evans's sitting room the radio was on. A man was giving a traffic report. Mickey was lying in his basket. He had a bald patch and a scar where the operation had taken place, but apart from that he looked fine. He purred softly as they all bent to stroke him.

The word 'Abersyn' on the radio made Mandy suddenly prick up her ears. The traffic report was focused on that area. Something about roadworks and traffic delays on the road between one of the big towns and the village. It must be local radio.

Local radio! She suddenly had an idea. If they could broadcast the news on the radio that the whale rescue was to take place at six-thirty, people might hear it in their cars on the way home from work.

'Hey,' she said to James and Jenny. 'I've just had a brilliant idea!' She explained quickly.

'I'll ask Mrs Evans if we can use her phone,' Jenny said, dashing out.

James had spotted a phone directory and was busy looking up the number.

Jenny was back within seconds. 'She said it's fine.'

James quickly found the number. 'You do it, Mandy,' he said.

Mandy was put through to the news desk. The news editor listened carefully.

'Right,' he said, when Mandy had explained. 'We broadcast news on the hour, every hour, so that's three times we can give out the appeal before six-thirty.'

'Oh, thank you so much,' Mandy said.

'And we'll send someone down to report the story,' the news editor told her.

'That's great,' Mandy said. 'Thanks again.' Her eyes were shining as she put down the phone. 'Well,' she said. 'That's it. Now all we can do is wait.'

'Nordica is really going to be famous,' Jenny said. 'TV, newspaper and now local radio!'

James chuckled. 'She's going to be the most famous whale in Wales.'

They said goodbye to Mrs Evans and Mickey and went back to the harbour. Several people were standing at the railings with binoculars. They weren't looking at Nordica but had their field glasses trained on something further out to sea.

Mandy, James and Jenny stopped to stare out across the water.

'Here,' a woman said, handing her binoculars to Mandy. 'Take a look.'

Mandy adjusted the binoculars then drew in her breath. 'Wow!'

'What is it?' James said, fidgeting impatiently beside her.

'A school of whales,' the woman told him. 'There must be about fifty of them.'

Mandy was still staring through the glasses. The woman was right. There must be fifty at least. She could see their great backs rising and falling with the ocean swell. Now and then jets of steamy gas rose into the air and fell like misty rain back to the surface.

Mandy scanned the whole length of the school, anxiously searching for a smaller whale . . . Nordica's calf. There was no sign of it. She suddenly felt scared. Supposing it had died? Supposing the wait to try to rescue Nordica had been *too* long for the young creature and it had perished? She could hardly bear to think about it.

'Look, James.' She handed the glasses to him.

There was one thing she was relieved about, however. If the Jacksons *had* gone out to scare away the whales then they certainly hadn't succeeded.

'Can you see Nordica's calf?' Jenny asked impatiently, dying to have a look herself.

James shook his head. 'No, 'fraid not.'

'Nordica's the one in the harbour,' Mandy explained, when the woman looked puzzled.

'Oh,' the woman said. 'I've brought my dinghy to help with the rescue.' She looked around. 'I hope a few more people than this turn up.'

'Yes,' Mandy replied. 'So do we.'

'She's got a calf, has she?' the woman asked.

Mandy nodded. 'We're really worried about it.'

'The others will have been looking after it, don't worry,' the woman said.

'Yes, but they won't feed it, will they?' Mandy said sadly.

The woman shook her head. 'I don't know about that. We'll just have to wait and see, won't we?'

'And we haven't got very long to wait now,' Jenny reminded her.

Mandy knew she was trying to cheer her up. But if Nordica's calf was dead it would spoil the whole thing.

They left the woman with the binoculars and went to find Ivor.

He was on *Seaspray* checking the engine. 'The TV people want to come out with us,' he told them, as they went on board. 'They're coming back at six o'clock.'

They told him about the local radio station and its promise to put out an appeal.

'That's great,' he said. 'I hope it works.'

Mandy sat down on a box and put her chin in her hands. 'If not enough boats turn up,' she said, 'then there won't be anything for the TV people to film.'

Ivor must have seen how downhearted she was. He patted her shoulder. 'It'll be OK, don't you worry.'

They went down to the shop to tell Jenny's mum about the rescue.

'Get yourselves an early tea,' she told them. 'It doesn't do you any good to go sailing on an empty stomach.'

They ran home, made a few hasty sandwiches and took them down to eat on the beach. They'd also raided the kitchen cupboards for saucepans, and spoons, and metal bowls . . . anything they could bang to make a noise with.

'My rattle!' Jenny had exclaimed suddenly. 'I almost forgot.' She rushed upstairs and came down with a wooden football rattle. She wound it round and round in the air.

Mandy and James covered their ears.

'If that doesn't scare Nordica,' James said, 'nothing will.'

On the beach they sat in the shelter of the wall and ate their peanut butter sandwiches and crisps.

They counted the boats. Three or four were already on the slipway ready to launch, although their owners just seemed to be hanging around, not quite knowing what to do.

'Dad'll be there to get things organised, don't worry,' Jenny said.

Mandy looked at her watch. Five-thirty. Her stomach turned over with excitement. 'Come on,' she said, getting to her feet. 'Let's get down to the harbour and see what's going on.'

When they got there, Ivor was talking to Bryan Jackson. The two men parted, and Bryan went aboard *Sea Jewel* and disappeared inside the wheelhouse.

Ivor came to greet them.

Mandy said close to his ear, 'What did he say?'

'What did who say?' Ivor looked puzzled.

'Mr Jackson.'

'We were just talking about the rescue. He volunteered to help,' he told her.

'Oh.' Mandy said. 'But I thought they hated the whales.'

Ivor grinned. 'They don't hate them,' he said. 'They just thought they were a nuisance. They've got some distress flares to let off in case the other noises don't do the trick.'

Distress flares. They were like rockets . . . explosives . . .

'Oh dear . . .' Mandy suddenly felt guilty. She had been jumping to the most terrible conclusions. Thank goodness she hadn't done any more snooping around their boat.

'Time to get on board,' Ivor glanced at his watch.

Muffin ran up the gangplank first. Jenny suddenly gasped and put her hand over her mouth. 'Muffin – I should have left him at home. Mum'll go mad if he smells of fish again.'

'Never mind,' Mandy said. 'You'll just have to bathe him as soon as we get back.'

They settled themselves on deck. Muffin sat with Mandy. She stroked his rough fur. Her touch seemed to calm him down and he sat quietly beside her, tongue hanging out, watching the activity down below. James was in the bow, unpacking the bag of pots and pans and laying them out ready.

'Well, Muffin,' Mandy said, giving him a hug, 'it's now or never.' She still felt worried. Half a dozen or so small boats were waiting to be launched from the slipway. Some were already in the water. There still didn't seem to be enough.

She suddenly realised someone was calling from the quay, and when she looked, the television crew were there. Ivor beckoned them aboard.

Then there was a shout from Jenny. She was standing on the other side, watching for the whales through Ivor's binoculars. 'Hey, you two . . . come and look!'

And when Mandy and James ran to her side they saw a sight Mandy knew she would never forget. A whole flotilla of boats was sailing round the headland. Large ones, small ones, some with sails, some with outboard engines . . . several pleasure cruisers gleaming white in the sun, their sharp hulls cutting through the waves like knives.

More cars with trailers had turned up along the harbour road. Some were unloading, others waiting patiently to launch their boats from the slipway. There were too many even to count.

Ten minutes later, the coastguard launch appeared, with Uncle Thomas standing in the cockpit, a loudhailer in his hand.

'Right.' Ivor shouted down to a man on the quayside to untie the ropes. 'Time to go, you three,' he shouted. 'Get ready.'

Seaspray's engine gunned and at last they were on their way.

In the bow, Mandy jumped up and down with excitement. She simply couldn't help it.

The coastguard vessel had gone from boat to boat, with Uncle Thomas shouting instructions as they went. Everyone took their craft in as close to the beach as they dared, forming a semicircle from the breakwater to the rocks – a barrier between Nordica and the shore. She *could* dive underneath the boats, but hopefully she would be too scared to come that close.

James and Jenny were standing in *Seaspray*'s bow. Jenny had Muffin in her arms. He was watching the waves with his head on one side, his ears cocked.

He suddenly began barking, just as James yelled: 'Mandy . . . here she is!'

Mandy rushed to the side. Nordica was rising up above the waves. Mandy felt James shove a saucepan and spoon into her hands. She banged it as loudly as she could, shouting and yelling at the top of her voice. That seemed to be a signal for everyone to do the same.

Mandy had never heard such a noise in all her life. Trumpets blowing, drums and saucepans banging, horns hooting, people shouting. *Poor Nordica*, she thought. *She'll be frightened out of her life*.

Nordica *was* frightened. She let out a powerful jet of steam, then dived beneath the surface. Suddenly everything went quiet. Then, to Mandy's immense relief, she appeared again, swimming not far away and heading towards the harbour entrance.

'She's going!' James yelled, as the boats slowly closed in on the whale and the noise rose to a crescendo. Closer and closer . . .

Then, to their horror, Nordica suddenly turned and dived, her huge tail hitting the water with a loud smack. Clouds of spray rose in the air and for a moment or two she couldn't be seen at all. But when the mist cleared she was there . . . swimming *towards* the flotilla of boats.

'Oh, no,' Mandy groaned. 'The other way, Nordica . . . the other way!'

Surely she wasn't going to brave the onslaught and dive underneath?

The boats closed in again, hooting, banging, booming, crashing. Mandy's heart was in her mouth. She wasn't sure it was working at all. In fact the din seemed to be confusing Nordica more than ever.

Suddenly, Muffin leaped from Jenny's arms on to the deck. Jenny flung out her hand but it was too late. Muffin had gone, leaping high over the boxes and fishing gear. He jumped up on the winch and balanced there like a circus performer, the breeze flowing through his long coat. Mandy gasped. If the ship suddenly rolled he would be tossed into the water.

Then the little dog began barking. Louder than

anyone had ever heard him bark before. Nordica looked in *Seaspray*'s direction for a second, then turned, dived, came up again and began swimming rapidly out towards the ocean.

The noise continued as the boats followed, honking and cheering until at last Nordica found the narrow inlet between the rocks. With one last farewell jet from her blowhole she joined the waiting whales.

A huge cheer rose from every boat. Everyone was jumping up and down and waving like mad. Then, for good measure, one of the Jacksons let off a couple of flares. They whizzed up into the sky with an arc of colour.

Ivor revved *Seaspray*'s engine and followed Nordica out into the deeper waters. *Sea Jewel* and a couple of the other fishing vessels were behind. They all wanted to make sure the whales had really gone.

Mandy felt tears streaming down her face. She turned to James and threw her arms round him. He wriggled, red in the face, but let her hug him just the same. Jenny ran from the other side and hugged them too.

'It was Muffin who clinched it.' Mandy wiped her face. 'He's the best dog in the world.'

Then a shout went up from the *Sea Jewel*. 'Look out, they're coming back.'

Mandy, James and Jenny turned in horror. Heading towards them were three whales. Mandy knew exactly who they were. Nordica and her mate, together with their calf. Reunited.

A strange silence seemed to settle over the waves as Nordica and the other two swam alongside *Seaspray*.

In the wheelhouse, Ivor was holding his breath. Whales *had* been known to turn boats over. And if Nordica was still in a panic after all that noise . . . ?

But Mandy knew there was no danger. Nordica and her family had come to say goodbye . . . and thank you. She leaned over the side and stretched out her arm. *Goodbye, Nordica, safe journey. I won't ever forget you.*

Nordica met her eye for a moment then, with a huge flick of her tail, turned and, with the other two following in her wake, swam back to join the others.

James was sitting down. 'Wow!' He took off his glasses, rubbed them on the knee of his jeans and put them back on again. 'Wait until we tell everyone back home about *this*!'

Mandy swallowed a great big lump that had come to her throat and couldn't say anything more at all.

'Right, everyone,' Ivor called from the wheel-house. 'Let's go home.'

When *Seaspray* was safely moored and the television crew had gone back to the studio to edit their film, Mandy, James, Jenny, Ivor and Muffin made their way down to the cafe for hot drinks and something to eat.

Mrs Evans cooked everyone a slap-up meal. Mandy and James, Jenny, Uncle Thomas and Auntie Gwyn, Gillian Orpin, and Kim from the *Herald*, who had cadged a ride in someone's boat, all sat down to eat together.

Will and Bryan Jackson turned up too. Bryan sat next to Mandy and gave her such a knowing look she really began to wonder if he could read her mind.

'Thanks for all your help,' Uncle Thomas said to Mandy, James and Jenny. 'If it wasn't for that last minute radio appeal, Nordica might still be swimming in the harbour now.'

Looking at the faces around her, Mandy knew she would never forget her holiday in Wales and all the new friends she had made. But now their adventure was over, and she felt a sudden pang of homesickness. In fact, now she thought about it, Mandy simply couldn't wait to get back to dear old Welford and tell them all about the whale in the waves!

Bantam Books is proud to present
SEASON OF VENGEANCE
by W. W. Southard

**Winner of the $25,000
Bantam Books/Twentieth Century-Fox
First Western Novel Contest**

Here is the exciting new Western author selected by the judges from approximately 1,000 manuscripts entered in this nationwide search for the previously unpublished Western writer who could carry on the great tradition of the fast-moving, authentic frontier entertainments written by such popular masters as Zane Grey, Ernest Haycox, Luke Short and Louis L'Amour.

In addition to Bantam Books publishing this winning first Western, Twentieth Century-Fox has purchased the film rights to W.W. Southard's novel.

We hope you enjoy
SEASON OF VENGEANCE.

SEASON OF
VENGEANCE

W. W. Southard

SEASON OF VENGEANCE
A Bantam Book / April 1981

ISBN 0-553-14741-2

Published simultaneously in the United States and Canada

Bantam Books are published by Bantam Books, Inc. Its trade-
mark, consisting of the words "Bantam Books" and the por-
trayal of a bantam, is Registered in U.S. Patent and Trademark
Office and in other countries. Marca Registrada. Bantam
Books, Inc., 666 Fifth Avenue, New York, New York 10103.

To my wife

Chapter
ONE

In the doorway of the little adobe house, Jessie Ramming kissed Anna long and hungrily and held her against him in a gentle, careful embrace. Then he swung into the saddle and reined his gray horse away, past the shed and the pole corral, toward the dry creek bed beyond.

He looked back once and saw her still standing there shading her hazel eyes against the early sun. Jessie had to smile. If she lived to be ninety, her face would always have the trusting innocence of a little girl.

His heart grew big in his chest. How could providence have been so generous to Jessie Ramming? First, to give him Anna; and now, after eight barren years, to give the two of them the promise of a child. It was perfect.

Too perfect. At the back of his mind, a warning sounded—a warning no louder than the dry whisper of a hidden rattlesnake. He resolved to stick closer to the house in the future, until the baby came. After today. After he had located the missing heifer.

To the west a half-day's ride across the rolling, infinite prairie, rode another man. Like Jessie he was tall and lean. But there the resemblance ended. This man rode in a slouch, his shoulders hunched high above the base of his neck, giving him the predatory look of a vulture. A tangle of black beard, streaked here and there with tobacco juice, concealed his face from his cheekbones to the grimy collar of his shirt. Below the shapeless gray hat only his eyes were visible. And they were not pleasant to look into, those eyes.

1

Beneath him, under a rundown saddle, was a raw-boned sorrel, ewe-necked and gaunt-ribbed, a horse with a treacherous temperament. They were a well-matched pair.

The sun stood squarely overhead when the bearded man caught his first sight of the two immense cotton-wood trees that marked Jessie Ramming's place. He rode for another hour before he smelled the odor of burning mesquite roots and lye soap from Anna's washing. He spurred the sorrel mare into a thicket of mesquite trees, dismounted, and withdrew a rifle from the scabbard lashed beneath a stirrup leather.

Stooping low, until his long arms almost touched the ground, he moved carefully up the ridge that concealed the house from view. Near the crest of the rise he flattened himself against the ground and continued on, crawling awkwardly on elbows and knees. High above, in the azure blue of the cloudless sky, a brace of turkey buzzards circled silently, watching.

The man waited for a long time. A single bead of sweat slid down the bony ridge of his nose, hesitated an instant, then splattered against the scarred butt of the rifle. Finally he saw her come into view.

Excitement shot through him like a fever. Smiling Jack Sluder had never killed a woman before.

He reckoned it was two hundred yards down the slope to where she was hanging out clothes behind the little house. When he squeezed the trigger, she didn't pitch backward as he expected, but jerked forward against the shock of the heavy bullet. The faded blue shirt she had been reaching to hang on the line fluttered to the dirt.

From where he lay, Sluder couldn't tell where the bullet struck, but he saw blood and flesh and bits of bone mushroom from her back. He knew, as surely as the sun was blistering the back of his neck, that she was dead.

He watched without expression as she lay on her side in the alkali soil, her knees drawn up against her belly. Her mouth was opening and closing, but he was too far away to hear the words she was saying.

Without conscious thought, his left hand crept to the

side of his head. The thin fingers played along a deep, ragged scar that began at the remnants of an ear and ran down into the tangled blackness of his beard. He turned his head and spat tobacco juice into the hard-caked earth, sending a horde of red ants into an aimless frenzy.

After a time, he backed away on his elbows and knees, cursing now and again in a ragged whisper as a knee or forearm impaled itself on a goathead thorn.

At last he rose stiffly, not bothering to dust his trousers, and walked with his stoop-shouldered gait down the slope to the sorrel. There he paused and looked for a long moment at the battered rifle in his hands. Then he shoved the weapon into the boot, mounted the restive mare, and rode westward, the way he had come. Behind him the woman still jerked occasionally in the dirt.

Jessie Ramming was whistling a song about a red-haired girl and a sailor when the shot sounded. The report came first to the ears of the gray gelding and he tossed his head, startling the heifer a few yards ahead.

The sound was the flat, angry slap of a rifle shot, not the thunder of a shotgun. Of that Jessie was certain. He drew the gelding to a halt, cocked his head to one side, and squinted his deep-set eyes.

The heifer saw her chance and lunged for the breastwork of mesquite trees lining the creek bed. Ramming didn't bother to glance after her. He was hoping that his ears were playing tricks. The only weapon he owned was his goose gun, fourteen pounds of eight-gauge thunder. The shot he had heard came from something else.

Abruptly he pulled his hat down tight and sent the gelding up the gulley at a dead run, toward the scant collection of buildings that comprised his home, a quarter-mile away.

But there was nothing to see, nothing out of the ordinary. Near the front door a wisp of steam rose from the heavy black wash pot that squatted in a bed of coals. The door itself was open, an invitation to any chance breeze on that warm autumn day.

"Anna!" he called, his deep voice unnaturally loud in the stillness of the afternoon.

3

In the corral a cow stopped licking the week-old calf at her side and lowed plaintively. It was the only answer to his call.

Quickly, and with growing urgency, he unsaddled the horse and strode toward the house. Ducking instinctively, he stepped through the doorway into the cool interior of the adobe. Only a meager shaft of light squeezed through the single tiny window and he squinted against the dimness.

"Anna?"

Fear was dammed behind the word.

He thought he heard a sound from somewhere in back. He moved through the single room that served as kitchen and sitting room into the bedroom, his boots booming hollowly on the rough planks of the floor. Returning to the kitchen he saw a covered pot on the stove and smelled the tanginess of stewing cottontail rabbit.

He was just outside the door when he heard the sound again. It was a weak sound, barely audible, and it made him think of a rabbit caught in a snare. The nerve endings along his spine grew cold and prickly. He stepped quickly to the corner, but all he could see was one end of the crude clothesline he had made for her.

An instant later he was at the rear corner of the house. When he saw her lying there his breathing stopped. His movements as he went to her seemed slow and measured, and everlasting.

She lay on her side, facing away from him. Her brown and white polka dot dress was powdered with gray from the alkali soil.

Where one shoulder blade had been there was now a large, ragged circle, stained a deep crimson.

Jessie knelt beside his wife and put one big, rough hand gently against the tumble of auburn hair lying along her temple.

"Anna! Anna!" he whispered.

Her eyelids fluttered weakly and she looked into his ashen face.

"I knew you'd come," she murmured. "I waited for you, Jessie."

As effortlessly as if she were a child, Ramming picked

4

up the limp form. As he held her in his arms he saw that it was already growing late. The setting sun was staining the western horizon with rich shades of orange and purple. It was the time of day she loved best.

Walking slowly, almost on tiptoe, he carried her into the house and laid her on their bed. Blood, thickly dark, oozed onto the muslin sheet.

Ever so gently, he cut away the brown and white cloth from her chest. There, just where the swell of her left breast began, was the bullet hole. It wasn't a large hole, Jessie thought numbly. Only a small, black circle surrounded by waxen flesh that was already turning a cold shade of blue.

He turned her on her side and cried aloud. Where the soft lead projectile had exited was an angry mass of shattered flesh and fragmented bone. The mushrooming bullet had carried away a segment of her shoulder blade as broad as his hand, leaving nothing but a cavern of ragged membranes and shredded muscle tissue.

Like a man sleepwalking, Jessie gathered clean rags and liniment and began to cleanse the wound. He went outside to the big cottonwoods and stripped off quantities of bark for a poultice. Afterward, in the light of the coal oil lamp, he pulled a chair to the side of the bed and took her hand in his.

In the night she roused once. "If it's a boy, we'll call him little Jessie," she murmured softly.

Jessie went outside to the corral and cried.

Daylight brought a faint hope. Ramming freshened the bandage covering the great wound in her back. He bathed her forehead, talking to her in his deep voice, assuring her that all would be well.

Despite a sense of foreboding, he tore himself from the room. Behind the adobe house where she had fallen, he surveyed the slope for a time, then climbed the ridge to its crest. His search was brief. In minutes he had found the tell-tale sign.

Angrily, he wiped away a mist of tears and studied the unnatural furrow in the earth. The sign was elementary. There were the two indentations where the rifleman's elbows had rested when he sighted down the barrel of the gun, and two more gouged by the toes of his boots. A

5

few inches to one side was the ragged pattern of brown where the man had discharged a mouthful of tobacco juice.

The rays of the morning sun touched an object all but hidden in the coarse blades of buffalo grass. As a man might handle a gem of inestimable value, Ramming picked it up carefully and deliberately. It was an empty brass shell casing, the scars of an imperfect breech girdling its lethal shoulder.

At last he stood and moved down the slope, away from the house. The faint succession of footprints led him to the cluster of mesquite bushes. There he spent another half-hour, painstakingly examining every scar in the soil, every track left by man and horse.

Finally, he followed the horse's tracks until there could be no question of its direction. Then he turned and hurried back up the slope, dread growing into a hard lump in his chest.

Chapter
TWO

He found Anna weakened. The skin of her face was drawn and sallow. Her breathing was quick and labored. He cursed himself for having left her alone.

Time became an indistinct, shadowy tunnel. One instant the tiny window would be aflame with the noonday sun; the next it would be a black rectangle with nothing beyond. Sometime during the pre-dawn darkness of the fourth day, Jessie laid his head against his forearm at the kitchen table and slept. When he awoke and looked into her little girl's face, he realized that she looked old. There were dark circles about her eyes. Her mouth was a white line, drawn down at the corners.

He dropped to one knee beside the bed and took her face between his big hands. Her flesh was cold, like clay.

He held her hand in both of his until daylight. Then he went outside to dig her grave. He chose a spot among the towering cottonwoods and with a heavy-headed grubbing hoe attacked the earth like a man possessed. Three long years of swinging a pickaxe in a Trabajo gold mine had taught him that skill very well.

It was done quickly. He buried her deep, so the coyotes and badgers couldn't reach her, and went back to the house.

He strode purposefully to the bedroom and, reaching up, removed the shotgun from the pegs that held it above the door. Seating himself on the edge of the bed, he drew the gun from its oiled sheath and held it out before him.

It was a massive weapon, a breech-loading eight-gauge of French manufacture. The dual, thirty-six-inch barrels could reach out and bring down a goose flying as high as the clouds. Or so his Grandfather Asa had said when he bestowed the gun on Jessie's father. And no one argued with Captain Asa Ramming, not even after the anchor chain of his packet ship snatched off his leg and fed it to a hungry mako shark through the hawsehole.

But Jessie's father never fired that shotgun. Francis Ramming was a bookish man, a schoolteacher, to the everlasting disappointment of Captain Asa. And when Francis made a gift of it to his son Jessie he did so contritely, as he would an object of the devil's own design.

The shells were in a corner of the steamer trunk. Jessie opened the box to fill his pockets and saw that not a cartridge was missing. He had never quite gotten around to shooting Captain Asa's goose gun. Now, testing its weight in his hands, he felt an eerie chill, the sensation that comes with inevitable peril.

Outside, at the corral, he dropped the bars of the gate and watched the cow and calf trot away to freedom. Coyotes would have that little one before the sun rose tomorrow.

The gray horse whinnied as he approached, and pushed its head against his chest. Ramming shoved the muzzle aside roughly and set about saddling. When he spoke, his voice had a tone that made the gelding shift uneasily.

"The world's not big enough to hide that man, Gray."

For the span of a deep breath, Ramming rested his head against the gray horse's neck, then he swung into the saddle and rode toward the ridge behind the house. At its crest he pulled up and turned in the saddle. It looks exactly as it always has, he thought. Except for the fresh mound of earth there beneath the cottonwoods.

Then he spoke to the gelding and they moved down the far slope, cutting through the mesquite thicket. Jessie didn't pause to search out the tracks of the other horse.

There was only one possible destination in the direction he had taken—the town of Trabajo.

It was late afternoon when he pulled the gray to a stop and reached for the canteen hanging from his saddle horn. Abruptly, a pang in his stomach reminded him that he'd had nothing to eat all day, and he hadn't thought to collect provisions when he walked out of the adobe house for the last time.

At that instant, a lean jackrabbit sprang from his covert beneath a ragged beargrass and darted up the slope away from the man on horseback. A moment later the big rabbit stopped and squatted on his haunches, his long ears scissoring with curiosity.

Ramming drew the shotgun from its scabbard beneath his leg and levered the breech open. Then he fished a pair of shells from his pocket and dropped them into the gaping chambers, realizing as he heard the hollow metallic echo that he had never even loaded the weapon before.

The rabbit had not moved. Jessie placed the butt of the shotgun against his shoulder and cocked the hammers of both barrels. If he missed with one, a second shot would be ready.

When he pulled the trigger, several things happened at once. The jackrabbit disappeared from view, swallowed up in a sudden eruption of dust. The recoil of the gun butt against his shoulder caused him to jerk the second trigger, firing the other barrel. The gray horse, as though stung in his tenderest regions by a bumble bee, gathered himself into a ball of startled sinew and sprang sideways half again his own length.

Ramming left the saddle cleanly, landing on the ground in an ungraceful heap. The gelding stood with trembling legs a dozen paces away, his ears cast forward in apprehension.

Jessie Ramming had almost forgotten that he could smile. He grinned and shook his head.

"Yeah, Gray. It makes a heap of noise. I'm afraid you and I don't know just a whole hell of a lot about this manhunting business."

He caught up the reins and, with the horse trailing,

9

walked up the slope toward the spot where the rabbit had sat on its haunches. But the rabbit wasn't there. At first he thought the charge of buckshot had gone wide of its mark. But then his gaze fell on a few shreds of hair and flesh; part of a long, hind leg, and some scraps of tissue that had once been ears.

Jessie contemplated the bloody remains and shook his head. The eight-gauge had disintegrated his supper.

He rode another hour, until the sun sank from sight and daylight became the velvet purple of dusk. He found an outcropping of sandstone near the crown of a small hill, unsaddled the horse and poured half the remaining water from the canteen into his hat. The gelding sucked up the moisture noisily.

Ramming then built a fire, and sat for a long time staring into the dancing flames. At last he spread his buffalo-hide chaps on the ground, pulled the still-damp saddle blanket over his shoulders, and closed his eyes.

It was well past midmorning when he rode the gelding into Trabajo. His first stop was the livery stable, where he saw to the feeding of his horse. Then he headed on foot along the boardwalk toward the sheriff's office.

The jail sat by itself at one end of Main Street, as though its designer had wished a measure of privacy. In truth, the sheriff who had chosen the location did so with an eye to defending it against would-be jailbreakers. He wanted a clear field of fire in all directions.

Ramming shouldered through the heavy-timbered door and drew up a step inside.

"I need to talk to the sheriff," he said to the hawk-faced man who sat back in a chair behind the desk.

The sitter kept his booted feet crossed on a stack of papers at one corner of the desk.

"You're talkin' to the law."

"I mean the sheriff." Something about the face of the man at the desk was troublesomely familiar. "I've got to see Sheriff Dunn."

The eyes of the other man held no warmth.

"Well, that's tough, mister. The sheriff ain't been seen for quite a spell." He thumbed the six-pointed badge out from his shirt front so Ramming could read the word

10

"Deputy" emblazoned across its face. "You'll have to settle for me. Now get on with it and quit wasting my time."

The nagging familiarity of the man's face remained, but Ramming pushed the thought away.

"Someone shot my wife."

The words came out without expression. Jessie could hardly believe the past five days could be summed up in such a paltry collection of sounds.

"Someone shot your wife, huh?" The deputy could have been talking about the weather. "How bad's she hurt?"

"She's dead."

"Well, now. That's too bad." The hawk-faced man drew his lips back in a grimace, biting into a match stick. "How'd it happen? Somebody get careless with a gun?"

Ramming was fighting a tempest inside him. He spoke through clinched teeth.

"She was killed. On purpose!"

For the first time, the deputy appeared to become interested in the conversation. He dropped his boots to the floor and leaned forward, shoving aside the clutter of papers on the desk top.

"The hell you say?" he drawled. He shifted the match to the other side of his mouth and pushed his hat to the back of his balding head. "You tell me what happened and I'll decide if it was done a'purpose or not."

In a few words, Ramming told it. Then he reached into his shirt pocket and drew out the scarred brass shell casing he had found there in the grass at the crest of the ridge.

The deputy reached across, took the metal object, and turned it over and over in his hand. At last he put it to his nose and sniffed at the open end.

"Hell this ain't fresh. It was fired a long time ago."

"Friday," Ramming said. "She was shot Friday, along toward sundown."

The deputy's head snapped up.

"You're tellin' me she was shot last Friday? And here it is Wednesday? What kind of crap are you tryin' to pull?"

Rage was knotted in Ramming's belly, but he forced his voice to remain even.

"She didn't die right away. I buried her yesterday."

The other man stood up, and recognition came suddenly to Jessie. He wondered how he could have failed to remember. The deputy was a man of average height, heavy-shouldered and thick-necked, with long, powerful arms. But his proportions were all wrong. His trunk from shoulder to midsection was abnormally long, the torso of a much bigger man. But from the waist down, he was a freak. His legs were ludicrously short, the stunted, bowed legs of a midget.

The mismatched parts of two men had been joined in Stub Heckman. The result was grotesque. And behind those close-set eyes was a deep bitterness, a characteristic Jessie had had occasion to measure a decade earlier when they had shoveled ore together in the bowels of the Miss Mable gold mine.

The deputy read the look in Jessie's face.

"Yeah, that's right. I'm Heckman. It's been a few years, but I ain't about to forget what you did to me that day at the mine."

Ramming's gaze was unwavering.

"You would have killed that kid, Heckman. He was half your size. And all he did was play a little joke . . ."

The deputy's fist came crashing down on the desktop. His face was livid.

"You just be damned sure of one thing. I ain't forgettin' it!"

Abruptly he stopped. He dropped his eyes to the badge on his chest as though reminded of unaccustomed authority, and sat back down. His booted feet went back to the stack of papers on the desk, where they had rested earlier. He spoke around the matchstick.

"I'll do some inquirin' around. But don't expect a whole hell of a lot at this late date. I ain't no damn magician."

Suddenly, Ramming had an immense urge to get out of that office and back into the fresh air. But there was one more question he had to ask.

"What happened to Sheriff Dunn? His term wasn't up."

Heckman had drawn a sack of tobacco from his shirt pocket. His eyes avoided Ramming's for half a minute while he rolled the cigarette. Finally he shifted his eyes to the other man's face.

"You ain't heard, I guess. The sheriff just up and cleared out one night without so much as a by-your-leave to nobody. Did write a note, though. Something about headin' over toward Silver City to get in on that new streak they found. Nobody's heard a word since."

He took the frayed match from his teeth, lit the cigarette, and flipped the stem toward the pot-bellied stove across the room. Then he turned back to Ramming.

"Like I told you. I'm the law in Trabajo now. You'd be smart to keep that in mind, mister."

Jessie reached over, plucked the shell casing from the litter on the desk, and pivoted toward the door. The deputy's voice broke loudly:

"Hey! That empty shell stays here, hombre. That's evidence."

But when Heckman looked up into the cold eyes of the tall man at the door, the shell didn't seem so important. He shifted his gaze away and began pawing through the papers on the scarred desk.

Chapter
THREE

Ramming stood on the boardwalk outside the sheriff's office, his fists clenched into knots of sinew. There was a terrible gnawing in his belly that had nothing to do with hunger. It was the pain of hopelessness, the futility of knowing there was no one else he could turn to for help. He hadn't realized how deeply he had counted on telling his story to Sheriff Wiley Dunn.

He was a rancher, not a gunman. Even if he somehow managed to track down Anna's killer, what could he do? His experience with the shotgun and the jackrabbit should be warning enough that he was a stranger to the world of gunfighters and shoot-outs.

It was with an almost physical effort that Jessie shut his mind to the impossibility of the task he faced. And with that thought came another. He didn't really care if the price he had to pay was his own life, so long as he could send Anna's killer to hell.

The torment in his breast slowly began to subside, as he realized that he was fully committed to that goal. No man nor barrier could turn him from it.

He let his eyes wander along the main street of Trabajo, taking in the Hotel Royale, about which there was no longer any aura of regality; and a few doors down the Western Mining and Land Bank, which once had held so many payrolls and gold shipments that its sides still bulged outward like barrel staves. It held memories he preferred to forget.

Farther on along the dusty street was the Mother

Lode Saloon, the dim coolness behind its batwing doors beckoning cow-punchers and miners and drifters—as long as there was a coin or an ounce of metal in their pokes.

At last Jessie forced his gaze across the street to a big, false-fronted store with a jumble of merchandise displayed on the walk under its awning. It was where he had met Anna, at a time when her father had been filled with grand hopes for his fine mercantile in the booming town of Trabajo. Before the ways of the savage West had driven him in despair back to his native Pennsylvania.

Only the sign of the store had been changed. "Heinsohn's Mercantile," it said now, the scrolled letters already fading beneath the sun's intensity.

Jessie procured the gelding from the livery and crossed the street to the mercantile. He didn't recognize the face of the proprietor, a fat and perspiring man who sat in a wicker chair near the counter, beside a barrel of dried beans.

The fat man made a half-hearted effort to rise as Ramming entered, then changed his mind and grunted an indifferent greeting. He was chewing a mouthful of beans from the barrel at his elbow. Jessie could hear them cracking between his teeth.

Moving woodenly, Ramming set about gathering provisions—some hardtack, salt pork, a little coffee, a small sack of dried fruit, some canned tomatoes. He gave little thought to the items. The hunger he had felt when he rode into town had vanished, burned out by the bitter frustration of his fruitless encounter with the deputy.

The proprietor heaved his bulk from the wicker chair and shuffled around the counter. Ramming studied the face as the fat man frowned at the ciphering before him.

"I'm looking for a man," Jessie said quietly. "A tall gent, worn-out boots, riding a mare. He'd have come through Trabajo three, maybe four days ago."

Heinsohn looked up quickly, but an instant later his eyes were veiled, empty.

"Nope. Ain't seen nobody fittin' that description."

15

He spread his huge hands in an elaborate gesture of ignorance.

Ramming gathered up his purchases, paid for them from the handful of coins in his pocket, and went on outside. It was clear he wasn't likely to get any help in Trabajo. Not with Sheriff Dunn out of the picture.

There was nothing to do but ride west. The mountains would be the place to find the sort of man he was looking for. He had heard tales when he worked in the mine, about how many an outlaw on the dodge had extended his life expectancy by taking refuge in the rugged vastness of the Rocky Mountains.

In the saddle once more, Ramming headed the gelding toward the other end of the street, where the stores and houses dwindled to shacks and outbuildings before surrendering entirely to the ruthless world of desert beyond.

He was passing the Mother Lode Saloon when, on impulse, he reined in to the hitching rail. If there was information to be had in this town, it would be here.

For a long minute after he stepped inside from the sun's brilliance, Jessie could see nothing except his own silhouette in the cheaply ornate mirror behind the bar. The odor of damp sawdust and tobacco smoke was strong in his nostrils.

He had taken a step forward when a hard voice sounded from the dimness and a shoulder slammed into his, sending him staggering against a table.

The voice came again, loud and grating and only inches from his ear, but the words were not directed at him.

"If there's anything I can't stand it's the smell of goat," the angry voice barked. "Next time take a bath before you come in amongst white folks. Or better yet, just don't come in a'tall."

The shadowy forms had moved nearer the batwing doors and Ramming could see more clearly. An old man, a Mexican with hair the color of freshly picked cotton, stood with his back against the hinged doors. An arm's length in front of him was the squat, gorilla-like figure of Deputy Stub Heckman, his lips drawn back in a mocking grin.

16

"You got it now, goat-herder? You'll give the saloon a bad name. To say nothin' of a bad smell."

With hardly any effort, the deputy picked up the slight Mexican by his shirt front and heaved him backwards through the slatted half-doors. Ramming heard the old man fall heavily on the wooden walk outside, then tumble down the steps.

Heckman swung around, wiped his hands in exaggerated fashion on his shirt front, and waddled back toward the bar while a burst of laughter ran through the cluster of men gathered there.

"Atta way, Stub," a voice bellowed. "Come on. Next one's on me."

The deputy must have come directly to the saloon after their confrontation in the sheriff's office, Ramming mused. But the lawman, preoccupied with his own heroics, had failed to notice him.

Jessie skirted the tangle of tables and chairs and found a place near one end of the mahogany bar, away from the deputy and his friends.

"What'll it be, mister?" the bartender asked indifferently.

"Beer," said Ramming, not really wanting it.

He caught the mug of tepid beer as it slid toward him and leaned forward, keeping his voice low:

"I'm looking for a man."

"So?" The bartender didn't interrupt the circular movement of the dingy rag on the bar's surface. "Ain't everybody?"

"The man who killed my wife."

"Killed your wife?" The bartender's voice rang loudly in the dimness. "What the hell fer?"

Jessie became aware that the rumble of conversation at the other end of the bar had subsided.

"Maybe you've seen such a man come through in the past three or four days. He'd be my height, six feet or so. Chews tobacco. Clothes probably ragged. Toes of his boots worn out. He'd be riding a mare with a split hoof on the off side. And carrying a Peabody .45 rifle, an old one."

The bartender was leaning across the shiny surface of the bar now, giving his full attention to Ramming.

17

"What'd he look like in the face? Was he a white man? Or a Mex, maybe?"

"I can't say," Ramming replied. "I didn't get a look at him."

He heard bootheels thumping on the wooden floor and turned to see Stub Heckman pushing through the line of cowboys, miners, and saloon hangers-on along the bar.

"Well, well. If it ain't the pilgrim. It don't look like you remember so good, Ramming. I told you I'm the law around here." He rubbed the deputy's badge on his chest with the heel of his hand in an almost subconscious gesture. "So you just let the law do the investigatin'. Hear?"

The bartender was slouched with his hairy forearms on the lip of the bar, watching the proceedings with great interest. Suddenly he saw an opportunity to curry favor with the temperamental deputy.

"Hey, Stub. Don't that sound kind of queer to you? This here feller can tell you everything about the hombre that did the shootin' except where his birthmark is at. And he didn't even get a look at him. Don't that sound pretty damn queer?"

Heckman had moved almost against Ramming, and now he put out a hand and poked a thick finger against Jessie's chest.

"You got a piece of evidence I want. Hand over that empty shell."

Ramming looked down at the finger pressing against his chest and then stared into Stub's eyes. The deputy let his hand drop but then he remembered that every man in the saloon was watching. Abruptly both of his broad hands shot out and caught Ramming's shirt front, forcing him back against the bar.

"I'm tellin' you one more time. Hand over that piece of evidence or I'll turn you upside down and shake it out of you. This time it ain't going to be like it was out at the Miss Mable, when you caught me by surprise."

Jessie's face didn't change expression. He reached up and clamped both of his hands around the deputy's wrists. A grin started on Stub's face. There was going to be some sport in this encounter after all.

But the swell of muscle along Ramming's forearms
18

grew rigid. His hands were the jaws of a vice, closing relentlessly on the bones of Heckman's forearms. Little by little the grin slipped from the deputy's face. The pain crept up his arms, into his eyes, and spread through his belly. His numbed fingers opened of their own accord.

Heckman's knees were beginning to buckle when Ramming at last released his grip. White of face, the deputy turned a venomous glare on the crowd that had gathered around. The men moved back a cautious step. Not a face registered emotion. They recognized the look in his eyes.

Regretting the action Heckman had forced on him, Ramming turned and began retreating toward the swinging doors. He was a pace from them when Heckman's voice split the silence.

"Right there, damn you! Hold it right there!"

Stub's voice trembled with rage. He had a hand outstretched, index finger aimed like a gun barrel.

For half a breath, Jessie considered the odds against reaching the doors. Then he turned slowly and regarded the deputy calmly. Heckman's right hand moved downward toward the gun on his hip. His hunger to use it was written plainly on his face.

"Nobody makes a fool out of me ... out of the law ... in this town, Ramming. I'm placing you under arrest for withholding evidence and interferin' with duly constituted authority. A few days in jail ought to learn you that you can't go around taking the law into your own hands."

A sudden desperation knifed at Jessie. He couldn't afford to be locked up while Anna's killer drifted farther and farther away. But if he made a move to escape, the deputy would cut him down. He had already set the stage for it.

Heckman pulled a pair of handcuffs from a hip pocket and tossed them to a puncher at the edge of the crowd.

"Put them cuffs on him, Red," the deputy commanded. "There ain't no tellin' what a bird like him will try."

Red took the handcuffs and advanced a step toward Ramming. He was directly in front of Heckman and two steps from Jessie when a quick shadow, like a bird

19

taking sudden flight, sliced across the doorway. Instinctively, Ramming reached and caught the long object flying toward him. The feel of it warmed his heart. Someone had tossed the eight-gauge goose gun squarely into his hands.

The heavy double barrels of the weapon swung of their own weight until they came to a focus on the paunchy midsection of the carrot-haired man moving toward him. It was not a time for calm reflection. Red dived to one side, splintering a chair in his haste to get clear of the yawning muzzles.

Heckman's hand had begun its move toward the Colt on his hip when he realized what was happening, but Red had blocked his view for the hundredth part of the second it took Ramming to swing the shotgun about. Now he knew that his standing as Trabajo's top dog was on the line. He had schemed long and hard to establish his reputation as a tough gunslinger, a man who could look death in the eye and smile. And he had fooled most of the townspeople. They didn't know his courage was a sham; that his knees trembled and his mouth became too dry to swallow when a showdown was imminent.

But that carefully contrived reputation had come home to roost. When he spoke he tried to make his voice low and even. He didn't quite succeed.

"You're gettin' in over your head, mister. You just throw that bird gun down and we'll forget about you threatenin' the law. Up to now you've only bought yourself a little jail time. But if you ain't put that gun down by the time I count to three, you're gonna have more trouble than you can say grace over."

Maybe, just maybe, the bluff would work, Heckman told himself. After all, he was the law. And, hell. It was just a woman that'd got shot. Why would a man get so worked up?

The detonation of the eight-gauge shot shell, trapped inside the walls of the saloon, slammed against eardrums with the impact of a flattened palm. The charge of double-ought buckshot screamed through the vacuum-like stillness, exploded in a shower of rosewood splinters against the ornately carved piano, shattered a fancy

20

lamp hanging low above it, and blew the door to a storeroom from its hinges.

For a long moment, the only sound in the saloon was the hum of piano strings. Three men lay flat on the floor, as still as death. An instant later, they began to scramble away on hands and knees like startled cockroaches.

Deputy Stub Heckman, white-lipped and weak of knee, was backed against the bar, his long arms extended above his head as far as he could reach. His eyes were riveted to the muzzles of the shotgun, but now and again, as though he couldn't quite control them, they darted toward the wreckage of the piano and the devastated storeroom door.

A grim smile tightened Ramming's face.

"I've got better things to do with my time than palaver with a tinhorn deputy sheriff, Heckman. If you haven't shucked those clothes you're wearing by the time I count to ten, I'm going to sic the other barrel of this scattergun on your belly button. And then there won't be any law at all in Trabajo."

A weak grin started on the other man's face, but withered as quickly as a morning glory blossom at high noon.

"You ain't serious about that, Ramming?"

"One . . ." Jessie said gently.

The count was at nine when Stub pulled off the second sock. He stood in soiled, ragged underwear, moving his hands uncertainly as if searching for pockets to hide them in.

"Out!" Ramming said, gesturing toward the swinging doors with a jerk of the long, blue-black barrels.

"Aw, hey. You wouldn't make me do that?"

The sound of the second hammer reaching full cock was sharp and hard in the saloon. Stub jerked erect and went toward the door.

"You've got another ten to get out of range of this shotgun," Ramming told him. "Down the middle of Main Street."

He walked out behind the deputy, into the blistering heat of the sun, and pointed the twin muzzles toward the far end of the dusty street. A whimper escaped from

21

Heckman's throat, but he broke into a run, a waddling, duck-like sort of gait. Jessie watched until the ludicrous figure turned and darted into the sheriff's office. Along the sidewalk a half-dozen townspeople had stopped in midstride to follow the deputy's progress. Laughter echoed across the false-fronted buildings.

Chapter
FOUR

Jessie moved to the gelding's side and slid his long gun into the saddle boot. An urgency prodded him, an urgency that had nothing to do with the fact he had made a fool of the law in this town. It sprang from the realization that, with the passing of every hour, the odds against his catching his wife's murderer grew longer.

He had a foot in the stirrup, preparing to swing into the saddle, when a heavy hand fell on his shoulder. An icy prickle of alarm pulsed down his spine. There was no way he could spin around and grab the owner of that arm before a finger could tighten against a trigger.

"Maybe I can give you a bit of help, after all," the gruff voice spoke beside his ear. "That coyote has had it comin' for a long time. You'd have done us all a favor to've perforated his innards with a load of buckshot."

Ramming turned. The fat face of Heinsohn, proprietor of the mercantile, was stretched wide in a generous grin.

"The man you asked about when you was in my store. A tall hombre, riding a sorrel mare? I seen such a gent here in Trabajo early this week. He stayed around town a couple of days, soakin' up whiskey over at the Lode most of the time."

Jessie felt his heartbeat quicken.

"When did he leave town?"

"Wal, he come over to my place and picked up some grub—and some cartridges, some of them .45 Peabody rimfires, as I recollect. That was ... let's see—yesterday morning, I believe."

"You said he rode out of town," Ramming interrupted. "Which direction?"

Heinsohn waved a fleshy arm in the general direction of the Rocky Mountains, stretching in a dim, blue line along the western horizon.

"Looked to me like he made a beeline for the hills. There sure ain't much between here and there to interest a man."

"Can you describe him?"

"To tell you the truth, there wasn't a whole lot a man could see. Had a beard that covered everything except his eyes and his nose. His clothes had seen better days, I can tell you for certain."

His bushy brows drew together.

"One other thing that a feller couldn't miss. He had a gosh-awful scar along the side of his head."

Ramming hardly heard. He was gazing into the distance, impatience goading him. But he had to ask one final question.

"Did you happen to see who was standing outside the door of the saloon a little while ago? Just before the shooting started?"

Heinsohn frowned.

"Nope. Wasn't nobody around. Just that old Mexican that runs a few goats over that rise yonder."

Jessie reached out and took the hamlike hand of the mercantile proprietor.

"I'm much obliged to you," he said.

Then he climbed astride the gray and headed him in a fast lope past the tumble-down fringe of Trabajo. A short distance beyond the last shack, Main Street became a trail which quickly became fainter as it angled upward toward the crown of the ridge.

It was clear that few travelers left town by this route. And when Jessie reached the top of the incline the reason became clear. Before him stretched an expanse of desert so immense it caused him to suck in his breath. Westward, the earth was as smooth and unbroken as a table top; as featureless as the surface of an ocean in a great calm. It must have been just such a sight that

24

caused men of past centuries to reason that the world was flat, he mused. The only impediment to that conclusion was the uneven band of blue that told of the mountains against the far horizon.

He rode on, paralleling the dim trail. Following it with his eyes, he saw that it ended a few hundred yards farther on. There, almost lost in the sun's raw glare was a tiny adobe shack, its color blending with the colorless desert around it. Behind the crude shack was a pole corral, inside of which were a dozen or more animals of varying hues and patterns: whites, grays, blacks, browns, and random combinations. It was obvious the goats were not confined by the fence. It was their home, where they came and went as their impulses dictated.

Ramming was still a distance from the shack when the sagging front door was drawn open on its leather hinges. Out stepped the white-haired Mexican who had been hurled through the doors of the Mother Lode Saloon by the swaggering deputy.

Jessie reined the gelding in.

"*Amigo*, I suspect I'm in your debt. Wasn't it you who threw the shotgun to me in the saloon?"

The old man shrugged. A smile pulled at his leathery face until it was seamed with a thousand wrinkles.

"If the shotgun came to you at a good time, I am glad, señor. That deputy is a bad one. There is more compassion"—he waved a gnarled hand toward the corral a few steps away—"in my children here."

Jessie leaned down from his saddle.

"Let me shake your hand, friend. He was looking for an excuse to blow my light out. Maybe someday I can return the favor."

He turned the horse away.

"It's time I was moving on. Again, *mil gracias* for the helping hand."

He put the gray into motion and was a hundred yards away when a thought came to him. He pulled up and looked over his shoulder. The old man still stood where he had been, shading his eyes with a knobby hand as he watched the departing rider.

Ramming swung the gelding about and loped back.

"Do you have a horse?"

25

"No, señor. But I have a fine mule. You are welcome to him."

"No, I don't need him, but I'm thinking you need to make yourself scarce for a few days. It won't be hard for Heckman to find out who gave me the shotgun, and he won't look kindly on the man that did it. I'd be pleased to have your company."

A broad grin, devoid of teeth, creased the old man's face.

"*Un momento, por favor*," he murmured, and disappeared around the corner of the adobe shack. In less than a minute he had returned, leading the saddled jack.

"That didn't take long," Jessie observed.

The Mexican lifted his white eyebrows in a silent, eloquent response.

"You were maybe expecting the invitation?" Ramming grinned.

"I have lived enough years to know a man cannot afford to be unprepared," the old man said gravely.

He swung agilely onto the back of the small brown mule and spoke to the long-eared animal in rapid Spanish. The mule moved out in a quick trot, switching his short tail spiritedly. There would be no waiting on that pair.

Jessie contemplated the shimmering expanse that lay before them and asked, "How far to the mountains?"

"With luck, four days."

"You've crossed it, then?"

"Many times," said the old man. "It's a journey you won't forget, *compadre*."

Ramming frowned.

"Maybe I didn't do you any favors inviting you to come along. This doesn't look like a part of the world a man would pick for a pleasure ride. And I don't have any idea when I might be headin' back this way."

The old Mexican took off his hat, reaching up to catch the back of the brim as his people had done for generations. He drew a forearm across his brow to wipe away the dampness.

"There is no one except my goats to worry about my absence," he said evenly.

For the first hours they moved along at a good pace, their hat brims pulled low against the afternoon sun. But little by little the heat and a steady, searing wind against their faces drained their vitality. The horse and the mule plodded ahead, but Jessie had the sensation that they were walking in place on some giant treadmill that started at the horizon behind them and ran on until it fell off the world somewhere ahead. He found himself gazing anxiously into the distance for the sight of a withered clump of buffalo grass or a stunted yucca plant.

He was relieved when the sun turned blood red and vanished from their view. It grew dark quickly after that and they stopped to make camp. On a meager fire of buffalo chips they cooked a simple meal, hobbled their mounts, and fell into exhausted slumber. They were up long before dawn, pricked into wakefulness by a desert cold that was as uncomfortable as the noonday heat at the other end of the spectrum.

"Those mountains don't look a step closer than they did yesterday," Ramming said after they had traveled silently for some time. "If we don't reach water today we're liable to find ourselves afoot."

The aging Mexican, a gray stubble beginning to show against his swarthy face, studied Ramming's horse with a critical eye.

"What you say is partly true. That fine horse you're riding will lay down and die if he doesn't get water. But my *amigo* here"—he patted the lathered neck of the jack—"will go until I tell him to stop. He would try to walk even after his heart quit beating."

Jessie grinned. It was a brag, the first evidence he had seen that his companion shared the usual human frailties. But, on the other hand, Jessie knew about mules, too. Their stamina and stubbornness were three times that of an ordinary cowpony. What they lacked in beauty they more than made up for in iron-willed obstinacy.

The Mexican was talking again.

"I believe we'll have water before the sun sets today, if fate finds us deserving. Your eyes are much younger than mine. Tell me what you see in the distance ahead."

Ramming shaded his eyes and stared. He looked until the tears came.

"Nothing. There's nothing ahead. Only the damned mountains, which I figure are moving in the same direction we're traveling. They're sure not getting any closer."

The old man grunted to acknowledge the comment, but said nothing. Jessie wanted to ask what it was that he should see in that eternal void, but he gritted his teeth and kept his peace.

Their shadows shrank beneath them as the miles unfolded. Sometimes, Jessie would see a spiral of dust moving toward them, such as a knot of horsemen might kick up. But then it would become a dust devil, a heat-kindled whirlpool that rose like a long rope from the earth to disappear against the sky.

Their shadows and the spirals of dust were the only movements in the entire universe, he decided. Those, and the quartet of turkey buzzards that drifted overhead on silent wings, waiting with grisly patience for a life to end below.

He jerked a thumb upward.

"Tell me. Why would carrion-eaters like those buzzards waste their time hunting in this godforsaken no-man's-land? There's sure no life in this desert."

The oldster's face crinkled in a toothless grin.

"I think you might be surprised, señor. There are a great number of creatures which make their home here. But you have to know their ways."

He nodded over his shoulder, in the direction they had come.

"Already today I have seen the tracks of many coyotes crossing our trail. And a land that has coyotes has rabbits and mice and lizards and insects, for they make their meals from any of these. But there is yet other life, if your eyes know what they see."

A few steps further on the old man pointed to a single smooth, looping track that cut across their path.

"There is the signature of one you should know. A sidewinder. It is only a small rattlesnake, but it can kill a cow or a horse. Or a man."

Jessie grunted.

"I've heard of 'em. But over in my country it's the diamondback a man has to look out for."

28

He frowned and glanced at the old man's face.

"I saw another track a little while ago. It wasn't a snake, but some sort of critter that had legs and dragged its body. Of considerable size, too."

The old Mexican's forehead furrowed until his white brows were almost touching.

"I know what that one is. And pray you never meet him. That is a Gila monster, a poisonous lizard that must have been designed by the devil himself. His body is not covered with scales, like the rattlesnake, but with tiny beads, beads of orange and black, so that a child might think he is a toy."

The old man hunched his thin shoulders.

"Some say even his breath is poison. I know only that his jaws carry enough venom to kill."

Despite the oppressive desert heat, Jessie felt a chill along his backbone.

"How big do they grow?"

"As long as your arm. And almost as big around when they are storing fat for the winter."

The Mexican shook his head.

"I wouldn't be concerned, *amigo*. Although the desert is his home, he is a rare creature."

Ramming was suddenly very glad the old man had come along.

"My apologies, friend. I clean forgot my manners. My name's Ramming. Jessie Ramming. I owe that much to the man who saved my neck."

The other gestured with his hand as if to wave away any such thought.

"You give me too much credit, señor. You're the one who was *muy hombre* back there in the saloon." He gestured again, making his next words unimportant. "I am called Juan Guillermo Campos y Sotelo. For my friends, Juan is sufficient."

Ramming studied the Mexican's face.

"You seem to know this country pretty well."

Juan swung his arm in a motion that took in all the eye could see.

"What you say is true. I have ridden these plains and mountains since before you were born, my friend."

"Prospecting?"

"*Sí*. Searching for that miserable yellow metal."

"Ever find anything worthwhile?"

The old man was so long in answering that Jessie thought he had failed to hear the question. When at last he spoke there was such intensity in his voice that Jessie felt a stirring in the hair along his neck.

"There, a week's ride away." He pointed to the southwest. "I found a mountain with a vein of gold that would take away your breath. In an instant, I became an *hombre rico*, a wealthy man. But believe this, too. Not a day has passed since then that I have not cursed the fate that led me to that mountain."

It was not a time for questions. Ramming waited.

"I had a beautiful young wife then, a kind and gentle woman whose father owned a ranch in Mexico. He begged me to stay and become his partner, but I was too proud. I had to bring his daughter to this wretched land to prove my manhood."

He cleared his throat.

"When I found the gold I was filled with pride. She would see the great man that I would become. I left her in the little house I had built for her, there at the foot of the mountain, and went back to dig out the precious metal."

His voice was almost a whisper. Ramming had to strain to catch the words.

"I had intended to return in two days, but I couldn't make myself leave the riches I had found. It was almost a week later when I rode back to our *casita*, leading two pack mules laden with the fine, rich ore. With such wealth even her father would have to pay honor to Juan Campos y Sotelo."

Again he was silent. At last Jessie said gently, "You don't have to tell me."

But the old Mexican was listening only to memories.

"The Apaches had not been gone long when I returned. Only a few hours. They had taken what they could carry from the house. It was not even burned."

He drew a forearm across his eyes.

"I found her a short distance up the canyon from the house. She was tied by her hands and feet, and stretched between two trees. They had taken her clothes and had

30

used her until they tired of that. Then they had practiced with their arrows.

"I prayed that death had come quickly to her."

There was no sound but the rhythmic beat of hooves and the creak of saddle leather. From the corner of his eye, Ramming saw a teardrop glistening on the old man's cheek. He turned and looked away. There was no appeal for sympathy in the Mexican's voice. He had relived the agony of his wife's death too many times to hope for any relief.

The gray gelding and the mule plodded steadily on, their heads hanging low and their ears flopping in time to their steps.

Finally Juan broke the silence.

"I have burdened you with a tale of grief that should be long buried and forgotten, Señor Ramming. Forgive me. I know your own sorrow burns like a red chili pepper in a fresh wound. I heard what you said in the saloon, that a man shot and killed your wife."

He cast a look of sadness at the man on the horse.

"Why would a man do such as that? Or is it yet too painful to speak about?"

Jessie drew a deep breath.

"I still have trouble believing it happened. Anna and I didn't have anything except that little patch of ground and a few head of cows. Nothing that would give anybody a reason to kill."

"Could it have been a band of renegade Indians? There are still those who hate the white skin enough to kill."

"No," Ramming said. "Not Indians. I found the sign on a ridge behind the house. It was a white man. He chews tobacco and wears boots."

Juan glanced sharply at him.

"Then it has to be an enemy of yours, Jessie Ramming. Someone who hates very deeply, enough to take the one thing you valued the most."

Ramming swept his hat off and ran a hand through his sandy hair.

"I've gone over it a hundred times in my mind. There's no reason. Not one damned reason."

A vague thought touched his mind.

"There was one thing. Right after Anna and I were married. But that was eight years ago."

Suddenly his companion pointed. He was standing in the stirrups of his saddle.

"There! Just to the left of the sun. It is God's way of apologizing for this unhappy land."

Ramming followed the extended finger. Ahead, still a considerable distance, was a strange formation of stone, shooting up unexpectedly from the face of the desert like a giant ship, the bow reaching toward the sky and the stern sinking into the sand.

"You mean there's water there?"

"A spring," replied Juan. "Fed by an underground river, I think. I've never known it to be dry. It is the only way a man can make this crossing."

Excitement rose in Ramming.

"Then the gent I'm looking for must have come this way."

The unusual formation was even more impressive as they rode nearer. Along the sloping spine of the mountain of stone sprang a handful of hardy desert shrubs, drawing sustenance from roots that went deep into the porous stone. The point of the rock rose a hundred feet into the air. Encircling the limestone mass was a small thicket of mesquite bushes and grama grass, and in the middle of that jungle, tucked beneath the overhanging ledge of stone, was a pool of the sweetest-looking water Jessie Ramming had ever seen.

Cautiously, allowing just a few swallows at a time in the beginning, they let the horse and mule drink. Then the two men lay on their bellies and drank their fill of the clear, cool water.

"This is twice you've saved my skin, oldtimer," Ramming said. "And one day I'll repay you. But I can't ask you to ride with me any longer. This is a score I've got to settle myself. And I would sure hate to have you get hurt in the process."

The white haired old man spread his hands in a gesture of concession.

"I understand, my friend. Even though you are not a man of violence like the one you are seeking, I believe you will be the victor. Your courage gives me strength.

32

Mañana, I will return to Trabajo, to confront the deputy who so enjoyed humiliating Juan Campos."

He smiled.

"Perhaps, when you have finished with your business and have returned, they will tell you that the one who smelled of goats was not a spineless coward after all."

Ramming studied the seamed face in the failing light.

"I'm afraid you've picked the wrong gent to set your compass by, *amigo.* It's not courage you see. I'm scared half out of my wits just thinking of what will happen when I meet up with the man I'm after. But it's something I've got to do."

The other nodded and smiled his toothless smile.

"That, my son, is courage."

They circled the edge of the little pool, looking for tracks that might tell them who had passed this way before them. They found, not an occasional hoofprint, but scores of them.

"Must have been a dozen or more riders," Ramming observed. "Indians?"

"Not these," replied Juan, kneeling beside the tracks at the water's edge. "A band of wild horses, I am thinking. Even the redskin would not allow his pony to foul the water so. In this infernal land, an *agua ojo* is far too precious a thing."

"Well, we won't learn anything from the tracks, then," Jessie grunted. "If I can find a way to climb that rock I'll take a look around before daylight is completely gone."

He slid the eight-gauge from its boot on the saddle and set out around the bluff, looking for a point where the mammoth triangle of limestone might be scaled. It was not until he had reached its backbone, a ridge that could have been the spine of some giant, petrified reptile, that ascent became possible.

It was a steep climb, but not overly difficult. The rock was broken by deep fissures which gave ample foothold, and the stunted trees gave him additional purchase. In a matter of minutes Jessie had reached the highest point. The view was stunning. The sun, slipping beyond the western rim of the world, left in its wake a haze of deepening purple that gave a look of featherbed softness to the expanse of rugged desert before him.

33

A coyote howled in the near distance, setting off answering cries from a half-dozen points of the compass. Ramming heard the quick wings of a nighthawk whisper through the dusk—and then he heard another sound. It was a rasping, scraping noise that didn't fit with the hush of descending darkness. He started to turn. But his footing was uncertain, and his movement came too late.

As though in slow motion, he saw an arm coming down. It held a rifle and behind it was a vague, shadowy face. The yell of warning to Juan Campos that started in Jessie's throat died before it was uttered. His knees folded beneath him, his arms went numb, and the double-barreled shotgun slipped from his grasp.

Chapter
FIVE

Consciousness was a long time returning. Jessie's mind spun in sickening convolutions, slowing gradually until he realized that the flashes of light in his brain were the flickering rays of a campfire. Instinctively, he tried to move but his arms wouldn't respond. He was lying flat on his back, his arms and legs spread-eagled outward and anchored securely.

Jessie's head was free, though, and he turned it to one side. On a large stone a dozen paces away sat a man, his lean body hunched forward while he fed small sticks into the blaze. Although he was facing away, Jessie knew the man heard his movements. But there was no answering glance in his direction. The man beside the campfire seemed oblivious to all about him.

Jessie rolled his head away and in the pale light of the fire found himself looking into the face of Juan Campos, stretched on his back a few feet away. Ramming's left hand and the old man's right were hardly more than a foot apart, each bound to the ankle-thick trunk of the same stubby mesquite bush by a leather thong. Thongs cut from his own saddle, Ramming reflected bitterly.

His head felt as though it had been split from front to back with an axe. He closed his eyes and willed his senses to stop spinning. After a time he opened them again and looked at the old man.

"Are you hurt, Juan?"

"Only my pride, *amigo*. I am sick with shame. He came without noise behind me and placed a gun to my head. There was a time when no man, not even the most skillful of Apache braves, could do that to Juan Campos y Sotelo."

He took a deep breath and sighed in despair.

"Do you know this man?"

Jessie swiveled his head again and studied the lean figure seated as still as a hunting owl on the rock beside the dying fire. There was nothing about him that evoked recognition. His face was turned away but Jessie could see the outline of a heavy beard. His neck was long and skinny, barely big enough to support his head. There! It was something about the bullet head that prodded worrisomely at Ramming's memory, but only for an instant.

"No, I guess not. But everything about him matches up with the sign I found behind my house. And what I heard in Trabajo."

Juan managed to shake his head affirmatively.

"Aye. It is the same man I saw in town in recent days. A strange one, I think."

"What did he do? He must have talked to someone."

"He stayed to himself. Even when he was drinking in the saloon he was alone." His eyebrows lifted at a sudden recollection. "Ah! I remember now. Three times, at least, I saw him go into the office of the sheriff."

The muscles along Ramming's jaw danced.

"It's got me buffaloed. Only thing I can figure is, he's mistaken me for someone else." He looked again at the face beside him. "I'm sorry as hell I got you into this *loco* situation, Juan. It's a mighty poor way to repay you for what you've done for me."

"Ah, Señor Jessie," the old man said gently. "Don't concern yourself about me. You didn't hold a gun to my head and force me to ride with you. And consider. We get to rest here on this fine, soft earth. Isn't that what we would be doing anyway?"

Ramming grinned back at the face outlined dimly in the uncertain light.

"Okay, Mister Campos. We'll play it your way. Let's get some sleep. Our silent friend over there will surely let us know if he has need of our services."

The night air in the high desert country had begun to cool with the setting of the sun. The ground on which they lay still held the day's warmth and it was only a matter of minutes before Ramming slept, disturbed only by the occasional need to flex his limbs.

Once when he awoke he saw by the light of a pale moon that the old Mexican stretched out beside him was sleeping peacefully, as if he had not a worry in the world. Turning his head, Jessie searched in the dimness for their captor. There was nothing to see in that direction but a soft orange glow from the last embers of the campfire.

Ramming slept again, and dreamed that he and Anna were lying together in the grass beside a quiet stream, watching the approach of a man on horseback. Abruptly, in the fitful way of dreams, Anna was galloping away on the horse while the stranger stood above him and stared down with cruel, cold eyes.

When he opened his eyes he saw that daylight's first pink flush was spreading across the eastern sky. By slow degrees, he became aware of a ragged form silhouetted against the murky dawn, and a moment later comprehension came. The cadaverous man with the scar was standing at his shoulder.

"Are you the man?" Jessie had to stop talking to draw a quivering breath through clenched teeth. Fear and rage battled for mastery in his breast. "Are you the man who shot her?"

The eyes that regarded him, half hidden in the shadows, were cold and impassive. They held no more expression than those of a corpse. After a time, he deliberately placed the muzzle of the rifle he held against Ramming's forehead and cocked the hammer. Jessie stopped breathing and closed his eyes. He wondered if there would be a great deal of pain.

He waited. Nothing happened. After what seemed an infinite age, he opened his eyes. There was only the indigo sky above, and the sound of hoofbeats. He was surprised to be still alive.

He lay without moving, regarding the purity of the early dawn sky and tasting the crisp, chill morning air.

37

Back there, when Anna had died, he had decided his own life was of little importance to him. Now, the sweetness of it was overwhelming.

He heard a rustle of sound and turned to the man on the ground a few feet away.

"Juan Campos, our friend with the beard has lit a shuck. And taken our mounts, of course. He has decided to let us lie here under the sun and shrivel up like a watermelon rind. But he can't be very smart. We'll be loose from here before long. . . ."

"Ah, Jessie Ramming, *mi amigo.* I'm afraid you and I are not to have a great deal of time. Turn your head and look this way."

Ramming lifted his head an inch and squinted his eyes, trying to penetrate the dusky blackness that still clung to the dew-dampened earth. After a minute he could see, at a point midway between them, a small, nondescript mesquite bush. There was nothing about it that seemed out of the ordinary.

Then, as the first grains of daylight settled like particles of dust on the wind, he saw an object near its base. A rock, he thought. But the rock had unusual markings. And the color. Almost a pretty hue. An instant later recognition came to him with the impact of a physical blow.

It was not a rock. It was the thing that Juan had described earlier, in tones of fervent dread.

A Gila monster!

The creature was tethered to the trunk of the tiny mesquite by a slender thong. The ribbon of leather had been forced through a slit in the lizard's heavy stump of a tail.

Jessie stopped breathing. His stomach churned. The Gila monster, what he could see of it in the meager light of false dawn, was repulsively sinister. The striking orange and black beads which covered its ungainly body merely accentuated its ugliness. It had none of the grace of a diamondback rattler, but all of its lethal repugnance.

The huge lizard lay flat on its belly against the sandy soil, its stubby, grotesque legs cocked outward at awkward angles.

38

"Juan," Jessie whispered. "I can't see any movement, any breathing. Maybe it's badly hurt. Or dead."

The negative movement of the old Mexican's head was barely perceptible.

"I'm afraid not. The ground is cold. He cannot move until the sun warms his body."

"And then what?"

"And then he will be very, very angry because of the wound in his tail."

Ramming squinted at the strip of leather anchoring the reptile.

"Is that piece of leather long enough . . . ?"

"For him to reach you or me? I have no doubt of it," Juan said wryly. "But we will know with certainty in a very short time. Already the air grows warm."

Frustration tore at Jessie's vitals. He had to fight. It was not in him to lie helplessly inert while death drew near moment by moment. He lay back and tightened the muscles of his arms repeatedly, forcing the numbness from them. Then he closed his eyes and set himself against the straps that held his wrists.

Nothing happened, except that the leather cut more deeply into the flesh of his forearms. Again he relaxed, and again he tensed every tendon in his body against the innocent thongs.

Given the proper circumstances, Jessie knew he could break any one of the leather straps that held him. But now he had no leverage, no way to use the strength of his powerful shoulders. All he had succeeded in doing was to tear the skin about his wrists. He felt his own blood oozing warmly into his hands.

He became aware that he had a tiny bit more movement in his arms. He had gained an inch of slack in the bonds.

The old man had said nothing while Jessie strained against the straps. Now he nodded slightly.

"The leather. It is stretching because of the dampness, the dew. But I'm afraid it won't be enough. The scar-faced one knew what he was about."

Ramming's breath was coming in shuddering waves. His forearms were afire with pain. And the bit of slack he had gained from his struggles was a false hope. Moist leather would be many times harder to break than the same leather when dry.

"Juan," he said with bitterness in his voice. "I can't do it. There's no way . . ."

The old man's tone changed subtly. Now it had a biting edge.

"You are going to let the killer of your wife get away with his deed, then? While you lie here and die like a rabbit waiting to be skinned, he will go unpunished. And he will laugh when he remembers your helplessness."

The words went like a dagger point to Jessie's heart. He had looked into the eyes of the man who had shot Anna down in cold blood, and now that man was riding away, beyond vengeance. The thought burned into his mind, more painful by far than the hurting in his wrists.

But too much time had passed. The sun had appeared, riding now above the horizon. The heat from its rays was intensifying, breath by breath.

Jessie Ramming gathered his strength to pull once more at the straps, but the baleful eyes of the Gila monster recorded that movement. The blunt nose lifted from the ground and the heavy body began to move, the stubby legs propelling the ungainly form forward with surprising agility. An angry hiss spewed from the reptile's gaping jaws and Jessie could smell the fetid odor of its breath.

Abruptly, he became aware that Juan was moving. Even though his arms and legs were still secured tightly, the old man's torso was thrashing wildly about on the ground.

The Gila monster's head, poised a hand's breadth from Jessie's shoulder, snapped suddenly about. In a flash of orange and black motion, the lizard launched itself toward the twisting body and an instant later the jaws were fastened in the flesh of Juan's neck.

Ramming watched in horrified fascination. It wasn't like the strike of a snake, a quick stab of the fangs and withdrawal. Instead, the hideously ugly head clung to the flesh, the jaws grinding their venom into the bloodstream of the old man.

Juan's movements had stilled. He lay tensely quiet, his eyes closed.

Anger exploded in Ramming's brain. With a surge of strength that he thought had been exhausted he pulled against the strips of leather. Pain radiated from his wrist and sped along his arm, but it served only to sting him to greater effort. An instant later, the thong holding his left hand burst apart.

As quick as Jessie's motion was, the Gila monster's reaction was quicker. Before he could jerk his arm away, the teeth of the reptile had cut a furrow across the back of his hand. At the end of its tether, the beaded lizard continued to hiss angrily as Ramming drew away.

"Barely in time," Juan Campos said huskily and Jessie realized the old man didn't know the monster had left its poison in his flesh, too. He turned the wound on his hand away from the other man and looked at him sorrowfully.

"*Viejo*, why did you do it? Now I have killed you."

Juan squinted his eyes, as though to bring them into focus.

"Please, my son. Don't condemn yourself. You have a trail to follow, and a black deed to balance. As for me, I will go to join the woman I have sorrowed for these many years."

The final words were slurred. The old Mexican rolled onto his back, looking skyward. His body tensed, fighting the multiplying pain.

"The sky," he mumbled hoarsely. "It is becoming yellow, the color she loved. It is her summons to me."

The gaunt body went limp. Ramming could see that his breathing had quickened. Life was slipping away from Juan Guillermo Campos y Sotelo.

Jessie was able to turn his body away from the lizard, until he was a bare few inches out of reach of the terrible jaws. But still, because his legs were pinioned, he could not put two hands to the strap that held his right arm. He watched in helpless, blind fury while his friend of three days grew still.

The sun moved higher and its heat increased in the airless pocket of desert growth around the stone butte. Careful to keep his shoulder drawn away from the Gila monster's range, he turned his head and looked into Juan's face, now cast with a yellow hue, the color of a man suffering from the final stages of malaria. But as he

41

watched, the weathered skin of the aged face stretched into a thousand wrinkles.

Juan Campos was smiling!

It lasted for a few seconds, no more, then the waxen flesh relaxed. Jessie saw the narrow chest heave twice with short, shallow breaths. Then he was still. The reptile's venom, injected at a vital point in his neck, had done its work quickly.

A bitter dryness clawed at Ramming's throat. He could feel his heartbeat quicken, his breathing accelerate. Swallowing was becoming increasingly difficult. He had received a larger dose of the lizard's venom than he had thought. His vision began to blur and he abruptly realized a new danger. If he passed out his body would inevitably roll back where it had been. Within the range of those lethal jaws!

Jessie closed his eyes again, grasped his right forearm with his left hand, and set himself against the leather shackle. Pain rose like a fiery curtain behind his eyes. He wanted desperately to relax, to let fatigue and blackness swallow him up. It wouldn't be so bad. Juan had not suffered long.

He looked at the face of the man beside him. It was serene, untroubled now. Ramming cursed bitterly at his own impotence, and struggled against the length of leather until he thought his spinning head would burst open and spill his brains onto the hot sand.

Then, at the peak of the effort, a fraction of a second before he made the decision to give up, something shifted. Almost in disbelief, he jerked again. The roots of the mesquite were giving up their purchase in the hard earth.

He tugged until the plant had moved close enough to allow him the use of both hands. In another minute he had torn the bush from the ground. With his jackknife he quickly slashed the thongs that held his feet spread-eagled outward.

The Gila monster watched sullenly, knowing its prey was beyond reach.

When he had freed his limbs, Ramming rose clumsily, fighting muscles that had stiffened through the long night. He deliberately avoided looking at the man on the ground as he cast about for a weapon. There it was, the stone on which their captor had sat before his campfire during the night.

Ramming raised the rock above his head and slammed it down squarely in the middle of the Gila monster's spine. Then he placed a booted foot on the neck of the reptile and sliced off the head with the blade of his knife. The lizard's stubby legs clawed futilely for a few seconds, then became still. But the mouth of the disembodied head continued to open and close, instinctively lethal to the last.

A spasm of dizziness sent Jessie suddenly to his knees, reminding him like a kick to the belly that his system was still fighting the effects of a small measure of the Gila monster's venom. When the spell had passed he gathered his courage and looked toward the old Mexican man still stretched grotesquely between the mesquite trees. The body now seemed as dry and shriveled as a broken stalk of corn. Jessie wondered that Juan Campos y Sotelo's frail form could have housed such a giant of a spirit.

He sat beside it for a long time, looking into the distance, beyond the desert to the far-off range of mountains, now as unattainable as the shores of another planet.

Later, when the sun moved high and sent its rays down to sear the desert for another day, Jessie scraped out a grave in the crusty earth, in the shade of the stone overhang that sheltered the little water hole.

Gently, he placed the slight body of Juan Campos in the depression, covered the seamed face with the big-brimmed hat of woven fiber, and buried the old man beneath a cairn of stones. It was the second time in a week he had covered the remains of someone he loved. He stood beside the crude grave with his own hat in his hand.

Aloud he said, "He will pay, *amigo*. He will pay."

Chapter
SIX

A rising impatience goaded Jessie. He wanted to be moving, on the trail of his quarry. But the gray gelding was gone. And Juan's little mule, hardened to survival in the badlands, had slipped out of his hobbles and vanished during the night, knowing somehow that his master wouldn't need him anymore.

No mount. And no weapon. Jessie thought dully that his problems might have been better resolved if the Gila monster had finished him, too. The poison was still working in him, making him light-headed, nauseous, and turning the saliva in his mouth to ash. But he had to have water, and he lay on his belly beside the water hole and drank until he was overfull. There would be no more water holes where he was heading.

Jessie was in the act of getting to his feet when his eyes fell on a long, slender object in the crystal clear water. He had already turned away, supposing it to be the limb from a mesquite tree, when a nudge from his mind's eye provoked another look.

It was the goose gun! It had plunged unnoticed into the pool when the bearded man's rifle barrel had knocked him senseless.

Wading out to recover it, Jessie felt a glimmer of hope, but it endured no longer than a shake of his head. How was he to carry a supply of water when he walked away from this oasis? Without it, the desert and the buzzards would have him in a day's time. Of what value was a shotgun to a man dying of thirst?

He had no answer to the question, but he went on anyway, breaking open the shotgun to replace the water-soaked cartridges with fresh loads. Glancing through the big double bore of the barrels he saw a shaft of light reflected from the pond, and an idea struck him with such force that he grunted aloud. Quickly he drew out his jackknife and began carving a pair of wooden plugs to fit the muzzles. When he was satisfied with their fit, he held the shotgun under water, letting the barrels fill. Then he wedged the plugs into the eight-gauge openings.

Less than a pint in each barrel, he judged. Not really very much, and chances were the taste would be something less than agreeable. But that bit of water might very well make the difference in whether Jessie Ramming was still alive when the sun went down forty-eight hours hence.

That burning orb was now edging toward the western horizon and when it sank from sight there would be no early moon, no light to guide his steps. He thrust the thought aside. Every moment that he wasn't moving toward the mountains was a wasted moment. He gazed around him once more, at the scuffed earth where he and his gentle old companion had lain, and then at the pile of stones on the far side of the water hole. His debts were piling up.

It required a definite effort of will to turn his back on the oasis and confront the hostile terrain of the desert. The vast prairie he and Juan Campos had set out across three days earlier had been ominous enough, but this land was like nothing he had ever encountered. Criss-crossed by deep, ragged ravines and populated with nothing but dagger-like cactus and lonely century plants, it was a place even the keeper of purgatory would shun.

He gazed across the harsh, treeless plain and remembered with aching clarity how he had stood at the back door of the Ramming home in the little Ohio town when he was a boy and listened to the rain drumming on the roof. In the yard the water glistened on the carpet of tall grass and, a little beyond, on the thick stands of timber.

But he had been ready for the new adventure when Francis Ramming had announced to his family that they were moving west, to a climate where Jessie's mother might have a chance to defeat the consumption that had wasted her body. But Francis Ramming had not truly comprehended the enormity of that decision. A schoolteacher, in a time when men raised their eyebrows at such work for a man, he saw the world through the rose-colored spectacles of a scholar, oblivious to the everlasting disappointment his sensitive nature had wrought in his stalwart, seafaring father.

When their Ohio neighbors had asked, "Where are you heading?" Francis Ramming's heartbeat had quickened. "West!" he announced. And, once committed to the move, he began to feel like a bold adventurer. Unhappily, nature had not equipped him for such a role. The long, arduous wagon journey to the new world was a series of calamities.

Not yet a man in years, Jessie had a far better aptitude for horses and wagons, directions and weather, than ever his father had had. Watching the ocher rim of the sun disappear now, Ramming hunched his shoulders against the recollection of how the Ramming family's homesite came to be chosen.

"Poppa," Jessie had said to his father. "The horses can't go much farther without rest. Blackie is hurting bad. We're going to have to stop here."

"I decide when we stop, son. Those animals will be all right." His father spoke sternly. "And Jessie. You must remember what I've taught you. Blackie is hurting badly. Not bad."

But Blackie was indeed hurting, bad or badly. The aging animal began to tremble in his harness. A tortured rumble erupted from his lungs. As they watched, he sank slowly to the ground. His eyes rolled wildly as the final tremor wracked his gaunt carcass. Then he was still.

There was no going on. On a windswept knoll in the middle of a vast sea of buffalo grass, devoid of trees and miles from the nearest natural water supply, their journey ended. But it was "The West," and Francis Ramming was blissfully content. Until he looked about for something with which to build a shelter. He was struck dumb

46

when he realized there were no trees to cut, no towns where lumber could be purchased, no neighbors from whom to borrow.

It was Jessie who asked, "Can't we dig a hole and cover it with the bed of the wagon?" And it was Jessie and his three sisters who constructed the dugout, all the while trying not to notice their father's ineffectual attempts at manual labor.

Two days later Jessie had to stop work on the dugout to dig a grave for his mother, and from that time on Francis Ramming was never quite in touch with the real world. He became withdrawn and silent, sitting for long periods staring vacantly toward the horizon. His dreams of conquering the frontier lay in shambles about him.

But life went on for Jessie and his sisters. He found a tiny spring a half-day's ride from the dugout, with water enough to keep them alive, although never enough for bathing. Buffalo chips were the fuel for their fire and their victuals were an unchanging round of wild berries or cactus apples, Mormon tea, and birds or cottontail rabbits caught in Jessie's snares.

The savage land gave no quarter. The nightly whimpering of Jessie's youngest sister finally broke through Francis Ramming's last defenses. One night, in the blackness of the dugout, he began raving, shouting curses his children had never heard from his lips, and shaking his fist toward the makeshift roof. Jessie managed to quiet his father and after a time the haggard, hollow-eyed man slept again.

But when they awoke the following morning his pallet was empty.

Jessie found him in the afternoon, wandering shoeless across the windswept prairie, lecturing to a classroom that existed only in his memory. That night he died in his sleep and Jessie hacked out another grave, beside that of his mother.

There were other families in the New Mexico territory whose disillusionment with the raw, uncivilized country was no less intense than the Rammings'. It was with one of these that Jessie's sisters were able to return to Ohio, to the home of an aunt. They begged Jessie to go with them. He would never survive in this untamed wilderness, they pleaded. But Jessie had become a man. And this was a man's domain.

The solitude of the dugout and its sea of prairie was absolute. Many a man would have fled in search of companionship, but the desolation suited Jessie perfectly. It was only after an interlude of several months that he finally admitted he had to leave it behind and find a way to make a living. So he climbed on the aging horse and headed westward, toward the mining town that lay at the far edge of the Staked Plains.

They called it Trabajo now, but its name was really *Mucho Trabajo*: Much Work, in Spanish. An early inhabitant of the townsite, one who had expected to find his fortune in gold lying about on the ground, had named it that after a cruel stint in a mine shaft.

Jessie Ramming had no difficulty finding work, and for three years he had labored in a mine euphemistically called the Miss Mable. There, swinging a pick and hefting a shovel for twelve hours a day, his strength grew to its fullest. And because he was a strong-willed man, he could work any two miners into exhaustion.

But life in the Miss Mable taught him something else: That even a healthy wage paid in gold was no substitute for fresh air and sunlight and the freedom to move about. When the vein began to play out he went looking for a likely piece of ground on which to stake his claim. He wanted to return to the solitude of the prairie, to be alone with his few animals and his thoughts. But fate had other ideas.

He made a trip to Trabajo for supplies, the last he would make for six months. He was at the counter in the mercantile, ready to settle his account, when he saw Anna. It wasn't the first time he had seen her. But the other times he had glimpsed her only from a distance. Now, seeing her close up, close enough to hear her soft voice and smell the woman sweetness of her auburn hair, his senses began to reel. Jessie became tongue-tied, hardly able to respond to her polite comment about the heat of the late spring day.

When he walked away, there was a single thought in his mind. He would have Anna for his wife. And typical of his tenacity, he proposed before autumn touched the

18

High Plains. It was none too soon, either. Anna's father sold the mercantile and moved back to Pennsylvania before the year was out. But she recognized the strength and depth and determination in the quiet man who asked for her hand, and she accepted.

And every day for eight years after, Jessie Ramming asked himself how fortune could have blessed him with such a woman.

Chapter
SEVEN

Jessie Ramming stumbled in the darkness and fell again. His hands were scraped raw and despite the buffalo-hide chaps that covered his legs, his knees were a mass of bruises. He had walked through the night with only the uncertain light of the stars to show him the way. Sharp-sided gulleys, ridges ledged with stone, low-growing cactus plants that waited in ambush, had battered him until there was scarcely any area of his body that did not ache. And now even the stars were growing dim.

Suddenly a dark, unnatural shape rose out of the ground before him. He stumbled and fell to one knee and froze there, straining his eyes to see if the strange hulk moved. The shotgun in his hand wouldn't help. It contained only water. If the object were an animal and it chose to attack, he would be helpless.

But the strange lump of soft darkness didn't move. Then Jessie's nose detected a hint of decomposing flesh. He moved cautiously nearer. It was the carcass of a horse, lying on its side.

The animal had been dead for no more than a couple of days, but the sun's heat had already started the decaying process. Buzzards and coyotes, too, had begun their grim work on the tender parts of the beast. Abruptly, Ramming knelt and inspected the feet of the horse. One hoof was badly split. He knew then what had happened.

This was the sorrel mare, the one that had stood

tethered to the mesquite bush on the ridge behind the adobe house, on the day that death came to Anna.

Ramming nodded to himself in the blackness. The killer had ridden this way a few days earlier, but had been left afoot when the mare became too lame to travel. He moved around to the horse's head and ran his fingers over the broad skull. At a point between the eyes he felt the hole where a rifle bullet had been fired into the mare's brain. That didn't exactly fit, Jessie mused. The man he was trailing didn't seem to be the kind who would waste a bullet on a crippled horse.

He sat down a few yards away and considered his discovery. The scarfaced man had been left with no choice but to return to the water hole on foot and wait there in the hope that someone would come along to provide him with another mount. Jessie bit his lip in disgust. He and Juan Campos had been very accommodating, two unsuspecting flies alighting in a spider's web.

But there was a crumb of consolation in finding the horse. This was the direction his quarry was heading, whatever his reason might be for riding toward the mountains.

After a time, Ramming got stiffly to his feet and walked on, trying not to think of the uncertainty ahead, of the odds against finding his wife's murderer.

Daylight came all in an instant, it seemed. One minute it was too dark to see where to place his foot, the next the world around him was aflame with brilliance. He enjoyed the warmth and the light for only a short time before the heat of the sun made him wish for a return to the chill cloak of darkness.

His determination to keep moving failed him before the sun reached its zenith. He crept into a sliver of shade beneath a rocky ledge, slept a miserable sleep until midafternoon, and awoke desperately craving a drink. He pried the wooden plug from a barrel of the shotgun and tasted the water. It was scalding hot and bitter with cordite but he forced himself to drink it.

Weaving on his feet like a drunk, he set out again, using the merciless sun once more as his guide.

Time lost meaning. The sun vanished but the harsh, searing light continued to burn in Jessie's mind. The cold came again, and wrapped around him like a shroud of ice. In the blackness of night he began to shake. His teeth chattered until that became the only sound he could hear. Again and again he fell in the rocks and the cactus spines, and each time it took him longer to regain his feet.

Once, after he had fallen among the rocks, he struggled to his feet and walked on for a half-hour before realizing that he had forgotten to pick up the shotgun. He sat down and cried, the whimpering cry of a pup begging not to be kicked again. Then he went back and found the weapon, but lost nearly two hours in the search.

Thirst came again, a terrible force that drove everything else from his mind. He had determined to save the second barrelful of water until the heat of the following day but at last he gave in to the craving.

He wrenched the plug from the muzzle of the shotgun and found that the water was frozen!

His body numb and his mind a kaleidoscope of thought fragments, Jessie staggered on. The sun pushed up and drove the chill from his bones and he saw that in the darkness he had walked through a vast sagebrush-carpeted plateau. He was at the first level of the foothills. Before him the terrain pitched steeply upward. Not far up there, the sagebrush and greasewood gave way to a belt of thick, sprawling piñon trees.

He climbed until his legs refused to function. Then he collapsed beneath one of the trees, rolled over on his back, and was asleep before his eyelids closed. His final thought was that it would all end right here.

A noise woke him. He opened his eyes to see a mule deer buck and two does standing not fifty feet away, watching him in hair-trigger hesitation. He reached for the shotgun but remembered too late that it was not loaded. The deer bounded away on spring-driven legs while the pangs of hunger sounded in Jessie's belly.

Something crunched beneath his feet. He looked down to see that the ground was carpeted with tiny brown nuts, fallen from the piñon tree above him. He had no idea if

52

the nuts were edible but he had nothing to lose. He ate one and then another. And then began gulping down the rich meat of the nuts by the handful. When he had gorged himself he drank the second cylinder of acrid water.

The muscles of his legs were stiff and sore but he felt the old urgency gnawing at him again. If Juan Campos had guessed correctly, that Scarface was heading for the mountain town of McSween, then he still had a great distance to cover. Behind him, the desert stretched in a brown wave to infinity. Ahead, the mountain range he had seen as a soft, blue haze for so many days had now become a fortress of jagged peaks, framed by a canopy of dark, angry clouds.

But Ramming didn't need those storm clouds to remind him that winter would be nearer at the higher elevations. The wind was steadily growing stronger and colder as he fought his way up the mountain slope.

It seemed to have no end. The piñon trees fell behind, giving way to regal ponderosa pines and pyramiding spruce trees. Where the trees thinned, ragged ledges of stone sprouted. The sun was well past its midpoint when he finally reached the crest of the mountain and gazed beyond into a deep, rugged canyon.

Jessie slumped down with his back against the dead stump of a lightning-felled pine and looked with sinking heart at the view before him. The slope he had climbed was insignificant in comparison to the fierce country ahead. The walls of the vast canyon at his feet shot almost straight up from the valley floor a dizzying distance below. A forest of conifers, interrupted by patches of autumn-yellowed aspens, made an impenetrable jungle as far as he could see.

Ramming was gathering his feet beneath him when a strangeness caught his eye. He studied the floor of the canyon for several minutes before he saw it again. In a small clearing in the very bottom of the chasm, almost hidden in the dense mountain growth, was a tiny cabin.

He watched it for a long time but saw no movement, no tell-tale ribbon of smoke coming from the chimney. He surmised it was a prospector's cabin, long since abandoned. But there was always the chance he might find a sign of the scarfaced man there.

It took him much longer than he had expected to reach a point on the mountainside above where he judged the cabin to be, and the sun was already crowding the peaks to the west when he spotted the little shack through the thick stand of timber.

Jessie hunkered on his heels for several minutes, studying the cabin. The door on its leather hinges stood wide open, swinging fitfully to the gusting wind. Still there was no sound, no light, no smoke from the chimney. He shrugged. So much for having company tonight.

He stood up and took one step down the mountainside. The sound of the shot rushed in at him from every direction. He dived for the trunk of a big ponderosa pine, hoping he had guessed which side would protect him. He didn't hear the second shot. His knees buckled under him and he pitched down the steep incline, tumbling over and over until his lifeless body crashed into a small evergreen.

Chapter
EIGHT

Jessie's senses returned slowly, a degree at a time. He would start to remember, then the blackness would blow in around him again like swirling dust. It was the pain that finally brought him to the surface. It pounded against his head like a pickaxe driving into granite.

At last he forced himself to open his eyes. He saw the rough walls of a cabin, and guessed it was the one he had approached so stealthily—the thought made him grimace—some hours before. He was lying on his back on a cot against one wall.

Slowly, gritting his teeth against the throbbing ache, he turned his head toward the center of the room. He made out the fireplace, a log burning cheerily in its midsection, and a few steps away a rough table on which sat a lighted coal oil lamp.

He saw the barrel of a rifle, lying across a pair of knees. But the knees were wearing gingham. Jessie squeezed his eyes shut for an instant, then looked again.

The long-barreled, single-shot rifle rested across the lap of a woman whose face he couldn't discern. But in the yellow lamplight her hair was a tousled gold. Her head was dropping forward. She was on the verge of falling asleep.

Ramming started to sit up but a stab of pain with the impact of a giant fist slammed against the side of his head. Dizzily, he lay back and put one hand up to explore his head above his right ear. His fingers discovered a thick swath of bandages, and a tenderness that made him gasp for breath.

His movement roused the woman with the gun. He saw her rise and take a step toward the cot on which he lay. The trouble, whatever it was, must still be out there, judging from her wariness.

"What happened?" Jessie's words were a dry whisper.

"You were shot," she said. Her voice was unsteady but still it was a strong, resolute voice.

"I suspected that." He attempted to smile. "Feels like I've been kicked by a mule."

She turned enough that he could see in the lamplight a sprinkling of freckles across the bridge of her small nose, but there was no hint of an answering smile.

"The bullet just grazed you. You'll be all right," she said evenly. Ramming had the unpleasant feeling that she wasn't particularly pleased about it.

"Did you get a look at who did it?" he asked anxiously. "Did you happen to see another man, a man with a scar . . . ?

The sudden tightening of the woman's shoulders, and the ashen look in her face, made him stop.

"Yes. I saw your friend. But he went away."

She was trying desperately not to cry and it made Jessie want to offer her comfort. Until, with a shock, he realized what she had said. She had called the scarfaced man his friend!

Fighting against the pulsing agony in his skull, he struggled to sit up. She swung the long barrel of the rifle up until he was staring into its muzzle.

"You stay where you are or I'll shoot you again!"

"Again!" Momentarily he forgot the pain. "You've got it all wrong, ma'am. That hombre's not my friend. I've been on his trail for the better part of a week."

His voice died as another onslaught of light-headedness enveloped him. He was barely able to comprehend her next words.

"Don't try to lie out of it. I ought to kill you like he . . ."

Sobs convulsed her slender body and the muzzle of

the rifle sagged to the floor. Ramming shook his head to clear the mist of pain from his eyes. Then, in one long stride, he caught the barrel of the rifle and pulled the heavy weapon from her hands. Quickly he slammed the breech open to unload the gun. But the old rifle was empty.

She stood behind the chair, gripping its back with whitened knuckles.

"I won't let you . . . do what he did," she said through clenched teeth. "You'll have to kill me first."

Steadying himself with a hand on the table, Jessie looked at her and shook his head.

"Ma'am, that man—if he's who I think he is—is the reason I'm here, all right. But you can be sure of one thing. He's no friend of mine."

She wiped at a tear with the heel of a hand. The gesture was an angry one, implying shame at the weakness it represented.

"Why should I believe you?"

He didn't have an answer. The giddiness had returned and he barely managed to stay on his feet long enough to reach the other chair. After a time the room stopped spinning and he looked at the woman again. She hadn't moved, but stood rigidly alert, her blue eyes as wary as those of a deer.

"My name is Jessie Ramming," he said slowly. "I have a place on the plains the other side of Trabajo. At least I did. Until I started on the trail of that man."

Not really knowing why, he stopped short of telling her about the death of Anna. He could explain that later, when he had gained her trust.

"You mean you've been chasing him?"

"Yes. I'm pretty sure it's him. Tall, skinny fellow. Has a bushy black beard?"

"And a scar? Here?"

She indicated the side of her face with long, delicate fingers.

He nodded, encouraged by her response.

"Yes. That would be him. That's the man I'm after."

Her voice had been even, without emotion. Now it bore a hostility that made him wince.

"So you're the reason he came through the mountains. He was trying to get away from you." Her lips were a white line across her face. "It's too bad I didn't shoot straighter."

Ramming's brow furrowed involuntarily, drawing the skin painfully tight against the wound high on his head. She was determined to be unreasonable.

"I don't know what you mean," he said sharply. "But that man thinks I'm dead. He came across these mountains for his own reasons, not because he was running from me."

He could tell by the unyielding look in her eyes that she was going to take a lot of convincing. At that moment he didn't feel like arguing the point.

"Where's your man?" he asked suddenly.

She waited a long time without answering. He thought she was simply going to ignore the question. But her eyes shifted to a muslin-draped doorway leading from the room. When they came back to his face they were filled with tears.

Still she said nothing. He took the lamp from the table and went to the little opening covered by the cloth. Warily, he pulled it aside and held the lamp before him. He was looking into a small lean-to storeroom built against the back wall of the cabin. A few provisions lined a shelf that ran along the back wall.

He glanced down. A ragged sheet covered an object on the floor beneath the shelf. A pair of scarred shoes and the worn legs of a pair of trousers protruded from beneath the fabric.

He knelt down and pulled back the sheet. In the yellow light of the coal oil lamp he saw the face of a man, gray-haired and gray-whiskered. Jessie gritted his teeth. There were two bullet wounds. One bullet had gone into his mouth and blown away part of his cheek. The other was in his chest. A big wound, where the slug had exited after entering the man's back.

He drew the cloth over the cold, white face and went back into the room where the woman still stood.

"I'm sorry," he said quietly. "Your father?"

"My husband."

58

"Oh." Jessie was flustered. "He was a lot older. I thought . . ."

"Emil was a good man," she said, and as she talked he had the feeling she wasn't saying it for his benefit. "He could write fine letters. I came out here from the East. I'd never met him before. But he was good to me. He didn't deserve to die."

After a time Ramming said, "Do you want to tell me what happened?"

She shook her head from side to side, telling him no, but she began to talk and the words came tumbling out.

"It was early yesterday morning. Emil had already left, to work the mine. That's when the man came. He was in the cabin before I knew anything. He grabbed me, and held a knife to my throat."

Her voice broke. She wiped at her nose with her apron. In the lamplight her face was a picture of torment. She wasn't very old but Jessie suspected what she was telling him had cost her a lifetime of suffering.

"What did he say?" he asked gently.

"Nothing, I never heard him say a word."

She was quiet for a long time, both her hands clutching at the neck of the gingham wrapper.

"And then?" Jessie prompted.

But whatever it was, she was pushing the memory away, back into a remote corner of her mind. She only turned her head slowly from side to side.

"He heard Emil coming. I started to scream. He hit me and knocked me down again."

Ramming had thought it was a shadow on her cheek, caused by the uncertain light from the lamp, but now he could tell it was a bruise. It started at the delicate swell of her cheekbone and spread into the tendrils of straw-colored hair above her temple.

"Look," he said. "You don't have to . . ."

But there was agony in her face. She had to go on.

"He had hidden his horse back there in the trees. Emil came to the door and he . . . just shot him in the mouth. Emil tried to get away. He ran after him and shot him again. I ran and hid."

The tears had quit. Her eyes were dry and her voice was stronger. But it was flat, toneless.

"He looked for me for a long time. I could hear him in the brush and rocks up on the mountain. After he left I came down and got Emil's rifle. All night I was afraid he would come back. Then I saw you."

She had slumped into the chair and had one arm resting on the table. Jessie said, "I'm sorry," and leaned forward to put his hand over hers. She drew her hand away quickly, then got up and walked to the fireplace. Facing away from him, she put her hands over her face and stood there for a long time.

Finally Ramming asked, "Do you have a horse, Mrs. . . . ?"

"Bucklin. Christina Bucklin," she murmured, her mind not really on the words. "We had a horse. But he's dead. He killed him, too."

"The scarfaced man?"

Her eyes were closed again.

"He just shot him in the head."

She drew a shuddering breath.

"I watched him from up on the mountain. He went to the corral behind the cabin. Emil's horse was there. It was a stallion, a beautiful black thing. Emil thought ho was really getting a bargain when he bought that horse.

"But then he found out what was wrong. The black was gentle until someone got on him. Then he went crazy. No one could ride him."

"What happened?"

"I knew what the horse would do when that terrible man got on him. The black threw him in two jumps, and broke the cinch, I guess. Anyway, the saddle came off. He grabbed his rifle but the gate was still open. The horse almost made it to the trees before he got off a shot. I saw the horse fall. I think he was dead before he hit the ground."

Ramming thought of the sorrel mare he'd found in the darkness, the bullet hole between her eyes. Scarface hadn't shot the animal out of compassion.

Abruptly she turned about. Jessie saw defiance in her eyes, and anger at herself.

60

"I would appreciate it if you'd forget what I've said," she declared stiffly. "It was not my intention to seek pity, Mr. Ramming."

She was on the knife-edge of breaking. He knew that any response he made would be the wrong one. He looked at her calmly.

"I'm half-starved. You suppose you could find something for me to eat?"

Her breath escaped in a long sigh. She stoked the fire and in minutes the aroma of venison stew filled the small cabin. Jessie sat at the table while she ladled an ample portion into a bowl. He devoured that helping, and a second and a third, and drank great tin mugs of steaming coffee.

He paid her no attention while he ate but he was aware that her blue eyes were watching his every movement, weighing his nature, and his intentions. There was little trust left in Christina Bucklin.

Finished with the meal, Ramming sat a moment watching her put things in order. She was a small woman, almost delicate, but she moved with the grace and sureness that come with inner strength. She felt his eyes on her and a flush of crimson brushed the whiteness of her cheeks.

Embarrassed at his own preoccupation with her, Ramming moved to the fireplace and added a few pieces of wood. He became aware of a sound outside the cabin, a sound that increased in intensity as he listened. He stepped to the door, swung it open, and had it snatched from his hand by the wind. Far above, in the crowns of the ponderosa pines surrounding the cabin, the wind cried out at the needle-sharpness of the icy mountain air.

He closed the door and went back to stand by the fire. His next words were spoken carefully.

"Mrs. Bucklin, something will have to be done . . . about your husband. The ground is going to freeze tonight."

She kept her face turned away. A tear fell from her cheek and hissed against the hot iron stew-pot in her hand.

61

"In there." She nodded toward the door to the lean-to room. "There's a shovel. And a lantern."

He procured the shovel and the coal oil lantern, avoiding the sheet-draped body with his eyes. "Do you have any particular place in mind?"

"Just . . . not too far from the cabin."

He fired the lantern and went outside. The sudden biting cold snatched the breath from his lungs. He chose a gentle rise in a circle of blue spruce trees fifty paces from the cabin and set to work. The ground was soft and the digging easy, except for the tree roots, and in a matter of minutes he no longer felt the cold.

He went back inside, dreading what was to come. But she seemed to have braced herself for the task. She held out a blanket, thick and warm but beginning to ravel at the edges. At the questioning look on his face, she said, "He liked to put this around him and sit by the fire when it was cold."

In the lean-to storeroom Jessie stooped to pick up the rigid form. It was surprisingly light. Emil Bucklin had not been a big man. Carefully he wrapped the body in the blanket and secured it with a length of heavy twine, then stooped through the small door with his awkward burden.

Christina Bucklin was not in the cabin. When Jessie stepped outside he saw her beside the grave he had dug, the lantern on the ground beside her. He knew the raw wind was chilling her to the bone but she gave no sign that she felt it.

He knelt down in the freshly turned soil and lowered the body into the grave with careful deliberation. Then he looked at Christina. There was only blankness in her features, so he proceeded to fill the excavation as quickly as he could. When he had finished, he took a step back and stood with bowed head.

A long time later he heard her say, "Thank you, Mr. Ramming."

They walked side by side back to the cabin. Seeing the hurt in the lines of her face, Jessie reached out to take her arm. She neither looked at him nor made a move to avoid his hand, but he felt her withdraw from the touch. He let his hand drop.

62

He built up the fire in the fireplace again and they stood silently, looking into the flames.

At last he asked, "What will you do?"

"I don't know. I hadn't thought about it."

"You'll want to go back East, to your people, I guess."

She shook her head, the cornsilk softness of her hair swaying gently in the flickering light.

"I don't have anyone. That's why I came out here."

It was a disquieting turn for Jessie.

"You'll need to go to town. Find a place to stay."

She didn't answer.

"I'll be leaving for McSween in the morning. You can come along."

Her head snapped up. The look she gave him was fiercely defiant.

"Don't worry about me. I'll manage."

Her obstinacy irritated him. For the past several hours his own purpose had been virtually forgotten in his concern for her. And now she was turning her back on his offer of help. To hell with it, he told himself. He had his own problems. He couldn't afford to waste time and sympathy on someone who didn't appreciate those commodities.

Ignoring her, he picked up the lantern and pushed through the door, bracing himself against the cutting edge of the mountain gale. It would have helped to ask directions from the woman but he stubbornly rejected the idea.

Holding the lantern high, he walked directly away from the door of the cabin, toward the base of the forested mountainside that shot up toward the cloud-shrouded sky. He climbed through the trees until he reached a level he thought was about right. Then, using the faintly illuminated smoke from the cabin chimney as a guide, he moved in a zigzag pattern across the steep slope.

The cold was growing more intense and he had no coat. He was almost ready to make the concession and go ask her where he should search when he found the little tree that had stopped his fall. He moved downhill from the blood-spattered sapling and a few minutes later found what he was seeking. The double-barreled shotgun was almost hidden beneath the mat of pine needles.

The cold, heavy steel felt good in his hand. It was like finding an old friend.

The woman watched him warily as he entered the cabin with the gun in his hands. Disregarding her stare, he went to the cupboard behind the table, searched through the scant collection of utensils for a moment, and took down a wooden bowl of congealed grease. He found a piece of cloth left from the bandage she had fashioned for his head, took a chair at the table, and laid the shotgun across his knees.

She continued to watch as he worked the tallow through the action of the big gun. When she spoke he couldn't tell if it was conciliation or suspicion in her tone.

"If you don't have a horse, how did you get here, Mr. Ramming?"

"I walked, Mrs. Bucklin."

"You couldn't have walked over the desert and the mountains. Emil said . . ."

"Believe what you like," he interrupted, and went on lubricating the weapon.

She started to say something, but instead closed her lips tightly. After a time she moved to the bed where he had lain unconscious and withdrew an armful of bedding from beneath it. Atop the pile of blankets was a huge buffalo robe.

She spread several of the blankets on the bed and turned to him.

"You're hurt. You can sleep here. I'll make a pallet for myself."

"No." His voice was toneless. He stood the shotgun in a corner, wiped the grease from his hands, and took a step across the room, reaching out toward her.

The sharp intake of her breath was loud in the tiny cabin. She drew back against the wall, holding the buffalo robe like a shield against her bosom.

"I should have known." She was shaking her head from side to side, her eyes wild as she watched his advance. "I thought you might be different . . . I should have expected it."

Jessie stopped. His sandy eyebrows came together in a frown.

"I don't know what you're talking about, Mrs. Bucklin. Just give me the buffalo robe. I'll make do in a chair over there by the fire."

She half fell onto the bed. Ramming took the heavy robe from her unresisting hands and moved over to the fireplace. He could hear her whimpering as he drew the robe about him, tilted his chair back against the wall, and closed his eyes. If she ever moved to get into bed he didn't hear the sound.

Chapter
NINE

Jessie awoke as the first faint light of day was showing at the cabin window. He added lengths of wood, heavy with pine pitch, to the fire in the fireplace and turned to warm his back. He looked at the bed where the blonde woman lay. Her eyes were open, regarding him steadily.

"Good morning," he said, not expecting her to reply. She didn't. He went to the door and stepped outside, wanting to give her a chance to dress.

He expected to meet a sharp, wind-driven cold. Instead, the dawn's chill was mild, with only a hint of the frigid temperature he had felt a few hours earlier when he went to dig the grave for Christina Bucklin's late husband.

Above the mountain to the east there was a faint, pink tint coloring the sky. The only clouds were a few high, uncertain mare's tails. The lack of cold puzzled Jessie. He had been sure a winter storm was building.

Taking his time, he moved to the grave and saw that the site he had chosen was a good one. The circle of spruce trees made it a natural cathedral.

With his jackknife he cut two limbs from an aspen and fashioned a cross, then drove it into the earth at the head of the grave. He stood away and looked for a long time at the mound of fresh soil. It was the third grave Scarface had bequeathed him.

Impatience pushed at him again and he walked quickly back to the cabin. He started to rap on the door but for a reason he didn't quite understand he opened it instead and went on in. She was up and dressed and gathering food to tie up in a bundle. He saw some dried venison, cornmeal cakes, dried fruit.

"You don't have to do that," Ramming said.

"I know that," she replied, without looking up.

He took two coins from his pocket and laid them on the corner of the table.

"I'm not doing it for money. Take it back."

He was angry and frustrated. The woman had rejected everything he had tried to do for her.

"I need a coat." He didn't try to keep the irritation from his voice.

She went to the lean-to room and came back with a plaid wool coat that fit too tightly across his shoulders and chest. But he put it on, and strapped on the buffalo-hide chaps. Then he picked up the bundle of food she had prepared and started toward the door. When he turned she was facing away from him, staring into the fire.

"Are you sure you don't want to go with me?"

There was no reply.

He closed the door behind him and turned up the canyon, past the pole corral where the killer had tried to ride the black stallion. A hundred yards farther on, at the very edge of the trees, he came upon the horse. The bullet had struck behind one ear.

Ramming went on, paralleling the dry creek bed that notched the very bottom of the canyon. The ground was covered with a carpet of reddish-brown needles from the towering ponderosas and for the first mile the going was easy. The air was damp and heavy but not nearly as cold as it should have been. Jessie felt an uneasiness he couldn't fathom, a disquieting sense of impending disaster.

Maybe it was the woman. She should have more sense, he grunted. With her husband dead, she was absolutely alone. There wasn't a chance in a million that another human being would pass this way during the long months of winter that lay ahead. When spring came someone would stumble on the cabin but it would likely be too late then.

He stopped on the faint game trail he was following and turned to look back. He could force her to go with him and probably save her life.

Involuntarily, he shook his head, remembering the knife-edge of her voice: "Don't worry about me. I'll manage."

Jessie trudged on, finding now that the trail he was following slanted sharply upward. Far ahead, through the tall pines, he could see the notch in the mountains where the trail would lead. And lying along those mountain peaks was a mass of angry, black clouds.

He hurried on, his labored breathing testifying to the thinness of the atmosphere and the elevation he had gained since leaving the cabin. The air was no longer mildly chilly. It was raw and cold, its edge honed by the wind.

A rock rolled from beneath his foot, jerking him to the ground. For a moment he propped himself up on an elbow, trying to catch his breath. But abruptly he quit breathing, straining his ears to catch the sound again. Something larger than a squirrel or rabbit was moving through the junipers below him, dislodging pebbles along the water course that formed a ragged trail up the mountainside.

Ramming moved off the trail, slipping behind the debris of a dead pine. He checked the loads in the eight-gauge, cocked both hammers, and slid the twin barrels through the dead branches until they were pointing back along the path he had come. It could be a bear or a hungry mountain lion. Or a lean scarecrow of a man with a black beard.

The first thing he saw was a mass of brown fur. His forefinger tightened against the forward trigger. Then he saw a tumble of blonde hair that had worked loose from the scarf around her head. Christina Bucklin, the buffalo robe wrapped about her shoulders, stepped into view between the trees.

Jessie's breath left his lungs in a rush. She heard the sound but still hadn't seen him. She stopped and scanned the brush ahead and Ramming thought again of a deer moving warily through the forest.

He sat and watched her for a full minute, taking in the crimson flush of her cheeks and the lithe movement of her body, a fluid grace that even the bulk of the robe couldn't conceal.

Finally he stood up, and took a perverse pleasure in the startled look on her face.

"Mr. Ramming." Her breath was coming in bursts of sound. "If your offer still holds, I would like to come with you."

He knew the price she was paying to say it, and he also knew that if he even hesitated in his answer, she would turn around and go back down the mountain.

"On one condition," he said, keeping his face stern.

"What?" She was holding her breath.

"That you drop the mister. My name is Jessie."

He grinned, and saw relief flood her eyes.

"Would you accept an apology?"

"No need for that."

"Yes. I wasn't very nice to you. I'm sorry. It was just that ..."

"Don't worry about it," he broke in. "Anyway, I suspect you and I are going to have our hands full up there."

He waved an arm toward the ragged skyline ahead, where the heavy clouds were spreading a premature darkness over the mountains.

"Let's get going."

He started up the trail again, feeling somehow comforted by the knowledge that the woman was following a few feet behind. He hadn't realized how much he had been troubled at leaving her.

Every step they took was a steep one. In the rarefied atmosphere their breathing whistled in their throats, sending little spurts of steam ahead. The junipers and stately ponderosa monarchs fell behind, their places taken by the high altitude growth—bristlecone pines and subalpine fir.

As they moved nearer timberline the wind grew stronger. Soon Ramming could feel the biting sting of sleet against his face. Glancing over his shoulder, he saw only Christina's eyes and forehead through the folds of the buffalo robe.

Gradually the sleet became thicker, softer, whiter, and soon it was clinging to the rocks and stumps along the faint game trail they were following. Jessie stopped and waited until she caught up. Leaning close, he shouted above the shriek of the wind: "How much longer before we start down?"

She shook her head inside the brown cocoon.

"I don't remember. A long time, I think."

She was right. The trail snaked up and down and around jagged outcroppings of rock, but always it climbed higher. The crest of the mountain pass was still somewhere ahead. The snow had thickened until the patches of stunted trees along the trail were concealed behind a curtain of white. It was getting deeper on the ground, too, accumulating so quickly that each step required a greater effort.

Ramming looked back just as Christina slipped and sprawled face down in the snow. He went back and helped her to her feet and held her arm as they went on. He knew she must be near the limit of her endurance.

"We'll find a place to stop for a while," he shouted in her ear.

She shook her head.

"I'll be all right. I can go on."

But as she took another step her legs buckled. Jessie grabbed for her arm but she toppled away from him, collapsing in a shapeless brown heap in a drift of snow. With one arm under her shoulders and the other beneath her knees, he picked her up and moved back to the trail. Tears sprang to her eyes and began to freeze as he watched.

She said something he couldn't understand. He lowered his head until his ear was close to her lips.

"I'm sorry," she said. "I shouldn't have come. Just ... leave me and go on."

He made his voice confident.

"We'll make it. Both of us. You hear?"

But even as he spoke fear was welling up in his throat.

70

And the wind, as if infuriated by his words, rose suddenly to a screaming pitch. He staggered backward, fighting to maintain his balance. Everywhere he looked there was stinging, drifting, driving snow. The blizzard was erupting into full fury.

Chapter
TEN

Sheriff Ben Slaughter belched contentedly, eased his bulk into a cane-bottomed chair on the hotel veranda, and whittled a match to a toothpick point. McSween was his town and he made it a daily practice to survey the comings and goings of its citizens from a vantage point on the porch of the hotel. It was Ben Slaughter's philosophy that there was more than an ounce of prevention in a conspicuous badge.

He looked for a time toward the bank of sullen clouds spreading like a pall of black smoke across the Capitan Mountains to the northeast and grunted with satisfaction. He had read the signs of a hard winter a long time ago. The horses had started putting on their winter hair earlier than usual and the deer had already begun to move down from the higher elevations to the forage and protection of Walnut Valley.

He grunted again, this time at the recollection of a note he had been handed while having his noon meal in the McSween Hotel. He hadn't bothered to read it then. It took more than a little scrap of paper to cause Sheriff Slaughter to interrupt a meal of roast beef and boiled potatoes.

He withdrew the note and unfolded it. A four-letter word, one he hadn't used in a long time, issued from his lips.

The note was brief: Be at the shack. Midnight." That was all, except for a crude mark after the last word that
72

vaguely resembled an egg with the tail of a fish attached to one end.

He cursed again, this time at length. Not many men in that part of the New Mexico territory could command Ben Slaughter. He had almost forgotten there was anyone who had that power over him. He shoved the note back into a pocket and bit the match stem in two.

The meal he had eaten wasn't setting so well. He felt a case of heartburn coming on.

He went home early and went to bed long before his usual hour. When he crawled out from the covers a few hours later, his wife didn't ask where he was going. She merely said, "Remember to wear your gloves, Ben. It's getting colder." He grunted but made no other comment. In the nearly ten years she had been married to Ben Slaughter, Bess had never questioned him about his comings and goings as the law of McSween and Walnut Valley. Her trust of him was complete.

Now, as he went about saddling the big red dun horse, Slaughter swore under his breath. Cursing was a habit he thought he had broken. He went to church, sometimes as often as once a month, and occasionally caught himself feeling sorry for the cowboys and miners who got wobbly legged drunk on Saturday night and woke up Sunday morning in the McSween jail with heads three sizes too big for their sombreros.

"You knew them chickens was going to come home to roost some day, Ben Slaughter," he muttered under his breath. "It couldn't last forever. You ought'a figured that, you jackass."

He jerked the latigo so tight the dun horse grunted in surprise and turned his head to give his master a puzzled look. Slaughter put a foot in the stirrup and stopped there, thinking about what would happen if he simply ignored the summons and went back to bed. The picture that came to mind was even more unpleasant than the unpleasant thing he was about to do. He swung into the cold saddle seat and turned up the road along the canyon, away from town.

There was no moon, or even the glimmer of a star. The

clouds he had seen earlier in the day had choked off all the sky over the broad expanses of Walnut Valley and the Capitan Mountains, all the way to the backbone of the Rockies to the west. The dun gelding didn't seem to mind the darkness, though. He single-footed along the narrow wagon road as surely as he would have in broad daylight. He, too, had an unwavering faith in the big man astride his back.

The road crossed a ravine that grew into a canyon that reached back toward the range of mountains bordering the northern reaches of the valley. There the sheriff swung his horse from the trace, across the trickle that was Walnut Creek, and headed in a northerly direction, following the shadowy line of the ravine toward the black hulk of the Capitan peaks.

There was no trail here and the ground was uneven and littered with boulders. The sheriff let the dun horse take his time. The wind had risen and the chill night air penetrated the jacket he wore. Bess had been right. It was colder. And he had forgotten his gloves.

Trees closed in around the horse and rider, making the blackness even more impenetrable. A ponderosa limb, as big around as a man's arm and quite invisible in the heavy darkness, struck the sheriff high on the forehead, knocking his hat to the ground and gouging a painful furrow across three inches of scalp.

Ben Slaughter didn't bother to swear. He was beyond that. The mere fact that he was here on the mountain in the middle of the night heading for a rendezvous that could only yield unwelcome news, left him silent with rage. And the worst part was that the anger was directed at himself.

After what seemed half a night of riding, he caught the scent of wood smoke. Angling up the steep, wooded slope toward it, he came to a small clearing. At its far edge he could see a faint glow, the light seeping from the cracks of a cabin that was all but invisible against the backdrop of trees.

The gelding had hardly moved into the clearing when a voice shattered the blackness: "Who is it?"

The high-pitched voice magnified Slaughter's irritation. He ignored the question and continued on toward the cabin, forcing the man in the clearing to step hastily aside.

The sheriff dropped the reins to the ground and went on inside. The other man followed. There was a candle on a three-legged table and a fire in the fireplace, although much of its warmth was leaking away through the cracks in the walls.

The man who had challenged him outside leaned his rifle against the door frame and shuffled toward the fire.

"You're late, sheriff."

Slaughter stood just inside the door, searching the shadows beyond the meager light from the candle.

"If you've got something to say to me, spit it out, Fish. I didn't come here to listen to you bellyache."

Fish sent a glance toward a distant corner of the shack and Slaughter followed his gaze. He saw the glowing end of a cigarette and his right hand dropped to the butt of the .45 Colt on his hip.

The sound that came from the darkness was like no voice he'd ever heard. It was a mixture of a whisper and a grunt. The kind of grunt a man makes when he's punched in the stomach. But Fish seemed to understand the words.

"Now don't you go gettin' nervous with that six-shooter," Fish said tensely. "Ain't nobody gonna cause you no bother."

"I'm already bothered by havin' to get out of a warm bed and ride to hell and gone up a mountain that's as black as the inside of a cow," Slaughter growled. "Get on with it."

"We gotta have your help," said Fish.

"Who's 'we'?"

The voice came again from the dark corner and a prickle of apprehension crawled down the back of Ben Slaughter's neck. It sounded like a name he should remember, but there was something terribly wrong with the voice that spoke it.

"What happened to you?" the sheriff asked, his irritation forgotten for the moment.

The man concealed by the darkness grunted a string of curses. The sound reminded Slaughter of someone choking on a fish bone.

"Okay. That's your business," he said. "But I didn't come here on no social call. And I'm ridin' out of here in another minute if I don't get some answers."

Obviously gaining courage from his companion in the shadows, Fish spoke up.

"Just you hold on, sheriff." He made the last word heavy with derision. "You'll stand fast 'til we have our say. Your memory ain't all that bad."

"What's that supposed to mean?" Slaughter demanded.

"That means if the good folks of Walnut Valley was to find out their fine sheriff had onc't been an outlaw, why his days of easy livin' would likely come to a sudden and uncomfortable end."

Slaughter had known it was coming. But he couldn't stop the flush of crimson that spread over his face and made his big ears burn.

"That's a damned lie and you know it! One night of ridin' to steal a few head of cows don't make a man an outlaw for the rest of his life. Especially when he's no more than a wet-eared kid."

There was a hoarse chuckle from the deep shadows in the corner of the room. Fish said, "Yeah, them folks around McSween might understand about them cows. But what about that old rancher that got shot in the gut and died of blood poisonin'?"

Fish finished on a high, nervous giggle that made Slaughter want to slap the barrel of his pistol against the man's mouth.

"It wasn't my bullet, and you know it. I wasn't even carrying a gun." He took a step toward Fish. "Now get it over with. What do you want with me?"

Fish backed away a step, then gestured toward the other man, who was leaning toward the fire to get a burning twig for his smoke. An unkempt mass of beard hid the face from Slaughter's view, but the bullet head above it left no doubt about the man's identity, even after all these years.

"My friend here needs some help," said Fish, trying to put authority in his voice.

"Forget it," Slaughter snapped. "I ain't breakin' the law. Not while I'm wearing this badge."

"Well, now. Just you hold on," Fish squeaked. "You don't have to do a thing. Just be a little careless with the keys to your calaboose."

The sheriff frowned.

"There ain't but one hombre in jail right now. You wouldn't have no reason to be interested in that no-good half-breed."

Fish grinned, his long, yellowed teeth glinting dully in the firelight.

"It just happens that that half-breed knows these mountains better than anybody in the whole New Mexico territory."

Slaughter shook his head doggedly.

"It just happens that half-breed took a knife and carved up a citizen of McSween 'til his own mother couldn't recognize the pieces. He's due to hang before the week's out."

Fish shot a glance toward the darkness that hid the third man, then turned back to Slaughter.

"Well, the hangin' will have to wait. We need him."

The sheriff's brow was a picture of black anger.

"You'll play hell. That murderer stays right there in my jail until the rope is ready."

Fish pushed out his thin chest.

"Now don't go boxin' yourself into a corner, sheriff. A man with your past ain't in much of a position to be talking tough."

Curiosity made Slaughter check his wrath.

"What do you want with a sorry polecat like Romero Red Feather?"

"Just never you mind," said Fish smugly. But at a sound from the shadows he turned and stepped toward his companion. Slaughter could hear a whispered conversation and a few moments later Fish was back standing before the fire.

Shrugging as if to indicate it wasn't his decision, he said, "The man says Romero Red Feather is the only gent living who can find a certain rock bluff he's looking for."

The sheriff remained silent, calculating that Fish's predisposition for shooting off his mouth would provide an answer to the question he wanted to ask.

"Guess it won't make no difference to tell you, sheriff. You ain't about to take a chance on spillin' the beans." He gestured toward the corner that concealed the bearded man. "He hid the loot from a bank robbery up in these hills eight years ago. A posse was a quarter-mile behind him and he didn't have no time to look for landmarks when he hid the money. He figures Romero Red Feather can locate it with the signs he recollects."

Ben Slaughter shook his big head slowly back and forth. A sickness was spreading through his ample belly. He was standing in the same room with a man who had just admitted robbing a bank. The thought burned in his mind like a glowing coal. His right hand dropped to the walnut butt of the low-slung Colt on his hip. But there it stopped. He was caught like a coyote in a trap. A few hours of youthful wildness on a night a dozen years ago, when he had ridden with a band of rustlers, had now returned to haunt him like an evil spirit.

The sheriff wasn't a man to waste time on regrets, but at that instant he would have traded all his worldly possessions for a chance to live that one night over again.

Fish saw the battle going on in the sheriff's face. He grinned his grotesque grin.

"Don't you get no righteous idees, sheriff. Out of the half-dozen gents that was along on the cow stealin' raid, there's just you and me and him"—he nodded toward the dim corner—"that's still drawin' breath. And if you haven't already guessed it, I'll spell it out for you. If you don't turn the half-breed loose, the folks in McSween are not only going to know about your cattle rustlin' past, they're also going to get the word that it was you who gut-shot old man Prather on that raid."

The sheriff had to get some air. He was choking in the small cabin, choking on the words spilling from Fish's twisted mouth. He spun on a heel and lunged toward the door. Behind him the high-pitched voice of Fish whined, "Hey, come back here. We've gotta have an answer." But Slaughter wasn't about to stop. A half-minute later he was on his horse and heading for the timber.

He rode hurriedly, gigging the big red dun with his spurs down the mountainside through the crush of pine
78

trees and shinnery. He could still hear the high, brittle voice of Fish, chuckling as the vise grew tighter and tighter. For a minute, the sheriff let himself think how it would be to turn his horse westward, toward the wildness of the big mountains, and leave behind the world he had made for himself among the folks of Walnut Valley.

He knew he couldn't do it, though. There was Bess, waiting for him with blind trust, never believing the man she had married could ever have had a dishonest thought.

And there were the hundreds of people in the town and up and down the length of the valley, good people who had trusted Ben Slaughter with their lives and property for more terms as sheriff than any other man had ever served. They deserved more than a rat who would turn and run when his back was against the wall.

Slaughter felt the ground level out beneath the hooves of the dun. He pulled the big horse to a walk, hearing the breath whistle through his nostrils and feeling his barrel swell as he sucked in great lungfuls of air.

The cold wind, laced with sleet, stung the sheriff's face, clearing his head of the mad whirl of terrible thoughts. A coyote howled high up on a ridge of the Capitans, reminding him that most things remained as they had been before. At that moment, Ben Slaughter pledged to himself that he would somehow square the misdeeds of his past with the oath he had taken when they pinned the badge on his chest. He would choose his own time but he would make it right.

The sheriff felt better for having made the decision. When he unsaddled the gelding he gave him an extra measure of grain, a tacit apology for having mistreated the faithful horse. But when he had undressed and crawled into the warm bed beside his sleeping wife, Slaughter lay for a long time, staring with unseeing eyes into the darkness.

Chapter
ELEVEN

Jessie's eyelashes were coated with ice. When he blinked his eyes he sometimes couldn't get them open again. He kept moving through the white, quicksand drifts long after exhaustion turned his legs into weak, unfeeling stumps.

The woman in his arms had been no heavier than a child when he first picked her up, but now her weight pulled at his arms until they were numb. Even the buffalo robe that was wrapped about her had become a tangible burden.

Ramming had long since lost sensitivity to the cold. There was no feeling in his feet. His face was heavy and swollen. The labored breaths he drew burned with scalding fire deep into his lungs. He looked toward the sky as he had done a dozen times. But the suffocating blanket of white gave no sign of slackening. There was no longer a trail to follow. The world looked the same in all directions.

He argued with himself. A minute, even a half-minute, of rest couldn't hurt. He would sit down in the soft pillow of snow and catch his breath; let his numb limbs regain circulation. Why not? But a deep, calculating logic wouldn't permit it. It drove him on like a cowboy quirting a horse.

Jessie had no idea how long he had lurched forward through the snow when it happened. One instant his feet were meeting the relatively solid substance of packed snow, the next instant he was falling through space. The only thought he had was to somehow shield Christina's body. He turned in the air, clutching her to his chest, and hit squarely on his back. Only the depth of the drifts where he landed saved him from a broken back or a crushed skull.

He looked about, trying to penetrate the thick screen of snowflakes, but as before it was like trying to see through a cabin window frosted over by a winter storm. The world beyond arm's length was totally obscured.

He stooped to pick up the figure in the buffalo robe and would have resumed the torturous walk but a small cry from within the robe stopped him. He laid her on the mound of snow again and drew the corner of the robe aside. What he saw brought a stabbing fear to his throat. The only color in Christina's face was the blue of her lips. It was the face of a woman without a heartbeat. He thought surely that she had died; that the sound he heard was his own moaning. But her eyes fluttered open and she looked blankly into his face.

Jessie looked away, anger swelling through him at his helplessness. He saw again the face of the old Mexican, Juan Campos, dying in the first light of dawn while he, powerful Jessie Ramming, lay impotently watching. It was that upward glance, a look of no greater duration than a pulsebeat, that showed him the outline of a specter standing out from the dimness about it.

He picked up the body of the woman and stumbled toward the dark oval a few yards away. It had vanished again behind the blizzard's veil and he feared for a moment that he had only imagined it. But then he was there, inside the mouth of a cave, carved by nature's elements from the sheer wall of a granite mountain.

He could smell the sharp odor of cat. The cave was the lair of a mountain lion. Numbly, Ramming wondered what he would do if a startled cougar came charging at him from the depths of the chamber. He took another step inside. The feline occupant of the cavern had been caught away from home when the blizzard struck.

The still air inside the cave gave an illusion of warmth but Ramming knew he had to build a fire quickly. Otherwise, Christina would die.

He placed her gently against a wall of the cave and

dropped to his hands and knees, feeling in the dimness for twigs or tree bark or pine needles. He gathered a tiny mound of the debris and drew a match from its leather pouch. The prickly pine needles caught quickly and in the light of the flame he found other scraps of tinder.

Jessie's inspection of the cave took only a few glances. It was not a deep cave, and frequently an errant gust of wind cut through, whipping the flames of the fire and reminding him that the blizzard howled unabated a few paces away.

Here and there on the floor of the cavern were the bones of an animal that Ramming took to be a deer, a meal the mountain lion had dragged inside to consume at leisure. Among the scattering of bones were the dead limbs from high-altitude conifers, but the supply was disappointingly scant.

The stone walls of the cave threw back the heat from the fire he had built and in a matter of minutes the cavern had become relatively warm. Jessie moved the woman nearer the blaze and opened the buffalo robe. She was dreadfully still. He leaned close and placed an ear near her lips. She was still breathing, although she gave no sign that she heard him utter her name.

He rubbed her arms briskly, and then her feet and legs. He knew the danger of frozen toes and he removed her shoes to encourage the circulation in her feet. Their smallness surprised him. She was a tiny thing. He wondered how he could have been so weakened that she had seemed almost too heavy to carry.

Then his eyes fell on the shotgun leaning against the rough rock wall. He had not even been aware of its weight. He had carried the eight-gauge gun so long it had become a part of him.

Christina was stirring. She moved a hand to her face. Her eyes opened slowly and reluctantly, like the eyes of a person who has slept so deeply the climb back to consciousness is long and tiresome.

"How do you feel?" he asked.

She started to speak, then glanced down and saw that he was cradling her foot in both of his big hands. Momentarily disconcerted by her expression, he hurriedly replaced her shoe and pulled the robe back over her.

After adding a few more twigs to the fire he moved to the opposite side of the small chamber and sat down with crossed legs.

When she spoke Jessie was startled at the animosity in her voice.

"Why didn't you leave me? You could have been off the mountain by now."

The question rankled, for a reason that wasn't quite clear to him. But what was clear in his mind was the hopelessness he had felt in the moments before a merciful fate had shown him the mouth of the cave.

"That's a dumb question," he said, not trying to hide his annoyance. "I wouldn't leave any human being behind in a blizzard like this."

When she spoke again, her voice was stronger, with a defensive edge.

"All right. I understand."

He looked sharply at her.

"Now what the devil does that mean?"

"Nothing."

His irritation grew. He hadn't expected any gratitude from her, but neither had he expected hostility. The storm and the ordeal they had so far survived together should have given them a common bond. Instead, she was behaving with hardly more warmth than she had shown in the first few moments of his return to consciousness at the cabin.

"I don't know what's eating you," he said tiredly. "If you don't like my company why didn't you stay at the cabin instead of following me up the trail?"

Her answer was slow in coming.

"Because I . . . decided I want to live."

It was not an answer he had expected.

"Why wouldn't you want to live? Because your husband had been killed?"

She nodded without looking at him.

"Partly that."

He waited, watching the dying fire color her blonde hair a deep, golden orange. He wanted to hear her finish the answer, but he waited in vain.

After a time Ramming glanced toward the mouth of the cave. Darkness, the absolute darkness of a night without a heaven, had descended in the minutes since they had been inside the shelter. Quickly, he set about gathering the bits of fuel inside the cave. There, at the very back, what he had taken for more bones was a collection of dead tree limbs, washed in by a mountain torrent.

He built up the fire, and sat with his back against the warm granite wall beside it. In an instant, it seemed, all his vitality drained away. Fatigue settled around him as thickly as the snow falling outside. He fought to keep his head from dropping onto his crossed forearms. The effort was too much. He decided he would doze for a few minutes.

He awoke with a start, realizing he was lying on his side. A yard away the fire was burning steadily but despite it a chill still wracked his body from time to time. He was looking for the woman in the shadows across the fire when he felt a heavy, furry object settle over him. Then a warm softness moved against his back and a different kind of chill sent an electric tingle through him. She had spread the buffalo robe over both of them and was lying nestled against his back. He could smell the woman scent of her, a fragrance caught and held beneath the folds of the robe.

With an effort he controlled his breathing.

"I'm all right. Don't worry about me," he said.

But she made no effort to move away, lying as she had been, pressed against the curve of his back and legs.

For the first time in days—it seemed vastly longer to Jessie—he felt himself beginning to relax. The tension that had lain coiled inside him for so long began to melt, receding like sun-warmed snow.

"Jessie."

He felt the warmth of her breath against the back of his neck.

"Yes?"

"Why are you chasing him?"

"The man with the scar? The man who shot your husband?"

"Uh huh."

His mind spun back to the instant when he saw Anna lying on her side in the dust beneath the clothesline.

84

Strangely, it seemed almost too long ago to recall clearly.

"I wanted him ... I still want him ... because he killed my wife."

She caught her breath in an audible whimper.

"You don't have to tell me."

"There's not much to tell," he said. "I had been away from the house most of the day. I was coming back when I heard a shot. I found her behind the house, where she had been hanging out the wash. She didn't die right away. I kept her alive almost four days."

There was no emotion in his voice. It made her shudder as she listened.

"I buried her and went looking for him."

"What was her name?"

"Anna. She was going to have a baby."

A tear rolled down her nose, dampening his shirt.

"Why? Why did he do it?"

"I wish I knew the answer to that."

She waited for him to say more but he was silent. Finally she asked, "Why didn't you tell me about her before?"

"You had your own troubles," he said.

Jessie had rolled onto his back, cradling his hands behind his head. Christina shifted, finding a more comfortable position. Her head was close enough to rest on his shoulder.

"We won't live through this, will we? We'll die right here."

He put an arm around her shoulders. A shiver raced through her body.

"We'll know in the morning," he said. "If the blizzard dies ..."

He was talking to hide the rapid beating of his heart. He tried to picture the scarfaced man in his mind, to push her softness out of reach. But it wouldn't work. He could smell her hair and feel her warm breath against his ear.

Abruptly, Jessie turned on his side, away from her.

"We'd better get some sleep while we can," he grunted.

She lay quietly for a time, still huddled against his

85

back. At last she asked, "What will you do when you find him?"

He thought about the answer for a long time. When he had finally framed a reply, he realized from her steady breathing that she had fallen asleep.

Chapter
TWELVE

Jessie awoke cramped, stiff, and cold clear through. He tucked the buffalo robe about Christina's sleeping form and built up the fire. In a short time the deeper recesses of the cave were visible and he saw that daylight was filtering in through the small hole formed by the drifting snow at the cave's entrance. They might even see the sun.

He turned and let his eyes linger for several minutes on the woman wrapped in the bulky robe. Something was eating at her. Something besides the shock of seeing her husband shot down.

He spoke her name.

"We've still got a long way to go," he said. "Let's have some breakfast."

Christina looked around, disbelief on her face. Like someone surprised to still be alive, Jessie thought. He unwrapped the dried meat and crumbled cornmeal cakes and fruit she had prepared back at the cabin, not really noticing that she had moved away until the fire was once more between them.

They ate in silence. Afterwards Ramming kicked the snow away from the cave's mouth and stepped outside into a world of dazzling sunlight. Squinting against the glare, he looked about him, and sucked in his breath. Six feet from the opening where he stood, the world simply disappeared. The ledge on which he had fallen with Christina during the blizzard was no wider than two good strides. Had he taken a single step after picking her up from the spot where they fell there would be no today. Their lives would have been crushed out on the jagged sea of boulders and shattered tree stumps two hundred feet straight down.

He didn't want her to see it but when he turned she was standing at his shoulder, looking into the nothingness beyond the lip of the cliff. She backed against the rock wall and huddled there. Her small, even teeth bit into her lower lip.

"Don't think about it," Ramming said. "Someone was looking out for us."

They had no difficulty getting off the ledge. It ran along for fifty yards, then broadened out until it became part of the ridge that sloped downward from the mountain pass. Only the depth of the new-fallen snow impeded their progress.

Ramming broke the trail, sometimes having to force his way through waist-deep drifts. She came a few steps behind, never complaining, speaking only when he asked a question. It was in that manner that Jessie Ramming and Christina Bucklin left the craggy, snow-shrouded peaks and descended two thousand feet to the broad canyon floor, and a gentle, easy trail.

But even then it was almost sundown when they came to the last ridge above the town.

They stood for several minutes drinking in the sights of civilization, watching lamplights blossom and hearing the barking of dogs and the lowing of cows waiting to be milked. Then Jessie abruptly realized that he had no plan, not even a shred of strategy, to follow when he reached McSween. It would be simply a matter of stumbling about, asking questions at random, hoping someone would drop a word that would give him a direction to follow.

He refused to consider the possibility that his quarry had bypassed McSween altogether and headed toward another settlement—like White Oaks, maybe; or Silver City. Or even El Paso.

A prolonged sigh at his elbow reminded him that he had another, and more immediate, problem. For all her stubborn determination, Christina Bucklin was still a widow, and would have no one to turn to when they reached the town. He had put off confronting that dilemma, hoping a solution would somehow materialize. It hadn't.

"You've spent a good deal of time in McSween, I suppose," he said.

"This is where I met Emil. He was waiting for me when I got off the stage. That's the only time."

"You mean you never came to town? You stayed there at the cabin?"

She looked at him blankly.

"Emil just had one horse. He came to town three or four times a year. To get what we needed."

Jessie looked at her and shook his head. The next question was out of his mouth before he could stop it.

"Didn't you ever get . . . lonely?"

"Yes," she said. That was all.

"Let's go to town," Jessie grunted. He moved out down the trail, almost hidden now in the early dusk.

Night had settled in by the time they reached the main street of McSween, a town not much larger than Trabajo, Ramming judged. But he saw signs that told him this town was on the way up, drawing new life daily from the veins of precious metal in the surrounding mountains. They saw evidence of new prosperity in the bunches of cattle and the orchards and the patches of cultivated land up and down the valley as they approached the town.

They walked side by side in the dust of the street, seeing by the light of an occasional storefront lantern the dry goods stores, dress shops, a furniture store with a pine coffin displayed in the window. They smelled the smells of town—freshly baked bread, new clothes, the aroma of barbershop bay rum, the earthy odor of a livery stable, the sharp smells of cigar smoke and hops from a noisy saloon.

And people. Miners, cowboys, Mexicans with green chili breath, moved along the rough boardwalk. Some among them showed signs of patronage of the saloon, stumbling, weaving uncertainly, and kicking up little clouds of dust from the rutted street. More than one turned to leer at the woman.

Christina moved closer to Jessie's side, walking with

89

hurried steps as though she would break into a run at any moment.

"We'll have to have a place to stay," Ramming said, scanning the false-fronted buildings along the street. "It'll have to be the hotel, I suppose."

She hesitated in midstride, falling behind so that he had to stop and turn.

"What's the matter?"

"I don't have any money."

"Okay," he said. He led the way up the wooden steps to the veranda of the two-story McSween Hotel. They had to wait until the aging clerk came from somewhere in the rear of the building, wiping the back of his hand across his mouth. The smell of whiskey was strong.

"Yep?" he greeted them. "You'll be wantin' a room?"

Ramming nodded. He didn't turn his head but he felt Christina's eyes on him, almost a physical force.

The clerk produced a key with a palsied hand and spun the register around on the counter. Ramming took the pen he offered, then hesitated. Using his own name seemed somehow unwise, but pride would have it no other way. He wrote, "Mr. and Mrs. J. Ramming" in the dog-eared register, picked up the gun, and started for the stairs. Christina seemed unable to move.

He reached the room near the end of the dim hallway and unlocked the door. She came in after him, slowly, suspiciously.

He was at the window, looking down at the after-dark comings and goings of the inhabitants of McSween, when she spoke.

"All right," she said tonelessly.

"All right what?" he asked, still gazing out the window.

"I won't argue. You'll be paid."

He turned and looked at her, standing stiffly erect just inside the door.

"I thought you didn't have any money."

"I haven't. I wasn't talking about money. You know that."

Her eyes went to the bed. He couldn't tell if it was an act of reflex or a deliberate one. But her meaning hit him full in the face.

90

"You mean because I rented one room? You think that . . . ?"

Her face was feverishly crimson, but there was no mistaking the misery in her eyes.

Ramming stepped nearer, so the lamplight fell on his face.

"I don't understand you at all, Mrs. Bucklin. We spent a night together on that mountain, with about as much privacy as anybody could hope for, and I . . . Well, nothing happened. Now, all of a sudden, you figure I'm trying to pull a fast one by registering us as man and wife."

She stood rooted beside the door, her mouth a thin line across her face. He shook his head, not bothering to hide the rancor in his voice.

"Okay. I'll explain it so you won't have any doubts. A man and a woman walking into a hotel and registering under different names is going to cause talk that will be all over town by the time we get the door unlocked. If the man with the scar is anywhere in this part of the world we'd be mighty dumb to announce our arrival."

He waved a hand toward the far side of the room, toward a parlor sofa from which most of the maroon color had faded.

"I'll sleep there. You don't have a thing to worry about."

If there was a lessening of the defensiveness in her face, Ramming couldn't detect it. He stepped to the door and swung it back.

"The rest of it is, I don't have enough money to rent an entire suite of rooms, Mrs. Bucklin." He let the anger fire his voice. "If you think you just can't stand to have me in the same room, I'll go down the street and sleep in the livery stable."

She didn't move.

"Well?" he demanded.

She moved woodenly to the bed and slumped on its edge.

"I can't help it." Her eyes weren't on him, but on the window, and the blackness beyond.

"I don't know where you get your ideas about men,"

he said, his tone softening. "You must have had some mean treatment, I guess. If your husband ..."

She interrupted before he could finish the sentence.

"No. Not my husband. I just ... can't talk about it.

Ramming shrugged. The gulf between them was growing wider, and nothing he said helped. He picked up the shotgun and walked to the door.

"Don't," she said. "You don't have to."

"It doesn't seem as if we're going to get along, Mrs. Bucklin. I'll see you in the morning. If you're still here."

She was on her feet, her hand lifting toward him, when he closed the door behind him.

Chapter
THIRTEEN

The hostler at the McSween Livery was a Mexican lad of no more than eighteen years. He was a young man who took his job seriously.

"I am sorry, señor," he said to Ramming in soft syllables. "I cannot permit you to stay the night here. It is against the rules. My *patrón* would be most unhappy."

Anger rose in Jessie's throat but subsided almost instantly. The earnestness in the face of the youth was sincere. If he was to get any sleep on this night, a different strategy would have to be found.

"What's your name, my friend?" he asked innocently.

"Martín," replied the youth.

"Martín," said Jessie, in the conspiratorial tone of a man sharing a secret with a trusted companion, "I can see you are wise beyond your years. There will be many hearts broken by Martín the handsome one."

A light sprang to the dark eyes of the Mexican.

"No, señor. There is only one. But, ah . . . she is such a one!"

He rolled his eyes heavenward, his hands tracing a voluptuous figure in the light of the stable lantern.

"Yes, I can see she has great esteem for you," Jessie said fervently. "She is not one to question the wisdom of her Martín. Eh?"

Martín grimaced and shook his head sorrowfully.

"Only last night, señor. My Consuela became very angry when another girl spoke to me. And the other girl? She is like a sister to me. I swear it to you."

Jessie put a hand to the young man's shoulder.

"They are very difficult to understand. Take my woman, for instance. It was only a little while that I stayed at the cantina. And the money I spent? It was nothing. But she screams and throws pans and won't let me in the house. A house, mind you, that I built with my own hands." He spread his broad hands in a gesture of futility. "Now I will have to sleep outside on the ground, like a dog. Ah, why do I let her . . . ?"

He turned and took a step toward the open double doors of the livery.

"Señor," the youth said quickly. "If a man came in while I was not looking, and went to the very back stall where I have just this minute placed fresh straw, how could I know he is there?"

Ramming smiled.

"My bones will be grateful to you for a soft bed, *amigo*. I wish you much luck with your Consuela."

"Aye, it is *suerte* I will need, señor. *Buenas noches.*"

It was early the following morning when Jessie located the shop of the gunsmith. He laid the heavy, engraved eight-gauge on the counter in front of the man and asked, "How much will you give me for it?"

Scowling, the gunsmith picked up the heavy weapon and examined it with minute care. At last he looked up, the scowl deepening.

"There ain't much call for these scatterguns, mister. Most of the folks that do business here would druther have themselves a Colt revolver, or one of them long-shootin' Winchester repeaters."

"How much?"

"Ten dollars."

"Nope. Twelve."

"Eleven. That's tops."

Ramming took the money and went outside into the early chill. He felt strangely vulnerable without the weight of the big goose gun in his hand. It was a sorry fate for Captain Asa Ramming's treasured weapon.

He was still thinking about the shotgun when he knocked on the door of the hotel room. Twice more he knocked, starting to wonder if she had already gone.

"Who is it?" The voice was thin, apprehensive.

"Open the door," he snapped, irritation rising in him.

The door opened a crack, then swung wide. He walked in and placed the small box of food on the scarred dresser.

"I didn't . . . I didn't know if I would see you again."

It might have been relief in her voice. Jessie wasn't sure.

"Where did you sleep?" she asked.

Unaccountably, he was angry. He said nothing.

"Where did you get the money for this?"

Then he knew what it was. The night in the livery stable wasn't what was eating at him. It was the shotgun. Somehow, its loss seemed a bad omen. As though the trail that linked him to the killer had suddenly been severed, like a wagon road washed out by floodwaters.

"Never mind," he growled. Turning to face Christina, he said without sympathy, "Look, you'll be okay here until you can find work. I've got business elsewhere and I know you'll feel a sight better when I'm gone. We'll just say adios now."

Christina was watching him with a stunned expression.

"Your gun! You sold your shotgun!"

"Don't worry about it. You'll have something to eat. I'll pay the room for a couple more days."

He didn't want to look at her blue eyes, shimmering moistly in the light from the window. He took a step backward, toward the door.

"Jessie."

He had his hand on the knob. He was irked at himself for hesitating.

"Could I tell you something before you go?"

"Why not?" he shrugged.

"I want you to understand. It's not you. I know I've acted crazy. It's because . . . It's because of what happened at the cabin."

Jessie, his back against the door, frowned. They'd been through this before.

"I didn't tell you everything about it." She walked to the window and stood looking into the distance, where the sawtooth peaks pushed up against the sky. "That man. He came in and threatened me with his knife."

"I know. You told me."

She didn't hear him.

"He came toward me. I was against the wall. I wanted to scream then, but he put the point of the blade here." She placed a trembling hand to her throat. "Then he . . . then he began to cut the buttons from my dress."

The porcelain knob of the door turned suddenly cold in Jessie's hand.

"He just went on and cut them off. My dress . . . and everything. I refused to get on the bed. I was going to let him kill me. But he knocked me down with his fist."

Her breath was coming in tiny spasms, between the words. She was still turned away from him.

"Emil finally came. But it was too late."

"Christina, I didn't . . ."

She shook her head violently from side to side.

"I still feel dirty. I'll never get it out of my mind. Up there, on the mountain with you, I thought we were going to die, and that made it easier. But it came back."

Ramming eased the door shut behind him and went to her. He didn't touch her but he said, "I wish you'd have told me before."

"You can go now." Her voice was barely audible. "I won't blame you."

"I've changed my mind."

"No, I want you to go. I don't want your pity. I'll be all right."

He took her arm and pulled her around until she faced him.

"Christina, if I thought pity would help you, I'd offer it. But I know it won't." He backed away a step. His big hands were balled into hard fists. "Up on that mountain, you asked me what I would do when I caught up to him. I'll tell you now. I've never killed a man and I don't want to. But there are some things a man has to do whether he wants to or not. This is one of them. I'll see him dead before I rest."

He said it without emotion. But there was no doubt in her mind that it would be so.

Jessie guided her to the faded sofa. Then he brought

96

food to her from the box on the dresser. When he had seated himself on the floor, with his back against the wall, they ate hungrily, in silence. Once he glanced up and caught her studying his face. She looked quickly away, flushing.

After they had finished eating Christina said, "I would like it if you would sleep here tonight. I kept hearing voices and footsteps last night. I was afraid someone would come in."

"Sure," Jessie nodded. There was no premonition to warn him that he would never keep the promise.

He got to his feet.

"I'm going out and do some asking around. You stay in the room. If he's in town, you sure don't want to be seen. He figures you're still back there at the cabin, helpless or dead."

"But what about you?"

"I'm not even sure he could recognize me in the daylight. It was night when he staked me out in the desert. Me and old Juan. You get some rest. No one will bother you now."

She got up and took a step toward him, then stopped.

"Be careful, Jessie."

It was only the second time she had used his given name. The sound of it from her lips was still with him when he left the hotel.

He went directly to the sheriff's office. Inside, he found a man with a badge seated at a battered desk and through his mind flashed the picture of a similar scene in Trabajo. But this lawman was different. Even the desk was tidy.

The man got up slowly, grimacing behind a graying, tobacco-stained beard.

"You'll have to excuse me, mister. This rheumatiz don't like for me to get up in a hurry."

"Are you the sheriff?" asked Ramming.

"No sirree," the old man cackled. "I wouldn't have the job fer all the yeller stuff in them hills. I just help out when Sheriff Slaughter wants me to. Right now I'm keepin' an eye on that wuthless breed back yonder in the lock-up."

"Where can I find the sheriff?"

"At the other end of town. In church."

"In church?"

"Yep. They're havin' a funeral."

"A relative of the sheriff?"

"Nope. A feller he had to shoot."

Ramming went back down the street and up the incline at its far end, where a tiny, weathered church stood off by itself on a rocky knoll. As he approached he heard singing. A few minutes later the doors opened and four somber-faced men came out, carrying a coffin between them. Behind them was a thin woman dressed in black, a handkerchief pressed to her mouth. A big man with a big paunch held a gentle hand on her arm as they followed the coffin-bearers down the steps.

On the big man's chest was a badge.

Jessie followed at a distance as the small group of mourners climbed the hill behind the church to the graveyard. The proceedings there were over in a matter of minutes, but the sheriff remained for a time, talking to the woman in black. Ramming saw him take something from his pocket and press it into her hands. Then he put on his hat and came down the hill.

"Sheriff Slaughter?"

"What can I do for you, son?"

"I'd like to ask you a couple of questions."

"Sure thing. I'm headed to the hotel to get a bite to eat. You're welcome to join me."

They walked down the street in silence.

Finally Ramming asked, "Was that the widow?"

"Yeah. 'Fraid so."

"Your deputy said you had to shoot the man. Seems a bit strange you and she would still be on speaking terms."

The sheriff looked at Ramming from beneath heavy brows.

"I shot him because I had to. He was ravin' drunk and killin' mean. She understands."

In the dining room of the McSween Hotel, Jessie declined the sheriff's invitation to join him in the meal, and watched as the lawman began to put away huge forkfuls of steak and biscuits and beans.

98

"What can I do for you?" Slaughter inquired around a mouthful.

"I need some help."

"That's what I'm paid for," the sheriff replied. Abruptly, he stabbed the fork toward Ramming. "Don't believe I've seen you in these parts before, mister. Not that it makes any difference. Everybody gets an equal share of the law around here."

"I'm from over around Trabajo."

"Trabajo? Why, sure. Me and Sheriff Wiley Dunn go back a long ways together. How's he been?"

Jessie shook his head.

"I haven't seen him in some time. They tell me he just picked up and moved on pretty sudden."

"Well, now. That don't sound much like Wiley Dunn. Where did he head for?"

"Silver City, they say. There's supposed to be a new strike over there. I guess he decided he'd get in on the ground floor."

Sheriff Slaughter chewed meditatively for a time.

"Nope," he grunted at last, his shaggy brows drawn together. "Dunn ain't one to go off half-cocked like that. He's been a lawman too long. Who told you that cock 'n bull story?"

"A fella that's wearing a deputy sheriff's badge in Trabajo. A gent that sure would like to see me again, I imagine. Behind the bars in his jail."

Slaughter peered at him quizzically.

"Care to tell me what happened?"

For a moment Jessie started to sidestep the question. But there was an openness, an honesty, in the big man's countenance that changed his mind.

"It started when somebody gunned down my wife."

Slaughter stopped with a knifeful of beans halfway to his mouth.

"I sure would like to hear the story, if you don't mind tellin' it, mister."

"Name's Ramming. Jessie Ramming. I had a place a couple days' ride east of Trabajo. Somebody laid up on a rise behind the house and picked off my wife with a rifle a little more than a week ago."

"There ain't many men in the whole territory low-down

99

enough to shoot a woman." The sheriff's voice was drawn tight with repressed rage. "How did he come to do it?"

"I don't have the answer to that. But I'll find out when I meet up with him. That's how I got tangled up with that deputy. He didn't want me doing the law's work, he said."

"Well, Mister Jessie Ramming. If it was me whose wife had been shot, I wouldn't let nobody, law or otherwise, get in my way until I had that jasper's hide stretched and dryin' on the barn door. Now, how can I help?"

In spite of himself, excitement prodded at Ramming. This keeper of the law looked plenty willing. And plenty capable.

"I believe the man I'm after came to McSween. It would have been a couple of days ago, maybe three."

Slaughter had stopped eating and was giving all his attention to the other man.

"Tell me everything you can about this hombre. What kind of horse would he be riding? Did you get a look at his face? There ain't hardly anybody that comes through McSween, or Walnut Valley, for that matter, that I don't know about."

"You wouldn't forget him. He'd be riding a good-sized gray gelding that he stole from me. But the thing you'd notice right off is the scar on the side of his face. Left ear is all chewed up. Looks sort of like a dried-up chunk of rawhide. The scar runs from his ear down across his throat. He's got a heavy beard, too. Trying to cover it up, I guess. And doesn't talk much, best I can tell."

An icy wind blew suddenly across the table where the two sat. Ramming saw the change come over the big lawman. The friendliness vanished. Jessie's first thought was that the sheriff had bitten down on a bad tooth.

"Does that description ring a bell?"

Sheriff Slaughter went on putting food into his mouth but he wasn't tasting it. He knew his face was getting red and he cursed himself bitterly. With a great effort he looked into the other man's face.

"Well, yeah. I might have seen such a gent. Came through here a couple or three days ago. Yeah, I recol-

100

lect. Three days, it was. But he didn't hang around long. Looked to me like he was headed for the other side of the mountains. White Oaks, maybe."

Sheriff Ben Slaughter didn't lie well. He had had very little practice. The words he spoke hung heavily in the air, their fraudulence crying aloud. He wouldn't have been surprised if the other man had called him a liar.

"Well, I was sure hoping I'd catch up with the illegitimate son here in McSween," Ramming said grimly. He started to go on, telling about the death of Emil Bucklin and the ordeal of Christina, but something in the sheriff's face stopped him. The invitation that he had seen earlier in the level gray eyes was now gone.

Ben Slaughter was in terrible agony. He was reliving the scene in the cabin on the mountaintop two nights earlier. He had sold his soul to Fish and the scarfaced man for a silver badge and his standing in the community. He hadn't expected Satan to call in his markers so soon.

Then the sheriff's mind dealt him its cruelest blow. Only that morning, before going to the funeral, he had set in motion the machinery that would allow Romero Red Feather to walk out of his cell to freedom! Slaughter had slipped an extra cell key into the malodorous enameled pot that stood in a corner of the half-breed's cell. He had thought he would make the breed's escape as unpleasant as possible. It was almost laughable.

"Did you get a look at the horse he was riding?" Ramming was asking.

"Can't say as I did," Ben Slaughter grunted sourly. He didn't want to talk anymore. He wanted to get away from this quiet-spoken man with the steady blue eyes who kept driving stakes into his heart.

"One more thing, sheriff," said Ramming. "I'll follow him to White Oaks or to El Paso or to hell if I have to. But I've got to have a horse and I'm flat broke. How can a man make some quick money? Without breaking the law?"

There was no humor left in Sheriff Slaughter. He just shook his big head, grunted something unintelligible, and shoved back his chair.

"Yeah, I'd head for White Oaks, if I was you," he said numbly.

Taking a coin from his pocket, he dropped it on the table beside his still half-full plate and wheeled toward the door. Jessie stood, too, but something told him it would be pointless to pursue his conversation with Sheriff Ben Slaughter.

The sheriff didn't look back. He walked out with his shoulders hunched, as a man will do to protect his head against painful blows. A fat, red-faced youth, tacking a poster to the porch pillar beside the steps, said around the tacks in his mouth: "Howdy, Sheriff Ben. How're y'all?" The sheriff walked on by as though the voice were nothing more than a gust of wind. He untied his horse from the tie rail, swung heavily into the saddle, and rode frozen-faced out of town.

Ramming walked back to the hotel, meditating about his talk with the sheriff of McSween. It had started well enough. The lawman had been concerned, even sympathetic. What had caused him to suddenly become disinterested? Or, more accurately, cool to the point of unfriendliness? Jessie was still chewing on the question when Christina unlocked the door for him.

He told her about his talk with the sheriff, but he left out Slaughter's abrupt change of attitude.

"What are we going to do now?" she asked.

"Head for White Oaks. As soon as I can get enough money together to buy a horse."

Then he realized what she had said.

"No. You're not going with me."

She didn't say a word, but stood looking solemnly into his eyes.

He watched her a moment, then walked to the window and gazed toward the west, where the majestic Rockies shot skyward in ragged stairsteps until their peaks wore mantles of white.

"I could get work in the mines. But I can't afford to wait for two or three weeks. He could be halfway to California by then."

"I'm sorry you had to sell your shotgun," she said, moving up beside him. He didn't let her see that she had touched a still-raw nerve.

She pointed toward the street below.

"He's certainly excited about something."

Jessie followed her gaze. An old man came limping in fitful haste down the middle of McSween's main street, waving his hat above his head and shouting. They could see his mouth working but the distance and the window kept the words from reaching their ears.

Jessie's mind was still on the matter of acquiring a saddle horse. He had already taken his eyes from the frantic figure in the street below when his memory summoned him back as clearly as the snapping of fingers. He looked down again. Sure enough. It was the grizzled old deputy with the rheumatism, the one who had been minding the jail and its half-breed inmate while the sheriff went to a funeral.

Down the side of the old man's head streamed a dark rivulet, the color of blood. Ramming grabbed the handle of the sash and threw the window wide. Now they could hear what he was shouting.

"Jailbreak! Help! Jailbreak! The breed's excaped!"

Chapter
FOURTEEN

The breed had indeed escaped.

It wasn't altogether clear to Romero Red Feather why someone would want him out of jail instead of dangling from a new rope on the freshly built gallows out behind the jail. But he wasn't in the habit of asking questions when fortune stubbed her toe and fell across his path.

A face at the window of his cell, a face with teeth that reminded him of a beaver, had whispered in the darkness and told him there would be a key in his cell. He had searched the small enclosure until daylight without success, deciding at last that it was some drunk paleface's idea of a joke.

Then, quite by accident, he found it, laying in the filth of the chipped and corroded pot, the only piece of furniture in the tiny cubicle if you didn't count the wall bunk.

Red Feather would have preferred the deepest shadows of night for his flight but a small risk at midday was a much more savory choice than dropping through a trapdoor at sunrise. The trouble was, he had no idea what he'd find when he stepped into the sheriff's office just beyond the cellblock. Suppose his "escape" was some impatient citizen's way of speeding him on his way to the happy hunting ground?

But the man with the beaver teeth had said there would be a horse saddled and waiting for him in the stand of trees a short distance up the hill, and hadn't Red

Feather's sharp eyes seen the hind legs of a gray horse in those very trees?

The key turned with a frightening clank in the massive iron lock of the cell door. He stood frozen for a full minute, but no one opened the heavy-timbered office door to investigate.

He swung the barred door open and tip-toed along the wooden flooring, his steps sounding deafeningly loud in his own ears. Ever so slowly he turned the knob of the solid oak door, forcing his muscles to move with the deliberate speed of the hands of a clock.

Through a crack no wider than the blade of a knife, he looked into the sheriff's office. Directly before him, less than two paces away, sat the old deputy. His back was to the door through which the glistening black eye of Romero Red Feather was peering.

At that moment the half-breed would have given a fair portion of whatever life remained to him for a weapon. A gun would do, but far sweeter still would be his exquisitely balanced knife, with its edge so sharp that, of its own weight, it could cut to the bone.

Soundlessly he slipped his boots from his feet and hefted one in his hand. The heavy leather heel of such a boot had been known to crush a man's skull. Without hesitation he slid through the door, took a long step forward, and swung the boot with all the strength in his shirtless, sinewy arm. The old man never knew what hit him. He slumped forward against the desk, then with a long, shuddering sigh slipped sideways to the floor.

Red Feather dropped to one knee beside the shriveled form of the deputy, his hands going automatically to the other's waist.

The old fool didn't even have a gun!

The half-breed cursed silently and fervently for the period of two deep breaths, then slipped his boots on and stepped toward the ancient desk. In an instant he had gone through its half-dozen drawers. Nothing! No knife. No gun. Not even a single bullet, or a matchstick. Someone had carefully cleaned it out.

For one more moment Red Feather looked longingly at the rifles chained securely in the rack against the far

105

wall. No time to search for a key. The thoroughness with which the desk had been cleared out told him it would take more than a few minutes to find that key.

Besides, the gray-whiskered deputy was already stirring. He must have a head as hard as the knot in an oak tree, Red Feather thought bitterly. Stepping with the quickness of a big cat, he glided out the front door, around the corner of the jail, and in ten seconds was moving through the thick copse of trees toward the horse tethered there. He felt a quick stab of disappointment at the emptiness of the rifle boot on the saddle. But in another moment he was astride the horse and moving through the trees toward the even thicker jungle of underbrush that marked the deep "V" of a canyon cut into the towering mountain range.

Romero Red Feather smiled a small, satisfied smile to himself. The chill air was sweet with the smell of freedom and the big gray horse beneath him was a good, strong animal. He had only to do a small chore for a friend of the beaver-toothed man, and he would be free. Perhaps he would ride to Mexico, to get a taste of real tequila, and señoritas who knew how to appreciate a man with the fiery blood of a Mexican and the heart of an Indian brave.

It was a simple thing for a warrior with a fox's cunning to keep out of sight of the thick-skulled, slow-witted white eyes in the town at the base of the mountain. Only once did Red Feather allow the gray horse to choose the easiest path as he climbed toward the peaks that rimmed the southern extremes of Walnut Valley. It was only a small clearing, hardly larger than the cell his rider had just left behind, that the gray chose to cross.

No one in McSween could have seen the gray horse and its bronzed, shirtless rider climbing that mountain, unless he had a vantage point some distance above ground level. Jessie Ramming, standing at the second-story window of the McSween Hotel, had just such a vantage point.

Jessie couldn't have said what drew his eyes upward to that particular clearing among the trees at that particular instant, while every other set of eyes along the street was drawn to the shouting, hurrying deputy with the

106

blood-spattered head. But glance upward he did, and his eyes were suddenly filled with the sight of a gray gelding he could have picked from a score of gray horses at any distance within rifle range.

"It's him!" Ramming breathed.

"Who?" Christina asked at his elbow.

"My gray horse! I saw him there. On the side of that mountain. A man, an Indian, was riding him away!"

She looked where he pointed.

"Jessie, how could you tell?"

"I know that horse, I know how he moves. It's him!"

He was at the door in three long strides.

"Christina, stay here. Don't leave the room."

In the next instant he was gone. Her words, "But you don't have a gun," echoed hollowly in the room.

Ramming pounded down the stairs and out the front door, hoping to find the sheriff in the crowd that was gathering around the deputy down the street. But the overwhelming bulk of Ben Slaughter was nowhere to be seen. As a matter of fact, the street toward the jail had emptied completely of McSween's citizens. They were drawn like bits of flotsam in a whirlpool toward the old lawman. And he, realizing abruptly that he had the stellar role, told his story again and again. With each telling, the courageous manner in which he had fought to hold the desperate escapee grew in dimension.

Ramming sprinted up the street toward the jail. The sheriff had to be there. But a glance inside told him the hope was in vain.

He turned away, his heart a heavy lump in his breast. And there, tied at a hitch rail in front of the blacksmith shop, was a saddled horse, its owner somewhere down the street in the tangle of people straining to hear the old deputy's dramatic narrative.

It didn't look like much of a horse. It was a thick-necked, Roman-nosed, faded roan beast built too lightly in the shoulders and too heavily in the hindquarters. But Ramming's mind held only a single thought. He had to catch that gray gelding.

The roan wanted to buck when Jessie's considerable weight settled in the saddle, but he hauled the horse's head up and gouged him painfully in the ribs. The roan

107

forgot his foolishness and lined out toward the upper reaches of the timbered slopes.

Jessie saw quickly that his choice of a horse, arbitrary as it had been, couldn't have been better. The roan understood mountains. Where a horse unused to steep slopes wants to run until he reaches the crest of every hill he confronts, a mountain-bred animal knows better. The roan's pace up the mountainside was a steady, ground-eating effort.

Ramming studied the skyline as the horse moved through the timber. The Indian (it had to be an Indian; no white man would head for those snow-capped heights without even a shirt) would be looking for the easiest and quickest way to put distance behind him. That meant he would make for the first deep cleft in the fortress of mountains rimming the valley's southern boundary.

Standing in the stirrups astride the roan, Jessie spotted the passage he knew would have to be somewhere up ahead. It was a narrow notch between two massive pillars of stone that shot upward to heights where eagles would have their aeries. There was no other pass through those mountains within a half-day's ride.

The Indian on the gray would head straight for that notch. Once beyond it, he could laugh at any pursuit.

Jessie Ramming didn't take pleasure in what he had to do, but he knew if he lost the gray now, and the man riding him, he might as well abandon his quest for the scarfaced killer. The single link to that devil was somewhere up ahead in the jungle of pine trees. Ramming would have to beat the Indian to the top by risking an alternate steeper route.

He kicked the roan into a run. That sturdy animal hunched his back and clawed at the steep slope like a mountain goat, never missing his footing and never pausing to choose a path. His instinct for mountain-climbing was scarcely less keen than that of a mule deer.

Up and up they climbed. Just when Ramming was certain he had reached the final plateau, he found another slope shooting upward. That one fell behind him and still another sheer slope rose up to take its place.

The hammer-headed roan poured out all his strength on that mountain and called on his reserves. And when his reserves were exhausted he kept climbing, drawing strength from his great heart. He would have slowed but the voice of the man in the saddle was constantly in his ear, talking to him as to a friend, coaxing him on.

Jessie knew he had asked too much of the roan horse. They would never reach the mountain pass in time. But at that instant he looked up and saw the spires of stone towering above him. He was at the entrance to the defile, a passage barely wide enough to admit a man on horseback.

He pulled the roan to a stop and slid to the ground. There were some cloven tracks of deer but no horse tracks leading into the cut. He had won. But even as he sighed in relief he heard the movement of another horse and knew the gray gelding and his rider were almost upon him.

He led the roan quickly into a thick stand of junipers and dropped the reins. That good mount wouldn't be wanting to move for a long time.

Then the sound of the roan's labored breathing reached his ears as he crouched behind a boulder and he knew that sound would carry a great distance in the thin air at that elevation. How could the Indian fail to hear it?

Hardly daring to allow himself a breath, Ramming waited behind the massive boulder that swelled from the side of the mountain, into the crevice through which the rider would have to pass. He heard the hooves of the approaching horse on the rocky ground and heard, too, the gray's heavy breathing as he labored up the final slope. The Indian couldn't hear the roan horse wheezing for the sound of his own mount sucking air.

Cautiously, Jessie peered around the boulder that concealed him. The horse and rider were only a few paces away. The sight of the gray so close made his throat tighten. Caution left him and he leaped from the ledge toward the man on the horse.

It was a mistake. He had jumped too soon. Romero Red Feather was twisted about in the saddle, looking at the trail behind him, when his nerve-endings triggered a

109

warning. He swung about, in time to see the big, sandy-haired man descending on him like a tawny puma.

Instantly, Red Feather kicked his feet free of the stirrups and flipped backwards off the gray horse's rump.

If the gray had stood his ground, Ramming would have lost his quarry in a footrace in the thick stands of pine and stunted spruce that marked the edge of the timberline forest. But the gelding, as startled as though Ramming were in fact a cougar in a mortal leap, wheeled about. The momentum of his spin slung the Indian to the ground directly beneath Ramming's plunging form.

Red Feather went down with a sudden explosion of air from his lungs, but he was up in an instant, ready to spring away into the trees. He never completed the first stride. A grip like the jaws of a steel bear trap clamped around one ankle.

This was Red Feather's game. He gazed for the hundredth part of a second into the gunmetal blue eyes of the stranger who held him, then let his muscles go limp. He felt the big man shift his grip and in that period of half a heartbeat Romero Red Feather found his chance. Instantly he drew a knee up and slammed it into the forearm that pinioned his right wrist. The hand that held his wrist was forced loose.

The Indian's free hand closed on a rock the size of a horse's hoof. He brought it around toward the head that hovered above his own. The stone would have crushed the skull of the blue-eyed man but at the last instant he threw up an arm and deflected the blow.

Jessie's left arm from his wrist to his elbow went suddenly numb. The Indian, squirming like a drowning cat, was breaking free. He rolled to his stomach, drawing his feet beneath him.

Romero Red Feather was made of sinew and gristle and rawhide. From the time he was old enough to outrun his Mescalero Apache mother, he had kept himself alive with his strength and his quickness of hand and eye. Seldom had he fought a man he could not either overpower or elude. In another second he would be free of the crazy one who had leaped on him out of nowhere.

But something was wrong. Red Feather found himself struggling to draw a breath. Flashes of painful red light burst in his brain. His neck was in the crook of the arm of the sandy-haired paleface. With both of his hands he pulled at that arm, but he might as well have been clawing at the trunk of a tree. The harder he squirmed and fought, the tighter the arm closed about his throat.

Then the blue sky above turned the color of blood and Romero Red Feather lost consciousness.

When he came to he was seated with his back against the base of the stone pillar that guarded the defile through the mountain. His hands and feet were securely bound. And his head ached terribly.

"Where did you get the gray horse?"

The other man was seated on the ground in front of him. His blue eyes bored into the ebony eyes of Red Feather until the Indian felt strangely apprehensive.

But he made no answer.

"I said, where did you get the horse?"

The paleface moved closer. He put out a hand and caught the Indian by the jaw, turning his face toward him.

Romero Red Feather spat in the white man's face.

Instantly, so quickly the movement was no more than a blur, a hand struck him across the ear. His head rang with the sound of brass bells.

"The horse. Where did you get him?"

It was the voice, not the words, that made Red Feather uneasy. This was not a man asking about a horse; it was a man whose spirit was troubled far beyond mere words. And he had said nothing about capturing an escaped murderer.

It was some kind of trick, Red Feather decided. He clamped his lips together and stared blankly off into the trees.

The paleface with the probing blue eyes walked away. For the space of a few seconds, Red Feather thought about trying to get away. But something about the set of the other man's shoulders as he disappeared into the brush drained the Indian's resolve.

Shortly the big man returned, leading a roan horse that was lathered with sweat from his thick neck to his heavy hindquarters. He dropped the reins of the roan and went to the gray gelding that was cropping at the sparse clumps of grass.

The Indian watched in fascination. Clearly the gray horse recognized the man. He threw up his head and whinnied as the man approached. When a hand went to his ears he nuzzled at the man's chest with comradely warmth. A smile pulled at the mouth of the blue-eyed one.

Romero Red Feather watched the scene in bewilderment. This man apparently had not caught him and battered him to the ground because he was a fugitive from the McSween jail. There was another reason.

When the man came back leading the roan Red Feather spoke.

"It is not because of the jail that you came for me?"

Ramming studied the Indian's face.

"What do you mean?"

"The sheriff did not send you?"

"I don't know what you're talking about. But I do know that's my gray horse. Where did you get him?"

The half-breed was tempted to tell the truth. He felt somehow that his captor wasn't particularly interested in what he had done. But he kept his tongue still. There might yet be a chance to slip away from the powerful grip of this crazy white eyes.

Ramming untied the Indian's feet and hoisted him into the saddle on the roan horse. Red Feather's heart sank at the ease with which he was lifted from the ground. He could still feel the painful crush of that forearm around his throat.

Bleakly, the would-be warrior sat astride the roan and watched as the other man took down a lariat from the fork of the saddle at his knee and fitted a noose over his head. Red Feather had expected that. But he didn't foresee what the paleface did next. He slipped the bridle from the roan's head and threw it into the brush. Then he swung into the saddle on the gray and moved out through the trees. The rope tightened around Red Feather's neck.

"Hey, you crazy man," he yelled at Ramming. "You'll get me killed. You got to lead this horse."

112

Ramming didn't look back. He merely took a dally around the horn of his saddle and rode on.

Romero Red Feather frantically kicked the tired roan into motion. His hands were tied behind him and his neck was in dire peril of being stretched beyond redemption. The horse beneath him was stiff and sore from the awful scramble up the mountainside and he didn't want to move. But the Indian gouged him brutally in the ribs, all the while filling the thin, pure air with Mexican curses.

Red Feather had figured he would find a way to regain his freedom as they rode down the mountain. But the plan was now forgotten in his struggle to maintain slack in the lasso around his neck.

Chapter
FIFTEEN

They rode into McSween that way. Shouts from a half-dozen throats rang out as Ramming headed the gray along the main thoroughfare, the roan still wanting to fall behind but kept in grudging motion by the urgent heels of Romero Red Feather.

At the far end of the street, in front of the jail, a dozen heavily armed men were in the process of mounting their horses. Looks for all the world like a posse, Jessie decided. Then he saw Sheriff Ben Slaughter stepping through the door, out onto the boardwalk.

He was still several paces away when the sheriff became aware of the clamor and glanced in his direction. The look that crossed Slaughter's heavy-jowled face defied description. It was the look of a man witnessing a personal calamity, Jessie thought, but then he decided it was simply surprise that caused the sheriff's mouth to twitch open and closed like that of a dehydrating catfish.

A moment later the big man with the badge strode toward Ramming with a broad smile while the posse members, laughing and clapping each other on the back as if they had had a hand in the enterprise, gathered around.

"Well, well," Ben Slaughter boomed. "What have we got here? A genuine one-man army, it appears like. Would you mind telling us ordinary mortals how you managed to corral this murderin' polecat?"

Ramming stepped down from the saddle.

"I don't know why you're so interested in this hombre,

sheriff, but it was my horse he was heading for the tall timber on." He stroked the gray's muzzle and got an affectionate nudge in return. "I just got lucky."

At that moment, the crowd that had gathered separated to provide a path for a little man in a tall, beaverskin hat. His hurrying steps almost carried him into a collision with Jessie's chest. He started talking in rapid, clipped words. The smell of whiskey spread around him in a little cloud.

"Luckier than you figured, my friend," he beamed, breathing noisily through his mouth. "There's a standing fifty-dollar reward for the apprehension of anybody that breaks out of the McSween jail and, as mayor of this here town, I just doubled that tidy little plum not more'n a half-hour before you come draggin' this half-breed scoundrel back so's we could stretch his neck all legal and proper."

The hand he held out was puffy and white, hardly strong enough, it seemed, to hold the five big gold coins he dropped into Ramming's palm.

"Now you just let the sheriff take charge of that Injun, friend, whilst we all go down to the Antlers and have us a drink. This here calls for a first-class celebration."

Jessie's head was spinning. He was being clapped on the shoulders and men were reaching out to shake his hand. He was conscious of the weight of the gold coins pulling at his pocket. His luck had taken a decided turn for the better.

He searched the faces in the crowd, then abruptly realized he was looking for a particular one. One with a tiny nose, a sprinkling of freckles, and a frame of tousled, golden hair. He spotted her at the edge of the gathering, not pushing through to him but holding back as though she was not sure that he, a sudden hero, would know her.

Ramming was about to call her name when he heard a loud, high-pitched voice overriding the murmur of the crowd. The voice was coming from the sidewalk near the front door of the jail office, beside the towering form of the sheriff.

And Jessie suddenly became aware he was the subject of that abrasive discourse.

"I tell you, sheriff, that's him!" The speaker was a man of medium height, dressed in the same manner as most everyone else in that crowd. But it was his face that set him apart. It was a narrow, hatchet-like countenance that seemed to pull back in embarrassment from a tier of teeth so long and prominent the lips were never quite able to conceal them.

The man with the remarkable teeth was pointing toward Ramming while he continued shouting into the ear of the sheriff.

"I seen him at the window of the jail just this morning, sheriff. Looked like he was talking through that back window to the half-breed. Then I seen him leading that gray horse there."

Sheriff Ben Slaughter held up both hands to stop the torrent of words. His expression wasn't pleasant.

"What are you trying to say, Fish? This man is the one who captured the breed. Ain't you heard?"

Fish's voice went an octave higher. It rang shrilly across the now-silent gathering.

"I'm sayin' he's the one that turned the killer loose in the first place, sheriff!"

Slaughter had his hat in his hand while he scratched at the thinning patch of hair above his ear.

"Now you tell me why in hell the man would break Romero Red Feather out of jail and then go catch him and lead him back at the end of a rope. You ain't makin' any sense at all."

"Didn't we just see him put a hundred dollars in his pocket? That ain't bad pay for a couple hours of ridin' through the hills."

Although Ramming had not moved a step, the sheriff swung around and pointed a finger at him.

"Just you stand fast 'til we get this straightened out, mister. Seems I do recall you sayin' something about needin' some quick money."

He turned back to the buck-toothed man.

"Anybody else see what you seen? Otherwise, it's your word against his."

Fish frowned, as though pondering the question.

"No, I guess not, sheriff," he said resignedly. But then he looked up with a gleam in his close-set eyes. "There's

116

maybe a way we can settle it. Didn't he say the gray is his horse? Didn't he say that right out so's everybody could hear it?"

Two or three hat brims bobbed in the crowd, denoting agreement by their owners.

"Just hold it a minute," the sheriff boomed. "This gent ain't had a chance to open his mouth." He motioned with his big hand. Ramming, stepping up on the sidewalk, fixed the hatchet-faced man with a cold stare. Fish's eyes wavered, then returned to the sheriff, who was scowling at Ramming.

"You did say the gray is your cayuse?"

"That's what I said. He was stolen from me, just like I told you this morning. I happened to see him heading away from town, up that mountain. It was pure luck that I spotted him."

The sheriff's eyes narrowed.

"That half-breed murderin' son has been cooling his heels right here in my jail for more'n a week. Now how do you suppose he managed to steal your horse while he was locked up in that cell?"

There was a chuckle from the knot of onlookers. Jessie could sense a change in their mood. It was no longer a warm, friendly crowd.

"Why would I tell you my horse had been stolen if I planned to use him in a jailbreak?"

The sheriff grinned, but there was no humor in it.

"Maybe so's you could come back at me with that very question."

Fish saw his opening.

"Sheriff, there's one way to get your answer. This gent admits the horse is his. Why don't you take a look around the jail? Or maybe in that patch of trees up the hill a'ways. If that there gray horse was staked out for the breed to use, then the tracks will be hereabouts somewhere. If they ain't, why I guess I'll just have to apologize."

It didn't take the band of zealous volunteers long to extend their search to the stand of trees. the only cover within a reasonable distance of the jail. Like a small army, they swept up the slope, the sheriff leading the way and Jessie at his side. Behind them came Fish,

117

followed by the wheezing, puffing mayor, and then the aggregation of McSween citizens: members of the erstwhile posse, storekeepers, miners, saloon hangers-on. They were in a holiday mood now, Jessie thought wryly. Like a crowd prepared to enjoy a hanging.

The sheriff had remembered to send someone down to get the gray gelding. In a matter of a few minutes he had the answer.

"No doubt about it. These tracks were made by your horse, mister. What've you got to say for yourself?"

"I've told you what happened, sheriff. Someone else must have tied my horse here for the Indian to escape on."

A rumble of skeptical murmuring rose from the crowd. Fish was at the sheriff's side, stretching up to talk intently in the bigger man's ear. Ramming looked over the heads of the throng of townspeople, into the eyes of Christina. She was standing a little distance off, her lower lip caught in her white, even teeth. He thought he saw a tear glistening on her cheek.

A voice growled at his elbow. It was Ben Slaughter, a black scowl clouding his face like a man bracing himself to do a job he doesn't relish.

"You'll be wantin' to come along with me, son."

Chapter
SIXTEEN

Thomas O. Fish leaned a shoulder against the rough trunk of a ponderosa pine and watched the backs of Sheriff Slaughter and his new prisoner move down the slope toward the jail. Fish's face was stretched in a wide grin, in the kind of tautness a drying pelt has. He was smiling at the shrewd way he had maneuvered the owner of the gray gelding into a jail cell. He was reasonably sure there was a certain man who would pay him well for the trick.

The crowd had drifted on down the hill toward the Antlers Saloon, doubtless following the mayor's lead. Pushing his hat back, Fish sauntered after them and abruptly found himself in step beside a small, blonde woman. He had seen her before, at the edge of the gathering that had witnessed the downfall of the sandy-haired man. She was lagging behind the others, her eyes on the broad-shouldered man walking beside the sheriff.

"Why, howdy, ma'am," Fish said genially, bobbing in front of her so that she had to look his way. "Too bad that gent turned out to be a crook. You just never can tell by their looks."

The glare she turned on him sent a surge of annoyance through Fish. He had felt the same look from other women.

"He's no crook," she said flatly.

"Oh?" Fish said in mock surprise. "You know him, I take it."

119

"Yes, I do." The words were barbed. "You were wrong. I know he didn't help that man escape."

He was suddenly defensive.

"Looks like the sheriff has other ideas. Especially after them horse tracks matched up like a pair of new nickels."

She turned and fixed him with a cold look.

"The sheriff didn't listen to anyone but you, Mr. Fish. I'm going in there and tell him what kind of man he has arrested."

She stepped up on the boardwalk in front of the sheriff's office, hesitated, then turned to him again.

"You seemed awfully anxious to accuse someone of helping with the jailbreak. And the sheriff seemed awfully ready to believe your story."

She was uncomfortably close to the truth. But the contempt in her voice stung him even more. His face grew a deep red.

"That high and mighty friend of yours is going to rot in this here jail. You just take my word for it." He was almost shouting. "We don't take kindly to the likes of him in McSween."

Her eyes bored steadily into his, until his gaze wavered. Then she turned and marched to the door. He had an almost uncontrollable urge to leap on her and pound her to the ground with his fists. But he fought down the impulse and watched her disappear inside. He had urgent business elsewhere, anyway. He could take care of her later.

A dozen steps down the street, Fish met the old deputy, his head now encased in a bulky bandage on which his hat balanced precariously. Fish reached out and grabbed him roughly by the arm.

"Tell the sheriff I'll look after the gray horse."

He didn't wait for a reply but untied the gelding and climbed into the saddle. He pushed his anger at the blonde woman into the back of his mind. Things were going better than he had figured they ever would when he saw that fool come riding back into town leading the half-breed. But now he had everything tied up in a tight little bundle. He had possession of the horse again, and maybe more important, he had the man who claimed to own it safely tucked away behind bars.

He shook his head. There was something about that gray horse he didn't savvy. If it was Scarface's horse in the first place, how come the sandy-haired gent kept making noises like it was his cayuse? Right out in public, too.

He rode down Main Street until it made a swing eastward. There it became the stage road that followed Walnut Creek down through the foothills to the plains and, ultimately, to the infant town of Roswell in the northern reaches of the Pecos Valley.

Fish's place was a half-mile from town. The shack in which he lived was a ragged little structure with a perpetual tilt obliging the prevailing southwesterly winds. There was a barn of similar fettle, containing a few bales of moldy prairie hay and a carpet of pigeon droppings.

On the ground in front of the house, a quarter-moon shaped patch of earth was swept as clean and free of stones and trash and other debris as one might expect of a kitchen floor. Fish uttered an oath as he rode the gelding across the yard and tied him to a peeling pillar supporting the tiny front porch.

"Estella!"

Out of the house came a Mexican woman of indeterminate age and extreme corpulence, her movements a waddle of gelatinous flesh.

"Dammit, woman," shouted Fish. "How many times I got to tell you to quit wasting your time sweeping the damn yard? That's about the dumbest thing I ever heard of."

"*Sí, Señor* Feesh," she said, a broad smile crinkling her face until her small black eyes all but disappeared.

"Ah, hell," he muttered. "Ain't you never going to learn English?"

As he went past her he slapped her hard on a fat buttock, hard enough to make her grimace with pain. Into his thoughts stole a small, graceful woman with blonde hair, and a lecherous smile pulled at his caricature of a mouth. But then, remembering her damning gaze, he scowled blackly.

121

"Get me some grub together," he snapped at the Mexican woman. Seeing the blankness of her expression, he cursed again and slapped his hands together: "*Comida*, dammit! *Ándale!*"

He felt an urgency pulling at him. The man they called Smilin' Jack was not a patient man. When a thing was expected at a certain time, it was unwise to be the one who caused the delay. Fish had felt the tongue of the scarfaced man on more than one occasion. And he had also felt the cold sweat of fear when that one's temper flamed out of control.

Fish was not a courageous man. He preferred to do his works in the shadows of the nighttime, or behind his adversary's back. Dealing with trouble face-to-face wasn't his style. And the man with the shriveled ear and whiskey voice was trouble, in spades, for any jasper foolhardy enough to cross him.

He slung the sack of rations across the skirt of the saddle, lashed it down, and swung astride the gray horse. Had he bothered to look into the tiny black eyes of the woman watching him he would have been astonished at the emotion which burned there. But he ignored her and sent the gelding out of the antiseptically clean yard at a gallop. He smiled grimly to himself. When he had collected his modest share of the bank loot from Smilin' Jack Sluder, he would still have enough wealth to pick and choose. And it damn well wouldn't be no fat sow of a woman like Estella who would get to help him spend the money.

His destination was the weather-beaten little cabin high up against the Capitan peaks where he and Smilin' Jack had had their little palaver with the sheriff. But he didn't take the shortest route to it, which would have been back through town and out along the White Oaks road. Instead, he spurred the gray north across the shallow, noisy waters of Walnut Creek, then straight up a heavily wooded ridge for a long distance before beginning his cut back to the west.

The sun was already worrying at the tops of the mountains on the horizon when he came to the clearing. It spooked him to approach that shack. It was as though the bearded, stoop-shouldered man had a sixth sense

122

that warned him when anyone was coming. Fish had never found him inside. He was always a distance away, that damnable rifle a hair's breadth from spitting lead.

It was that way now. Fish was halfway across the clearing when he saw movement in the deep shadows to one side of the cabin. Sluder stepped out into the sunlight, his weapon resting in the crook of an arm.

Fish rode toward him. Sluder gave no sign of recognition or acknowledgment, but stood in his slightly stooped manner and watched the horse and rider draw near. Fish made up his mind that this time he wouldn't be the first to speak. He was always the one to do it, and it always made him feel second-rate, like he wasn't quite man enough to be in Sluder's company.

He pulled the gray to a halt. The man on the ground didn't move, but watched him without expression. Fish tried to look elsewhere, for a moment fixing his eyes on the dried-up piece of gristle that had been an ear. But in spite of himself his eyes were drawn to those of Sluder. They were like the eyes of a timber wolf he had once seen in the mountains, sitting on its haunches at the far edge of light from a campfire.

He fought down a shiver that touched the back of his neck, and gave in.

"Howdy, Jack. I've brung you some grub and some whiskey."

Sluder put a hand to his throat, as though anticipating pain.

"What the hell are you doing on the gray?" The voice that came from his lips was a wheezing, raspy whisper. But Fish had no difficulty understanding the words, nor their temper.

"The breed's back in jail. He was . . ."

He wanted to hurry on and explain but the look on Sluder's face stopped him.

"Damn your eyes! He was supposed to be out by now, and ridin' that gray horse."

The muzzle of the long-barreled rifle swung an insignificant degree toward Fish's chest. He saw the movement, and swallowed.

"Hold on, Jack. Let me tell you what happened."

Fish was off the horse now, and he took a step backwards.

"I got him out, like you said to do, Jack. The sheriff took care of his part okay. But we had some bad luck."

"Bad luck be damned!" Sluder's voice was a raw snarl.

"The breed got away and was nearly across the south ridge. But some crazy yahoo rode after him. Caught him bare-handed and drug him back to town. There wasn't nothin' Slaughter could do but throw Red Feather back in jail, what with that crowd gathered around."

Sluder stepped nearer, until his face was a hand's breadth from that of the other. Fear drained the color from Tom Fish's features.

"Do you take me for a fool? No man could catch that half-breed in the mountains."

Fish backed up another pace.

"Well, this gent did."

"Who is he? What's his name."

"Why, I never did hear his name. But he claimed this gray horse belongs to him."

Fish wasn't prepared for Sluder's reaction. He saw the dark eyes flicker for the barest instant toward the trees through which he had just ridden. A quiver jerked that lean, stooped body as though the man had experienced a sudden chill. The rifle that had hung at arm's length was at once high against his chest, the thumb of one hand tight on the hammer.

Fish could barely understand the words that snapped like a whip's end from the twisted mouth.

"You lie! The man that owned that horse ain't alive! You hear?"

"Wait a minute, Jack," Fish implored. "I'm just tellin' you what he told the sheriff. He claimed it was his horse, but maybe he was lyin'. Yeah, that's it. He was just lyin' about it being his horse."

Fish became aware that Smilin' Jack Sluder had moved to one side, into the deeper shadows of the thick pines.

"Where is he now?"

"Let me tell you about that, Jack. You'll get a kick out of . . ."

124

"Damn it to hell! Quit running off at the mouth and say it. Where is he?"

"In jail. Like I was tryin' to tell you, he come sashayin' back into McSween, leadin' the breed at the end of a rope like he was leadin' a goat. The sheriff and everybody was there. The mayor gave him a hundred dollars for bringing in the escaped prisoner. Why, you'd have thought he was a stud duck the way they was takin' on over him. 'Specially that woman of his."

He felt the eyes of the other man burning into him. He held up both hands, palm out.

"Okay, I'll get to it, Jack. While everybody was standing around, I calls out to the sheriff and tells him this hombre must have been the one who helped Romero Red Feather break out because it was his horse the breed rode off on."

Sluder was silent, his heavy black brows drawn down in deep thought. Fish hurried on.

"There wasn't much Slaughter could say, not with the corner you've got him boxed into. I tell you, Jack, you're a slick one, you are."

"Shut up! Give me that bottle and go put the grub in the shack. I've got to think."

"Sure thing, Jack," Fish nodded eagerly. He led the horse away toward the cabin. He was glad to leave the presence of the scarecrow-looking man with one ear. He was bad enough when he was only being mean. Throw in a little fear and he was like a keg of blasting powder with a lighted fuse.

It was a new experience for Fish. He had known Jack Sluder most of his life, all the way back to when the two were kids growing up, when they had graduated from stealing watermelons to stealing cows and payrolls. Sluder had always been the strong one, the leader, the one who gave the orders. And Fish hated him with a passion reinforced by the certain knowledge that he didn't have the courage, and never would have it, to challenge Sluder's authority.

Now that little inkling of fear he had seen in the other man's eyes made him chuckle to himself. By damn, it was worth a cussin' out to find out that the bastard had a little human blood in him.

125

He jumped and spun about as a footfall sounded at the door, then cursed at his fright. It was Sluder.

"I want that half-breed out of jail," he whispered. "But more than that I want that other sonofabitch dead."

The intensity of his voice, even muffled as it was by the great scar down the side of his neck and across his throat, gave Fish a prickly feeling.

"What you got against him, Jack?"

Sluder took a flask from his pocket and drank deeply. Then he put a hand to his neck. "He's the reason I've got this."

Fish started to speak, but a sharp movement of Sluder's hand cut him off.

"His string has run out. This time I'll make sure."

"Are we talkin' about the same man?" Fish asked worriedly, his brow wrinkled.

"I'm talking about the man that said he owned the gray horse you're ridin', dummy."

"Yeah, sure. The man that brung the breed back," Fish agreed eagerly. "Don't he have a name?"

Jack Sluder gazed through the front door, toward the rim of mountains to the east, where another storm was building.

"Ramming! Jessie Ramming!" The words had the bitter sound of an oath.

"Who's Jessie Ramming?"

"A hard man to kill. That's who." Suddenly he snapped his long, thin fingers. The sound was startlingly loud in the tiny cabin. "I think I got it figured."

"Hold on a minute, Jack. I ain't going to walk up to that jail and gun down a man in his cell. We've already pushed Sheriff Slaughter as far as we can push him. He wouldn't stand for it. Besides, I hear there's a territorial marshal out of Santa Fe heading this way."

"Shut your face. All you've got to worry about is following orders. You have an extra six-shooter?"

Fish shook his head.

"Uh-uh. Just the one I'm packin'."

Sluder reached into his pocket and withdrew a leather pouch. From it he took a gold piece.

"Go buy a six-gun someplace. It don't have to be new but it had damn well better shoot. Then tonight you take it over to the jail and slip it through the window to Romero Red Feather. Do it while the sheriff's still there, before he goes home. But just be sure he don't see you."

"I don't get it," Fish said, shaking his head. "Slaughter has to figure he's got to turn the breed loose again. Why worry about him seein' me?"

Sluder's eyes were cold.

"I think we've got about all the use we can get out of Sheriff Ben Slaughter. Tell the half-breed to put a slug in him."

Fish had a stunned look.

"Them McSween folks would string us up if they was to find out."

"They won't," Sluder snapped. The whiskey had taken some of the hoarseness from his voice.

"What about this Ramming feller? You gonna just let him be?"

The light that sprang into Sluder's eyes brought the old fear back to Fish.

"Tell the breed I'll double what I've already promised him if Ramming is dead as a wedge before he leaves the jail."

A broad grin pulled at Fish's lips.

"Why, I just imagine Romero Red Feather will be more'n happy to oblige, 'specially considering the fact that Ramming's the cause of him bein' back in jail."

He turned toward the door. Sluder's voice stopped him.

"You said something about a woman. She with Ramming?"

Fish shrugged.

"I guess so. Leastways she was sure talkin' up for him." He ran his tongue over his thin lips. "She's some looker, too."

Swift as a striking snake, Sluder's hand shot out and grabbed a fistful of Fish's red checked shirt.

"You keep your damn hands off her. I'll take care of Ramming's woman."

Chapter
SEVENTEEN

Jessie Ramming stood at the tiny window of his cell and gazed out past the newly built gallows to the intense blue of the autumn sky and the crazy quilt of reds, yellows, and browns with which nature had imbued the mountain slopes. It gave him a sickness in the pit of his stomach to think how unattainable was the freedom on the other side of the jail's heavy log walls, a freedom he had possessed until an hour ago. He would never again make the mistake of taking it for granted.

He heard the door leading from the office into the jail corridor swing open but he didn't turn to see who had entered. Doubtless someone to see Romero Red Feather, in the cell across the passageway. Well, whoever it was would have to awaken the half-breed. He had wasted no time on regrets after his return, but had wrapped himself in a blanket and was now stretched out on the puncheon floor, sound asleep.

"Jessie."

He spun around. Christina Bucklin stood outside the barred door of his cell, a look of deep despair etched on her lightly freckled features. If anything, it made her prettier. He stepped quickly across the tiny cell to the bars that separated them.

"Christina, what are you doing here? This is no place for you."

"Nor you, Jessie Ramming," she said, trying to keep the tremor from her voice. "I talked to the sheriff. I told him you were with me, and couldn't have helped that man escape."

"What did he say?"

"Well, he looked kind of funny. Sick, really. But he said it was too late to do anything else now. That you'd have to stay locked up here until the circuit judge rides through from Las Cruces."

"How long?"

"A week, maybe, the sheriff said."

"Damn!" It was the first time she had heard him swear. "The man with the scar hasn't gone to White Oaks. He's here, in McSween! I'd bet on it. It's the only way to explain why my horse is here."

He had reached up and gripped the bars until his knuckles turned white. She could see the sinews working in his powerful forearms.

"Jessie, do you know the man who accused you of helping the Indian escape?"

He shook his head, his blue eyes gray-black with anger.

"No. I've never seen him. And a man wouldn't likely forget that face. I don't know what his game is, but he and I are going to have a long talk when I get out of this place."

He paced back and forth in the small enclosure while Christina stood silently, the knuckles of one hand against her mouth.

"Christina, I've got to talk to the sheriff. I think I can convince him to let me out. He seemed reasonable enough when I talked to him earlier."

She looked crestfallen.

"Jessie, I asked him to talk to you. But he wouldn't hear of it. He was not very nice about it. It was like he was afraid of something."

She sent a glance toward the door at the end of the corridor.

"He warned me not to stay very long."

Ramming reached into his pocket and withdrew the five twenty-dollar gold pieces. They glinted dully in the palm of his hand.

"They forgot about these. Take them and buy what

129

you need. But first I want you to go to that gunsmith across the street from the hotel and buy back my shotgun. He gave me eleven dollars for it. You'll probably have to pay twelve to get it back. But I want that gun."

"Yes, Jessie," she said, and put her small hand on the big square fist that gripped the steel bar.

"Get whatever else you need, then go directly back to the hotel. And stay there until you hear from me."

She looked at him as though there was something else she wanted to say. But after a moment she turned and walked quickly to the door. Jessie's throat tightened as he watched her walk away. The silence was suddenly heavy with foreboding.

When Christina stepped into the sheriff's office she saw that the big lawman was standing at a window, his broad back to her. She hesitated, another appeal on her lips. But he didn't turn. She went on outside, into the gathering darkness.

Walking down the sloping, dusty street toward the center of McSween, Christina tried to close her mind to what she had seen during the afternoon. But it wouldn't work. The picture that haunted her was of the strong, gentle man in the center of that hostile, bloodthirsty crowd. She found herself wondering what kind of woman his wife had been, to set him on a trail of such uncompromising vengeance.

She located the building with the sign that said *Reb's, Gunsmith*, across the street from the hotel, and went inside. Reb scowled at her in the lantern light, and the scowl deepened when she told him what she wanted.

"Hey," he growled. "Ain't that the shotgun that belonged to the varmint up there in jail? The one that helped the Injun escape?"

Christina glared at him.

"Just tell me how much for the gun."

"Well, now. A shotgun like that is pretty hard to come by, ma'am. They's lots of folks would be mighty proud to have it. I figger I could get twenty bucks out of it, easy."

"I'll give you twelve," she said, her mouth a tight line across her face.

130

"I couldn't hardly do that, ma'am. Wouldn't be good business. Tell you what, though. I'll take eighteen. That's bottom."

She stepped closer and leaned over the counter, until her face was inches from his.

"When the sheriff finds out who's been killed with that shotgun, he'll take it from you to use for evidence and you won't get a cent out of it."

Reb's mouth dropped open. He started to say something, then stopped. He handed the shotgun across the counter.

"Gimme the twelve dollars."

Christina was disappearing inside the hotel across the street when Fish stepped around the corner of the gun-smith's shop. Even in that uncertain light he recognized her full figure. It had been in and out of his thoughts on the long ride down to town from the cabin where Jack Sluder was holed up.

Now, the mere glimpse of her made the muscles of his belly tighten. His eyes became narrow slits. He stood for a long moment and watched the empty door through which she had gone.

"Just you wait," he grunted aloud, and spat into the dust. Then he went on into Reb's gunshop.

In the sheriff's office, Ben Slaughter stood as he had when the woman had walked out. A fire burned deep inside him. All day the feeling had been building, ever since he had dropped the key into the pot in Romero Red Feather's cell. It was a fuse burning and hissing in his gut, and it was going to explode. The blonde-haired woman had made it worse, with her eyes cutting into him as she struggled to hold back the tears. He thought of Bess. If it were he in trouble, Bess would be in there fighting, too.

Suddenly he spun on a heel and headed for the door to the cells. Maybe it would ease his mind to talk to the prisoner. If he could find a flaw in Jessie Ramming's story, or in the man himself, the guilty fire inside him might subside.

Slaughter didn't run his jail for the comfort and convenience of prisoners. There was no light in the cell compound. But he left the door slightly ajar, so that a thin shaft of lamplight from the office sifted along the corridor.

"Ramming," he growled.

"Yes," said Ramming from the darkness of his cell.

"You understand how it is. I got to hold you until the circuit judge can hear the facts. It might be that he'll decide in your favor."

Jessie was silent.

"Dammit, man," said Slaughter. "You ain't makin' it any easier."

The voice that came from the cell was granite-hard.

"I told you what happened, sheriff. The man who killed my wife stole the gray gelding from me. I have no idea how the half-breed came to be riding my horse."

The sheriff stood for a time rubbing at the stubble of whiskers along his heavy jaw. Maybe he had found that flaw he was looking for.

"Tell me something, Mr. Jessie Ramming," he said coldly. "If your wife was killed no more'n a couple of weeks ago, how come it is that you're already hooked up with another woman."

"I started to tell you this morning. But you didn't seem too interested. I was following the trail across the mountains from Trabajo when I came on a cabin. I found a woman there. The blonde woman."

"By herself?"

"The man I was trailing, the man with the scar, had been there ahead of me."

Ramming stopped, his thoughts going back to the terrified woman in the little cabin, her husband's cold body lying covered in the lean-to room.

"Get on with it," Slaughter commanded harshly. But a premonition of disaster clutched at his chest.

"He had mistreated her something terrible."

The sheriff spoke too quickly.

"What about her man?"

"Shot in the back by the hombre with the scarred face. I buried her husband."

"Aw, hell."

The words left Slaughter's mouth in a sick whisper. In that fraction of a second, he made up his mind. No more would he drag his honor and integrity through the filth.

132

He had made a terrible mistake, but he would set things straight even if he had to spend the rest of his life doing it. Even if it meant going to prison for that foolish, long-ago episode of cattle rustling.

Quickly, Slaughter unlocked the door to Ramming's cell. And it was that moment that a capricious fate chose for Tom Fish to peer over the sill of the rear window into the dimness of the cellblock.

Fish could make out the big form of the sheriff and he could see that he had unlocked the door of the cell—the cell where Fish had whispered his message to Romero Red Feather in the darkness of an earlier night.

Fish's mind wasn't usually occupied with more than a single thought at a time. But in that instant, several thoughts came rushing into his head simultaneously. The first was that the sheriff, keeping his unspoken promise to Sluder, was turning Romero Red Feather out of jail again. The second was that, in another few moments, the half-breed would be gone, leaving the sheriff and Ramming alive and healthy.

And the third notion that crowded into Fish's faltering brain had to do with money. Sluder had promised the half-breed a goodly share of the bank loot for killing the sheriff and the owner of the gray horse. The idea came to Fish with an almost painful suddenness. He would do the breed's job and collect the extra share of money!

It was not in Fish's nature to weigh the pros and cons of an idea. He aimed past the shoulder of the man in the cell nearest him and shot the sheriff squarely in the chest. Across the corridor, in the other cell, another figure sprang up at the sound of the shot. Fish could see only the dimmest outline in the scant light but there was no question in his mind. It had to be Jessie Ramming. He pulled the trigger five more times, as rapidly as he could thumb the hammer back. Even after the man had fallen to the floor he continued to shoot.

At the first explosion Ramming threw himself to one side. As the firing continued he pressed against the wall, trying to see the face of the man at the window. But the darkness was impenetrable. All he could distinguish was the outline of a man's head.

The shooting stopped. The smell of burning gunpowder hung thickly in the cramped cell. He heard the sound of a gun falling to the floor inside the window and quick footsteps fading into the distance.

A moan came from near the cell door, now standing open. Moving with caution, Jessie crept toward the uncertain shaft of lamplight that split the darkness along the corridor between the cells.

The sheriff was lying on his back, his right hand clutching the butt of the long-barreled .45 Peacemaker that had never cleared leather. Ramming caught up his forearm and felt for a pulse. He found it, but even as he pressed his fingers against the limp wrist he knew the heart of big Ben Slaughter was failing.

"Sheriff?" he said gently.

He was aware of the other man biting back deep pain.

"Yeah. I'm cashing in, Jessie Ramming." Slaughter's breath was coming in short, shallow gasps. A hand reached up and caught Jessie's shoulder, pulling him down until his ear was inches away from the other's face.

"I want you to know, Ramming. I'm sorry as hell. I know you didn't help the breed get away."

In the darkness Ramming shook his head.

"Why, sheriff? If you knew, why did you lock me up?"

The big man's booming voice was fading now, like thunder rolling away into the distance.

"That's a long story, friend. Longer than I have time to tell." He coughed, a hollow, bubbling echo that left no doubt where the slug had gone. "Tell Bess ... tell my wife I was thinking about her."

Ramming swallowed at a lump in his throat.

"Sure, I'll do that." He leaned closer to the sheriff's ear as a tremor shook the big hand lying in his. "Can you tell me who's behind it? A name. Give me a name."

"Yeah. He's a mean one, all right. The devil himself ain't ..."

Jessie saw that reason was slipping from Slaughter's grasp.

"Sheriff," he interrupted harshly. "Who is he?"

Slowly, like a man lying back to rest after a long day's labor, Ben Slaughter sighed a great sigh, and lay still.

Ramming placed the lifeless hand gently across the sheriff's chest, where the worn badge showed faintly in the lamplight. Then he stood, hearing for the first time the total silence in the dimness of the cellblock.

He stepped across the corridor to the other cell. Crumpled against the bars was the half-naked body of Romero Red Feather. Blood still oozed onto the wooden floor in an ever-widening circle. Ramming knew before he reached in to feel for a heartbeat that the half-breed wouldn't be worrying any longer about the new gallows waiting behind the jail.

It seemed a long time since the last shot had been fired but Jessie knew it had been hardly more than a minute. He started moving toward the office, wondering who would take over the duties of the law when McSween learned its great sheriff was dead.

He had stepped through the front door, into the darkness of the upper end of the town's main street, when he heard the sound. It reminded him of a swarm of bees. In the fragments of light from stores and homes along the thoroughfare, he saw a collection of hurrying figures, heading in his direction. The sound he had heard was voices, the voices of men stirred to frenzy by the shots booming through the thin mountain air.

Jessie had already taken a step in the direction of the approaching cluster of men when a sudden, chilling thought froze him into immobility. When they rushed in and saw Ben Slaughter's body, and realized Jessie Ramming was no longer behind bars, their conclusion would be drawn in an instant. And the gun that had been dropped into his cell by the killer! Why hadn't he had the presence of mind to grab it up?

Abruptly, Ramming spun on his heel and in three quick steps was around the corner of the building, out of sight of the townsmen pouring up the slope. He didn't stop to listen to their reaction to the grim scene inside but moved quickly and quietly toward the thicker blackness of that damnable patch of trees where the hooves of his own horse had convicted him.

* * *

Easing quietly down the hill behind the row of wooden buildings that fronted main street, Tom Fish felt a foot taller. The instant the last shot was fired, when he knew he had wrought an end to two lives, a feeling of power began to swell within him. It was a sensation of mastery, of superiority, the kind of feeling he had when he was drinking, between the first moment the whiskey sent its hot message through his bloodstream and the time when it finally numbed him into insensibility.

He chuckled aloud. Smilin' Jack Sluder wouldn't be kicking him around no more. No sirree! Why, ol' Tom Fish might just have himself about half of that bank loot Sluder had stashed away somewheres back in the hills. Just as soon as the breed could help 'em locate it.

Once he had his slice of the money, look out, El Paso! The señoritas on both sides of the Rio Grande wouldn't be forgettin' Tom Fish for quite a spell.

Fish's thoughts were pursuing that pleasurable path just as he came abreast of the McSween Hotel. He looked toward the big, two-story structure and remembered vividly the contemptuous look with which Ramming's woman had scalded him a few hours earlier.

And there she sat, across the street in the hotel, waiting for her man to show up. Well, it was going to be a long wait. Tom Fish and Colonel Colt had seen to that.

He laughed again. It was purely something, how a couple of little old .44 caliber slugs could change so many lives. And that sassy blonde ought to be told who it was that had turned her square-jawed manfriend into six feet of cold corpse.

Fish stepped out onto the rough plank walk. As he did, a freckle-faced youngster of no more than ten years came running full tilt along the walkway. Fish's hand shot out and grabbed the suspenders that crossed at the center of the boy's back.

"Hey!" the lad shouted. "What did ya' do that for?"

"I wanna talk to you," said Fish.

"Hey, mister. I cain't stop. I'm already late as all get out. My pa is going to take the hide off'n me with a razor strap soon's I get home, but I just had to see what all the fuss was up at the jail."

136

Fish pulled a hand from his pocket and held it out, palm up. In it lay a silver coin.

"How'd you like to take this home?"

The boy caught his breath in a sharp gasp.

"Would I? You bet! What do I hafta do?"

Fish pointed toward the hotel.

"You go over there and find out from the clerk what room is registered to a gent named Ramming. Then you go find that room and give the woman there a message. She's kind of a little woman. Has blonde hair." Even in that skimpy light the boy caught the sly wind. "A good-looker. Understand?"

"Sure," he said. "What's the message?"

"You tell her to come down the back stairway of the hotel. Tell her that a man named Jessie is waitin' at the bottom of the stairs. And he's in a hurry."

The boy grinned knowingly.

"Mister, I'll have it done before you kin say Jack Robinson."

He caught the coin in the air, and was gone in a blur of churning legs.

Fish stood there and smiled his grotesque smile. Wouldn't old Jack Sluder be surprised when he turned up at the cabin with Ramming's wench?

Chapter
EIGHTEEN

The footing was treacherous in the blackness of the dense woods and Jessie had to move slowly. He had no plan, except somehow to get word to Christina that he was no longer in jail. After that, and after he once again had Captain Asa's goose gun in his hands, he would start trying to put together the pieces of a puzzle that so far went nowhere. Despite the seemingly disconnected events, there still had to be more than coincidence in the fact that his gray horse had turned up in McSween; had, in fact, been part of someone's plot to break the half-breed out of jail.

And the sheriff? What had he meant with those last words about knowing that Ramming had nothing to do with the escape? Jessie's head was spinning. It was like a looking glass that didn't give you back your own reflection.

There was little activity along Main Street. The crowd was still at the jail, every man reading the signs and coming up with a different conclusion as to what had occurred there. They would be in agreement on one thing, though. The absence of one Jessie Ramming was as good as any confession you could find.

Jessie pulled his hat down tight above his eyes and shuffled across the street, kicking clouds of dust ahead of him. He wandered aimlessly, nonchalantly toward the front of the hotel, then appeared to remember some urgent errand that took him out of the lantern light of the hotel veranda.

138

At a darkened corner of the two-story structure he sent a quick glance down the street, then slid along the side of the hotel toward the jumble of sheds and make-shift corrals hidden in the dimness behind it.

A sharp sound, like a man cursing, reached his ears as he came to the rear corner. He stopped abruptly and hugged the wall, peering cautiously into the shadows. There was no stray shaft of light to help, only a sprinkling of stars above. It wasn't enough. It could have been a pair of drunks leaning against each other as they weaved away from the rear stairway of the hotel, or it could have been a man and a woman quarreling. There was disagreement between the two but the voices were too far away.

The couple was swallowed up in the sooty blackness. Jessie moved carefully through the weeds and discarded boxes until he found, more by feel than sight, the outside stairs down which the two apparently had come. His breath escaped in an audible rush, and he realized he had barely been allowing himself to breathe. Had there been no outside access to the second floor of the hotel he couldn't have contacted Christina without giving himself away. And by now everyone in McSween, including the clerk in the hotel, would know that Jessie Ramming was wanted for murder.

Slowly, keeping tight against the wall so the steps wouldn't creak, he climbed to the second floor. The door was ajar, as though someone had departed in a hurry. Ramming nudged it open and found himself looking down the dimly lighted hallway that gave on to the second-floor rooms.

Her room—their room—was the third one along the corridor. Softly, quickly he moved down the uncarpeted hall to the door and started to knock. But at the last instant he drew his hand away. Every occupant of every room on the top floor would hear that knock. Instinctively he reached down and tried the knob. The door was unlocked!

He frowned. Christina must have forgotten to lock it after she returned from the jail. He would have to caution her about that. She couldn't afford unlocked doors so long as Scarface was at liberty.

The lamp on the dresser was still burning. But Christina was gone. He scowled. Something was definitely wrong.

For the barest instant he considered the possibility that she had taken the five twenty-dollar gold pieces and left. Then he shook his head sharply, angry with himself. She might leave, but she wouldn't do it without returning the money to him. That was the kind of woman she was.

Then he saw the buffalo robe, rolled up and lying across the foot of the bed. Wherever she had gone, she planned to return. He picked up the thick robe. It was unnaturally heavy. In a single motion he unrolled it across the bed. Out tumbled the mammoth goose gun! Fondly, he stroked the checkered walnut stock and ran his fingers along the smooth blue steel of the yard-long barrels. He smiled.

Beside the robe lay Christina's wool shawl. He picked it up and heard the soft clink of coins.

He was in the act of turning toward the door when he heard the noise. It was the sound of footsteps pounding along the hallway, and the sound of restrained voices. Jessie was suddenly very glad he had closed the door. He was hidden from the sight of anyone walking to other rooms along the hall.

But instead of fading down the corridor, the footsteps stopped abruptly. Whoever it was had stopped outside the door to his room.

Ramming stood frozen, his hand still outstretched to take hold of the knob. It wasn't Christina. He could hear male voices, barely muffled by the thin door.

"Yeah, this is the room he rented, marshal." It was the voice of the elderly clerk. "His wife came up a while ago. I ain't seen her go out. I figger she don't know he broke jail."

The voice that answered was a deep rumble.

"Don't bet on it. It's my guess she's the one who slipped him the gun he killed the sheriff with. And the breed."

There was the rattle of a key against the metal lock of the door. The clerk's voice came again.

"Sure lucky for us McSween folks that you showed up

140

when you did, Marshal Beaulieu. We ain't got no law at all, now that Sheriff Slaughter's been gunned down. It's a crying shame."

The key turned. But the clerk, assuming the door was locked, had merely shot the bolt. There was a moment of swearing while he rattled the knob in an attempt to open the door. It was in that period of a few seconds that the fugitive gathered his wits. The conversation confirmed what he had feared. He, Jessie Ramming, had murdered Ben Slaughter and the half-breed. There was no question about it in the minds of the town's inhabitants. If they caught him now, that new gallows out back of the jail, intended to accommodate the late Romero Red Feather, would not go begging after all.

Jessie was across the room quickly and silently. He shoved the window up, slid the awkward length of the heavy shotgun through his belt, and climbed outside. There was no ledge, nothing which would give him a toehold. He let himself down to the full length of his arms, his fingertips clutching the windowsill.

Below him, a few splinters of lamplight merely accentuated the darkness. He had no idea what was down there. But at that moment the door to the room swung open. He let go.

Directly beneath the window through which Ramming had made his exit was another window, this one at the hotel kitchen. It was a convenient opening for the cook, one he had used for years to dispose of kitchen waste. The pile of cans and boxes there reached almost to the sill of the bottom-floor window.

Ramming landed with a great noise in the middle of that collection of refuse. Magnifying the din was the sudden yowl of a departing cat, caught unawares with its head inside a can.

Ramming was trying to stand up when he heard a shout from above.

"There he is! That's him, marshal! You kin put lead in him if you hurry!"

Jessie had reached the edge of the wedge of light from the kitchen window. He wasted a split-second in an upward glance. He saw the head and shoulders of a big man leaning out from the second-floor window as he

141

dived into the shadow. The movement saved his life. The angry bellow of a Colt shattered the chill night air. Bits of gravel stung his leg. In another heartbeat the blackness had swallowed him up.

He ran. He ran away from the hotel, away from McSween, toward the blackly forested mountains beyond. A quarter-mile was behind him when he finally slowed, his breath whistling in his throat. Reason returned. He could travel all night on foot but, come daylight, their horses would run him to the ground with ease. He had to have a horse himself.

It was late, though. The horses that had been tied at hitchrails along Main Street were gone now, stabled for the night. The street was empty. Lights showed at only a handful of places: the jail; the furniture store, where the corpses of Ben Slaughter and Romero Red Feather were doubtless being fitted for pine boxes; and the livery stable, whose lantern burned at all hours.

It was toward that last pinpoint of light that Jessie began to move. With the right kind of luck, he just might find his own gray gelding.

It took him the better part of an hour to work his way down the ridge and through the network of shacks and buildings and barking dogs to the livery's rear entrance. Through a crack between the double doors he scanned the interior in the limited illumination from the lantern. A flicker of movement caught his eye, but it was only a blaze-faced bay horse shifting his weight in the stall at the rear of the sprawling structure. The very stall, Jessie thought ruefully, that had served him as a bed.

Disappointment knifed through him. He should have known better than to hope his own horse would be waiting so conveniently for him.

The night's chill was biting through his coat, but he made himself stand motionless for a full five minutes, peering through the crack into the dimly lighted interior of the livery. He couldn't afford to take a chance of stumbling into the hands of the marshal now. Not until he had solid evidence that would prove the sheriff and the Indian had not died by his hand.

In the darkness, Jessie bit his underlip. That was not all that concerned him. There was the mystery of Christina's whereabouts. That worry had gnawed at his mind through the past hour a great deal more than he cared to acknowledge. He had tried to tell himself she had left the hotel on some innocent errand. A shopping trip, maybe. She would have to have something to eat. But it was no good. With a sickening certainty, he knew Christina was in trouble.

Finally, Jessie slipped the blade of his jackknife through the crack and lifted the bar that held the double doors closed. Slowly, slowly he swung the door open, enough to allow himself to slide inside. Once there, he stopped and listened, scarcely daring to breathe. But there was no movement or noise, except the comfortable sounds of well-fed horses drowsing in the warmth of the stable.

He grinned a humorless grin. It was almost too easy. Stealing a horse was the simplest thing in the world.

Ramming ran his eyes over the bay with the blaze face that stood in the rear stall. He was a good-looking animal, deep-chested and long-bodied; a runner. But he still had the rugged look of the cowhorse about him. Some cowboy would swear the air blue come morning when it became time to fetch his mount.

Across the partition that separated the stalls rested an almost-new saddle, with a bridle hanging from the horn. In the space of a half-minute, Ramming had the bay bridled and was tightening the cinch of the saddle. He never heard the footsteps on the straw behind him.

A shower of lights exploded in his brain. He knew he was falling, but there was no pain. That came several minutes later, when he opened his eyes. The throbbing in his head was a deep-rooted agony, the wrenching pain of toothache.

Clarity returned gradually to his vision. Above him stood the young Mexican, Martín, the youth who had been so accommodating on the night Jessie had sought a place to sleep. Now his expression was anything but sociable.

"So!" the young man hissed through his teeth. "It is the *hombre malo* who lies so convincingly. The one who shoots down men in the dark, like a sneaking coyote."

Ramming's mind was spinning slowly to a stop. As he

143

started to raise himself on his elbows, he felt a sudden painful stab over his heart. He blinked his eyes and looked down. The needle-sharp tines of a pitchfork were pressed against his chest. Three small circlets of blood showed through his shirt, where the tines had pierced the flesh.

"I should do it! I should kill you there where you lay in the straw." The youth's voice was high-pitched and brittle, almost as though he were on the verge of breaking into tears. "But no. It would be too easy, Señor Ramming. Better that you have a day or two to look into your heart before they hang you on the gallows where my . . ."

A sob escaped his lips. He wiped angrily at a tear with the back of his hand.

"Martín!" Ramming's voice slashed through the air like a whip cracking. "Listen to me! I didn't kill the sheriff. Or the other man. Someone else did it. Someone who shot through the window of my cell."

The Mexican youth shook his head as though he were shaking away a wasp.

"It is a lie! I went to the jail. I saw the gun, where you had dropped it after all the bullets had been fired. And there was the body of Sheriff Ben, without life." His face was distorted with grief. "And I saw Vicente. With five wounds. Dead . . ."

He began to cry unashamedly. Jessie's tone softened.

"You mean the half-breed? Romero Red Feather?"

The Mexican nodded, his voice shuddering as he caught his breath.

"Sí. His name wasn't Red Feather. That was only a name he called himself. He was Vicente Romero."

"You knew him well?"

The youth dipped his head in the barest of nods.

"My name is Martín Romero. He was my half-brother."

The words cut across Ramming's thoughts like a whiplash, intensifying the throbbing ache that had begun to subside behind his eyes.

"I'm sorry."

Anger flashed again in the youth's dark eyes.

"Why didn't you kill him on the mountain? Instead of bringing him back to jail, and shooting him there like a mad dog in a cage?"

Jessie started to speak but Martín went on, speaking almost to himself.

"Vicente would have preferred to die in the mountains. They were his home. He loved them, like a wild animal loves the wilderness. When I was just a *muchachito,* he would take me with him into the mountains. We would sleep under the stars and trap the little animals to eat and follow the tracks of the deer and bear. There was not a tree or a rock or the faintest trail that I did not learn from Vicente."

His voice trailed off as the memories flooded his mind.

Quietly, Ramming said, "I went after him and brought him back to town because he was riding my horse. A horse that was stolen from me a long time ago. By another man. But I didn't shoot your brother."

Martín glared at him in the lantern light.

"Then why did you run away?"

"Who would believe the words of a man who had been locked up for helping a murderer escape?"

The youth winced at the blunt description of his half-brother. But then he nodded, ever so slightly.

Jessie got to his feet. The pitchfork was still in the hand of the young Mexican, but it was forgotten.

"Martín, maybe you know something about the man who talked the sheriff into locking me up. A thin-faced hombre, with no lips and teeth that are too long. Why would he want me in jail? I've never seen him before today."

Martín's expression was an eloquent characterization.

"He is no good, that one. He has no job, only a little place out of town a short distance. I wouldn't trust him to water my horse."

The words suddenly brought Ramming's thoughts back to his own problem.

"*Amigo.* Where is my gray horse? What did the sheriff do with him after he took me to jail? I thought I would find him here."

The Mexican boy's heavy, black brows shot upward in sudden recollection.

"I saw your gray horse today. After Sheriff Ben took you away. This same man. This Fish. He was the one who was riding the gray." He shook his head remorsefully. "At that time I gave no thought to it. He and the sheriff were *compadres*, I think."

Ramming's eyes narrowed.

"You mean Sheriff Slaughter was thick with that piece of trash?"

Martín shrugged.

"I have seen them talking together as though they knew each other very well."

Jessie's look was so intense the youth took an involuntary step backward.

"That could explain it," Ramming said. "That's why the sheriff was so quick to buy that wild story Fish spun about me and the jailbreak."

He reached out a hand and grasped the young man's shoulder.

"Tell me how to get to his place. I'll have a little chat with that hombre. It's the only hope I have of running this thing to the ground. And getting out of the trap somebody laid for me when they gunned down the sheriff and your brother."

Sorrow returned to the dark eyes of the Mexican.

"It would please me to know who cheated Vicente out of his life, even though there was only a little life left to him."

He gestured with an arm toward the east.

"Fish's *casa* is a short ride in that direction, Señor Ramming. A half-mile, no more. It is a poor place. Only yesterday I heard a man bet with another that the house will fall to the ground at the first snow this winter."

Jessie took the hand that Martín Romero extended toward him.

"It is time I got moving. If lady luck is with me, I will find this man with the name and face of a fish. I pray he will lead me to another man. And that man is the one I want, more than a starving man wants a drink of cold water."

146

He started to turn away but Martín's next words stopped him.

"If you don't mind, señor. To tie me up would be a favor. Otherwise, when they find a horse missing I have no job. And without a job how can I marry my beautiful Consuela?"

It brought a smile to Ramming's face, the first one in a long time.

With a length of soft rope he bound the hands and feet of Martín and, at the youth's insistence, tore a piece from his shirt and stuffed it into his mouth.

"They're still on my trail, so they'll find you before long," Jessie assured him. He took a twenty-dollar gold piece from his trousers and slipped it into a pocket of the youth. "Many thanks, my friend."

The youth, an urgent look in his dark eyes, grunted and shook his head as Ramming took up the reins of the blaze-faced bay.

"No, *amigo*," Ramming said. "You've earned that money, and more. Some day I'll finish paying the debt I owe you."

The Mexican, lying on his side in the straw, was still shaking his head as Jessie led the gelding outside. He closed the door and stepped up into the saddle. His appraisal of the bay had been accurate. He moved out quickly, smoothly, falling immediately into a ground-consuming canter.

The cold light of a full moon bathed the roofs of the town and gave ghostly shapes to the mountains that rose in ragged waves along either side of Walnut Valley. Ramming headed the bay in a lope toward the nearest neck of timber, where curious eyes were less likely to spot him. The fact that he was absolutely innocent of the murders of the two men at the jail would remain his secret if the good citizens of McSween caught up with him. They'd have a noose about his neck before he could take a deep breath. Especially if they found him riding a stolen horse.

Another thought weighed heavily on Jessie's mind as he rode, causing him to push the bay faster than was prudent through the moonlight-streaked timber. Christina would never have left the hotel room unless she believed she was helping him. But he had to give first priority to clearing his own name. Without that, he wouldn't be of any help to either of them.

Chapter
NINETEEN

Christina was startled when she heard the quick knock at her door. She laid the bundle containing the goose gun and what remained of Jessie's one-hundred-dollar reward on the bed.

"Who is it?" she whispered.

"Message for you, ma'am."

It was obviously the voice of a child. She unlocked the door and looked into an animated, snaggle-toothed face.

"Yes?"

"Do you know a man name of Jessie, ma'am?"

She nodded, holding her breath.

"He said to tell you he was waitin' at the back of the hotel and that you was to go down the back stairs."

Relief flooded through Christina. She managed to nod her head in understanding. The boy turned and darted away.

Christina sent one quick glance around the room, decided she couldn't afford to waste a second, and slipped through the door. Stealthily, she crept along the hall and through the door to the tiny second-floor landing at the head of the outside stairway. The stars were dim. The ground below her was black.

Regretting that she had not taken time even to grab up a shawl, she felt her way cautiously down the rickety, creaking stairs. Halfway down she heard a movement below and whispered: "Jessie?"

There was no reply. Abruptly she realized that, if Jessie Ramming had somehow escaped from jail, any sound could jeopardize his life. She bit her lip, wishing she hadn't spoken his name.

She was on the bottom step, with one hand on the stairway railing, when she felt a hand close roughly about her wrist. Her first impulse was to jerk away, but she fought down the urge.

"Jessie, is that you? How did you get ... Did the sheriff let you go?"

Suddenly she was spun around by the hand that grasped her wrist, and another hand closed roughly over her mouth. A scream rose in her throat but her head was jerked back so violently the scream was choked off. A nauseating odor of tobacco and perspiration clogged her nostrils.

"You just be nice and quiet, little lady," a vaguely familiar voice grated at her ear. "Jessie ain't comin'. Ever! And if you don't hanker to have a broken neck you'll do exactly like I tell you. Hear?"

Christina's head was spinning. The words didn't make sense. If Jessie wasn't here, he had to be in jail. The terrible voice beside her, that sent chill bumps down her spine, made it sound as though something terrible had happened.

But she couldn't ask a question. She could barely breathe. The man was forcing her ahead of him through the tangle of weeds and clutter of boards and boxes behind the hotel. Once she kicked backwards, her heel sliding down his shin. She heard a sulphuric explosion of cursing and her arm was jerked upward behind her back. She had to walk quickly or risk having her shoulder dislocated.

They walked that way until even the occasional lights of Main Street had receded to dimness. When they stopped at last and the hand was removed from her mouth, Christina knew that any scream would be futile.

She felt the rough, prickly loop of a rope pulled tightly about her wrists and a strangely high-pitched voice command. "Get on that horse, and don't try nothin' foolish."

Then she knew. It was the voice of the man called Tom Fish, the man who had persuaded the sheriff to put

Jessie in jail. She remembered the things she had said to him outside the jail, after the sheriff had taken Jessie away. And she remembered the look in his eyes. The bitter taste of fear crowded into her throat.

"On the horse," he demanded again, jerking at a handful of her hair. Awkwardly, she climbed on the horse. In another moment he was mounted behind her and they were moving through the cold night, away from the warm, reassuring refuge of McSween.

Christina was shivering violently, as much with fright as with the cold, when they reached a collection of nondescript buildings that even the soft rays of the emerging moon couldn't enhance. Fish pulled the horse up at the steps of the dilapidated house and stepped to the ground.

"Get down," he grunted, and jerked the rope that bound her wrists.

She slid to one side in the saddle, and would have fallen to the ground, but he caught her about the waist. Instead of releasing her, he held her tightly for a long moment, letting his hands wander over her body.

Christina shuddered.

"Get your filthy hands off me!"

Fish spun away and pulled roughly on the rope.

"Come on! You ain't gonna be so damned uppity when ol' Fish gets through with you."

He pushed her hard as she stepped through the door and Christina fell heavily to the floor. In the next instant, in the scrap of light from the moon, she saw his leering face bending toward her. Slowly, as though enjoying the prolongation of her terror, he moved his hands to the neck of her dress and began deliberately to unfasten the buttons.

Christina closed her eyes, willing her mind to shut out the ugly lust in his face.

Abruptly she felt his hands stop their movement. She opened her eyes and became aware that the light of a lamp was illuminating the room.

"What the hell are you doing up?" she heard Fish snarl. "Get your butt back in the bedroom."

Christina twisted her head and looked across the kitchen. There, standing in the doorway to another room, a lamp held high in her hand, was a fat Mexican woman in a tattered wrap. Her brows were drawn together in disapproval and her head was swiveling from side to side on a neck hidden somewhere in pyramiding folds of flesh.

"No, no, Meester Feesh," the Mexican woman was admonishing. "It is bad what you do."

"I told you to get the hell out of here!"

Fish was on his feet, his hands curled into angry fists at his side.

The woman took a step toward him, still rocking her head from side to side in stubborn rebuke.

"No, señor. You cannot do that. It is bad. Very bad."

Christina saw the sudden insanity in Fish's face. Saliva ran from a corner of his mouth and dripped from his chin. As the obese woman moved toward him he snatched up a butcher knife from a scarred sideboard and took one step toward her. The knife was low at his side and hidden from Christina's view, and for a long moment Christina didn't understand the look of disbelief on the other woman's face. Then she felt something splatter warmly against her arm and saw a dark stain spreading rapidly across the broad abdomen above her.

The Mexican woman turned, carefully placed the lamp on the rickety kitchen table, and lowered her vast bulk into a chair. Christina wondered if the chair would sustain that enormous weight. She wanted to scream, or cry, or shout, but her throat tightened of its own accord, closing off any sound. Dumbly, she watched as the fat woman looked down and tried to stem the widening stain with her stubby fingers.

Fish reached down, grabbed Christina's wrist, and pulled her to her feet. The madness was gone from his eyes. Instead, they held a perverted satisfaction. He had gained his pleasure when the knife blade sank into the folds of flesh.

There was a worn coat hanging beside the door. He took it down, threw it around Christina's shoulders, and with a hand on her upper arm propelled her through the door. He looked back once, where Estella was sitting at the table, staring in bewilderment at the blood pulsing through the knife wound. Then he closed the door.

152

Silently he pushed her toward the horse and helped her mount. For the first time Christina recognized the animal. It was the same gray horse Jessie had ridden when he returned from the mountain with Romero Red Feather trailing behind him at the end of a rope. She tried unsuccessfully to stifle a sob. If only Jessie could be here!

After that, time stood still. They rode into the forested mountains, climbing always higher. They rode until Christina's legs burned with raw misery, and they kept riding, until her muscles and bones could no longer send their signals of agony to her brain. She would have fallen out of the saddle more than once if Fish hadn't put a hand out to catch her.

At last, through chattering teeth, she asked, "Where are we going?"

"To see a man," he said shortly, and after that there was silence, except for the rising wind, wailing like a distant banshee through the crowns of the conifers.

Chapter
TWENTY

The moon was beginning its slide toward the blackness of the mountaintops when Jessie Ramming came in sight of Tom Fish's place. He inspected the house and barn and corrals in the pale light and grinned a humorless grin. Martín's description was unerring. There was no mistaking this homestead. The man who had bet that it would cave in at the first snow had put his money on a sure thing.

He reined the blaze-faced horse at an angle toward the barn, keeping that ramshackle structure between himself and the house as he moved nearer. He half-expected to see the gray gelding in the corral, but the only sign of life was a gaunt jersey cow, languidly chewing her cud. She gave no sign that she was aware of the horse and rider.

Easing the bay past the corner of the barn, Ramming saw the yellow light of a lamp shining faintly from a window. He frowned. The absence of a horse meant Fish was gone. But then who was inside? Martín had made no mention of a wife and children.

Jessie slid the big shotgun from the boot on the stolen saddle and let the twin barrels rest in the crook of an elbow as he advanced toward the house. The hooves of the bay echoed loudly on the packed earth.

He pulled the horse to a halt at the edge of the fragile porch and shouted: "Fish! You in there?"

A prickly sense that something was wrong prodded

Jessie. He would make a fine target for a gun barrel concealed behind a darkened window. But then he shrugged. It wasn't on this night that Jessie Ramming's number was up. Fate had already let that opportunity slip by.

He stepped down from the saddle, still holding the eight-gauge in the crook of his arm, and went up the steps of the porch. The boards squealed in protest, announcing to anyone inside that a visitor was at the door.

Through the door's dingy glassine covering Jessie looked inside. On the table sat a lamp. Beside it, in a chair, was the shapeless figure of a woman. Her head had fallen forward on her breast and Ramming supposed that she was asleep. But as he studied the scene a tiny flicker of movement caught his eye. From her midsection slid a droplet of a dark, thick substance that traveled to the floor and joined a syrupy pool of similar fluid already gathered there.

He shoved the door open and in two strides was beside the woman. She heard his steps and opened her eyes. Pain screamed silently at him from beneath the half-closed lids.

"Is Fish here?" he demanded.

Her lips moved but no sound came. Then she answered his question with a slight turn of her head.

He picked up the lamp and held it out so that its rays illuminated the woman's abdomen. The front of her wrapper was slick and shiny with blood. As Ramming watched, more of the dark red substance welled out through a slash in the cloth.

"Who did this?" He couldn't keep the harshness from his voice as his eyes fell on the butcher knife, its broad blade mottled with the same crimson stain that was spreading on the floor.

Her dark eyes, dulled with pain and shock, were glued to his face, as though afraid he might turn and walk away. But still she did not speak.

Impatience tore at him. The territorial marshal would have gathered his posse by now, and quite likely would have picked up his trail. He needed to be gone.

The woman read his thoughts. With a great effort she lifted her head and murmured, *"Por favor,* señor. Help me."

Jessie shook his head sharply. What was he thinking about? He couldn't ride away and leave this poor wretch. Quickly, he snatched up the lamp and looked into the bedroom, intending to carry her to the bed. He stopped and let his eyes measure her bulk. She would die before he could wrestle her to the bed.

In another instant he had stripped the bed and with the corn husk mattress and blankets prepared a pallet on the floor beside the chair where she sat. Slowly, carefully he began to ease the massive body onto the makeshift bed. She tried to help, but the loss of blood had weakened her gravely.

Groaning with pain, she at last lay stretched out on the pallet. Without hesitation, Ramming pulled back the wrapper and inspected the wound in her bulging midsection. His hands curled into fists against his thighs. He had yet another reason to find the man called Fish.

He packed the wound with flour from the cupboard, watching sadly as blood welled through the poultice. Tearing strips from a sheet, he contrived a bandage for the awkwardly placed gash, glancing occasionally into her face. Silently, she watched his movements, wincing now and again.

He dampened a rag and wet her lips, then knelt down and said slowly, deliberately: "I will send someone. *Comprende?"*

Her head moved in the barest nod of understanding. He got to his feet but her voice brought him back to one knee beside her.

"Señor, I am grateful."

"Don't talk," he said. "Save your strength."

She went on as though she hadn't heard.

"You are looking for Señor Feesh?"

"Yes."

"He is bad. A bad man. He has killed me, only because I tried to help the woman."

Jessie tensed.

"What woman?"

"The leetle woman. With freckles, and hair like corn-silk."

The words were like a kick to the pit of his stomach.

"He has her? The blonde woman? Christina?"

"Her name I did not hear. But she is his . . . how do you say . . . preesoner?"

Her eyes closed for a moment. Ramming knelt closer.

"Where has he gone. Where has he taken her?"

Her eyelids fluttered open.

"To the mountain, I think. To a cabin I have heard him speak about."

"How can I find it?"

Her voice was weaker now. He had to strain to catch the words.

"Do you know the high mountain? With the rock face? The cabin is close by there."

He nodded. He had seen such a peak, dominating the range of mountains along the northern rim of Walnut Valley, when he had ridden along the opposite slope with his half-breed captive. The same rock-ribbed peak which had dominated his view from the jail cell.

"I will find it," he said. "But first I will send someone to help you."

She was looking at him and Ramming tried to smile reassuringly. Then he saw that she had died with her eyes open.

"Damn him!" he breathed, and covered her face with the remnants of the torn sheet.

The long, lean bay horse moved easily along the canyon floor. At a gentle pressure on the reins he crossed the noisy shallows of Walnut Creek and turned without hesitation up the incline that would take them to the upper reaches of the mountain bulwark.

Jessie pounded the saddle horn with his fist. The lead he was following was too slim. The odds of finding the cabin were nothing to brag about. And even if he did, how could he be sure the ugly man called Fish would be there, with Christina? Beyond that was the ultimate question: Was he following a trail to Scarface, or was he pursuing a counterfeit track his mind had invented?

He struck the swell of the saddle with his fist again. Somewhere up ahead was his quarry. It had to be!

He shivered and pulled his coat tighter about him. The thought of meeting at last with the bearded, ghost-like figure made the hair stand stiffly along the back of his neck. If their meeting meant death for himself, so be it. He could no more abandon this trail of vengeance than he could will his heart to stop beating. When a man had been wronged as Jessie Ramming had been wronged, no reason on earth was reason enough to abandon the pursuit.

He saw through the trees that the moon was touching the horizon. Swinging about in the saddle he found the bright face of the North Star and set his course by that old acquaintance. There could be no waiting for daylight. The urgency that had chafed steadily at him since he had found the hotel room empty now screamed through his veins like a ravenous cougar. The gods might punish him with yet another death but it wouldn't be because he didn't try.

In quick succession, like the lunatic nightmares that swarm through a fevered mind, memories of his losses crowded into his head. Guilt lay like a bitter lump in his breast. Everyone he touched had died a brutal, wanton death—his beloved Anna; the brave *viejo*, Juan Campos; and big Sheriff Ben Slaughter and the man of two bloods, Romero Red Feather. And, within the past hour, the fat, harmless Mexican woman, whose life ran out through a knife slash in her belly while he, a total stranger, lent the only ears to hear her final words.

For a moment, the old sickness welled up in Jessie's throat. Only once in his adult life, before Anna's death, had he confronted violence face-to-face. It was when they had been married only a few months. He had driven the wagon to Trabajo for supplies—seeds for a garden, a few pounds of nails, beans, and flour, some dress material for Anna. His surprise to her.

The wagon had the good grace to wait until he reached town before it broke down, disabled by a sheared wheel pin. He was lying on his back beneath the front axle when he heard the gunshots. He rolled onto his side and looked toward the doors of the Western

158

Mining and Land Bank, in time to see two masked men burst through the doors.

Running for their lives, the two gunmen had to skirt Ramming's wagon to reach their horses. One didn't make it. He fell two strides from where Jessie lay, half his head blown away by a 400-grain Sharps bullet fired from inside the bank.

The other, a lean, angular man with prominent ears and a hawk nose, paused only long enough to scoop up the gunny sack from his partner's lifeless hand. When he straightened, the bandanna mask slipped from his clean-shaven face. Ramming looked directly into his eyes.

In another instant the bank robber had vaulted into his saddle and vanished in a cloud of dust, toward the desert wasteland and the savage mountains beyond.

It took Sheriff Wiley Dunn's posse ten days and the lives of seven good horses to run the desperado to earth. Ramming cursed the accident of fate that had placed him in a position to see the man's face but he couldn't turn down the sheriff's plea that he take the witness stand.

It was his testimony that got the bank robber a life sentence in the territorial prison at Santa Fe, and as the sheriff led him away in manacles the cold-eyed prisoner said to Jessie: "That'll cost you, you son-of-a-bitch!"

They never did find the money.

When he had thought these thoughts, Ramming smiled. But it was not a pleasant smile. He knew he was no longer the same gentle man of peace who had stood and trembled at those bitter words. Violence and death had left their indelible scars.

Almost without conscious thought he slid the huge shotgun from its leather casing, broke open the breech, and checked the double loads. He wanted to pull the triggers on that murderous weapon, to feel its powerful recoil against his shoulder, and know that the double charge of buckshot was speeding toward its target.

He swept off his hat and threw his head back, filling his lungs with the cold, high-elevation air. It wasn't the pungent odor of conifers that stung his senses, however, but the reek of danger, hanging like brimstone about him.

159

Chapter
TWENTY-ONE

There was light inside the cabin but Fish's cautious hail brought no response. He swung stiffly to the ground and caught Christina as she slid from the saddle. This time he made no move to take advantage of the closeness, but steadied her with one hand as they went inside.

On a table in the center of the room burned a candle, its wax oozing down the sides of an empty whiskey bottle. But it was the fireplace toward which Christina crept. Its warmth made her want to sink to the floor and lie there. Doggedly, she dragged herself to a log bench positioned against the wall beside the fire. She couldn't suppress a groan as she collapsed on its rough seat.

After a time she looked up. Fish was standing with his back to the fireplace. His eyes never left the door.

Involuntarily her glance followed his. Someone was coming in from the blackness outside.

She held her breath, praying that whoever it was would command that she be freed. A figure came toward her, until the light from the fireplace was full on his face. Her mind refused to accept what her eyes told her.

Then Christina screamed, a feeble cry that was instantly whipped away by the wind that pounded at the cabin walls.

The voice she heard was a guttural whisper.

"What the hell is she doing here?"

Fish was nodding his head as though the affirmative gesture might influence the other's disposition.

160

"This here's Ramming's woman, Jack. Didn't you say you wanted to take care of her?"

The bushy black beard that masked Sluder's face trembled with the intensity of his words.

"You fool! This ain't Ramming's woman."

Fish's mouth stood open.

"It ain't? But I seen her . . ."

Sluder's fist slammed against the top of the makeshift table, threatening to collapse it.

"I say she ain't his woman!"

Abruptly the anger was gone from the scarred face. He placed the flask of whiskey he held on the grimy cupboard and moved in his shuffling gait to the bench where Christina sat huddled in dread.

"Yessir. I know who this purty thing is. Don't I, little lady?" The brutal gleam in his squinted eyes burned into hers. "She's a recent widder. Ain't that so, ma'am?"

She tried to choke it back, but a whimper, the sound a frightened puppy makes, escaped from her lips. The long fingers of Sluder's hand were suddenly clasping her chin. Then, slowly, they slid downward to her neck and moved in a rough caress. Christina shut her eyes tightly. But all that did was summon to her mind a picture of the horror in her cabin that other morning. She wanted to be sick.

As quickly as it had come, the impulse which drove him to put his hands on her faded. He spun around and fixed Fish with a scowl that caused the other man to freeze in the act of striking a match along his thigh.

"What about him? And what about the sheriff? Did the breed do his job?"

Fish, relieved that he was somehow forgiven for bringing along the woman, attempted a confident smile.

"Jack, you ain't gonna be disappointed. I took care of it better than you was figurin'."

"Just tell me what the hell happened!"

"Well, you see, I got to thinkin' that the breed might get too anxious to get out of sight of them new gallows and botch the job. So I took care of it myself." He glanced at Sluder from beneath uncertain brows. "I kind of figured that would be worth a bigger slice of that bank loot you got hid, Jack."

Sluder's rifle, propped against the table, was suddenly in his hands again. The unconcerned downward slant of the barrel was nevertheless enough to focus Fish's mind on the object of his narrative.

"I got to the jail just as the sheriff let the breed loose," he said. "It was pretty dark in there but I seen that the sheriff had opened his cell door. Well, that looked like a good time to take care of them hombres like you wanted, Jack."

He couldn't resist a pause to heighten the suspense of his tale. This time the bearded man waited without comment.

"Anyway, I put one right smack-dab into Slaughter's heart, jist about this far from that badge of his'n."

"And . . . ?" Sluder let the word drag out.

"I put them other five slugs into the gent you was so jumpy about, Jack. You can bet your bottom dollar that Ramming feller won't be doggin' your trail no more."

The sense of what Fish was saying came slowly to Christina. She shook her head, trying not to understand the words. Then, in a flood, the tears came. She sobbed uncontrollably, the sound not unlike the wail of the winter wind buffeting the crude cabin.

Sluder had turned and was watching her coldly.

"Now what the hell brought that on?"

"Like I told you, Jack. She acted like she was awful sweet on that Ramming jasper."

"There's something here I don't savvy," grunted the scarfaced man. He walked over to the bench where Christina was slumped, caught a handful of her yellow hair, and jerked her head back.

"What do you know about Jessie Ramming? How come you're gettin' all slobbery about him bein' blowed away?"

She only turned her head from side to side, oblivious to the painful strain against her hair.

Sluder chuckled. It was the most dreadful of all the sounds he had made.

"Well, well. It sure looks like they was acquainted, don't it?" His rasping tone grew threatening. "How come you to know him? And I don't want none of your lying, neither. Hear?"

162

She nodded. What difference did it make now? Now that Jessie was dead.

"He came to our cabin. After you left."

"Wait a damn minute!" Sluder yanked at the handful of hair again. "What kind of horse was he ridin'?"

She winced.

"He didn't have a horse. He was on foot."

This time his jerk was so forceful the woman cried out.

"You lie! There ain't no man alive that could've walked across the desert and the mountains from where I left him."

Abruptly he stepped back. Again, there was that terrible belching chuckle.

"Well, now. I guess that's about right, ma'am. There sure ain't no man *alive* that could do it. Maybe Jessie Ramming got lucky and reached your place on foot, but he ain't going to have that kind of luck no more. Ain't that so, Fish?"

Fish was enjoying the woman's anguish. It was what he had wanted to do to her.

"That's a sure enough fact, Miz High and Mighty. That friend of yours ain't going no place except to boothill." He was bobbing his head up and down as he remembered the scene. "Yessir. It was like shootin' squirrels in a cage. I stood right there at the back of the jail and poked that ol' .44 through the little window of the breed's cell and, Bam! I put that first one dead center of the sheriff's wishbone. He went down like a pole-axed steer."

Fish's story was carrying him now. He had forgotten his listeners as he recreated the killings.

"Even in that bad light ol' Fish didn't miss a shot. When I seen that the sheriff was down, I quick as a flash opened up on the gent in the other cell. He didn't make no noise a'tall. Jist laid right there on the floor and kicked a time or two afore he died."

He giggled excitedly.

"Ya see, Jack? There wasn't nothing special about that Ramming feller after I put five slugs into him." He cleared his throat nervously. "I was thinkin' you and me might split that bank money down the middle."

163

Christina had tried to close her mind to Fish's rambling recital, but when he stopped talking she had the feeling that something was not right about his story. A piece didn't fit. It was the slimmest of threads to grab, but she clutched frantically at it.

"You were at the back of the jail? Where they built the gallows?"

"That's right, ma'am," he smirked. "The one they was going to string the breed up on. But they'll never catch him now. He ought to be walkin' through that there door any minute."

The intensity of her voice was lost on Fish, but Sluder caught the change in her tone.

"Shut your damn mouth a minute," he broke in. "Now, how come you to ask that question, little lady?"

She was remembering what she had seen in the dimness of the cellblock area in the jail. Her reply wasn't to Sluder's question, but to clear her own frenzied thoughts.

"It wasn't the Indian in that rear cell. It was Jessie."

Fish still didn't grasp the significance of her words.

"Them McSween folks are gonna be talking about this day for a long time, Jack. Ain't that so?"

Sluder's arm swung in a wide arc that ended against the side of Fish's head. He stumbled backwards, barely catching himself short of the fireplace.

"Hey, Jack. What did you want to go an—?"

Sluder raised his fist and Fish bit off the sentence before it was completed.

"Now you tell me what you was thinkin'," he growled, his hairy face so close to Christina she could smell the whiskey on his breath. Then, like the snap of fingers, she realized what her revelation would mean.

"Nothing," she said tensely.

Sluder's hands caught the front of her dress. He lifted her to her feet until she was on tiptoe. A knife appeared in his hand, the blade flashing orange in the light of the fire. It was the same blade he had held against her throat before, when the nightmare had had its beginning.

She swallowed dryly.

"The sheriff put Jessie in the back cell. I went to see him after he was locked up."

164

Sluder's words were barely distinguishable.

"And the breed? Where was he?"

"He was in the cell at the front of the jail. The one with the window facing Main Street."

There was a little cry from across the room. Fish had slunk into the shadows and was trying to be inconspicuous. The suddenness with which his fortunes had changed made him want to throw up.

"That ain't so, Jack," he cried. "It was Ramming I shot. I swear it!"

Sluder had released Christina. Now he stood silhouetted against the dancing tongues of flame from the fireplace. For a terrifying instant, it was not Sluder's face that Fish saw there. It was that of Lucifer!

But it was Sluder's gravelly voice that spoke.

"Fish, you knew that I was counting on that breed to help me find where I hid that bank money. You knew that, didn't you?"

Fish couldn't speak. Sluder's tone was almost gentle, the tone of a parent reasoning with a child.

"But more than that I wanted that man Ramming dead. You knew that, too, didn't you? That's why I told you to have the breed do the killin'. So there wouldn't be any slip-ups."

Fish had both arms extended before him. Desperation choked his voice.

"I tell you she's lyin', Jack. I seen it was Ramming before I pulled the trigger. You don't think I'd make a mistake like that, do you, Jack?"

Slowly, deliberately, Sluder took up the rifle and elevated the muzzle. Christina watched in horrified fascination as the reflected firelight traveled along the octagonal steel barrel. It was like reliving the insane moment when she had watched that same rifle blast away part of Emil Bucklin's face.

She could see, in the shadows, that Fish had fallen on his knees.

"No, Jack! No, Jack!" He was repeating the words over and over, a litany of fear. When the shot exploded in the little cabin, Christina closed her eyes tightly. She heard the sound of a body falling to the floor, and the fitful scrape of boot soles against the rough wooden floor.

Jessie Ramming, less than a quarter-mile away, might have heard the shot even above the sound of the rushing wind and been warned. But it was at that instant that a young buck deer in rut, listening tensely to the horseman's approach, wheeled and bolted away through the brush. All the rider knew was that the source of the wood smoke coming to him on the wind had to be somewhere up ahead.

It was not long afterwards that he reached the edge of the clearing and saw slivers of firelight leaking through the weathered split-log walls. The relief that he felt warmed his entire body. Whether he was closer to the scarfaced man or not didn't, at that moment, matter as much as knowing that Christina had to be there, a few yards away across the clearing.

Jessie's impulse was to rush to the cabin, throw open the door, and blast away at anyone who stood between him and Christina. But he gritted his teeth until his jaws ached and forced himself to sit upon his horse quietly for a long time, watching the dim outline of the cabin and the gray horse tied to a stunted spruce nearby.

At last he got down, secured the bay, and slid the shotgun from its boot on the saddle. He was surprised at his own calmness. His pulse was steady, his breathing quiet and even. Despite the certain knowledge that he would have to kill a man in a matter of minutes.

It took Jessie the better part of a half-hour to work his way across the clearing, even though there was no sign that anyone inside the cabin was keeping watch. The gray gelding had his ears thrown forward, recognizing the man's familiar scent, but at a word from Ramming the horse returned to his half-slumberous state.

Moving like a stalking cat, Jessie reached the wall of the cabin. There, a few feet away, was the outline of a window frame. He eased towards it but found that it had been boarded up. A foot beyond it he found a crack between the hand-hewn boards that was wide enough to afford a view inside.

The fire in the fireplace was sinking but the candlelight showed him that his caution was unnecessary. On a bench against the wall lay Christina, her hands bound at her sides and a cloth tied tightly about her mouth. A few feet away, in the center of the room, was her captor. He sat in a chair at the tiny table, his head resting on his forearms. Sound asleep, Jessie concluded.

He smiled to himself. In his mind he had created a menace vastly out of proportion to the unwary enemy who slept inside.

He went to the front door, unlatched it, and pushed it inward. Deep within his subconscious a tiny warning bell sounded, triggered by something about that door. But Jessie was too anxious. He wanted to be inside, to challenge his adversary, to ensure that Christina was unharmed.

Chapter
TWENTY-TWO

Christina's heart leaped into her throat when he came through the door. The sound she made was nothing more than a moan, muffled as it was by the gag drawn painfully tight across her mouth. Jessie heard it but his attention was focused on the man sleeping at the table.

All those signals came together for him an instant later. The man at the table wasn't sleeping. He was dead. Christina's moan was not a message of welcome. And the latch at the front door! It had been fastened on the outside!

Jessie knew, even as he tensed his muscles to spin toward the door, that his movement was too late. He felt the presence of the man there as surely as though he had touched him.

"Put the gun down," the guttural voice commanded, and all the apprehension that had dogged Ramming from the moment of Anna's death came rushing back to numb his senses.

Carefully, without turning, he laid the shotgun across the table, between the candle and the mop of unkempt hair on Fish's head.

"Over there. Beside the fireplace."

The order came quietly, without emotion.

Ramming moved to the smoldering fire, shot a quick glance at Christina's ashen face, and turned. Recognition came in a chilling tide. It was the face in the campfire at the desert oasis, the face that had looked along the

168

gunbarrel against his forehead, when he had been ready to die.

"Let the woman loose," whispered the voice from the bearded, indistinct face.

Ramming untied her hands and worked the gag loose. Unsteadily she got to her feet, then put her arms around him and clung tightly, her cheek against his chest. She was trying hard to control her sobs.

"Now ain't that touching?" grunted Smiling Jack Sluder.

Jessie pushed her gently to the bench and fixed his gaze on the man with the rifle.

"Who in hell are you? What are you after?"

"Well, now. I'm a mite disappointed that you ain't figured that out after all this time, Mister Jessie Ramming. I took you for a man with a fair amount of brains. Looks like I was wrong."

"You're the man . . . You're the man who killed my wife. Why?"

Sluder laughed. Christina winced at the sound. He went to the table, put a hand against the lifeless shoulder of the man slumped there, and shoved. Fish's still-warm body flopped from the chair and sprawled on the floor, face up. His long, yellowed teeth gleamed dully in the flickering light.

Sluder moved the chair around until he was facing Jessie and the woman. On the table, beside the big shotgun, he placed the rifle, its deadly muzzle centered on Jessie's chest.

"So you don't remember?"

Sluder's left hand crept upward to the side of his head and touched the ragged stump of his left ear.

"It's been more than eight years but I remember you, Jessie Ramming, just like it was yesterday. I ain't never going to forget you sitting there on the witness stand and pointin' your finger at me and telling how you seen me come out of that bank. No sirree! Not if I live to be a thousand."

As clearly as a key springing a lock open, recollection came to Jessie. This was the man he had seen running from the bank in Trabajo, the man who had paused to snatch up his dead partner's sack of stolen money. The face a perverse fate had revealed so clearly to Ramming.

Sluder talked hurriedly on in his rasping tone, as if he had looked forward to this moment for a long time.

"Do you remember what I said to you when that damned mule-headed sheriff was taking me away with my hands chained? After the judge had said I was going to spend the rest of my life in prison? I told you it was going to cost you. But I don't suppose you remember that."

He paused to roll a cigarette and light it with the candle. Ramming and the woman watched his eyes glinting like polished ebony in the yellow light.

Sluder nodded smugly at his own memories.

"Yeah, I ain't a man to forget little favors like you done me, Ramming. But you did more than just send me to the pen for life. You also cost me this."

His left hand rose again to the side of his head, not against the scarred ear but cupped inches away as though the wound were still painful to the touch.

"Yeah, this here little scar messed up my ear and fixed it so I can barely talk. But it sure did help my memory— of you sittin' there spillin' your guts to the jury.

"It was one of them lousy prison guards that done it. I got caught trying to bust out of that hell-hole and the bastard hit me across the side of the head with his rifle. The hammer damn near tore my head off."

He flipped his cigarette stub into the fireplace. They could see his grin, even behind the heavy beard.

"Well, that guard won't be using his rifle on any other poor sucker. I fixed his bacon permanently when I busted out the last time."

Sluder picked up the heavy goose gun and hefted it in his bony hands. He put it to his shoulder and looked along the twin barrels to Ramming's chest.

"So this is what you come huntin' me with, is it? I've always sort of fancied these cannons."

Jessie wanted the scarfaced killer to keep on talking. The coals in the fireplace a few inches from him had planted the seed of an idea.

"What did you do with the money from the bank?" he asked quietly.

170

Sluder was silent a moment, then he grunted agreeably.

"Sure. Why not? It won't hurt none to tell you the whole story, Jessie Ramming. Because it's not going to be like it was out there in the desert. I ain't walking away from here 'til you're dead meat.

"You ain't the only one that got paid back for sending me to prison. Sheriff Wiley Dunn's bones are rotting in an old mine shaft over there a few miles from Trabajo. All I had to do was promise that short-legged deputy of his a slice of the bank loot and he did the job for me. He'll get a bonus, too. That town'll be afraid not to hand him the sheriff's badge come election time."

Ramming's insides were knotted in torment. Not just at the thought of the death of an honest lawman, but at the knowledge that Stub Heckman would reap the fruits of that deed.

"You still haven't told me what you did with the money," he said, shifting on the bench so that his right hand was hidden from Sluder's view. "Must be something wrong or you wouldn't be poking around up here on top of this mountain."

He saw immediately that his random guess had touched a nerve. Sluder's fist came down hard on the table, making the candle on its whiskey-bottle stand totter unsteadily.

"Damn that buck-toothed idiot, anyhow," he snarled, glaring at the lifeless form of Tom Fish as though the corpse could feel his wrath. "The half-breed you hauled back to jail was supposed to help me find it."

"Somewhere up in these peaks, I guess," Ramming said evenly.

"Yeah, up in there someplace." Sluder waved a hand toward the mountain range beyond the cabin. "I slung the sack of money into a little rock cave, no bigger'n that fireplace, five minutes before Dunn's posse caught up to me. It was at the base of a big, rust-colored bluff that had some Injun signs chiseled on it, but it would take me a month to find it without help. That's where the breed was to come in. He could've taken me right to it."

He looked down at the body on the floor, then spat through his teeth.

171

"But that jackass there had to screw up the works by killing the wrong man."

Jessie glanced at Christina, gauged her angle from the fireplace, and stood up. His right hand slid out of his pocket in a natural movement as he stepped in front of the fire. With an all but imperceptible flick of his hand he had sent an eight-gauge shotgun shell squarely into the glowing coals.

Sluder had tensed visibly when Ramming got to his feet. His hand had been on the butt of the shotgun, caressing the intricate carving along its walnut stock. Now he snatched up the massive weapon from the table and held it cradled across his chest.

"Stay put, hombre. Unless you're in a big hurry to say goodbye to your lady friend."

Ramming wanted to get nearer to the man holding the shotgun, so he would have a split second to act when the shell exploded. But the bed of red-hot coals did its work too well. He had no time to reduce that distance before the powder in the shot shell reached the ignition point.

The explosion was an avalanche of sound in the little room. Coals from the fireplace flew in every direction, like a fireworks display. Ramming knew, even as he lunged toward Sluder, that the distance was too great. His outstretched hands clawed at empty space as he fell to his knees.

There was surprise on Sluder's face, but there was no sign of unsteadiness in the long barrels of the shotgun, aimed squarely at Ramming's head.

"Stand up!" Rage made Sluder's voice almost unintelligible.

Jessie got to his feet. Now the shotgun was centered on his belt buckle.

"You're too damned smart to live, Ramming. That was the last chance you're going to get. I'm gonna blow you smack in two with this cannon and while you're dying you can think about what I'm doing with that purty little yellow-haired woman there."

"Jessie!"

It was Christina's voice, rugged with despair. It ended with a little cry, drowned in the sound of Sluder drawing back the gracefully lethal hammer to full cock. In a

172

strangely detached way, Jessie saw the bearded man's long, grimy finger slide around the front trigger and begin its curl. His time was up. Captain Asa Ramming's goose gun was going to have its man after all.

Perhaps it was that sudden picture of his stubborn, courageous forebear that fired Jessie's resolve, or maybe it was the brutal image of Sluder having his way with Christina that spurred him to take the gamble. As quick as the paw of a cat, his hand swept round in a short arc that began at the fat candle on the table beside him and ended at the yawning muzzle of the eight-gauge. The wax was warm and pliable. It slid as easily and snugly into the right-hand gunbarrel as a hand into a glove.

Smilin' Jack Sluder couldn't have stopped the movement of his forefinger if he'd wanted to. He pulled the trigger.

Ramming flung himself to one side as a sheet of fire belched from the breech of the shotgun. The entwined steel of the barrel, its stress point exceeded many times over by the incredible pressure, curled backward in a half-dozen jagged tentacles. Like an icicle shattered by a sudden blow, splinters of steel sprayed in a deadly shower across the room.

Sluder's right thumb vanished in bloody shreds, but it was of no concern to him. A fragment of exploding gunbarrel, a piece no larger than the button on a shirt, had already drilled through his left eye and buried itself deep within his brain.

Crouched behind the stiffening form of Tom Fish, Ramming saw Sluder take two steps backward and crumble to the puncheon floor, a scarecrow with all its straw sucked suddenly away.

After a time, he got to his feet and went to where Christina sat on the bench, still holding her hands spread against her face.

"He's dead," Jessie said quietly. "Sluder's dead."

She looked at him between her fingers and shook her head. She wasn't yet ready to accept it.

He drew her to her feet and held her against him for a long time, until her trembling subsided. She continued to cling tightly to his arm as they both looked down at the body of the bearded man, the disfigured features a grim

173

reminder of the malice his mind had bred. Ramming stooped and picked up the ruined shotgun, one barrel blown apart and the other warped into uselessness.

"Cap'n Asa would sure be aggravated," he said wryly.

Christina started to ask what he meant, but then decided to keep silent.

Chapter
TWENTY-THREE

Daylight was conceding vague shape to the trees that ringed the clearing by the time Jessie had wrapped the bodies in tattered blankets and secured them across the back of the gray horse. Remembering with a start that some cowboy down in McSween would just now be finding out his horse had been stolen, Ramming had decided it would look better for him and Christina to ride the gray and let the blaze-faced bay carry the two dead men. But the bay horse would have none of it, bucking and squealing and fighting the tie rope when Jessie came near with a corpse.

Christina had made some coffee from Sluder's meager store of provisions and they stood looking into the fireplace while they sipped it, their backs to the twin bloodstains on the floor.

"Do you think they'll believe you?" she asked after a time.

"Believe me about what?"

"When you tell them about these ... men. That they're the ones who killed the sheriff."

Ramming took a long moment to answer her question. Finally he nodded.

"Yeah. I thought about that. With both of them dead there's no way to prove it."

"You could leave them here. And ride away," she said, her voice even, emotionless.

He glanced sharply at her and saw what he knew he

would see in her face. She didn't mean it. Unless it was the choice he wanted to make.

"We both know that wouldn't work," he said. "In a few years of running from the law I'd begin to look like our scarred-up friend hanging across the saddle out there."

She shuddered, gripping her upper arms.

"Yes."

Later she said, hesitantly, "I suppose you'll be going back to the other side of the mountains. To your place."

She let the sentence hang in the air, for him to finish. But he didn't speak, instead gazing distractedly into the dying fingers of fire.

At last he said, "We'd better get started."

Snow flurries had whipped across the mountaintops before dawn, but the scattered patches of white were already beginning to melt under the eye of the sun. Sitting behind the saddle with her arms around the big man's waist, Christina felt strangely at peace, as though some great, protracted burden had been lifted from her breast. Even the knowledge of the dead men on the horses a few paces behind couldn't dull the edge of her contentment.

She studied the broad shoulders of the man in front of her and felt an almost irrepressible desire to tighten the grip of her arms and lay her cheek against that sturdy back. She put the thought away quickly, reminding herself that Jessie Ramming wasn't hers at all. It was only circumstance that had mingled their lives for a time, and now that circumstances was coming to an end.

That thought caused her elation to suddenly vanish, as quickly and completely as the steam that spurted momentarily from the nostrils of the horses.

"There it is," she heard him say.

Far below, like miniature houses constructed for child's play, she saw the stores and homes and outbuildings that made up the town of McSween. It was a reassuring sight where for the most part ordinary people went about their ordinary business, working and laughing and raising their families and never knowing the

176

stark terror of looking into the eyes of a madman named Jack Sluder.

Jessie must have been thinking the same thing.

"Looks mighty peaceful."

At that instant, the boom of a big-bore rifle crashed against their ears, echoing in diminishing waves through the canyons beyond. From the wall of trees ahead burst a dozen horsemen, every hand that wasn't holding reins gripping a rifle or a handgun.

"Hold it right there!" came a thundering command, and a moment later they were surrounded by the posse and its cavvy of blowing, foam-flecked mounts.

There was no question about who was the leader of that posse. He was a lean, ramrod-straight horseman whose sun-browned face had the texture of a pine plank too long in the weather. A man didn't need to see the badge on his vest to recognize the authority in him. But his blue eyes were the open, frank eyes of a man who clings stubbornly to a hope of finding a grain of good in the most villainous of adversaries.

"You'd be Jessie Ramming?"

"Yes," Ramming nodded.

"My name's Beaulieu," the other man said, the slightest hint of a Southern accent drawing out the words. "I'm the territorial marshal." He touched his hand to the brim of his big hat as he turned his gaze toward Christina. "And you must be Mrs. Ramming?"

"No. My name is Christina Bucklin."

The marshal's eyebrows twitched upward in a barely perceptible movement before his gaze returned to Jessie.

"You see this fine buckskin I'm riding?"

Ramming glanced at the big horse on which the marshal sat.

"Yes," he answered, puzzlement clear in his voice.

"Do you have any idea why I'm riding this horse?" the marshal asked, his tone pleasantly conversational.

"Why, no. I guess I haven't," Jessie replied, wondering if the lawman had suddenly taken leave of his senses.

"I borrowed this good horse," said Beaulieu, his voice still innocently casual, "because that's my horse you're riding."

A picture of Martín Romero, wanting desperately to talk around the gag in his mouth, came instantly to Jessie's mind. That's what the young Mexican had wanted to tell him.

Jessie grinned in spite of himself and looked into the soulful blue eyes of the marshal.

"Outside of being a little skittish around dead men he's one hell of a fine horse," he said.

The posse was getting restless but Marshal Beaulieu sent a glance over his shoulder along the line of horsemen. The murmuring quieted instantly.

"You want to tell me what happened down there in the jail?" Beaulieu asked.

Ramming frowned. He had expected a prompt and not-too-gentle escort back to jail in the hands of the posse, but here was the marshal chatting about the killing of the sheriff as though he already had the answers. Or thought he did. Jessie's throat was suddenly tight and dry. If they took a notion to string him up to the nearest ponderosa, there was no one to intercede.

"The sheriff had decided to let me out." Even to Jessie's ears the words sounded contrived. "He had just unlocked the cell when a gun went off behind me. Someone had stuck a pistol through the window of my cell and shot the sheriff. I ducked. The rest of the slugs went for the half-breed."

The marshal's face was exasperatingly empty.

"How come he didn't put a bullet in you?"

It was a question that had prodded at Ramming's mind a hundred times.

"I don't know."

"I do." It was Christina's voice, sounding as out of place in that talk of murder and mayhem as a meadowlark's call at midnight.

Every eye in the posse swung toward her.

"We'd be mighty happy to hear it, ma'am," the marshal drawled.

"Those men there . . ." She nodded her head toward the gray gelding and the blanket shrouded bodies.

"I was gettin' around to them," said the marshal. "Kindly go on with your tale, ma'am."

178

She swallowed dryly.

"It was the one named Fish who shot the sheriff. I heard him tell the other man about it. He meant to kill Jessie but he was in the wrong cell. So after he shot the sheriff he shot Romero Red Feather. By mistake."

The marshal's eyebrows rose.

"That's a pretty far-fetched yarn, ma'am. Who might the other gent be?"

Ramming broke in.

"How about taking a look, marshal?"

Beaulieu grunted.

"Presuming those two didn't die of natural causes, I reckon it's my bounden duty to find out what caused 'em to expire."

At a wave of his hand the posse dismounted. The marshal followed Jessie to the side of the gray gelding and watched silently while he untied the ropes.

Fish was the first that Ramming laid on the ground. He pulled back the blanket to expose the waxen, grinning features.

"This one probably died of ugly," the marshal grunted.

Then Jessie stretched the long, slender form of the other man on the ground beside Fish and turned back the blanket. He heard a sound at his elbow, as though someone had punched the marshal in the pit of his stomach.

"I'll be a son-of-a-bitch!" Beaulieu muttered incredulously. He knelt beside the bearded man's body and with some difficulty twisted the stiffened neck until the ragged remnant of gristle, resembling more a walnut than an ear, was exposed.

"It's him. Sure as water runs downhill," he nodded. "No mistakin' that scar."

He straightened his lean frame until his height dominated the men gathered around.

"You know who this jasper is?" he asked Ramming.

Jessie nodded.

"He said he escaped from prison."

"He told it right. That's Smilin' Jack Sluder, all right. He's why I'm here. Been trailin' that polecat ever since he cut the throat of a prison guard and high-tailed it south from Santa Fe."

Suddenly he swung around and fixed Ramming with a flinty stare.

"How did you get mixed up with the likes of him?"

Jessie was suddenly very, very tired. It had been two long, punishing days since he'd slept. He heard his own voice from a distance.

"I testified against him over in Trabajo eight or nine years ago, when he went to prison for robbing the bank. He came to my place when he broke out."

Beaulieu was listening intently.

"How come he didn't kill you?"

Jessie looked out across the rugged sweep of mountains that fell away to the east, toward a heavy mass of clouds gathering blackly along the horizon. There would be rain on the prairie today.

"He killed my wife instead."

The cowboys and store clerks and miners in the posse suddenly found that they, too, needed to look off into the distance. Then one by one they moved away to their horses, checking cinches and retying slickers. It was Beaulieu who finally broke the silence.

"Guess I should have told you at the start, Ramming. We found the gun on the floor of your cell. Reb, the gunsmith, told us that Fish here had bought it right before the shooting started. We also found the Mexican woman that someone had opened up with a knife. Was hoping maybe you could shed some light on that."

Christina's voice had the brittle tremor of a steel wire drawn to breaking.

"I saw Fish do it. For no reason. She was just trying to help me."

"It figures," nodded Marshal Beaulieu. "Tom Fish and Smilin' Jack were two of a kind. Sluder just had a bit more of the rattlesnake in him." He nudged Sluder's body with the toe of his boot. "Dammit, anyhow. I sure did want to have a little palaver with him before he cashed in."

Jessie's head came up.

"He said some things, marshal. When he thought it wouldn't make any difference. He said the deputy over at Trabajo killed old Sheriff Dunn and dumped his body down a mine shaft. Name's Heckman. Stub Heckman."

Beaulieu's mouth had become a thin, hard line.

"It'll give me a fair amount of pleasure to peg that coyote's pelt to the wall. Wiley Dunn was a fine lawman."

"One other thing," Ramming said. "The reason he wanted Romero Red Feather out of jail was to get the breed's help in locating a cave where he dumped the bank loot."

The marshal's seamed face grew long.

"Yeah. It was too much to hope. With Sluder finished, there ain't one chance in hell of finding that money."

"Maybe one chance," said Jessie.

Beaulieu's head snapped around.

"How's that?"

"Sluder told us he threw the sack of money into a cave at the foot of a big rock bluff."

"There probably ain't more than four or five hundred bluffs just like that in these here mountains," growled the marshal.

"This one's different. It has some old Indian markings on it."

For an instant the marshal's face lighted up, but a moment later his optimism faded.

"Sounds fine. Except that old Smilin' Jack was probably right. It would take a man with Romero Red Feather's savvy of the country to find that particular rock bluff."

Jessie knelt to wrap the blanket around Sluder's body, but stopped abruptly.

"There's one other man who could find it," he said. "A kid at the livery stable. The breed's half brother."

But fatigue had slipped a noose over Jessie's mind. His thoughts were coming with molasses slowness. What was it that Martín had said? About himself and Red Feather and the mountains?

He heard the marshal talking again, but the words ran together until they had to be repeated.

"I said that pretty well takes care of the loose ends, pardner." Then Beaulieu grinned until his big, sun-baked ears had to move out of the way. "I do have one more official chore. That's to tell you that you've got a considerable reward coming for nailing this murdering son.

181

Upwards of five hundred dollars, as I recollect. And a heap more from the bank, if your hunch about finding the stolen money pays off."

Ramming looked at the tall lawman blankly.

Beaulieu put out a big, hard hand.

"Now that you've come into some money, *amigo*, I figure you'll be wantin' to buy yourself another horse. Well, it just so happens I'm looking to sell a fine, blaze-faced bay for twenty dollars, saddle throwed in."

Before Jessie could reply, the marshal spun around and singled out two of the posse with a quick wave of his hand.

"You boys can ride double. Hoist them two stiffs onto a hoss and let's head back to town."

Jessie and Christina watched them ride down the slope and disappear into the trees. Behind them the blaze and the gray were cropping at the short mountain grass.

Christina waited in silence as long as she could. Then she said, "When you go back to your place..." She stopped. She couldn't think of anything more to say.

Jessie was looking into the distance, across the mountains and beyond the desert to where the plains spilled over the horizon.

"This mountain country sort of grows on a man," he said. "I could settle down in this valley. Run some cows. Plant an apple orchard, maybe."

He turned and looked into her blue eyes, where tears had started to gather.

"I couldn't do it alone, though."

Christina moved against his broad chest and felt his powerful arms close around her. There was still the bitter taste of dread from a nightmare memory that refused to die. But she knew, as surely as Jack Sluder was cold and stiff and dead, that time and Jessie Ramming would bury that, too.

About the Author

Writing Westerns is, for me, a natural reaction to the Southwest's infinite blue skies and majestic mountain-desert landscape, the kind of country that spawned a special breed of men: bold and self-reliant, rawhide tough, and big-hearted to a fault. If you look closely, you can find traces of those qualities even today among the oldtimers who inhabit New Mexico, the setting for *Season of Vengeance*.

New Mexico was also the setting for my boyhood, years spent hunting, fishing, exploring on horseback, and helping wrest a living from land that was more hostile than fertile.

Following an unremarkable performance in high school, I enlisted in the Navy in time to catch the final act of the Korean conflict, serving as a radar operator aboard an amphibious assault ship.

After a four-year hitch, I returned to New Mexico and enrolled at Eastern New Mexico University, ultimately earning a bachelor's degree in journalism and a master's in political science.

Newspapering has been my life's work since. I've had stints on dailies in Texas, New Mexico, and Kansas, and for the past decade I have served as managing editor of the Clovis *News-Journal* situated at the heart of New Mexico's High Plains region and an hour's drive from the site where Sheriff Pat Garrett fed Billy the Kid Bonney a fatal dose of lead barely one hundred years ago.

I grew up in a world of Westerns. On my tenth Christmas, I was suffering from a head and neck injury caused by a spill from a horse and I was supposed to be resting my eyes. Therefore, I had to hide in a closet because I was so eager to read my gift—one of Graham M. Dean's juvenile Westerns. Years later I worked for the old gentleman, as editor of a newspaper he owned.

I read most of the great Western writers: Zane Grey, Max Brand, Luke Short, Clarence Mulford, Ernest Haycox and, in later years, that master of Western storytelling, Louis L'Amour. For a youngster whose earliest ambition was to become a cowboy, they provided a wealth of enjoyment and, quite probably, the seeds of a yen for writing.

Such were the stepping stones that led me to write *Season of Vengeance*. In it I have tried to give readers a picture of that New Mexico about which I spoke, of the men and women who tamed it, and of those who died trying.

In my typewriter now is a second novel set in the New Mexico Territory of the 1800s, a time when cattlemen fought renegade Indians, merciless elements, and sometimes each other, to build their empires.

Despite a degree of bondage to a typewriter, I make time for my wife and three children, and a recalcitrant gelding that regularly forgets he's broke to ride.

W. W. Southard
Clovis, New Mexico
September, 1980

"REACH FOR THE SKY!"

and you still won't find more excitement or more thrills than you get in Bantam's slam-bang, action-packed westerns! Here's a roundup of fast-reading stories by some of America's greatest western writers:

☐	14207	**WARRIOR'S PATH** Louis L'Amour	$1.95
☐	13651	**THE STRONG SHALL LIVE** Louis L'Amour	$1.95
☐	13781	**THE IRON MARSHAL** Louis L'Amour	$1.95
☐	14196	**SACKETT** Louis L'Amour	$1.95
☐	14183	**PAPER SHERIFF** Luke Short	$1.75
☐	13679	**CORONER CREEK** Luke Short	$1.75
☐	14185	**PONY EXPRESS WAR** Gary McCarthy	$1.75
☐	14475	**SHANE** Jack Schaefer	$1.95
☐	14179	**GUNSMOKE GRAZE** Peter Dawson	$1.75
☐	14178	**THE CROSSING** Clay Fisher	$1.75
☐	13696	**LAST STAND AT SABER RIVER** Elmore Leonard	$1.75
☐	14236	**BEAR PAW HORSES** Henry	$1.75
☐	12383	**"NEVADA"** Zane Grey	$1.95
☐	14180	**FORT STARVATION** Frank Gruber	$1.75

LOUIS L'AMOUR 1

BANTAM'S #1
ALL-TIME BESTSELLING AUTHOR
AMERICA'S FAVORITE WESTERN WRITE

THE SACKETTS

Meet the Sacketts—from the Tennessee mountains they headed west to ride the trails, pan the gold, work the ranches and make the laws. Here in these action-packed stories is the incredible saga of the Sacketts —who stood together in the face of trouble as one unbeatable fighting family.

☐	14868 SACKETT'S LAND	$2.25
☐	12730 THE DAY BREAKERS	$1.95
☐	14196 SACKETT	$1.95
☐	14118 LANDO	$1.95
☐	14193 MOJAVE CROSSING	$1.95
☐	14973 THE SACKETT BRAND	$2.25
☐	20074 THE LONELY MEN	$2.25
☐	14785 TREASURE MOUNTAIN	$2.25
☐	13703 MUSTANG MAN	$1.95
☐	14322 GALLOWAY	$1.95
☐	20073 THE SKY-LINERS	$2.25
☐	14218 TO THE FAR BLUE MOUNTAINS	$1.95
☐	14194 THE MAN FROM THE BROKEN HILLS	$1.95
☐	20088 RIDE THE DARK TRAIL	$2.25
☐	14207 WARRIOR'S PATH	$1.95
☐	14174 LONELY ON THE MOUNTAIN	$2.25

Buy them at your local bookstore or use this handy coupon for ordering:

FOR HIS EYES ONLY

BY
LIZ FIELDING

Liz Fielding was born with itchy feet. She made it to Zambia before her twenty-first birthday and, gathering her own special hero and a couple of children on the way, lived in Botswana, Kenya and Bahrain—with pauses for sightseeing pretty much everywhere in between. She finally came to a full stop in a tiny Welsh village cradled by misty hills, and these days mostly leaves her pen to do the travelling.

When she's not sorting out the lives and loves of her characters she potters in the garden, reads her favourite authors, and spends a lot of time wondering, *What if...?*

For news of upcoming books—and to sign up for her occasional newsletter—visit Liz's website: www.lizfielding.com

This and other titles by Liz Fielding are available in eBook format from www.millsandboon.co.uk

DEDICATION

With thanks to Kate Hardy and Caroline Anderson
for their never-failing belief.

And to Gail McCurry Waldrep for the fudge frosting.

CHAPTER ONE

'WHAT'S GOT MILES'S knickers in a twist?' Natasha Gordon poured herself half a cup of coffee. Her first appointment had been at eight and she'd been on the run ever since. She had to grab any opportunity to top up her caffeine level. 'I was on my way to a viewing at the St John's Wood flat when I got a message to drop everything and come straight back here.'

Janine, Morgan and Black's receptionist and always the first with any rumour, lifted her slender cashmere-clad shoulders in a don't-ask-me shrug. 'If that's what he said, you'd better not keep him waiting,' she said, but, shrug notwithstanding, the ghost of an I-know-something-you-don't smile tugged at lips on which the lipstick was always perfectly applied.

Tash abandoned the untouched coffee and headed for the stairs, taking them two at a time. Miles Morgan, senior partner of Morgan and Black, first port of call for the wealthy flooding into London from all corners of the world to snap up high-end real estate, had been dropping heavy hints for weeks that the vacant 'associate' position was hers.

Damn right. She'd worked her socks off for the last three years and had earned that position with hard work and long hours and Janine, who liked everyone to know how 'in' she was with the boss, had casually let slip the news on Friday afternoon that he would be spending the weekend in the country with the semi-retired 'Black' to discuss the future of the firm.

'Down, pulse, down,' she muttered, pausing outside his office to scoop up a wayward handful of hair and anchor it in place with great-grandma's silver clip.

She always started out the day looking like a career woman on the up, but haring about London all morning had left her more than a little dishevelled and things had begun to unravel. Her hair, her make-up, her shirt.

She tucked in her shirt and was checking the top button when the door opened.

'Janine! Is she here yet?' Miles shouted before he realised she was standing in front him. 'Where the hell have you been?'

'I had a viewing at the Chelsea house first thing,' she said, used to his short fuse. 'They played it very close to their chests, but the wife's eyes were lit up like the Blackpool illuminations. I guarantee they'll make an offer before the end of the day.'

The prospect of a high five-figure commission would normally be enough to change his mood but he merely grunted and the sparkle of anticipation went flat. Whatever Janine had been smiling about, it wasn't the prospect of the office party Miles would throw to celebrate the appointment of the new associate.

'It's been non-stop since then,' she added, and it wasn't going to ease up this side of six. 'Is this urgent, Miles? I'm showing Glencora Jarrett the St John's Wood apartment in half an hour and the traffic is solid.'

'You can forget that. I've sent Toby.'

'Toby?' Her occasionally significant other had been on a rugby tour in Australia and wasn't due home until the end of the month. She shook her head. It wasn't important, but Lady Glen... 'No, she specifically asked—'

'For you. I know, but a viewing isn't a social engagement,' he cut in before she could remind him that Lady Glencora was desperately nervous and would not go into an unoccupied apartment with a male negotiator.

'But—'

'Forget Her Ladyship,' he said, thrusting the latest edition of the *Country Chronicle* into her hands. 'Take a look at this.'

The magazine was open at the full-page advertisement for Hadley Chase, a historic country house that had just come on the market.

'Oh, that came out really well…' A low mist, caught by the rising sun, had lent the house a golden, soft-focus enchantment that hid its many shortcomings. Well worth the effort of getting up at the crack of dawn and driving into the depths of Berkshire on the one day in the week that she could have had a lie-in. 'The phone will be ringing off the hook,' she said, offering it back to him.

'Read on,' he said, not taking it.

'I know what it says, Miles. I wrote it.' The once grand house was suffering from age and neglect and she'd focused on the beauty and convenience of the location to tempt potential buyers to come and take a look. 'You approved it,' she reminded him.

'I didn't approve this.'

She frowned. Irritable might be his default mode but, even for Miles, this seemed excessive. Had some ghastly mistake slipped past them both? It happened, but this was an expensive full-page colour ad, and she'd gone over the proof with a fine-tooth comb. Confident that nothing could have gone wrong, she read out her carefully composed copy.

'"A substantial seventeenth-century manor house in a sought-after location on the Berkshire Downs within easy reach of motorway links to London, the Midlands and the West. That's the good news. The bad news…"' She faltered. Bad news? What the…?

'Don't stop now.'

The words were spoken with a clear, crisp, don't-argue-with-me certainty, but not by her boss, and she spun around as the owner of the voice rose from the high-backed leather armchair set in front of Miles Morgan's desk and turned to face her.

Her first impression was of darkness. Dark hair, dark clothes, dark eyes in a mesmerising face that missed beauty by a hair's breadth, although a smile might have done the business.

The second was of strength. There was no bulk, but his shoulders were wide beneath a crumpled linen jacket so old that the black had faded to grey, his abdomen slate-flat under a T-shirt that hung loosely over narrow hips.

His hand was resting on the back of the chair, long cal-loused fingers curled over the leather. They were the kind of fingers that she could imagine doing unspeakable things to her. Was imagining…

She looked up and met eyes that seemed to penetrate every crevice, every pore, and a hot blush, beginning somewhere low in her belly, spread like wildfire in every direction—

'Natasha!'

Miles's sharp interjection jolted her back to the page but it was a moment before she could catch her breath, gather her wits and focus on the words dancing in front of her.

…the bad news is the wet rot, woodworm, crumbling plasterwork and leaking roof. The vendor would no doubt have preferred to demolish the house and re-develop the land, but it's a Grade II listed building in the heart of the Green Belt so he's stuffed. There is a fine oak Tudor staircase but, bearing in mind the earlier reference to wet rot and woodworm, an early viewing is advised if you want to see the upper floors.

Her heart still pounding with the shock of a sexual attraction so powerful that she was trembling, she had to read it twice before it sank in. And when it did her pulse was still in a sorry state.

'I don't understand,' she said. Then, realising how feeble that sounded, 'How did this happen?'

'How, indeed?'

Her question had been directed at Miles, but the response came from Mr Tall, Dark and Deadly. Who *was* he?

'Hadley,' he said, apparently reading her mind. Or maybe she'd asked the question out loud. She needed to get a grip. She needed an ice bath…

She cleared her throat. 'Hadley?' His name still emerged as if spoken by a surprised frog, but that wasn't simply because all her blood had apparently drained from her brain to the more excitable parts of her anatomy. The house was unoccupied and the sale was being handled by the estate's executors and, since no one had mentioned a real-life, flesh-and-blood Hadley, she'd assumed the line had run dry.

'Darius Hadley,' he elaborated, clearly picking up on her doubt.

In her career she'd worked with everyone, from young first-time buyers scraping together a deposit, to billionaires investing in London apartments and town houses costing millions. She knew that appearances could be deceptive but Darius Hadley did not have the look of a man whose family had been living in the Chase since the seventeenth century, when a grateful Charles II had given the estate to one James Hadley, a rich merchant who'd funded him in exile.

With the glint of a single gold earring amongst the mass of black curls tumbling over his collar, the crumpled linen jacket faded from black to grey, jeans worn threadbare at the knees, he looked more like a gypsy, or a pirate. Perhaps that was where the Hadley fortune had come from—plundering the Spanish Main with the likes of Drake. Or, with the legacy now in the hands of a man bearing the name of a Persian king, it was possible that his ancestors had chosen to travel east overland, to trade in silk and spices.

This man certainly had the arrogance to go with his name but, unlike his forebears, it seemed that he had no interest in settling down to live the life of a country gentleman. Not that she blamed him for that.

Hadley Chase, with roses growing over its timbered Tudor heart, might look romantic in the misty haze of an early summer sunrise, but it was going to take a lot of time and a very deep purse to bring it up to modern expectations in plumbing, heating and weatherproofing. There was nothing romantic about nineteen-fifties plumbing and, from the neglected state of both house and grounds, it was evident that the fortune needed to maintain it was long gone.

On the bright side, even in these cash-strapped days, there were any number of sheikhs, pop stars and Russian oligarchs looking for the privacy of a country estate no more than a helicopter hop from the centre of London and she was looking forward to adding the Chase to her portfolio of sales in the very near future. She had big plans for the commission.

Miles cleared his throat and she belatedly stuck out her hand.

'Natasha Gordon. How d'you do, Mr Hadley?'

'I've been stuffed, mounted and hung out to dry,' he replied. 'How do you think I feel?' he demanded, ignoring her hand.

'Angry.' He had every right to be angry. Hell, she was furious with whoever had meddled with her carefully worded description and they would feel the wrath of her tongue when she found out who it was, but that would have to wait. Right now she had to get a grip of her hormones, be totally professional and reassure him that this wasn't the disaster it appeared. 'I don't know what happened here, Mr Hadley, but I promise you it's just a minor setback.'

'A minor setback?' Glittering eyes—forget charcoal, they were jet—skewered her to the floor and Tash felt the heat rise up her neck and flood her cheeks. She was blushing. He'd made her blush with just a look. That was outrageous... 'A *minor* setback?' he repeated, with the very slightest emphasis on 'minor'.

His self-control was impressive.

Okaaay... She unpeeled her tongue from the roof of her mouth, snatched in a little oxygen to get her brain started and said, 'Serious purchasers understand that there will be problems with this type of property, Mr Hadley.'

'They expect to be able to view the upper floors without endangering their lives,' he pointed out. He hadn't raised his voice; he didn't have to. He'd made his point with a quiet, razor-edged precision that made Miles's full-blown irritation look like a toddler tantrum.

'Natasha!' Miles prompted, more sharply this time. 'Have you got something to say to Mr Hadley?'

'What?' She dragged her gaze from the seductive curve of Darius Hadley's lower lip and fixed it somewhere around his prominent Adam's apple, which only sent her mind off on another, even more disturbing direction involving extremities.

Do not look at his feet!

'Oh, um, yes...' She'd tried desperately to get her brain in gear, recall the notes she'd made, as she stared at scuffed work boots, jeans smeared with what looked like dry grey mud and clinging to powerful thighs. He'd obviously dropped whatever he was doing and come straight to the office when he'd seen the ad. Did he work on a building site? 'Actually,' she said, 'there's more than one set of stairs so it isn't a problem.'

'And that's your professional opinion?'

'Not that I recall there being anything wrong with the main staircase that a thorough seeing to with a vacuum cleaner wouldn't fix,' she added hurriedly when Miles sounded as if he might be choking. Come on, Tash…this is what you do. 'I did advise the solicitor handling the sale that they should get in a cleaning contractor to give the place a good bottoming.'

A muscle tightened in his jaw. 'And what was their response to that?'

'They said they'd get the caretaker to give it a once-over.'

Some property owners did nothing to help themselves, but this probably wasn't the moment to say so.

'So it's just the woodworm, rot and missing lead flashing on the roof that a potential buyer has to worry about?' Darius Hadley raised his dark brows a fraction of a millimetre and every cell in her body followed as if he'd jerked a string.

Amongst a jangle of mixed messages—her head urging her to take a step back, every other part of her wanting to reach out and touch—she just about managed to stand her ground.

'Actually,' she said, 'according to the paperwork, the woodworm was treated years ago.' Something he would have known if he'd taken the slightest interest in the house he'd apparently inherited. 'I think you'll find that it's the cobwebs that will have women running screaming—'

Behind Hadley's back, Miles made a sharp mouth-zipped gesture. 'Mr Hadley isn't looking for excuses. What he's waiting for,' he said, 'what he's *entitled* to, is an explanation and an apology.'

She frowned. Surely Miles had already covered that ground? She assumed she'd been called in to discuss a plan of action.

'Don't bother; I've heard enough,' Hadley said before

she could get in a word. 'You'll be hearing from my lawyer, Morgan.'

'Lawyer?' What use was a lawyer going to be? 'No, really—'

Darius Hadley cut off her protest with a look that froze her in mid-sentence and seemed to go on for an eternity. Lethal eyes, a nose bred for looking down, a mouth made for sin... Finally, satisfied that he'd silenced her, his eyes seemed to shimmer, soften, warm to smoky charcoal and then, as she took half a step towards him, he nodded at Miles and walked out of the office, leaving the room ringing with his presence. Leaving her weak to the bone.

She put out a hand to grasp the back of the chair he'd been sitting in. It was still warm from his touch and the heat seemed to travel up her arm and spread through her limbs, creating little sparks throughout her body, igniting all the erogenous zones she was familiar with and quite a few that were entirely new.

Phew. Double phewy-phew...

'He's a bit tense, isn't he?' she said shakily. A sleek, dark Dobermann to Toby's big, soft Labrador puppy—to be approached with caution rather than a hug. But the rewards if you won his trust...

Forget it! A man like that wasn't a keeper. All you could hope for was to catch his attention for a moment. But what a moment—

'With good reason,' Miles said, interrupting a chain of thought that was going nowhere. Dark, brooding types had never been even close to the top of her list of appealing male stereotypes. Far too high-maintenance. *Rude* dark, brooding types had never figured.

A barrage of hoots from the street below distracted her, but there was no escape there. Apparently oblivious to the traffic, Darius Hadley was crossing the street and several people stopped to watch him stride down the road in the direction of Sloane Square. Most of them were women.

It wasn't just her, then.

Without warning he stopped, swung round and looked up at the window where she was standing as if he'd known she'd be there. And she forgot to breathe.

'Natasha!'

She jumped, blinked and when she looked again he'd gone and for a moment she was afraid that he was coming back. Hoped that he was coming back, but a moment later he reappeared further along the street and she turned her back on the window before he felt her eyes boring into the back of his head and turned again to catch her looking.

'Have you spoken to the *Chronicle*?' she asked; anything to distract herself.

'The first thing I did when Mr Hadley's solicitor contacted me early this morning was to call the *Chronicle*'s advertising manager.' Miles walked across to his desk and removed a sheet of paper from a file and handed it to her. 'He sent this over from his office. Hadley hasn't seen it yet but it's only a matter of time before his lawyer contacts them.'

It was a photocopied proof of the ad for Hadley Chase— exactly as she'd read it out—complete with a tick next to the 'approved' box and her signature scrawled across the bottom.

'No, Miles. This is wrong.' She looked up. 'This isn't what I signed.'

'But you did write that,' he insisted.

'One or two of the phrases sound vaguely familiar,' she admitted.

She sometimes wrote a mock advertisement describing a property in the worst possible light when she thought it would help the vendor to see the property through the eyes of a potential buyer. The grubby carpet in the hall, the children's finger marks on the doors, the tired kitchen. Stuff that wouldn't cost much to fix, but would make all the difference to the prospects of a sale.

'Oh, come on, Tash. It sounds exactly like one of your specials.'

'My "specials" have the advantage of being accurate. And helpful.'

'So you would have mentioned the leaking roof?'

'Absolutely. Damaged ceilings and pools of water are about as off-putting as it gets,' she said, hating that she was on the defensive when she hadn't done anything wrong.

'What about the stairs?'

'I'm sure they'd be lovely if you could see them for the dust and dead leaves that blew in through a broken window.' The house had been empty since the last occupant had been moved to a nursing home when Alzheimer's had left him a danger to himself a couple of years ago. 'The caretaker is worse than useless. I had to find some card and fill the gap myself but it's just a temporary solution. The first serious gust of wind will blow it out. And, frankly, if I were Darius Hadley I'd put a boot up the backside of the estate executor because he's no help.' He didn't reply. 'Come on, Miles. You know I didn't send this to the *Chronicle*.'

'Are you sure about that? Really? We all know that you've been putting in long hours. What time was your first viewing this morning?'

'Eight, but—'

'What time did you finish last night?' He didn't wait for her to answer but consulted a printout of her diary, no doubt supplied by Janine. No wonder she'd been smiling. This was much more fun than an office party. Gossip city... 'Your last viewing was at nine-thirty so you were home at what? Eleven? Eleven-thirty?'

It had been after midnight. Buyers couldn't always fit into a tidy nine-till-five slot. Far from complaining about the extra hours she put in, that they all put in—with the exception of Toby, who never allowed anything to interfere with rugby training, took time off whenever he felt like it and got away with murder because his great-aunt was married to Peter Black—Miles expected it.

'They flew from the States to view that apartment. I could hardly tell them that I finished at five-thirty,' she pointed out. They'd come a long way and wanted to see every detail and she wasn't about to rush them.

'No one can keep up that pace for long without something suffering,' he replied, not even bothering to ask if they were likely to make an offer. 'It seems obvious to me that you attached the wrong document when you emailed your copy to the *Chronicle*.'

'No—'

'I blame myself.' He shook his head. 'I've pushed you too hard. I should have seen it coming.'

Seen *what* coming?

'I didn't attach the wrong anything,' she declared, fizzing with indignation, her pulse still racing but with anger now rather than anticipation. How dared anyone tamper with her carefully composed ad? 'And even if I had made a mistake, don't you think I'd have noticed it when the proof came back?'

'If you'd actually had time to look at it.'

'I made time,' she declared. 'I checked every word. And what the hell was the *Chronicle* thinking? Why didn't someone on the advertising desk query it?'

'They did.' He glanced at the ad. 'They called this office on the twentieth. Unsurprisingly, they made a note for their records.'

'Okay, so which idiot did they speak to?'

He handed her the page so that she could see for herself. 'An idiot by the name of Natasha Gordon.'

'No!'

'According to the advertising manager, you assured them that it was the latest trend, harking back fifty years to an estate agent famous for the outrageous honesty of his advertisements.' His tone, all calm reason, raised the small hairs on the back of her neck. Irritable, she could handle. This was just plain scary. 'Clearly, you were angry with the executors for not taking your advice.'

'If they didn't have the cash, they didn't have the cash, although I imagine their fees are safely in the bank. Believe me, if I'd been aping the legendary Roy Brooks, I'd have made a far better job of it than this,' she said, working hard to sound calm even while her pulse was going through the roof. 'There was plenty to work with. No one from the *Chronicle* talked to me.' Calm, cool, professional...

'So what are you saying? That the advertising manager of the *Chronicle* is lying? Or that someone pretended to be you? Come on, Tash, who would do that?' he asked. 'What would anyone have to gain?'

She swallowed. Put like that, it did sound crazy.

'You are right about one thing, though,' he continued. 'The phone has been ringing off the hook—' her sigh of relief came seconds too soon '—but not with people desperate to view Hadley Chase. They are all gossip columnists and the editors of property pages wanting a comment.'

She frowned. 'Already? The magazine has been on the shelves for less than two hours.'

'You know what they say about bad news.' He took the ad from her and tossed it onto his desk. 'In this instance I imagine it was given a head start by someone working at the *Chronicle* tipping them off.'

'I suppose. How did Darius Hadley hear about it?'

'I imagine the estate executors received the same phone calls.'

She shook her head, letting the problem of how this had happened go for the moment and concentrating instead on how to fix it. 'The one thing I do know is that there's no such thing as bad publicity. I meant what I said to Mr Hadley. Handled right…'

'For heaven's sake, Tash, you've made both the firm and Mr Hadley into a laughing stock. There is no way to handle this "right"! He's withdrawn the house from the market and, on top of the considerable expenses we've already incurred, we're not only facing a hefty claim for damages from Hadley but irreparable damage to the Morgan and Black name.'

'All of which will go away if we find a buyer quickly,' she insisted, 'and it's going to be all over the weekend property pages.'

'I'm glad you realise the extent of the problem.'

'No…' She'd run a Google search when Hadley Chase had been placed in their hands for sale. There was nothing like a little gossip, a bit of scandal to garner a few column inches in one of the weekend property supplements. Unfortunately, despite her speculation on the source of their wealth, the Hadleys had either been incredibly discreet or dull beyond imagining. She'd assumed the latter; if James Hadley had been an entertaining companion, his money would have earned him a lot more than a smallish estate in the country. He'd have been given a title and a place at Charles II's court.

Darius Hadley had blown that theory right out of the water.

Forget his clothes. With his cavalier curls, his sœurring, the edge of something dangerous that clung to him like a shadow, he would have been right at home there. Her fingers twitched as she imagined what it would be like to run her fingers through those silky black curls, over his flat abs.

She curled them into her palms, shook off the image—this wasn't about Darius Hadley; it was about his house.

'Come on, Miles,' she said. 'You couldn't buy this kind of publicity. The house is in a fabulous location and buyers with this kind of money aren't going to be put off by problems you'll find in any property of that age.' Well, not much. 'I'll make some calls, talk to a few people.' Apparently speaking to a brick wall, she threw up her hands. 'Damn it, I'll go down to Hadley Chase and take a broom to the place myself!'

'You'll do nothing, talk to no one,' he snapped.

'But if I can find a buyer quickly—'

'Stop! Stop right there.' Having shocked her into silence, he continued. 'This is what is going to happen. I've booked you into the Fairview Clinic—'

'The *Fairview*?' A clinic famous for taking care of celebrities with drug and drink problems?

'We'll issue a statement saying that you're suffering from stress and will be having a week or two of complete rest under medical supervision.'

'No.' Sickness, hospitals—she'd had her fill of them as a child and nothing would induce her to spend a minute in one without a very good reason.

'The firm's medical plan will cover it,' he said, no doubt meaning to reassure her.

'No, Miles.'

'While you're recovering,' he continued, his voice hardening, 'you can consider your future.'

'Consider my future?' Her future was stepping up to an associate's office, not being hidden away like some soap star with an alcohol problem until the dust cleared. 'You've got to be kidding, Miles. This has to be a practical joke that's got out of hand. There's a juvenile element in the front office that needs a firm—'

'What I need,' he said, each word given equal weight, 'is for you to cooperate.'

He wasn't listening, she realised. Didn't want to hear what she had to say. Miles wasn't interested in how this had happened, only in protecting his firm's reputation. He needed a scapegoat, a fall guy, and it was her signature on the ad.

That was why he'd summoned her back to the office—to show the sacrifice to Darius Hadley. Unsurprisingly, he hadn't been impressed. He didn't want the head of some apparently witless woman who stammered and blushed when he looked at her. He was going for damages so Miles was instituting Plan B—protecting the firm's reputation by destroying hers.

She was in trouble.

'I've spoken to Peter Black and he's discussed the situation with our lawyers. We're all agreed that this is the best solution,' Miles continued, as if it was a done deal.

'Already?'

'There was no time to waste.'

'Even so… What kind of lawyer would countenance such a lie?'

'What lie?' he enquired blandly. 'Burnout happens to the best of us.'

Burnout? She was barely simmering, but the lawyers—covering all eventualities—probably had the press statement drafted and ready to go. She would be described as a 'highly valued member of staff'…blah-de-blah-de-blah… who, due to work-related stress, had suffered a 'regrettable' breakdown. All carefully calculated to give the impression that she'd been found gibbering into her keyboard.

It would, of course, end with everyone wishing her a speedy return to health. Miles was clearly waiting for her to do the decent thing and take cover in the Fairview so that he could tell them to issue it. The clinic's reputation for keeping their patients safe from the lenses of the paparazzi, safe from the intrusion of the press, was legendary.

Suddenly she wasn't arguing with him over the best way to recover the situation, but clinging to the rim of the basin by her fingernails as her career was being flushed down the toilet.

'This is wrong,' she protested, well aware that the decision had already been made, that nothing she said would change that. 'I didn't do this.'

'I'm doing my best to handle a public relations nightmare that you've created, Natasha.' His voice was flat, his face devoid of expression. 'It's in your own best interests to cooperate.'

'It's in yours,' she retaliated. 'I'll be unemployable. Unless, of course, you're saying that I'll be welcomed back with open arms after my rest cure? That my promotion to associate, the one you've been dangling in front of me for months, is merely on hold until I've recovered?'

'I have to think of the firm. The rest of the staff,' he said with a heavy sigh created to signal his disappointment with her. 'Please don't be difficult about this.'

'Or what?' she asked.

'Tash… Please. Why won't you admit that you made a mistake? That you're fallible…sick; everyone—maybe even Mr Hadley—will sympathise with you, with us.'

He was actually admitting it!

'I didn't do this,' she repeated but, even to her own ears, she was beginning to sound like the little girl who, despite the frosting around her mouth, had refused to own up to eating two of the cupcakes her mother had made for a charity coffee morning.

'I'm sorry, Natasha, but if you refuse to cooperate we'll have no choice but to dismiss you without notice for bringing the firm into disrepute.' He took refuge behind his desk before he added, 'If you force us to do that we will, of course, have no option but to counter-sue you for malicious damage.'

Deep, deep trouble.

'I'm not sick,' she replied, doing her best to keep her voice steady, fighting down the scream of outrage that was beginning to build low in her belly. 'As for the suit for damages, I doubt either you or Mr Hadley would get very far with a jury. While the advertisement may not have been what he signed up for—' she was being thrown to the wolves, used as a scapegoat for something she hadn't done and she had nothing to lose '—it's the plain unvarnished truth.'

'Apart from the woodworm and the stairs,' he reminded her stonily.

'Are you prepared to gamble on that?' she demanded. 'Who knows what's under all that dirt?'

She didn't wait for a response. Once your boss had offered you a choice between loony and legal action, any meaningful dialogue was at an end.

CHAPTER TWO

How DARED HE? How bloody dared he even suggest she might be suffering from stress, burnout? Damn it, Miles had to know this was all a crock of manure.

Tash, despite her stand-up defiance, was shaking as she left Miles Morgan's office and she headed for the cloakroom. There was no way she could go downstairs and face Janine, who'd obviously known exactly what was coming, until she had pulled herself together.

She jabbed pins in her hair, applied a bright don't-care-won't-care coating of lipstick and some mental stiffeners to her legs before she attempted the stairs she'd run up with such optimism only a few minutes earlier.

She'd been ten minutes, no more, but Janine was waiting with a cardboard box containing the contents of her desk drawers.

'Everything's there,' she said, not the slightest bit embarrassed. On the contrary, the smirk was very firmly in place. They'd never been friends but, while she'd never given Janine a second thought outside the office, it was possible that Janine—behind the faux sweetness and the professional smile and ignoring the hours she put in, her lack of a social life—had resented her bonuses. 'It's mostly rubbish.'

She didn't bother to answer. She could see for herself that the contents of her desk drawers had been tipped into the box without the slightest care.

Janine was right; it was mostly rubbish, apart from a spare pair of tights, the pencil case that one of her brothers had given her and the mug she used for her pens. She picked it up and headed for the door.

'Wait! Miles said...'

In her opinion, Miles had said more than enough but, keeping her expression impassive, she turned, waited.

'He asked me to take your keys.'

Of course he had. He wouldn't want her coming back when the office was closed to prove what havoc she could really cause, given sufficient provocation. Fortunately for him, her reputation was more important to her than petty revenge.

She put down the box, took out her key ring, removed the key to the back door of the office and handed it over without a word.

'And your car keys,' she said.

Until that moment none of this had seemed real, but the BMW convertible had been the reward Miles had dangled in front of his staff for anyone reaching a year end sales target that he had believed impossible. She'd made it with a week to spare and it was her pride and joy as well as the envy of every other negotiator in the firm. Could someone have done this to her just to get...?

She stopped. That way really did lie madness.

No doubt Miles would use those spectacular sales figures to back up his claim of 'burnout', suggesting she'd driven herself to achieve the impossible and prove that she was better than anyone else. *So very sad...*

He might even manage to squeeze out a tear.

All he'd have to do was think of the damages he'd have to pay Darius Hadley.

Taking pride in the fact that her fingers weren't shaking—it was just the rest of her, apparently—she removed the silver Tiffany key ring Toby had bought her for Christmas from her car keys and dropped it in her pocket, but she held on to the keys. 'I'll clear my stuff out of the back.'

'I'll come with you,' Janine said, following her to the door. 'I need to make sure it's locked up safely.'

She wasn't trusted to hand over the keys? Or did the wretched woman think she'd drive off in it? Add car theft to her crimes? Oh, wait. She was supposed to be crazy…

'Actually, you'll need to do more than that. I'm parked in a twenty-minute zone and it'll need moving before— Oh, too late…'

She startled the traffic warden slapping a ticket on the windscreen with a smile before clicking the lock and tossing the keys to Janine as if she didn't give a fig. She wouldn't give her the pleasure of telling everyone how she'd crumpled, broken down. It was just a car. She'd have it back in no time. Just as soon as Miles stopped panicking and started thinking straight.

She emptied the glovebox, gathered her wellington boots, the ancient waxed jacket she'd bought in a charity shop and her umbrella and added them to the box, then reached for her laptop bag.

'I'll take that.'

'My laptop?' She finally turned to look at Janine. 'Did Miles ask you to take it?'

'He's got a lot on his mind,' she replied with a little toss of her head. In other words, no.

'True, and when I find out who's responsible for this mess he won't be the only one. In the meantime,' she said, hooking the strap over her shoulder and patting the soft leather case that held her precious MacBook Pro, 'if he should ask for it, I suggest you remind him that I bought it out of my January bonus.'

Janine, caught out, flushed bright pink but it was a short-lived triumph.

'There's a taxi waiting to take you to the Fairview,' she said, turning on her heel and heading back to the office.

Tash glanced at the black cab, idling at the kerb. Even loaded as she was, the temptation to stalk off in the direction of the nearest Underground station was strong, but there was no one apart from the traffic warden to witness the gesture so she climbed aboard and gave him her address.

The driver looked back. 'I was booked for the Fairview.'

'I have to go home first,' she said, straight-faced. 'I'm going to need a nightie and toothbrush.'

Darius strode the length of the King's Road, fury and the need to put distance between himself and Natasha Gordon driving his feet towards the Underground.

A minor setback? A house that she'd made unsellable, and a seven-figure tax bill on a house he couldn't live in—what would merit serious bother in her eyes?

Cornflower-blue, with hair that looked as if she'd just tumbled out of bed and a figure that was all curves. Sexy as hell, which was where his thoughts were taking him.

Once on the train, he took out the small sketchbook he carried with him and did what he had always done when he wanted to block out the world. He drew what he saw. Not the interior of the train, the woman sitting opposite him, the baby sleeping on her lap, but what was in his head.

Dark, angry images that had been stirred up by a house he'd never wanted to set foot in again but just refused to let go. But that wasn't what appeared on the page. His hand, ignoring his head, was drawing Natasha Gordon. Her eyes, startled wide as he'd confronted her. The way her brow had arched like the wing of a kestrel hovering over a hedgerow, waiting for an unsuspecting vole to make a move. The curve of hair drooping from an antique silver clasp, the tiny crease at the corner of her mouth that had appeared when she'd offered him a smile along with her hand. It was as if her image had burned itself into his brain, every detail pinpoint-sharp. The blush heating her cheeks, a fine chain about her neck that disappeared between invitingly generous breasts. Her long legs.

Was he imagining them?

He couldn't remember looking at her legs and yet he'd drawn her shoes—black suede, dangerously high heels, a sexy little ankle strap...

He did not fight it, but drew obsessively, continuously, as if by putting her on paper he could clear his mind, rid himself of what had happened in that moment when he'd stood up and turned to face her. When he'd looked back, knowing that she'd be there at the window. Wishing he'd taken her with him when he'd left. When he'd hovered for a dangerous moment on the point of turning back...

Wouldn't Morgan have loved that?

He stopped drawing and just let his mind's eye see her, imagining how he'd paint her, sculpt her and when, finally, he looked up, he'd gone way past his stop.

Tash sat back in the cab as the driver pulled away from the kerb, did a U-turn and joined the queue of traffic backed up along the King's Road.

A little more than twenty minutes—just long enough to get a parking ticket—that was all it had taken to reduce her from top-selling negotiator at one of the most prestigious estate agencies in London, to unemployable.

'It's a beautiful house, Darius.' Patsy, having dropped off some paperwork and made them both a cup of tea, had discovered the *Chronicle* in the waste bin when she'd discarded the teabags. 'Lots of room. You could make a studio in one of the buildings,' she said with a head jerk that took in the concrete walls and floor still stained with oil from its previous incarnation as a motor repair shop. 'Why don't you just move in? Ask me nicely and I might even come and keep house for you.'

'You and whose army?' He glanced at the photograph of the sprawling house, its Tudor core having been added to over the centuries by ancestors with varying degrees of taste. At least someone had done their job right, taking time to find the perfect spot to show the Chase at its best. The half-timbering, a mass of roses hiding a multitude of sins. A little to the right of a cedar tree that had been planted to commemorate the coronation of Queen Victoria.

The perfect spot at the perfect time on the perfect day when a golden mist rising from the river had lent the place an ethereal quality that took him back to school holidays and early-morning fishing trips with his grandfather. Took him back to an enchanted world seen through the innocent eyes of a child.

'It's got at least twenty rooms,' he said, returning to the armature on which he was building his interpretation of a racehorse flying over a fence. 'That's not including the kitchen, scullery, pantries and the freezing attics where the poor sods who kept the place running in the old days were housed.' Plus half a dozen cottages, at present occupied by former employees of the estate whom he could never evict, and a boat house that was well past its best twenty years ago.

She put the magazine on his workbench where he could see it, opened a packet of biscuits and, when he shook his head, helped herself to one. 'So what are you going to do?'

'Wring that wretched girl's neck?' he offered, and tried not to think about his hand curled around her nape. How her skin would feel against his palm, the scent of vanilla that he couldn't lose… 'Subject closed.'

He picked up the *Chronicle* and tossed it back in the bin.

'It said in the paper that she'd had some kind of a break-down,' Patsy protested.

A widow, she worked as a freelance 'Girl Friday' for several local businesses, fitting them in around the needs of her ten-year-old son. She kept his books and his paper-work in order, the fridge stocked with fresh milk, cold beer, and his life organised. The downside was that, like an old time travelling minstrel, she delivered neighbour-hood gossip, adding to the story with each stop she made. He had no doubt that Hadley Chase had featured heavily in her story arc this week and her audience were no doubt eagerly awaiting the next instalment.

'Please tell me you don't believe everything you read in the newspapers,' he said as, concentration gone, he gave up on the horse and drank the tea he hadn't asked for.

'Of course I don't,' she declared, 'but the implication was that she had a history of instability. They wouldn't lie about something like that.' She took another biscuit, clearly in no hurry to be anywhere else.

'No? She was in full control of her faculties when I saw her,' he said. 'I suspect the breakdown story is Morgan and Black's attempt to focus the blame on her and lessen the impact on their business.' Lessen the damages.

'That's shocking. She should sue.'

'She hasn't bothered to deny it,' he said.

'Maybe her lawyer has advised her not to say anything. What's she like? You didn't say you'd met her.'

'Believe me,' he said, 'I'm doing my best to forget.' For-get his body's slamming response at the sight of her. The siren call of a sensually pleasing body that had been made to wrap around a man. A mouth made for pleasure. The feeling of control slipping away from him.

Precious little chance of that when his hands itched to capture the liquid blue of eyes that had sucked the breath out of him, sent the blood rushing south, nailing him to the spot. A look that eluded his every attempt to recreate it.

It was just as well she was safely out of reach in the Fairview, playing along with Morgan's game in the hopes of hanging on to her job. Asking her to sit for him was a distraction he could not afford. And would certainly not endear him to his lawyers.

'I wonder if it was anorexia?' she pondered. 'In the past.' Patsy, generous in both character and build, took another biscuit.

'No way.' He shook his head as he recalled that delicious moment when, as Natasha Gordon had offered him her hand, the top button of her blouse had surrendered to the strain, parting to reveal the kind of cleavage any red-blooded male would willingly dive into. 'Natasha Gordon has all the abundant charms of a milkmaid.'

'A milkmaid?'

Patsy's grandparents had immigrated to Britain in the nineteen-fifties and she'd lived her entire life in the inner city. It was likely that the closest she'd ever come to a cow was in a children's picture book.

'Big blue eyes, a mass of fair hair and skin like an old-fashioned rose.' There was one that scrambled over the rear courtyard at the Chase. He had no idea what it was called, but it had creamy petals blushed with pink that were bursting out of a calyx not designed to contain such bounty. 'Believe me, this is not a woman who lives on lettuce.'

'Oh…' She gave him an old-fashioned look. 'And did this milkmaid apologise with a pretty curtsy?' she asked, confirming her familiarity with the genre.

'She didn't appear to have read the script.' No apology, no excuses… 'She suggested that the advertisement was little more than a minor setback.'

'Really? You're quite sure the poor woman is not cracking up?'

'As sure as I can be without a doctor's note.' But there was a distinct possibility that he was.

Milkmaids, roses…

Forget wheeling her in to apologise. If it was possible to be any more cynical, he'd have said they were hoping that she might use her charms, her lack of control over her buttons, to distract him from taking legal action.

He shouldn't even be thinking about how far she might go to achieve that objective. Or how happy he would be to lie back and let her try.

'Dad's really worried about you, Tash. You've been working so hard and all this stress…well…you know…' Her mother never actually said what she was thinking out loud. 'He thinks you should come home for a while so that we can look after you.'

Tash sighed. She'd known that whatever she said, they'd half believe the newspaper story, convinced that they had been right all along. That she would be safer at home. No matter how much she told herself that they were wrong, it was hard to resist that kind of worry.

'Mum, I'm fine.'

'Tom thinks a break would do you good. We've booked the house down in Cornwall for the half-term holiday.' So far, so what she'd expected. Her dad the worrier, her brother the doctor prescribing a week at the seaside and her mother trying to please everyone. 'You know how you always loved it there and you haven't seen the children for ages. You won't believe how they've grown.'

Twenty-five and on holiday with her family. Building sandcastles for her nieces during the day and playing Scrabble or Monopoly in the evening. How appealing was that?

'I saw them at Easter,' she said. 'Send me a postcard.'

'Darling…'

'It's all smoke and mirrors, Mum. I'm fit as a flea.'

'Are you sure? Are you taking the vitamins I sent you?'

'I never miss,' she said, rolling her eyes in exasperation. She understood, really, but anyone would think she was still five years old and fighting for her life instead of a successful career woman. This was just a hiccup.

'Are you eating properly?'

'All the food groups.'

When the taxi had delivered her to her door, she'd gone straight to the freezer and dug out a tub of strawberry cheesecake ice cream. While she'd eaten it, she pulled up the file on her laptop so that if, in a worst case scenario, it came to an unfair dismissal tribunal she had a paper trail to demonstrate exactly what she'd done. Except that there it all was, word for word, on the screen. Exactly as printed. Which made no sense.

The proof copy she'd seen, approved and put in her out tray had been the one she'd actually written, not the one that was printed.

Either she really was going mad or someone had gone out of their way to do this to her. Not just changing the original copy, fiddling with the proof and intercepting the phone call from the *Chronicle*, but getting into her laptop to change what she'd written so that she had no proof that she'd ever written anything else.

Okay, a forensic search would pull up the original, but there would be no way to prove that she hadn't changed it herself because whoever had done this had logged in using her password.

Which meant there was only one person in the frame.

The man who hadn't let her know he was back a week early from a six-week rugby tour. The man who hadn't come rushing round with pizza, Chianti and chocolate the minute he heard the news. Who hadn't called, texted, emailed even, to ask how she was.

The man who was now occupying the upstairs office that should, by rights, be hers.

Her colleague with benefits: Toby Denton.

She wouldn't have thought the six-foot-three blond rugby-playing hunk—who'd never made a secret of the fact that he saw work as a tedious interruption to his life and whose only ambition was to play the sport professionally—had the brains to engineer her downfall with such cunning.

His cluelessness, off the rugby field, had been a major part of his appeal. When there was any rescuing to be done—which was often when it came to work—she was the one tossing him the lifebelt. Like giving him her laptop password so that he could check the office diary for an early-morning appointment when, typically, he'd forgotten where he was supposed to be.

The announcement of his appointment as associate partner had appeared on the company website the day after she'd been walked to the door with her belongings in a cardboard box. Photographs of the champagne celebration had appeared on the blog a day later. It was great PR and she'd have applauded if it hadn't been her career they were interring.

'Tash?' her mother asked anxiously. 'Are you baking?'

'Baking? No…' Then, in sheer desperation, 'Got to go. Call waiting. Have a lovely time in Cornwall.'

Call waiting… She wished, she thought, glancing along the work surface at the ginger, lemon drizzle and passion cakes lined up alongside a Sacher Torte, waiting for the ganache she was making.

She *had* been baking. She'd used every bowl she possessed, every cake tin. They were piled up in the sink and on the draining board, along with a heap of eggshells and empty sugar, flour and butter wrappers and a fine haze of icing sugar hung in the air, coating every surface, including her.

It was her displacement activity. Some people played endless computer games, or went for a run, or ironed when they needed to let their brain freewheel. She beat butter and sugar and eggs into creamy peaks.

Unfortunately, her mind was ignoring the no-job, no-career problem. Instead it kept running Darius Hadley on a loop. That moment when he'd turned and looked at her in Miles Morgan's office, his face all dark shadows, his eyes burning into her. His hands. The glint of gold beneath dark curls. The air stirring as he'd walked past her, leaving the scent of something earthy behind.

That moment when he'd stopped in the street and looked back and she'd known that if he'd lifted a hand to her she would have gone to him. Worse, had wanted him to lift a hand...

Her skin glowed just thinking about that look. Not just her skin.

Madness.

Her skin was sticky, her eyes gritty; she had no job and no one was going to call. Not Miles. Not any of the agencies that had tried to tempt her away from him. Last week she was the negotiator everyone wanted on their team, but now she was damaged goods.

If she was going to rescue her career, this was going to have to be a show rather than tell scenario. She would have to demonstrate to the world that she was still the best there was. Her brain hadn't been dodging the problem; it had been showing her the answer.

Darius Hadley.

She was going to have to find a buyer for Hadley Chase.

A week ago that had been a challenge, but she'd had the contacts, people who would pick up the phone when she called, listen to her when she told them she had exactly the house they were looking for because she didn't lie, didn't waste their time. Matching houses with the right buyers was a passion with her. People trusted her. Or they had.

Now the word on the street was that she'd lost it. She was on her own with nothing to offer except her wits, her knowledge of the market and the kind of motivation that would move mountains if she could persuade Darius Hadley to give her a chance.

She was going to have to face him: this man who'd turned her into a blushing, jelly-boned cliché with no more than a look.

In the normal course of events it wouldn't have been more than a momentary wobble. It had been made clear to her by the estate's executor that the vendor wanted nothing to do with the actual sale of his house and if he'd let her just get on with it she would never have seen him again. Apparently her luck had hit the deck on all fronts that morning.

At the time she hadn't given the reason why Darius Hadley was keeping his distance any thought—it had taken all her concentration not to melt into a puddle at his feet—but the more she'd thought about him, the more she understood how it must hurt to be the Hadley to let the house go. To lose four centuries of his family history.

If there was no cash to go with the property, he would have no choice—death meant taxes—but it was easy to see why he'd been furious with them, with *her*, for messing up and forcing him to confront the situation head-on. Maybe, though, now he'd had time to calm down, he'd be glad of someone offering to help.

Selling a country estate was an expensive business. Printing, advertising, travel, and she doubted that, in these cash-strapped days, he'd be inundated with estate agents eager to invest in a house that had been publicly declared a money pit.

Hopefully she'd be all he'd got. And he, collywobbles notwithstanding, was almost certainly her only hope.

Fortunately she had all the details of Hadley Chase on her laptop.

What she didn't have were the contact details for Darius Hadley.

She'd had no success when she'd searched Hadley Chase on Google hoping for some family gossip to get the property page editors salivating. She assumed it would have thrown up anything newsworthy about Darius Hadley, but she typed his name into the search engine anyway.

A whole load of links came up, including images, and she clicked on the only one of him. It had been taken, ironically, from one of those high society functions featured in the *Country Chronicle* and the caption read: 'Award-winning sculptor Darius Hadley at the Serpentine Gallery...'

He was a sculptor? Well, that would explain the steel toecaps, the grey smears on his jeans. That earthy scent had been clay...

His tie was loose, his collar open and he'd been caught unawares, laughing at something or someone out of the picture and she was right. A smile was all it took to lift the shadows. He still had the look of the devil, but one who was having a good day, and she reached out and touched the screen, her fingertips against his mouth.

'Oh...' she breathed. 'Collywollydoodah...'

CHAPTER THREE

THE NARROW COBBLED backstreet was a jumble of buildings that had been endlessly converted and added to over the centuries. All Tash had was the street name, but she had been confident that a prize-winning sculptor's studio would be easy enough to find.

She was wrong.

She'd reached a dead end and found no sign, no indication that art of any kind happened behind any of the doors but as she turned she found herself face-to-face with a woman who was regarding her through narrowed eyes.

'Can I help you?' she asked.

'I hope so... I'm looking for Darius Hadley. I was told his studio was in this street,' she prompted.

The woman gave her a long, thoughtful look, taking in the grey business suit that she kept for meetings with the property managers of billionaires; she had hoped it would cut down on the inexplicable electricity that had sparked between them in Miles's office. A spark that had sizzled even when he was outside on the pavement looking up at her.

Okay, maybe she should have worn a pair of sensible, low-heeled shoes, added horn-rimmed spectacles to make herself look *seriously* serious. Hell, she *was* serious, never more so—this was her career on the line—but there was only so far she could stretch the illusion. As for her favourite red heels, she'd needed them to give her a little extra height, some of the bounce that had been knocked clean out of her. Besides, Darius Hadley wouldn't be fooled by a pair of faux specs. Not for a minute.

She'd experienced the power of eyes that would see right through any games, any pretence and knew that she would have to be absolutely straight with him.

No problem. Straight was what she did and she had it all worked out. The look, the poise, what she was going to say. She was going to be totally professional, which was all very fine in theory but first she had to find him. She'd called in a big favour to get his address but now she was beginning to wonder if she'd been sold a fake.

The woman, her inspection completed, asked, 'Is Darius expecting you?'

'He'll want to see me,' she said, fingers mentally crossed. 'Do you know him?'

'Sure,' she said, a slow smile lighting up her face. 'I know everyone. Even you, Natasha Gordon.'

Tash, still dragging her chin back into place, followed the woman back down the street towards a pair of wide, rusty old garage doors over which a sign suggested someone called Mike would repair your car while you waited. She produced a large bunch of keys and let herself in through the personnel door.

'Darius?' she called, leaving the door open. Tash, grabbing her chance, stepped in after her. 'How are you feeling about the milkmaid today?'

Milkmaid?

There was a discouraging grunt from somewhere above her head. 'Not now, Patsy.'

She looked up. Darius Hadley was standing on a tall stepladder, thumbing clay onto the leaping figure of a horse.

'Do you still want to wring her neck?' Patsy persisted.

'Nothing has changed since last week,' he replied, leaning back a little to check what he'd done, 'but, to put your mind at rest, that damned house has given me enough trouble without adding grievous bodily harm to the list.'

'So it would be safe to let her in?'

Now she had his attention.

'Let her…' He swung around and her heart leapt. He was so high… 'She's *here*?'

'She doesn't have a milking stool, or one of those things they wear across the shoulders with a pail at each end, but other than that she fits the description. Abundantly,' she added with a broad smile. 'Of course it helped that you've been drawing her on any bit of paper that comes to hand for the last few days.'

'Patsy…'

'I found her wandering up and down the street looking for your studio. Your name on the door would be a real help,' she said, apparently not the least bit intimidated by the growl.

'That would only encourage visitors. People who interrupt me while I'm working,' he said, looking over Patsy's head to where she was hovering just inside the doorway.

Maybe it was just the sunlight streaming in through the skylight above him, but today his eyes were molten slate, scorching her skin, melting the starch in her shirt, reducing her knees to fudge frosting.

It wasn't just his eyes. Everything about him was hot: the faded, clay-smeared jeans hugging his thighs, midnight-black hair curling into his neck, long, ropey muscles in his forearms. And those hands…

She had tried to convince herself that she'd imagined the electricity, the fizz, the crackle… There had been a shock factor when she'd seen him in Miles's office, but he'd been in her head for days and not just because he was her only chance to get back to work.

She'd been dreaming about those hands. How they'd feel on her body, the drag of hard calluses against tender skin…

'I know I'm the last person on earth you want to talk to, Mr Hadley,' she said quickly before he could tell her to get lost, 'but if you can spare me ten minutes, I've got a proposition for you.'

'Proposition?'

The word hung in the air.

Darius looked down at the shadowy hourglass shape of Natasha Gordon, backlit by sunlight streaming in over the city rooftops.

It was just a word. Morgan couldn't possibly be using her as a sweetener. But then again, maybe it was her idea...

'If you could spare me ten minutes?' From above her he could see straight down the opening of her blouse, the way her luscious breasts were squished together as she raised her hand to shield her eyes from the light pouring in from the skylights. 'Maybe we could sit down,' she suggested, lifting her other hand a little to show him a glossy white cakebox, dangling from a ribbon. 'I've brought cake. It's home-made. I'll even make the tea.'

He picked up a damp cloth and wiped his hands, giving himself a moment to still his rampaging libido. He should send her packing but how often did a man receive a proposition from a sexy woman bearing cake? And now she was here he'd be able to capture the look that had eluded him, draw her out of his head.

'I hope you or your mother can cook,' he said and Patsy nodded, apparently satisfied that it would be safe to leave him alone with her, and left them to it.

'Would I come bearing anything less than perfection?' she asked.

Not this woman, he thought. She'd pulled out all the stops... 'How did you find me?'

'Does it matter?' she asked, the wide space between her brows crumpled in a tiny frown that didn't fool him for a moment. Not many people knew where he worked. She'd had to work hard to locate him.

'Humour me,' he suggested, taking a step down the ladder, and she caught her breath, muscles tensed, barely stopping herself from taking a step back. She was nowhere near as cool as she looked. Which made two of them.

'I did what anyone would do. Ran an Internet search,' she said quickly, 'and there you were. Darius Hadley, award-winning sculptor, presently working on a prestigious commission to create a life-size bronze of one of the greatest racehorses of all time.' Lots of details so he'd forget the question. He was familiar with the technique. His grandfather had been a past master at diverting him whenever he'd asked awkward questions. 'There was a photograph,' she added.

'Of me?' He took another step down. She swallowed, but this time stood her ground.

'Of the horse. It was in the *Racing Times*. Photographs of you are scarce. You don't even have a website.' She made it sound like an accusation.

'I seem to manage.'

'Yes…'

She turned away, giving them both a break as she looked around at the dozens of photographs taken from every angle of the horse—galloping, jumping, standing—that he'd pinned to the walls. She paused briefly at the anatomical drawings of the skeleton, the muscles, the blood vessels and then looked up at his interpretation of the animal gathered to leap a jump.

'If I'd known who you were when the house came on the market,' she said at last, 'I could have used the information to get some editorial interest. Racehorse owners are among the richest men in the world and Hadley Chase is close to one of the country's major racehorse training centres.'

'You managed an excessive number of column inches

without any help from me,' he said, 'but that's who, not where,' he said, refusing to be sidetracked.

A rueful smile made it to a mouth that was a little too big for beauty, tugging it upwards. 'The where *was* more difficult. And the address was only half the story. If it hadn't been for Patsy I'd still be looking for you.'

'So?' he insisted.

'I'm sorry, Mr Hadley. An estate agent never reveals her sources.'

'A journalist?' No, the piece in the newspaper had not been kind. Reading between the lines, anyone would be forgiven for assuming her 'collapse' had been the result of a coke-fuelled drive for success. Something in her past... Journalists would not be flavour of the month. 'An art dealer?' he suggested. Who would be vulnerable to those big blue eyes and a loose top button? No... Who had moved recently? 'Freddie Glover threw a house-warming party a few months back,' he said.

She neither confirmed nor denied it and, satisfied, he let it rest.

'If you've come to apologise...' She seemed bright enough so he left her to fill in the blank.

'I was sure Miles would have performed the ritual grovel but I could go through the motions if you insist,' she offered.

A little movement of her hand, underlining the offer, sent a barely discernible shimmer through her body—a shimmer that found an answering echo deep in his groin. Yes...

She waited briefly, but he was too busy catching his own breath to answer.

'I'm sorry about what happened, obviously, but that's not the reason I'm here.'

'Why are you here?' he demanded. He hated being this out of control around a woman. Could not make himself send her away. 'For heaven's sake, come in and close the door if you're staying. I won't eat you…'

She didn't look entirely convinced, but she closed the door, took a breath and then walked towards him with the kind of mesmerisingly slow, hip-swaying walk that had gone out of style fifty years ago. Around the same time as her hourglass figure.

No longer backlit from the street, the light pouring in from the skylights overhead lit her up like a spotlight and he could see that she'd made an attempt to disguise its lushness beneath a neat grey suit. Or maybe not. The skirt clung to her thighs and stopped a hand's breadth short of serious, leaving a yard of leg on display, always supposing he'd got past the deep vee of her shirt. She really should try a size larger if she was serious.

As for her hair, she'd fastened it in a sleek twist that rested against the nape of her neck; it was a classically provocative style and his fingers, severely provoked, itched to pull the pins and send it tumbling around her face and shoulders.

She'd stopped a teasing arm's width from the ladder, looking up at him. Near enough for the honeyed scent of warm skin, something lemony, spicy, chocolatey to reach him but, maybe sensing the danger, not quite close enough to touch. Clearly her instincts were better honed than his because every beat of his pulse urged him to reach for her, pull her close enough to feel what she was doing to him…

Forget the cake. Eating her, one luscious mouthful at a time, was the only thing on his mind.

'Well?' he snapped. Angry with her for disturbing him. No one was allowed to disturb him while he was working. Angry with himself for wanting to be disturbed. For the triumphant *Yes!* racketing through him at her unexpected appearance, despite the certainty that this was some devi-

ous scheme of Morgan's—sending in the sex bomb to persuade him to drop his claim for damages.

Tash ran her tongue over her teeth in an attempt to get
some spit so that she could answer him. Lay out her offer
like the professional she was.

She was used to meeting powerful men and women but
she was having a tough job remembering why she was in
Darius Hadley's studio. The concrete floor and walls made
the space cold after the sun outside, but a trickle of sweat
was running down between her breasts and an age-old instinct was telling her to shrug off her jacket, let her hair
down, reach out and run her fingers up his denim-clad
thigh, perched, tantalisingly, at eye level.

'What do you want, Natasha Gordon?'

She looked up and saw her feelings echoed in Darius
Hadley's shadowed features and for a moment it could have
gone either way.

She was saved by the crash of a pigeon landing on the
skylight, startling them both out of the danger zone.

'I don't want anything from you, Mr Hadley,' she said
quickly. Could this be any more difficult? Bad enough that
he thought she'd sabotaged the sale of his house without
acting like a sex-starved nymphomaniac. 'On the contrary.
I'm going to do you a favour. I'm going to sell your house
for you.'

'Miss Gordon…'

'I know.' She held up her hand in a gesture of surren-
der. 'Why would you trust me? After the debacle with your
ad,' she added, and then wished she hadn't. Having found
him, got through the door a darn sight more easily than
she'd expected and survived that first intense encounter,
reminding him why he should throw her out was not her
brightest move.

'Is there any hope that you're not going to tell me?'
he asked.

Phew… 'Not a chance.' She slipped the strap of her laptop bag from her shoulder and let it drop at her feet, anchoring herself in his space. Then she placed the glossy white cakebox on his workbench alongside his neatly laid-out tools—most of which appeared to be lethal weapons. Most, but not all. She picked up a long curved rib bone.

'That belonged to the last person who annoyed me,' he said, finally stepping off the ladder.

'Really?' Apparently there was a sense of humour lurking beneath that scowl. Promising…

'What did he do?' she asked, looking up at the sculpture rearing above her, heart swelling within its ribcage as the horse leapt some unseen obstacle. From what she'd seen of his work on the Net, it appeared that visceral was something of a theme. 'Did he throw you? Is this you getting your own back?'

'Anyone can make a pretty image.' He took the bone from her, replaced it on the bench. 'I want to show what's behind the power, the movement. Bones, sinews, heart.'

'The engine rather than the chassis.' Eager to avoid close eye contact, she walked around the beast, examining it from every angle, before looking across at Darius Hadley from the safety of the far side. 'That's what you do, isn't it? Show us the inside of things.'

'That's what's real, what's important.'

'I saw your installation outside Tate Modern. The house.' That had been stripped back to the bones, too.

'You've done your homework,' he said.

'I was just walking past. I didn't realise it was yours until I looked you up online. I thought it was…bleak.'

'Everyone's a critic.'

'No… It was beautiful. It's just…well, there were no people and without them a house is simply a frame.'

'Perhaps that was the point,' he suggested.

'Was it?' He didn't answer and she looked back up at the horse. 'This is…big.'

'I'll cast a smaller version for a limited edition.'

'Just the thing for the mantelpiece,' she said flippantly. Then wished she hadn't. His work was more important than that. 'I'm sorry; that was a stupid thing to say. I'm a bit nervous.'

'I'm not surprised. Does Miles Morgan really think he can buy me off with a glimpse of your cleavage and a slice of cake?'

'What?' She checked her top button but it was still in place. Just. She'd worn her roomiest shirt but working ten, fourteen hours a day didn't leave much time for exercise, or a carefully thought-out diet. And she'd moved less and eaten more in the last week than was good for anyone; it was definitely time to get out of the kitchen and back to work. 'Miles didn't send me. As for the cleavage…' She lifted her shoulders in a little shrug that she hoped would give the impression that she was utterly relaxed. She was good at that. The most important thing she'd learned about selling houses was to create an image. Set the stage, create an initial impact that would grab the viewer's attention then hold it. This time she was selling herself… 'I've been on a baking binge and eating too much of my own cooking.'

'And now you want to share.'

'I thought something sweet might help to break the ice.' Ice?

There was no ice as she bent forward to tug on the gauzy bow that exactly matched the shade of her lipstick, her nails; only heat zinging through his veins, making the blood pump thickly in his ears.

He'd been drawing her obsessively for a week, trying to get her out of his head, but while the two-dimensional image had been recognisable it lacked the warmth, the sparkle of the original.

Right now all he wanted to do was peel away her clothes, expose those rich creamy curves to the play of sunlight and shade.

He wanted to draw her from every angle, stripping away layer after layer until he could see her core. Until he could see what she was thinking, what she was feeling; transmute that into a three-dimensional image exposing the heart of the woman within.

He wanted a lot more than that.

'What have you got?' he asked.

'I wasn't sure which you'd like so I brought a selection,' she said, looking at him. For a moment the air seemed to crackle and then she was looking down at the box, her eyes hidden by silky lashes. 'There's lemon drizzle, chocolate, coffee, sticky ginger and, um, passion cake.'

The scent of vanilla rose enticingly from the box, taking him straight back to his childhood—that sweet moment when he'd been allowed to lick the remains of the mixture from the spoon; when he'd sunk his teeth into a cake still warm from the oven.

He was no longer a boy but he resisted one temptation only to look up and find himself confronted by the reach-out-and-touch-me lure of warm breasts.

Was this how it had been for his father? An obsessive urge to possess one woman wiping everything from his mind. One woman becoming his entire world.

Stick to the cake…

'You weren't kidding when you said you'd been on a baking binge, Miss Gordon,' he said, taking the first piece his fingers touched, anything to distract him. 'Did the Fairview recommend it as occupational therapy?'

'Tash, please. Everyone calls me Tash.'

'I prefer Natasha,' he said, sucking the icing from his thumb, and she blushed. Not the swift suffusion of heat that rose to her face in that moment when they'd confronted

one another in Morgan's office and seen how it would be
if they ever let their guard down, but a real girlish blush.

'Nobody calls me that,' she said. 'Only my mother.
When I've done something to exasperate her.'

'That would be your mother and me, then.'

'Point taken.' The corner of her mouth tilted upwards in
a wry sketch at a smile. 'I'd be annoyed with me if I were
you. I'm pretty annoyed myself, to be honest. It wasn't
much fun having to phone my parents and warn them that
they and their neighbours and everyone they knew would
be reading about my breakdown in the evening paper. Warn
them that they'd probably have reporters ringing them at
home, knocking on the door. Which they did, by the way.'

'No comment.'

The smile deepened to reveal a small crease in her cheek.
She'd once had a dimple…

'It's not true, by the way. About the Fairview. In case
you were in any doubt. Just so that we're on the same page
here, Miles Morgan and I parted company less than fifteen
minutes after you left the office.'

'He fired you?' He should have waited. Gone back. Followed his gut instinct to grab her hand and take her with
him… 'I'm not big on employment law but I'm fairly sure
he can't have it both ways. He can't dismiss you when
you're on sick leave.'

'You're probably right,' she admitted, 'but I refused to
cooperate with his plan to have my sanity publicly questioned and hide away in the Fairview in the cause of
saving the firm's reputation.'

'I saw the paper.'

'Everyone saw the paper,' she said. 'I'm supposedly giving my brain a rest in the Fairview while I consider my
future.'

'You didn't deny it,' he pointed out.

'Like that would have helped.' She clutched at her throat

with both hands. '*I'm not mad. It wasn't me. I was framed!*' she croaked out, rolling her eyes, feigning madness.

He was expected to laugh, but it was taking all his concentration just to breathe because she'd forgotten not to look at him. And then she remembered and he could see that it wasn't just him. They were both struggling with the zing of lightning that arced between them.

'Since Plan B was a threat to sue me for malicious damage…' Her voice was thick, her pupils huge against the shot-silk blue; what would she do if he reached out and took her hand and held it against his zip, if he sucked her lower lip into his mouth? '…I didn't think there was much point in hanging around.'

He turned away, crossed to the kettle, picking it up to make sure there was some water in it before switching it on. Any distraction from the thoughts racketing through his head. The same thoughts that had driven him from Morgan's office amplified a hundred times.

He had no problem with lust at first sight. Uncomplicated, life's-too-short sex that gave everyone a good time and didn't screw with your head. This was complicated with knobs on. He should never have let her stay.

He could not have sent her away…

'It's a bit like denying Hadley Chase is riddled with woodworm,' he said, tossing teabags into a couple of mugs, making an effort to bring the conversation back to the house—as effective as any cold shower. 'Once it's in print, who's going to believe you?'

'Exactly… Not that it is,' she said, as eager as him to get back to business, apparently. 'Riddled with woodworm. The house has been neglected in recent years, the roof needs some work, but the structure is sound and the advertisement did get people talking about the house,' she stressed earnestly, as if that were something to be welcomed. 'My photograph was reprinted in all the weekend property supplements.'

'Your photograph?' He waved her towards the ancient sofa that he sometimes slept on when he'd worked late and he was too tired to stagger the hundred yards home. 'Didn't Morgan employ a professional?'

'Oh, yes, and he did his best with the interior, but it was raining on the day he was there so, despite his best efforts with Photoshop, his exteriors weren't doing the house any favours,' she said, sinking into the low saggy cushions. 'We were running out of time so, when the weather changed at the weekend, I grabbed the chance to dash down the motorway early on Sunday and take some myself.'

'You've got a good eye.'

'Oh, I took hundreds of pictures. That one just leapt out at me.'

It was more than that, he thought, getting out the milk, keeping his hands busy. She'd taken the trouble to go back in her own time. Given it one hundred per cent... 'It's a pity the property pages didn't just stick to the photograph.'

'That was never going to happen. It was too good a story to pass up on and it was a fabulous PR opportunity. If Miles hadn't panicked...' She paused, as if something was bothering her.

'What? What would you have done?'

'Oh... Well, first I'd have got in a firm of cleaners at the firm's expense. Then I'd have invited the property editors to lunch at the Hadley Arms and, once I'd got them gagging at the perfect picture postcard village, I'd have driven them up to the house, slowly enough so that they could appreciate the view, that first glimpse as the house appears.'

'And then?'

'Well, obviously,' she said, 'I'd have got you an offer within the week.'

Her smile was bright and as brittle as spun sugar. He

wanted the real thing. Not just mouth and teeth, but those eyes lit up, glowing…

'Despite the dodgy staircase and the leaking roof?' he pressed.

She tutted but it earned him a hint of what her smile could be. 'It hasn't rained all week.'

'This hot spell can't last.'

'No, which is why we need to get cracking. Hadley Chase has so much *potential*,' she continued. 'I hadn't re- alised the extent of the outbuildings until I went down by myself. The stables, the dairy and how many houses have got a brewery, for heaven's sake?'

'It was standard for big houses back in the day, when drinking small beer was safer than water. It hasn't been used in my lifetime. Nor has the dairy.'

'Maybe not, but they're ripe for conversion into work- shops, holiday accommodation, offices. Miles isn't usually so slow…' She let it go, a tiny frown buckling the smooth skin between her brows. 'My mistake.'

'Surely it was his?'

'It's a little more complicated than that.'

She propped her elbow on the arm of the sofa, chin on hand, giving him another flash of her assets. By way of distraction, he picked up the cakebox and offered it to her.

'You do still want to sell the house?' she said as she leaned forward and did an eeny-meeny-miny-mo over the cakes with a dark red fingernail before choosing one.

Some distraction.

'I assumed you'd been sent by Morgan to persuade me to drop my suit,' he said, helping himself to another look straight down the front of her shirt. She was wearing one of those lace traffic-accident bras and all the blood in his brain went south.

She looked up when he didn't say any more. 'Do you still think that?'

Thinking? Who was thinking... He shook his head. 'No. You're pitching for the business.'

She looked up, no smile now, just determination. 'This isn't business, it's personal. What you do about Morgan and Black is your own affair, but my expertise won't cost you a penny.' She gave another of those little shrugs and, as she recrossed her legs, he switched from imperial to metric. A metre...

It had to be deliberate, but he didn't care.

'Of course, if you'd rather sit back and wait a year or two for the fuss to die down...?' she offered before biting into a small square of lemon drizzle cake, her teeth sinking into the softness of the sponge. White teeth, rose petal lips...

Forget the inner woman, he wanted to draw her naked, wanted to mould that luscious body in clay, learn the shape with his hands and then recreate it. Wanted to taste the tip of her tongue as it sought out the sugar clinging to her lip...

'You *might* be lucky,' she said, cucumber-cool, apparently unaware of the effect she was having or of the turmoil raging within him. 'It might be a big news week in the property business and they won't dredge up the story all over again. Reprint the original advertisement.' She finished the tiny square of cake, sucked the stickiness off a fingertip. It was deliberate and he discovered that he didn't care. Just as long as she went on doing it. 'I'll leave you to imagine how likely that is.'

'You seem to forget, Natasha, that I've seen your expertise at first hand.'

'What you've seen, Mr Hadley, is me being stitched up by a man who wanted the promotion I'd worked my socks off for without the bother of putting in the hours.' A fine rim of sugar, missed by her tongue, glistened on her upper lip.

'Darius,' he said, aware that a film of sweat had broken

out above his own lip. Whatever it was she was doing, it was working. 'Only my accountant calls me Mr Hadley.'

He expected her to come back with *your accountant and me*. Instead, she said, 'I'm sorry, Darius. When I said it was a bit more complicated than you thought, I meant really *complicated*.' She looked up, her eyes intent and just a touch desperate. 'The mess-up with the advertisement wasn't a mistake.'

'Not a mistake?'

'Not a mistake,' she repeated, 'but *I* was the target. You were just collateral damage.'

CHAPTER FOUR

'COLLATERAL…?' DARIUS REPEATED, rerunning what she'd said through his head. 'Are you saying this was all about some internal power play at Morgan and Black? That it was deliberate?'

'I really am sorry,' she repeated.

'Not half as sorry as I am.' Or Miles Morgan would be if it was true. 'Did he get it? Your promotion?'

A sigh of relief rippled through her. 'My promotion, my car and, as the icing on the cake, my reputation down the drain.'

The desperation had been fear, he realised. She'd been afraid that he would laugh out loud or call her a liar. The truth of the matter was that he didn't know what to think. It seemed preposterous and yet he'd already half convinced himself that she hadn't messed up the ad. Apparently Freddie Glover wasn't the only one susceptible to a pair of blue eyes and a great pair of—

'The kettle seems to have boiled. Shall I make the tea?' she asked.

'You did volunteer.' Tea was the furthest thing from his mind, but it gave them both a moment and, besides, he wanted to watch her move. The lift of her head, the unfolding of her legs, the muscles in a long shapely calf as she fought the clutches of the sofa. 'Why did he want to destroy your reputation?' he asked, reaching on automatic for his sketch pad, a pencil, working swiftly to capture the image. The lines of her neck, her shoulders as she clicked the kettle back on. Her back and legs as she bent to open the fridge. 'Wasn't your promotion enough?'

'There was no other way of being certain I'd be history,' she said, concentrating on opening a carton of milk. 'I'm really good at my job.'

After an initial wobble when she'd looked as if she wanted to tear his clothes off, Natasha Gordon was doing a very good job of presenting herself as a woman totally in control of her emotions but her eyes betrayed her. A pulse was visible at her throat and if he slid his hand inside the open invitation of her shirt, laid his palm against her breast, he knew he would feel her heart pounding with rage.

The pencil he was holding snapped…

'So are you looking for revenge?' he asked.

'I have my revenge,' she said, losing patience with the carton and jabbing the end of a spoon into the seal as if stabbing whoever had done this to her through the heart. Milk shot over the sleeve of her jacket and, embarrassed, she laughed. 'Okay, maybe I do have issues, but Miles Morgan was panicked into grabbing the first answer that presented itself. No doubt with a little prompting from…' Catching herself, she slipped off the jacket and used a piece of kitchen paper to mop the milk from her sleeve.

'From?'

Right at that moment he didn't much care about the who or the why, he simply wanted to keep her looking like that, and the stub of his pencil continued to work as she shook her head and a wisp of hair escaped the prim little knot, floating for a moment before settling against her cheek.

She frowned. 'I can't be sure. It all happened so fast… Someone had it all worked out in advance and knew exactly which buttons to press.' She pulled a face. 'There's nothing like a champagne celebration to show the world that it's business as usual.'

'Does this someone have a name? I'm sure my lawyer would like to know.'

'No doubt, but I'm not here to help you bring them down,' she said. Nevertheless, the tiny frown persisted. She wanted answers, too.

'So you do want your job back,' he pushed.

'That's not going to happen.'

'You won't work for the man who took your job?'

She shrugged, managed a smile of sorts. 'Never say never. Who knows how desperate I'll get…? How do you like your tea?' she asked, glancing across at him. 'Weak, medium, stand up your spoon…' She stopped. 'Are you drawing me?'

'Yes. Do you mind?'

'I'm not sure.'

'I'll stop if you insist,' he said. 'And strong. Dash of milk. No sugar. You think Morgan will regret it?' he asked, dragging his gaze from his contemplation of her long upper lip just long enough to commit it to paper. 'Grabbing the easy option?'

'Who knows? Toby's bright enough, but he's never allowed work to interfere with his weekends on the rugby field. He's always put that first. To be honest, I never thought he was that interested in property sales and management. I had the impression that his family had pushed him into the day job.'

Toby. He logged the name to look up later. 'I'm surprised he got the job at all if that's his attitude.'

'His great-aunt is married to Peter Black.'

'Oh.'

'He's just turned twenty-three,' she said thoughtfully. 'Maybe he's realised he's not going to get a professional contract.'

'He lost his dream so stole yours? It demonstrates a ruthless streak. That's vital in business, or so I'm told.'

'It's a trait he kept well hidden. I still find it hard to believe…' She shrugged, letting whatever it was she found hard to believe go. 'Lazy and ruthless is a bad combination, Darius. Would you want him at your back in a crisis? More to the point, would you want to work for a man who'd thrown you to the wolves without a proper hearing? Without any kind of investigation? Forget Toby Denton. He might have my promotion, but it'll always be second best as far as he's concerned. It's Miles I can't forgive. It'll be a cold day in hell before I work for him again.'

'Never say never,' he reminded her and got a reprise of the smile for his pains.

'Maybe if he offered me a full partnership,' she said, 'which is undoubtedly his version of a cold day in hell at the moment.'

'Okay, I get it. It's not going to happen, but if you don't want revenge,' he asked, 'and you don't want your job back, what do you want?'

Natasha's shoulders dropped a fraction. Darius knew that he'd asked the right question, but didn't know whether to kick himself or cheer as her lips softened into the smile he'd asked for. The one that reached her eyes.

His body was divided on the issue; his brain was definitely up for the kicking while the rest of him was responding like a Labrador puppy offered a biscuit.

While he distracted himself by capturing her mouth on paper, Natasha cupped her hands around her warm mug, leaned her hip against the arm of the sofa, making herself at home.

'A week ago I could have walked into any real estate agency in London and been offered a job,' she said. 'Since I've become available, my phone has remained ominously silent.'

'Are you surprised?'

'No, and I haven't embarrassed anyone by reminding them of their generous offers.'

'I'm sure they're all extremely grateful for your tact,' he said, unable to resist a smile of his own. Forget the allure of a body made for sin, he was beginning to like Natasha Gordon. She'd just had the feet knocked out from under her but she'd come up fighting.

'I don't imagine they've given me a second thought. I'm history, Darius. I'll have to restore my hard-earned reputation before anyone will give me the time of day.' She paused, evidently hoping he'd chip in at this point. He drew the line of her jaw. Firm, determined... 'The only way I can do that is by selling Hadley Chase,' she said, offering him the opportunity to help her out.

'Then you really are in trouble.'

'That makes two of us,' she said, taking a sip of her tea. 'I admit that it will require a certain amount of ingenuity and imagination to pull it off, but who has a bigger incentive?' She looked sideways at him, blinking as she caught him staring at her, but this time she didn't look away. 'Who would work harder to find you a buyer?' she asked. 'And for nothing?' she added as a final incentive.

'For nothing? You'll be drummed out of the estate agents guild,' he warned.

Her lips twitched into another of those little smiles. Parts of him twitched involuntarily in response. His head didn't have a chance.

'Believe me, it's a once-in-a-lifetime offer. What have you got to lose?' Energy, excitement at the challenge poured off her in an almost physical wave. 'We're a match made in heaven.'

He shook his head, afraid that he'd already lost it. He shouldn't even be having the conversation. The lawyers would have a fit.

'An estate agent no one will employ and a house no one can sell? That sounds more like hell to me,' he said, but he was unable to stop himself from laughing. She was bright, intelligent and, under other circumstances—the uncompli-cated, no strings, hot sex circumstances—would no doubt be a lot of fun. Unfortunately, this was getting more com-plicated by the moment.

'I'm not promising heaven,' she protested, 'but it won't be hell. Honestly.'

That he could believe… 'I bet you say that to all the poor saps trying to sell a house in a recession.'

'I do my best to give it to them straight,' she replied. 'And I do everything I can to help them to make the best of the property they're selling. That's my job.'

'Paint it magnolia and hide the clutter in the cupboards?' he suggested.

'Getting rid of the clutter so that you can open the cup-boards is better. Storage space is a big selling point.' She looked at him over the mug. 'Giving the place a good clean helps. Brushing out the dead leaves. Fixing broken win-dows.'

He frowned. 'Are you telling me that there's a broken window at the Chase?'

'You didn't know? I did point it out to your caretaker. He said he'd mention it to the executors.'

And they hadn't bothered to mention it to him. Well, he'd made his position clear enough. Not interested…

'Look, I'm not pretending that it's going to be easy,' she said. 'You're not selling a well-kept four-bed detached house in an area with good schools.'

'I wouldn't need you if I was.'

It was an admission that he did need her and they both knew it.

'What I'm promising, Darius, is that you won't have to be personally involved in any way.' She reached out a sympathetic hand, but curled her fingers back before it touched his arm. Even so, his skin tightened at the imperceptible movement of air and the shiver of it went right through him. 'I do understand how difficult this must be for you.'

'I doubt it.' Nobody could ever begin to understand how he felt about the Chase. The complex mix of memories, emotions it evoked.

'No, of course not, but Hadley Chase has been in your family for centuries. I can see how it must hurt to be the one who has to let it go.'

'Is that what you think?' he asked, looking up from those curled-up fingers, challenging her. 'That I'm ashamed because I've failed to hold on to it?'

'No! Of course not.' The blush flooded back to her cheeks. 'Why should you be? This is the fault of preceding generations.' The possibility that by criticising his recent ancestors she might be digging an even bigger hole for herself must have crossed her mind and she moved swiftly on. 'I'll do everything possible to make this as painless as possible,' she promised. 'All you have to do is let the caretaker and your lawyer know that I'll be handling things on your behalf, then you needn't give it another thought.'

This time his laugh was forced, painful. 'If you could guarantee that you'd have a deal.'

'I can guarantee that I won't disturb you again without a very good reason,' she assured him.

Too late. Natasha Gordon was the most disturbing woman he'd ever met, but the Chase was a millstone around his neck, a darkness at the heart of his family, his grandfather's last-ditch attempt to regain control of a world he'd once dominated, ruled. To control the future. To control him. The sooner he was rid of it, the burden lifted, the better.

'Suppose I agree to let you loose on it,' he said, as if it wasn't already a done deal, 'do you have a plan?'

'A plan?'

'You don't have an advertising budget,' he pointed out, 'or a shop window for passers-by to browse in, or even a listing in the *Yellow Pages*.'

'No, but I do have the Internet, social media.'

Oh, shit…

'Did you say something?'

Not out loud, he was almost certain, but his reaction had been so strong that she had undoubtedly read his mind. 'You can't use my name,' he warned, gesturing around the studio, 'or any of this to generate publicity.' This was his world. He had created it. No one else. He wouldn't have it touched by his family or the Chase.

'It'll be a low-key approach,' she assured him, far too easily. 'Nothing flashy, nothing to embarrass you. You have my word.'

'Your word, in this instance, is worthless. Once it's on the Net you'll lose control.'

'Only if I get it right.'

'Is that supposed to reassure me?'

She frowned, obviously confused by his attitude. 'It's just a house, Darius.'

She was wrong, but he couldn't expect her to understand his love/hate relationship with the place. With his family. 'You've got all the answers,' he said dismissively.

She shook her head. 'If I had all the answers, I wouldn't be here,' she said, 'I'd be at Morgan and Black, lining up viewings with the property managers of the kind of men and women who can afford to buy and maintain an English country house to use for two or three weeks in the year. During the shooting season,' she added, in case he didn't get the point, 'or maybe for Christmas and the New Year, before they move on to Gstaad or Aspen for the skiing.'

'That's…'

'Yes?'

'Nothing.'

He shouldn't care who bought it, or how little they used it… He didn't. And he had no reason to trust her, or to believe that she'd lost her job for anything other than sheer incompetence. Only the fact that Miles Morgan had lied about a breakdown, publicly humiliating her in a way that even if she had been grossly negligent would still have been unforgivable. And that he'd disliked the man on sight.

What Natasha Gordon had done to him on sight was something else. The fact that he wasn't thinking with his brain was reason enough to stay well clear of any harebrained idea she came up with, but the Revenue would not wait forever for the inheritance tax he would have to pay on the estate. The truth of the matter was that he couldn't afford to wait until the fuss died down.

'Okay.'

Tash was used to being looked at. She had no illusions about being any kind of a beauty, but—cosseted and nurtured on all that was good and nourishing by a mother who'd nearly lost her—she'd developed from a skin-and-bones kid into an unfashionably curved lushness that men seemed to find irresistible.

She'd quickly learned to keep both flirtatious vendors and buyers at a distance, but Darius Hadley had not flirted with her. The connection was something else, something visceral, and now he was looking at her with an intensity that heated her to the bone.

With each stroke of his pencil on the paper she became increasingly conscious of her body. Every line he drew felt like a fingertip stroked across her skin. It was as if she was coming undone; not just her top button, but every part of her was unravelling as she became exposed to him.

Far from keeping her distance, she'd barely stopped herself from reaching out, laying her hand on the solid muscle of his arm, sliding a finger along the dark hair gathered in a line along his forearm. But one touch would never be enough; it would be lighting the blue touchpaper, setting off a chain reaction that nothing could stop. And the problem with that was…?

'Did you hear me? I said okay.'

'Okay?' The breath hitched in her throat as she repeated the word. He'd agreed? 'Is that okay as in yes?' she asked. 'You'll give me a chance?'

There was a seemingly endless pause and for a moment he seemed to be somewhere else. Possibly thinking of all the reasons why it was a bad idea. What his lawyer would say. It would undoubtedly compromise his case against Morgan and Black…

'A conditional yes.'

Uh-oh…

'I'll give you a chance to sell Hadley Chase on one condition.'

'Anything,' she said.

'You're that desperate?' he asked, with a look that warned her she should have asked what condition.

'Anything that's legal, decent and honest,' she said, scarcely daring to breathe. Make that legal and honest. She was prepared to negotiate on decent…

'Desperate, but not stupid.'

Probably… 'What is it?'

'I want you to sit for me.'

'Sit?' For a moment she couldn't think what he meant but, as he continued to look at her, hold her fixed to the spot with no more than the power of his gaze, she knew exactly what he meant.

Her mouth dried and her hand fluttered from her shoulder to somewhere around her thigh in a gesture that took in all the important bits in between.

'As in *sit*?' she asked. 'Pose? Model for you?'

'If you're asking whether I'd want you naked, the answer is yes,' he said bluntly. 'It's your body that I want to draw, not your clothes.'

'Oh…' She blinked as a rush of blood heated her skin, her lips, and something deep within her liquefied. Appalled by how much she wanted to do it, she curled her fingers into her palms to stop herself from reaching for her buttons right then and there.

Misunderstanding her silence, he said, 'You're asking me to take you on trust, Natasha. That's a two-way deal.'

'Trust is important,' she agreed, 'but the thing is, I'm not asking you to take your clothes off.'

'I will if it will make it easier for you,' he said.

'Yes… No!' What on earth was she thinking? It was outrageous. She should be outraged, not tingling with excitement at the thought of exposing her ample curves to his molten gaze. So much for keeping this professional… 'Would you have asked if I was a man?'

He shrugged. 'Possibly. The right man, one with more than good muscle definition to commend him, and, like you, Natasha, he would have assumed I wanted more than a model.'

'I'm assuming nothing,' she declared, despite the betraying heat lighting up her cheeks that an artist, a man who saw more than most, would pick up in an instant, 'but I've just been handed a very painful lesson about mixing business with pleasure.' He said nothing so she continued. 'My fault. I broke the work/life balance golden rule.'

'With Morgan?' he asked.

'Miles? Good grief, no!'

'Then it has to be Toby Denton, the guy who's occupying your desk, driving your car. Did he get a hat-trick?'

'I'm sorry?'

'Did he break your heart, too?'

'Oh… No…' She shook her head. 'We didn't have that kind of a relationship.'

'What was it like?'

'A bit like a starter home,' she said. 'Something you know you're going to grow out of sooner rather than later. I was too busy for anything serious and, while he might look like perfect boyfriend material, there aren't many women who will play second fiddle to a rugby ball. The occasional night out, plus one do, sleepover suited us both.'

'Colleagues with benefits? It was still a betrayal.'

'Yes.' Worse, she would never know whether it had been a spur-of-the-moment thing or planned from the start and she had been duped, taken for a fool.

'Well, thanks for the vote of confidence,' he said after a moment, 'but sitting isn't a pleasure. It's uncomfortable, tedious, muscle-aching work. And you're right. Business and pleasure is a bad combination. Good models are hard to find, which is why I don't complicate the relationship with sex.'

'Does that mean…' She stopped. Of course it did. He'd just said so. Which was good. Really good. 'Can I see?' she asked, holding out her hand for the sketch pad, no longer so knicker-wettingly eager to get her kit off. 'What you've drawn?'

He handed it over without a word and she studied the small details he'd put down with little more than the stroke of a pencil.

Her mouth, fuller, sexier than she'd ever seen in the mirror when she'd grabbed a second to slide lipstick over it. The curve of her neck emerging from her collar, the line of her leg, her skirt stretched across her backside as she'd bent to search the fridge for milk—it was definitely time to get on the treadmill. Her eyes, giving away the feelings that vibrated through her whenever she looked at him.

'I understand why some primitive people thought the

camera stole away their soul,' she said, shaken by what he'd seen in those few moments, fixed on paper with so few lines. How much more would he see if he was being serious? She would be utterly exposed—and not just because she'd be stripped to her skin. 'It's not what I was expecting.'

Darius leaned back against the stepladder, folding his arms. 'Did you imagine I was drawing your internal organs?'

She swallowed, managed a wry smile. 'Well, that is more your style. This is just me.'

'What's on the surface. The image you show the world. I'll go deeper.'

'You won't find much muscle definition,' she warned him.

'You have a lot of everything, Natasha.'

'I was sick as a kid,' she said. 'My mother spent my childhood trying to fatten me up. I ran away from home to escape the egg custard.' She glanced up at the skeletal horse, then at the sketch pad, flipping back through the pages to see what else was there—anything to avoid looking at him, betray her eagerness for him to draw her, sculpt her—and discovered that every page was filled with drawings of her. Far more than he could have done in a few minutes. 'I don't understand. You couldn't have done all this today.'

'No.' His face was expressionless.

'But the other day… You only saw me for a minute or two and this is—'

'I've only scratched the surface.'

The room seemed to darken as their gazes locked, acknowledging the raw, subliminal connection in that moment when they'd faced one another across Morgan's office.

A shiver ran through her and she closed her eyes. When she opened them again, the sun was pouring in through the skylights and Darius was still waiting for her answer. He knew it would be yes…

'Will I be a limited edition bronze?' she asked. 'On display in a gallery window? Like the horse.'

'It's possible. If your interior lives up to the promise of the packaging.'

'My packaging!'

'It's very attractive packaging.'

'An excessive amount of packaging, I think you just said. Will you give me a couple of months to shed ten pounds?'

'Don't even think about it,' he said, taking the pad from her. 'Are you concerned that you'll be recognised?'

'Recognised?' The tension evaporated as she laughed at the idea of any of his subjects being recognised in the finished sculpture. 'Unlikely, I'd have thought.' She hoped. If anyone found out, she knew what interpretation they'd put on it. 'I might have to make it a condition.'

'It's all about trust,' he said, not joining in, and for a moment she was afraid that she'd offended him. 'So? Do you have any more problems?'

Problems?

Only one. The fact that she was more interested in the man than his house. She'd forgotten why she was here, that her future depended on getting this right. That problem.

'How about the fact that you'll be making money out of your side of the bargain while I'll be working for nothing?' she suggested in an attempt to bring them both back to the reason she was here.

'We might both be wasting our time, Natasha,' he said, pushing away from the stepladder, suddenly much too close. 'But if I discover depths in you that are worth exploring I'll…' His eyes suggested that his thoughts were a long way from art.

'Yes?' The word was thick in her throat. Not just his thoughts—her own were on a much lower plane…

'I'll give you a first casting.'

'So that I can put my "depths" on the sideboard for everyone I know to look at?'

'You'll love every minute of it,' he said. 'All those horny men running their hands over cold bronze, imagining the warm, living flesh.'

'No…' There was only one man she wanted running his hands over her flesh and he was right there, in front of her.

'Every woman longs for something in her past with which to scandalise her grandchildren,' he said. His face was all shadows, his eyes leaden, his voice so soft that it was barely audible.

'How would you know that?' she whispered.

He lifted his hand in what felt like slow motion and grazed her cheek with the roughened tips of his fingers and, as he drew them down the line of her jaw, a jolt went through her body as if it had been jump-started.

Her nipples tightened, puckering visibly beneath the heavy silk of her shirt, sending twin arrows of heat to the apex of her thighs, a bead of sweat trickled down her back and Darius, his thumb teasing the corner of her mouth, smiled darkly.

Question asked and answered.

She was finding it difficult to breathe, speech was beyond her; they both knew that she couldn't wait to have her depths thoroughly explored in every conceivable way, so she did the only thing left to her.

He didn't take his eyes from her face as she slipped the tiny pearl buttons of her shirt one by one until the silk parted and then, her eyes never leaving his, her parted lips swollen, burning, she turned her head to suck his thumb into her mouth.

Her tongue swirled around it, licking it, tasting clay and cake, sugar and something spicy that hadn't come out of a jar. She whimpered when he took it from her. Whimpered again when he dragged its moist, broad pad across her lips.

'Shush...' he murmured and there was a moment of perfect stillness when the world centred on that small contact, balanced on a knife-edge. Then he slowly lowered his mouth to hers, retraced the path of his thumb with his tongue and she nearly fainted from the hot burst of pleasure that flooded through her. It was only his arm supporting her that kept her on her feet as her lips parted and his tongue embarked on a meltingly slow dance of exploration.

She reached for him, cradling his head as the kiss deepened and her senses were bombarded from all directions. His hair tangled in her fingers, stubble tickled her palms. The scent of metal and clay and the oiled wooden handles of the tools he used clung to him, earthy and elemental. His hands tugged her shirt from her waistband and slid up her back, his thumbs nudged her breasts. The hard bulge of his erection butted into her hip.

He leaned back to look at her as he swept aside silk and lace, his calloused fingers lifting her breasts free of her bra, grazing the tender skin. And then his tongue swept over the rock-hard tip of her breast and her knees buckled.

There was a crash as he swept bones, tools aside and, without apparent effort, lifted her bodily onto the bench.

Yes...

The word spiralled through her, triumphant, exhilarating, liberating. She might have shouted it, but all she could hear was the sound of blood pounding in her ears as her pulse went off the scale. All she could feel was the heat of his mouth trailing moist kisses down her throat, his teeth, razor stubble grazing the swollen, sensitive skin of her breast, his suckling tongue sending a lightning bolt to her throbbing, swollen core.

'Darius...' It was a breathless, desperate plea and his hand was between her thighs, pushing aside the flimsy barrier to greet the liquid fire that flashed to meet first one and then two of those deliciously long fingers driving into her.

She reared to meet them, wanting more, demanding more as the furnace, lit in the very first moment she'd set eyes on him, hit meltdown. She'd wanted it then, wanted it as she'd beaten butter and sugar into submission, wanted him inside her...

She clutched at hard shoulders, her nails digging into his flesh through the soft cloth of his shirt as his knuckle hit the sweet, screaming spot. She had no breath to scream, urge him on; all she could do was make small desperate sounds as she arched upwards, demanding more, as he made her wait, taking his time, stroking, tormenting, teasing her throat, her breasts, her stomach with his teeth, his tongue, keeping her on the limit of endurance with his fingers, the subtle pressure of his thumb until her body, lost in bliss, slipped from her control and became entirely his. Only then did he release her in a shattering orgasm that went through her like a tornado, lifting, spinning, dumping her dazed, slicked with sweat and clinging to him like a life raft.

Her head was a dead weight against his shoulder, her limbs like sun-warmed putty, and if he hadn't been holding her she would have slithered to the floor in a boneless heap.

CHAPTER FIVE

FOR A LONG moment the only things moving in the room were dust motes dancing in the sunlight streaming in from above. Then Darius eased back a little.

'Are you okay?' he asked.

Okay? *Okay*?

'Give me a minute to locate my bones and I'll let you know.'

'Hang on…' He slid an arm beneath her knees and, lifting her clear of the bench, carried her to the sofa.

'Mmm…' She let out a contented sigh as she stretched out on the cushions, looking up at him from beneath lids too heavy to lift. She reached for his belt, planning to hook her fingers under it and pull him closer so that she could get at that deliciously flat belly beneath the baggy T-shirt, do a little nibbling on her own account. Ease the pressure of what had to be a very painful bulge against the zip of his jeans.

He caught her, wrapping his hand around her wrist, keeping her from her goal.

His eyes were burning her up and he held her tightly for a moment before, with a visible effort, he released her and then, taking care not to let his fingers touch her skin, lifted the lace of her bra and carefully replaced it over her breasts.

'Darius?'

He didn't answer but began to refasten her shirt buttons

with all the concentration of a bomb disposal officer defusing an unexploded bomb. One wrong move, one touch…

'What are you doing?' she demanded. Then, as the reality began to sink in, 'No…'

'I work here, Natasha, and I meant it when I said I don't have sex with my models.'

'I'm not a model…'

'No.' A faint smile tugged at the corner of his mouth. 'A professional model would never undress in front of an artist but, unless you're carrying a stash of condoms in that bag, we're done.'

The implication that she went to work armed and ready for action was like a bucket of cold water. Did he think she did that with everyone who needed a little encouragement to use her services?

Well, why wouldn't he? He knew she was desperate—desperate enough to sit naked so that he could draw her.

She'd completely lost the plot, forgotten that this was just business…

'Sorry,' she said, swinging her legs to the floor and forcing him to step back. 'You're not the only one who doesn't get down and dirty on the job,' she said, frustration making her snippy. 'Sex with a client is definitely off the agenda.'

'Just as well I'm not a client, then. Unless you've changed your mind about waiving your fee for selling the Chase?'

'No,' she said. 'A deal's a deal. I'll settle for the perks.'

'Perks?'

'The chunk of bronze to go on the mantelpiece, the hand job. Thanks for that, by the way; it's been too long…' The words were out before her brain was engaged… 'Give me a call when you want me to strip naked for you,' she added, putting some stiffeners in her legs so that she could stand up. Get out of there. 'You'll find my number inside the lid of the cakebox.'

'Most people find a business card more convenient,' he

said, flipping it open and glancing at the label on which she'd printed her name, telephone number and email address as he searched for a phone amongst the scattered tools and bones on his workbench and programmed in the number. 'You can carry more than one at a time.'

'Unfortunately, my card is out of date and since I had no way of knowing if you'd listen to me...' She swallowed. He'd done a lot more than listen and she'd done a lot more than talk. 'In my experience, men don't throw away home-made cake, no matter where it's come from.'

'You were confident that once I'd tasted it I'd want more?'

The scent of sex hung in the air as thick as paint and they both knew that the taste he was referring to had nothing to do with confectionery.

No, no, no... 'Oh, please!' she said. 'When I have all those horny men queuing up at my front door for my lemon drizzle.'

Take that, Mr Hadley...

'Really?' He sucked on the tip of his thumb. 'Personally, I prefer my sugar light on the lemon, heavy on the spice.' A hot flush raced from her navel to her scalp as she realised that he was tasting her. 'Sticky ginger...' he said, volley intercepted and returned. Point won... 'I've sent you my number. In case you run into any problems.'

'Problems. Right.' There wouldn't be any problems. She'd make sure of that. But first she had to get out of here before she spontaneously combusted.

Jacket...

Where was it?

She looked around, knowing that she should be grateful that she wasn't crawling around on her hands and knees looking for her underwear.

She should.

Really.

Darius spotted her jacket lying on the floor beside the sofa and, beating Natasha to it, scooped it up. She took a nervous step back, keeping him at arm's length. She was mad at him. The condom remark had been crass, deliberately so—a bucket of cold water on an overheated situation that had got out of hand. Unfortunately, all it had done was create steam. They were both still on a hair trigger and playing Russian roulette which was why, instead of following her excellent example and tossing it to her, he shook her jacket out and held it up, inviting her to turn around and slide her arms into the sleeves.

She could have ignored him, said she'd carry it, but after the slightest hesitation she turned, holding her arms towards him so that he could ease it on. She smelled of spice and sex and, with a groan he couldn't stifle, he slid his hands down from her shoulders to cup her lovely breasts, pulling her against him while he breathed a kiss against her neck. She leaned back into him with a whimper that was half despair, half bliss and for a moment he just held her, before summoning the willpower to give her a gentle push towards the door.

'Go,' he said.

She turned in his arms and looked up at him, her eyes liquid, appealing.

'Now,' he said, his forehead touching hers, her breasts brushing against his chest. He was wood and there was nothing he could do about it. 'Please.'

She took a breath. 'Right. Yes… This was so not what I intended.' She took a step back, picked up her bag, made it as far as the door, then paused. 'I won't bother you again until I have some news.'

'I won't be holding my breath.'

Wrong on both counts.

He'd been bothered the minute he'd set eyes on her. Unable to get her out of his mind. And breathless ever since she'd walked into his studio with that mesmerising sway of her hips.

'How will you get there?' he asked. A tiny frown puckered her smooth forehead. 'The Chase. Now that the devious Denton is driving your Beemer?'

'Oh…' She shook her head, as if clearing it. 'I'll hire something.'

'A waste of money. You'd be better off putting a deposit on a van,' he said. 'That way you can put your name on the side and use it as free advertising. Sell the house and I'll design you a logo.'

Things were safer than feelings…

'If I sell the house,' she pointed out, 'I won't need one.'

'If you sell the house, Natasha, you won't need to work for anyone else. It won't only be eager estate agents, and horny men pining for you, but desperate vendors who'll be beating a path to your door.'

'Thanks, but self-employment doesn't figure in my five-year career plan.'

'I think we've established that right now you don't have a career or a plan.'

'The career is temporarily on hold. The plan is a work in progress,' she said and, as if to underline the fact that—perks notwithstanding—this was strictly business, she offered him her hand.

Despite the danger to his simmering libido, he was unable to resist taking it. Small, soft, with perfectly groomed nails, it lay like a touch of velvet against his clay-roughened palm evoking X-rated thoughts and he needed to get her out of his studio before common sense went to hell in a hand basket.

'Please go,' he said.

Her lips parted as if she was going to say something. Clearly she thought better of it and, having opened the door, she stepped through into the street and closed it behind her without another word.

He slipped the latch before Patsy decided to pop in and give him the third degree, leaning his forehead against it while he called the estate executor to update him on the situation.

Brian Ramsey spluttered and protested at the inappropriateness of allowing Natasha access to the house, but Darius cut him short.

'You chose Morgan and Black to handle the sale. They messed up,' he said. 'Now we'll do it my way. Please make sure that Gary Webb is available tomorrow to let her in.'

'Mr Webb is on sick leave and really, in the light of recent events, I have to insist that Miss Gordon is accompanied by someone responsible. Tell her that if she comes in the office later this week I'll check the diary and see when someone is available.'

Oh, right. Next month some time. Maybe. This was the man who'd conspired with his grandfather to ensure that a Hadley remained at the Chase for another generation.

'What's the matter with Gary?' he asked.

'He had a fall.'

Tash walked away on legs that were all over the place, her stomach churning with every kind of emotion imaginable.

She needed to sit down. Needed coffee. Ice cream...

For heaven's sake, she was a grown-up and smart enough to know that leaping on a man you barely knew was never going to end well, especially when it was supposed to be strictly business. *Especially* when her entire life plan depended on it being strictly business.

What on earth had she been thinking?

Scratch that. No one had been thinking, least of all her. Apparently she still wasn't because she couldn't wait for the return match and next time she'd have more than cake in her bag…

She was grinning, helplessly, at the thought when her phone began to ring. She checked the number, ultra cautious since her name had been plastered all over the evening papers. Journalists might believe that she was safely tucked up out of harm's way in the Fairview where they couldn't get at her, but it hadn't stopped them trying her number, leaving sympathetic messages, wanting her side of the story. As if she was going to fall for that.

It wasn't a journalist. It was Darius.

'Text me your address,' he said, before her brain could unscramble itself and deliver a simple hello.

'Excuse me?'

'The caretaker is in hospital and the legal lot insist that you're accompanied by a responsible adult.'

'That's very, um, responsible of them.' She'd bet the house that wasn't all they'd said. They would have had a dozen good reasons why he should pull out of their deal. Given a minute, she could probably come up with at least that many herself. But he hadn't… 'What's the matter with Mr Grumpy?'

'He fell off a ladder. Broken leg, broken wrist, bruises.'

'Oh…' How to go from feeling great to feeling about two inches high in ten seconds. 'I'm so sorry.' And she was. He'd been a grouch but he didn't deserve that. 'Is he going to be okay?' Then, as an awful thought struck her, she said, 'He wasn't trying to fix that window, was he?'

'Is that a guilty conscience I can hear, Miss Gordon?' Darius asked. 'Maybe you should take him some of your cake.'

'Darius!'

He laughed. 'Relax, Sugarlips. This is not your fault—he was clearing a blocked gutter at the village hall, but you're right, it needs fixing. I'll get it sorted.'

Sugarlips? Oh, cripes…

'I could arrange that for you,' she offered, doing her best not to think about what had made him pick on that particular endearment. She should definitely not think about him sucking the tip of his thumb. She could still taste him, smell him on her… 'I have a first-class honours degree in estate management.'

'Well, bully for you. Call the National Trust; maybe they'll give you a job.'

'They did,' she said. 'I turned it down.'

There was a brief silence which told her that she'd finally managed to surprise him, then he said, 'I'll pick you up at eight tomorrow morning.'

'You?'

'I'm the only responsible adult available at short notice.'

'Oh…' Her heart, already going like the clappers, hit warp speed.

'Of course you could wait for Brian Ramsey to find some free time in his diary but he isn't particularly happy with my choice of sales agent so he won't be in any hurry.'

'No, thanks. I talked to Brian Ramsey about cleaning up the house. He was barely polite when I was representing an agency he had engaged.'

'Then I'll see you tomorrow. You can bring lunch.'

'Blokes do windows, women do food?'

'You could take me to the pub if you'd prefer, but I was thinking of your budget.'

'A picnic it is. Any allergies?' she asked. 'Anything you won't eat?'

'Just save the wussy lemon cake for your legions of admirers. You know what I like.'

He disconnected before she could reply and Tash had to fight the insane urge to run back to the studio and write her address in lipstick on his sketch pad. On his chest. Across his stomach…

'Are you all right, dear?' A woman waiting for the bus was looking up at her with concern.

'Um… Yes… Thank you.' She sat down on the bench beside her, flapped her shirt collar to create a bit of breeze around her face. 'I've just, um… It's a bit warm, isn't it?'

Darius was at the door on the dot of eight and despite a sleepless night—or maybe because of it—Tash was waiting for him. No short skirt, no dangerous buttons with a mind of their own, no sexy high heels. Today she was kitted out in a pair of comfortable jeans, a baggy T-shirt and a pair of running shoes, bought when she'd decided to get a grip on her weight and decided to go running with Toby. Once had been enough and any wear on the soles was down to the occasional dash to the corner shop for emergency baking supplies.

Her laptop bag was ready for business, lunch was packed; she hadn't left herself with a single excuse to delay so that she would have to invite him up while she gathered her stuff. No excuse to offer him coffee, or invite him to try the spiced cookies she'd been baking at three that morning.

There was work to do, her career to save, Hadley Chase to sell and when he buzzed from the front entrance she was ready to go.

Strictly business.

She ran down the stairs, swung through the door…

Oh, good grief.

He didn't say anything when she skidded to a stop on the pavement and the casual *hi* that she'd been mentally rehearsing died on her lips at the sight of him leaning back against the door of an elderly Land Rover.

If the vehicle was well past its prime, Darius, in a black polo shirt and faded denims that clung to his thighs, was looking like every kind of sin she'd ever wanted to commit.

He was just so damned beautiful that every one of her

nerve endings sent out a 'touch me' tingle and she was seriously wishing she'd gone for a shirt with unreliable buttons and a bra that pushed her boobs up to her chin. He might keep a poker face when he was looking down her cleavage but she knew exactly what he was thinking. Right now she hadn't a clue.

She'd run through this moment over and over as she was taking a shower, picking out what to wear for exploring a dusty old house, cutting sandwiches. Imagining what he'd say, what he'd do. Rehearsing every possible combination of responses.

Would it be a curt let's-forget-what-happened nod? Eminently sensible…

Her heart had skipped a little beat at the prospect of a let's-think-about-this kiss on the cheek. Sensible but with possibilities…

Or please, please, please, a let's-do-it kiss that would buckle her knees and have her melting on the pavement.

None of the above.

He kept his distance, one eyebrow slightly raised as he took in her passion-damping clothes, her hair fastened in a single plait that was held together with nothing sexier than an elastic band. Then, just when she thought it was safe to breathe, he reached out, ran his thumb over her mouth and said, 'Good morning, Sugarlips.'

His low, sexy voice vibrated against her breastbone and the carrier containing their lunch slipped through her fingers and hit the pavement.

An annoying little smile lifted the corner of his mouth as he straightened and opened the passenger door. 'I hope there was nothing breakable in there.'

'The flask is well padded, but I don't suppose it will have done the cake much good,' she replied before, blushing like an idiot, she scrambled up into the passenger seat, leaving him to pick it up.

She concentrated on fastening her seat belt as he climbed in beside her, filling the space with his presence, his earthy scent mingling with the smell of hot oil.

Her fingers were shaking so much that he took her hand, unpeeled her fingers from it and clicked it home.

'It was a bit stiff...'

'I know how it feels.'

She tried not to look, but was unable to help herself. Oh, cripes...

'I'm sorry the transport doesn't meet your usual standard of comfort,' he said, leaning forward to start the engine, ignoring the tension twanging the air between them; presumably a man who spent his life around naked women posing on a pedestal would have had plenty of practice.

She made an effort to focus her thoughts elsewhere. On the house with the puce living room that had been on the market for months and the owner's outrage when she'd suggested that a quick coat of magnolia might help...

Her breathing slowed, the pulse pounding in her throat became a gentle thud.

Better.

'No problem,' she said. 'As you pointed out, I'm working this job economy class.'

'You've got it,' he said, a wry smile creating a crease in his cheek and undoing all that effort. Fortunately the Land Rover, vibrating noisily, covered the shiver that rippled through her.

'So, what's the plan?' he said.

'Plan?'

'I assumed you'd been up half the night working on your plan to find a buyer for the Chase.'

'It shows, huh?' The expensive stuff that was supposed to conceal dark shadows round the eyes clearly wasn't doing the job.

'Just guessing,' he said, ratcheting up the smile, and

the swarm of butterflies in her stomach, which until then had at least been flying in close formation, went haywire.

Think about that hideous purple and yellow bathroom...

'Nearly right,' she managed. 'I was up half the night creating a media presence for Hadley Chase on Facebook and Twitter.'

Nearly right. Nearly true. She'd done that within half an hour of getting home. The major time had been spent finding and following media types—and the people they followed—journalists, the local Berkshire newspapers and county magazine. Anyone who had an interest in country houses, property, local history, social history. Anyone who might conceivably be interested in following Hadley Chase.

She'd spent the rest of the night trying to come up with a really convincing reason why she should call him and cancel. She needed to keep her distance, keep it professional.

She also needed to get to Hadley Chase this week, rather than at the convenience of a lawyer who thought she was poison, so here she was, on the dot of eight o'clock, her brain out to lunch and her stomach throwing a butterfly party while she drooled over the man.

Forget strictly business. She should have lured him up to her flat and invited him to shag her brains out. Maybe then she'd be able to concentrate on the job in hand.

He glanced back over his shoulder, giving his attention to the traffic. Giving her a moment to catch her breath.

She focused on the memory of a house with an orange front door. And that had been the best bit. A kitchen with every tile on both walls and floor a different colour. Heard herself saying, 'So jolly...'

Maybe he wasn't as cool as he looked either and needed a moment of his own because he didn't press her on the plan. Which was just as well. She wasn't getting paid so she couldn't afford to throw money at the problem; she was going to have to be inventive.

'How's Mr Gr…er…Gary?' she said, raising her voice above the noise of the engine when the silence had gone on too long.

'Comfortable, according to the nurse I spoke to.'

'I'm really sorry.'

'Not half as sorry as he is, I suspect.'

'I meant I'm sorry that you have to do this. You didn't want to be involved. In the sale.'

They were stopped in traffic and he looked across at her as if unsure how to answer her. His eyes were liquid silver in the morning sunlight, with a hint of steely blue. Then someone hooted impatiently from behind and once they were rattling along the motorway the noise of the engine, the tyres, the trucks rushing past, made anything but the most urgent conversation impossible.

Tash made an effort to focus on the problem ahead—she had no illusions about the Chase being an easy sell—but she was sitting within inches of Darius Hadley. Sunlight was glinting over the steel wristband of his watch, drawing attention to the hand wrapped lightly around the steering wheel, the fingers that had been inside her, driving her wild with pleasure less than twenty-four hours ago.

Who could focus on anything but the mesmerising flex of the muscles in his forearm, his thigh as he changed gear, switched lanes?

Swamped by lust, heated by the sun beating in through the windscreen on her breasts, thighs, she closed her eyes to shut out temptation. When she opened them again, her cheek was pressed against his shoulder, she was breathing in the scent of warm male and her first inclination was to close them and stay exactly where she was.

She felt, rather than saw, Darius glance down at her. 'It must have been a late night. Not many people can sleep in a Land Rover.'

Humbled, she reluctantly straightened. 'I was just resting

my eyes,' she said, using a yawn to surreptitiously check her chin for dribble. 'While I focused on the plan.'

'Sure you were,' he said, grinning.

'The brain does its best work while the subconscious is switched off,' she said, realising that they'd left the motorway. How long had she slept?

Her satnav had kept her on the main roads but Darius, on home ground, had ignored the dual carriageway that bypassed the village of Hadley and as she looked around, trying to figure out where they were, he slowed and turned down a track half hidden by the rampant growth of early summer spilling from the verges.

'I hope we don't meet anyone coming the other way,' she said as they bounced, very slowly, through a tunnel of fresh new summer leaves along a dirt track so narrow that the frothy billow of cow parsley brushed both the sides of the Land Rover.

'If we do, they'd better have a good reason for being here,' he said. 'This is estate land.'

'This is the back way in?' she asked, trying to recall a map she'd seen, orientate herself. A chalk stream, low after an unusually dry spring, was curling quietly around shingle banks just below them on the right, which put them at the lower end of the estate and, as she turned and looked up, she caught a glimpse of tall chimneys through a gap in the trees.

'The main road goes round in a long loop to bypass the village,' he said. 'This entrance is known only to estate residents, who have more respect for their suspension than to use it, and locals doing a little rough shooting for the pot.'

She looked at him. 'Do you mean poachers?'

'My grandfather would have called them that,' he said. 'I don't have a problem with the neighbours keeping the pigeon and rabbit population under control in return for the odd trout.'

'Well, that's very neighbourly, but people who buy this kind of property tend to be nervous of unidentified gun-fire,' she said, trying to pin down what exactly was wrong with the way he said 'grandfather'. 'If…when…I find you a buyer, someone had better warn the locals that they'll have to find their small game somewhere else.'

His jaw tightened, but all he said was, 'I'll make sure Gary passes the word. When…*if*…you find a buyer. Having burned the midnight oil and spent the drive down here leaving the work to your subconscious,' he said, 'have you got any further than creating a Facebook page?'

'It's a work in progress,' she admitted. Between reliving their close encounter in his studio and wondering how soon they could manage a replay, she hadn't been giving nearly enough thought to saving her career. 'What I need is a story.'

'A story?' He slowed almost to a stop, looking at her instead of the track.

'Relax, Darius, I've got the message. Your name is off limits. Cross my heart,' she added and then, as his eyes darkened, she drew her finger, very slowly, across her left breast in a large X.

His foot slipped from the accelerator, the engine stalled and only the ticking of the engine disturbed a silence so thick that it filled her ears.

'You are in so much trouble, Natasha Gordon,' he said, his face all dark shadows, his eyes shimmering with heat.

'Is that a promise?' she asked, her breath catching in her throat. 'Or are you all talk?'

The click of their seat belts being released was like a shotgun in the silence and then his hands were on her waist and, without quite knowing how she'd got there, she was straddling his thighs, her mouth a breath away from lips that had haunted her since the moment she'd first seen him.

She wiggled a little, snuggling her backside closer to the

impressive bulge in his jeans, and he groaned. 'Correction. *I'm* in so much trouble…'

'Talk, talk, talk…' she murmured against his mouth, cutting off any attempt at a response with a swirl of her tongue over his lower lip. There was a satisfying buck from his hips and, giving no quarter, she sucked it into her mouth.

Darius leaned back to give her more room.

There had been a bulge in his pants ever since she'd appeared on her doorstep in curve-disguising clothes, her hair in restraints, minimal make-up. She'd been doing her best to appear cool but she hadn't needed lipstick to draw attention to a mouth that had been hot, swollen, screaming *kiss me* at a hundred decibels.

He just about managed to restrain himself—if he'd kissed her they would never have left London and he wanted this over. He'd done a good job of keeping his mind on the road while he was driving along the motorway, but then she'd fallen asleep with her head against his shoulder, her lips slightly parted, wisps of escaping hair brushing his neck. Now the scent of hot woman was filling his lungs.

'You want action, Sugarlips?' he said. 'Help yourself.'

Needing no second invitation, she slid her hands through his hair, tangling it in her fingers, a little cat smile tugging at her lips as she made him her captive, teased him with her mouth, sucking, nipping, inviting him to come out and play.

He was in no hurry. Right now her breasts were snuggled against his chest, her backside was tormenting his erection, her mouth trailing moist kisses under his chin.

There was nothing more arousing than a woman intent on pleasure and, resting his hands on her hips, he did no more than support her, holding her steady so that she could concentrate on driving him wild.

It didn't take long. Her top, barely skimming her waistband, rode up as she leaned forward and he closed his eyes, memorising each curve of her lovely body as his hands, with a will of their own, slid up to graze the silk of her skin. Her waist dipped above the flare of her hips; there was nothing straight about her, he discovered, as his thumbs teased the edges of her stomach and she squirmed on his lap.

For a moment he was the one holding his breath but then he reached her ribcage and he felt the hitch of her breath under his hands as his fingers took a slow walk up her spinal column, kneading each vertebrae in turn, pausing only to release the catch on her bra, so that his thumbs were free to imprint the soft swell of her breasts in his memory. They had just reached her nipples when her tongue found the pulse throbbing in his neck.

With a roar, he pulled her top, bra over her head and tossed them behind him, then forgot to breathe as she leaned back against the steering wheel, eyes smoky, slumberous, only the tiniest rim of blue circling satin-black pupils.

'Perfect,' he said, filling his hand with her full, ripe breasts, thumbing her rock-hard nipples, stroking them with his tongue, sucking on them. Just perfect...

'Darius...' There was an urgency in her voice now and he popped the button at her waist, slid down the zip and eased his hands down inside the back of her jeans, a scrap of lace, easing them down as he cupped her peachy backside in his hands and lifted her towards his mouth.

He swirled his tongue around the dimple of her navel, mouthed soft kisses in the hollow of her pelvis, blew against the blonde fluff of her sex and she whimpered, wanting more. She was right—this wasn't enough. He wanted her naked. He wanted her out of here, lying on a bank of soft grass down by the stream with sunlight, filtered through the leaves, playing on her skin. He wanted to touch every inch of her, memorise her body. Be inside her...

'Let's get out of here,' he said, pushing open the door

and half falling with her into the verge, where they lay laughing, catching their breath amongst long grass, red campion, a few late bluebells that were a perfect match for her eyes. 'Come on,' he said, hauling her up, holding her close, not wanting to let her go even for the short scramble down the bank.

She clutched at jeans that were heading for her knees. 'Where are we going?'

'You're not going anywhere.'

'What the…?' He swung round and Natasha gave a little shriek as they were confronted by a helmeted, visored security guard. 'Where the hell did you come from?' he demanded.

Ignoring his question, the guard said, 'This is private property. You're going to have to leave.'

'What? No…' Then cursed himself for every kind of fool—Ramsey had told him that he'd employed a security firm to keep an eye on the place. Cursed again as he realised that Natasha was standing there without a stitch above her waist and not much below it and putting himself between them. 'Show a little respect,' he said, boiling with anger that the man hadn't had the decency to look away. More likely couldn't take his eyes off her.

Despite his helmet and a uniform designed to make him look as much like a policeman as possible without breaking the law, the man took a nervous step back, looked away.

'There's no need for that,' he said defensively. 'I'm just doing my job.'

'Hanging about like some Peeping Tom. You're the trespasser,' he said, wrenching off his polo shirt and handing it to Natasha, bundling her back into the seat they'd just fallen out of before turning furiously on the man. 'This is my land.' The words were out of his mouth before he realised what he was saying. 'I am Darius Hadley and I own this estate.'

'Good try, but Mr Hadley is dead,' he replied, 'and the house is being sold, so if you'd just get back in the vehicle. You can turn around about fifty yards ahead—'

'I know where I can turn. I know every inch of this estate,' he said, cutting him off, but clearly words weren't going to do it. Taking his wallet from his back pocket, he opened it and held it out so that the man could see his driver's licence. 'Darius Hadley,' he repeated, while the man checked the name and photograph. 'The previous owner was my grandfather.'

'Even so, sir, I'll have to check with the office.'

'Check with who you like. How did you know we were here?' It seemed unlikely that a patrol just happened to be passing at the exact moment he'd stalled his engine.

'There's CCTV on all the entrances, Mr Hadley. Apparently this one is something of a lovers'…'

'Get rid of it.'

'I'm sorry…'

'I want the cameras down now. Every one of them, is that clear?'

'I can't—'

Darius didn't wait for the excuses, but reached into the Land Rover for his mobile phone and called Brian Ramsey.

'Ramsey,' he said, before the man could do more than say his name, 'I understand that you've had security cameras installed at the Chase. Get rid of them. And the security company.'

'Darius…' he said, in what he no doubt thought was a soothing voice. 'The house is empty and this is the most economic…'

'It's intrusive. The tenants have a right to privacy.'

'I'm sure if you asked them they would tell you that there have been problems with trespassers, poachers. The trout stream is a selling point and the insurance company…'

'There's a public footpath across the estate and those

poachers are not just keeping down the rabbit population, they're local people and they do a better job of keeping an eye on the place than any security firm. No arguments. I own this estate and I want the cameras gone. Today.'

He ended the call without waiting to hear more and turned to the man. 'You heard me. You're fired.'

CHAPTER SIX

'ARE YOU OKAY?'

'There's nothing wrong with me,' Natasha said as Darius climbed in beside her. 'You could do with a few lessons in reality, though.'

'What?' About to reach for the ignition, he sat back, dragged his fingers through his hair. Far from okay, she was furious. 'I'm sorry. That was—'

'Don't apologise to me,' she snapped. 'What on earth were you thinking?'

He glanced at her, aware that he was missing something but not sure what. 'I was thinking that perhaps you might just be a little bit upset at being seen half-naked by a total stranger,' he said.

'Really? And how would that be different from you making a bronze of my entirely naked body for the entire world to stare at?' He wasn't deceived by the mildness of her tone. She was mad and actually he didn't blame her. On a stupid scale of one to ten that had to be a nine. She might have been up there with him, reaching for ten, but he'd started it. Clearly some serious grovelling was in order, but she wasn't done. 'I am not made of porcelain, Darius; I won't break if some bloke gets an eyeful of my tits, but that man probably has a wife and family to support.'

What? He was apologising to her, but apparently her only concern was some lout who'd leered at her breasts.

'How do you suppose his employers will react when they're told they've lost their contract because someone—a man who was just doing his job keeping Hadley Chase safe from intruders—hacked off the high and mighty Darius Hadley?'

High and mighty?

'I'm not—'

'No? You should have *heard* yourself. *"This is my land!"* Really? Because I got the strong impression that you don't give a tuppenny damn about the place.'

'I give a damn,' he said.

'About selling it as quickly as possible with the least possible inconvenience to yourself.'

'No...'

'When was the last time you actually set foot on the place?'

'You have no idea—'

'So tell me.'

Tell her? What? That his father had sold him? Share the shrivelling knowledge that his value had been counted in sterling. That his grandfather had forced his own son to choose between the woman he loved beyond reason and his infant son.

He was still holding his cell phone and, instead of answering her, he hit redial.

'Ramsey...I'm sorry,' he began before the man had a chance to say more than his name. 'You're right, the house must have a security presence and the company are doing an excellent job. Please ask them to pass on my apologies to the guard I met this morning. He took me by surprise but he was simply doing his job and it has been pointed out to me that I behaved like a jerk.'

He didn't wait for an answer, but disconnected, tossed the phone back on the shelf and reached for the ignition.

Natasha cleared her throat. 'Do you want your shirt back?'

'Keep it,' he said. 'I'll wear your top. Now you've cut me down to size, it'll be a perfect fit.'

'Oh, I think you fill this one pretty well,' she said, pulling it over her head and handing it to him, before turning behind to recover her top and bra from the back seat. By the time she was straight he had pulled up in front of the house.

To the right the parkland fell away to the river; then, beyond it, the Downs offered a breathtaking view for miles around.

Tash sighed. Beside her, Darius had that same locked-away look that he'd had when she'd first set eyes on him, except now she knew that it was not simply about the advertisement. For a moment, before he'd called Brian Ramsey, told him to apologise to the security guard, she'd seen the darkness, a pain like a knife in his heart.

There was something about this house, what had happened here, that hurt bone-deep, and yet he'd brought her here. She'd like to think it was because he wanted to spend the day with her, maybe fool around a little—fool around a lot if the last few minutes were anything to go by. Now she realised that she had simply provided him with a hook, that her need had given him an excuse, a way back.

The minute he came to a halt, she climbed down, grabbed her bags from the back seat but, instead of going straight to the door, she walked to the edge of the lawn where there was a strategically placed bench, giving him breathing space to come to terms with being here before he had to go inside.

Meanwhile, she had a job to do and she'd better jolly well stop lusting after Darius; she took out her mini camcorder and began to create a panorama to post on Facebook.

The crunch of his boots on the gravel warned her that he had followed her. 'The house might have a few shortcomings, but the setting is perfect,' she said, not looking up until the view was blocked by his broad chest. She didn't stop filming but, instead of panning from left to right, she lifted the lens until his face filled the screen.

'Here are the keys. The alarm code is 2605.'

'You're leaving me to it?' she asked, letting the camera fall to her side, a little hollow spot of disappointment somewhere below her waist that he was ducking out. 'I thought you'd been appointed responsible adult?'

'Apparently I failed at the first hurdle. Don't worry. I'll ask that security guard to frisk you for the family silver before you leave,' he said.

'You were wrong, Darius.'

'Totally.' He met her gaze head-on. 'I lashed out because I felt guilty.'

'I realise that, but I'm an adult; I knew where I was, what I was doing. The responsibility was equally mine.'

'But you didn't know what I knew.'

'Oh? And what was that?'

'Ramsey told me he'd employed a security company; it just never occurred to me that they would be monitoring the place so closely.' He shrugged, summoned up the ghost of a smile. 'Forget that; I wasn't thinking about anything except getting you naked.'

She resisted the urge to fling herself at him again and, keeping her own smile low-key, said, 'Ditto.'

His own smile deepened a fraction, but he shook his head.

'Shall I tell you why I liked being with Toby?' she asked.

'No—'

'He never patronised me,' she said. 'He never doubted that I knew what I was doing.' Okay, he wasn't that bright. If she knew what she was doing, she wouldn't be this close to a man who made her self-preservation hard drive crash whenever she thought about touching him. About him touching her. 'He never felt the need to protect me.'

'He stole your job!'

'He was paying me the ultimate compliment, Darius. He knew that I was strong enough, smart enough, to survive.'

'Maybe, but I wasn't patronising you. I was just doing that macho shit…'

'I know.' About to reach out, touch him, reassure him, she tucked the house keys in her pocket, sat down on the bench, took a flask out of her bag, keeping her hands busy.

She'd wanted him to share his pain. Maybe, while she had him on her hook, she could show him how.

'I spent the first twenty-one years of my life being protected, Darius. It gets old.' She unscrewed the cups from the top of the flask, looked up. 'Have you got time for coffee?'

Darius recognised his moment to make his excuses and walk away. It was what he always did when things became complicated, involved—walking away from emotional entanglement. Something he'd been signally failing to do ever since he'd set eyes on Natasha Gordon in Morgan's office.

He'd walked, but he'd hardly made it across the road before he was looking back, hooked on that luscious body, those eyes. Now, layered on that first explosive impact, was her sweet, spicy, delicious scent, the taste of her skin, her mouth entwining itself around him, binding him to her.

He should be running, not walking away, but he'd been running since he was seventeen years old. Running from the house behind him and yet here he was, because Natasha had needed him. Or maybe he'd needed the excuse she gave him to return, face it. Whichever it was, he barely hesitated before joining her on the bench, taking the coffee she'd poured for him.

'Thanks.'

'You're welcome,' she said, but didn't follow it up with an offer of something sweet to go with it. Just as well—

'cake' would, in his mind, forever be a euphemism for sex and even he balked at a garden bench with half an acre of lawn in front of them.

'Okay,' he said, 'I'm hooked. Tell me about the first twenty-one years of your life.'

'All of them?' she asked. 'I thought you had to be somewhere.'

He leaned an elbow on the back of the bench, making it clear he was going nowhere. 'Hospital visiting.' Another hurdle to face. 'Gary isn't going anywhere.'

She took a sip of her coffee.

'Come on,' he said, waggling his eyebrows at her. 'You know you want to tell me.'

'But do you really want to hear?'

He was beginning to get a bad feeling about this, wishing he'd gone with his first thought and walked away. 'How about a quick rundown of the highlights?' he suggested.

'Lowlights would be more accurate,' she said.

'Were they that bad?'

'No…' She reached out as if to reassure him and for a moment her fingers brushed his arm. 'But highlights are all sparkle and excitement. Champagne and strawberries.'

'And lowlights are egg custard?'

She laughed. 'Give the man a coconut. My first twenty-one years were all wholesome, nourishing, good-for-you egg custard when I longed for spicy, lemony, chocolatey, covered-in-frosting, bad-for-you, sugar-on-the-lips cake,' she said.

'Thanks for the coconut, but I don't deserve it,' he said. 'I have absolutely no idea what you're talking about.'

'Of course not. No one ever does.'

'Try me.'

She looked at him over the rim of her cup, then put it down. 'Okay. It's taking quiet beach holidays in the same cottage with my family in Cornwall every year, when I dreamed of being in a hot-air balloon floating across the Serengeti, bungee jumping in New Zealand, white water rafting in Colorado like my brothers.'

'Why?'

'Given the choice, wouldn't you have preferred hot-air ballooning?'

He thought about it for a moment then said, 'Actually they both have a lot to commend them and Cornwall does have surfing.'

Tash, who was finding this a lot harder than she imagined, grabbed the distraction. 'You surf? In one of those clinging wetsuits?' She flapped a hand to wave cooling air over her face. 'Be still my beating heart.'

'You don't?' he asked, refusing to be distracted.

'Surf? I can't even swim. The most dangerous thing I do at the seaside is paddle up to my ankles with my nephews and nieces. Build sandcastles. Play shove ha'penny down the pub.'

'And again, why? You mentioned that you were sick as a kid, but you look pretty robust now.'

'Robust?' She rolled the word round her mouth, testing it. 'Thanks for that. It makes me feel so much better.'

'No need to get on your high horse; you have a great body—one that I guarantee would cause a riot in a wetsuit—but that wasn't the "why" I was asking. Why were your parents so protective?'

And suddenly there it was. She'd lived a lifetime with everyone knowing what had happened to her, looking at her with a touch of uncertainty, of pity.

She'd left all that behind when she'd left home. She hadn't told anyone in London, not even Toby, but when Miles had introduced a private health scheme for the staff late last year, the insurance company had put so many restrictions on her that he'd called her into his office, convinced she was a walking time bomb. She'd told him everything and now the bastard had used it against her.

Had it played on his mind when he was thinking of promoting her? Because it stayed with you, stuck like dog muck on a shoe. Telling Darius was harder than she'd imagined when she'd blithely set out to show him how to trust someone so totally that you exposed yourself in ways that had nothing to do with getting naked.

Their relationship was purely physical and she never saw it being anything else. He had 'loner' stamped all over him, but she didn't want to alter the image he had of her. To have the 'attractive packaging' undermined by that darkness he would find in her inner depths and exposed in bronze. But he'd given her his trust when not many men in his situation would have given her the time of day and if she could get him to open up she would have repaid him whether she sold Hadley Chase or not.

'I had cancer—' There it was, the great big nasty C-word. 'Leukaemia—'

'Leukaemia?' Well, that put a dent in his smile. 'Oh, God, I'm sorry. I thought…'

'What?'

'From what you said about being force-fed egg custard…'

'What?'

'The newspaper hinted at some psychological problem…' He looked distinctly uncomfortable. 'Patsy wondered if you might have had some kind of eating disorder.'

'You've got to be kidding!' The tension erupted in a burst of laughter. 'Look at me!'

Darius looked and he wanted to laugh, too. 'I told her she was way off beam,' he said. 'I'm beginning to have a very warm regard for egg custard.' His fingers lightly traced the outline of her face from temple to chin. 'That is a very healthy glow.'

'I think the word you're looking for is pink and over-weight,' she said, 'which actually is pretty ironic.'

'Pretty' was too bland a word for Natasha. She was no pretty milkmaid... 'It is?'

'I'm told that people suffering from anorexia look at themselves in the mirror and see fat even when they're skin and bones. Well, my parents look at me and see skin and bones despite the fact that I'm—'

'Luscious.'

'Nicely fielded,' she said, turning away, but he hooked his finger around her chin, forcing her to look him in the eyes.

'I know what I mean, Natasha.'

'Do you?'

'Believe me. I can usually wait to get a room.'

'Are you saying that you don't usually toss women into the nearest verge?' she teased, laughing now as the tension of telling her story left her and he added a whole raft of other words to describe Natasha Gordon. Ripe, earthy, soft, warm and unbelievably sexy... 'That you'd rather have a safe double bed?'

'Safe?' There was nothing safe or comfortable about this relationship. He had no idea what Natasha would say or do next. What he would do. His fingers seemed to burn when he touched her. He had no control over his responses... 'You will live to regret that.'

'Promises, promises...' For a moment they just looked at one another, then she turned away from the intensity of it and he allowed her to break the contact between them. 'Actually, robust is good. My family still treat me as if I've been stuck back together with some very dodgy glue and might fall apart at any moment.'

'No swimming, because pools are a germ factory and who knows what's in the sea?' he suggested.

'That's pretty much how it went.'

'It must have been difficult for them to truly believe that you've made a full recovery,' he said. 'I imagine you never quite trust the fates once you've been through something like that.'

'It wasn't just my parents. I've got three older brothers and they lived through it, too. Tom, the eldest, became a doctor because of what happened to me.'

'What about the other two?'

'James is a vet; Harry is a sports teacher. He's nearest in age to me and appointed himself my personal bodyguard when I started school. If anyone got too close, too rough, watch out.'

He knew he'd have been the same, but he could see it wouldn't be much fun to be on the receiving end of that kind of protection. 'How did you cope with that?'

'I regret to say that I loved it. I was a proper little princess,' she admitted ruefully, 'and, with three gorgeous brothers, everyone wanted to be my friend. It was only when I was fifteen and Harry discovered that I had a crush on a boy in the lower sixth that it all got out of hand.'

He grinned. 'I suppose he warned him off his little sister?'

'Oh, it was worse, far worse than that. The poor guy obviously didn't have a clue that he was the object of my desire. He always smiled at me in the corridor—probably because I *was* Harry's sister—and I'd just built up this huge fantasy. As you do…' He glanced at her and she rolled her eyes. 'Teenage girls.'

'An alien species,' he agreed. 'And?'

'And my sweet brother asked him, as a personal favour, to take me as his date to a school disco.'

'You're kidding?'

'I wish,' she said, 'but Harry was captain of sport and played under-eighteen rugby for the county. A request from him was in the nature of a decree from Mount Olympus.'

'So you had your dream date?'

'Bliss city.'

'But?'

She sighed. 'There is always a "but",' she agreed. 'I discovered what Harry had done, which was a total nightmare, but worse, much worse, I discovered that everyone else knew.'

'Before? After? During?'

'During. The classic overheard gossip in the loo… The girl he would have taken if Harry hadn't stuck his oar in was giving vent to her feelings about the spoiled, fat little cow who'd got her brother to twist her boyfriend's arm.'

'Ouch,' he said, flippantly enough, but deep down he was imagining what that must have been like for an over-protected fifteen-year-old girl. The embarrassment, the shame… 'What did you do?'

'I waited in the cubicle until they'd gone, then I slipped out of school and walked home.'

'Of course you did. How far was it?'

'A couple of miles. It wouldn't have been a problem, but I'd abandoned my coat because I didn't want anyone to see me leave.'

'Coat? What time of year was this?'

'It was the Christmas disco,' she said, and he let slip a word that he immediately apologised for.

'No, you're okay.' She held up her hand and began to count off the reasons why that word was just about perfect. First finger… 'There was the no-coat thing, which on any level was pretty dumb.' Second finger… 'There were the sparkly new shoes which weren't made for long-distance walking and fell apart after half a mile.' Third finger… 'Then it began to rain.'

'Your date didn't miss you?'

'Not for a while. When a girl disappears into a cloak-room who knows how long she'll be and I don't suppose he was in any hurry…' She shrugged. 'Anyway, my feet hurt, my dress was ruined and my life was over. Worse, I knew my parents would be waiting up for me, wanting to hear about my date. I couldn't face all that concern, all that sympathy, so I hid in the garden shed.'

'Oh, I can see where this is going. No one knew where you were. They organised a search party, called the police, dragged the river?'

'All of the above.'

'You're kidding?'

She laughed at his horrified reaction. 'Okay, not the river. Tom came looking for a torch and found me before it got that far. I was given a severe talking to by the local constabulary on the subject of responsibility and Dad grounded me for the whole of the Christmas holidays. No parties or holiday outings for me. Not much of a punishment, to be honest. I wanted to hibernate.'

'He knew that. He was making it easy for you.'

'Oh… Of course he was.' She shook her head. 'I never realised.'

'You were upset.'

'It got worse. School insisted that I had "counselling",' she said, making quote marks with her fingers, 'because obviously anyone who behaved so irrationally, so irresponsibly, had problems and needed help.'

Hardly irrational, he thought. More like a wounded animal going to ground. Something he knew all about.

'Not a Christmas to remember, I'm guessing.'

'White-faced parents, Harry in the doghouse with everyone. A total lack of ho-ho-ho. On the upside, by the time the holidays were over there were other scandals to talk about.'

'And the downside?'

'I'm still trying to prove that I can put one foot in front of the other without one of them holding my hand. Proving to my brothers that their broken little sister is all mended.'

Darius, thinking that if they'd seen her laying into him they might be convinced, said, 'Any luck?'

'The nearest I came was last Christmas when I drove home in the BMW.'

'Ho-ho-ho!'

She dug him in the ribs with her elbow. 'Men are so shallow. If I'd known how easy it was to impress them I'd have saved my bonuses for a flash car instead of putting down a deposit on my flat.'

'The fact that you didn't proves how smart you are.'

She sighed. 'Not smart enough to see this coming. Every morning I wake up and, just for a moment, everything is normal.'

Ten seconds, he thought. You had about ten seconds when you thought life still made sense before that jolt as you remembered and it was like the first moment all over again.

'I just feel so stupid.'

'Only someone you trust, someone you love can betray you, Natasha. It always comes out of left field.' He felt, rather than saw her turn to look at him. There would be a question mark rippling the creamy skin between her brows and he held his breath, waiting for the questions.

How did he know? When had his world come crashing down? Who had betrayed him? For what seemed an age the only sound was a blackbird perched high in the cedar tree. It was one of those long silences that the unwary rushed to fill and, even though he recognised the danger, he found himself tempted to tell her anyway.

She stirred before he could gather the words. Begin...

'The real downside was the guilt,' she said. 'I was old enough then to see what it did to my mother, to understand what she must have been through when I was little, so when Dad suggested I take my degree at Melchester University...'

Conflicting emotions twisted his gut. Relief that she'd let him off the hook, regret that he'd missed his chance.

'You wanted to make it up to them,' he said.

'It was okay, actually. Melchester has one of the best estate management courses in the country and, with all those lads living away from home for the first time, I was never short of a date.'

He doubted her mother's cooking was the only lure but he didn't want to think about that. 'So what made you toss away the dream job with the National Trust and run away to London to work for Miles Morgan?'

'I live in a small town. I was the little girl who'd had leukaemia. My sickness defined me. No one could see past it, not even my family.'

'So you finally made the break.'

'No... I lied to them, Darius.'

'Lied?'

'I knew that if I took the National Trust job, just down the road, I'd never leave. Never do anything. I'd marry someone I'd known all my life, who knew everything I'd ever done...'

'You told them you didn't get it?'

She nodded. 'It felt like breaking out of jail.' She tossed away the dregs of her coffee, staring out over the neglected lawn. 'I'll be honest. This isn't where I saw myself five years on from my degree, but I've worked harder than anyone so that I wouldn't have to go home and prove them all right.' She turned to look at him. 'You think I'm terrible, don't you? That I don't know how lucky I am to have a family who cares about me.'

Close. Very close. Apparently he wasn't the only one reading body language, studying inner depths. She must have learned a thing or two watching the men and women trying to hide their reactions to the houses she showed them, playing their cards close to their chest.

'I have no family,' he said, 'so I'm in no position to judge.'

'None?' And in a moment her expression turned from inward reproach to concern. 'I'm so sorry, Darius. That's really tough. What happened to your parents?'

Yes, well, that was the thing about trusting someone with your secrets; it was supposed to be a two-way deal but his moment of weakness had passed and he was already regretting this excursion into her past. Why complicate something as simple as sex?

'I have no parents.' He drained his coffee, screwed the top back on the flask and put it back in her bag. 'Did you ever tell them the truth?' he asked before she could push him for details. 'About the job?'

She shook her head.

'Maybe you should,' he advised. Clearly she was harbouring the guilt.

'They'd be devastated. And now, after all that horrible stuff in the paper, all those between-the-lines insinuations that I'm mentally unstable, they're out of their minds worried again.'

Her eyes were shining, but the tears were more of anger than anything else, he was certain. Was that how it was? Love? This complicated mishmash of guilt, anxiety, the desperate need not to hurt, to protect? Add in passion, sacrifice, the world well lost and you were well and truly stuffed... Or maybe blessed beyond measure.

Natasha blinked back the threatening tears and he put his arm around her, drew her close. There was a moment of stiffness, resistance and then she melted against him. 'My mother is desperate for me to go with them on the annual trek to Cornwall so that she can look after me,' she said. 'Heal me with sea air, walks on the beach, evening games of Scrabble.'

'Instead, you're playing hide the sausage in the woods with a disreputable sculptor who's going to put your naked body on display for the entire world to see,' he said.

She snorted, buried her face into his shoulder and suddenly, sitting there, his arm around her, both of them shaking with laughter, felt like a perfect moment.

Above them the swallows swooped just above head height, the scent of roses was drifting on a warm breeze and the temptation to stay there, looking out over the heat-hazed valley, almost overwhelmed him.

CHAPTER SEVEN

'DARIUS?'

He stirred and Natasha lifted her head, looked up at him. 'I'm sorry I shouted at you.'

'I'm not.' Tears of pain and laughter had clumped her eyelashes together. He used the pad of his thumb to wipe away one that had spilled over, kissed lips that were raised in what felt like an invitation. 'You can tell your family from me that they don't have a thing to worry about. You are strong in every way and I'm really glad you're on my side.'

Really glad as he kissed her again and, lost in the sweetness of her mouth, for once in his life not thinking about an exit strategy. It should be scaring the wits out of him, but the connection between them had an honesty that overrode any fear of commitment. Natasha needed him on her side to re-establish her career, didn't know that security guard from Adam and yet she had instantly empathised with him and she hadn't hesitated to give it to him with both barrels when she thought he was wrong. How many women in her situation would have done that?

When he was with her, he had no sense of losing himself, but of becoming something greater.

Blessed.

It was Natasha who moved.

'Enough of this maudlin self-pity,' she said. 'I've got work to do.'

He looked back at the house. Huge, empty... 'Are you going to be all right on your own?'

She gave him a warning look and he held up his hands. 'Sorry...'

'No... I shouldn't be so defensive.' Then, as he made a reluctant move, 'Actually, there is one thing.'

'Yes?'

Tash had felt the exact moment that Darius had wanted to move. For a blissful few minutes he'd been still, utterly relaxed and his kiss had been so tender that tears had once again threatened to overwhelm her.

After such an emotional exchange most men would have said *anything* but that shuttered 'yes' was warning enough, if she'd needed it, not to get too deeply involved with Darius Hadley. He wasn't a keeper and no one could protect her from that kind of pain.

'If I find any diaries, can I borrow them?'

'Diaries?'

'I imagine there are diaries, letters?' she prompted. 'Something interesting must have happened in three and a half centuries. You've got a ballroom, so presumably there were country balls? The occasional drama over a little inappropriate flirting? Maybe a duel?' she added, just to get a response.

'I have no idea,' he said stiffly, all his defences back up.

'Oh, for goodness' sake, Darius, lighten up,' she said crossly. 'If there had been any scandal to be dug up, the newspapers would have been all over it when that blasted ad became a news item.'

It didn't mean there wasn't a family skeleton rattling around in the cupboard because it was obvious that something wasn't right. He'd changed the subject faster than greased lightning when she'd asked him about his parents.

She lifted an eyebrow, inviting him to come clean, but even yesterday, with a bulge in his pants that had to have hurt, he'd been unreadable, hiding whatever he was thinking, feeling. What had it taken to build that mask?

What would it take, she wondered, to shatter it?

No, no, no…

'A house that grand, that old, must have hosted some interesting people over the centuries?' she persisted. It was all very well to casually toss out the words 'social media', but posting pictures of the house on Facebook and flinging 'buy this' Tweets around like confetti wasn't going to do the job.

'Not interesting in your sense of the word. The Hadleys were riding, shooting, fishing country squires with no pretensions to high society.'

'More Jane Austen than Georgette Heyer,' she said with a sigh. 'I don't suppose she ever came to tea? Jane Austen,' she added. Much as she loved Georgette Heyer's books, a visit from her wouldn't arouse the same kind of interest. 'I need a way in, something to grab the attention, create interest, start a buzz going.'

'Why don't you make up a story?'

'Excuse me?'

'Most family history is based on Chinese whispers— expanded and decorated with every retelling. Our story is that James Hadley was given the estate by Charles II for services rendered during his exile. How much more likely is it that he bought it cheap for a quick sale from one of Cromwell's confederates who, come the Restoration, decided the climate in the New World might be better for his health?'

'You're such a cynic, Darius Hadley.'

Off the dangerous territory of recent history, he grinned. 'A realist. Who's going to challenge you if you say Jane Austen stayed one wet week in April and, confined to the house, spun a story to keep everyone amused?'

'I have no doubt that some obsessive Janeite would know exactly where she was during that particular week.'

'Really?'

'I'm afraid so. They didn't have email or Skype or television to keep them amused so they wrote long detailed letters to their family and friends telling them where they were, what they were doing. And instead of blogging, they kept *diaries*…' She lifted her hands in a *ta-da* gesture.

'Being caught out in a blatant lie might grab the house another headline. *Mad Estate Agent Lies About Austen Connection*?' he offered. 'You did say any publicity would be good publicity.'

'I think you've had all that kind of "good" publicity you can handle and I'm trying to restore my reputation, not sink it without a trace so, unless you can point me to an entry in one your ancestors' diaries along the lines that "Mrs Austen visited with her daughters, Cassandra and Jane. It rained all week, but Jane kept the children amused acting out scenes from a little history of England she has written…" we'll save that as a last resort.'

'You're the expert,' he said. 'You'll find the diaries in my grandmother's room. She was writing a history of the house. I don't know if she ever finished it.'

'A history?' She was practically speechless. 'There's a history! For heaven's sake, Darius, talk about pulling hen's teeth!'

He grinned. 'I've made the woman happy. If there's nothing else?'

'No… Yes…' She fished in the picnic bag and produced a small plastic box. 'Take Gary these cookies from me. They're not as healthy as grapes, but they'll help a cup of hospital tea go down.'

Tash let herself into the house, dealt with the alarm and then, as the Land Rover rattled into life, she turned and watched it disappear as the drive dipped and curved through the woods. It seemed a little early for hospital visiting, but he'd shown no interest in going inside the house and she suspected that it served as a useful excuse to avoid whatever it was that he didn't want to talk about.

Despite her airy assurance that she would be fine, it was a huge old place, undoubtedly full of ghosts and, as she opened the glazed doors that led from the entrance lobby into the main reception hall, what struck her first was the stillness, the silence.

Out of the corner of her eye she saw something move, but when she swung round she realised that it was only her reflection in a dusty mirror.

Heart beating in her throat, she looked around but nothing stirred except the dust motes she'd set dancing in the sunlight pouring down from the lantern fifty feet above her and, just for a moment, she was back in the studio with Darius holding her, limp, sated in his arms. Reliving the desperate frustration when that wretched guard had turned up.

They were so not done.

No, no, no… Concentrate…

Beneath the mirror, an ornate clock on the hall table had long since stopped. Dead leaves had drifted into the corner of each tread of that dratted staircase. All it needed was a liveried footman asleep against the newel post and she would have stepped into the *Sleeping Beauty* picture book she'd had as a child.

As the germ of an idea began to form, she began to film the scene in front of her, panning slowly around the grand entrance hall with its shadowy portraits, an ormolu clock sitting on an elegant serpentine table thickly layered with dust, paused on the room reflected in soft focus through the hazy surface of the gilded mirror.

She opened doors to shuttered rooms where filtered light gave glimpses of ghostly furniture swathed in dust sheets, climbed the magnificent Tudor staircase—not a woodworm in sight—and explored bedrooms in varying stages of grandeur.

There was a four-poster bed that looked as if Queen Elizabeth I might have slept in it in the master suite. Next door was a suite for the mistress of the house—a comfortable, less daunting bedroom, a dressing room and bathroom and a small sitting room with a chaise longue, a writing desk and a bookshelf filled with leather-bound journals. Research material for his grandmother's history.

The desk had just one wide drawer and nestling inside it was a heavy card folder tied together with black ribbon and bearing the title *A History of Hadley Chase by Emma Hadley*. She had just untied the ribbon and laid back the cover to reveal a drawing of the Tudor house that had been added to and 'improved' over the years when her phone pinged, warning her of an incoming text.

It was from Darius.

Darius stopped twenty yards from the main gate and the gatehouse cottage that Gary shared with his grandmother.

Mary Webb had been his grandmother's cook and the nearest thing to a mother he'd ever had. She'd given him the spoons to lick when she was making cakes, stuck on the plasters when he'd scraped a knee, given him a hug when his dog died. And, like everyone else in this place, had known his history and kept it from him.

When he'd learned the truth he'd walked away from the house and everyone connected with it and never looked back. That had been his choice, but while he had a home, a career, there was no guarantee that Gary, a few years older, who'd made him a catapult, lain in the dark with him watching for badgers, taught him to ride a motorbike, would have either when the estate was sold.

This is my land...

The words had come so easily. But they were hollow without the responsibilities that went with it. *Noblesse oblige*. Natasha hadn't used those words, but when she'd rounded on him that was the subtext.

She'd asked him how long it had been since he'd set foot on this estate. Almost as long as he'd lived here. An age. A lifetime. He would never have come back if he'd had his way and yet, because of her, he was here. Not for the land, but for a woman. The irony was not lost on him.

He took out his phone, sent her a two-word text and when he looked up Mary Webb was standing on the doorstep. Seventeen years older and so much smaller than he remembered.

Sixteen years.

The text was unsigned, but it came from Darius and could only mean one thing. She'd asked him how long it was since he'd last set foot on Hadley Chase. He hadn't answered, but he had been listening.

Sixteen years…

The article she'd read about his commission for the sculpture of the horse had mentioned that he'd been at the Royal College of Art and from the date she'd been able to work out that he had to be thirty-one, maybe thirty-two. That meant he'd have been sixteen or seventeen when he left the Chase, long before his grandfather became sick or he'd left for art school. It suggested a family row of epic proportions. A breach that had never been healed. Scarcely any wonder he hadn't wanted her digging around, poking in the corners stirring up ghosts.

But this was a tiny crack and through it other questions flooded in. Not just what had caused the rift, but where could a hurting teenage boy with no family have gone?

She tried to imagine herself in that situation. Imagine

that instead of hiding out in the shed, she'd run away. It happened every day. Teenagers running away from situations they couldn't handle.

Where would she have run to? How would she have lived?

How would she have felt returning home after sixteen years, a stranger, changed beyond recognition from the cossetted girl who'd painted her nails, pinned up her hair, put on a new dress and sparkly shoes to go to a school disco?

He'd shown no interest, no emotional attachment to the property until that security guard had ordered him to leave but then the claim had been instinctive. Possessive.

'This is my land...'

She looked around her. Darius had lived here while he was growing up, going to school. All his formative years had been spent roaming the estate. In this house. It had made him who he was, given him the strength to survive on his own. She would have expected a photograph on the desk, on the bedside table. There was nothing, but there had to be traces of him here. His room...

When she'd visited the Chase in order to prepare the details for the kind of glossy sales brochure a house of this importance demanded, there had been a team of them from Morgan and Black, walking the land, detailing the outbuildings, the cottages, the boathouse. Inside, she had concentrated on the main reception and bedrooms while junior staff had gone through the minor rooms, the attics.

She arranged the desk to look as if the writer had just left it for a moment, took photographs of that and the view from the window, then picked up the folder and went in search of the room which had been Darius Hadley's private space.

She found it at the far end of the first floor corridor. Grander than most bedrooms, with a high ceiling, tall windows looking out over the park and furnished with pieces that had obviously been in the house for centuries. And yet it was still recognisable for what it was. A boy's bedroom. Unchanged since he'd abandoned it.

Her brother Tom was about the same age and he'd had the same poster above his bed, the same books on his shelves.

The similarity ended with the books and posters. Tom had always known what he wanted to do and by the time he was seventeen he'd had a skeleton in his room, medical diagrams on the walls.

Darius, too, had been focused on the future. There were wall-to-wall drawings, tacked up with pins, curling at the edges.

One of them, the drawing of a laughing retriever, each curl of his coat, each feather of his tail so full of life that he looked as if he was about to bound off the paper after a rabbit.

On a worktable lay a folder filled with watercolours. Distant views of the house, the hills, the birds and animals that roamed the estate. The faint scent of linseed oil still clung to an easel leaning against a far wall. She opened a wooden box stacked beside it. Brushes, dried up tubes of paint. He'd moved on from sketches and watercolours to oil, but none of those were here.

She turned to the wardrobe and a lump formed in her throat as she saw his clothes. A pair of riding boots, walking shoes, battered old trainers bearing the shape of his youthful foot lined up beneath shirts, a school uniform, jackets, a suit and, in a suit bag from a Savile Row tailor, what must have been his first tux, never worn.

What kind of a life had he had here? Privileged, without a doubt, and yet he'd apparently walked away from it, leaving everything behind. His clothes, his art, his life.

She'd been seven or eight when Tom was that age and he'd seemed like a god to her then, but when she'd been sixteen, seventeen, the boys in her year had seemed so immature, so useless. She couldn't imagine any of them coping without their mother to do their washing, put food in front of them, provide a taxi service.

She sat on the narrow bed, rubbed her hand over the old Welsh quilt that he'd slept under, then kicked off her shoes, leaned back against an impressive headboard, putting herself in his place, looking out of the window at the view he'd grown up with, trying to imagine what had been so bad that it had driven him away. And failing. It was so beautiful here, so tranquil.

She sighed. No doubt her home life would have looked enviable to an outsider and in many ways it was. But she'd been older, an adult when she'd left. He'd been a boy.

She let it go and, propping the folder against her thighs, began to read his grandmother's history of Hadley Chase.

Darius was right—nothing important had happened, no one of great significance was mentioned—and yet his grandmother had edited the journals, adding her own commentary and illustrations on events, providing an insight into the lives of those living and working in the house, on the estate and in the village since the seventeenth century. The births, marriages, deaths. The celebrations. The tragedies, changes that affected them all. Tash had reached the late eighteenth century when her phone rang.

'Hi…' she said, hunting for a tissue.

Darius, pacing Mary's living room while she packed a bag, heard the kind of sniff that only went with tears.

'Natasha? What's happened? Are you hurt?'

'No…' Another sniff. 'It's nothing.'

'You're crying.'

'I was just reading about an outbreak of smallpox in the village in 1793. Seven children died, Darius. One of them was the three year old son of Joshua Hadley. He wrote about him, about the funeral. It's heartbreaking…'

She'd found the history. It had figured heavily in his

education as the heir to the estate and the death of small children had been a fact of life before antibiotics.

'It was over two hundred years ago,' he reminded her.

'I know. I'm totally pathetic, but your grandmother drew a picture of his grave. It's so small. This isn't just a history; it's a work of art.'

'And full of smallpox, floods, crop failure.'

'Full of the lives of the people who've lived here. Not just the bad bits, but the joys, the celebrations. Your grandmother's illustrations are exquisite. Clearly it's in the genes,' she prompted.

He ignored the invitation to talk about his grandmother. 'You'll find Joshua's portrait in the dining room.'

'Actually, I'm looking at some of your early work right now,' she said, not giving up. 'Watercolours.'

'Chocolate-box stuff,' he said dismissively.

'That's a bit harsh. I love the drawing of your dog. What was his name?'

What was it about this woman? Every time he spoke to her, she churned up memories he'd spent years trying to wipe out. The only reason he was even here, being dragged back into the past, was because of her.

He should have just signed the whole lot over to the Revenue and let it go. It wasn't too late… Except there were things he had to do. People he had to protect.

'Darius?'

'Flynn,' he said. 'His name was Flynn.'

'He looks real enough to stroke.'

Even now, all these years later, he could feel the springy curls beneath his fingers. Smell the warm dog scent. Leaving him behind had been the hardest thing, but he'd been old—too old to leave the certainty of a warm hearth and a good dinner.

He'd mocked her sentimentality over a child who'd died

two hundred years ago but now he was the one with tears stinging at the back of his eyes.

'Darius, are you okay?'

He cleared his throat. 'Yes…'

'So, can I use all this stuff?'

'Will a smallpox outbreak help to the sell the house, do you think?' he asked.

'I'll probably miss out that bit.'

'Good decision.'

'So that's yes?'

'That's a yes with all the usual conditions.'

'You've already got me naked,' she reminded him.

He'd meant the ones about keeping his name out of it but, just as easily as she could dredge up the sentimental wasteland buried deep in his psyche, she could turn him on, make him laugh. 'You're naked?' he asked.

'Give me thirty seconds.'

He gripped the phone a little tighter. The temptation was there, but the thought of walking back into that house was like a finger of ice driving into him. 'Not even thirty minutes, I'm afraid. I've hit a complication.'

'Where are you?' she asked, as quick to read a shift in tone as body language.

'I stopped at the gatehouse to visit Mary Webb, Gary's grandmother,' he explained. 'He lives with her.'

'Oh… That was kind.'

'It was a duty call. She used to be my grandparents' cook. I couldn't just drive past.' He'd thought he could. He'd spent the last seventeen years mentally driving past.

'Kindness, duty, it doesn't matter, Darius, as long as you do it.'

'I'm glad you think so. She's five-foot-nothing and frail as a bird these days but it hasn't stopped her from reading me the riot act.'

'Give her a cookie,' she said, not asking why she was

angry. No doubt she understood how a woman would feel who'd lost—been abandoned by—a child she'd cared for, loved since infancy. Who, as a result of what happened that day, had lost her own grandson. His grandfather had not been a man to cross… 'People from the village are keeping an eye on her, doing her shopping, but she needs more than that so I'm taking her to see Gary, then driving her down to stay with her daughter in Brighton.'

'That should be a fun drive.'

'I'll blame you every mile of the way.'

'If it helps,' she said.

No, but thinking about her might. 'I'll survive,' he assured her. Probably. 'But I have no idea how long I'll be.'

'Don't worry about it. You take care of Mrs Webb. I can sort out some transport for myself. There's a bus to Swindon and I can catch a train from there. Don't give it a second thought. It's not a problem. Piece of cake—'

Her mouth was running away with her as she tried to hide her disappointment. It should have been an ego boost but all he wanted was to reach down the phone and hold her. Helpless, he waited until she began to repeat herself, finally ground to a halt, before he said, 'I'm taking her in Gary's car. I'll leave the Landie keys under a flowerpot in the porch for you.'

'Oh.'

'That's it?' he asked. 'You're finally lost for words?'

'No. I was just thinking that if you're bringing Gary's car back, I might as well stay here and wait for you.'

'It'll be late.'

'We might have to stay the night,' she agreed.

Not in a million years… 'I've got a better idea. Let's meet halfway at your place. We can have that picnic you promised me.'

'Oh? And what will you bring to the party?'

'A bottle of something chilled and a packet of three?' he offered.

'Three? That's a bit ambitious, isn't it?'

'One for yesterday, one for this morning, one for fun?' he suggested.

Her laugh was rich and warm. 'Talk, talk, talk…' she said, and ended the call.

He was grinning when he looked up and saw Mary watching him.

'My suitcase is on the bed,' she said primly. Then, as he passed her, she put her hand on his arm. 'It was the motorbike, Darius. That's why he told you about your Dad. Gary never cared about any of the other stuff you had, but that motorbike…'

'I know…'

It was Gary, with a battered old machine that he was renovating, who'd taught him to ride on the estate roads, so when he'd come down and found a brand-new silver motorbike waiting for him on his seventeenth birthday, the first thing he'd done was fire it up and drive it down to show him.

Cock-of-the-walk full of himself, too immature to understand how the one who'd always been the leader might feel when he saw him astride a machine so far out of his own reach. The understanding, in that split second, of the reality of their friendship; how, from that moment on, every step would take them further apart. For him there would be sixth form, university, the eventual ownership of this estate. For Gary, who'd left school at sixteen with no qualifications, there would be only a life of manual labour on little more than the minimum wage. And he'd used the only weapon he had to put himself back on top.

'He didn't do anything wrong. He told the truth, what he knew of it, that's all.'

'He was a stiff, proud man, your grandfather. He broke

your grandmother's heart, barring your father from the house while he stayed with your mother. The poor lady was never the same after. It wasn't that she didn't want to love you, Darius, just that she'd lost so much that she couldn't bear the risk.'

'Everyone lost, Mary. My grandfather most of all.'

Tash rolled off his bed and crossed to the window to look out across the park in the direction of the gates, rubbing her arms briskly to rid herself of the tingle of excitement that, just hearing the sound of his voice, riffled her skin into goose bumps.

Silly. She couldn't see the gatehouse cottage for the trees, but she was still grinning. She'd taken their relationship a step beyond a place Darius was comfortable with, hoping it would help him open up. Maybe it had. He'd stopped to talk to Gary's grandmother and the fact that she was angry with him suggested a strong emotional bond.

You only got angry with people you cared about. The fact that he'd mentioned it suggested that it mattered; he hadn't just called in, done the minimum, but had seen a need and acted on it. The journey might not be a comfortable one, but she doubted it would be silent; Mary Webb knew his secrets and he would be able to talk to her.

The fact that he'd felt able to tell her that she'd been angry suggested...

Stop it. Right there. The last thing she needed right now was a load of emotional complications messing with her head. Keep it simple.

Darius pressed the bell and Natasha's voice, distorted by static, said, 'Who's there?'

'You'd better not be expecting anyone else.'

'My cake is in great demand,' she said.

'Sugarlips!'

'First floor, the door on the right,' she said, and buzzed him up.

'I'm in the kitchen,' she called as he opened the door, and he kicked off his shoes alongside hers and followed her voice.

Her top, something silky in a rich chocolate, slid from her shoulder, a short pink skirt in some floaty material rose up, drawing attention to her long legs, bare feet, as she reached for a couple of wine glasses and, without saying a word, he put his arms around her and buried his mouth in the delicious curve between her shoulder and neck, sucking in her flesh, nipping at the sweet spot at the base of her neck.

A shiver of pleasure went through her as his hands found her breasts and she relaxed into him. It was the thought of this moment that had sustained him through an emotionally fraught day. The thought of holding her, breathing in the scent of her hair, her skin…

'Hello, you,' she said, laughing as she turned in his arms, reaching up to put her arms around his neck. Her hands didn't quite make it, her smile fading as her eyes searched his face and instead she cradled his cheeks in her palms, her thumbs wiping the hollows beneath his eyes as if to brush away dark shadows that only she could see. 'You've had a rough day…'

'No talking,' he said roughly. His ears were ringing with sixteen years of history as they'd talked about about everything, about every*one* but his mother. And now when Natasha would have answered him he cut her off with an abrupt, hungry kiss. For a heartbeat she was shocked into stillness and then she wrapped her arms around his neck, one of those long legs against his thigh and melted against him, her hot silk mouth the entrance to paradise.

He kissed her slow and deep while his hands reacquainted themselves with the feel of her skin, the already familiar shape of her curves, spreading wide around her waist, pushing up her top as his thumbs caressed the hollows of her stomach, his fingers teasing out all the little hotspots in her ribs.

Her fingers tangled in his hair, hanging on to him as she responded with little moans against his tongue and he fed on her sweet, spicy nectar that blotted out memory, blotted out everything but this moment, this need.

She uttered a soft cry as he broke off to get rid of her top, her bra and then leaned back with a sigh of contentment as he took his mouth, his tongue on a slow exploration of her body.

Definitely no talking…

CHAPTER EIGHT

TASH WAS INCAPABLE of coherent speech as Darius, his hands cradling her backside, sucked on the sensitive spot beneath her chin, curled his tongue around the horseshoe bone at the base of her throat, trailed hot, moist kisses between her breasts.

She whimpered as he ignored them and kept on going down, down, then he hit her navel and his tongue did things that had her gasping, breathless, climbing up him with her legs.

He propped her on the counter without missing a beat, then, with his hands free, he pushed up her skirt and slid his hand beneath the scrap of lace, pressing his thumb against the hot, swollen little button screaming for attention, then slowly circled it, in time with his tongue.

'Unngh…' she said, grabbing the collar of his polo shirt and hauling it, hand over hand, until it was over his head, then swallowed as she got the full impact of his powerful shoulders, arms moulded by the heaving of tons of clay, stone, metal, his broad chest arrowing to a narrow waist, hips, a mouth-watering bulge…

'Want to do it here?' he asked, his eyes burnished coal, teasing her with the tip of his finger before plunging it deep inside her.

'Unngh uuuunngh,' she urged, tightening around it, wanting more, wanting everything.

'Or would you rather move this to a nice safe bed?'

Safe...

There was nothing safe about this except the leaving-nothing-to-chance protection she'd stowed in the tiny seam pocket of her skirt and she answered him by taking it out, holding it between her teeth as, never taking her eyes from his, she tugged on his belt, flipped the button...

She looked up and, taking the condom from between her lips, he lowered his mouth to within a breath of hers and said, 'Don't stop now.'

He closed the gap, taking the word 'kiss' to a whole new meaning as, fingers shaking, she lowered his zip with the utmost care, eased her hands inside his jeans and pushed them down, releasing him. Clung to his hips as he disposed of her underwear, sheathed himself.

Then he looked up, straight into her eyes. 'Ready?' he asked.

'No talking,' she whispered and he was inside her with a thrust that went to her toes, held it while she caught her breath, opened her eyes. 'Don't stop now,' she murmured, wrapping her arms around his neck, her legs around his waist, taking in everything he had to give.

He gave it slowly, totally focused on her, reading her response to every thrust, every touch, taking this most basic of all acts and, instead of snatching for swift satisfaction, raising it into something new, something extraordinary, only taking his own release when he'd brought her to the point of incoherent howling meltdown.

Tash, shaking, shattered, wasn't sure which of them was supporting the other, only that they were holding each other, her cheek pressed into the hollow of his shoulder, listening to his heart return to a slow steady thud, breathing in the arousing scent of fresh sweat. All she knew was that she was glad she'd shut the kitchen window. That it was double-glazed...

* * *

Darius was the first to recover, straightening, lifting Natasha to the floor, holding her until he was certain that she could support herself. Or maybe holding on to her so that she could support him.

That was so not how it was meant to be.

Wound up by a day that had been filled with memories he'd spent half a lifetime trying to eradicate, he'd come looking for a hot, fast, cleansing release. Basic sex. What had just happened was something else...

He cleared his throat. 'I don't know about you, but I could do with a drink.'

She lifted her head, kissed his cheek. 'Sounds perfect.' She spotted the bottle he'd put on the kitchen table, picked up the glasses and handed them to him. 'Bring them through to the bathroom.'

There was no way they could both cram into her tiny shower cubicle so Tash filled the tub, added some bubbles, lit scented candles. He brought two glasses half filled with a pale chilled wine, set the bottle on the ledge and climbed in. She settled between his legs, leaning back against his chest, sipping the wine in restful silence as she relived each moment, each touch.

So much for the keep-it-simple sex. That had been as far removed from the simple gratification of a basic need as she'd ever experienced. No one had ever concentrated so completely on her in that way. Given so much...

His skin, golden in the candlelight, was too tempting and she turned her head, found the tender spot behind his knee with her tongue. He rescued her glass as, spurred on by his instant reaction, she half turned to take her mouth on an exploration of the smooth silk of his inner thigh, then turned to face him.

'Here or in a nice safe bed?' she asked.

'No bed is ever going to be safe with you in it but I'll

risk it,' he said, drawing her up his body so that he could kiss her. 'And this time I'm going to lie back and let you do all the work.'

Not work... All pleasure.

Tash woke to the early-morning sun, her body all delicious aches, and the night came flooding back. How she had made him the centre of their lovemaking, focusing on him so intently that she could read his response to every touch, giving herself in a way that she had never imagined and discovering a whole new level of pleasure in doing so.

She turned to reach for him but she was alone but for a sheet a paper on the pillow beside her. He'd drawn her as she'd slept—her breasts exposed, the curve of her buttock visible above the sheet tangled around her thighs, her hand extended towards him as if calling him back to bed.

Anyone looking at it would know that she had spent the night making love to the artist. If it had been anyone else, she'd have said that it was beautiful, but looking at herself, so vulnerable, so exposed, was disturbing. And why had he left it? Did he leave a picture for all his lovers? Something for the scrapbook? Something to scandalise the grandchildren?

Coffee. She needed coffee. Peeling herself off the bed, she tucked the drawing away in a drawer, pulled on a wrap and went through to the kitchen.

There was a note propped up against the kettle.

Sorry to kiss and run, but the horse is booked in at the foundry next week. Keep the Land Rover and the house keys for as long as you need them. D.

Next week? The horse had looked a long way from finished when she'd seen it and yet he'd taken a precious day to drive her to Hadley Chase. Of course this was a Darius

Hadley sculpture. What she thought was finished and what he considered finished…

She reached for her phone to text him…what? Thanks for the keys? For his time? For everything? There had been a lot of 'everything' to thank him for.

Keep it simple, she reminded herself, keying in the words:

Thanks for yesterday. N.

That covered it. Then she realised that she'd used N instead of T, which made it a lot more complicated. He was not a keeper and she was Tash, not Natasha. This was no more than a bit of a fling while she sorted herself out, she reminded herself.

So why did it feel like so much more?

Because she was all over the place. Because her life had been turned upside down. Because he was so much more…

She hit send before her brain fried tying itself in knots avoiding the truth.

Tash spent the next few days building up a media presence for Hadley Chase. She scanned some of the watercolours and used one that Darius had painted of the house as the header for the Facebook page, the ready-made web page she'd invested in and the Twitter account. It was very similar to the photograph she'd taken. No wonder he'd said she had a good eye.

Once it was all in place, she scheduled one-hundred-and-forty-character 'bites' from the history on the Twitter feed, adding his grandmother's exquisite illustrations, and then she did the same thing with the rest of his paintings. She linked it to the Facebook page and to the webpage where she'd laid out the house details.

She recorded a voice-over for the 'Sleeping Beauty'

video that she'd made inside the house and posted that on YouTube, linking each room to something from the history.

By the following week, she was gathering quite a following, getting lots of shares and re-Tweets, but most of the people who commented were less interested in the house than the artist and the history.

Who had painted the watercolours? Where could they buy them? Were prints available? Was the house open to the public? Where could they buy the book?

So far, no one had connected the paintings with Darius Hadley—hardly surprising considering the sculptures that had made his name. She considered sending a link to the Facebook page to Freddie Glover. She knew he'd get it, and no doubt wet himself in his rush to get his hands on the pictures. But Darius had dismissed the pictures as chocolate-box stuff and, besides, she'd given him her word.

There was no word from Darius—well, he was busy— but whenever the doorbell rang she rushed to see who it was.

'Tash?'

'Hi, Mum,' she said, buzzing her up, quashing her disappointment as she reached for the kettle. 'This is a surprise. I thought you'd be busy cooking and packing for the holiday.'

'Cooking,' she said, taking a casserole dish from a basket and popping it into the fridge. 'I ran out of room in the freezer.'

As you do…

'And you came all the way to London to give it to me?' she teased.

'Not just that. I thought, since you aren't working, we could spend the day together. We could go shopping… maybe have afternoon tea at Claibournes? Dad offered to treat us.'

Oh, right. This wasn't just food, it was the entire take-your-mind-off-it scenario.

'Actually, Mum, I'm a bit busy.'

'You're working? Has Miles Morgan—?'

'No. I'm handling a private sale for a client,' she said quickly, ignoring the fact that the definition of a client was someone who paid for your services. After all, a first casting Darius Hadley bronze would be worth a bob or two. Assuming he was still interested. 'So, what are you shopping for? You've left it a bit late for holiday stuff.' And her mother never left anything until the last minute. Obviously, she'd decided on a little face-to-face persuasion to join them.

'The holiday is off.'

'Off?'

Her mother sighed, laid out a couple of cups and saucers, heated the teapot. 'We had a call last night. Apparently the water tank overflowed, a ceiling came down and the cottage is uninhabitable for the foreseeable future. The kids are devastated.'

'Oh…I'm sorry.'

She cracked a wry smile. 'Really?'

'Absolutely. I know how much you enjoy it.' It might not be her idea of a good time, but Cornwall was a spring half-term tradition that went way back, rain or shine, and as a child she'd loved it. When she had children of her own she would love it again. 'Can't you find somewhere else?'

'For nine adults and seven children at half-term? And it's the bank holiday.'

'Eight adults,' Tash reminded her, getting down the cake tin. 'Lemon drizzle?' she offered, putting it on a plate. 'What will you do?'

'Organise some day trips, I suppose. We'll manage.' She took a piece of cake, rolled her eyes in appreciation 'You could open a cake shop,' she said. 'Or maybe an Internet home delivery service? Lots of demand for good home-made cake.'

'I could, but I won't.'

'Just a thought. Tell me about this private sale.'

'Actually, it's Hadley Chase.'

Her mother frowned. 'Isn't that the house—?'

'Yes. I've promised the owner that I'll find him a buyer.'

'And he agreed?'

'Why wouldn't he? I have a terrific track record.'

'With an agency behind you,' she said. 'Glossy brochures, ads in the *Country Chronicle*…' She stopped, realising that wasn't the most tactful thing to say. 'Advertising costs the earth.'

'Not necessarily.'

She showed her mother the Facebook page and got an unimpressed *humph*. 'People who buy stately homes aren't going to see this,' she said.

'It's all about getting a buzz going. Getting noticed by the media.' Getting them to follow you was the hardest part. They apparently took the view that they were there to be followed.

Her mother took another look. 'Well, you do seem to have a lot of comments.'

'Most of them asking who painted the picture of the house.' The one thing she couldn't tell anyone. 'Or if the history has been published and where can they buy it.' Maybe she should be following publishers. Art dealers.

'It is a lovely picture. Who did paint it?'

Yes, well, there was the rub.

'I found it in the house. It wasn't signed.'

'Well, someone who lived there was very talented.' She took another forkful of cake, then said, 'What you need is a plan.'

'This is the plan,' she admitted. 'Well, one of them. I've made a sort of *Sleeping Beauty* story. Pictures of the stairs covered in leaves, furniture shrouded in dust sheets, cobwebby attics, glimpses of the view through dusty windows, matching the room with sound bites from the history, and put it on YouTube.' She played it through.

'It's very…atmospheric.'

'Thanks. That's exactly what I was going for,' she said.

Her mother sighed. 'This is all very arty and interesting but what would you have done if Miles Morgan hadn't…' She made a vague gesture, clearly not wanting to say the words. 'To recover the situation?'

'Well, I would have suggested…' She stopped. Keep it simple… Okay, she couldn't afford to hire a firm of contract cleaners but maybe, just maybe… 'Mum, can I offer you a proposition?'

'You can offer me another piece of that cake,' she said, pouring out the tea, adding a splash of milk. 'What kind of proposition?'

'Well, you can see for yourself that Hadley Chase is a beautiful country house set in amazing grounds. It has a chalk stream with trout fishing for Dad and the boys, rods included,' she added. She'd seen them hung on racks in one of the storerooms. 'There are views to die for, and Hadley is a classic English village with thatched cottages, a centuries-old pub and a village green. I know it's not Cornwall,' she said quickly, 'but it will be free.'

'Well, that sounds delightful and incredibly generous of you, considering it's not your house,' her mother replied, suspicious rather than enthusiastic, 'but you seem to have glossed over the delightfully atmospheric cobwebs. And didn't it say in the paper that the staircase was about to fall down?'

'There is nothing wrong with the staircase that a vacuum, a duster and a little elbow grease won't fix.' She waited for the penny to drop. It didn't take long.

'So when you say "free", what you actually mean is that we'll be spending our holiday dealing with the dust and the leaves and whatever else is lingering in the corners. In other words, giving the place a thorough scrub?'

'Not all of it,' she protested. 'Just the main rooms.'

'And the bedrooms, unless we're going to camp on the lawn. And the bathrooms. And the kitchen.'

'I'll do the kitchen before you get there. Really, it's not that bad.'

Her mother sipped her tea.

'Seven days, eight adults,' she prompted. 'All I'm asking is an hour a day from each of you and in return you get to stay in an ancient and historic manor house. I promise,' she continued before her mother could raise any other objections, 'that no one at the WI will have holiday pictures to beat yours. Not some pokey little cottage, not even an apartment in a stately home, but the whole place, four-poster beds and a ballroom included, to yourselves.'

'I don't know, Tash—'

'You should read Emma Hadley's history. I've scanned it and printed it so you can take a copy with you. The illustrations are beautiful,' she said. 'You could give a talk. I'll make a PowerPoint presentation for you.' A tiny giveaway muscle in the corner of her mother's mouth twitched and, confident that she was hooked, Tash sat back. 'Of course, if it's too much for you, I could give Harry a call. If he and Lily have got nowhere booked for half-term I'm sure he would love to help...'

'You will be staying with us?' her mother asked, matching her guilt play and trumping it. 'Not just cleaning up the kitchen and then running away back to London?'

That was the thing with mothers. They could see through you, right down to the bone. A bit like a sculptor she knew...

'Oh, I'll have to be there,' she said. 'I'll be holding an open day on the last Saturday. With afternoon tea. Is there any chance of a few of your scones?'

'Is there any chance that you will be coming to Cornwall next year?'

She was a mere amateur compared to her mother.

'You can count on it. I've decided to take up surfing.'

Her mother, ignoring that, stood up. 'I suppose I'd better go home and get everyone organised. We'll bring our own bedding. And towels,' she added. 'Mice will almost certainly have made nests in the linen cupboards.'

Oh, joy…

'I'll ask one of the boys to pick you up on Saturday morning.'

'No need. Darius…Mr Hadley has loaned me his Land Rover.'

'*Darius* Hadley?' Her mother frowned. 'That name rings a bell. Would I have seen him in *Celebrity*?'

'I couldn't say,' she said truthfully.

Tash still had the keys and she had Darius's permission to do whatever it took to sell the house. No need to disturb him when he was so busy. Except, of course, someone would have to inform the security people that he would be having house guests.

And an open day on the Saturday.

What should she do? Text, phone and leave a message or go and see him? Her mother would not be amused if the police arrived mob-handed to evict them. She had to be sure he'd got the message and if he was working flat-out he might not check his phone.

She would just have to go and see him.

It was quicker to take the Underground than drive across London or take the bus and, since there was a truck completely blocking his street, she'd clearly made the right decision.

There was quite a crowd watching the drama and she spotted Patsy among them. 'What's going on?'

'They're loading up the horse. Darius!' she called. 'You've got company.'

He appeared from behind the truck, sweaty, dusty. There was clay in his hair and smeared across his cheek where he'd wiped away sweat with the back of his hand and a week's worth of beard only added to the piratical look.

'Hang on,' he said, 'I just need to see this on its way.'

'Take your time.'

His face split in a wide grin. 'I always do.'

Oh, yes...

She caught Patsy's eye and hoped she hadn't said that out loud. Judging by the eye-roll, she didn't need to. 'Have you sold the house yet?' she asked.

'No, but I'm working on it.'

'If there's anything I can do—' she produced a business card '—give me a call.'

'I can't afford help,' she said. 'That's why I'm here. I've offered my family a week in the country in return for their help cleaning the place up.'

'Well, now, I can't afford to take my boy away this half-term. If you need more hands, I'll work for board and country air.'

'Well, thanks. The more the merrier.'

'Clear it with Darius and give me a ring,' she said, glancing at her watch. 'See you later.'

Tash pressed herself against the wall as the truck started up and Darius joined her as it slowly pulled away, the crated horse lashed down in the back. They watched it pull out into the main road and disappear, then he looked down at her.

'You look like ice cream. I'd kiss you,' he said, 'but I stink.'

'It's a good stink.' Earthy clay, freshly sawn pine mingled with the sharp scent of honest sweat and, lifting a hand to his face, she rubbed her palm against his beard. 'And I want to try this.'

He lifted her hand, touched it to his lips. 'That's all I've got,' he said, tucking her arm around his waist and, with his arm around her shoulder, headed up the street. 'I haven't been to bed since I got out of yours.'

She stopped. 'You took time out to take me to Hadley Chase when you were that pushed?'

'Don't…' He touched the space between her brows. 'Don't frown. I was already struggling. The house, a whole lot of mess being dragged up from the past… You fired me up.' He unlocked the door to a small mews cottage at the end of the street. 'How do you feel about being my muse?'

His muse? For just a moment the image of herself as his inspiration sparkled in her imagination. She forced herself back to earth. 'It sounds a bit Pre-Raphaelite to me. I'm getting images of scantily dressed women lounging around a cold and draughty studio while louche men discuss their vision. I think I'll pass.'

'I didn't say becoming my muse, I said being her.'

'I don't get a choice?'

'Neither of us do, apparently.'

'Oh… Well, I'm glad to have helped,' she said, leaning against him briefly. 'Have you eaten?'

'Patsy kept me fuelled up. Have you been trying to get hold of me?' he asked, taking a phone out of his back pocket. 'The battery on this is flatter than a pancake.'

'I did leave a message, but I thought if you were working you wouldn't pick it up.'

'It's that important?'

'I haven't sold the house,' she said quickly, 'but it was too important to leave to chance.'

'Scrub my back and you'll have my full attention,' he assured her, kicking off his boots in the tiny lobby, peeling off his T-shirt and letting it lie where it fell.

On the outside, the cottage fitted with the rest of the

street. Inside, it was bare polished wood floors, white walls, spare steel lamp fittings and old rubbed leather chairs.

He slipped the buckle of his belt, let his jeans fall, stepped out of them and, naked, walked up the open staircase that led to a sleeping loft, not stopping until he reached a granite and steel wet room.

'If you're going to scrub my back you'd better lose the clothes or they'll get soaked,' he warned as he flipped the tap. His eyes gleamed wickedly. 'Or you could leave them on. Either way works for me.'

'Behave yourself.' She hadn't come dressed down. She'd wanted to make an impact, wanted him to notice her and even before she reached for the hem of the clinging cross-over top she was wearing she could see that she had. 'I have to go home on the Tube.'

She unhooked the swirl of printed chiffon that stopped six inches above her knee, kicked it away and stepped out of her shoes.

'Stop right there,' he said when she was down to the champagne lace bra and panties that she'd bought with birthday money and even in the sale had cost twice anything else she wore next to her skin. 'I really want to see those wet.'

'When you can do more than kiss my hand,' she said, but took her time over removing them since he appeared to like them so much. 'Turn round.'

His eyes were focused on her breasts. 'Do I have to?'

Oh, boy. That was a tough one. His thick dark curls, the streaks of clay on his cheeks, his chest, water sluicing over his skin gave him the elemental look of some tribal chieftain who'd battled the elements and won through.

Every primitive instinct was urging her to take a step forward, press her body against his and go for it but the dark hollows in his temples, beneath his eyes warned her that it was the last thing he needed.

She picked a gel off the shelf, made a circular gesture with her finger and after a moment he turned, placed his hands flat against the granite, bracing himself, or more likely propping himself up.

His finely muscled back, narrow waist, taut buttocks were, if anything, even more distracting.

Get a grip, Tash. You can do this…

She applied the gel to his hair, stretching up on her toes to ease out the dried-in clay with her fingers, leaning into him to massage his scalp—her body, breasts sliding against him as the soap cascaded down his back.

He groaned as she repeated the process. 'Dear God, woman, what are you doing?'

'Torturing myself,' she said as she applied gel to a sponge and began working it into his shoulders.

'That makes two of us. If you have something important to tell me you'd better get on with it, while I can still think.'

'I've organised a cleaning party for the house. We'll be staying there from Saturday for the entire week.'

'Staying?' He half turned to look at her.

'Relax. It's just my family.' She worked the soap down his back, into the hollow above those gorgeous tight buttocks.

'No…' he began, then caught his breath as she used her hands to work the soap between his thighs.

'The Cornwall holiday fell through so I offered them a week in the country in return for a little light housework.'

'I can't ask your family to clean my house,' he said.

'You didn't—I did,' she said, getting down on her knees and working the foam behind his knees, over his totally gorgeous calves. 'Patsy's volunteered, too.'

'Patsy?'

'I saw her in the street. She said I should run that by you.'

'The whole damn street will know every detail within an hour of her coming home.'

'It's just an old house,' she reminded him. 'A lot of dull portraits, a couple of four-poster beds and a kitchen out of the Ark. I just need you to tell Ramsey and the security people that we'll be there,' she said. 'Now you can turn around.'

He turned and for a moment the breath stopped in her throat. He might not have been to bed in a week, but one part was still wide awake and ready for action.

Everything slowed down as she dropped the sponge and used her fingers between his toes, his ankles, the tender spot behind his knees, the smooth skin inside his thighs. Then she stood up and soaped his chest, his stomach.

At one point he reached for her but she tutted. 'No touching...'

His legs were trembling by the time she reached the parts that did not know when to lie down and quit.

'Sweet heaven,' he said, leaning back, clutching at a rack holding a pile of towels, his eyes closed as she took him in her palm, stroking him until, with a shuddering sigh, he spilled into her hand. And then she flipped off the water, put her arms around his neck and kissed him very gently. 'Now, go to bed.'

Darius, dazed, barely able to speak, reached up and pulled a towel down from the rack, wrapped it around her and pulled her warm, wet body against him. 'Stay with me,' he begged.

'Is that what a muse would do?' she asked, looking at him, her eyes dark, intense, searching. A smallest of frowns defeating her smile. 'Be there so that when you wake up you can draw her sated, replete, every desire satisfied?'

'I left a note,' he said. 'I left the picture...'

'Why?'

'You were sleeping. Taking it would have been as if I was stealing something intimate from you.'

'Oh.' She leaned her forehead against his chest so that

he shouldn't see her eyes. See what she had been thinking. 'If you want it, Darius, take it. It's yours.'

He took a step back, lifted her chin, reading her as easily as most people read headlines. 'You thought it was a kiss off?' he asked. 'A Darius Hadley sketch in return for some hot sex?'

'No! Maybe.' Her shoulders dropped. 'I don't know you, Darius.'

'No, you don't,' he said, pulling another towel from the rack, wrapped it around his waist. 'If I ever did anything that skanky I would sign and date it so that it would be worth something. A realisable asset.'

'Darius…'

He didn't wait for her mumbled apology. She hadn't trusted him and that was a deal-breaker. He picked up the receiver of the landline beside the bed, punched in a fast-dial number.

'Ramsey? Darius Hadley.' He didn't bother with the courtesies. 'My agent has organised a clean-up of the house. Please inform the security people that they will be resident on site from…' He looked across at Natasha, hovering in the doorway of the wet room, a towel clutched to her breast.

'Today,' she said on a gasp. 'I'm going down there today to turn on the water, clean up the—'

'From today,' he said, despite everything, unable to take his eyes off her as Ramsey droned on about the inadvisability of letting a group of strangers into the house. The damp strands of hair clinging to pink cheeks, creamy shoulders and it was all he could do to stop himself from going to her. Begging forgiveness…

This was the madness. The same madness that had seized his father. Wanting a woman beyond sense, beyond reason.

'Your objections are noted but, to tell you the truth, Ramsey,' he said, cutting him off, 'I don't actually care what you think. The only reason I don't just sign the whole lot over to the Treasury is because someone has to protect the tenants and I know that won't be you.' He cut off Ramsey's protest. 'Is there anything else?' he asked, returning the receiver to the cradle, but leaving his hand on it, anchoring him to the spot.

Tash swallowed. His face was shuttered and the apology bubbling up in her throat died unspoken.

Shouting at him when he'd behaved like a jerk had been a momentary bump in the road, no more than a shake-up. Doubting his honour was, apparently, a damned great rock. She'd crossed some invisible line and the damage was terminal.

'There's just one more thing,' she said, clutching the towel to her breast. Being naked had, in an eye blink, gone from the most natural, most perfect thing in the world to the most awkward.

This definitely came under the 'never mix business with pleasure' rule but, despite the lack of encouragement to continue, there was still business to be done.

'Unlike Morgan and Black, I can't afford to put on a three-course lunch at the Hadley Arms, so I'm holding an open day on Saturday week,' she said. 'I'll be serving afternoon tea. On the lawn if the weather holds, in the ballroom if it doesn't.' There was still no response. Not even a sarcastic comment about cake. He just kept his hand on the phone as if waiting for her to go so that he could make another call. 'While I have no doubt that potential buyers and the property press would like to meet you, it's not essential.' Not one word. 'That's all.'

She gathered her clothes, made it downstairs on rubber legs, pulling them on over still damp skin as she headed for the door, banging it hard shut behind her. So that he'd know she'd gone. So that she couldn't go back.

Damn, damn, damn… How could she have got it so wrong? How could she have got herself so involved?

Involved was for the future, when she was established, with a man who was ready to settle down, raise a family. It wasn't for now and it certainly wasn't with a man who had heartbreak stamped all over him. She'd known from the first moment she'd set eyes on him that he wasn't a man made for happy ever after. This was supposed to be a fling. Hot, fast, furious and, like the bronze of an anonymous nude figure, something to rub your fingers over in passing when you were old and remember with a smile.

Okay. The bronze wasn't going to happen. Her career, on the other hand, still needed to be rescued. That deal was still on. It was back to strictly business.

Which was what she'd wanted in the first place. Until she didn't.

'Natasha?' She'd reached the corner of the street without being aware how she'd got there and practically bumped into Patsy as she came out of the corner shop carrying a bundle of files. 'Are you okay?'

'Oh, um, yes… Just in a hurry,' she said, suddenly aware of damp strands of hair clinging to her cheek and neck, that her top, pulled on over damp skin, was twisted, telegraphing what had just happened as loudly as if she'd posted his drawing on Facebook. 'There's so much to do. I, um, told Darius you had volunteered to join the clean-up party.'

'Let me guess. He said no.'

'No.' He hadn't. He'd muttered about gossip but he hadn't actually said no. Why would he? She'd been posting pictures of Hadley Chase all over the Net and there was nothing Patsy could tell the neighbours that they couldn't see for themselves. 'I'll be glad to have you if you're still up for it.'

'I'll be there, rubber gloves and dusters at the ready.'

'It won't all be work,' she assured her. 'Does your boy like fishing?'

She grinned. 'I guess we'll find out.'

Tash opened her bag and took out one of the new business cards she'd ordered off the Net—*Natasha Gordon, Property Consultant*—and offered it to Patsy. 'Email me if you have any special food requirements. And everyone is bringing their own bedding. Is that okay?'

'None and no problem. I'll come tomorrow afternoon straight after school if you like? Help you get the bedrooms ready.'

'You are such a star!'

'We'll be there at about six.'

'Great.' She was halfway around the corner when Patsy called, 'Natasha…' She half turned. 'Your skirt is caught up in your knickers.'

CHAPTER NINE

THE FIRST THING Tash did when she arrived at Hadley Chase was hunt down the stopcock in the scullery and turn the water on. It was, of course, stuck fast, so her next task was to brave the cobwebs and spiders in the toolshed to find a wrench so that she could shift it.

Someone had left all the taps open, which was obviously the right thing to do, but meant that once the tank had filled and the water was flowing she had to tour the house, turning them all off, mopping up leaks and making a note of where they were so that they could be fixed. A job for her dad, and she fired off a text to him, asking him to bring some plumber's mait.

She paused on the first floor landing, aware that something had changed but for a moment unable to think what it was. Then she realised that it was the window.

Despite working day and night to finish his sculpture, Darius had remembered his promise to get it fixed and for a moment she leaned her forehead against the cool surface of the glass. She had wanted him to trust her with the darkness that lay at his heart but she'd been so quick to leap to the conclusion that he was about as deep as an August puddle. And if he was, wasn't that what she'd expected? Gone into with her eyes wide open? Except he'd been angry, because… Well, because didn't matter.

Without trust there was nothing. And that was what she had. Nothing.

With a throat full of dust and desperate for a cup of tea, she plugged in the electric kettle. It blew a fuse. She mended it with the wire and screwdriver she'd brought with her. Next job, lighting the ancient solid fuel range cooker...

By the time she'd got it going, she was coated in smoke and black dust and more cobwebs from the fuel store, her knuckles were sore and she was seriously considering her mother's suggestion of an alternative career in the confectionery business.

Unfortunately, having spent the previous night emailing individual invitations to the open house and afternoon tea—spiced with the painting of the house and extracts from the history as attachments—to everyone she could think of, partners and children included since it was the weekend, any career change would have to be put on hold until she'd shifted two years' worth of dust.

The first job was the fridge. She washed it down, then switched it on. Another fuse blew, tripping all the electrics for the second time.

This time she went through them all, changing the wire in three that looked a bit dodgy. That done, she toured the house again, checking every light switch. The last thing she needed was to have them go pop when it was dark.

It was dark by the time she'd wiped down the last surface in the scullery. She picked up the bowl of water to tip down the sink and then screamed as she caught sight of a face in the window, slopping water down her filthy jeans and over her shoes in the process. Belatedly realising that it was her own face, smudged with coal dust, she laughed a little shakily. Then a second face appeared beside it.

This time the scream wouldn't come.

She opened her mouth, but her throat was stuffed with rocks and no sound emerged, even when the back door opened and a black-clad figure put his head around the door.

'Sorry, miss, I didn't mean to startle you.'

It was the security guard who'd tried to move them on.

'Mr Hadley called the office to tell us you'd be here and asked if I would look in on you and check that you were all right. He thought you'd be easier if it was someone you knew by sight.'

Since the rocks were taking their time to budge, she tipped the remaining water down the sink.

He shrugged awkwardly. 'I'm sorry about the other day.'

'No problem… Just doing your job… I'm fine,' she said, sounding unconvincing even to herself. 'Would you like a cup of tea?' she offered, peeling off her rubber gloves and squelching her way into the now gleaming kitchen.

'I can do better than that,' he said, placing a carrier on the table from which emerged the mouth-watering scent of hot fried food and the sharpness of vinegar.

Until that moment she hadn't thought of food but, suddenly assailed by sharp pangs of hunger, she said, 'Please tell me that's fish and chips.'

He grinned. 'Mr Hadley thought you might be glad of something hot to eat.'

Darius… Her heart, just about back to normal, missed a beat. She'd said she didn't know him, but it seemed that he knew her.

'There appear to be two lots,' she said, peering into the carrier.

'Well, I haven't had my supper yet. I was going to have it in the van, but why don't I put the kettle on while you dry off?'

It was barely light when Darius woke, fully aroused—he'd been dreaming about Natasha. One moment she'd been a vision in something floaty, looking and smelling like a summer garden, the next she'd been pressed up against him, naked, soapy wet, her fingers kneading his scalp, her breasts against his back. And when he'd turned round and she'd taken him in her hand...

He closed his eyes, wanting that moment back. Wanting her to be there with him. He'd asked her to stay, but then...

Then he'd done what he always did with any woman who got too close, who he wanted too much; he'd used the first excuse that offered itself to make it impossible for her to stay.

She was so easy to read. Every thought, every idea was right there in her lovely face and she knew it. The fact that she'd buried her face in his chest was enough to warn him that she was hiding something and damn it, of course he was mad that she could think such a thing of him. But why wouldn't she?

She'd just been betrayed in the worst possible way. Her confidence had to be shaky. And he'd made all kinds of excuses not to wake her because she could read him, too. Would have seen what he could not hide. That it had been a panic run.

What he'd felt, what he'd drawn, had terrified him. He'd had to leave her a note so that she knew about the Land Rover and keys, but it had been bare of emotion. He'd left mixed messages and she'd interpreted them just as he'd hoped she would. Until he'd walked around that truck and his heart had practically leapt out of his chest with joy.

He knew what he felt was senseless. And he'd acted senselessly.

He took a cup of coffee out into the tiny yard he shared with a couple of randy pigeons and a pot of dead daffodils, watching the sun turn the sky from a pale grey to blue, stirring only when there was a long peal on the doorbell.

It was Patsy with a large cardboard envelope. It was addressed to him c/o Patsy and when he turned it over, saw it was from Natasha, he didn't have to open it to know what it was.

'*I don't know you...*'

Of course she didn't. He'd never let anyone close enough to know him. He didn't know himself.

'Why did she send it to you?' he asked. 'How did she know your address?'

'I don't keep it a secret,' she said, looking pointedly at his door. The cottage, like the studio, bore no number. 'She's a nice woman, Darius.'

'No...' There were a dozen words rushing into his head to describe Natasha, but 'nice' wasn't one of them. Vivid, fun, kind, thoughtful, vulnerable, hot, glorious, spicy sweet... He realised that Patsy was looking at him a little oddly. 'Sorry, yes, of course you're right.'

'I'm going to Hadley Chase as soon as school is out this afternoon. When will you be coming down?'

'I have to go to the foundry today,' he said. 'Take the horse apart so that they can start making the moulds.' Dozens of intricate parts, every one of which had to be checked for imperfections through each stage of the process.

'And tomorrow?' she asked.

'It's going to take weeks,' he said, but she knew that. That wasn't what she was asking.

She didn't press it. 'Any message?'

He shook his head. 'No, wait.' He took a card out of his wallet and handed it to her. 'Pay for the food. And whatever's needed for the open house party. Tell them to help themselves to whatever wine is left in the cellar.'

'Is that it?'

'Michael will find it very different,' he said, reluctant to let her go, disapproval in every line. She knew how he was. That he never got involved.

'That's the point of a holiday,' she said and—for the first time since he'd known her—she refused the opportunity to talk at length about her son, about anything and left him standing on his doorstep.

He closed the door, opened the envelope, took out the drawing and traced every line of Natasha's spicy sweet sleeping body with his finger.

Sated, replete, every desire satisfied...

'Not just you, Sugarlips,' he murmured. 'Not just you.'

Natasha opened her eyes and lay quite still, not sure for a moment where she was. Then, as everything came into focus and she saw the distant hills through a tall window, she remembered. She was at Hadley Chase, lying in the bed that Darius Hadley had slept in as a boy.

She'd crawled into it some time after midnight, every limb aching, too exhausted to bother with the curtains— nothing but a passing owl would see her—and curled into his pillow, wishing he was there with her.

No chance.

For a while she'd been warmed by the fact that he'd asked the security people to check on her, bring her something hot to eat—he must have known that the old range cooker wouldn't deliver on day one—and she had sent a text, thanking him. Nothing fancy.

Thanks for supper. Most welcome. T

No more, no less than any well brought-up woman would do.

There was no response. Of course not. You didn't expect a reply to a bread-and-butter thank-you note. The food, she reminded herself, had been no more than a courtesy. She might have mortally offended his sense of honour, but she had organised a freebie clean-up of his house: *noblesse oblige* and all that.

She reached for her phone, kidding herself she was

checking the time—hoping that he might have unbent sufficiently to ask if she was okay in the empty silence of the night.

Nothing. No texts. No missed calls.

She sighed, rolled out of bed, winced a little as she stood up. Her knees creaked and her shoulder hurt from all the stretching and bending and scrubbing, but at least there was hot water for a shower.

She stoked up the oven, took a cup of tea out into the garden and sat on a bench beneath a climbing rose massed with creamy buds. A small muntjac doe with a tiny fawn wandered across the lawn within feet of her. She took a photograph with her phone and Tweeted it—there was nothing like cute animals to get a response—not forgetting to add the website URL.

Her mother and sisters-in-law would arrive with a ton of food, she knew, but ten adults and eight children were going to take a lot of feeding so she headed to the village to make the day of the butcher and the couple who ran the village store and farm shop. Orders placed, she treated herself to coffee and a muffin at the pub while she took advantage of their free Wi-Fi to check her Facebook and Twitter pages.

There were a couple of messages on Facebook asking her to get in touch, one from a publisher, the other from the features editor of a magazine, both asking her to ring them.

They were both interested in Emma Hadley's history of Hadley Chase so she invited them to the open house on Saturday. Maybe she should invite Freddie, the art dealer, too. If she could sell the book, the paintings and the house in one day she would become a legend.

Meanwhile, acceptances to the open house were coming in; even the regional television news magazine were hoping to send a team. No response yet from the *Country Chronicle* despite personal notes to both the editor and the advertising manager who, in her opinion, owed Darius a two-page feature at the very least.

She checked a missed call from her mother, a response to the text to her Dad. She'd left a voicemail expressing disbelief that her daughter had spent the night alone in a house that was miles from anywhere. If she'd known, if she'd *told* her, she stressed, she would have come on ahead of her father.

Normally the suggestion that she couldn't cope would have infuriated her. Instead, she found herself in total agreement. Last night, she would have totally welcomed her mother's company. She was smiling at that thought when she realised that someone was standing on the far side of the table.

Expecting it to be the girl wanting to clear her coffee, she said, 'I'm done.' Then, when she didn't begin to clear she looked up and her heart stopped.

'Darius…' Her vocal cords seemed to be in some disarray, too. 'I…um… How did you get here?'

'I took a train to Swindon,' he said, 'and then caught the bus. Piece of cake.'

He should have smiled then, but he didn't.

'You've still got Gary's car,' she said as her brain, buffering the emotion dump, the rush of sensations, images of him racing through her memory like a speeded-up film, finally caught up.

'It needed servicing.'

'Don't tell me,' she said, 'you're not just Darius Hadley, sculptor. You moonlight as Mike, the man who repairs cars while you wait.'

Smile now. Smile, pull out a chair, sit down, tell me why you're here. Please…

'I spotted the Land Rover as I drove through the village.' No smile. Still standing.

'I've been organising supplies for the week and stopped

to use the Wi-Fi.' She gestured vaguely at the open laptop. 'If you're stopping, will you sit down? I'm getting a crick in my neck.'

He pulled out the chair opposite and one of his knees brushed against hers as he sat down but he moved it before she could catch her breath and shift hers.

'Would you like some coffee?' she asked.

He shook his head.

Could this be any more awkward?

'I've…um…got a publisher interested in your grandmother's history,' she said, her legs trembling with the strain as she tucked her feet back as far as they would go so that she didn't accidentally touch him.

'Then my troubles are over.'

Sarcasm she could do without. This she could do without.

'Why are you here, Darius?'

'Why did you send the drawing back?'

Oh, shoot. That was so complicated, so mixed up, such an emotional reaction…

'Why didn't you just tear it up?' he insisted, looking straight into her eyes. 'Throw it in the trash with the teabags and potato peelings.'

She blew out her cheeks, tucked a strand of hair behind her ear. 'It was a beautiful drawing, Darius. There was no way I could have destroyed it.'

The truth, plain and simple.

'You could have taken it to your friendly art dealer,' he said.

'Unsigned?'

'With a letter from you as provenance, he would have snatched your hand off.'

'No!' Her protest was instinctive. She could never share such an intimate moment with Freddie, or any other art dealer.

'You could have simply kept it,' he persisted.

'Something to shock the grandchildren?'

It was the second time she'd offered him a chance to smile at the memory of an earlier, happier moment. For the second time he did not take it, but simply waited, demanding total honesty, the exposure of feelings she'd been unwilling to even think because once you'd thought them…

'You left me something of yourself, Darius. A memory to treasure.' Explaining this was like tearing away layers of flesh. Total exposure of the inner depths he talked about. But infinitely safer than thoughts that even now were rushing in. 'I lost the right to anything so precious when I destroyed that with my lack of trust.'

'Trust is a two-way thing, Natasha.'

'You took me on trust, no questions asked.'

'That was business. This…'

She'd asked herself what it had taken to build that impenetrable façade. What it would take to shatter it. Suddenly, in that hesitation, she had a glimpse into the darkness. Trust. It was all about trust.

'This?'

He shook his head. 'You shared your past with me, Natasha, offered me the chance to open up to you, but I didn't have your courage.'

'No…' She instinctively reached out a hand to him, grasped his fingers. 'It's hard. It wasn't the moment. I understood.'

'And I understand about the drawing. If it hadn't mattered, you'd have either kept it as a souvenir of a hot night, or you'd have been checking out the value with Freddie Glover.'

'If it hadn't mattered,' she replied, 'you wouldn't have been so angry.'

And for a moment they both just sat there, looking at each other, aware that they had just crossed some line.

Then he turned his hand beneath hers so that their fingers were interlocked.

'I've been walking away from people since I was seventeen years old,' he said. 'I keep trying to walk away from you.'

'Why?'

'Is there anything in the Land Rover that will spoil if it's left for an hour or two?' he asked, ignoring the question. She shook her head. He stood up, closed up her laptop and took it across to the bar. 'Will you look after this, Peter?'

He nodded. 'It's been a while, Darius.'

'Too long,' he said, heading for the door. 'We'll catch up later.'

'Darius…' she protested. 'My entire life depends on my laptop!'

'It'll be safer there than left in the car. I'll come back for them both later.'

'Yes, but…'

'I walked away from Hadley Chase. I have to walk back.' He'd reached the doorway, looked back, held out his hand to her. 'Will you walk with me?'

'Why me, Darius?' she asked, taking it.

'I don't know,' he said, and finally there was the hint of a smile. 'Only that no one else will do.'

He said nothing more until they were through the open gates of Hadley Chase and walking down the path that led to the river.

'The Clarendon family used to live over there,' he said, pausing at a gap between the trees and looking across the river to where a four-square Georgian house nestled beneath a rise in the Downs. 'The families were very close. My father and Christabel Clarendon were practically betrothed in their prams.'

His father… 'The house is the headquarters of an IT firm now,' she said. 'Steve told me.'

'Steve?'

'The security guy. They had a false alarm there last night.' She turned to look up at him. 'Betrothed?'

'They were both only children,' he said, moving on. 'There was land and money on both sides and it was the perfect match.'

'It takes a bit more than that.'

'Does it? Arranged marriages are the norm in other cultures and they'd known one another since they were children. There would be no surprises.'

'There are always surprises.'

'Yes...' They were climbing now through the woods and he stopped before an ancient beech tree that had once been coppiced and had four thick trunks twisting from its base. He looked up. 'It's still here. The tree house.'

He put a foot on a trunk that had been cut to form steps and, catching a low branch, pulled himself up to take a look, then disappeared inside.

'Is it safe?' she asked, following him. 'Wow... This is some tree house.'

'Gary built it for me,' he said.

'Gary?' The floor was solid planks of timber, the roof a thick thatch where swallows had once nested, the sides made from canvas that rolled up. There was a rug and a pile of cushions, faded, torn, chewed or pecked. 'Why?'

'His dad worked on the estate. Gamekeeper, gardener, whatever needed to be done. When Gary left school, he became his dad's assistant and did odd jobs around the estate. One of those odd jobs was to keep me amused during the school holidays. One summer he amused me by building this.'

'He did a great job.'

'It was more than a job. He was like an older brother,' he said. 'The kind that teaches you all the good stuff. The stuff that adults tell you is bad for you.'

'Drinking, lads' mags, smoking the occasional spliff? I've got brothers,' she reminded him when his eyebrows rose. 'You can't know how much I wished I was a boy.'

'Can I say, just for the record, that I'm glad you're not?'

'Oh, me too,' she assured him. 'Men wear such boring shoes.'

He looked down at the purple ballet pumps she was wearing. 'Pretty.'

For a moment she had a vision of him bending down, taking one off, kissing her instep... She cleared her throat. 'What did you do up here?'

'When I was younger I used it the way any kid would. Hideout, den, a place to keep secret stash. We used to sit up here watching badgers at dusk.'

'Brilliant.'

'It was... Of course, Gary never put that much effort into anything without an ulterior motive. When I was away at school, he brought girls here.' He shrugged. 'I did too, when I was older.'

'The young master seducing the village maidens?' she teased.

'Rather the opposite,' he said and his sudden grin sent a lump to her throat for a magical youth that had been somehow blighted. 'I'll check it out, clean it up for your nephews and nieces.'

'Does that mean you're staying?'

'I've put off the foundry until Monday but they can't start without me. Is there room?' he said, sliding his arms around her waist, drawing her close, and the down on her cheeks stood up as if she were a magnet and he was the North Pole.

'No problem, I'll share. Your room is pretty much as you left it, give or take a few things. I borrowed some of the chocolate-box pictures for the blog. I've had a lot of interest,' she rushed on, to cover just how important his answer was. 'There's a greeting card manufacturer...'

'That's the take,' he said, ignoring the throwaway distraction. 'What's the give?'

'Me,' she said. 'If there's still a vacancy for a muse?'

'So when you said share...?'

'I could bunk in with Patsy, but I barely know her, while we're—'

He groaned, pulling her into his arms, kissing her with a hot, sweet, haunting tenderness that could rip the heart out of you. It was the perfect kiss you saw in the movies, the kiss a girl dreamed about before life gave you a reality check, the kiss you'd remember when every other memory had slipped away into the dark. When he finally drew back, rested his forehead against the top of her head, he was trembling.

'Darius...' She cradled his face in her hands, wanting to reassure him, to tell him... 'You kept the beard,' she said shakily.

She felt him smile against her palms. 'You said you liked it.'

'As I was saying, we're compatible in practically every way.'

'I doubt your parents would be impressed with our, um, compatibility,' he said, climbing down the tree, lifting her after him. 'And then there are those three over-protective brothers of yours. I'm seriously outnumbered.'

'That's ridiculous, Darius. It's your house.'

'No. I'll get a room at the pub.' He took her hand and began to walk up the path towards the house. 'I thought we might go back to the beginning, slow things down a little. Maybe date?'

'Date?'

'An old-fashioned concept, involving the back seat of the movies, Sunday lunch in a country pub, dancing.'

'You dance?'

'I can learn.'

'Well, perfect, but what about the muse thing?'

'Getting naked? Inspirational sex?' He grinned. 'We can do that too.' They had reached the edge of the lawn and they both turned to look at the house. 'We appear to have company,' he said as they spotted the small red car at the same moment that the woman leaning against it spotted them.

'Brace up, Darius. It's my mother.'

CHAPTER TEN

'Mum!' Tash gave her a hug. 'How lovely! Can I introduce Darius Hadley, the owner of Hadley Chase?'

'Mr Hadley.' Her mother's eyebrows remained exactly where they were. It just felt as if they'd done an imitation of Tower Bridge.

'Darius,' he said, offering his hand with a smile Tash recognised from the pages of the *Country Chronicle*. Protective camouflage that he wore in public, but never with her. 'I can't tell you how grateful I am to you for pitching in and helping like this.'

'I'm helping my daughter,' she said. 'I thought you were on your own, Tash, or I wouldn't have been so concerned.'

'I was and, believe me, if you'd had any idea you would have been a lot more concerned. Three electrical blowouts, a gazillion spiders and the fright of my life when the security guard peered in through the window.'

'Well, really! How thoughtless.'

'No...thoughtful. Darius was concerned about me, too, so he called their office and asked if Steve could bring me some fish and chips. He was perfectly sweet. He made up the Aga, made sure I knew how to set the alarm and checked all the outbuildings before he left.'

'I'm really glad you're here, Mrs Gordon,' Darius said before she could comment. 'I didn't think I'd be able to get away, but I've put back the project I'm working on until Monday. I met Natasha in the village just now when I stopped to book a room at the pub.'

'He's just shown me the most amazing tree house, Mum,' she said, taking out the keys and unlocking the front door and, just like that, they were through it and in the hall; no drama about the big moment when he stepped back into the house. 'The kids are going to love it. I'll make some coffee. Why don't you show my mother the portrait of Emma Hadley, Darius?' she suggested, pushing him in a little deeper. He glanced at her, the only sign of tension a touch of white around his mouth. 'She's going to give a talk to the Women's Institute on the history of this place.'

'Of course. It's in the library, Mrs Gordon,' he said.

'Laura,' she said. 'I don't understand. Why are you staying in the village?'

'Well, obviously I'll be here, doing as much as I can, but this is your holiday. You won't want a stranger—'

'Nonsense! Of course you must stay here.'

Tash grinned, *Bazinga*...

'Mum, Mum, we've found a boathouse! There's a single scull!'

Patsy rolled her eyes. 'I told you not to go near the river without an adult, Michael.'

'Tom and Harry and James are down there, river dipping with the little kids.'

'Are you interested in rowing, Michael?' Darius, who was cutting the lawn, had stopped for a drink of the fresh lemonade Patsy had brought out.

'He's been desperate to try it ever since the Games,' she said.

'Well, let's go and take a look at it. I'll need a hand to get it down. Any volunteers?' He glanced around at the women stretched out on the grass, soaking up the sun, studiously avoiding looking at Natasha, who took the view that the one-hour rule didn't apply to her and was busy washing down the external doors and windowsills.

'Take Tash,' Patsy suggested. 'Please. She's making us feel guilty.'

'Natasha?' he prompted. 'Do you want to give these women a break?'

'They're on holiday, I'm not.' But she peeled off her rubber gloves and joined him.

'Did you sleep well?' he asked as they followed Michael down to the river.

'Not especially,' she admitted. 'You'd think in a house of this size we might manage a few minutes on our own. If the kids had been ordered to chaperone us, they couldn't have done a better job of it.'

'Your mother knew what she was doing when she insisted I stay,' he said. 'If it's any consolation, I'm not getting much sleep, either.'

'Memories?' she asked.

'More the fact that my childhood bed no longer smells of dog, but of you. Which is very disturbing, especially when I've spent the last twenty-four hours under the close-eyed scrutiny of your three very large brothers who, let me tell you, are nowhere as easy to charm as your mother.'

'Maybe you should stop being so charming to their wives,' she suggested, a little tetchily, he thought.

'You want me to be charming to you?'

'No! That is so not what I want and you know it.'

He knew but they'd reached the boathouse and Michael was dancing with impatience, waiting for the slowcoach adults to catch up.

'Anticipation only increases the gratification,' he said.

'That had better be a promise.'

'Cross my heart,' he said, drawing a cross over his chest, just as she had, and she groaned.

'Come on!'

'Okay, let's see.'

The buckles on the straps were rusted but they finally managed to free them and lower the scull into the water and then watch as it filled with water.

'I'm sorry, Mike; the hull is cracked.'

'Can it be fixed?' he asked once they hauled it out of the water and Darius had located the damage.

'Maybe, but it's a fibreglass hull and will have to go to a special workshop.' Seeing his disappointment, he said, 'You know, if you're really keen on trying this, Michael, I'll find you a club in London where you can get some proper training.'

The boy's mouth dropped open. 'Wicked!'

'You'd better go and ask your mother. Tell her that it's my contribution to the medal tally in 2020,' he called after him.

Natasha was grinning. 'He's a great kid.'

'Patsy worries about him. I think that's why she volunteered for your work party. She can't watch him twenty-four-seven and he's getting to the age for trouble.'

'Sport is a good alternative.' She looked at the scull. 'Was this yours?'

'It belonged to my father. He was a rowing blue. When I was a kid like Michael, I used to sit in that seat, put my feet and hands where his had been and try to feel him.'

'You never knew him?' she asked.

He shook his head. 'He was a lecturer at the School of Oriental and African Studies. He lived there during the week and came home to the estate cottage where he and Christabel had set up home for the weekends and during the holiday.'

'That doesn't sound like a great way to start a marriage.'

'It was her choice, apparently. She didn't like London.'

'What happened?'

'Not a what—a who. An Iranian student of such shimmering beauty that one look was all it took for my father to lose his head, his reason, his sanity.'

'Your mother.' And, when he glanced at her, 'The name is the giveaway.'

He nodded. 'My father abandoned Christabel and his unborn child without a backward glance and went to live in France with Soraya.'

Unable to bear the musty boathouse, the memory of that boy trying to reach out to a father he'd never known, he walked out into the clean air, kicked off his shoes and sat on the crumbling dock. These days his feet trailed in the water, soaked into the bottom of his jeans.

Natasha picked her way carefully over the boards and sat down beside him, her toes trailing in the water, waiting for him to continue or not as he wished.

'My grandfather cut him off without a penny, hoping it would bring him to his senses,' he said. 'But he was senseless.'

'And Christabel? What did she do?'

'She took it badly, lost the baby she was carrying. A boy who would have been the heir to all this.'

'Poor woman...'

'Her parents sold the house across the river and moved away. Gary told me that she'd killed herself.'

'No!'

'My grandfather denied it but I was never sure so I did a search a few years back.' He plucked a piece of rotten wood from the plank beside him, shredded it, dropping the pieces in the water. 'She lives in Spain with her husband, three children.'

'Did you get in touch with her?'

'I wanted to. I wanted to talk to someone who'd known my father so I went to the house, hoping to see her. They were just going out...' He shook his head. 'Rumour always has a grain of truth. She might have tried something desperate and she didn't need me descending like a black crow in the midst of her lovely family, raking up the past.'

Tash felt tears sting the back of her eyes and the lump in her throat was so big that she couldn't say anything. Instead, she squeezed his hand.

He glanced at her. 'Is that approval? I got something right?'

'Absolutely.' She slid her arm around his waist and he put his arm around her shoulders so that her head was resting against his shoulder. 'What happened to your parents?' Something bad must have happened or he wouldn't have been living with his grandparents.

'When I was a few months old, Soraya's mother became desperately ill and she had to go home. She left me with my father, which seems a little odd, but they weren't married and maybe she was afraid to tell her family that she was living with a married man. That they had a child.'

'I think I'd find that pretty difficult, to be honest.'

'It seems they already knew. Two days after she left, my father received a message from her father. He wanted to bring his family to Europe and, to get exit visas, they needed money to bribe officials. A lot of money. The bottom line was that if he wanted to see Soraya again he would have to pay.'

'But…that's appalling!'

'My father, beside himself, went to my grandfather, begged him for help and the old bastard gave it to him, but at a price.'

'You…' She'd known there was something, but could never have guessed anything so desperate. So cruel.

'He'd lost his heir. His son was unfit in his eyes. I wasn't the golden child of the perfect marriage, but I was all he had left.'

'You were the price he had to pay to rescue your mother.'

'Ramsey drew up a legally binding document surrendering all parental rights to them. I was to live with my grandparents, they would have full control of my education and upbringing and I would be my grandfather's heir on the condition that my parents understood that they would be dead to me. And my father signed it.'

'Of course he signed. How could he do anything else? He loved your mother, Darius; he couldn't abandon her.'

'No. I was safe and she needed him.'

A kingfisher flashed from a post into the water. A duck rounded up her fluffy brood. Somewhere along the riverbank a child shrieked with excitement. All bright, wonderful things, but what had been a charmed day now had a dark edge to it.

'What happened?' she asked.

'My grandfather handed over the cash, my father left for the airport and that's the last anyone ever heard of him or my mother. Not that anyone was looking.'

'I'm so sorry.'

'When he died, I insisted that Ramsey carry out a proper search for them before the house was put on the market. If either of them were alive this belonged to them.'

'Was there nothing in the house you could sell?'

'Unfortunately, the Hadleys weren't great art collectors. No one had the foresight to commission Gainsborough to paint the family portraits, buy Impressionists when they were cheap, snap up a Picasso or two.'

'Ancestors can be so short-sighted. What about land? Or the cottages?'

'The land is green belt and can't be built on. The cottages are occupied by former members of staff. I'll use what's left from the sale to rehouse them.'

'And the London flat?'

'When he was diagnosed with Alzheimer's, Ramsey insisted my grandfather sign a power of enduring attorney in my name. I sold the flat to finance his nursing care. There's some money left, but not enough to pay the inheritance tax.'

'Your grandfather might have raised you, Darius Hadley, but you are nothing like him.'

'At seventeen I was halfway there. Arrogant, spoilt, thought I owned the world. If I'd stayed here, I would have been exactly like him.'

She wanted to tell him he was wrong. She just tightened her hold around his waist and for a moment he buried his face in her hair. After a while, he said, 'My grandmother came to my first exhibition. She was dying by then, but she defied him that once. I went to her funeral but when my grandfather saw me he thought I was my father and began ranting at me...'

'Did Ramsey discover any more about what happened to your parents?' she said, desperate to distract him from the horror of that image.

'Only rumours. That the family had been caught trying to leave the country and they were all either rotting in jail or dead. That my father had made the whole story up just to get his hands on the money and he and Soraya were living somewhere in the sun. That my father was the victim of a honeypot trap and once he'd handed over the money he was disposed of. Take your pick.'

'No. Not the last one.'

And for the first time the smallest hint of a smile softened his face. 'You know that for a fact, do you?'

'One hundred per cent,' she said. 'Maybe, for a passion so intense that nothing else mattered they might have surrendered their son. Considered it their penance. But if it had been a con, Soraya would have got rid of you the second she realised she was pregnant.'

Totally focused on him, on his pain, she saw the gone-in-a-moment swirl of emotion deep in his eyes; scudding clouds of joy, sorrow, dark and light, every shade of grey.

'You didn't know any of this? Growing up?' He shook his head. 'Gary. Gary told you.' Who else? 'Was it one too many beers on one of your owl-or badger-watching adventures?'

'It wasn't beer that loosened his tongue. It was a motorbike. He had an old bike that he'd rebuilt from scrap and he taught me to ride when I was barely tall enough to reach the pedals. When I got a brand-new bike for my seventeenth birthday he was the first person I wanted to share it with.'

'Oh…' She could see what was coming.

'Young, brash, spoilt, it never occurred to me how he would feel. Obviously, I'd always had more than him, but this was grown-up stuff, stuff he wanted and could never afford on the pittance my grandfather paid him. Stuff I didn't have to work for, but would come to me just because my name was Hadley. It was like a chasm had opened up between us and he lashed out with the only weapon he had to put himself back on top. It just came out. How my father had sold me so that he could be with his whore.'

'Chinese whispers,' she said, perfectly able to imagine how gossip whispered in the village had been distorted, twisted with every retelling. Garbled, warped…

'He was already back-pedalling, trying to take it back before I'd fired up the bike to go and confront my grandfather, but nothing could unsay those words. I demanded to know the truth and the old man didn't spare me. He said I was old enough to know the truth and he laid it out in black and white. My father had betrayed his wife, abandoned his unborn child for a—'

'Darius…'

She'd cut in, not wanting him to repeat the word, but he raised his hand to touch her cheek, looked down at her. 'Let me finish. Get it out in the light.' He made a gesture that took in the sagging boathouse, the house out of sight behind the trees. 'This is all he really cared about. Preserv-

ing the house, preserving the name. Nothing that was real.'
He took his wallet from his back pocket, opened it, handed
her a photograph. 'This is what my father cared about.'

'She's beautiful, Darius.' The snapshot was of a young
woman laughing at something the photographer had said,
her eyes filled with so much love that it took her breath
away. To be looked at like that… 'Where did you get this?'

'It arrived in an envelope after my grandmother came
to the exhibition. No note.'

'A smile like that against four hundred years of history. No contest.' She looked up at Darius, at the same
dark eyes… 'She would have come for you. Crawled over
broken glass. No piece of paper would have stopped her.'

'Yes. I've always known, deep down, that they're dead
but I hoped…'

'Where did you go? How did you live?' she asked.
'When you left?'

'Not in a cardboard box under Waterloo Bridge,' he said,
apparently reading her mind. 'I went to Bristol, sold the
bike, rented a room, signed on at a sixth form college and
got a job stacking supermarket shelves.'

'The *bike*?' she said. 'You told me you walked out!'

'Metaphorically,' he said, but the darkness had been replaced with the beginnings of a smile. 'I wanted…I needed
you to walk with me.'

'All you had to do was ask.' For a moment they just
looked at one another until it was too intense, too full of
the unspoken words in her head and she scrambled for another thought. 'What happened to Gary?' she asked, her
voice catching in her throat.

'You always go straight to the heart of what's important, Natasha. I'm banging on about ancient history and
you bring me crashing back to earth with what's real. The
human element.'

'I wasn't dismissing what happened to you. But you said

it, Darius. You had everything going for you while he had nothing and I can't imagine your grandfather was a man to overlook such an indiscretion.'

'You're right, of course. I didn't betray Gary but it couldn't have been anyone else. Mary told me that my grandfather gave him a choice—he left the estate and never returned, or his father and grandmother would lose their jobs and the cottages that went with them.'

'Hurting, angry, lashing out… He made them all pay.'

'If I'd stayed I could have stopped that.'

'How? By bargaining with him? What would you have surrendered to save him?' He had no answer to that. 'He would have had you at his mercy, Darius. You were both better off away from here.'

'Right again. My mistake was not stopping to pick up Gary on the way out. I'll always regret that.'

'I don't imagine you were thinking very clearly,' she said, untangling herself from his arms. 'Come on,' she said, standing up, picking up her shoes. 'There's grass to cut, doors to be washed…'

Darius caught her hand. 'Thank you.'

There was nothing she could think of to say, so she stood on her toes and kissed him. It was supposed to be brief, sweet, over in a moment, but neither of them wanted it to stop. Even when the kiss was over they didn't want to let go.

'If we don't go back soon, they'll wonder where we are.'

'You wanted to take a good look at the boathouse, check if it will have to be pulled down or whether it can be restored,' he offered.

'Right,' she said, leaning her forehead against his chest before forcing herself to step away, get back to washing down paintwork. When she turned around her brother James was leaning on the wall of the boathouse, arms folded over the fishing rod he was holding. He'd clearly been there for some time.

CHAPTER ELEVEN

DARIUS WAS THE first to recover. 'Did you manage to catch supper?' he asked.

'With half a dozen children screaming and splashing about? They've scared away every fish within five miles so we thought we'd leave the women to sort out lunch while we walk down to the village and test the local ale. It's a Sunday holiday tradition. There'll be a pint waiting when you've finished checking out the structural integrity of the boathouse.'

He didn't wait for an answer.

'Did that sound like a friendly invitation,' Darius asked, 'or am I going to be pinned to the dartboard?'

'The pre-Sunday lunch trip to the pub is a mysterious male tradition,' she replied, 'from which mothers, wives and sisters are excluded. All I can tell you with any certainty is that you're the first man I've kissed who's ever been invited by my brothers to join them.'

'So that's good?'

'Probably, but if they do pin you to the dartboard by your ears I'll give them all particularly noxious jobs tomorrow.'

'I'll want pictures,' he said.

'I'll post them on Facebook,' she promised. 'When are you leaving?'

'After lunch. I've got to do what I should have done on Friday before the foundry starts up on Monday morning.

I can't promise to be here on Saturday. Once we start, we don't stop until it's done.'

'I didn't expect you to come this weekend. It's been...'

'Fun, Natasha. It's been fun.'

'Even getting beaten by my mother at Scrabble?' He said nothing. 'You let her win? Go!' she said, laughing, pushing him away. 'Before your beer gets warm.'

Before she dragged him under the nearest bush.

Darius, pausing for a break, checked his phone. There was a text from Natasha.

Needs full structural survey. Xxx

She'd attached a photograph of the boathouse.

Grinning, he took a selfie and sent it back with a text.

Needs total scrub down. Xxx

Natasha had kept in touch, sending pictures of the house emerging from its cocoon, but it was her suggestive little texts that made him smile. He'd replied with pictures of bones emerging from moulds. No comment needed.

Tash sighed with pleasure. Hadley Chase was gleaming, as perfect as she could have hoped, brought back to life, not just by sunlight and polish, but the laughter of children, the smell of baking, the armfuls of flowers from the long neglected cutting garden supplemented by cow parsley, willow herb gathered by her sisters-in-law to create huge free-form flower arrangements.

Tables had been laid in the conservatory for tea, the hired water boiler and teapots lined up and ready, the doors thrown open to the lawn, where the children were playing croquet with a set Harry had found in one of the outbuildings as the first cars began to arrive.

'It looks magical, Tash. If Darius were here he wouldn't be able to let this go,' Patsy said.

'Maybe that's why he's staying away.'

'Or not. Isn't that his Land Rover?' Patsy had offered to drive her home so that he could take the Land Rover back to London. 'Go and say hello,' she said as he drove straight round to the back of the house.

'Too late,' she said as the editor of the *Country Chronicle* advanced towards her, hand outstretched.

'Tash! I'm so glad to see you looking so well.'

'As you can see, Kevin, rumours of my breakdown were not just exaggerated but completely untrue.' She took his hand. 'Thank you for coming today. It means a great deal to me.'

'You have Peter Black to thank for that. He is so angry with you that he threatened to withdraw all Morgan and Black advertising if I covered the Hadley Chase open day.'

'A bit of a hollow threat, I'd have thought. There is nowhere else for this kind of property.'

'Hollow or not, I can't allow advertisers to dictate what we print.' He looked around. 'I have to congratulate you, my dear; your campaign has caused quite a stir. The children are a nice touch, by the way. Can we photograph them with the house in the background for our feature?'

'Feature?'

He smiled. 'Two pages? Maybe more if Darius Hadley will talk to me. I don't like being threatened.'

Darius stood back, watching Natasha greet visitors, delegate various members of her family to show them around the house, confident, professional, totally focused on the task she'd set herself. She'd told him she was the best and she was right. For a while she'd been entirely his but after this her world would reclaim her.

It was what he'd wanted, he reminded himself. It was the way he always wanted things. A hot flirtation and then move on. No emotional engagement.

Too late. It had been too late the moment he'd set eyes

on her, too late the minute he'd allowed her to stay. Kissed her. He'd let down his guard, done what he'd sworn he'd never do. He'd fallen hopelessly, ridiculously in love and where once he would have thought that made him a fool, he now knew that it made him a better man.

The thought made him smile and he was just going to her, to tell her that, when Morgan appeared on the doorstep. He instinctively took a step forward to protect her, but she had it covered, her voice clear, calm, composed.

'Miles? This is unexpected.'

'I'm here to apologise, Tash. I've been made a fool of.'

'Really?' She didn't step back to let him inside.

'That idiot Toby has gone.'

'Gone?' That rattled the cool.

'He's signed a contract to play professional rugby in Italy. It seems that's where he was last month. Not on a tour, but having trials, medicals, negotiating a deal. When his parents found out they were furious so they cooked up this scheme to cause a crisis, get rid of you and force him to forget the sports nonsense and put the company, his family first. He arrived at the reception not knowing what the hell was going on, but his mother cried and he was cornered.'

'Why on earth couldn't they just let him be happy?'

'Families, inheritance…' He shrugged. 'You know how it is.'

'Yes…' she said. 'Yes, I know.' She cleared her throat. 'Was Janine involved?'

'She and Peter were always…close. Let's just say that she's currently seeking alternative career opportunities.'

'And what about Morgan and Black?' she asked.

'There is no Black. That is the second reason I'm here. I'm looking for a new partner, Tash. I would like it to be you.'

Darius didn't wait for her answer. He'd just heard the

sound of hell freezing over and he'd felt the chill to his bones.

He hoped to escape unnoticed but Laura was in the kitchen, loading up a trolley with sandwiches, cakes, scones.

'Darius! How lovely to see you. Does Tash know you're here?'

He shook his head. 'She's busy.'

'Is it going well out there?'

'There seem to be a lot of people. Can I give you a hand?'

'I've got it covered. Why don't you take a last look around while the house is looking at its best? The way it must have been when you lived here.'

'It might have looked like this, Laura. Polished within an inch of its life, flowers everywhere, but it never felt like this. It had no heart. You and Derrick, your family, Natasha…'

He stuck his hands in his pockets, stared up at the ceiling, struggling to find words that would convey how they'd transformed this place. Made it somewhere he wanted to come, could walk in and not feel that he was somehow wanting. A want he'd understood when he'd learned the truth. He was a second-best replacement for the boy who'd died in the womb.

There was only one word… 'Love… Love has done this. Your family came together to do this for Natasha because you love her. That's the difference.'

Laura put a sympathetic hand on his arm.

'You're tired, Darius. Working all hours at the foundry and selling a house is as stressful as death or divorce, even when you've only lived there a few years. Four hundred years…' She shook her head. 'I can't begin to imagine how you must be feeling.'

'No…'

He'd had a window, a few hours, and he'd grabbed it,

wanting to be here, to stand by Natasha, but she didn't need him. This was what she'd been working for. The prize. She had everything she wanted.

'Sit down. I'll get you a cup of tea and something to eat. Something to keep up your blood sugar levels. There are cucumber sandwiches, scones, or I've made some Bakewell tarts?'

'Try spiced ginger.'

Natasha was standing in the doorway, flushed, laughing, and his heart leapt as it always did when he saw her. And each time it was different. That first time it had been purely physical, like a rocket going off. The rocket was still there, but now there was so much more. She was so much more. But her laughter, her joy was for something else.

'Well, I'm sure you could do with a break, too,' her mother said, 'so why don't you get it for him while I take the trolley through to the conservatory?'

Natasha walked across the kitchen, sat on his lap, put her arms around his neck and kissed him. 'How are your blood sugar levels now?' she asked, her eyes sparkling, the pulse in her throat thrumming with excitement.

'Up. Definitely up…' he said. 'In fact, this might be a very good time to check out the structural integrity of the boathouse.'

'Tash…' She slid off his lap, tucked a stray strand of hair behind her ear and was four feet away by the time her father appeared in the doorway. 'There's a Mr Darwish asking for you. I've put him in the library.'

'Yikes! Major property buyer.' She stopped at the door, leaned back. 'By the way, we're getting a double page spread in the *Country Chronicle*. Kevin Rose, the editor, knows you are *the* Darius Hadley. I'm afraid you're busted.'

'It was only a matter of time before someone made the connection,' he said. 'Will it help if I talk to him?' he asked, as if he hadn't heard their conversation.

'Darling, if you talk to him we'll be on the front cover.'

'Great,' he said as she flew out of the door. 'I'll do that, then.'

They both watched the space where she'd been for a moment. 'Her career is her world, Darius. She had a bad start in life and maybe we overprotected her.'

'She told me. All of it.'

'She threw up a job that had been her dream to get away. Be independent. Prove something to us.'

'To herself, I think.' That she wasn't that kid lying in a cancer ward, or a basket-case teenager. And she'd done it, becoming the top-selling agent for her company with a bright red BMW sports coupé to prove it. And when she'd been knocked back she'd proved it all over again. 'You knew she turned down the National Trust job?'

He smiled. 'She told you about that too.' He crossed to the fridge. 'I play golf with the man she would have worked for. He asked me why she'd turned the job down—a first, apparently. I never told her mother. Beer?'

'No… Once I've talked to Kevin Rose, I have to get back to London.' She'd given him so much; the least he could do for her was deliver the front page of the *Country Chronicle*. With that very public demonstration of her ability to turn disaster into triumph, she would be able to name her price when she was negotiating terms with Miles Morgan. 'This was just a flying visit. I'm installing a sculpture in Lambourn in a week or two and I had to come down to look at the site.' It was a pathetic excuse by any standards, but Derrick accepted it at face value. 'If I don't manage to catch Natasha before I go, tell her…' What? What could he say? 'Tell her she's better than the best.'

'Darius? Can you talk?'

'If you're quick.'

Tash frowned. Nothing had seemed quite the same between them since the open day. Okay, she'd been busy, he had to be somewhere else, but he'd left without saying goodbye and something was missing. The sex—snatched in brief moments when he wasn't working—was still stunningly hot, but the perfect focus that made her believe that she was the only woman in the world had gone. And those fun 'dates' had been forgotten. It was as if the shutters had come down and she was afraid that the reality of the sale had cut deeper than he'd anticipated. In which case he wasn't going to want to hear this.

Or he was ready to move on. In which case he would.

'I'm working,' he prompted impatiently.

'Yes… Sorry… I just wanted you to know that I've got two firm offers for the house on the table.'

'Two? Are we going to have a bidding war?' He sounded bored rather than excited by the prospect.

'Behave yourself. One is from an overseas buyer who's looking for a small country house to complement his London apartment. He's offering the guide price.'

'Take it.'

'The second offer is lower. I've negotiated them up from their opening bid but it's still half a million below the guide price.'

'So why are we talking about it?'

'Because it's a better package.'

'Can you keep this short? They're waiting to weld the heart in place.'

'Really? You're that close?'

'Natasha, please…'

'Sorry. The second offer is from the IT company across the river. They're expanding and need more space but there are planning restrictions on their own site. The thing is, most of the staff live locally and their children go to the village school so they don't want to move.'

'Then maybe they should up their offer.'

'It's lower, but it's actually worth more. I've managed to exclude the estate cottages, which means you won't have to rehouse the tenants and you'll have more disposable income from the sale. Sitting tenants will also affect the resale value of the properties so it will help reduce the inheritance tax bill. Repairs and maintenance can be offset against tax and the cottages will be realisable assets in the future. Finally—'

'There's more?'

'Finally,' she said, 'they know Gary; he's done jobs for them in the past and they will keep him on as caretaker and odd job man with a salary and company benefits that he could never have hoped to achieve from your grandfather's estate.'

She could have simply presented Darius with the easy offer, job done. They both had what they wanted. House sold, reputation restored and she'd always known that there was no future in this relationship. It wasn't his fault that she'd got four-letter-word involved and she wasn't about to drag it out to the bitter end. Better let go while they were still friends.

But when the first bid had come in from the IT company she'd immediately seen the possibilities—the value to the village, to the people Darius felt responsible for—and she'd hammered out the best deal she'd ever put together. One she would always be proud of. Not only did it ensure that Hadley continued to thrive, but it would keep a link for Darius with the village that bore his name.

'Their surveyor has just left,' she said. 'Say yes and the money will be in the bank by the end of the month.' She waited. 'Hello? Am I talking to myself here?'

'No...' He sounded hemmed. 'I'm simply speechless. You are an extraordinary woman, Natasha Gordon. Nothing left to prove. To anyone.'

'Thanks…' Her voice caught in her throat. 'I'll, um, let Ramsey have the details, then, shall I?'

'I suppose so.'

'Darius? Is this what you want? Only if you've changed your mind about selling, tell me now.'

'Why would I do that? Hadley Chase is the last place on earth I'd ever live.'

'I don't know. It's just that you seem a little scratchy.'

'Do I? Why don't you come over and smooth me out?'

Smoothing him out was something she'd taken great pleasure in doing on numerous occasions while he'd been working twelve-hour days, but there was something decidedly off in that invitation. As if he wanted her, but hated himself for it. Or maybe he wanted her to hate him. Whatever it was, all the pleasure drained out of her day.

'I thought you were working,' she said. An alternative to the flat *no* that she knew was the right response. That she couldn't quite bring herself to say.

'You've got me,' he said. And that had sounded like relief.

'I'll call Ramsey now,' she said. 'Get things underway.' He didn't answer. 'Darius? Is this it?'

'Yes,' he said. Abrupt. To the point. 'Job done. Time to think about your fee.'

'The bronze…'

Tash swallowed. No. He'd said it. Job done. And they both knew that they weren't talking about the sale of a house but, after all they'd been through, shared, there was no way she could sit for him like a model being paid by the hour.

'You've done enough. Your interview with Kevin Rose was above and beyond. Do you need any help clearing the house?' she asked. 'There are some lovely pieces of furniture here.' She was sitting at his grandmother's desk and if she could have afforded it she'd have made an offer.

'No. There's nothing there I want. Ramsey will deal with it.'

Nothing? Really? She sat back. Where had the photograph of his mother come from? It could only have been his grandmother. She stroked her hands across the lovely desk. She'd seen one very like it on an antiques programme on the television. That one had had a secret drawer.

Darius stared at the phone for a long time before he hit end call. He'd lied about working. The horse was finished, delivered to the man who'd commissioned it and awaiting positioning in the place where it would forever be leaping over an unseen fence.

He tossed the phone on the sofa where Natasha had sat on the day she'd come to see him, promising him a whole lot more than the sale of his house when she'd looked at him with those big blue eyes and invited him to try her cake.

Senseless. Except that he hadn't lost his senses. He'd found them. Found something he'd never truly known as a boy. Found whatever it was his father had found, because family history suggested that the 'perfect marriage' had been his grandfather's idea. His way of controlling the future.

It was something he'd been running away from as a man, afraid that, like his father, he'd lose himself to something he couldn't control. But he'd been so wrong. You didn't lose yourself; you found yourself in love. Became whole.

He walked across to the clay sculpture that he'd begun the day he drove back from Hadley Chase, knowing that it was over. He'd worked in the foundry in the day, worked on this at night, capturing for ever that moment when she'd reached out to him in her sleep.

He hadn't needed the drawing. His hands had worked the clay, formed the well-known curves, her shoulders, the bend of her knee, her hair tumbled against the pillow.

His fingers curled around the hand extended towards him, that he couldn't see for the tears blinding him.

'Darius…'

'Natasha?'

'I need to see you. Can you spare me half an hour?'

'I'm at the studio. Come over.'

Tash ended the brief call. One last time, she promised herself. One last time.

It was late by the time she arrived at the studio. The studio door stood open and she looked through but the sun was low and the interior was dim. 'Darius?'

He was taking down the photographs of the horse, clearing the decks and, as she hesitated in the doorway, he half turned and it was all still there and more. The heart-leap, the joy, only a hundred times more powerful, underscored by every touch, every kiss, every memory they had made together.

'No cake?' he asked.

'No time,' she said. 'I've been rushed off my feet with work. It's dark in here.'

He flicked a light switch and illuminated the area by his desk, sofa, and she walked across, put down the thick envelope she was carrying.

'More paperwork?' he asked.

'No. I…' This was going to be the last time she saw him and she didn't want it to be like this… 'I was looking at your grandmother's desk and it occurred to me that I'd seen one very like it on an antiques programme. On the television.'

'You're here to tell me that it's worth a fortune?'

'No. I'm here to tell you that it had a secret drawer.'

He became very still. 'That was in it?'

'No, it was empty, but it's what got me looking through the rest of the house. I knew there had to be more than that one photograph. I found this in the attic.'

She opened the envelope, tipped out the contents. Photographs, letters that had come from his parents' flat in Paris. The report of the car accident where they'd died, fleeing across the border with her family. Their death certificates. A letter his father had left for him in case anything went wrong. He'd known the danger…

'I'll leave you to look at them.'

'No!' His hand gripped her arm, holding her there beside him, and he picked up a photograph of his mother holding him in her arms, his father standing beside him with such a look of love on his face that it had brought tears to her eyes when she'd seen it.

And suddenly the stiffness, the self-protective armour melted and she was in his arms, holding him, wiping the tears from his cheeks, murmuring hush sounds as he thanked her.

'Did you ever see your grandfather again?' Tash asked a long time later, after he'd read the letter, looked at the photographs. 'After your grandmother's funeral?'

'That was when Ramsey realised how sick he was. He wouldn't have it, of course, and it was only after a fall and a stay in hospital that we were able to move him into a nursing home for his own safety. I used to go and visit him. Mostly he had no idea who I was; occasionally he thought I was my father and asked me how Christabel was. How long before the baby was due.'

'It's a terrible thing, Alzheimer's,' she said. 'It robs you of the chance to end things properly. Tell people that you love them.'

'Say the words while you can?'

'I…' How could she say yes and not tell him that she loved him? How could she load him with that emotional burden? 'It's complicated.'

'That's what I thought, but I'm going to make it simple.'

He stood up, took her hand and led her across the studio and switched on the floodlights above his work plinth, lighting up a sculpted figure, a scene that was imprinted on her heart.

She took a step closer, looked at herself as Darius had seen her. The figure lying semi-prone amongst a tangle of sheets was sensuous, beautiful, and he hadn't had to reveal her ribs or her organs to show her inner depths. Every thought, every feeling was exposed. Anyone who looked at it would know that this was a woman in love.

The detail was astonishing. In the modelling of the hands, the tiny creases behind the knee, the dimples above her buttocks. They hadn't been in the drawing. He'd done this from memory.

When she turned he was there, watching her.

'She's beautiful, Darius,' she said a little shakily, 'but she's going to be a bit of a tight fit on the mantelpiece.'

'She won't leave here. She's not for display in a gallery window. This was personal, Natasha, for me, an attempt to hold on to something rare, something special. But once it was done I realised that only the real flesh-and-blood woman will do. Tomorrow it will be nothing but a lump of clay.'

'You're going to destroy this?'

'Why would I keep it? Every time I looked at it I'd know what kind of fool I was for sitting back and making a sketch instead of responding to that invitation and getting back into bed with you. For not saying the words. A statue won't laugh with me, cry with me, knock itself out making the world right for me.'

'No.' It could never do that. 'But it will always be perfect. Never grow old. Never demand anything of you—'

'Never give anything back,' he said. 'Never...'

'Never?' she prompted.

'Never love me back.'

He'd said the words as if he was tearing lumps off his flesh.

Not just hot, gorgeous sex but something bigger, something deeper. The one thing that in his privileged youth he'd never known. The one thing that in his successful career he'd never allowed himself.

'Love?'

'The biggest four-letter word in the dictionary,' he said. 'You're right; you should say the words rather than live with regret. I love you, Natasha Gordon, with all my heart. That's it. No claim, no expectation and absolutely no regret.'

Now she was the one with tears stinging her eyes. 'I told myself I didn't want you to feel guilt, Darius, that I wanted you to remember me with pleasure, but I was afraid to put myself on the line... Your courage shames me, you deserve more but I love you, Darius Hadley. With all my heart.' His expression was so intense that for a moment she couldn't speak. Then, never taking her eyes from his, she made a gesture in the direction of the sculpture. 'It's there, on display, for all the world to see.'

For a moment neither of them moved, breathed, and then he kissed her so tenderly, holding her as if she were made of glass. It was a shatteringly beautiful moment, nothing to do with sex, but a promise...

When he drew back, resting his forehead against hers, he said, 'There are a couple of other things I have to say. I need a plus one at the unveiling of the horse next week. The Queen is doing the honours so you'll need a hat.'

She blinked back the stupid tears and began to smile. 'A hat? Right.'

'I've looked up dancing classes but I need a partner. And how do you fancy seeing the new James Bond movie?'

'That's three things.'

'Is that too demanding? Only the thing is, Natasha, I'm looking for more than high-octane no-commitment sex. I'm looking for a grown-up full-time relationship with a woman who knows what she wants—a woman who will have time for me and a family as well as a career. So I'm asking—is that something you can fit around your new job?'

'New job?'

'Didn't hell just freeze over?' he asked. 'I overheard Morgan offer you a partnership.'

And suddenly everything fell into place. 'Is that why you've gone all moody on me?' she asked.

'Moody?'

'Moody, shuttered, closed-up, just like you were when we first met.'

'It's what you wanted.'

'Absolutely.'

'So why didn't you tell me?'

'Maybe because you got all moody, shuttered, closed up,' she said, turning to him on legs that were shaking as she realised how close she'd come to losing this. 'No time for anything but a quickie. Running away. If you'd been talking to me I'd have told you all about it. And that I turned him down.'

'But…' His frown was total confusion. 'You weren't even tempted?'

'I told you, Darius, I could never trust a man who treated me the way Miles did, but it wasn't just that. I like being my own boss. Tailoring my sales pitch to meet individual needs. Looking for the right house for a client who appreciates good service. I like doing things my own way.'

'I like doing things your way, too,' he replied as she began slipping her buttons one by one.

'I have to get up,' Tash protested, making an effort to wriggle out of Darius's warm embrace. 'I've got an appointment at eleven.'

'Where are you going?' he asked, his hand on her belly

spooning her against him as he nuzzled the tender spot behind her ear.

'Sussex. I've found the perfect house for a client and she's flying in from Hong Kong to see it.' She bit her lip as his hand moved lower.

'Is this the one you've been raving about?'

'Mmmm... Can I tempt you to a day out in the country?' she asked in an attempt to distract him. Distract herself. She really, really had to get going... 'Once the viewing is over we could take a walk on the Downs, have lunch at a country pub. Can you spare the time?'

'No,' he said, moving so that she flopped over onto her back and was looking up at him. 'Can you?'

No! The answer was definitely, almost certainly, maybe *nooooo*, but his lips were teasing hers, his hand was much lower and the word never made it beyond a thought.

Damn it, he always did that! She woke in plenty of time to get where she had to be and then he ambushed her. She grinned as her little van pulled out of the mews and she headed south towards the Sussex Downs. It was just as well that she'd started putting the alarm forward half an hour or she'd be permanently late.

As it was, she needn't have worried. She picked up the keys from the selling agent in good time but when she pulled up outside the gates there was no sign of her client, only a voicemail message on her phone saying that she'd been held up, but would she go ahead and take photographs for her of the garden and especially of the grotto.

Terrific. She just hoped it wasn't a wind-up. Over the last few months there had been a few of those—wasted journeys to see non-existent clients, non-existent houses. Rivals who resented the splash of publicity following her sale of Hadley Chase. The feature on her new consultancy in the *Country Chronicle*. She'd got smarter about checking before she wasted time or money on them, but this one had checked out.

She took her camera and her camcorder, filming the walk up the drive to the sprawling house, smothered in an ancient wisteria that would look so pretty in the spring.

It was absolutely perfect—and not just for her client.

There was room for an office, a cottage in the grounds for Patsy—who was working for her now—and Michael. And a small barn tucked away at the rear.

It was a house where two people could grow their lives, their family, and there was no use kidding herself. The only reason she'd wanted Darius to come with her was so that he would see it and fall in love with it too.

The mews cottage was great, but there was no room for an office for her, no room for anything except the two of them indulging in a lot of that high-octane sex. She swallowed. He was the one who'd said he wanted more—commitment, a family.

She didn't need to tour the house to take photographs. She'd done that, leaving them where Darius could see them, hoping… She'd taken a few of the garden but, with a sigh, she set off to take more.

The low sun was gleaming through grasses, scarlet dahlias that were making the most of a lingering autumn. The leaves in the hidden woodland dell that housed a grotto created in the bole of what had once been a huge tree.

She'd seen photographs but hadn't been down there. Today, though, she followed a narrow rill that fell in steps before dropping into a natural stream that trickled into a pool within the grotto. Light was filtering from above and more than just water gleamed in the darkness.

None of this had been in the agent's photographs and, curious, she stepped down. For a moment she couldn't believe what she was seeing and then, as she did, she caught her breath.

It was a bronze of the figure Darius had made, that he'd said he was going to destroy. She was here, lying on a bed, surrounded by a pool—a woodland nymph reaching out for her lover.

She didn't need the tingle at the base of her spine, didn't have to turn around, to know Darius was there with her.

'It's beautiful,' she said.

'Yes.'

She turned. 'How did you know?'

'I didn't. I gave you a description of the house that would be perfect for us. Five bedrooms, room for a home office, an outbuilding of some sort, a staff cottage, and I waited for you to find it.'

'But what about Mrs Harper?'

'There is no Mrs Harper. I'm your client.'

'You? But…' She shook her head. 'But how did you organise this?' she demanded, flinging out a hand in the direction of the sculpture.

'The owner indulged me. Unfortunately, the downside to that was his insistence that it stay, whether we buy or not.'

'But…but…but…' she spluttered. And then she knew. 'You've already bought it, haven't you?'

'It seemed wise, just in case he got a better offer. I've leased out the studio. You decide whether we keep the mews or your flat for our London bolthole; you can find a tenant for the other, which leaves only two questions.'

'Two?'

'The first is: will you marry me?'

She swallowed.

'What's the second question?' she asked.

'I think you'll find that your mother is hoping for a Christmas wedding. Are you happy with that?' He waited as she struggled with a throat that was Sahara dry. 'If you need a hint, yes and yes are the correct answers.'

She flung herself into his arms, laughing and crying a

little at the same time. 'Yes, and yes, and yes, and yes…'
And then she threw a punch at him. 'You discussed it with
my mother!'

'Let's just say there was some heavy hinting going on
the last time we went for Sunday lunch.'

'Oh, good grief. It's not compulsory, you know!'

'Too late. We've booked the church.' And then he was
kissing her and she said nothing more for a very long time.

Wedding bells, fairy lights glistening over a white frost.
Red berries and ivy twisted around pew ends and around
the Christmas roses in her bouquet. White velvet and her
grandmother's pearls. And Darius.

Darius waiting for her at the altar. Darius holding out
his hand to her, folding it in his and holding on tight, then
smiling as if this was the best day in his life. And Natasha
smiling back because it was the best day of hers. So far.

* * * * *

A sneaky peek at next month...

MODERN™
tempted

**FRESH, CONTEMPORARY ROMANCES TO TEMPT
ALL LOVERS OF GREAT STORIES**

My wish list for next month's titles...

In stores from 21st March 2014:

❑ One Night with Her Ex – Lucy King

❑ Flirting with the Forbidden – Joss Wood

In stores from 4th April 2014:

❑ The Secret Ingredient – Nina Harrington

❑ Her Client from Hell – Louisa George

Available at WHSmith, Tesco, Asda, Eason, Amazon and Apple

Just can't wait?

0314/3

APR 14 *B*

"I need to return to Zeena Sahra. The cancellation of my engagement will have long-reaching consequences for our country."

Feeling unaccountably bereft at the thought of Sayed's abandonment, Liyah nevertheless nodded. "I understand."

"Good. It is unfortunate you will not be able to work out your notice, but it is fortuitous that you already made your plans to leave."

"What? Why won't I work out my notice?"

"I've told you, we must leave for Zeena Sahra immediately."

"You said you had to leave."

He gave her a look that said she wasn't following him. "Naturally you must come with me."

"Why?"

"You may carry my child."

"But we don't know that."

"And until we do, you stay with me."

D0681635

Lucy Monroe

Sheikh's Scandal

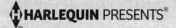

Recycling programs
for this product may
not exist in your area.

ISBN-13: 978-0-373-13239-3

SHEIKH'S SCANDAL

First North American Publication 2014

Copyright © 2014 by Harlequin Books S.A.

Special thanks and acknowledgment are given to Lucy Monroe for
her contribution to The Chatsfield series.

NORTON PUBLIC LIBRARY
1 WASHINGTON SQUARE
NORTON, KANSAS 67654

HARLEQUIN®
www.Harlequin.com

Printed in U.S.A.

All about the author...
Lucy Monroe

Award-winning and bestselling author **Lucy Monroe** sold her first book in September 2002 to the Harlequin Presents® line. That book represented a dream that had been burning in her heart for years—the dream to share her stories with readers who love romance as much as she does. Since then she has sold more than thirty books to three publishers and hit national bestseller lists in the U.S. and England, but what has touched her most deeply since selling that first book are the reader letters she receives. Her most important goal with every book is to touch a reader's heart, and when she hears she's done that it makes every night spent writing into the wee hours of the morning worth it.

She started reading Harlequin Presents® books when she was very young and discovered a heroic type of man between the covers of those books...an honorable man, capable of faithfulness and sacrifice for the people he loves. Now married to what she terms her "alpha male at the end of a book," Lucy believes there is a lot more reality to the fantasy stories she writes than most people give credit for. She believes in happy endings that are really marvelous beginnings, and that's why she writes them. She hopes her books help readers to believe a little, too...just as romance did for her so many years ago.

She really does love to hear from readers and responds to every email. You can reach her by emailing lucymonroe@lucymonroe.com.

Other titles by Lucy Monroe available in ebook:

MILLION DOLLAR CHRISTMAS SURPRISE
PRINCE OF SECRETS *(By His Royal Decree)*
ONE NIGHT HEIR *(By His Royal Decree)*
NOT JUST THE GREEK'S WIFE

For my editor, Suzanne Clarke. It's always a little bit terrifying changing editors, but you've made it a really lovely experience and I'm thrilled how well our creative visions mesh. I'm also delighted to find we are kindred spirits in other areas. I feel as if we're a destined team. Thank you!

CHAPTER ONE

NOT EASILY IMPRESSED, Liyah Amari very nearly stopped to gawp upon entering the Chatsfield London for the first time.

Flagship of the Chatsfield family's hotel empire, the lodging preferred by Europe's elite was magnificent.

San Francisco's property where her mother had worked since before Liyah's birth was beautiful, but nothing compared to the opulence of this hotel. From the liveried doormen to the grandeur of the ballroom-size lobby, she felt as if she'd stepped into a bygone era of luxury.

A decidedly frenetic air of anticipation and preparation was at odds with the elegant surroundings, though. One maid rushed through the lobby—which Liyah was certain was anything but a normal occurrence—while another polished the walnut banisters of the grand staircase.

It looked like an impromptu but serious meeting was happening near the concierge desk. The desk reception staff were busy with the phone and computer, respectively, checking in an attractive elderly couple.

"Welcome to the Chatsfield London, Mr. and Mrs. Michaels. Here is your room key," the young man said, "and here is your complimentary hospitality pack. We very much hope that you enjoy your stay."

Both staff were too busy to pay attention to who might be entering the hotel. Behind reception, Liyah saw a row of photographs depicting the Chatsfield London's staff. Something in her chest tightened as she caught the image of Lucilla Chatsfield staring back at her from within a frame.

One of the Chatsfield siblings Liyah admired and wished she could get to know, Lucilla was too far up the hotel's ranks for that to ever be likely.

A noise from behind her dragged her attention to where maintenance was replacing a bulb in the giant chandelier that cast the saffron walls with an elegant glow. Ecru moldings and columns added a tasteful but subtly lavish touch and the faint but lingering smell of fresh paint indicated they'd had a recent tidying up.

Liyah's sensible shoes made no noise as she crossed the black-and-white marble-tiled floor, heading directly for the elevator as she'd been instructed to do.

A man stepped in front of her. "May I help you find someone?"

His tone and expression were polite, but it had to be obvious to him that Liyah in her well-fitting but conservative black gabardine suit was not a guest at the Chatsfield.

"I have an appointment with Mrs. Miller." As was her usual habit, Liyah was fifteen minutes early for her meeting with the senior housekeeper.

The man's eyes lit up. "Oh, you must be the maid from Zeena Sahra."

No. That had been her mother. "I am familiar with Zeena Sahran culture, but I was born in America."

Liyah had been hired as a floor supervising chambermaid on the presidential level with special concierge services, just below the hotel's penthouse suites. With hospitality as well as housekeeping duties, she would be working in tandem with the concierge team in a new initiative designed to increase customer satisfaction.

It would be a much more satisfying job for Liyah than

the one her mother had held for almost three decades and Hena would have approved wholeheartedly.

"Yes, of course. The elevator is right this way." The man started walking. "I will have to key your access to the basement level."

"Thank you."

Liyah was still a few minutes early when she knocked on the senior housekeeper's office door.

"Enter," came from within.

Mrs. Miller was a tall, thin woman who wore a more severe version of Liyah's suit with a starched white blouse buttoned all the way up.

"I'm pleased you are here, Miss Amari, but I hope you've come prepared to begin work immediately," she said after the pleasantries were out of the way.

"Yes, of course."

"Good. Your concierge floor has been booked for the sheikh's harem." Mrs. Miller gave a disdainful sniff with the word *harem*.

"Excuse me? A sheikh from Zeena Sahra is coming to stay?" And he needed an *entire floor* for his harem?

No wonder they'd wanted to transfer her mother from the Chatsfield San Francisco.

"Yes, Sheikh bin Falah will be staying with us for two weeks. His fiancée will be joining him for the second one."

Liyah schooled the shock from her features. "Sheikh al Zeena, or Sheikh bin Falah al Zeena, but he would not be referred to as Sheikh bin Falah. To do so would cause offence."

Liyah wasn't sure about correcting her boss, but she assumed this sort of knowledge was why she'd been hired.

At least now she understood the need for her *expertise*. Not just a tribal sheikh but the crown prince of Zeena Sahra was coming to stay at the Chatsfield London.

Probably the single most gorgeous man alive, he could

easily be an international playboy with a string of super-models hanging on his arm. However, he had a reputation for being buttoned-down and focused entirely on his duties as emir of Zeena Sahra.

"I see. I'll make a note of it. I presume addressing him as Your Highness is acceptable."

"It is, though from what I have read, since Zeena Sahra is an emirate, he prefers the title of *emir*."

Mrs. Miller's mouth pursed. "Why didn't we know this?"

"It's a small thing, really."

"No," Mrs. Miller said sharply. "There's nothing small about this visit from the sheikh. Every detail must be seen to with absolute attention. If not, mistakes happen. Only last week someone wanted to send silk napkins to the Chatsfield Preitalle with the inscription 'Princess Maddie.' Can you believe it? For a royal wedding? This is why each detail *must* be perfect."

"I will do my best."

"Yes. In addition to your usual duties, for the duration of the sheikh's visit, you will also personally oversee the housekeeping staff for his suite and the adjoining rooms for his security people."

Nothing like being thrown in at the deep end, but Liyah didn't mind. She thrived on a challenge.

Nevertheless, it was a good thing Liyah had gotten her degree in hospitality management. It didn't hurt either that she'd cleaned rooms at the Chatsfield San Francisco every summer break through high school and college, not that her mother had encouraged Liyah to make her career there.

Quite the opposite, Hena had been adamant that her daughter *not* work for the Chatsfield. And now that she knew what she did, maybe Liyah understood that better.

After a somewhat harried orientation, during which staff members she met asked as many questions of Liyah about Zeena Sahra as she asked them about the Chatsfield London, she returned to her newly rented bedsit.

About the size of a college dorm room with an efficiency kitchen and miniscule bath tacked on, it was a far cry from the two-bedroom apartment with a balcony she'd shared with her mother in San Francisco. An apartment she'd been only too happy to move out of when she got the floor supervisory position with the Chatsfield London.

The job offer was a brilliant coincidence that Liyah's mother would have called destiny. But then Hena Amari had had a romantic streak her daughter did not share.

Although her outlook on life was decidedly more pragmatic, once Liyah had seen the contents of her mother's safety-deposit box and read Hena's final letter, she'd known she had to come to England.

The new job had allowed her to do so without dipping too deeply into what was left from the proceeds of her mother's life insurance policy. The money had been welcome if entirely unexpected. The policy had been one of the many profound shocks Liyah had found in that safety-deposit box.

Shocks that had ultimately ended with her working for the Chatsfield London.

The hotel had been looking specifically for someone with knowledge of Zeena Sahran culture and hospitality norms. Ironically, they had contacted the San Francisco property's senior housekeeper, Stephanie Carter, in hopes of transferring Hena Amari.

With Hena's sudden death, Stephanie, knowing about Liyah, had suggested her instead. Even though Liyah had not worked for the Chatsfield San Francisco since the summer before her last year of university, her education and experience had made her uniquely eligible for a newly created position.

The irony that a job with the hotel would make it possible for her daughter to fulfill Hena's final wish was not lost on Liyah.

Liyah did not resent her mother's silence on any front, but only superb emotional control had allowed her to take one stunning revelation after another without cracking.

On the outside.

The most stunning revelation of all had been that the extremely wealthy English hotelier Gene Chatsfield was Liyah's biological father.

After years of seeing the exploits of his legitimate children in the tabloid press, Liyah found it nearly impossible to believe his blood ran through her veins. What did she, a woman who had worked hard for everything she had, have in common with this notorious, spoiled family?

She had an almost morbid curiosity to discover what kind of man raised his children to be so profligate while sending the most meager of stipends to Hena on Liyah's behalf.

The answer might lie in the very fact of Liyah's existence, the result of Gene's indulgence in numerous affairs with his hotel maids. Affairs that did *not* make it into the press.

Hena hadn't known about the hotelier's wife, much less his propensity for seducing the chambermaids, until after he left San Francisco and a pregnant Hena behind. It had all been in the final letter Hena had left Liyah.

She'd never told another soul the identity of Liyah's father. Hena's shame in the fact he'd been a married man colored the rest of her life and yet she'd written in her letter that Liyah needed to forgive him.

Hena had claimed that Gene Chatsfield was not a villain, not a demon, not even a very bad man. But he had been a man going through a very bad time. Her final request had been for Liyah to come to London and make herself known to her father.

Liyah would respect her mother's last wishes, but she was happy to have the opportunity to observe the man incognito—as an employee, not the daughter he'd never acknowledged.

Her uniform crisp, her long black hair caught in an impeccable bun, Liyah stood tucked away in a nook near the grand staircase. She'd been in London two weeks and working at the Chatsfield ten hectic days, but had yet to catch a glimpse of her father.

Word had come down that the Honorable Sheikh Sayed bin Falah al Zeena was arriving today, though. Liyah had no doubts her father would be on hand to greet the sheikh personally.

One thing that had become patently obvious in the past ten days: the sheikh's stay was incredibly important to the hotel, and even more significant to the Chatsfield's proprietor.

Apparently, in another ironic twist of fate, Gene Chatsfield currently resided in the Chatsfield New York, leaving his new and highly acclaimed CEO, Christos Giatrakos, alone to handle operations from London. However, Gene Chatsfield's arrival in London to *personally* oversee the emir's visit said it all.

Knowing how key this high-profile guest's stay was to her father, Liyah was determined to do her job well. When she made herself known to Gene, there would be nothing to disappoint him in *her* work ethic.

Her floor was in impeccable order, each of the rooms to be occupied garnished with a crystal bowl of fruit and a vase of fragrant jasmine. She'd arranged for a screen to be placed at the elevator bank on her floor, as well, effectively blocking the harem quarters from curious looks.

She'd made sure the sheikh's suite was similarly taken

care of. There was nothing to offend and a great deal to appreciate in her setup of his rooms and the floor below.

Thoughts of her work faded as an older man walked with supreme confidence across the lobby. His air that of a man who owned all he surveyed, he acknowledged the numerous greetings by his employees with a regal tip of his head. Her father.

Stopping in front of the reception desk, he was clearly prepared to welcome the sheikh upon arrival.

Gray hair shot with silver, his blue eyes were still clear, his six-foot-one frame just slightly stooped. Garbed in a perfectly tailored Pierre Cardin suit, his shoes no doubt handmade, he looked like a man who would fit right in with the fabulously wealthy people his hotel catered to.

Gene smiled and said something to the head of desk reception. And all the air expelled from Liyah's lungs in a single whoosh.

She'd seen that smile in the mirror her whole life. His lips were thinner, but the wide smile above a slightly pointed chin? That was so familiar it made her heart ache.

His eyes were blue, hers were green—but their shape was the same. That hadn't been obvious in the publicity shots she'd seen of him.

She'd gotten her mother's honey-colored skin, oval face, small nose and arched brows, not to mention Hena's black hair and five-foot-five stature. Their mother-daughter connection had been obvious to anyone who saw them together.

Liyah had never considered she might also share physical traits with her father.

The resemblance wasn't overly noticeable by any means, but that smile? Undeniably like hers.

This man was her father.

Hit with the profundity of the moment, Liyah's knees

went to jelly and she had to put her hand against the wall for stability.

Unaware of her father's moderate financial support and way too aware of the Amari rejection of any connection, Liyah had spent her life knowing of only one person in her family.

Hena Amari.

Her mom was the only Amari who had ever recognized Liyah as a member of that family. A family who had cast her out for her *disgrace*.

And since her mom's death, Liyah had been alone. In that moment, she realized that if this man accepted her—even into the periphery of his life—she wouldn't be alone any longer.

Her father's face changed, the smile shifting to something a lot tenser than the expression he'd worn only seconds before. He stood a little straighter, his entire demeanor more alert.

Liyah's gaze followed his, and for the second time in as many minutes she went weak in the knees.

Surrounded by an impressive entourage and dressed in the traditional garb of a Zeena Sahran sheikh stood the most beautiful man Liyah had ever seen. Known for his macho pursuits and outlook, despite his supreme political diplomacy, the emir wouldn't appreciate the description, she was sure.

But regardless of…or maybe *because of* his over-six-foot height, square jaw and neatly trimmed, close-cropped facial hair, the sheikh's masculine looks carried a beauty she'd never before encountered.

No picture she'd ever seen did him justice. Two-dimensional imagery could never catch the reality of Sheikh Sayed bin Falah al Zeena's presence. Not his gorgeous looks or the leashed power that crackled in the air around him like electricity.

Nothing about the unadorned black *abaya* worn over Armani, burgundy *keffiyeh* on his head and black triple-stranded *egal* holding it in place expressed anything but conservative control. The Zeena Sahran color of royalty of the *keffiyeh* and three strands of the *egal,* rather than the usual two, subtly indicated his status as emir.

Wearing the traditional robe over a tailored designer suit with the head scarf implied supreme civilization. And yet, to her at least, it was obvious the blood of desert warriors ran in his veins.

The first melech of Zeena Sahra had won independence for his tribe—which later became the founding people of the emirate of Zeena Sahra—through bloody battles western history books often glossed over.

Inexplicably and undeniably drawn to the powerful man, Liyah's feet carried her forward without her conscious thought or volition. It was only when she stood mere feet from the royal sheikh that Liyah came to an abrupt, embarrassed stop.

It was too late, though.

Sheikh Sayed's espresso-brown gaze fell on her and remained, inquiry evident in the slight quirking of his brows.

Considered unflappable by all who knew her, Liyah couldn't think of a single coherent thing to say, not even a simple welcome before moving on.

No, she stood there, her body reacting to his presence in a way her mother had always warned Liyah about but she had never actually experienced.

Part of her knew that he was surrounded by the people traveling with him, the Chatsfield Hotel staff and even her father, but Liyah could only see the emir. Discussion around them was nothing more than mumbling to her ears.

The signature scent of the Chatsfield—a mix of cedarwood, leather, white rose and a hint of lavender—faded and all she could smell was the emir's spicy cologne blending with his undeniable masculine scent.

Her nipples drew tight for no discernible reason, her heart rate increasing like it only did after a particularly challenging workout and her breath came in small gasps she did her best to mask with shallow inhales.

His expression did not detectably change, but something in the depths of his dark gaze told her she was not the only one affected.

"Sheikh al Zeena, this is Amari, our chambermaid floor supervisor in charge of the harem floor and your suite," the head of desk reception stepped in smoothly to say.

Being referred to by her last name was something Liyah was used to; meeting a crown prince was not.

However, her brain finally came back online and she managed to curl her right hand over her left fist and press them over her left breast. Bowing her head, she leaned slightly forward in a modified bow. "Emir. It is my pleasure to serve you and your companions."

Sayed had a wholly unacceptable and unprecedented reaction to the lovely chambermaid's words and actions.

His sex stirred, images of exactly *how* he would like her to serve him flashing through his mind in an erotic slide show of fantasies he was not aware of even having.

The rose wash over her cheeks and vulnerable, almost hungry expression in her green eyes told him those desires could be met, increasing his unexpected viscerally sexual reaction tenfold. Hidden by the fall of his *abaya,* his rapidly engorging flesh ached with unfamiliar need.

Sayed's status as a soon-to-be-married man, not to mention melech of his country, dictated he push the images aside and ignore his body's physical response, however. No matter how difficult he found doing so.

"Thank you, Miss Amari," Sayed said, his tone imperi-

ous by necessity to hide his reaction to her. He indicated
the woman assigned to tend his domestic needs. "This is
Abdullah-Hasiba. She will let you know of any requirements we may have. Should you have any questions, they
can be taken directly to her, as well."

Miss Amari's beautiful green gaze chilled and her full
lips firmed slightly, but nothing else in her demeanor indicated a reaction to his clear dismissal.

"Thank you, Your Highness." Dipping her head again in
the tradition of his people, she then turned to his servant. "I
look forward to working with you Miz Abdullah-Hasiba."

With another barely-there dip of her head, the much-
too-attractive hotel employee did that thing well-trained
servants were so good at and seemed to just melt away.

Sayed had a baffling and near-unstoppable urge to call
her back.

CHAPTER TWO

STILL GRAPPLING WITH the fact she'd forgotten her father in the presence of the emir, Liyah knocked on Miz Abdullah-Hasiba's door.

She hadn't even taken the chance to meet Gene Chatsfield's eyes for the first time. How could she have missed such a prime opportunity?

She was here to observe her father and ultimately make herself known to him. Liyah had not come to the Chatsfield London to ogle a Zeena Sahran prince.

Aaliyah Amari did not *ogle* anyone.

The door in front of her swung open. The unexpectedness of it, even though she'd been the one to knock, further emphasized how disconnected from her normal self Liyah was.

Wearing a dark apricot *kameez* embroidered around the neck and wrists with pale yellow thread, the emir's personal housekeeper clasped her hands in front of her and bent her head forward. "Miss Amari, how may I be of service?"

"I wanted to make sure you and the emir's other female traveling companions have found your accommodations acceptable."

"Very much so." The older woman stepped back and indicated Liyah should enter her room. "Please, come in."

"I do not want to take you from your duties."

"Not at all. You must share a cup of tea with me."

With no polite way to decline, and frankly not inclined to do so, Liyah followed the other woman to the small sofa on the other side of the deluxe room. As much as it might bother her, Liyah could not deny her fascination with the emir.

At least, not to herself.

The Middle Eastern tea service Liyah had purchased on behalf of the hotel—along with the ones for the sheikh and his fiancée's suites—sat in the center of the oval coffee table.

Miz Abdullah-Hasiba poured the fragrant hot drink from the copper-and-glass pot into the short, narrow matching cups with no handles. "This is a treat."

"Yes?"

The housekeeper nodded with a smile. "Oh, yes. We do not travel with glassware as it is too easily broken."

"Naturally." Liyah waited for the housekeeper to take a sip before following suit, enjoying the sweetened warm beverage and the bittersweet memories it evoked.

Her mom had insisted on beginning and ending each day with a cup of mint tea augmented by a touch of honey.

"Nevertheless, the Chatsfield is the first hotel on the emir's current European travel itinerary to have thought to provide the traditional tea service."

"They will only be found in your room, the emir's suite and that of his fiancée, I'm afraid."

The older woman smiled. "Your grasp of our culture is commendable. Most hotel staff would have put the tea set in the room for the emir's secretary."

Liyah did not shrug off the praise, but neither did she acknowledge it. She was more aware of the Zeena Sahran culture than the average Brit or American, but anyone observant would have taken note that the housekeeper had been booked in the most deluxe room beside the emir's fiancée's suite.

"His secretary is actually junior office staff, I believe," Liyah observed.

"She is. The emir follows the old ways. By necessity, his personal administrative assistant is Duwad, a male."

"Because your emir cannot work late hours in his suite with a woman, married or otherwise," Liyah guessed.

"Precisely."

"So, this is a business trip?" Very little had been said in the media about the nature of the emir's current travel plans.

"For the most part. Melech Falah insisted Emir Sayed enjoy a final European tour as it were before taking on the mantle of full leadership of our country."

"The king intends to abdicate the throne to his son?" She'd read speculation to that effect, but nothing concrete.

"One might consider that a possible course of events after the royal wedding."

Liyah approved the other woman's carefully couched answer and did not press for anything more definite. "Our head of housekeeping was scandalized at the thought of booking a separate floor for a sheikh's harem."

"Ah. She assumed he would be bringing a bevy of belly dancers to see to his *needs,* no doubt."

"That may have been her understanding, yes." Liyah herself had assumed something similar, if not quite so fanciful when first told of the harem.

The Zeena Sahran housekeeper laughed softly. "Nothing so dramatic, I am afraid. The emir is ever mindful of his position as a betrothed man."

Not sure she believed that, but having very little practical experience with men and none at all with their sex drives, Liyah didn't argue. She did know the rooms she'd prepared had all been for different female staff members of the prince's entourage.

Most of the rooms that would ultimately be occupied were slated to house the emir's fiancée and her mostly female traveling companions. Her brother was supposed to be accompanying her, as well, and had booked a suite on the presidential level near the emir's.

Not quite as grand, it was nevertheless impressive accommodation.

After a surprisingly enjoyable visit with Hasiba—as she insisted on being called—in which the housekeeper managed to convey unspoken but clear reservations toward the future emira of Zeena Sahra, Liyah left for a meeting with the concierge.

He and his staff expected her input on a finalization of entertainment offerings to make to the sheikh over the next two weeks.

Liyah came out of the royal suite, pleased with the care the chambermaid assigned to the emir's rooms had taken.

The vases of purple iris—the official flower of Zeena Sahra—Liyah had ordered were fresh and perfectly arranged. The bowls with floating jasmine on either side of the candelabra on the formal dining table did not have a single brown spot on the creamy white blossoms.

The beds were all made without a single wrinkle and the prince's tea service was prepped for his late-afternoon repast.

She headed for the main elevator. While staff were encouraged to use the service elevator, she was not required to do so. The busiest time of day for housekeeping and maintenance usually coincided with light use on the guest elevators.

So, as she'd done at her hotel in San Francisco, Liyah opted to use them when she wasn't carrying towels or pushing a cleaning cart. Something she rarely had to do in her position as lead chambermaid, but not outside the realm of possibility.

The doors slid open with a quiet whoosh and Liyah's gaze was snagged by espresso-brown eyes.

The emir stared back, his expression a strange mixture of surprise and something else she had very little experience interpreting. "Miss Amari?"

"Emir Sayed." She dipped her head in acknowledgment of his status. "I was just checking on your suite."

"The service has been impeccable."

"I'm glad you think so. I'll be sure and pass your kind words on to your suite's housekeeping staff."

He inclined his head in regal agreement she doubted he was even aware of.

She waited for him to step out of the elevator, but he did not move. His security detail had exited first with a smooth precision that came off as a deeply ingrained habit, followed by the emir's administrative assistant and the junior secretary.

They all waited, as well, for their sheikh to move.

Only he didn't.

He pressed a button and the doors started to close. "Are you coming?" His tone implied impatience.

Though she didn't know why. Her brain couldn't quite grasp what he was doing on the other side of the doorway. If he was going back down again, wouldn't his security be on the elevator with him?

One thing she did know: she wasn't about to commit the faux pas of joining the emir. "Oh, no. I'll just go to the service elevator."

"Do not be ridiculous." He reached out and grabbed her wrist, drawing shocked gasps from his staff and an imprecation in the Zeena Sahran dialect of Arabic from his personal bodyguard.

Liyah had little opportunity to take that in as she was pulled inexorably into the elevator through the shrinking gap between the heavy doors.

They closed behind her on another Arabic curse, this one much louder and accompanied by a shocked and clearly disapproving, *"Emir Sayed!"*

"Your Highness?"

"There is no reason for you to take another elevator."

"But your people…shouldn't you have waited for them?"

His elegant but strong fingers were still curled around her wrist and he showed no intention of letting her go. "I am not accustomed to being questioned in my actions by a servant."

The words were dismissive, his tone arrogant, even cold, but the look in his eyes wasn't. She'd never heard of brown fire before, but it was there in his gaze right now.

Hot enough to burn the air right from her lungs.

Nevertheless, her professional demeanor leaned toward dignified, not subservient. By necessity, she pulled the cool facade she'd perfected early in life around her with comfortable familiarity.

"And I am not used to being manhandled by hotel guests." She stared pointedly at his hold on her wrist, expecting him to release her immediately.

It wasn't acceptable in the more conservative culture of Zeena Sahra for him to touch *any* single woman outside his immediate family—and that did not include cousins—much less one that was a complete stranger to him.

However, his hold remained. "This is hardly manhandling."

His thumb rubbed over her pulse point and Liyah had no hope of suppressing her shiver of reaction.

His heated gaze reflected confusion, as well. "I don't understand this."

He'd spoken in the dialect of his homeland, no doubt believing she wouldn't know what he was saying. She didn't disabuse him of the belief.

She couldn't. Words were totally beyond her.

For the first time in her life, she craved touch worse than dark chocolate during that most inconvenient time of the month.

"You are an addiction," he accused, his tone easy to interpret even if she hadn't spoken the Zeena Sahran dialect fluently.

Suddenly embarrassed, wondering if she'd done something to invite his interest and reveal her own, she pulled against his hold. He let go, but his body moved closer, not farther away, the rustle of his traditional robes the only sound besides their breathing in the quiet elevator.

With shock she realized there was no subtle sound of pulleys because he'd pushed the stop button.

She stared up at him, her heart in her throat. "Emir?"

"Sayed. My name is Sayed."

And she wasn't about to use it. Only she did, whispering, *"Sayed,"* in an involuntary expulsion of soft sound.

Satisfaction flared in his dark eyes, a line of color burnishing his cheekbones. For whatever reason, the emir liked hearing his name on her lips.

He touched the name badge attached to her black suit jacket. "Amari is not your name."

"It is." Her voice came out husky, her throat too tight for normal speech.

"Not your given name."

"Aaliyah," she offered before her self-protection kicked in.

"Lovely." He brushed the name tag again and, though it was solid plastic, she felt the touch as if it had been over bare skin. "Your parents are traditionalists."

"Not exactly." Liyah didn't consider Hena's decision to

make an independent life for herself and her illegitimate daughter *traditional*.

Hena had simply wanted to give Liyah as many connections to the country of her mother's birth as she could. Hena had also said she'd wanted to speak hope for her daughter's life every time she used her name, which meant *high exalted one*.

It was another example of the deceased woman's more romantic nature than that of her pragmatic daughter.

Liyah doubted very much if Gene Chatsfield had anything to do with naming her at all.

"Your accent is American," Sayed observed.

"So is yours."

He shrugged. "I was educated in America from the age of thirteen. I did not return to Zeena Sahra to live until I finished graduate school."

She knew that. His older brother's tragic death in a bomb meant for the melech had changed the course of Sayed's life and his country's future.

Further political unrest in surrounding countries and concerns for their only remaining son's safety had pushed the melech and his queen to send Sayed to boarding school. It wasn't exactly a state secret.

Nor was the fact that Sayed had opted to continue his education through a bachelor's in world politics and a master's in management, but having him offer the information made something strange flutter in Liyah's belly.

Or maybe that was just his nearness.

The guest elevators at the Chatsfield were spacious by any definition, but the confined area *felt* small to Liyah.

"You're not very western in your outlook," she said, trying to ignore the unfamiliar desires and emotions roiling through her.

"I am the heart of Zeena Sahra. Should my people and their ways not be the center of mine?"

She didn't like how much his answer touched her. To cover her reaction she waved her hand between the two of them and said, "This isn't the way of Zeena Sahra."

"You are so sure?" he asked.

"Yes."

"So you have studied my country." He sounded way too happy about that possibility.

"Don't take it personally."

He laughed, the honest sound of genuine amusement more compelling than even the uninterrupted regard of the extremely handsome man. "You are not like other women."

"You're the emir."

"You are saying other women are awed by me."

She gave him a wry look and said dryly, "You're not conceited at all, are you?"

"Is it conceit to recognize the truth?"

She shook her head. Even arrogant, she found this man irresistible and had the terrible suspicion he knew it, too.

Unsure how she got there, she felt the wall of the elevator at her back. Sayed's body was so close his outer robes brushed her. Her breath came out on a shocked gasp.

He brushed her lower lip with his fingertip. "Your mouth is luscious."

"This is a bad idea."

"Is it?" he asked, his head dipping toward hers.

"Yes." Was this how it had begun with her mother and father? "I'm not part of amenities."

No wonder Hena had spent so much effort warning Liyah against the seductions of men.

"I know." His tone rang with sincerity.

"I don't do elevator sex romps," she clarified, just in case he didn't get it.

Something flared in his dark gaze and Sayed stepped back, shaking his head. "I apologize, Miss Amari. I do not know what came over me."

"I'm sure you're used to women falling all over you," she offered by way of an explanation.

He frowned. "Is that meant to be a sop to my ego or a slam against it?"

"Neither?"

He shook his head again, as if trying to clear it.

She wondered if it worked. She would be grateful for a technique that brought back her own usual way of thinking, unobscured by this unwelcome and unfamiliar desire.

She did not know what else he might have said or how she would have responded because the telephone inside the elevator car rang. She opened the panel the handset resided behind and answered it.

"Amari here."

"Is the sheikh with you?" an unfamiliar voice demanded, and she wondered if Christos Giatrakos, the new CEO himself, had been called to deal with the highly unusual situation.

A shiver of apprehension skittered down her spine, until she realized that the tones had that quality that implied a certain age.

"Yes, the emir is here," she forced out, realizing in kind of a shocked daze that she might well be speaking to her father for the first time.

"Put him on."

"Yes, sir."

She reached toward Sayed with the phone, the cord not quite long enough. "Mr. Chatsfield would like to speak with you."

Sayed came closer and took the handset, careful not to touch her in the process.

She retreated to the other side of the elevator where she was forced to witness the one-sided conversation. Very little was actually said beyond the fact there was no problem and they would be arriving at the lobby level in a moment.

Even with her tendency to shut down, Liyah would have felt the need to explain herself, not so the emir of Zeena Sahra. If she had not witnessed his moment of shocked self-realization, she wouldn't believe he was discomfited in the least by their situation.

True to his word, the elevator doors were opening on the lobby level seconds later. Both the emir's personal bodyguard and Liyah's father were waiting on their arrival.

The conspicuous absence of anyone else to witness their exit from the elevator said more than words would have what everyone thought had been happening in the stopped elevator.

Offended by assumptions about her character so far from reality, Liyah walked out with her head high, her expression giving nothing of her inner turmoil away.

Making no effort to set her boss's mind at rest in regard to Liyah's behavior, the emir barely acknowledged Gene Chatsfield before waving his bodyguard onto the elevator with an imperious "Come, Yusuf."

"In my office," her father said in frigid tones as the elevator doors swished to a close.

The following ten minutes were some of the most uncomfortable of Liyah's life. Bad enough to be dressed down by the owner of the Chatsfield chain, but knowing the man was her father, as well, had intensified Liyah's humiliation at the encounter.

The short duration of her time in the elevator with the sheikh and her obvious lack of being mussed had saved her from an even worse lecture. However, Liyah had been left in no doubt that she was never to ignore hotel policy of employees vacating the main elevators when guests entered again.

Definitely *not* the moment in which to make herself known to Gene Chatsfield as the daughter he'd never met.

Sayed woke from a very vivid dream, his sex engorged and his heart beating rapidly.

It was not surprising the dream had not been about his fiancée. He had known Tahira, the daughter of a neighboring sheikh, since their betrothal when she was a mere infant. He had been thirteen and on the brink of leaving for boarding school in the States.

His feelings toward her had not changed appreciably since then.

The uncomfortable but also unsurprising reality was that the dream had centered on the beautiful Aaliyah Amari he'd met his first day in London. And thought about incessantly since.

He'd seen her in passing twice, once before the elevator incident and once since then. Both times his attention had been inexorably drawn to Aaliyah, but she'd done her best to pretend ignorance of his presence on the most recent occasion.

Understandably.

Nevertheless, even after the briefest collision with her emerald-green gaze, electric shocks had gone straight to his instant erection. And he'd almost stumbled.

Him.

Accused of being made of ice more than once, his disturbing reaction to this woman who had no place in his life bothered Sayed more than he wanted to admit. The elevator incident was still firmly in the realm of the inexplicable, no matter how much he'd tried to understand his own actions in the matter.

Sheikhs did not pant after chambermaids, not even those with additional responsibility. Aaliyah was of the servant class. He was an emir. He could not even consider an affair with her if he were so inclined.

Regardless, while Sayed had not been celibate for his entire adult life, he had been for the past three years.

Once Tahira had reached the age of majority and their betrothal had been announced officially, his honor demanded he cease sexual intimacy with other women. No one else seemed to expect it of him, but Sayed didn't live according to any viewpoint but his own.

However, his celibacy might well explain the intense and highly sexual dreams. Three years was a long time to go without for a thirty-six-year-old man who had been sexually active since his teens.

The knowledge that his sexual desert would end in a matter of weeks after he married Tahira gave him little comfort.

He could no more imagine taking the woman he still considered a girl, despite her twenty-four years, to bed than he could countenance giving in to his growing hunger for Aaliyah Amari.

CHAPTER THREE

LIYAH WATCHED HER father from the distance of the cavernous lobby.

If she wasn't sneaking in unnecessary glimpses of the emir, Liyah was straining for yet another impression of Gene Chatsfield. It was ridiculous.

Unable to deal with her attraction to Sayed in any other way than to avoid direct contact, she was no closer to coming to terms with the reality of her father, either.

And she felt like a coward.

Hena Amari had always been vocal in her praise of what she considered her daughter's intrepid and determined nature. Neither of which were at the forefront of Liyah's actions right now.

She needed to get her first meeting with Gene Chatsfield over with. If for no other reason than to tell him of her mother's death.

She sincerely doubted anyone else had done so. It wasn't something that human resources would have mentioned to the owner of the entire hotel chain.

The Chatsfield San Francisco had sent a beautiful bouquet of purple irises to the funeral; however, these were probably organized by Stephanie Carter and that was no indication their proprietor knew of his chambermaid's death.

Liyah watched as Gene stepped onto the elevator, no

doubt headed to the penthouse-level suite he always occupied when he was in London.

The empty suite. Because his fiancée was out shopping and not expected back until after teatime.

Now would be the perfect time for Liyah to make herself known to him. Things with the hotel were running smoothly; there had been no further complications with the sheikh's visit.

And what was Liyah doing here if it wasn't to fulfill her mother's final request?

Unlike her half sister Lucilla Chatsfield, Liyah didn't want to make her career at the family hotel and certainly not simply to please her father. He hadn't exactly been supportive of Lucilla's career, his one child who had made it clear she was not only interested in the welfare of the hotels, but worked hard for the Chatsfield. Instead, her father had hired a man with a ruthless reputation and, if the rumors were true, Giatrakos was extending his own personal brand of punishment not only to Lucilla, but to the remaining Chatsfield siblings. The man was a dinosaur when it came to workplace ideals.

Besides, Liyah had no fantasies that Gene Chatsfield would publicly acknowledge *her*. Not after a lifetime of him not doing so.

Theirs would always have to be a private relationship. The Chatsfield name had spent enough time in the tabloids. Gene would never willingly be party to dragging it through the red ink of more media scrutiny.

But that didn't mean he wasn't interested in meeting his twenty-six-year-old daughter.

His payment of support, as modest as it had been, all the way through her college years indicated he felt something toward Liyah. If only obligation.

Just like her obligation to Hena's memory.

Right. It was time.

Taking a breath to calm her suddenly racing heart-beat, Liyah untucked her mother's locket from beneath her blouse. She'd worn it every day since Hena had given it to Liyah on her deathbed.

Curling her fingers around the metal warmed by her skin, Liyah took courage from the love and memories that it would always evoke and keyed the elevator for the pent-house level.

A few minutes later, Gene Chatsfield opened his suite's door, holding a mobile phone against his chest and wear-ing a puzzled expression on his features. "Yes, Amari?"

Something cold slithered down her spine at her father's use of her last name. But what else was he supposed to call her? He probably didn't even know her first name.

That would change in the next hour.

Dismissing the inevitable nerves, Liyah schooled her features into her most comfortable mask of unruffled dig-nity. "Mr. Chatsfield, I would appreciate a few moments of your time."

"If this is about your employment here, I have to tell you I trust my human resource and senior housekeeping staff implicitly. It's no use you looking for special favors from the proprietor and, quite frankly, in very poor taste."

"It's nothing like that. Please, Mr. Chatsfield."

For a moment, Gene Chatsfield looked torn. "Come in," he said, "and sit down. I just need two minutes." After the briefest of gestures to the sofa in the lounge area, Gene hovered in the doorway to the room beyond.

"I'm sick of it, Lucca."

Faintly embarrassed and very uncomfortable to be pres-ent for such a clearly personal conversation between Gene and his son, Liyah looked around the room. Beside a large, comfortable chair was a side table that held a glass of what looked like whiskey and a newspaper. The headline screamed across the room. Lucca Chatsfield Does It Again!

What might have once been the amusing antics of a world-renowned playboy—a stranger to her—it now sickened her to know that these scandalous exploits were from her own flesh and blood. She had unfollowed @Lucca-Chatsfield, wanting no more distractions or information about her family.

"Just keep it off the internet, and for all our sakes, stay the hell away from Twitter," Gene growled into the phone before cutting the call dead and turning his attention back to Liyah.

If anything, his frown turned more severe, clearly ready to tackle what he saw as another problem. "While I'm aware I must have a certain reputation among the chambermaids, my days of dallying in that direction are years in the past."

Liyah couldn't hide the revulsion even the thought of what he was implying caused. "That is *not* why I'm here."

Inexplicably, he smiled. "I'm glad to hear it. My fiancée is a possessive woman."

And he was a former lothario with a past he no doubt wanted to keep exactly where it was. Buried.

"You know, this was a bad idea. I'm sorry I bothered you." She couldn't promise it wouldn't happen again, but she was leaning toward the idea that maybe…really, *it wouldn't*.

No matter what Hena had wanted.

"Nonsense. You've interrupted my afternoon for a reason. Come in." He stepped back and indicated with an imperious wave of his hand that she should enter.

"Are you sure you're not the emir around here?" she muttered under her breath as she did as he bid.

Apparently, he heard her, because he laughed, the sound startled. "You are no shrinking violet, I'll give you that, Amari."

"My name is Aaliyah, though I usually go by Liyah."

It sounded more American, even if the spelling was pure Middle Eastern.

"We are not on a first-name basis," he replied with a return to his superior, if wary, demeanor of earlier.

She nodded acknowledgment even if she couldn't give verbal agreement. He was her father; they *should* be on a first-name basis.

He led her into a posh living room with cream furniture, the walls the same saffron as a great deal of the hotel. Recessed lighting glowed down from the arched ceiling and a fire burned in the ornate white marble fireplace.

"Please, sit down." He indicated one of the armchairs near the fire before taking the one opposite.

She settled into the chair, her hands fisting against her skirt-covered thighs nervously. "I'm not sure how to start."

"The beginning is usually the best place."

She nodded and then had a thought. Taking the locket from around her throat she handed it to him.

"This is a lovely, antique piece of jewelry. Are you hoping to sell it?" he asked, sounding confused rather than offended by that prospect.

"No. Please open it and look at the pictures inside." One was of Liyah on her sixteenth birthday and the other was of Hena Amari at the same age.

She wouldn't have looked appreciably different at eighteen, the age she was when she had her short affair with Gene Chatsfield.

He looked at the pictures, his puzzled brow not smoothing. "You were a lovely girl and your sister, as well, but I'm not sure what else I'm looking at."

"The other woman isn't my sister. She was my mother."

He looked up then. "She's dead?"

Liyah nodded, holding back emotion that was still too raw.

"I am very sorry to hear that."

"Thank you. She didn't tell me about you until just before she died."

He frowned, his expression growing less confused and more cautious. "Perhaps you should tell me who *she* is and why she would presumably have told you about me."

"You don't recognize her?" Even after having time to really look at the picture?

It was small, but the likeness was a good one.

"No."

"That's…" She wanted to say *obscene,* but stopped herself. "Disappointing."

"I imagine, if you are here for the reason I believe you are."

"You know why I'm here?" she asked, a tiny bud of relief trying to unfurl inside her.

"It's not the first time this has happened."

"What exactly?"

"You're about to claim I am your father, are you not?"

"That happens to you a lot?" she demanded, both shocked and appalled. "How many innocent chambermaids did you seduce?"

"That is none of your business."

No, really, it wasn't.

Eyes narrowed, Liyah nevertheless nodded. "While I find it deplorable you apparently never even bothered to find out my first name from Mom, don't try pretending you didn't know of my existence. She told me about the support payments."

"Your mother's name?" he demanded in a voice icier than *she'd* ever managed.

"Hena Amari." There, that should at least clarify things. Though how he hadn't already made the connection with her last name, Liyah couldn't figure out.

"And I supposedly had a fruitful tryst with this Hena Amari. Did she work for one of my hotels, too? She must have, I kept my extramarital activities close to home in those days."

"She was your chambermaid at the Chatsfield San Francisco."

"What year?" he demanded.

She told him.

He shook his head. "While I am not proud of my behavior during that time in my life, neither am I going to roll over for blackmail."

"I'm not trying to blackmail you!"

"You mentioned support payments."

"That you made until I graduated from university. They weren't large, but they were consistent."

"Ah, so now we are getting somewhere."

"We are?" Liyah was more confused than her father had seemed when she first arrived.

"You're looking for money."

"I am not."

"Then why mention the support payments?"

"Because they're proof you knew about me," she said slowly and succinctly, as if speaking to a small child.

Either he was being deliberately obtuse, or something here was not as she believed it to be. The prospect of that truth made Liyah pull the familiar cold dignity around her more tightly.

"I never made any such payments."

"What? No, that's not possible." Liyah shook her head decisively. He was lying. He had to be. "Mom told me you weren't a bad man, just a man in a bad situation."

Hena had refused to name Liyah's father while living, but she'd done her best to give her daughter a positive impression of the absentee parent.

As positive as she could in the face of undeniable facts. The man had been much older and married. Hena had been a complete innocent, in America for the first time and too-easy prey.

"She said the support proved you cared about me even if you couldn't be in my life." Though that had been his choice, hadn't it?

He'd kept his affairs secret; he could have kept a minimal relationship with his illegitimate daughter just as heavily under wraps.

"It sounds to me like your mother said a great deal, much of it fabricated." He sounded unimpressed and too matter-of-fact to be prevaricating.

Sick realization washed over Liyah in a cold, unstoppable wave that made her feel like she was drowning. She was breathing, but couldn't get enough air. Betrayal choked her.

Her mother had lied to her.

The one person in her life Liyah had always trusted. Her only family that mattered.

Something inside Liyah shattered, loosening feelings and entrenched beliefs like flotsam in the miasma of her emotional storm.

Liyah's entire reasoning behind following through on Hena's last wish was false. Her father didn't know about Liyah, wanted nothing to do with her and never would.

"I can only repeat, I never made any such payments." There was no compassion, no understanding, in his cold blue eyes. "If you really were my child and I had elected to help support raising you, you can rest assured the monetary stipend would not have been negligible."

She stood, her legs shaky—though she wasn't about to let him know it—her heart a rock in her chest. "I'm sorry I bothered you. I won't do so again."

"See that you don't. Your regret would far outweigh anything you might hope to gain." He rose, as well, towering over her, despite the slight stooping of age. "If you attempt to cash in on our supposed connection in *any way,* I won't hesitate to prosecute you to the fullest extent of the law."

She reeled back, feeling as if he'd struck her. "My mother was wrong."

"She certainly was to send you on this wild errand. Is she even dead? I doubt it?"

"Yes, the only parent that will *ever* matter to me died four months ago."

"And it took you this long to come find your supposed father? More like you worked out how to cash in on some convenient coincidences."

Drawing on the brittle exterior she'd had to show to the world too much in her life, Liyah lifted her head and looked at Gene Chatsfield like the worm he was. "The only convenience is the fact your hotel paid for my trip here."

"I will expect you to put in your notice tomorrow. I won't have a would-be blackmailer working in my hotel."

"I would leave right now but unlike some of the children *you* raised, I have a work ethic." With that, Liyah swept from the suite on legs that barely held her up.

Not that she'd let the man in the suite see her weakness. He'd gotten the single moment of vulnerability from her she would ever give him. The moment when she'd asked him in so many words to be her father.

She was on the elevator before Liyah remembered she'd left her mother's locket with Mr. Chatsfield. Only, when the elevator doors opened to the lobby, she found herself incapable of keying in access to the hotelier's floor again.

She stood there in a fugue of inner turmoil as two men got on the elevator with her. Liyah should have stepped off, not ridden it with guests.

She did nothing, turned away from them as one keyed access to the presidential level.

Realizing there was no way she was returning to the

suite, she managed to press the button for her concierge level, not at all sure what she was going to do when she arrived there.

She only knew one thing with certainty. Liyah wasn't asking Gene Chatsfield for the necklace. She wasn't ever going to ask that man for anything again.

He'd most likely see she got it back via employee channels, anyway. And if he didn't?

Liyah would let go of the memento the same way she'd had to let go of her belief Hena Amari would never lie to her.

Her entire childhood had been influenced by the deception that her father knew and cared about her in even some minimal way. The realization he did not shouldn't be so devastating, but shards of pain splintered through Liyah's heart.

Only then did she realize how much it had meant to her to believe she *had* a father, no matter how distant and anonymous.

Liyah tried to tell herself that her life was no different today than it had been yesterday. Gene Chatsfield had never been anything more than an ephemeral dream.

So, he denied his paternity? It didn't matter.

She wanted to believe that, but she'd never been good at lying to herself no matter how impenetrable the facade she offered the rest of the world.

Cold continued to seep through her, making her shiver as if she was standing at the bus stop in the winter's chill. Her usually quick brain was muzzy, her hands clammy, her heart beating a strange tattoo.

If she didn't know better, Liyah would think she was in shock.

Sounds came as if through a tunnel and colors were strangely sharp while actual details grew indistinct.

She felt like if she reached out to touch the wall, her

hand would go right through it. Nothing felt real in the face of a lifetime and what amounted to a deathbed confession marred by lies.

Deceptions perpetrated by the one person she would never have looked for it from destroyed Liyah's sense of reality, Gene Chatsfield's denial a blow she would have never expected it to be.

Despite her inner turmoil, clipped tones managed to draw Liyah's attention. Perhaps because they came from the one man who managed to occupy her thoughts more than her biological father.

Sayed spoke in Arabic to his personal bodyguard, the man she'd heard called Yusuf.

So furious he seemed unaware of Liyah's presence, she realized why as the import of his conversation hit her.

Apparently, Liyah wasn't alone in facing betrayal today. Unbelievably, the future emira of Zeena Sahra had eloped with a palace aid.

Another kind of shock echoed through Liyah. What woman would walk away from a lifetime with Sayed?

The doors whooshed open and she stepped onto the floor that had been blocked off for the harem of Sayed's entourage, one thought paramount. The no-longer-future emira's rooms would not be occupied. Not tomorrow, or any day thereafter for the next week.

Liyah's overwhelming need to be completely away from the potential of prying eyes had an outlet.

She kept her eye out for anyone in the hall, but it was blessedly empty. As much as she liked Abdullah-Hasiba, Liyah felt an almost manic fear of being forced to speak with the older woman, or anyone else related to Sayed.

She was barely handling her own destructive revelations; Liyah wasn't up to hashing out the prince's woes with his loyal staff.

Using her pass card, she quietly let herself into the former fiancée's room. Tears Liyah never allowed herself to shed in front of her mother for Hena's sake, much less before strangers, were burning her throat and threatening to spill over.

Once inside the lavishly appointed suite, Liyah had no interest in the mint-green walls and elegant white accents and furniture. Her focus was entirely on the fully stocked liquor cabinet in the alcove between the suite's sitting room and small dining area.

The request for the full accompaniment of alcohol had surprised Liyah, but it had come from Tahira herself, rather than through Sayed's staff.

It was Liyah's job to see that hotel guest's requests were attended to, not determine their appropriateness.

Though considering the fact Sayed's suite had no alcohol and neither was any requested for his support staff, Liyah had thought it wasn't a habit he was aware his future emira indulged in.

It was pretty obvious in the face of recent events that drinking wasn't the only thing Tahira had been hiding from her fiancé.

Liyah was on her third glass of smooth aged Scotch, without the dilution of ice, when she heard the telltale snick of a key card in the suite's door lock.

She watched with the fascination of a rabbit facing off a snake as the heavy wooden door swung inward.

The handsome but set face of Sheikh Sayed bin Falah al Zeena showed itself, along with his imposing six-foot-two-inch body clad in his usual designer suit under the traditional black men's *abaya*.

Dark eyes narrowed in shocked recognition.

CHAPTER FOUR

SAYED KNEW EXACTLY what drove him to his former fiancée's suite and it wasn't any form of sentimentality.

It was for the fully stocked liquor cabinet he could indulge in without witnesses.

He'd stopped in shock at the sight that greeted his eyes once inside, his body's instant response not as unwelcome as it would have been only two hours before.

Aaliyah Amari lounged on the sofa, a crystal glass in her hand, her emerald eyes widened in surprised befuddlement. The scent of a very good malt whiskey lingering in the air implied she'd come to Tahira's room for the same reason he had.

To drink.

On any other day, he would have been livid, demanding an explanation for her wholly unacceptable behavior. But today all his fury was used up in response to the betrayal dealt him by his betrothed.

"She's not here," Aaliyah said, her words drawled out carefully.

"I am aware."

Aaliyah blinked at him owlishly. "You're probably wondering why *I* am."

"It would appear you needed a drink and a private place to have it."

Her expression went slack. "How did you know?"

He shrugged.

"Have you been speaking to my father?" She leaned forward, her expression turning nothing short of surly.

The woman had to be inebriated already if she thought the emir of Zeena Sahra had taken it upon himself to converse with her parent. "If I have seen Mr. Amari, I am unaware of that fact."

Her lush lips parted, but the only sound that came out was a cross between a sigh and a hiccup.

He almost laughed. "You are drunk."

"I don't think so." Her lovely arched brows drew together in an adorable expression of thought. "I've only had three glasses. Is that enough to get drunk?"

"You've had three glasses?" he asked, shocked anew.

"Not full. I know how to pour a drink, even if I don't usually imbibe. I only poured to here." She indicated a level that would be the equivalent to a double.

"You've had six shots of whiskey."

"Oh." She frowned. "Is that bad?"

"It depends."

"On?"

"Why you're drinking."

"I learned someone I thought would never lie to me had done it my whole life, that I believed things that were no more than a fairy tale."

That sounded all too familiar. "I am sorry to hear that."

It was her turn to shrug, but in doing so she nearly dropped her mostly empty glass. "She said my father wasn't a bad man."

"She?" he heard himself prompting.

"My mom."

"You didn't know your father?" His life had not been the easy endeavor so many assumed of a man born to royalty, but he'd had his father.

A good man, Falah al Zeena might be melech to his

people, but for Sayed, the older man wasn't just his king. He was and had always been Sayed's loving father—papa to a small boy and his closest confidant now.

"Not until recently." Aaliyah's bow-shaped lips turned down. "I think Mom was wrong."

"He *is* a bad man?" Sayed asked, the surreal conversation seeming to fit with the unbelievable day he'd already had.

Aaliyah sighed, the sound somehow endearing. "Not really, but he's not very nice."

"I think many might say the same about me."

"Probably."

He laughed. "You are supposed to disagree. Do you not realize that?"

"Oh, why? I think's it's the truth. You're too arrogant and imperious to be considered *nice*."

"I am emir."

"Exactly."

"You do not think a ruler can be kind?"

"Kind isn't the same as nice and you're not ruler yet, are you?"

"As emir I have many ruling responsibilities." Which were supposed to increase tenfold when he became melech after his wedding to Tahira.

A wedding that wasn't going to take place now, not after she'd eloped with a man a year her junior and significant levels beneath her in status.

"Okay."

"Okay what?"

"I'm not sure." She looked at him like he was supposed to explain the conversation to her.

"You're smashed."

"And you want to be."

"You're guessing."

"My brain may be fuzzy, but it's still working."

"Yes?"

"You guessed I wanted a private place to drink because you do, too."

"That's succinct reasoning for a woman who probably couldn't walk a straight line."

"I'd prefer not to try walking at all right now, thanks." She waved a surprisingly elegant hand.

"I'll get my own drink, then."

She made a sound like a snort, putting a serious dent in any semblance to elegance. "You were expecting me to do it?"

"Naturally." He failed to see why that should cause her so much amusement.

But his response was met with tipsy laughter. "You really have the entitlement thing down, don't you?"

"Is it not your job to serve me?" He dropped ice in a glass and poured a shot's worth of ouzo over it

"You wanted to make this official?"

"What? No, of course not." He found himself taking a seat beside her on the sofa rather than settling into one of the armchairs. "You will tell no one of this."

She rolled her eyes at him and shook her head. "What is it with rich, powerful men assuming I have to be told that? Believe it or not, I don't need anyone knowing I was caught getting sloshed in a guest's room."

The mental eye roll was as palpable as if she'd done it with her glittery green gaze.

"Tahira won't need it." Not the room and not the liquor she'd ordered for her rooms. The words came out more pragmatic than bitter, surprising him.

Sayed might be undeniably enraged at Tahira's lack of commitment to duty, her deceptions and her timing, but it was equally undeniable that he felt no emotional reaction to her elopement with another man.

"That worked out conveniently for both of us."

That was drunken logic for you. "I would not be here if she had kept her promises," he pointed out.

"She ran off with someone else, right?"

"The press already have the story?" he demanded.

Things were going to get ugly very quickly, but for the first time in his memory, Sayed could not make himself care right at that moment. He'd lost his brother and the rest of his own childhood to politics and the violence they spawned in angry men.

Sayed had spent the intervening years taking on every duty assigned him, dismissing his own hopes and dreams to take on the welfare of a nation. He'd put duty and honor above his own happiness time and again, doing his best to fill an older brother's shoes he'd never been meant to walk in.

He was tired. Angry. Done. Not forever, but for tonight he wasn't emir. He was a man, a newly freed man.

"I spent my entire life being what and who I was supposed to," he offered, not sure why, but feeling the most shocking certainty that his confidences *were* safe with this woman.

Aaliyah drained the last bit of amber liquid from her glass. "Yes?"

"It was not as if I was attracted to Tahira. Marriage to a woman who seemed more like a little sister than a future wife did not appeal."

"But you never tried to back out of it."

"Naturally not."

"And that makes you angry now that she's taken off for the freedom of a life of obscurity."

"Are you sure you've had three doubles? You're very lucid in some moments."

Aaliyah giggled and then hiccupped and then stared at him as if she couldn't quite believe either sound had come from her mouth.

He found himself smiling when, ten minutes ago, he would have said that would be impossible. Even his fury was banking in favor of the constant burn of desire Aaliyah sparked in him.

She smiled tipsily. "You're both better off."

"That is a very naive view of the situation."

"Maybe." Aaliyah shrugged. "I was born to an amazing woman who gave up everything she knew of life to keep me, not a queen."

"My mother is amazing," he said, feeling strangely affronted.

"I know. I read about her. Melecha Durrah is both a gracious and kind queen. Everyone says so."

"Not *nice?*" he teased.

"I would not know. I've never met her."

"She is," he assured. "More so than either her husband or son."

"Nice can be overrated."

"Why do you say that?"

"My mother was too nice. If she'd ever just let herself get angry at the people who hurt her, she would have had a better life."

"Perhaps she enjoyed the peace of forgiveness."

"Maybe." Aaliyah stood, swaying in place. "I think I'll have another."

He jumped up and guided her back to the sofa. "After some water, I think."

"I don't want water."

"Yes, you do, you just don't know it." He wasn't sure *anything* would prevent a hangover at this point, but staying hydrated would help.

"You're awfully bossy."

"So I've been told."

"I'm sure you have."

He shook his head, filling two glasses with ice from the

bar. He snagged a couple liter bottles of water as well as the ouzo before carrying it all back to the sofa.

He put everything on the coffee table before pouring them both a glass of water and topping off his ouzo.

"You weren't even finished with your first drink," she commented after taking an obedient sip of water.

"You're five shots up on me."

"And you intend to catch up?"

Why not? "Yes."

"How did you know Princess Tahira had alcohol in her rooms?"

"I know everything about the people I need to." With one glaring exception.

"Not *everything*."

"No, not everything." Clearly, he hadn't known about the palace aid. "It would have been politic of you not to point that out."

Aaliyah shrugged. "I'm a lead chambermaid, not a politician."

"You don't act like any maid I've ever encountered."

"Gotten to know many of them, have you?" she asked with a surprisingly bitter suspicion.

"No, actually. That is precisely what makes you so different."

Her ruffled feathers settled around her. "Well, I don't usually work housekeeping. I was assistant manager of desk reception in my previous job."

"Why are you working as a maid now?"

"They wanted my mother, but she died."

"Your mother is gone, as well?" he asked, pity touching his heart as it rarely did.

"Yes. She was from Zeena Sahra."

"Did you come to London to be with the rest of your family?" There was a small community of Zeena Sahrans residing in the British city.

"The Amaris don't recognize me."

"But that's impossible." Family was sacrosanct in Zeena Sahran culture.

"Mom refused to allow someone else in the family to adopt and raise me. The Amaris refuse to recognize a bastard."

He frowned, inexplicable anger coursing through him. "Do not use such language to describe yourself. It is not seemly."

"Neither was offering to pay me off if I'd change my last name."

"They did that?" It boggled his mind.

Aaliyah nodded, an expression of deep vulnerability coming over her features he was fairly certain she was not aware was there. "No matter what Mom hoped, they were never going to accept me into the family. She is buried in the family plot. I won't be."

"It is their loss."

"I keep telling myself that, but you know? Sometimes it's hard to believe."

"Believe it."

"They're not alone. I am and I don't like it." She covered her mouth and stared suspiciously at him, as if he'd drawn the admission out of her rather than her offering it unasked for.

"No one should be abandoned by their family."

She tried to put on an insouciant expression that fell far short, but he wouldn't tell her so. He found he enjoyed seeing what he was sure others did not.

The true Aaliyah Amari.

"It happens." She shrugged and this time her glass tipped enough to spill its nearly full contents down the front of Aaliyah's inexpensive black suit jacket.

She didn't even jump, just looked down at the water-soaked jacket. "Oops."

"You are all wet."

"I am." She cocked her head to one side as if studying him and finally said, "You could offer to get a towel."

"Should I?"

Instead of answering, Aaliyah unbuttoned the front and started shrugging the black fabric off her shoulders.

"What are you doing?" he demanded, his body tightening in a familiar way.

"Don't worry, I'm wearing a blouse underneath, but if I don't get this off, that will be soaked, too."

Once she removed her jacket, Sayed couldn't hold back his gasp. She'd been too late. The white cotton was wet and clinging to the skin of her torso and the lace-covered curves of her breasts.

Aaliyah looked down and made a moue of distaste his mother would have been proud of, then she giggled. "Too late."

"My very thought."

"I guess I'd better take this off, too."

His conscience demanded he discourage her from that particular course of action, but he refused to listen, watching in lustful fascination as she removed her uniform tie and then the soggy blouse.

Her lacy bra was surprisingly revealing.

"You like pretty lingerie," he said with a blatant shock that would have indicated the ouzo had already hit his system to anyone who knew him.

Sayed was not blatant. He was subtle. Especially in delicate situations like this one.

Aaliyah nodded. "Why shouldn't I? I have to dress conservatively for the job, but that doesn't mean I can't be as feminine as I like underneath."

"Your uniform does not mask your womanliness."

"Are you sure?" she asked very seriously. "I always thought it did."

Very decisive, he shook his head. "No."

"This isn't very modest, is it?" she asked in that way that said her brain was catching up to her actions.

"It is all right," he heard himself say.

"You would say that. You're a man."

"I am." Despite what many thought, he was indeed a flesh-and-blood male.

"Well, I know what to do." She nodded with exaggerated movement.

Expecting her to put her damp jacket back on, he sat blinking in lust-ridden surprise as she lifted her hands to fiddle with her hair at the back of her head.

A moment later long, black, silky waves of hair cascaded down over her shoulders and breasts. She arranged it so the wavy strands created a black silk blanket over the tempting mounds of flesh of her breasts.

"There." She smiled with satisfaction, clearly proud of herself.

"You believe that is more modest?" he asked, his voice cracking on the last word in a way it had not done in more than twenty years.

She looked down, as if trying to figure out why he would ask. "It covers the important bits."

"It does." In a way guaranteed to send his libido into overdrive.

She poured herself another glass of water, managing to do so without spilling any of the liquid. Though it was a close thing.

Taking a sip, she gave him a look of expectation.

"What?" he asked.

"It's your turn."

"To spill on myself. I do not think so."

"You don't have to spill your drink, but you're supposed to take off your outer robe and stuff."

"I am?" Had he fallen through the rabbit hole and not realized it?

"It's only fair."

That made surprising sense.

He stood up, a little startled at how difficult that simple act had been. "It is called an *abaya*."

"I know."

He let it slide from his shoulders, laying it over the back of the sofa.

"The gold around the collar with burgundy embroidery means you're a big mucky-muck in Zeena Sahra," Aaliyah said sagely.

"Yes."

"So does your *egal*. I think you should take it off."

"Why?" He never removed his *keffiyah* and *egal* in front of strangers.

The head covering and triple-banded braided cord that bespoke his position as prince were as much a part of him as his close-cropped beard.

"I think you could do with a few hours of not being emir."

Aaliyah's words resonating through him, he stared at her. "I think you are right."

Isn't that what he'd decided himself not minutes ago?

She nodded, her hair shifting to reveal glimpses of honey-colored flesh he had a near-irresistible urge to taste. The reasons for resisting were melting away with other inhibitions that came with his place of state.

"My current thoughts are definitely not appropriate for an emir," he admitted.

"So, take it off."

"Removing my *egal* won't take away my role."

"We'll pretend it does."

The idea was very appealing. He gave in and pulled off both the head covering and *egal* holding it in place.

"Now the suit jacket," she instructed.

"Are you trying to get me naked?"

"I don't think so?"

"You don't sound very sure." And looked adorably confused by the idea.

CHAPTER FIVE

AALIYAH'S BROWS DREW together in thought. "You're supposed to be even with me."

"It doesn't work that way."

"Yes, it does." She nodded, her head only wobbling a little, her expression all too serious.

There was something flawed in her logic, but he couldn't identify what just then.

Besides, he liked the idea of stripping away another layer of the trappings that separated him from this woman. It was as satisfying as removing the *egal* and *keffiyeh*, letting go of his position for just a few hours in the privacy of the hotel suite.

Inexplicably, his fingers shook as he stripped out of his hand-tailored jacket, burgundy silk tie and gray pinstriped dress shirt.

Aaliyah didn't seem to notice, her eyes eating him up in a very flattering way. After the hours spent building his muscles while honing fighting skills passed down for generations in his family, he had no false modesty.

But the way she looked at him was not simply that of a woman attracted to his fit body; it was more intense than that.

She watched him with a powerful hunger more honest than any expression he'd seen on a lover's face.

She made a soft sound that went straight to his groin. "Your hair is too short to cover any skin."

"You do not sound bothered by that fact."

She shook her head.

"Perhaps you have noticed, but there is already hair on my chest," he pointed out.

Taking after his ancestors, it wasn't too plentiful, but enough he did not look like a boy.

"Yes." She audibly swallowed. "Your nipples are hard."

"I bet yours are, too." And lusciously tempting.

"They are," she breathed out.

He had to swallow a groan. "Drink more water. I'm having another ouzo." It tasted about a hundred proof and he rarely drank, but she wasn't outdoing him.

They both slammed their drinks back. Funnily enough, she choke-coughed on her water. His ouzo had gone down smooth as glass.

They sat in silent contemplation for long seconds.

"You wanted me," she said, her expression thoughtful. "That day in the elevator."

As if he needed reminding of when that might have been. He didn't because the desire had not left him since the first moment he'd seen Aaliyah.

"Yes," he said when it appeared she was waiting for him to reply in some way.

He still did. Intensely. Even painfully.

His sex was harder than any muscle in his body right now—and he had abs of rock that could withstand blow after blow from a sparring partner.

"I've never had sex in an elevator," she admitted like it was a deep, dark—even shameful—secret.

"I haven't, either."

"Oh."

"I am not certain it's as common an occurrence as romance movies would have us believe."

"You watch romantic comedies?" she asked.

He shrugged. "My mother enjoys them. My father and I usually defer to her when we have an opportunity to watch a movie as a family."

"That's sweet."

He was unaccustomed to being thought of as sweet and did not want to dwell on it. "Gene Chatsfield would have been very angry if there'd been evidence of sex that day, I believe."

"He was mad enough," she said dismissively.

"You don't sound too worried about that."

"I'm not." Her lovely features twisted in a scowl. "I'm leaving the Chatsfield."

He would have asked why, but Sayed's mouth went dry as she shifted to put her water glass down on the coffee table. Her hair fell away, exposing one breast. The dark nipple under champagne-colored lace as hard and delicious looking as he'd imagined it to be.

He cleared his throat and poured another glass of ouzo. "Three years is a very long time."

"Yes?" She blinked at him in more charming confusion.

"Yes." He tossed back the shot and put the glass down. "Without sex. It is a very long time."

"I wouldn't know."

"No?" She was sexually active? That was a good thing, considering the things he was thinking about doing.

"Nope." She hiccupped, covered her mouth and then laughed. "Sorry about that."

He shook his head, his focus on her seminudity, not her hiccups. "It is nothing."

"So, you're saying you've gone without sex for *three* years?" Her voice was laced with both disbelief and shock.

"I have." And considering Tahira's recent actions, he seriously doubted his ex-fiancée could say the same.

Aaliyah gave him a probing look. "Are you telling me the truth?"

"Why would I lie?" he asked with more genuine curiosity than offense, though he was unused to having his words questioned.

"Because you're hoping to talk me into bed?"

"I do not need to go for the sympathy vote to get a woman into my bed."

"No, you probably don't." She looked him over in a manner that was both innocent and lascivious.

He flexed his chest muscles for her and groaned when her beautiful green eyes grew dark and bottomless with desire as she inhaled sharply. "You probably have loads of women panting after you."

"I would not know. I spend very little time with single women these days." His own honor mocked him in ways he'd never share with another.

"Why?"

"I was a betrothed man."

"Oh." She smiled, appearing very happy with some thought she was having. "You really are one of those guys."

"What guys?"

"The ones who know how to be faithful, even before marriage."

"I am not perfect, but once Tahira came of age and our engagement was made official, it would have been wrong to continue having lovers."

"You never considered having sex with her…in *three* years? She never offered?"

"No."

"That's, um…"

"Proper."

Her full lips turned down in a frown. "Not what I was thinking."

"Pathetic?" Deluded of him? *Sad?*

He did not think that anything could cool his ardor, but the prospect that she pitied him proved extremely effective. He did not need pity sex, nor would his pride allow him to accept it, no matter how much he wanted her.

"I'm pretty sure *pathetic* is never a word anyone would use to describe you. I was going to say maybe you should have taken that as a warning."

Just like that, the craving was back, his sex pressing against the confinement of his trousers.

"Warning?" he asked, not understanding.

"Presumably, she was just as happy to remain celibate."

"At least with me, yes."

"So, neither of you were sexually attracted to each other?"

"It would appear not."

"You didn't think that was a problem?"

"Marriages among those in position are not made for the same reasons as in your world."

"Elitist much?"

He shrugged. He would not deny it. "Our worlds are barely in the same solar system."

"Wow. It's really true, *in vino veritas*. Although that's ouzo you're drinking, not wine."

"I assure you, I do not need spirits to tell the truth."

"Are you really that arrogant?"

"I'm not sure what you mean."

"Of course. Our worlds are too far apart for us to communicate." Her voice was laced with unmistakable sarcasm.

His wasn't when he said, "Right now, we're in the same space."

It was kind of amazing, really. That he would be alone in a place of privacy with this woman who was a maid, but whom he wanted more than he had any woman in his memory.

Her head tipped slightly and she looked up at him in unconscious sensuality. "We are, aren't we?"

"It is a moment out of time."

She laughed out loud. "Arrogant and cheesy. Why do I still want to kiss you?"

He did not understand what she found so amusing. This was a moment that would never be repeated, could never be repeated. Yet he was grateful that destiny had written their meeting—here in this room that would never see his ex-betrothed—into their stars.

"Why shouldn't you want to kiss me?" he asked, certain he wanted it enough for both of them but aware that if she didn't he would do nothing about his own desires.

That damnable honor again.

"You think you are too good for me."

"No." He was shocked. "I did not say this."

"What about the whole different-worlds thing?" she asked, sounding hurt.

Which had never been his intention. "That is reality, not a judgment on either of our values as human beings. There are emirs in neighboring countries I would prefer never to have to interact with again."

"Really?"

"Absolutely."

"And me?"

"It would be my great delight to be able to spend more time with you," he said with more honesty than he ever offered.

"But?"

"But an emir cannot have even a temporary relationship with a hotel maid. Life is not a fairy tale." No matter how much he might wish otherwise.

"And you are certainly no Prince Charming."

The fact she apparently found him lacking bothered

him, but he did not understand why it should. "No, I have never pretended to be anything but a man."

"Who is prince of his people."

"Exactly."

She looked at him strangely. "You really don't mean to be arrogant, do you?"

"No."

"You are, though. Just in case you ever wondered."

He found himself laughing. "Duly noted."

"You're not offended."

"Why should I be?"

"Because the opinion of a mere hotel maid doesn't matter, does it?"

"Of course your viewpoint is important." More important than he wanted to admit.

"You sound like a politician."

"I *am* a politician." Though not one that could be voted out of office.

Diplomacy was nevertheless very important in his life. He wasn't being diplomatic with her, however. He meant his words. For reasons he could not identify, her opinion mattered.

"You're very sexy for a politician." She sounded surprised by that fact.

Or perhaps it was her own admission of it.

Unable to bank the hunger any longer, he leaned forward. "I am glad you think so."

"You're going to kiss me," she whispered as his mouth was centimeters from hers.

He didn't bother to give a verbal reply, but pressed his mouth to hers. At first, she acted like she didn't know what to do, but then her lips softened and she let them mold to his.

And he understood her initial reticence. She'd said she

didn't do one-night stands; naturally, she would have reservations about what was about to happen between them.

With great reluctance, he pulled his lips from hers. "We cannot have more than one night," he felt compelled to point out one last time.

He was still a man of honor, no matter how inconvenient.

Liyah had to process Sayed's words and what they meant before she could reply. "I know."

He'd made their short-term incompatibility perfectly clear. And she didn't care. She'd spent her entire life listening to her mother preach against easy familiarity with men.

Liyah had not dated in high school and only rarely in college, but she'd never allowed anything beyond simple kisses. She'd maintained her virtue on behalf of Hena Amari, to prove something that was forever denied her.

Her daughter's worthiness to be recognized by the Amari family.

She would never know that acceptance, but she *was* worthy to carry the Amari name. More worthy than those who would turn their back on Hena because her love for her child was too great to let Liyah go.

Liyah had remained chaste to prove to them all, but most especially Hena, that her mother had raised her better than any of them could have. Proving something to a woman who was irrevocably gone from Liyah's life, or people who simply did not matter, seemed beyond ridiculous.

Even to her alcohol-addled brain.

She had an entire life of being alone to look forward to. For this night, she would experience intimacy she'd always denied herself and might never know again.

No matter how melodramatic she told herself the sentiment was, Liyah had the distinct feeling no other man after this one would ever suffice.

Was love at first sight real, or was this just lust?

Liyah did not know, but the feelings she had for this arrogant sheikh went beyond anything she'd ever experienced.

She'd always thought her mother had been doing some kind of penance in never dating or seeking out another relationship, but maybe it was even simpler. Maybe Hena Amari had never stopped loving Gene Chatsfield.

And he hadn't even remembered what she looked like, much less her name.

Pushing those disturbing thoughts away, Liyah focused entirely on the man before her, the one whose kiss had touched her more deeply than she thought possible.

Sayed breathed against her lips, the soft puffs of air brushing them in a gentle caress. "I want to kiss you again."

She sighed softly. "I'd like that." A lot.

He didn't ask again, but put his desires into action, this time placing one hand behind her head. She found the control inherent in the action entirely in line with the man's nature.

What surprised her was how much she enjoyed it. She *liked* the way he helped her angle her head for the best connection, but she burned with the way his mouth felt against hers.

It was amazing and sent more sparks of unfamiliar need along her nerve endings. She wanted so much more than just a simple kiss. Not that this kiss felt simple. Decadent, delicious and completely addictive—his lips were lethal to her restraint.

One kiss melted into another until she realized what he wanted as his tongue slid along her lips pressing gently at the seam of her mouth. Liyah let him in and shuddered as the intimacy of their connection went to a whole new level.

He tasted like licorice and...*another person*. Liyah had never had a man's tongue slide along her own, had never experienced this level of familiarity with another person's mouth.

It was erotic in a way she never would have expected, making her want more. More of what, she wasn't sure.

But definitely more.

He cupped her breast and then she knew. She wanted more of *that*.

The thin layer of her bra might as well not even be there. Everywhere his hand had contact tingled, sending bursts of bliss arcing through her.

Warm masculine fingers caressed her, kneading her curve and brushing across her nipple. Her entire body went rigid at the electric jolts going directly from her aching peak to the core of her being.

Was this normal? Could ecstasy be this easy to achieve?

All the women's magazines made it sound a lot more complicated.

He gently pinched her nipple between his thumb and forefinger, his tongue playing a mating dance with her mouth she'd never known but recognized nevertheless.

And she realized what she was feeling *wasn't* the ultimate in ecstasy. Because it kept building. One pleasure on top of another. Every sensation more intense than the last, her entire body heating as her blood rushed.

If this wasn't a climax, she wasn't entirely sure she was going to survive one.

But, oh, she was willing to try.

Sayed broke the kiss, the sound of their panting breaths loud to her ears. "Are you certain you want this?"

She nodded, unable to get a single word out.

"You understand, tomorrow I am again the emir of Zeena Sahra."

"But tonight you are just a man," she reminded him in a desire-laden whisper.

"Yes." The sound was closer to a growl than a word.

He kissed her again, this time his mouth devouring hers, his hold on her head implacably keeping her lips right where he wanted them. His aggressive passion might have frightened her but for the gentle way he continued to knead her breast and rasp her nipple.

Putting off a lifetime of restraint, she reached out to do some of her own sensual exploration. His skin was hot against her fingertips and smoother than she expected. The black curls of hair on his chest were also surprisingly silky, his small male nipples ridged.

There was nothing soft about the layers of muscle bunching under her touch, though.

Chest, biceps and abdomen cut with defined muscles.

His body was so different than hers.

Sure, there was the male/female thing. But it was so much more than that.

Wearing the *egal,* or not, Sayed exuded power. He would always be alpha, never the beta. His physical and mental strength was awe-inspiring and in this moment those traits inspired her arousal, as well.

So focused on experiencing his body, she didn't notice his hands moving at first.

But when he unclipped her bra with a single efficient movement and peeled the lace-and-silky fabric away from her body, she couldn't ignore that.

Her already-hard peaks pebbled tighter at the direct exposure to air. She'd felt that hundreds of times in her life, when she undressed for bed.

What she'd *never* felt was the corresponding throb between her legs she experienced now. Or this new need to be touched *there*.

A desire she could only express with wordless whimpers and the tilting of her pelvis in a wanton display that should have mortified her.

It didn't.

His big hands slid around her sides and up her rib cage, leaving prickles of arousal in their wake until he cradled both her breasts.

"Lovely." Approval laced his tone. "A truly sweet handful."

"You have big hands. So hot," she rambled.

It was only when his rich laughter washed over her that Liyah realized how her words could be taken.

"I didn't mean to say I'm…that's not…"

He brushed his lips over hers. "Shh. You are perfect. We will leave it at that."

She had no chance to reply as his thumbs swiped over her electrified nipples. She'd thought the thin barrier of silk had made no difference in how these caresses felt, but she'd been wrong. Very, very wrong.

While the sensation of emptiness and need grew in her core, the rest of Liyah's body grew increasingly sensitive. Heat washing over in wave after wave of unadulterated lust, her skin ached for his touch in a way she hadn't even known was possible.

He seemed to understand, because his caresses moved on from her breasts to brush over her stomach, along her sides and right up to her underarms. Usually ticklish, the only response this unexpected touch elicited was gasping shivers and a hope he would not stop.

Inundated by sensations so intense she couldn't hope to distinguish one from the other, she moaned long and low.

His hands tightened into a hold on her waist, his fin-

gers squeezing and releasing in quick succession. "You
are so responsive."

"You make me *feel*." Liyah had spent her entire life
hiding behind a buttoned-down facade which allowed for
almost no emotion.

Feelings were dangerous.

But she'd found an inexplicable, if temporary, safety
in this man's arms.

He kissed along the underside of her jaw, teasing her
skin with the edge of his teeth and sending shivers cascad-
ing along her nerve endings. "You are far more intoxicating than the ouzo."

"You, too." She wished she could be more eloquent, but
Liyah had no experience in this kind of talk and had no
response but bare honesty.

He didn't seem to mind her lack of dramatic articula-
tion as he intensified the sensual onslaught of his hands
and mouth on her body.

CHAPTER SIX

SAYED PULLED BACK, giving her a probing look with his dark brown gaze. "You are not drunk."

It was a statement, but there was a question in the espresso eyes that demanded her undivided attention.

Even inebriated, Liyah realized that if she admitted to how inexperienced she was with alcohol, never mind sex, he would stop. The man had an overdeveloped sense of honor.

But regardless if she *was* a little tipsy, Liyah knew what she wanted. And it wasn't for him to stop.

"No." She turned her head, brushing his strong jaw with her lips, inhaling his spicy masculine scent. "If anyone is taking advantage, it's me."

There, she'd managed to sound both sober and in possession of her faculties. And honest. Because it was the truth. She'd never been *all that* and she knew it, but this amazing man wanted to make love with her.

No matter how much he'd claimed to want Liyah before, he wouldn't have acted on that desire without this particular unbelievable set of circumstances. He'd said it himself.

Their worlds didn't overlap. Not even a little.

"Then no one is taking advantage," he stated very firmly as his hands moved to the fastening on her skirt. "I believe it is time to remove more layers of the lives we choose not to acknowledge tonight."

"Yes." She didn't want any reminders of her job at the Chatsfield or why she'd taken it.

Shockingly, Liyah felt no hesitation about taking off the rest of her clothes. Especially as it appeared Sayed was intent on helping her.

Though she'd never been naked with a man before, wasn't accustomed to exposing her body to anyone for that matter. Hena had raised Liyah to be extremely modest, even among her female peers at school.

A lifetime's modesty melted under the heat of his desire and she did her best to help him undress, as well.

When they were both completely nude, no outward sign of their usual roles, he nodded with satisfaction. "Perfect."

"You are."

He smiled, the expression somehow rapacious. "Thank you."

"You're welcome." She was barely aware of what she was saying.

Her mind so preoccupied with the sight of acres of muscular bronzed flesh, she relied on rote response.

He moved toward her with the grace of a predator. "I hope you are ready for this."

She did, too.

He stopped in front of her. "I am breaking a three-year fast. Prepare yourself. I plan to feast on you."

Managing a bare nod, she shuddered at the words, but even more at his expression.

With practiced ease, he swung her up into his arms, the naked skin all along one side of her body pressed to his front.

She gasped.

"Couch sex is for when the comfort of a bed is not available." He swung them around and started walking to the suite's bedroom.

She didn't argue, just leaned forward and started placing tasting kisses against whatever skin she could reach.

Salt and unexpected sweetness burst over her taste buds.

The thought of making love for the first and only time with Sayed in the bed reserved for the woman he had intended to marry resonated with a strange sense of rightness.

While Liyah had no hope of ever being that woman, for tonight she was undeniably *his*.

He managed to pull back the covers and lay her on the bed without dropping her, or even unduly jostling her.

"You're pretty good at this," she said as he released her, impressed.

Sayed straightened, giving her full view of his amazing body, his expression confused in a way she was pretty sure it never was. "I'm sorry?"

"The whole getting-me-into-bed thing," she explained. "You were smoother than jazz."

"Smoother than jazz?" he asked with humor. "Really?"

She shrugged, unworried if her metaphor came off as campy. It's exactly what she meant. "No music is smoother."

"Perhaps I should be happy you didn't compare me to custard." He stood up.

She giggled and covered her mouth at the unfamiliar sound coming from her. "Maybe."

He shook his head, but his look was indulgent. He moved to join her on the bed.

"I suppose you have loads of experience carrying women to bed."

He stopped, sitting on the edge of the mattress, and looked down at her. "Actually, not so much." His dark gaze smoldered. "You are an exception in more than one way."

"The whole not-bedding-a-lowly-hotel-maid thing?"

she teased, her confidence boosted by her certainty that was exactly what Sayed was about to do.

"Among other things."

"You're saying you don't usually carry your conquests to bed?"

"I cannot think of another instance."

At his admission, heat poured into places she wasn't used to feeling anything and she found it hard to continue their repartee. "For three years, anyway."

"Ever."

"Oh." That was…it was just…kind of amazing and more than she wanted to dwell on right now, if she wanted to keep her few working synapses continuing to connect in her brain. "I guess it's just instinct."

He laughed, the sound arresting and incredibly sexy. Her chest felt tight. "Sayed…"

He cursed, his humor disappearing in an instant, replaced by that power-driven intensity she was so drawn to.

"What?" she asked, not sure what she'd done.

"Say it again."

"I don't know what you mean?"

He put his hands down and leaned forward, pressing the pillow on either side of her head, his face only inches from hers. "My name."

His name? Her befuddled brain tried to make sense of his request. "Sheikh Say—"

"No," he said with quiet intensity. "Not my title. My *name.*"

"*Sayed.*" If the word held more emotion when she said it, she refused to acknowledge it.

Something flared in his espresso eyes and then his lips were on hers again. Though she'd been sure they'd reached the pinnacle of passionate kisses already, she realized quickly how wrong she'd been.

He shifted to lie beside her and pressed his body against

hers, his hardness rubbing along her thigh. Another set of new and wonderful sensations beset her.

Liyah moved restlessly, her legs falling open.

He laid one hand between them, covering her feminine curls and most private flesh. "This is mine."

She had no thought to deny him. "Yes."

"Tonight is ours and you will be mine in every way."

Her answer was a wordless cry as he shifted and put his mouth over one of her nipples.

It was the most incredible feeling she'd ever known—the wet sucking heat, the sizzling jolts of pleasure shooting outward and through her body from that swollen bit of flesh, unbelievable.

Then his finger dipped into that most intimate place and she realized once again she'd been wrong. There was definitely more she could feel, more she could experience.

And more.

And more.

And more.

One sensation blended into another, her need for his touch growing in exponential proportion to every caress he gave her.

His fingers rolled slickly over a bundle of nerves even more potent than her nipples and she cried out. She knew about her clitoris. She hadn't grown up in a cave, but she had been raised to *never* talk about sexual things.

Not with her mother. Not with the other girls at school. Not with anyone. Sex was an entirely taboo subject with Hena Amari and she'd made sure Liyah saw it that way, too.

Liyah had spent her life excelling in school and then her career. She was almost as much a virgin in purely social interaction as sex. Sayed's intimate touch was the first time Liyah had ever realized exactly *where* that particular bundle of nerves was.

And he knew *how* to manipulate it for maximum impact, which he proved with expert caresses. Delight filled her, pushing from the inside outward, making her feel like her skin was too tight for her body.

It built and built, making her wonder how much more intense it could get as her sense of time and even her own person drowned in a pool of bliss.

Then something shattered inside her, the ecstasy exploding in shards of sharp rapture and she screamed. His name.

A long, pleasure-laden wail.

His mouth came off her nipple as he lifted his head, those magical fingers still moving in gentle circles as their gazes met. Satisfaction mixed with untamed hunger in his.

Barely touching her, he continued to cause tremors and contractions throughout her body. "You are so beautiful in your passion, *habibti*."

His words and the endearment were as potent as his most intimate caress. Oh, she knew he didn't mean she really was his love, but Liyah's heart squeezed, anyway. He could have used *aashitii*, an endearment appropriate for an extramarital lover, but much less tender.

Tonight Liyah could be his *habibti*.

Tension still thrumming through her and unable to process the unfamiliar and overwhelming reactions of her body, Liyah's head rolled side to side on the pillow.

"Sayed." That was all she could say. Over and over again.

Despite imbibing copious amounts of alcohol and his easy use of *habibti*, Liyah did not have the courage to call him sweetheart, or lover, in English or Arabic.

And he *liked* when she said his name. So she did it again and again, her vocabulary shrunken to that single word.

He surged up over her, his big body settling between her legs. Sayed kissed her again, stealing his name right from her lips.

His rigid sex rubbed against her where his fingers had been, sending little shocks along her nerve endings, drawing forth a new kind of passion from her.

It wasn't just pleasure. It was the need to have him joined to her body in the most intimate way possible.

He broke the kiss, his breathing as heavy as hers. "We need a condom."

"A condom?" she asked, her mind hazy with drink and passion.

"Yes." He groaned. "You do not have one." He cursed, his body filling with a different kind of tension. "Of course you do not. This is not your room. You would not carry such a thing with you in your work uniform."

She was kind of impressed with how many thoughts he managed to string together. The gist of them finally penetrated her own muzzy focus. They needed a condom and he didn't have one.

"Look in the drawer beside the bed."

He stared down at her, his stillness almost scary. "Did Tahira request them?"

"No." Liyah didn't even try to stifle the alien need to comfort, reaching up with an appeasing touch. "She was your fiancée. It seemed an expedient item to provide."

"Presumptuous."

Liyah just looked at him.

He moved to get what they needed, never quite losing contact with her body. Moments later, he settled back into his intimate position between her legs after putting on a condom from the brand-new box she'd put there herself in anticipation of an engaged couple's stay at the hotel.

His smile could have melted ice a lot thicker than that around Liyah's heart. "Perhaps *expedient* is the right word."

Her answering smile was as inevitable as what came next.

Sayed shifted so he pressed against the opening to her

body. Everything inside Liyah stilled, her world shrunk down to this exact moment, this space, the breaths they shared between them. Nothing outside Sayed had a hope of registering.

Not with him on the brink of joining them in the most intimate way, an experience that if Liyah was honest with herself she'd never actually expected to have. With anyone, much less this prince.

"This is going to be hard and fast." The words were guttural and low. "I am too excited."

Despite their detour into the mundane, she was still floating on a cloud of bliss, pretty sure fast and hard would work for her. "It's all right."

She wanted—no, *craved for*—him to experience the same pleasure she had.

He shook his head. "You are too perfect, *habibti.*"

"Not per—" Her words choked off abruptly as he pressed for entry.

Even though he'd warned her he was going to go fast, he moved inside her body with measured deliberation.

Liyah stretched around him, feeling full and connected like she'd never been to another person. Then a sharp sting shot through her core, making her gasp.

He must have encountered the barrier to her body. Liyah didn't feel like she was tearing, more like a stabbing pain.

He looked down at her. "It is good?"

She doubted he realized he'd asked the question in Arabic.

"Yes." It *was* good, even if it hurt.

"You are so tight."

She could only nod, gritting her teeth against the searing ache.

He drew back a little.

Despite the pain, she whimpered in protest at his withdrawal. "No."

His own breathing labored, his jaw was clenched as tight as hers, his arms shaking. And she realized it was using all his control to hold back.

Unfamiliar emotion seeped past the barrier around Liyah's heart.

"I'm not going anywhere, *ya ghazal.*" He laughed, the sound sexy and dark. "Believe it."

Again, his endearment touched her more deeply than he probably meant it to, but Liyah's mother used to call her a gazelle. She'd claimed Liyah had the gracefulness and beauty of the animal so often used in Arabic poetry.

Sayed's addition of the possessive *my* only added to its impact, insuring this experience went far beyond the physical for Liyah.

He pressed forward again, the pain so sharp she couldn't breathe. She bit back a cry, terrified he would stop. And was infinitely grateful she had when the pain transformed into a whole new level of pleasure.

"That is it," he gritted out. "You have relaxed."

"More than," she managed to gasp out.

"You said you had not been on a sexual fast."

She just shook her head.

"Say what you like, *habibti,* but no woman is this tight and tense upon initial penetration when she has been sexually active regularly."

"I want you."

"I have no doubts." He thrust once, twice, three times.

Her body reacted with delight even as residual pain hung at the edges of pleasure.

"I admit I like knowing I am the first in a while."

She swallowed, trying to agree, unable to get another word out as he continued his slow, sure thrusts.

"Tonight, you are absolutely mine," he claimed a second time with an almost savage satisfaction.

And once again, she could only nod, the overwhelming ecstasy of the moment crashing over her.

For tonight, she wasn't just his.

He was hers.

Inside and surrounding her with his big body.

"Ready?" he asked her.

"Yes," she finally managed. Though she had no idea what she was supposed to be ready for.

Weren't they already making love?

He pulled back and then surged forward powerfully.

Oh. Yes.

All vestiges of pain drowned in ecstasy as he pistoned inside her body again and again. Here was the speed and intensity he'd warned her about.

Her body tightened under and around him as indescribable pleasure built again.

Her climax took her by surprise, the waves of bliss so intense she couldn't even cry out this time, her throat strained with a silent scream.

Moments later, Sayed went rigid above her, his shout ringing in the room around them.

And her pleasure was complete.

He collapsed down, but somehow managed to keep most of his weight from crushing her. "I am sorry, *ya ghazal*."

"Why?"

"That was too fast."

"But it felt incredible." A sudden thought worried her, and because her inhibitions were down, it came right out of her mouth. "Didn't you think so?"

"Oh, yes, *habibti*. But if I had lasted longer, it would have been mind-blowing."

He was still hard inside her.

She smiled up at him. "Show me."

He did.

* * *

Sayed woke to the pleasure of a warm, silken body against him. He opened his eyes cautiously, the early-morning sun revealing not his suite but another luxurious room.

Tahira's suite.

Tahira. Memories came crashing back. She'd eloped with a palace aid. And he'd come here to drown his sorrows in ouzo, only to end up experiencing the most intense and pleasurable night of his life.

Thankful he did not get hangovers, he tipped his head to see the top of Aaliyah's dark head peaking above the sheet. She was curled on her side, the Egyptian cotton sheet pulled up to cover her face, even as her body snuggled trustingly into his.

Which shocked him.

She might be used to sleeping with someone else, but he was not.

Sayed never took lovers to his own bed and had never spent the night in theirs.

Yet he'd slept more soundly last night than he had in months, even with the knowledge of Tahira's betrayal and its ramifications looming over him.

It must have been the ouzo.

He started to tug his hand back from where it rested against Aaliyah's stomach and she made a soft sound in her sleep, showing no signs of waking. For some reason he was loath to relinquish contact with her soft skin and he allowed his hand to settle again.

Just for a moment.

He could not make himself regret giving in to his desire for the beautiful Aaliyah Amari.

Nor could he allow himself to service the craving she elicited in him again.

Even if he could remain for the additional week in London he had planned, it would be a bad idea.

Regardless, he had to return to Zeena Sahra immediately.

The lack of a wedding between him and Tahira would have far-reaching political ramifications. Not least of which was the fact no emir had progressed to melech of Zeena Sahra while still a bachelor in the entire history of his country.

He and his father would have to find another suitable matrimonial prospect for Sayed, and very quickly, if they wished to minimize their international embarrassment.

His father.

Damn it.

Sayed should have called the older man the night before. He would have to do so very soon.

Should he wake Aaliyah before he left? It might be more comfortable for both of them to avoid the morning after.

However, it was inevitable, he realized.

Sayed wasn't about to do the walk of shame down the corridors of the hotel back to his suite in yesterday's no doubt hopelessly wrinkled suit.

With reluctance he could not deny but nevertheless had to ignore, Sayed removed the arm he had curled loosely around Aaliyah. She mumbled and stretched one leg so it brushed his provocatively but, once again, did not wake.

With more effort than it should have taken to make himself do it, Sayed moved so he was sitting on the side of the bed and reached for the phone.

Calling Yusuf, he instructed his personal bodyguard to bring him fresh clothing.

"Your parents both called yesterday."

"You handled it with tact and aplomb as usual, I am sure, Yusuf." The man was Sayed's personal bodyguard, not assistant, but he handled things too sensitive for Duwad or Abdullah-Hasiba.

Yusuf was the only person who had known where Sayed

had ended up the night before. In fact, the bodyguard had suggested it.

"I did."

"Good."

Aaliyah groaned, moving beside him.

"You are not alone, Emir?" Yusuf asked.

"No."

"Do you need me to take care of it?"

The idea of his old friend *handling* Aaliyah as he had others of Sayed's bed partners in the past was not acceptable. "No."

"She needs to sign a nondisclosure agreement."

"She won't say anything, Yusuf. She's not that type of woman." Sayed knew how hopelessly naive he sounded and he hadn't been that innocently trusting since his brother's assassination all those years ago.

Still, he was certain he was right.

"Keep her there until I arrive," Yusuf instructed.

"Did you forget who is emir here?"

Aaliyah's head came up from under the sheet at that and she stared at him with wide eyes.

"I never forget my duty to you, O' Emir." Sarcasm dripped from Yusuf's tone.

"It is not your duty I'm questioning." Just the other man's willingness to follow a direct order.

Not something either of them had high expectations of after all their years of friendship.

"Think with your big head here, Sayed," Yusuf almost pleaded. "If she is not there when I arrive, I will be forced to turn the matter over to Omar."

Sayed didn't bother to remind Yusuf that no name had been mentioned. Even if his bodyguard hadn't been keenly aware of Sayed's preoccupation with Aaliyah Amari, discovering the identity of the woman Sayed had spent the night with would not provide much of a challenge for the security team.

Sayed felt his own groan coming on.

"Is that what you want?" Yusuf asked when Sayed didn't reply to his statement.

No way would Sayed sic his father's *fixer* on Aaliyah. "That is not acceptable."

"As you say."

Which was not agreement. Not coming from the man who had grown up alongside Sayed and was almost as close as a brother.

Sayed had been trained to lead a country and Yusuf had been trained to protect the royal house of Zeena Sahra. They shared a common goal that had solidified the bond between them from childhood.

"I will see you shortly."

"As you wish, Emir."

Grinding his teeth at the additional sarcasm lacing his friend's tone, Sayed hung up the phone.

He turned to face Aaliyah. She'd scooted to the other side of the king-size bed and was sitting against the headboard, her long, dark hair in just-woken-up disarray, the sheet pulled up over her nudity.

The way it outlined her delectable curves, he did not think the cotton provided the barrier she thought it did.

There was no point putting off what he would rather avoid altogether. "My bodyguard insists you sign a non-disclosure agreement."

Aaliyah nodded and then winced. Pressing the hand not holding the sheet in a death grip against the side of her head, she let her eyelids slide shut.

"You do not mind?"

"No," Aaliyah said in a whisper. "Would you mind not yelling, though?"

"You've got a hangover?"

Her eyes snapped open, fire sparking in their narrowed green depths. "Thank you, Captain Obvious."

He laughed, when he was sure nothing could have made him do so today. Not when he faced one of the biggest political crises of his life.

CHAPTER SEVEN

AALIYAH'S FROWN TURNED into a full-on glare.

And Sayed's laughter increased, lightness pushing away a layer of his stress. "You are a breath of fresh air."

"Why? No one else frowns at you?"

"It *is* pretty rare." He stood up, unashamed of his nudity. "Come. You can have the first shower. It will help."

She stared at him like he'd lost his mind. "I'll wait until you leave."

"Don't be ridiculous." He started going through the drawers and cabinets in the room. "Are there any pain relievers in the suite?"

"Your fian...the princess requested we stock ibuprofen. It is in the bathroom cabinet."

"She's not a princess," Sayed remarked as he went in search of the pain reliever. "Her father is a very influential sheikh, but he is not a king. And now she is merely a *Mrs. Palace Aid*."

Which would not afford her any of the prestige or benefits life as *his* wife would have done.

"You're a little bitter there."

Coming back out of the bathroom with two pills and a glass of water, he shrugged. "She chose her life, now she will live it."

And he did not think the pampered daughter of a powerful sheikh would enjoy her newly humbled circumstances as much as Tahira clearly believed she would.

"Love makes up for a lot of deprivation."

"That is a sweet sentiment, but not very realistic." He handed Aaliyah the pills and water.

She frowned up at him. "My mother and I went without many luxuries you probably take for granted as necessities, but I never doubted her love and that made up for everything."

"She was no doubt an amazing woman," he said with sincerity.

Ms. Amari had raised Aaliyah, after all.

"She was." With a look of sadness, Aaliyah looked away as she swallowed the pills.

When she tried to hand him back the glass, he shook his head. "Drink it all. It will help."

"I don't think I can."

"Sip it."

She sighed. "It wasn't the alcohol, was it? You really are this bossy all of the time."

"It comes with the job." He smiled, the urge to laugh again not easy to stifle, but he did not think she would appreciate it.

She finished the glass of water and put it down.

"Good. Now, go take your shower." If he timed it right, Yusuf would arrive while she was in the bathroom.

Sayed didn't understand this need he had to protect her, but he had no doubts it would embarrass Aaliyah greatly to face Sayed's security staff the morning after.

She seemed discombobulated enough by her one-night lover's presence.

She took a tighter grip on the sheet, her expression mutinous. "I'll wait."

"I am not accustomed to having my instructions disregarded," he told her, lacing his tone heavily with censure.

"Poor you." She appeared anything but sympathetic. "I'm sure you will survive it."

"You were not this stubbornly shy last night."

She glared up at him. "I was drunk."

"You told me you were not."

"I wanted you to make love to me."

"So, you knew enough to make the choice," he said with some relief.

"Of course. I'm not a child."

He tugged on the sheet. "Are you sure?"

Affront was written all over her lovely face.

He shrugged, lifting one brow. "Only, your refusal to get out of the bed seems a bit childish to me. After last night."

Color stained her cheeks, but determination firmed her chin. "Fine. Get me one of the hotel robes from closet."

"I assure you, I saw everything last night." He did not know why he was teasing her, but couldn't seem to help himself.

"It's not the same."

"No. You are right. We do not have the luxury of time to do anything about our nudity and the inevitable reaction to it this morning." He indicated his semierect sex with a small wave of his hand.

"Sayed!"

"What? You will not pretend you did not enjoy our lovemaking."

"Stop talking about it!"

"But why?" he asked in genuine confusion. "I do not mind telling you, it was amazing."

Yanking the sheet with her, she jumped up from the bed and wrapped herself in it before he got much more than a glimpse of honey skin and a couple of well-placed love bites he had very fond memories of giving her.

His breath expelled in a telling but unstoppable whoosh. "You are quite beautiful."

The rose of her cheeks turned crimson and she scooted around him to storm across the room to the closet. Aaliyah pulled one of the aforementioned robes off its hanger and then stalked into the bathroom, attitude in every line of her body.

He watched her lovely form until it disappeared behind the firmly closed and—yes, he'd heard the snick—*locked* door.

His pang at the knowledge no woman in his life would react like she did was as inexplicable as it was undeniable.

A knock sounded on the door to the suite. Sayed donned the other robe from the closet, surprised when he realized that not only was it a man's robe with the dark blue hotel crest on the left breast, but it was his size.

Had the hotel anticipated him visiting his fiancée in the suite? The brand-new box of condoms in the bedside table would indicate a resounding *yes*.

Sayed let Yusuf in. "Leave my clothes in the other room and the agreement on the desk over there. She's agreed to sign it."

Subtle tension released from Yusuf's shoulders. "That is good."

"She did not balk at all."

"It would appear Miss Amari is a woman of principle."

"As I told you."

Yusuf disappeared into the other room as Sayed found himself gathering Aaliyah's clothing.

Considering her blushing reticence this morning, he did not think she would like to see their clothes strewn around the sitting room. They'd so clearly been yanked off their bodies in passion and with little finesse.

Yusuf cursed in the other room, a word usually reserved for serious screwups, which Sayed never indulged in.

The other man came storming back into the room. "Tell me the condoms are in the bathroom trash."

"What?" Sayed was used to the intrusiveness of constant security, but this was pushing the bounds of propriety. Yes, the condoms *were* in the bathroom trash bin.

That was something that Yusuf should take for granted. Sayed was not an idiot. "You forget yourself, Yusuf."

"No, *Emir*. That would be you."

"What are you talking about?" But even as he asked, Sayed's memory of the night before began to nag at him.

The final time they'd made love had been like waking from a dream. In fact, he was pretty sure that's how it had started. Bodies moving together in the dark before waking to an unhurried joining and slipping back into slumber.

Sayed's insides tightened with realization.

It hadn't been a dream and they hadn't used a condom.

"Since I doubt very sincerely you have suddenly developed an interest in rough sex, the blood on the sheets can only mean one thing. Miss Amari was a virgin."

What was Yusuf going on about? "What blood?" Sayed's annoyance with himself made his tone harsher than it needed to be.

"The smears in a single strategic spot on the bottom sheet of the bed," Yusuf said, each word an emphasized bullet.

Ignoring for a moment the other reality for this new one, Sayed rushed into the bedroom, his gaze falling on the telltale streaks almost instantly.

How had he missed them this morning? Oh, yes, because he'd been so busy watching Aaliyah. Nothing else in the room had registered.

"She must have started." That would explain her over-the-top shyness about exposing her body to him this morning.

One of the things Sayed had enjoyed the most about the night before had been Aaliyah's lack of inhibition.

"Her period?" Yusuf asked giving the bloodstain a jaundiced look.

"What else?"

"What else indeed?"

"Anyway, we used condoms thoughtfully provided by the hotel." Except that one time, which he had no choice but to disclose.

"How could you be that careless?" Yusuf demanded, not unfairly.

Sayed could barely believe his own lack of control. "I woke from a dream that wasn't a dream."

"She was touching you?" Yusuf asked, his expression unreadable.

Another man might be able to refuse to answer such intimate questions, but Sayed had responsibilities that required a level of truthfulness with Yusuf he would never have offered even the close friend he was.

"Yes."

Yusuf did not comment. He did not need to. It was all written on the bodyguard's face.

He believed Sayed had been duped in a con as old as time, by a *virgin*.

Liyah took longer in the shower than she usually did, blushing as she washed the traces of blood from between her thighs. Even though there was no one else to see it.

She could not believe how abandoned she'd been with Sayed the night before. She'd brazenly initiated intimacy, even going so far as to touch him to wakefulness that last time.

She didn't regret it. She couldn't. It had been the most amazing experience of her life.

Even so, she was astonished at how she'd responded to

Sayed. Yes, the whiskey she'd drunk had helped lower her inhibitions, but most of it was Sayed the man.

Not the emir.

She sighed. Her first waking moments had brought home very clearly that she no longer shared her bed with Sayed the man, but Sheikh Sayed bin Falah al Zeena, emir of his country.

Realizing she couldn't hide in the shower forever, she got out and dried off.

Bracing herself for another encounter with the emir, she wrapped her hair in a towel and donned the robe again. Liyah pulled the door open and came face-to-face with two men, not one.

Sayed's face wore a wary expression she didn't understand.

The other man was Yusuf, the same personal body-guard that had been on the elevator with Sayed. And he was scowling. At her.

"I'm sorry I took so long." Embarrassment crawled up her insides. She hadn't meant to keep the emir from his shower. "You did insist I bathe first."

"Aaliyah, do you need Yusuf to get supplies for you?" Sayed asked.

"Supplies?" Had she skipped a page in the book?

"For your monthly."

Make that a whole chapter. Why would he offer such a thing? "No."

"Do not be embarrassed, Miss Amari," Yusuf assured her. "It is no trouble to procure what you need."

"I'm not even due for two more weeks," she blurted out, extremely uncomfortable.

She didn't know if Sayed's other lovers were just really open, or what, but Liyah found it very disconcerting talking about such a personal matter with him, much less in front of a virtual stranger. And she really didn't understand why it was coming up now.

Sayed made a sound that had her turning her attention to him. "You were a virgin," he accused, like it was a major crime.

Liyah stumbled back from his inexplicable but palpable anger. She ran into the jamb, her gaze skittering back to Yusuf only to find his scowl had grown darker.

"Why does it matter?" She could understand if he'd been disappointed in the sex, but his reactions last night made that unlikely. "I didn't lie about anything."

"You implied you were sexually active."

"When?" And again, why would it matter?

"When I told you about my *fast*. You said you hadn't been on one."

"You can't fast from something you've never had," she said with some exasperation.

Things started making sense, though. They were men from Zeena Sahra, the country that had spawned the attitude of Liyah's Amari relatives and her mother's own self-castigation.

Well, they could just get over themselves. Liyah *wasn't* her mother and her virginity, or current lack thereof, was *her* business, no one else's.

She drew herself up, pulling cool dignity into every pore. She would not be bullied. "My choice to give my virginity was and is *my* business."

"Are you saying you had plans to lose your virginity?" Sayed demanded.

"Of course not." What was the matter with him this morning? She was the one with the hangover. "You're the one who came to the suite while I was drinking," she reminded him. "I didn't have some great assignation planned."

"I came for some time on my own."

"And you found me." She challenged him with a look. "You didn't seem to mind that last night."

"That is not the issue here," he said frigidly.

"No? Well, my virginity is off the table of discussion."

"Miss Amari?" Yusuf asked, sounding slightly thawed.

Maybe he realized policing her morals wasn't his job.

She wasn't feeling the defrost, however. "Yes?" she asked, her tone the one she reserved for her peers who had thought their parents' money made them better than her.

"Are you on birth control?"

"No." Why would she be? She'd been a virgin.

Yusuf's scowl was back. "And yet you initiated sex without a condom."

Liyah wasn't sure if even last night's pleasure had been worth this kind of embarrassment. "We used condoms."

"Not the last time," Sayed said.

She stared at him. "What? No, that's not right. You always put a condom on before..."

Her discomfort at this type of discussion was only growing the longer it lasted.

"You woke me, it felt like a dream." He said it like he blamed her for that.

"This conversation is extremely uncomfortable for me. I do not know how it is in your families, but my mother discouraged talking about this kind of thing."

"By 'this kind of thing' do you mean sex, or the classic mantrap?" Yusuf asked with derision.

Liyah stared first at the bodyguard and then at Sayed. "Mantrap?" she asked, fury overcoming her embarrassment.

"What would you call it?"

"A mistake. *On both our parts,*" she emphasized, speaking to Sayed, though it was his bodyguard casting the slurs.

"A very convenient mistake," Yusuf opined.

She glared at him, but whatever she'd been going to say was preempted by Sayed.

"That is enough, Yusuf. You will apologize to Miss Amari for making that kind of accusation, as will I for allowing it. As she said, the mistake was mutual, though more my own than hers, considering Liyah's undeniable lack of experience."

Both men apologized with a surprising sincerity that allayed Liyah's anger, but did nothing to help her acute embarrassment.

"I accept your apologies. Now, can I sign that nondisclosure agreement? Only, I'd like to leave." She wanted out of this hotel suite and away from the emir and his bodyguard in the worst way.

Even if it meant saying her final goodbye to Sayed.

"Unfortunately, it is no longer that simple." Regret laced Sayed's every word.

"Why not?"

"You might be pregnant," he said, as if spelling it out for a small child, and not sounding at all pleased by the prospect.

She frowned. "I'm not stupid, but isn't that very unlikely?"

"Considering where you are at in your cycle, no."

"But…" She really didn't know what to say to that. She wanted to deny his assertion, but she couldn't.

Women had sex all the time without getting pregnant. Couldn't she be one of them?

The idea that she could be following in her mother's footsteps after a single night's indiscretion both terrified and dismayed her.

"Could we stop talking about this now?"

"You're acting very repressed," Sayed said, censure in his tone.

Ding. Ding. Ding. Give that man a prize. "Because I don't want to talk about this!"

"Last night's transgressions cannot be ignored."

Any fleeting sense of romance still lingering in her wary emotions from the night before dissipated then. "I don't talk about sex."

"Never?" Sayed's disbelief was palpable.

"No."

"But you are twenty-six and your mother died only recently."

"So?" Where did he think she got her discomfort with the subject from?

"What about friends?" he pressed, like it mattered for some reason she could not fathom.

"I was a scholarship student surrounded by peers who drove Beemers and wore designer jewelry with their school uniforms. I had very few friends, none I would have talked about regarding such a taboo subject."

Sayed was now looking at her strangely. "Sex is taboo?"

"Yes, which is why I wish we could stop talking about it right now."

"But last night…"

"Alcohol is apparently very effective at lowering my inhibitions."

"And in college?" Yusuf asked, still harping right along with his emir on the whole who-had-she-talked-about-sex-to thing.

"What part of 'taboo subject' are you not getting?" she demanded with asperity.

He shook his head, his expression pitying.

Which she would not accept. She'd never allowed anyone to pity her and Liyah wasn't about to start now. "I have hardly been deprived."

She'd had things a lot more important than sex, or a romantic relationship, to think about. Namely, making

Hena proud and proving Liyah's value as a student and later employee.

"Condoms are not infallible as birth control." Yusuf's frown was for both her and Sayed.

Sayed winced in acknowledgment and faced Liyah, his expression too serious. "The fact is, the nondisclosure agreement is the least of our worries right now, *habibti*."

"Don't call me that." It brought the night before into today where it had no place.

Yusuf sighed and looked very tired all of a sudden. "Miss Amari, you have to face reality. You may well be pregnant with the next heir of Zeena Sahra."

"No," she cried before panic had her spinning back into the bathroom and locking the door behind her.

Nausea twisted her stomach, chills rushing up and down Liyah's arms and legs. She could *not* be pregnant.

She was not her mother. Liyah had worked so hard to build a life her mother would be proud of. Hena Amari would be devastated by this turn of events.

The knowledge her mother was no longer around to witness Liyah's fall from grace was no comfort.

The fact she had no one to turn to for advice, for support, even for a good lecture, sliced open the wound of her mother's death that had barely begun to heal.

This could not be happening. Liyah would not allow it to happen.

She charged back into the room. Yusuf and Sayed stopped talking and faced her, wearing twin expressions of surprise.

"I am not pregnant. Do you hear me? *I will not be pregnant.*"

Sayed's dark eyes widened, his features moving into lines of unwelcome sympathy. "It is not something you can will away, Aaliyah, nor do I believe you truly wish to."

"I was not setting some sort of *mantrap*," she all but shouted.

"I believe you. That is not what I referred to."

"What, then?" she demanded belligerently

"Would you will our child out of existence if you could?"

She staggered back a step, her earlier nausea returning. How could she answer that?

Of course she would never will a child out of existence. She'd spent a lifetime believing her father didn't want her, no matter what Hena had tried to convince Liyah. She could never visit that lack of acceptance on her own child.

Not even in the womb.

But there was another truth she could not ignore. "I do not want to be pregnant."

And she didn't care if those two attitudes seemed to be at odds. In her mind, one had nothing to do with the other.

If she were pregnant, she would make the best of it, but Liyah categorically *did not want to be* pregnant.

"Why did she have to die?" she asked of no one in particular, knowing only that she wanted to talk to Hena one last time with a pain that was tearing at her.

Sayed laid his hand on her arm. "I know you miss her, but your mother didn't leave you on purpose, *ya ghazal*."

Liyah jumped, not having realized he'd moved so close. She looked up at Sayed, unsure why his words, his very presence, was so comforting. It shouldn't be. "Everything has been so hard since she left. Everything."

"It will be okay."

Confusion, grief and pain a maelstrom of emotion inside her, Liyah shook her head. "No. It can't be. The Amaris will know they were right to reject me. They'll want to take my baby away, too. She'll grow up without her father like I did."

Send For
2 FREE BOOKS
Today!

I accept your offer!

Please send me two free novels and two mystery gifts (gifts worth about $10). I understand that these books are completely free—even the shipping and handling will be paid—and I am under no obligation to purchase anything, ever, as explained on the back of this card.

❏ I prefer the regular-print edition
106/306 HDL GEUX

❏ I prefer the larger-print edition
176/376 HDL GEUX

Please Print

FIRST NAME

LAST NAME

ADDRESS

APT.#   CITY

STATE/PROV.   ZIP/POSTAL CODE

Visit us online at
www.ReaderService.com

◀ Detach card and mail today. No stamp needed. ◀ © 2013 HARLEQUIN ENTERPRISES LIMITED. ® and ™ are trademarks owned and used by the trademark owner and/or its licensee. Printed in the U.S.A.

Send For
2 FREE BOOKS
Today!

I accept your offer!

Please send me two
free novels and two mystery
gifts (gifts worth about $10).
I understand that these books
are completely free—even
the shipping and handling will
be paid—and I am under no
obligation to purchase anything,
ever, as explained on the back
of this card.

❏ I prefer the regular-print edition
106/306 HDL GEUX

❏ I prefer the larger-print edition
176/376 HDL GEUX

Please Print

FIRST NAME

LAST NAME

ADDRESS

APT.#   CITY

STATE/PROV.   ZIP/POSTAL CODE

Visit us online at
www.ReaderService.com

HP-514-GF13

Liyah's thoughts spun with dizzying speed, no chance for her to take hold of one.

"But don't you ever accuse her of blackmailing you," Liyah demanded fiercely. "Don't you dare pretend you don't remember me. You don't have to acknowledge her, but you won't treat her like that, like she's garbage under your shoe. Do you understand?"

CHAPTER EIGHT

"PERHAPS I SHOULD get Abdullah-Hasiba," Yusuf said.

Liyah spun toward him. "No. You won't tell her. This is *my* business."

Her business. No one else's. She was alone now.

On one level, Liyah realized that she was flying apart, but she could do nothing to stop it. Her ability to repress her feelings and put on a cool front had deserted her completely.

After a wary glance at her, Yusuf looked toward Sayed for direction.

His emir ignored him, moving forward so Liyah had no choice but to back up until he had her pressed against the wall. She should have felt trapped, but her rampaging heart started to calm, her breathing slowing down to match his even inhalations.

He filled her vision and dominated her other senses, leaving no room for anything else, including her escalating panic.

Cupping her cheeks, Sayed waited until Liyah met his gaze and held it. "Listen to me, *ya ghaliyah ghazal*. If you carry my child, we will face this together. You are not alone."

If only that were true. He could call her his precious gazelle, but she *wasn't* his. She *wasn't* precious to him.

No matter how beautiful he found her, women who didn't

come from money or royalty, women like Liyah, who worked for a living, didn't exist for him in his world.

She almost laughed with gallows humor. "You don't even think I'm good enough for an affair. You aren't going to raise a child with me."

And why were they even talking like this. She *wasn't* pregnant. She couldn't be.

"I told you, the differences in our lives are just that. Not levels of superiority."

"Right. *Mrs. Palace Aid,* remember that?"

He huffed out a sound that was almost a laugh. "I believe that, after her betrayal, I am allowed a measure of leeway."

"I suppose."

"Just promise me this. We will take each day as it comes...together."

How could she promise that? How could she trust it?

"Promise me, *habibti.*"

"You called me that on purpose."

"Everything I do is on purpose."

"Not taking my virginity, it wasn't."

Instead of renewing his anger with the reminder, it made him laugh. "No, perhaps not, but taking you to my bed was."

"You were drunk."

"No, I was not."

"Oh."

"Were you too inebriated to know what you were doing?" he asked. "Tell me the truth."

"No. I told you."

"Then we will both accept the consequences of choices we knowingly made."

She nodded.

"Together."

"For now."

"As long as your pregnancy is a possibility."

She tried to read his eyes, but could see nothing beyond sincerity and determination that might give her stubbornness a run for its money. "Okay."

He smiled. "Good. That is a beginning."

Yusuf cleared his throat. "We need to consider procurement of the morning-after pill."

Sayed turned so he stood between Liyah and the bodyguard, his back to her. "What are you talking about?"

"Emergency birth control."

"No."

"It's not—"

"An option," Sayed insisted, interrupting his bodyguard.

"It might be," Liyah offered, remembering an article she'd read about the different types of after-the-fact birth control. "If it's the one that doesn't get rid of pregnancy, only prevent it."

"How is it possible you know this and yet are so uncomfortable talking about sex?" Sayed asked, turning to face her again, his expression searching.

She rolled her eyes. "I read." One of her secret vices was a long-standing subscription to a popular women's magazine. "I'm inexperienced, not ignorant."

"Tell me about this pill."

"Well, there's more than one, but I think…hope…the one Yusuf is talking about is safe. You know, if I'm pregnant already, it won't hurt the baby. Or me." She wanted to keep denying the possibility she was pregnant.

And truly, she couldn't believe she was, but she wasn't an ostrich. She wouldn't be burying her head in the sand in the face of a potential reality.

No matter how much she might want to.

Sayed nodded acknowledgment. "It cannot be one hundred percent effective."

"Not absolutely, no."

"So, our immediate plans must be the same regardless."

"You are right, of course," Yusuf answered. "I will begin making arrangements."

"I'll have to talk to the local clinic about getting the pill."

"No," Sayed and Yusuf said in unison.

"What? Why not?" How else were they going to get it?

"Too risky," Yusuf said baldly.

"In what way?" she asked, again feeling like she was missing something.

Sayed grimaced. "We cannot afford for word of this situation to leak to the press, particularly in the wake of the scandal Tahira's defection has caused."

Liyah wanted to protest at being labeled a *situation,* but understood Sayed's viewpoint. He was already facing major public scandal; she had no desire to add to it.

"Stealth mode. I've got it."

Sayed sighed. "If destiny has ordained you carry my child, then we will do our best to face that fate with courage and honor, but we will proceed with caution in the interim."

"You make it sound like we're going to war."

He smiled and shook his head, dropping his hands. "Life is a war of choices, Aaliyah. Last night, neither of us made the best ones, but that does not mean we rush headlong into rash decisions this morning."

She missed the touch of his hands, but told herself not to be a fool. "We look at our options and take responsibility."

Something Liyah believed in very strongly and couldn't help being glad he did, too.

Sayed was no Gene Chatsfield.

"Exactly." Sayed's tone was laced with satisfied approval, his gaze almost warm before he turned very serious. "However, some responsibilities carry greater weight than others."

"What do you mean?"

"I need to return to Zeena Sahra. Tahira's actions will have long-reaching consequences for our country."

Feeling unaccountably bereft at the thought of his abandonment, Liyah nevertheless nodded. "I understand."

"Good. It is unfortunate you will not be able to work out your notice, but it is fortuitous that you already made your plans to leave."

"What? Why won't I work out my notice?"

"I've told you, we must leave for Zeena Sahra immediately."

"You said *you* had to leave."

He gave her a look that said she wasn't following him. "Naturally you must come with me."

"Why?"

"You may carry my child."

"But we don't know."

"And until we do, you will be under my protection and care."

"But—"

"Come, do not tell me you would not love to visit the country of your mother's birth."

"I would, very much, but under different circumstances than these."

He shrugged. "We make of our circumstances what we wish them to be."

"Remember that when you're dealing with the fallout from Tahira's elopement." Liyah felt bad as soon as she said the words. "I'm sorry. I didn't mean to make light of what you're going through."

"Apology accepted. Now, let us prepare for our trip."

"I didn't say I was going."

"But you will." He smiled winningly. "What better guide to introduce you to the magic that is Zeena Sahra than its emir?"

"I don't remember you being this persuasive last night."

Bossy, yes, persuasive, no.

"It is another facet of my character for you to come to know."

As the jet taxied down the runway, Liyah marveled at how efficiently Sayed's people worked.

It was easier than thinking about *why* she was on this plane.

In the time it took Liyah to explain to the head house-keeper that an unavoidable circumstance had arisen which required Liyah to leave London immediately, they had packed her bedsit, paid off the lease and delivered her things to Sayed's jet.

She hadn't brought much more than clothes with her from the States to begin with, but still.

All this effort and near-frightening efficiency on behalf of the *possibility* she carried Sayed's baby.

Thankfully, her boss had been a lot more understanding than Liyah had expected. The head housekeeper had told Liyah that with her work ethic, the older woman knew her lead chambermaid would not be leaving if any other choice was open to her.

"My counterpart in San Francisco as well as your former employers had nothing but good things to say about you, Miss Amari."

The unprecedented warmth and affirmation from the usually no-nonsense woman had been a balm to Liyah's battered pride after her father's attack on her integrity the day before.

And it had made Liyah feel guilty because she wasn't telling the whole truth and her only reason for having to leave was the results of her own poor judgment.

It was a smooth takeoff and it hardly seemed as if any time had passed at all before the pilot announced they'd gained sufficient stability and altitude to move about the cabin and turn on small electronic devices.

"I wasn't expecting that on a private plane," she said to Sayed, who sat beside her.

"Air safety regulations must be maintained." The answer did not come from Sayed, but Yusuf, who now stood in the aisle beside their seats.

He and the rest of the security team were sitting toward the front of the plane. Two on either side of a table they'd been using to play cards on since the door had been closed for takeoff.

Other than the cabin attendant, there was no one else on the spacious private jet. Clearly, Sayed was taking pains to keep her presence on the plane under wraps.

She should have felt like his dirty secret, but his attitude toward her was too respectful. And as she'd told him earlier, she understood the need for stealth mode.

For now.

She wasn't Hena Amari; Liyah wasn't about to fade into the background to save the man she'd had sex with from facing up to his responsibilities.

Sayed, who had taken the seat beside her rather than sitting opposite, had papers spread on the table.

They looked like printouts of news articles. Since most of them had pictures of Tahira and a rather ordinary-looking man, Liyah assumed they were the media's response to the elopement.

The man in the pictures with the Middle Eastern beauty did not appear near middle age, but his hair was clearly already thinning. Though there were stress lines around his eyes, they still appeared kind.

And Liyah thought she might understand how a woman could trust her life to this man over one who had never shown the slightest physical interest in her despite their engagement.

Because for all Tahira's beauty, *she* looked extremely young and even more innocent than Liyah had been before last night.

Sayed noticed her interest in the articles and waved at them. "My former fiancée with her *palace aid*."

"You're going to have to stop putting that rather obvious emphasis on his job title if you don't want the media to label you an elitist."

Sayed frowned, but Yusuf said, "Miss Amari is right."

"You are not my public relations specialist," the emir reminded his bodyguard.

Yusuf didn't bother to answer, but held out a single pill blister pack. "As we discussed."

Sayed took it. "Thank you."

Yusuf nodded before returning to his seat.

Liyah did not watch him go; her focus was stuck on the silver packet in Sayed's hand.

"How effective is it?" she asked, her memory not very clear on that point.

"Dr. Batsmani said it is considered between eighty and ninety-five percent."

"Then why am I on this plane? Why didn't I just take it back in London and be done with it?"

"Five to twenty percent are hardly impossible odds." Sayed called the cabin attendant over for water with a wave of his hand.

When it arrived, Liyah opened the blister pack with inexplicable reluctance. Her head knew this was absolutely the right thing to do. She hadn't planned on motherhood at this point in her life, if ever.

If she were pregnant, Liyah would do her best, just as Hena Amari had done. That didn't mean she craved the opportunity to raise a child alone.

Although, according to Sayed, that was not one of the options she had to worry about.

Some little part of her heart disagreed with her head, telling her to forget the pill. Hadn't she wondered what kind of sane woman could let a man like Sayed go?

But no woman with honor would want to have him because he was trapped.

Besides, last night had been the first time she'd ever allowed her emotions to rule. And the aftermath had not been a resounding success.

"It has no effectiveness sitting in your hand," he teased.

She leaned toward him. "Shh…"

"It's just a pill. Nothing to be embarrassed about."

"You know what it's for," she whispered.

Humor, rather than the seriousness she would have expected, warmed his dark eyes. "Yes, indeed. I do know."

"I don't understand how you're so cavalier about…" She paused, looking for a word that wouldn't practically burn her mouth to say.

"Sex?" he asked, striving for innocent, but too amused to be anywhere close.

She glared at him. "You're from Zeena Sahra. You went without for three years. You should understand repressed."

"Suppressed, maybe. It's not the same. I am not ashamed to share a common physical need with an entire planet of people."

"It's different for you, you're a man."

"Do you think so?"

"Mom was pretty adamant that women had to remain chaste until marriage."

"And yet you decided not to."

"I doubt I'll ever marry," she admitted. "I'm too shy with men."

"Really?" He didn't sound doubtful, so she didn't take offense at his question.

"Most men. The combination of alcohol and you is a lethal combination."

"I would like to think the alcohol was unnecessary."

"It probably would be in future," she admitted with the honesty she seemed unable to suppress around him. "But last night? It definitely played its role."

"And yet you insist you were in control of your faculties when you chose to make love with me."

"I was, just not chained down by my usual inhibitions and introversion around men."

"You will be less nervous with the opposite sex in the future, I am sure." He didn't sound exactly pleased by that prospect.

"It didn't work that way for my mom."

"She had you."

"And a family who rejected her. I have no one left to reject me."

"That's a rather morbid thought."

"Sorry."

"I will reject you if it will make you feel better."

"Don't do me any favors." But she felt a small smile curving her lips.

She liked bantering with him.

Which scared her probably more than it should.

Determined to lead with her head, not her heart, she took a deep breath, tossed back the pill and swallowed it down with water.

CHAPTER NINE

As the minutes wore on, a need for the restroom broke through Liyah's consuming thoughts.

Loathe to interrupt Sayed in his furious typing on the computer he'd pulled out, she tried to ignore the growing urgency.

She grabbed a magazine from the pocket to the side of her chair and laid it on the table, hoping the glossy stories about other people's lives would keep her mind occupied and off her biological needs. She flipped through the pages, nothing catching her attention.

Shifting slightly from one side to the other helped, but pretty soon she was going to have to ask Sayed to move.

Suddenly, he stopped typing and leaned toward her. "Are you all right, *habibti?*"

"Yes, I just, um…" Liyah wasn't just repressed about sex, but found talking about any private bodily functions a trial.

Which was ridiculous, she realized. She was an adult woman, for goodness' sake.

"You should have told me you were a virgin." Sayed frowned at her. "I could have shown more restraint with you last night."

"Are you trying to undo a lifetime of repression in a single day, or something?" If asking him to move so she could use the restroom would have been embarrassing, this was mortifying. "I'm fine."

"You are clearly in pain."

"I need to pee," she huffed out in a furious whisper, frustrated by her own reticence and his insistence.

"Why did you not say so?" He rose, allowing her to exit her seat.

When she got back, she considered sitting across from him, but didn't gainsay him when he stood again so she could retake her seat by the window.

Once she was settled in again, he handed her an electronic reader. "It has most of the recent bestsellers, but if you want to download something else, the plane is set up with wireless internet."

"Thank you. The magazines would have been fine."

"Nonsense. Though, really, you should probably take a nap."

Startled, she asked, "I look tired?"

"Perhaps a little. It has been a full and wearing day."

He could say that again. "For you, too, but I don't see you dozing in your chair."

"The last time I napped, stuffed animals still decorated my bed." He smiled. "Getting six hours of sleep in a row is a luxury for me."

"But that's not healthy."

He shrugged. "Such is the life of an emir taking over the responsibilities of a melech with no younger brother to take over my own diplomatic duties."

"Why is your father abdicating? Does he have health issues?" she asked before realizing it was probably an invasive query. "Sorry, you don't have to answer."

"I never answer questions I do not wish to."

"Arrogance has its benefits."

He smiled. "I suppose so. I do not mind telling you my father is in excellent health."

"Is he tired of being king?" she probed, trying to understand the heavy responsibilities being thrust on Sayed.

"Not at all."

"Then why?"

"It is tradition."

"Will your father take over the diplomatic stuff once he's no longer acting melech?"

Sayed jerked, as if surprised by the question. "That would not be in line with Zeena Sahran tradition. I am not sure my father would find taking orders from his son a comfortable circumstance."

"But the melech dictates political policy?"

"With the help of a cabinet of counselors, yes. My father will act as one of my advisers, as well."

It still wasn't making sense to her. "So, what, your father is just going to retire and start golfing, or something? Won't he get bored?" How much time could it take to give Sayed advice every day?

Maybe she didn't understand working monarchies, but she could not imagine a former king content to sit home twiddling his thumbs.

"Honestly? I have wondered the same thing myself. My father is a very dynamic man and I do not think he would enjoy the pursuits that kept my grandfather busy in his twilight years."

"So, why retire now? Do you want to take over as melech?"

"No one has ever asked me that." He looked at her like she was some kind of rare species he'd never seen before.

"Maybe they should have. What's the answer?"

"My duty is clear."

"Yes, but is it one you want, or even need, to take on right now?"

"You question things you cannot hope to understand."

"Maybe." But he still hadn't answered the question and Liyah thought that was telling.

Sayed went back to his computer, dismissing her. Refusing to take it personally, Liyah skimmed his download of that morning's copy of *The Times*. He had probably been happy to note there was no mention of Tahira's elopement, but it would certainly be in tomorrow's edition.

After a while, she set the reader down, intending to take that nap he suggested.

But as soon as she closed her eyes, everything started pressing in on her. The argument with her father played over in her mind like an unpleasant reality show. When she managed to push those images aside, then pictures of the night before rose up to fill the void.

An unrelenting montage of the sensual and profound that uselessly fed her newly discovered love.

Sighing, she opened her eyes.

It didn't help. Her mind and heart were determined to dwell on emotions and experiences she would have been better off without.

Sayed turned from his work at his computer. "You are very pensive, Aaliyah."

"Don't you think I have reason to be?" She rubbed her temples. "I may not be an emir, but my whole life just took a ninety-degree turn."

"Perhaps you needed a detour."

"Do you think you know what's best for *everybody?*"

"It is in the job description."

"Right."

He smiled.

And she almost smiled back. Darn him.

That nap was sounding better and better. If only she could sleep, but then she'd probably dream about him. She'd done that *before* they'd made love. Now the dreams would probably be even more frequent and, with her new knowledge, definitely more graphic.

She expected him to go back to his work, but he didn't. "You said something yesterday about having a confrontation with your father being the reason you'd broken into Tahira's liquor stash."

Liyah opened her mouth to deflect, but she wanted to discuss the painful event with someone and Sayed was offering. "Yes."

"It did not go well?"

"No."

"You alluded to him treating you very poorly." Sayed's dark gaze probed hers.

"He did."

"You are being rather laconic." Sayed smiled, as if he found her amusing.

She didn't mind. She liked his smile. Too much. "I suppose I am."

She found herself grinning at his huff of obviously exaggerated exasperation, but then memories took away the lightness his humor had wrought. "It hurt that my father thought I was trying to work an angle, but that's not what was most painful."

"What was it, then?"

"When it became clear that my mom had lied to me my whole life." That had hurt so much. "She always told me that even though he could not have me in his life because he already had a wife and children, he cared enough to send a small stipend to help with my care and education."

"And this was a lie?"

"Yes. Oh, he was married, but he didn't even know I existed."

"That must have been quite a blow." Sayed laid his hand over hers, offering comfort she needed badly. "To learn your beloved mother had been dishonest with you, but also to be made aware that whatever concern you'd thought he had for you had no substance."

"You can't care about someone you don't even know exists."

"And then when he learned, he reacted badly."

"That's one way to put it."

Liyah wanted to lean into Sayed, but stopped herself from such a blatantly needy action. "The best I can figure out, the money Mom saved from not paying rent was what she pretended came from him."

It had been an elaborate but necessary ruse as Hena had insisted on teaching Liyah about finances from a young age. Her own parents had not been forthcoming with Hena and she'd made some bad monetary decisions in her ignorance.

She'd been determined her own daughter would not be put in the same situation.

Hena teaching Liyah about finances resulted in her daughter being very aware of their own. The pretense of support payments had worked to conceal both of the big secrets her mother kept from Liyah.

"Not paying rent?" Sayed asked.

"Another thing she hid from me. Her father owned our apartment and allowed us to live there rent-free as long as Mom promised not to bring me to Zeena Sahra."

"What?" Sayed's expression registered astonishment. "Why would he make such a stipulation?"

"So I wouldn't shame them with my existence."

"Because your mother chose to raise you," he guessed.

Apparently, he understood his own culture better than Liyah did. She'd never understand that kind of thinking. "Yes."

"Was that the reason you had no immediate plans to travel to Zeena Sahra?"

"Not on your life. Once I'd fulfilled my mom's last wish, I had every intention of visiting her homeland."

"You are very strong-minded."

"Another facet of my character for you to get to know," she said, facetiously repeating his words of the morning back to him.

He nodded quite seriously, though. "Yes, it is, and one I believe I like."

"Considering how bossy you are, that is difficult to believe."

He shrugged. "Nevertheless, it is the truth."

"You're surrounded by yes-men," she guessed, not sure she believed it.

"You've met Yusuf," Sayed said with meaning.

She felt another smile and gratitude for it. "He doesn't seem overawed by you, that's for sure."

"I assure you, he is not."

"That makes two of us," she said cheekily.

"I am wounded. A man hopes his lover esteems him."

"We're hardly lovers." They were more like a one-night stand with consequences.

His gaze heated. "I would like to be."

Suddenly tension thrummed between them.

"I find that hard to believe."

"I will not press my attentions on you, but I will also not pretend the thought of making love to you again does not dominate my thoughts far too much, particularly considering the issues facing me."

"You still want me?"

"Very much so."

"But won't that make the chances of pregnancy higher?"

"We will use condoms."

She blushed, as much at his frank speech as at the fact she hadn't immediately thought of that, as well. "Okay."

"Okay?"

"I want you, too." And any stored memory for the future she could manage to hoard, she would.

"I am glad."

"Me, too, I think."

They shared a look that made sitting in the luxury leather seat on the private jet uncomfortable.

She was pretty sure he would have done something about it right then, though she had no idea what it would have been considering their circumstances, but the flight attendant came over to set the table in front of them for dinner.

They were eating their braised lamb with potatoes and vegetables when he asked, "You discovered these things after your mother's death?"

Liyah found herself explaining how she'd found out her grandfather owned her apartment, how utterly devastating the funeral and meeting with the lawyer afterward had been when he had told her she must vacate her apartment.

"I didn't let them see it, though. I wouldn't give them the satisfaction."

"You have admirable emotional control."

If he realized the feelings she had for him she'd been unable to prevent or stifle, he wouldn't think so.

"Do you plan to return to San Francisco?"

"After we confirm I'm not pregnant?"

"If that is the case, yes."

"I don't know. Maybe I will travel for a while." She'd planned to save what was left of her mother's life insurance for the future, but to what end?

Liyah was twenty-six. If she didn't experience life now, when would she?

"Alone?" Sayed asked, disapproval evident. "Your mother would not encourage that, I think."

"I'm an adult and this is the twenty-first century, not the twelfth. A woman can travel alone."

"Not safely."

"Oh, please."

Sayed spent the next five minutes quoting statistics for crime against women traveling alone, particularly out of their home countries.

"Why do you know all this?"

"My cousin Samira wanted to go backpacking across Europe without bodyguard or chaperone a couple of years ago."

"How old was she?" He was thirty-six, Liyah knew. She couldn't quite picture a woman in the same age bracket wanting that kind of trip.

But then again, why not?

"Twenty-two. Her mother is my father's younger sister."

"And you said no."

"Actually, my father refused permission on the request of my aunt."

"Why not her own father?" Or Samira's mother, for that matter?

"Her father died in the explosion that killed my older brother."

"I'm sorry."

"It is an old grief."

"But not one that ever goes away completely."

"No."

"So, I bet Samira was mad." Or maybe being raised in the royal family had made it easier to accept restrictions for the woman who was four years younger than Liyah.

"We found her a well-trained female bodyguard team and a companion to travel with her."

"And they went backpacking?" Liyah asked in shock. "Seriously?"

"With a few travel compromises, yes."

"Let me guess, they rode first class on the trains and

had drivers in the cities they visited on a well-ordered travel itinerary."

He smiled winningly. "Something like that."

"So, is Samira your only cousin?"

"No, she has a younger brother. Bilal. My aunt was pregnant when she lost my uncle."

"Are you close?"

"He is twelve years my junior."

"I'm sure he looks up to you."

"I spent what time I could with him since moving back from the States, but he left for his own years at university. Bilal was to return to Zeena Sahra in time for my wedding." Sayed's lips twisted in a grimace.

"He is close with my father. He stepped in for his deceased brother-in-law from the beginning."

"Bilal is lucky to have you both."

Sayed shrugged. "He is family."

"So, why can't you train him for the emir responsibilities before taking over from your father as melech?"

"You do not think I will make a good king?" Sayed demanded, sounding hurt.

"That's not what I'm saying. I'm just pointing out there are options to tradition." Her mother's insistence on certain traditions had hurt Liyah more than helped her.

Hena's willingness to break with others had made Liyah's life what it was—in a very good way. Which was not to say that all tradition was bad, but being a slave to it was.

"Tell me about growing up in San Francisco," Sayed said in an obvious attempt to change the subject.

Liyah didn't hesitate, though. Because answering him gave her a chance to talk about her mom and that was something she'd been craving to do.

Sayed listened attentively to the stories of Liyah's childhood and time living with her mother as an adult.

"You clearly loved your mother very much."

"Yes."

"It is equally apparent that she loved you fiercely."

Suddenly choked with emotion, Liyah could only nod.

He narrowed his eyes in thought. "It sounds very much like each prevarication on your mother's part was done with the intent to protect your feelings."

"Then why ask me to find my father? She had to know once I realized the truth how devastated I would be, how his rejection would hurt."

"I can only theorize Ms. Amari expected a much different reaction from your father than the one he gave you."

"She died hoping her family would one day acknowledge me."

"She was an optimist."

Liyah smiled. "She definitely was. She tended to see the best in people and dismiss their flaws." Expelling a long breath, she admitted, "I also don't think she ever stopped loving my father."

And because of that love, Hena Amari had built Gene Chatsfield up in her head to be a man very different than the one he was in reality.

"While that love may have been misplaced, your mother's love for you was not. You were undoubtedly the most important person in her life."

"She sacrificed so much for me and she never once threw it back in my face."

"A truly astonishing woman."

"Yes, she was."

"I think, perhaps, her daughter is a great deal like her."

Liyah wasn't sure how true that was, but if she could share her mother's strength and willingness to sacrifice for others, she would count herself very blessed.

"You have already shown how deep your well of integrity goes," Sayed remarked.

"How so?"

"Many women would have tried to capitalize on what happened last night. You've done nothing but try to help me mitigate any possible negative consequences."

Liyah couldn't believe how much better she felt about everything that had happened since her mother's death after talking with Sayed. "Thank you."

"No thanks needed. We all need a friend now and again."

"Do you have friends? People *you* can trust enough to talk to?"

"I have my parents and Yusuf. Perhaps Bilal will become one now that he will be back in Zeena Sahra."

"That is a short list." Even with his cousin added to it.

"Trust for a man in my position cannot be offered on a whim."

She could well imagine. Last night would not have helped with that, either. "I'm sorry."

"For?"

"Last night."

"I am not." He shrugged. "I should be, but I enjoyed it too much to allow for genuine regret."

He sounded like he thought that was a terrible weakness.

"You're awfully hard on yourself."

"My father says I feel the weight of the world on my shoulders."

"Not carry?"

"No. He insists I do not need to carry the burden of responsibility that I do, but one day soon, I will rule in his place when I was never meant to do so. For his sake and that of my brother, I can offer nothing less than everything to my country."

A brother's death in childhood would have been devastating to any child, but for Sayed and the way it changed the course of his life? Even more so.

Looking into eyes filled with gravity to match his declarations, Liyah felt a twinge of emotion she refused to call love. "Maybe you *are* a little awe-inspiring, anyway."

"I am glad you think so." He grinned, the expression so unguarded it took her breath away.

CHAPTER TEN

"So Gene Chatsfield was your mother's lover?" Sayed asked, sounding pretty sure of her answer.

"Yes."

"I imagine he has reasons for his distrustful attitude," Sayed said mildly.

She still frowned. "But I wasn't lying to him."

"You and I know that, but he did not."

Sayed's belief in her honesty helped soothe the sting of her father's blatant rejection and hurtful accusations.

"He didn't even remember what she looked like," Liyah said, still unable to grasp that particular reality.

How could he have forgotten such a special, wonderful woman?

"It sounds like he was in a bad place in his life when they met," Sayed said, as if reading Liyah's thoughts.

"That doesn't excuse him seducing an innocent young woman and then forgetting about her as if she never mattered."

"Many errors in judgment cannot be excused, but that does not mean they can never be forgiven."

"So, you're going to forgive Tahira?"

"Eventually," he said, shocking Liyah. "But probably not until everything her defection has caused has been dealt with, and in a way that is not to the detriment of my people."

"Wow, you really are some kind of amazing." Though she had no doubt he meant his caveat for forgiveness one hundred percent.

He looked pleased by her declaration. "I have very good parents."

"I think your basic core has a lot to do with it, as well."

Sayed shrugged. "Perhaps, but even in that I must acknowledge the gift of good DNA."

She reached out and touched his face. She simply couldn't help herself.

He stilled, making no move to dislodge her hand. "What?"

"I just wanted to reassure myself you're real."

"I am flesh and blood like the next man."

"Emir."

"With you, I prefer to be a man only."

"Is that possible?" Her heart responded to the man, but her head reminded her that the emir was way out of her league.

"Right now, in this moment, it is."

Neither broke eye contact as the attendant cleared their dinner detritus from the table.

"Did you know there is a small bedroom in the back of the plane?" he asked when the attendant had moved away. "It is a necessary luxury for those times when travel and sleep schedules do not coincide."

Goose bumps were traveling up her arm from the circling of his thumb against her palm. "Um, that's nice?"

"Would you like to see it?"

Liyah was being propositioned. She wasn't sure who was more shocked when she accepted.

Herself, or Sayed.

Sayed led Aaliyah into the sleeping quarters. Although it was as superbly appointed as the rest of the plane, the bed was only a double size.

He would not allow the cramped quarters to prevent him from his current objective: giving Aaliyah an experience worthy of the gift of her innocence.

No matter how mind-bogglingly good the sex had been the night before, they'd both been under the influence of alcohol. And he hadn't known she was a virgin.

He'd entered her body completely unaware of the gift she bestowed. Without proper care many virgins experienced a great deal of pain their first time.

It was only by grace and benevolent genetics that Aaliyah had not.

The knowledge he was her only lover resonated in the most primal part of Sayed's psyche.

And he wanted more.

Desire riding him harder than a runaway camel in the desert, he reached for her the moment the door shut behind them. Sayed pulled Aaliyah flush with his body and into a kiss. Over half a foot shorter than him, she should not fit so perfectly, but she did.

Like their two bodies had been made just for this connection.

He demanded a response from her and she gave it, her passion a match for his, though expressed differently. Her lips melted under his, parting almost instantly. Without a second thought, he accepted the alluring, silent invitation.

Surprised and a little worried that it was every bit as stunning as the night before, he rubbed his tongue along hers.

She tasted so sweet, familiar in a way that should not be possible after only one night together.

Her hands came up and then his *egal* and *keffiyeh* were being tugged off in one motion and tossed away.

Amused despite the desire raging through his body, he broke the kiss. "You do not want the emir?"

Emerald eyes trapped his with the emotion glowing in

them. "Sayed, when we are like this, I will always want the man."

"No one wants only the man." Not since the day he became emir, not merely second son and sheikh.

"I do," she vowed, her musical voice vibrating with sincerity. "I did last night."

"No matter what we might wish, I never stop being the emir." It was a warning for him as much as her.

His future had been written in the stars the day his brother was killed. Sayed was not just a figurehead.

He had no choices about walking away from his responsibilities. There was no one to take his place and he loved his people too much to let them down.

She shook her head, looking up at him, her beautiful oval features set in serious lines. "You're right and you're wrong at the same time. Because right now, you *are* Sayed. Yes, you are emir, but that is not *all* you are."

He wished he could agree, but honesty forced him to shake his head in disagreement, even as his hands smoothed down her body, seeking the hem of her top.

"What do you call Melech Falah?" She shivered as he tugged her blouse out of her waistband.

"Father."

She rubbed her cheek against his affectionately. "So, he is not only a king, but he is your dad, too?"

"Yes, but his duty comes first."

"Are you sure about that?" she asked, shifting her lower body against his.

Did she expect him to focus on *conversation* right now?

She laid her hands against his chest, one landing unerringly over his heart. "You don't think it would have been better for Zeena Sahra's sense of country unity and its international consequence for their prince to be educated and raised within its borders?"

"My safety was necessary." There was no sentimentality in that.

"Oh, yes, absolutely, but your dad sent you away. The king would have just increased your security. How often did he and your mother come to visit you in the U.S.?"

"Several times a year." Though Sayed had only been allowed home a few times in all the years he attended school in the States.

They'd spent the summers together in Europe with his aunt and young cousins, their exact location kept from any but his father's closest advisers.

"Tell me again, your father was never more or less than melech."

"He was and is my *father*," Sayed said, never having denied it, but also understanding she had a point in what she said.

"And right now? You are my *man, rohi*. Even if it is only for the next hour, I won't give up a second of that and I won't let you, either."

"I am supposed to be the experienced one here, but you are seducing me utterly." He could not acknowledge the *my soul*.

No doubt she had heard it from her mother and did not realize the deeper connotations the endearment carried between lovers. Those implications were all too fitting between them, though he would probably never have the freedom to acknowledge.

But their souls fit, just like the rest of them.

"I like that." She pushed his outer robe off his shoulders. "Because everything about you makes me want you more."

He did nothing to stop the gold-trimmed black fabric from pooling at their feet.

She went directly for his suit jacket, taking time to lay it over a chair in the corner. "I may be repressed, but you dress like a monk."

"I do not think monks wear Armani." And she did not seem very repressed right now.

"Maybe not." She grinned up at him cheekily. "I'd rather you weren't wearing it right now, either."

Delighted by her, he laughed. "Your wish is my pleasure to grant."

He finished undressing, not minding in the least that she seemed intent on helping him.

When he was totally naked, his swollen sex jutting out from his body, he let her look her fill. He'd noticed how much she enjoyed it the night before. And having her gaze on him with such innocent hunger turned him on like nothing else.

She didn't even wait for him to suggest she join him in his nudity before she started stripping, too.

Primal masculine satisfaction coursed through him and he grinned, even as his body reacted to every inch of honey skin she revealed.

"What?" his undeniably proactive lover asked as she laid her oh-so-conservative skirt on the chair with his clothes.

"It is me, not the alcohol."

"What?" she asked, her expression confused as she unbuttoned her simple white blouse.

"Repressed Aaliyah has abandoned you for the present."

Her hands stilled, the blouse gaping to reveal the luscious curves of breasts in another very feminine bra while a blush climbed her throat and up into her face. Yet she didn't pull the open edges together.

"I feel free with you, like I can do anything and it's okay." She sounded astounded by that reality, but not unhappy.

He was delighted. "Exactly. Me. *Not the alcohol.*" He made her lose her inhibitions, no whiskey needed.

Her gaze sharpened in comprehension and she smiled. "Evidence would be in your favor."

"I am aware."

"Your arrogance is showing again."

"You say that like it's a bad thing."

Her smile made his heart pause in its beats.

He shook his head. "You have no idea what you do to me."

"I think I have a clue, *rohi*." She gave a significant glance downward.

Laughing, he bent and swept her into his arms, pulling her scantily clad body flush to his.

He had never had so much fun with a lover.

She gasped, then threw her head back and hooted, the sound of amusement so sweet it sent shivers through him.

"You sure you don't make a habit of this?" she asked, still giggling. "It's just that it feels like a habit."

"Only with you."

He arranged her on the bed, having pulled the bedding back much to her apparent amusement.

"You find this funny?" Arousal was his predominant emotion at the moment, his sex so hard it was already leaking preejaculate.

"This? As in making love? No. But seriously, it's like you're a professional at the suave lover thing."

"At least you didn't compare me to a musical genre again."

"I couldn't have been too drunk if I was able to come up with metaphors."

"Or only a very inebriated woman would make such a comparison."

"There is that." She winked at him. "I stand by it, though."

"Tonight, you are not under any influence but me."

"I'll tell you a secret," she whispered against his ear

as he settled next to her, leaning down with the intent to kiss her again.

"Yes?"

"You're a lot more intoxicating than that stuff I was drinking last night."

"And I will not leave you with a hangover."

"Just muscles sore in all the right places."

"I knew it." He sat up.

She grabbed his arm, like she thought he was going to leave. "What?"

"I *did* hurt you last night."

"What? No. Maybe a little, but isn't it always like that the first time?"

"Oh, no, it can be much worse. We were very lucky your body's barrier was not too stubborn." If it had been he might have noticed it, though.

All he'd felt was how tight she was, how good her silky, wet heat felt around his shaft.

"I wouldn't know about anyone else, I only know that last night was the most amazing experience of my life."

"Then the bar is high."

"For what?"

He worked on the remaining buttons of her blouse. "To make this time truly memorable and worthy of your first experience with a lover."

"Why?" she asked as she tugged on his arm.

Unable to deny her, he leaned down and took the kiss he'd meant to a moment ago. Her lips were soft under his, but she wasn't passive by any stretch, her mouth mobile and enticing.

He finished undoing her buttons and pulled her blouse from her body, lifting her to sit up so he could get it off completely. Feeling like he was opening a truly stunning gift, he took the opportunity to dispense with her bra, as well.

He loved the way her entire body shivered as her nipples were exposed to the air. She'd done the same the night before and he'd found it incredibly arousing. He still did.

Soft sounds came from her as he laid her back on the bed, this time coming down beside her fully. Naked skin slid against naked skin, building the intensity between them.

His hand resting possessively on her belly, he remembered her question and broke the explosive kiss. "Because that is what you deserve."

"Huh?" Unfocused green eyes looked up at him. "What?"

"Why I am committed to making this time better than last night."

"Oh, that's sweet," she said on a hitching breath as he began to caress her. "But unnecessary, not to mention unlikely."

"You think so?"

"Last night was pretty special."

"Tonight will blow your mind."

"You're kind of competitive, huh?"

He shrugged. He wasn't competitive so much as he always won. He was emir; he had to be the best at everything he chose to do.

It wasn't just built into his position; it was in his DNA.

"Can I touch you?" she asked, her voice husky with need.

"Of course."

She licked her lips. "Anywhere?"

"Yes." The word ended on a hiss as her small hand curled around his sex.

She made a hum of approval as her grip moved up and down the column of hard flesh, driving his arousal higher and higher.

"Do not stop," he instructed her as he began his own explorations.

He intended to drive her to the point of madness with desire.

Long pleasurable minutes later, he realized that every moan of pleasure he pulled from her, every restless movement of her body, drove him closer to the edge of losing his own control.

He'd never found it so hard to hold back, not even the first time he'd lain with a woman.

But Aaliyah Amari was some kind of sensual sorceress, every sexy whimper a powerful spell on his body.

Even when he pressed her legs apart and put his mouth on her, his own body reacted like she was touching him.

She cried out, tried to pull away. "No. That's…I don't think…"

He lifted his head. "Do not think, *habibti*. Feel."

He tasted her, the sweet tang of her arousal exploding on his tongue as the scent of almonds mixed with musk created a heady perfume around him.

Each woman had her own unique scent, but he had never found one so alluring.

He pushed his tongue inside her and pulled it out again, kissing her in ultimate intimacy.

She mewled, but when he shifted his head so he could flick her clitoris before circling it with the tip of his tongue, she screamed. Long and loudly.

Her responsiveness was addictive and he went back again and again for more of her taste, more of her reactions, using his tongue to lave and then caress with his consciously hardened tip. He added a finger to her passage, reveling in the slick wetness he found there.

She moved against him, her sounds growing more and more desperate, her muscles contracting and relaxing until she went rigid and came. Her thighs locked on either side of his head.

He did not mind at all. He had no intention of moving.

He softened the caress of his tongue, though, pulling his finger from inside her, drawing out her pleasure but not to the point of discomfort.

She went rigid once more and then completely boneless, her legs flopping down to leave her completely open to him.

It was time for the next step: rebuilding her sexual need until she was whimpering for release.

And that was exactly what Sayed did, touching his *habibti* all over with hands first, but then his mouth—using teeth and tongue to bring her back to the edge of exploding.

However, by the time he rolled on the condom he had to be careful not to come from his own touch, and that never happened to him.

He wished they didn't need the barrier. Making love with nothing between them had been one of the most profound experiences of his life, even if he'd thought it a dream at the time.

Perhaps it was better this way.

Sheathed to prevent the further sharing of his seed with her body and perhaps keep back some part of his soul from hers, he turned her onto her side and angled his body behind her.

"What are you doing?" she demanded, her voice heavy with passion. "I *need,* Sayed."

"And I will give you what you need." He pressed into her from behind, the position allowing him to touch her at will.

One arm tucked under her neck so he could reach her breasts, he reached down with his other hand to touch her clitoris as he began to move.

She gasped out sexy demands even as she moved her pelvis with instinctive rhythm.

This time they came together, their shouts mixing in a sexual song he could easily become seriously addicted to.

The thought was so disturbing, he did not let himself sink into afterglow. He took hold of the condom and carefully pulled out of her, but could not make himself move away completely.

She made a distinctly unhappy sound.

"Shh…" He kissed her sweaty brow, the affectionate gesture too natural to be comfortable for a man who knew his time with his love would be measured in days not years. "I need to take care of the condom."

He made his way to the efficiency-size en suite on unsteady legs.

The mirror showed him a face he'd never seen before, one with eyes far too soft with vulnerability.

He was emir. Not merely a man.

Not a man at all who could afford to crave a woman like he'd learned to hunger for Aaliyah after such a short time.

He needed to find himself and put this other man away. Sayed owed it to his people and to the brother who had died before getting the chance to lead them.

Sayed should have been working strategy the whole plane ride, but he'd spent hours talking with Liyah and then making love.

He had to put distance between them, or he wasn't going to be able to do what he needed to when the pregnancy test came back negative.

Let her go.

CHAPTER ELEVEN

QUEEN DURRAH ESCORTED Liyah to her quarters in the palace harem herself.

Even the melecha's personal attention could not mitigate Liyah's feeling of abandonment upon Sayed's nearly instant disappearance after their arrival to the palace, however.

Sayed had barely taken the time to introduce her to his esteemed parents before excusing himself to speak to his father privately. The monarchs had been surprisingly gracious, but Sayed's desertion had stung.

Coming on top of the way he'd been acting since they made love, it was doubly hurtful.

He'd walked into the bathroom a man and came out one hundred percent emir, focused on affairs of state.

Sayed had dressed in silence and then turned to her, his gaze set firmly somewhere beyond her left shoulder. "Nap now. I'll have the cabin attendant knock on the door in time for you to shower and dress for landing."

She might have argued if her eyes hadn't already been drooping, her body seconds from sliding into sleep regardless.

As he'd promised, she'd been alerted in time to shower and dress in clothes miraculously ironed while she'd been napping. However, even though she'd returned to her seat, Sayed had spent the entire descent and landing talking to Yusuf, who had joined them in one of the empty seats across the table.

Then Sayed had been fully occupied the drive to the palace with his smartphone.

Liyah knew he had important issues that had to be dealt with, but that hadn't diminished her sense of the growing distance between them.

A distance that should never have been bridged in the first place, her brain tried to remind her. Her emotions foolishly balked at that truth.

Liyah had never warred so much within herself as she had since meeting Sayed, not even when she'd been deciding about going to England to meet her biological father.

No matter how unreasonable, how hopeless, how *ridiculous,* her growing feelings for Sayed were, Liyah could not deny them. However, she had no intention of sharing them with anyone else, especially the man himself.

Not by word, or deed.

Which meant she maintained her outward dignity and self-possession with particular care as she kept pace with the queen.

She led Liyah up a grand staircase that made the one at the Chatsfield London seem simple and unassuming in comparison. A strip of plush red carpet ran up the center of the mahogany steps shined to a glasslike finish. The matching elegantly carved banisters were held up by over a hundred ornate three-foot-high crystal newels.

Everything about the stone palace complex located on the shore of Zeena Sahra's Bahir Sea was over the top and yet not in the least tacky.

After several turns and traversing a distance easily equal to a couple city blocks, they approached an imposing set of double doors. Liyah wasn't even surprised to find a man dressed in the manner she'd come to associate with Sayed's security detail standing to the left of the doors.

The queen nodded to him, but made no verbal greeting.

The guard opened the door on the right and Queen Durrah led Liyah through it, only the softest swishing sound indicating it closing behind them.

Queen Durrah smiled at Liyah, her amber gaze reflecting an impressive determination and confidence of spirit. "For the next five days, you will stay here as our honored guest, but your name and relationship to my son will not be revealed."

She did not ask if Liyah understood, or even agreed. Somehow that assumption of agreement was more intimidating than Sayed's bossiest moments.

"Five days?" Liyah asked.

"Perhaps six."

Liyah nodded, though not entirely sure why that exact length of stay was necessary.

"The definitive blood test can be performed five days after the *event* at the earliest." The queen waved her hand as if referring to something she would prefer not to address directly.

The pregnancy test.

"Do you want me to stay in my room?" So much for Sayed's promise to be her tour guide.

"My goodness, no." The queen opened a door on her right to reveal a lovely sitting room done in champagne with burgundy accents. "You are not a prisoner here."

Just a guest who had to remain anonymous.

Liyah could not quite suppress how impressed she was by her accommodations. They could have put her in the servants' quarters and she would not have minded at all. "This is the size of the living room in our old apartment."

"Our?" the queen asked in a way Liyah found she could not refuse to answer.

Not that she would have regardless. "I shared an apartment with my mother until her death four months ago."

Liyah managed to speak of her mother's loss without revealing what it cost her to do so, but she turned away to give herself a moment. Though she hoped her intent was not obvious. Liyah would not have Queen Durrah thinking she was some weak emotional mess.

"I am very sorry to hear about your mother." There was no mistaking the sympathy in the older woman's tone. "I remember losing my own mother. I miss her to this day."

"Thank you," Liyah replied, renewing her attempt to pull in her emotions.

"Aaliyah." There was a command in the queen's tone Liyah once again could not ignore.

She turned. "Yes, Your Highness?"

"I am not accustomed to speaking to the back of someone's head." The queen shook her head, her eyes narrowing. "Never mind. Did my son suggest you should stay in your room during your stay here?"

"No."

Queen Durrah nodded as if approving Liyah's response. "While you are not a prisoner, there are a few concessions we will all appreciate you making."

Liyah was impressed. The queen hadn't ordered her to make those concessions, but her wording made it clear she expected Liyah's cooperation.

"Whatever I can do," she promised the other woman.

"While your things have been delivered, during your stay here we would prefer you not wear the clothes you brought with you. You will discover traditional Zeena Sahran clothing in your wardrobe. You may consider it a gift and take it with you when you leave the palace."

"That is not necessary." She hadn't missed the queen's certainty Liyah wouldn't be staying.

"Nevertheless, the clothing is yours. We would appreciate it very much if you would wear it whenever you leave this room, including the hijab over your hair."

"Okay."

"You may notice I do not wear the hijab. It is by no means a requirement in our culture." The queen wore her hair in an elegant coif, a tiara that could have been a large hair ornament tucked into the dark tresses.

"I don't mind wearing the hijab." Though Liyah didn't really understand why Queen Durrah had asked her to do so.

"I am glad to hear that, but it is absolutely not a requirement." Sayed's deep masculine tones thrummed through Liyah, drawing her around to face him with inexorable pull.

"Sayed." Liyah was incapable of further speech at the moment.

"Do you like your suite?"

She nodded. "It's beautiful."

"But not her prison," Queen Durrah inserted.

"Of course not, Mother. What have you been telling her?"

"We have just been discussing how best to handle her visit."

"I believe I said I wanted to have that discussion with her?" he asked, irritation sparking in his dark gaze.

The queen shook her head. "You should not be here at all."

"And yet you knew I intended to come and speak to Aaliyah as soon as I'd talked to Father."

"Surely you could not be finished discussing your strategy for dealing with Tahira's little escapade already?" the queen prompted.

"We can finish after I've made sure Aaliyah is comfortable."

"Surely I am capable of doing that."

Tired of watching words being bounced between mother

and son like tennis volleys, Liyah went out on the balcony and left them to it.

Sayed joined her a few seconds later. "Are you all right, Aaliyah?"

"Do you want a polite lie, or the truth?"

"Truth, please." His hand landed on her shoulder and Liyah wondered what the queen thought of that.

"I'm a bit overwhelmed, and while this suite is gorgeous it *does* feel a little like a prison."

He turned her to face him and waited until she tipped her head back so their gazes met. "It's not meant to. If nothing else, I want you to enjoy your stay here, to truly come to know the country of your mother's birth."

"Will I see you at all?"

"You are seeing me now."

"That's not an answer."

"It's the best one I can give you." The glimpse she got in that second of Sayed the man, the very conflicted man, told Liyah she wasn't the only one struggling with their situation.

"You promised to be my tour guide."

"And so he shall be." The queen stood in the open French doors leading to the balcony.

"Mother, could you please give us some privacy?" Sayed asked in a pained tone that would have been funny if Liyah wasn't feeling so fragile.

More emotions she was doing her best to hide.

"I'll just call for some tea and wait for it in the sitting room." Whether it was the queen's not-so-subtle way of telling her son she wasn't leaving them entirely alone, or a simple peace offering, Liyah wasn't up to guessing.

"Aaliyah, please."

"What?" she asked, searching the depths of Sayed's brown gaze for something.

Even she couldn't say exactly what.

"Don't look like that."

"Like what?" She was doing her best not to look like anything.

He dropped his forehead against hers, breaking eye contact, but cocooning them in another type of intimacy. "Like you might break."

"I won't break."

"Promise me."

"I promise." Though she wasn't sure she was telling the truth. And she was an honest woman. "I'll try."

He made a sound that hurt to hear. "Taking it one day at a time, right?"

"Does that really work?"

"Yes." His hands cupped both sides of her neck, his thumbs rubbing softly against her skin.

Knowing if she didn't break contact she was going to say or do something she'd regret, she stepped away. "I suppose it's a good philosophy but not one I think you exercise very often."

He took a step toward her and then seemed to think better of it and moved even farther away.

"You would be surprised. No matter how much a planner you are, in the world of politics and running a country there is only so much you can control." He managed a contained tone, but his hands fisted the wrought-iron railing in front of him with white-knuckled intensity.

"Then you cannot blame yourself for what is beyond that control." She hoped he took the words as the absolution she meant.

He swallowed, and when he spoke again his tone was a little ragged around the edges. "Cultivating the patience to deal with challenges as they arrive instead of fighting against them is another thing my father taught me was essential."

They remained there, together but silent, until the queen

informed them that the tea had arrived and the king had requested his son join him to finish their discussion.

Seeming unable to help himself, Sayed kissed Liyah on the temple before leaving her suite.

Despite the fact even this small display of affection was not exactly acceptable by Zeena Sahran standards, the queen did not remark on it as she poured Liyah a cup of steaming jasmine tea.

"Now, about the hijab."

"Yes?"

"Wearing a scarf gives you instant access to an unremarkable assurance for privacy of identity should it become necessary." Queen Durrah smiled very much like her son. "Besides, there is less chance of you being recognized as a foreigner if you wear one."

"And the clothes?"

"Hiding in plain sight." The queen smiled. "I believe that is a well-known technique, yes?"

"Yes."

"The presence in the palace of a traditional Zeena Sahran woman would be cause for much less speculation than an obvious American."

Liyah didn't doubt it, having to bite back a smile at how much the queen reminded her of Sayed in that moment. They were both so certain they knew what was right.

"Unfortunately, there is nothing we can do about your Americanized speech."

"I'm perfectly happy to speak in Arabic while staying here at the palace," Liyah said in a perfect Zeena Sahran dialect.

The queen's eyes widened and then she flashed that smile so reminiscent of her son again. "How wonderful. Sayed did not mention your fluency in our language."

"I've never mentioned it." Liyah smiled herself as she

explained. "My mother spoke only the Arabic dialect of her homeland in our home and expected me to do the same."

"Perhaps we'll wait to apprise Sayed of this," the queen offered with a surprising glint of mischief in her eye.

Bewildered by the melecha's quicksilver mood change, Liyah nodded. "You're really different than I expected."

"Sayed did not get his propensity for impetuous action from a stranger." Queen Durrah winked. "I've decided I like you."

Ignoring the claim that could have little weight, Liyah stared at the older woman with an expression she knew revealed disbelief. "You believe your son is impetuous?"

"Less now than he was as a child, yes, but your presence here is proof he has not eradicated the trait entirely."

"You do not sound too upset by that." Another conundrum for Liyah's brain.

"I am not. Sayed is emir and will one day be melech, but he is still my son. His brother's death changed him so much, it changed all of us." For a moment grief shimmered in the depths of Queen Durrah's gaze. "It pleases me to see proof he has not changed completely."

"So, you're not upset about this situation?" Liyah found that hard to believe.

"What will be, will be."

"But surely you don't want me to be the mother of your grandchild." Though the older woman had already made it clear she didn't expect Liyah to be pregnant.

The queen reached out and patted Liyah's arm. "As to that, I cannot say. I may instinctively like you, but we have barely just met. One thing I'm certain of, your presence here will shake things up."

"And you think that's a good thing?"

"Oh, yes. Both my husband and son are still living in the shadow of Umar's death, though it occurred more than twenty years ago. I will miss my son every day until we are reunited in the afterlife, but it is time my family moved into the future."

Liyah understood that sentiment, though it had only been a few months since her mom's death. If Sayed hadn't come crashing into her life, Liyah was pretty certain her own life would have slid into marking time as she grieved a circumstance that could never be changed.

"Don't you think Tahira's elopement was enough of a shake-up?" Liyah had the temerity to ask.

"Certainly that was the catalyst for change. I find it very interesting that my son's response was to engage in shockingly unprecedented and personally perilous behavior with you."

Liyah had no answer to that.

Queen Durrah's beautiful face settled into thoughtfulness. "Honestly, I expected Tahira's betrayal to entrench him even more firmly behind the walls he erected so many years ago. I am very happy to be wrong."

Liyah paced her suite, having just returned from late-morning tea with Queen Durrah.

Who, despite her royal status and very definitive views on propriety, had turned out to be both likable and kind. And very much interested in her son's happiness.

Liyah had been astonished by the warm reception she'd received from both the king and queen. She threatened their well-ordered existence and Liyah's presence could do nothing but add to issues caused by Tahira's defection.

Yet both the monarchs had treated Liyah with nothing but respect. The king was a little more standoffish, but she didn't find that surprising. The fact he treated Liyah like a welcome guest to the royal palace did.

Queen Durrah had gone one step farther and taken pains to spend time each day with Liyah, however. Sayed's mother seemed intent on developing a friendship with the hotel employee her son had temporarily plucked out of obscurity.

The melecha had managed to ferret out the details of Liyah's estrangement from her Amari relatives in the mere two days since her arrival in Zeena Sahra. A very restful person with a smile very similar to her son's, Queen Durrah had found her way into Liyah's affections almost as quickly as Sayed had.

His mother had unequivocally denounced the actions of Liyah's relatives, remarking that someone needed to speak to them and bring them to awareness of the error of their ways.

The rather fervid gleam in Queen Durrah's amber gaze had given Liyah pause, but thankfully no rapprochement with the Amaris had been attempted.

Not that a queen would bother herself with the personal affairs of someone like Liyah, but for a moment there... well, Liyah had worried.

A knock sounded on the suite's door and she quickly pulled up the beautiful hijab that matched the pale green silk *dishdasha* she wore. The emerald-green embroidery around the hem and over her bodice was the exact shade as the chiffon of the hijab.

Liyah had never felt so feminine and pretty as she did since coming to Zeena Sahra. Gone were her conservative suits and boring white blouses, replaced by *dishdasha* gowns and *kameez* in vibrant colors Liyah never would have chosen for herself.

But she liked them. A lot.

She'd always dressed plainly, in clothes that did nothing to accentuate her feminine curves. While the traditional *dishdashas* and *kameez* were considered more modest than western clothing, the long dresses and long tunic-style tops with matching pants Liyah had found in her wardrobe were cut to emphasize the fact she was a woman.

The swish of silk that accompanied her every movement further increased her sense of femininity.

Not that Sayed had noticed. He hadn't had an opportunity to because she hadn't seen him for even the briefest glimpse in the past forty-eight hours. During the one
dinner she'd shared with his parents, he hadn't been there.

At her own request, she ate breakfast alone in her room
and lunch in the harem garden. But if he had invited her to
share one of those meals with him, she would have been
happy to do so.

Liyah wasn't surprised at the neglect. She'd seen Sayed's
war within himself on the day of her arrival. She thought
he might be the one person of her acquaintance less willing to give in to emotions than she was.

Adjusting the hijab, she pulled the door open and found
a familiar face on the other side. "Abdullah-Hasiba! Come
in."

Liyah stepped back to let the older woman into her suite,
but Hasiba shook her head.

Her expression did not reflect Liyah's delight in their
renewed acquaintance. "My melecha has requested your
presence."

"Yes, of course," Liyah replied.

Hasiba spun on her heel, walking away without another word and Liyah's happiness deflated as quickly as
it had come.

She followed the longtime family retainer in silence,
saddened by the clear end to a friendship with a woman
she admired.

Hasiba stopped outside a familiar set of double doors,
one of many in the palace complex she'd discovered. "My
melecha awaits you inside."

Liyah nodded, unable to speak. Why she should react
so strongly to this small rejection when she'd faced much

worse ones, she didn't know, but the loss of Hasiba's regard hurt.

Hasiba huffed, like she was annoyed, which she probably was.

Liyah reached for the door handle but the older woman's hand beat hers, covering the brass knob. "You took advantage of my emir."

"I didn't." Liyah had no defense but the truth.

"He was an engaged man."

"No. Tahira eloped."

"You could not have known."

Suddenly Liyah understood the root of Hasiba's disappointment in her. "I did know. I overheard the emir talking about it with Yusuf on the elevator."

"My emir would never show such a lack of discretion."

"They weren't conversing in English, but honestly? I don't think either of them realized I was there. You must realize how blindsided he was by Tahira's actions."

Hasiba's expression turned even darker. "So, you thought you'd trap yourself a sheikh now that he was single?"

Liyah opened her mouth to reply, anger overcoming her sadness, but a masculine voice beat her to it.

"I assure you, Abdullah-Hasiba, Miss Amari has in no way attempted to *trap* me," Sayed said, distaste for the idea ringing in his tone. "She could certainly have taken advantage, but did not and has done everything she could to diminish the consequences of *my* folly."

Liyah should have asserted claim to her part in their joint debacle, but she was too busy drinking in the sight of Sayed after a two-day drought.

"I apologize, my emir," Hasiba said with apparent sincerity. "I made assumptions I should not have." Then she proved her earnestness by turning to Liyah. "I am truly sorry, Liyah."

Liyah nodded. "Your reaction is understandable." Mostly. Liyah wouldn't lie to herself and pretend the assumption of such things about her character didn't hurt.

She hated the fact that because some people would take advantage of a man in Sayed's situation, anyone would just assume Liyah would, too.

"I do not agree," Sayed said, his tone icy.

Hasiba flinched, clearly upset she'd angered her emir.

Liyah gave the older woman a small smile. "Don't worry about it, really." She frowned up at Sayed. "Don't be cranky. Hasiba's heartfelt loyalty is a gift you should not take for granted much less criticize her for."

"Obviously you two are friends—does she not owe you loyalty, as well?"

"Over her dedication to your family? Not even. Be reasonable, Sayed."

Hasiba gasped at Liyah's familiarity with her sheikh, but she did not comment on it. Thankfully.

"I am always reasonable. My emotions do not rule me."

Liyah got the additional layer of message in his words and took it to heart, feeling inexplicably buoyed by the idea he felt something toward her, even if he did not intend to act on it. She was in the same frame of mind, wasn't she?

"Her Highness has requested Miss Amari's presence." Hasiba dropped her hand from the door and stepped back. "I will leave you to escort her inside."

Sayed frowned. "You called her Liyah just a moment ago."

"Yes, and in private consultation with your mother, I have leave to call her 'my lady,' but it would not be proper to refer to her with such familiarity in the company of others."

Looking unconvinced, Sayed nevertheless nodded and dismissed Hasiba. "Why did she call you Liyah?"

"That is what everyone calls me."

"You never gave me leave to do so." He made no move to enter his mother's private reception rooms.

"I like it when you use my full name."

"Oh, yes?" Again, he didn't appear completely convinced.

Liyah sighed and admitted, "Only my mother ever called me Aaliyah. It was special to me."

His handsome face filled with satisfaction. "Then I am honored to be in her company."

Sayed was grateful for the looser conventions in his country than many surrounding Zeena Sahra when Liyah laid her hand on his arm at his invitation.

Just that much connection helped soothe the ever-growing need to touch her, though what he really wanted was to kiss her senseless.

He opened the door to his mother's private reception room and led Liyah inside.

"Good, you have both arrived." His mother's pleased expression made him immediately nervous.

"Good afternoon, Queen Durrah." Aaliyah smiled at his mother, but did not step away from Sayed's side.

And with unfamiliar weakness, he was glad.

"Good afternoon, dear. I thought you might enjoy a tour of the capital today." His mother gave him a look of censure. "You have not yet left the palace."

"I thought it was for the best." Aaliyah's reply told him nothing of how she felt about that.

And though she was undoubtedly right, he did not like the fact she felt constrained to remain in the palace.

"You are not our prisoner, as I have stated before." His mother turned an expectant expression on Sayed. "Is that not right, my son?"

"Yes, of course."

"Good. You can accompany Aaliyah. Who better to

share the history and points of interest of our beloved city?" she asked, unconsciously echoing his unacted-upon invitation to Aaliyah.

"But I have—"

"Nothing on your calendar for this afternoon," his mother interrupted him with uncharacteristic lack of tact.

If his schedule was clear, this was the first he'd heard of it. Which meant his mother had arranged the break from meetings.

She was committed to this course of action.

Even knowing the futility of arguing, he still had to try. "I am the last person that should be seen with Aaliyah."

"You brought her as a guest to our home, did you not?" his mother asked, her tone a mixture of censure and steel-hard determination.

"You know I did and that I had little choice in it."

"Regardless, she is your guest and you have shamefully neglected her the past two days. You were not raised to display such a lack of consideration."

"This is hardly a normal circumstance."

"Circumstances are rarely *normal* in the life of a royal, Sayed, as you well know."

"And if we are seen together?" he challenged. This was not a good idea. She had to see that.

"What if you are? I am certain it will not be in a compromising position. It would do your image some good to be seen with such a lovely companion after Tahira's defection."

"But the media will speculate as to her identity."

"I would recommend taking an unmarked car on the tour," his mother said dryly. "And offering no one Aaliyah's name."

"My keeping company with a hotel maid will cause a scandal and we do not need another one of those." He'd spent the past two days working nonstop to put a lid on the one they were facing already.

"It was my understanding that she was a floor supervisor?"

"On the housekeeping staff." How could his mother not see what a disaster waiting to happen this outing was?

"Do not be a snob, Sayed. It is unbecoming."

He wasn't sure which bothered him more, his mother's words or the fact that Aaliyah had dropped her hand from his arm and taken several steps away from him.

"I am not." He turned to Aaliyah, uncaring for the moment if his mother understood his thoughts.

Aaliyah's feelings were uppermost in his mind right then.

She'd made an effort to school her features into an emotionless mask. However, it did not hide the hurt deep in her emerald eyes. Not from him, anyway.

He moved toward her, drawn by an irresistible need to wipe that pain from her gaze. "Aaliyah—"

"Don't." She put her hand up. "Whatever you think you need to say, don't. While I appreciate Queen Durrah's concern for my entertainment, I am *not* your guest."

Aaliyah sidestepped, managing to put more space between them and move closer to the door. "I am not your friend. You have absolutely no obligation to spend time with me. There is no reason for you to give up your afternoon."

"My son is a better host than that," his mother inserted firmly.

Aaliyah shook her head, giving his mother a sad little smile that made him want to swear. "While I appreciate your earlier offer of a car and driver and this latest attempt to provide me with a tour guide, in three days we'll do the blood test and discover I'm not pregnant."

Regardless of words that sounded heartless as his own

mind replayed them, Sayed wanted to protest. He was fighting what felt like a hopeless rearguard action to emotions he could not allow himself to feel.

Oblivious to his conflicted thoughts, Aaliyah continued, "Then I will move to a hotel and explore my mother's homeland to my heart's content. Until then, I am fine with not leaving the palace and making as little impact here as possible."

"There is no reason for you to be sequestered in the palace, much less the harem."

"I mean no offense, but I'm afraid I must disagree, Queen Durrah. Sayed is right. There is every reason. If you don't mind, I'll go back to my room now. I downloaded a new book on the reader Sayed gave me."

"How generous of my son to provide you with books to read," his mother said, sarcasm making her usually soft tones clipped.

Aaliyah just shrugged and left without waiting for either he or his mother to dismiss her from their presence.

CHAPTER TWELVE

"WELL DONE, SAYED," his mother mocked.

He turned quickly to face her, angry in a way he never was with his beloved parent. "Why would you suggest something so fraught with risk? And if you were going to do so, you could have at least given us both the courtesy to approach me without Aaliyah present."

His mother stood up, her expression filled with censure and unmuted disappointment. "Because it never occurred to me that you would lack any courtesy whatsoever and make it so obvious you did not want to spend time with that poor girl. She is here because of you, or had you forgotten that salient fact?"

"It was a one-night stand."

"Was it?"

"Of course, what else could it be?"

"A gift of fate?"

"How can you say that?" He spun away, his emotions in turmoil he did not want even his mother to see. Especially when she was voicing thoughts he'd done his best to suppress in his own mind. "There can be nothing between Aaliyah and me."

But the words rang hollow, even to his own ears.

"Because she doesn't come with a breeding certificate and border treaty as Tahira would have done?"

Shocked by his mother's attitude, he blurted, "I am an emir."

Though that mattered less and less with each passing day. Aaliyah had connected to Sayed the man and respected the prince. What more could he want from his emira?

His practical brain had no answer.

"I thought sending you to school in the States would curb some of that elitist mentality."

"I am no elitist." He didn't like the sensation of having the same argument with his mother as he'd had with Aaliyah.

"Perhaps not, though evidence would suggest otherwise. You are, however, undoubtedly an idiot." Affection in her tone dulled some of the sting of her denouncement.

He turned back to face her, only to watch as his mother left the room, throwing both doors wide.

"She always was good at the grand exit." His father stood near the door leading to an adjoining room.

Sayed dry-washed his face with his hand. "Yes."

"She has also always been very intuitive. If she is pressing you to spend time with Miss Amari, perhaps that is what you should be doing." Was it possible his father agreed with Sayed's mother?

Maybe the melech didn't realize how close to gone on Aaliyah his son, the emir, was. "Why? So I can get into yet another weeklong wait to discover my fate?"

"You are that attracted to her?"

"I wanted to snatch the birth control pill from her hand and throw it in the garbage rather than let her take it," Sayed admitted.

He'd wanted to just let destiny take its course, but a prince could not deny his responsibilities. Sayed thought Yusuf might have realized it, too, but like a true friend, he'd said nothing.

"I am surprised," his father admitted, sounding it.

"No more so than I."

"Your mother and I were betrothed in the cradle."

"I know."

"But I was in love with her before our wedding ever took place."

"You were?" Sayed could not stifle his shock. "You married so young."

"From the moment I began to notice the opposite sex, Durrah was the one I wanted. Discovering on our wedding night that she shared my affection was the happiest moment of my life to that point."

"You were very lucky."

"Blessed by fate," his father agreed with a rare genuine smile. "Yes, we were."

"Mother was everything that you could want in your queen." With nothing in her background for the media to feast on.

Not like Aaliyah, who not only came from the masses but whose mother had not been married to her father. Sayed did not care, but some would and she could be hurt deeply by the viciousness the media was capable of.

"Yes, she was and is."

"I barely know Aaliyah," Sayed claimed, though he wasn't sure he spoke the truth.

He felt like he already knew the important parts of her too well to forget easily.

"You knew Tahira your entire life."

Sayed wasn't sure what point his father was trying to make. "And I had no idea she was having an affair."

"You cannot be sure she was."

"She ran off with him."

"For love, if her note to her father is to be believed. I raised you better than to simply assume the worst on the basis of circumstantial evidence."

"Yes, you did."

"And I raised you better than to hurt someone the way you did Miss Amari arguing with your mother about spending time with her." His father frowned. "Didn't you tell me you promised to show her the country of her mother's birth?"

"It was a foolish promise to make."

"But a commitment nonetheless." The implacability of his father's tone and expression said this was not an argument Sayed had a hope of winning.

Especially when it meant fighting his own deepest desires.

As he went to leave his mother's receiving room, his father's voice stayed him at the door. "It may help to remember a salient truth, Sayed."

"Yes?"

"Both your mother and I have already committed to accepting and helping Aaliyah succeed in her role should she be pregnant."

"And if she's not."

"You know us well enough to answer that."

Sayed wasn't so sure. He'd only come to realize very recently how mistaken he'd been about himself. He'd thought he would have been content to marry Tahira and only now realized how miserable he would have been.

He thought he might even owe her a thank-you for the elopement.

Standing on the balcony overlooking the harem gardens, Liyah ignored the second knock on her door in less than hour.

Hopefully, if she didn't answer, whoever it was would take the hint and go away.

The sound of a door opening and soft footfalls across the carpet told her she had not been so lucky.

"I was an ass."

"Yes." She wasn't going to deny the obvious.

Nevertheless, Liyah did not react outwardly to Sayed's presence or his surprising admission, though her heart started beating faster.

Honestly, if she could ignore him completely right now, she'd prefer it.

But Sayed was a guy who took responsibility and apparently his mother believed he had some sort of obligation toward Liyah. Queen Durrah had apparently convinced her son of it, too.

So, here he was. To apologize? To invite Liyah on an outing?

Whatever it was, she wanted it over and him gone. Her defenses were always at her lowest around this man and she did not want him to see the tears tightening her throat.

He stepped up behind her, laying his hands on her shoulders. "I hurt you."

She shrugged, unwilling to lie and equally loath to admit to her weakness. It was too close to admitting why she was so susceptible to him.

Love hurt. There was no other name for the conflagration of emotion he sparked in her. She loved him.

She was pretty sure she always would, too. That one-true-love stuff she'd always thought a ridiculous fairy tale? She was living it. Only the happily ever after? It was still in the realm of fantasy and always would be.

"I am very sorry. It was not intentional." His right hand slipped down and around to press against her stomach, guiding her body back toward his.

"I never thought it was." She was just a one-night stand that wouldn't go away and his apology didn't change that, but she'd still liked hearing it. "Please let go of me."

She couldn't blame him for not wanting to spend time with her, but his touch brought her emotions too close to the surface. And that was something she couldn't deal with.

His lips brushed against her temple. "I want nothing more than to spend the afternoon with you."

"Right."

He gently but firmly turned her to face him. If she could believe the evidence of her eyes, his expression showed turmoil equal to Liyah's. And this time, he was doing nothing to hide it.

It shouldn't matter, but it did. Forcing her gaze straight ahead, she opened her mouth to demand again he let her go, but she could not make the words come out.

She wanted this closeness.

He sighed, his hands rubbing in circles on Liyah's back. "I have spent the past two days putting out fires Tahira's elopement sparked. We have two border countries offering a similar alliance, accepting either one of which would lead to a dangerous political imbalance and almost certain aggression on the part of the other."

Did he even realize he was still touching Liyah?

"Tahira's country should be offering reparations along with the previously agreed-upon treaty, but her uncle's current strategy is to lay blame for her defection at my door."

Liyah had stubbornly kept her gaze on his chest, but she had to see what he was feeling about that. She raised her head, their gazes clashing immediately.

A volatile mix of emotions poured through her, needing the smallest spark to send them burning sky-high.

Longing. Love. Desire. Need. Pain. And worry.

Because he had major stress lines around his beautiful brown eyes.

Of its own volition, her hand lifted to smooth away those lines. "Sounds tense."

"That's one word for it. I have others that aren't acceptable in mixed company."

"Is it going to be okay?" Was *he* going to be all right?

"Yes, because there is no other option."

"Are you going to marry someone from those other two countries?"

"No."

"What about Tahira's country. Maybe she's got a sister? A cousin?"

He shook his head. "Right now the idea of a politically motivated match is leaving a very bad taste in my mouth."

"That makes sense." Liyah did her best to ignore her heart's leap at his pronouncement.

"So, with all of this to occupy my thoughts, you'd think there was no room for anything else."

"You don't have to make excuses for not seeing me. Your mother is kind, but she's wrong. You don't owe me anything." Maybe if Liyah kept saying it, he'd realize she believed it.

No matter how much the truth hurt.

"I wasn't trying to excuse myself. I was admitting that even with everything else on my mind right now, I cannot stop thinking about you, craving you."

"You mean sex." Disappointing, but not unexpected. And it wasn't as if she'd say no. Surely he had to realize that.

"That's definitely part of it, but I *want* to take you sightseeing."

"You said—"

"A bunch of camel dung, because facing what I want doesn't mean I get to have it."

"You're kind of complicated."

"I'm an emir, complicated defines my life."

"Is there something we could do that wouldn't put us at risk for exposure?" She felt like a fugitive in witness protection asking, but as much as he was now disparaging his own arguments, he'd been right.

Having her recognized with him wouldn't do him any favors. Not because she wasn't good enough, but because—like he'd said before—she was just too different to fit in with his life.

She ignored the tiny voice that said she'd been fitting in pretty well with his family the past two days.

He smiled. "You are willing to spend time with me, even after I behaved like such an ass?"

"Yes." A smile played around her own lips. "But we have to stay in stealth mode."

If she had a chance to spend time with him before the inevitable and growing-closer expiry date of their association, she'd take it.

"We could go into the desert. Our family has been going to the same retreat since the first melech."

"Like your Camp David?"

"If Camp David stepped out of an *Arabian Nights* fantasy, yes."

"Really?" She made no effort to hide her enthusiasm.

"Absolutely. Will you come with me?"

The spark of uncertainty and steady burn of desire in his espresso gaze decided her. "Yes."

"Pack a bag. We'll spend at least one night."

"Can you afford to take this time off?"

"Taking myself out of the equation for the moment will actually make it easier for my father to effect his own form of diplomacy."

"That sounds ominous."

"Not really, but he yells a lot more than me. He can posture without me there as a witness to force the others to draw a line in the sand."

"Not a hard thing to do in the desert."

"But sandstorms have a habit of obliterating those lines."

"And Melech Falah is the sandstorm?" she asked.

"Yes."

"Then what are you?"

"The voice of rationality everyone will want to deal with after three days of my father's chest pounding."

"It's good cop/bad cop."

"On an international scale, yes." He grinned, clearly pleased with himself and his father.

She couldn't help returning the smile.

Sayed hadn't been exaggerating. The royal family's retreat *was* like a set from *Arabian Nights,* only every silk hanging and antique Turkish carpet was genuine.

They spent three days exploring the desert, Sayed showing Liyah the beauty of his country in his own unique way.

And they made love. Often and in romantic settings she would never have envisioned.

The last day, he took her to an oasis where he had a semipermanent tent set up. He said the herdsmen used it, but when he took her inside it smelled of sweet jasmine and was filled with silk blankets and pillows.

She twirled around, her silk *abayah* flowing gently around her. "This is no herdsmen's tent."

"No, today it is the tent for the emir and his lover."

She didn't deny the label like she might have three days before. Their affair might be short-lived, but she would never be the same and she didn't think he would, either.

They made love that night into the wee hours. Stars glittered in the cornflower-blue sky as they cuddled, facing the pulled-back curtains of the tent opening.

Security guards were in smaller tents around, but she'd learned to forget they were there. Strange how quickly a person could become adjusted to things like that.

She curled around his body, his arms holding her with fierce possessiveness and a sense of security no weaker for its lack of permanence.

"When is the blood test?" she asked.

"Dr. Batsmati will draw a sample tomorrow morning."

"And the blood test is one hundred percent accurate?"

"This one is, yes. It's why we had to wait a minimum of five days from making love."

"Then I guess I'll move to a hotel soon."

"You are assuming it will be negative."

"Aren't you?"

"No," he said, shocking her. "I've prepared for a positive result."

"What do you mean? What will happen if I am pregnant?" The question *was* academic as far as she was concerned.

Her body had already started responding as it usually did the week before her period.

"A royal wedding."

"What? What are you saying? We aren't getting married." Considering her feelings for him, she should have been thrilled at his words, but panic made her heart race instead.

She didn't want him trapped into marriage.

"If you are pregnant with my child, it is the only course of action open to us."

"But I took the pill. I'm not pregnant."

He shook his head. "One thing you learn in high-level politics is how real a chance even five percent, much less twenty, can be."

"But marriage? You can't be serious."

"Never more so." He looked down at her, his expression too shadowed to read in light provided by the moon and stars. "Don't you want to marry me?"

"That's not the point."

"No, it is not. The point is that you will not raise our child alone."

"Why can't we share custody? I could move to Zeena

Sahra." There was nothing to return home to. No one who would care if she made her life halfway around the world. "There are hotels there. I could continue to build my career."

"And be what to our child?"

Was that a trick question? "Her mother."

"How do you propose to do that without causing a great scandal?"

"And you don't think marrying me—a chambermaid—would do that?"

"Lead chambermaid," he said, proving he remembered their first meeting. "And something more when you weren't taking a job to provide you access to your father."

"You're still nowhere near my orbit, you said so yourself."

"There will be a media furor." He sounded way less bothered by that than he should be. "But nothing like the ongoing existence of a woman in my son's life who is not my wife."

"You can't want to marry me. I'm not princess material at all."

"I disagree. You have already proven to have more heart and honorable intent than Tahira ever did—at least where I am concerned. You are articulate and intelligent, self-controlled, as well. Once you have the proper training, the rest of the world will be able to do nothing but admire my choice in emira."

"Proper training?" she asked carefully, not liking the sound of that at all.

His thumb caressed her palm, sending shivers through her. "Consider it like going to university to get a degree in being a political figure."

"A political figure's wife, surely."

"Make no mistake, as my emira and ultimately melecha

of our country, you would have a political role, just as my mother does."

"How am I supposed to train for something like that?"

"With the teachers who served me best."

"You had tutors? I thought you went to boarding school in the States."

He smiled, the expression impacting her like it always did. "I'm referring to my parents. Both have already agreed to do their best to help you learn your new role, should it become necessary."

"I didn't think having sex with you was signing me up for a new career."

Sayed shrugged, his body shifting against hers. "Life is like that, full of curve balls, as one of my old professors was so fond of saying."

"This is crazy. You know that, don't you?"

"Difficult? Perhaps. Crazy? No."

"Stop talking about it." She wasn't pregnant and all this talk of marriage was only going to make it harder to leave him.

She couldn't afford dreams with so little substance.

"For now." Sayed turned over, pushing her onto her back and proceeded to blow her mind. Again.

If his lovemaking seemed to be tinged with desperation, she figured maybe her own feelings were simply reflecting back on her.

Sayed stormed into his father's office and threw the newspaper in his hand onto the king's desk. "Why didn't you tell me?"

"Once the story broke, there was nothing you could do." His father flicked a glance at the image of Sayed and Liyah in a passionate lip-lock—and not the first one in three days to run in their country's most widely circulated newspaper. "The only course of action left open was to wait and see how it was received."

"Pictures of Aaliyah and I kissing were on the Net hours after we arrived at the retreat."

"You did kiss her outside."

"In our private gardens!"

"Not that private." His father seemed a lot less angry than Sayed would have expected. "You know how dangerous a high-powered camera lens can be."

"How did they know we even left the palace?"

"You know we have media watching us all the time."

"Not this closely. Someone had to have leaked something."

His father shrugged. "Perhaps. Our people love the Cinderella angle. Have you noticed? Omar said it's all over the social media sites."

"And your *fixer* did nothing to kibosh it?"

"On the internet? Not going to happen."

"I doubt very sincerely the border countries looking for an alliance are nearly as caught up in the romance of it all," Sayed fairly growled.

"You would be surprised."

"What do you mean?"

"Apparently, none of them wanted us making such a firm alliance with the others. You marrying an outsider with no political agenda will actually work in our favor."

"Who said anything about marriage?"

"Do you really think anything else will suffice after that?" His father pointed to the second photo in the story.

It was of Sayed and Aaliyah leaving the oasis tent, his arm around her, their expressions and manner clearly that of a couple who had just made love.

"What if she won't agree?" Her reaction to Sayed bringing it up in response to her pregnancy had been a solid wall of negativity.

He hadn't realized how much he needed her to want it until she'd made it clear she *didn't*.

"You'll have to convince her. From the look of things, it shouldn't be that hard."

"You have no idea."

Liyah hung up with Dr. Batsmati, a tight band of disappointment squeezing her chest. They'd done a rush on the lab results.

He'd only drawn her blood a couple of hours ago. She wasn't pregnant.

Pretty soon, she'd be leaving the palace.

And she'd never see Sayed again.

Pain ripped through her as she'd only felt once before. When her mother died.

The rejection of her Amari relatives and her father hadn't been pleasant, but neither had caused this devastating depression to settle over her.

Even her mother's death hadn't made Liyah wonder if she would ever truly know joy again. Melodramatic?

Maybe, but she loved Sayed and she didn't care if it made sense. It didn't matter that she'd always thought it impossible to fall so deep so fast.

She'd done it and wasn't sure if her heart was going to survive the blow of losing Sayed.

And yet the temptation to leave without seeing him again was strong.

Only, she wasn't that person, the one who hid from the hard things in life. Hena Amari had set a better example than that.

Taking the time to change into a dark teal *dishdasha* Sayed had found particularly alluring, Liyah mentally prepared for the discussion to come.

She brushed her hair out until it shone and then draped

the hijab over it loosely, framing her face to its best advantage.

Okay, so maybe she wanted Sayed to be at least a little sorry to say goodbye to her.

Opening the door, Liyah jumped back with a surprised squeak at the sight of Sayed there already, his fist raised to knock.

"Surely the sight of me is not such a shock," he said with one of the smiles she'd started to think of as hers.

He never offered that particular expression to anyone else that she'd noticed. And Liyah had been looking.

"You know this is the harem. You aren't supposed to be here."

"I am emir."

"And you still have to maintain traditions. What, is there some kind of secret passage you use, or something?" She really didn't think Sayed walked by the door guard without a qualm.

Dark color slashed Sayed's cheeks above his closely cropped beard. "Yes, in fact, there is."

"What? Really? Where? Show me." She was perfectly willing to be sidetracked from the discussion they had to have.

He laughed and shook his head. "You are pretty irresistible when you're all enthusiastic."

"So, show me."

"After we talk."

All anticipation drained away and she turned from him. "Dr. Batsmati called you, too. I thought he would."

"Actually, I haven't spoken to the good doctor." Sayed's gaze probed hers, stripping her bare if he but knew it. "Is this rather depressed appearance because he told you there was no baby, or that you *are* pregnant?"

"I'm not depressed," she lied.

"Uh-huh."

She flopped down onto the settee, no longer concerned with presenting the best image of the "one that got away" and equally uncaring about the secrets of the palace.

Did any of it really matter? "I'm not pregnant."

"And you are unhappy about that," he said, as if feeling his way toward something.

She sighed, tempted to lie again, but the man knew her more intimately than anyone else living. He would be able to tell. "Yes."

"Because?"

"Does it really matter?"

"Oddly enough, it does. You see, we are in something of a predicament." He dropped a newspaper onto the open seat beside her. "If you are unhappy at the thought of never seeing me again, all may not be lost. If you're simply feeling baby fever, that's another thing. Although it could work to our advantage, too."

"What in the world are you talking about?"

He indicated the paper with a nod of his head. "Read that."

"More of the Cinderfella romance between Tahira and her palace aid husband?"

"Not exactly."

With a huff, Liyah started reading, hope and despair twisting together in a knot inside her with each new paragraph. Not Cinder*fella,* but a modern-day *Cinderella* fairy tale. Where Liyah played the role of servant elevated to princess by the love of her prince.

Only Sayed *didn't* love her and he had to be furious about this. "Oh, my gosh…what are we going to do? How did they learn my name? Can we get a retraction printed?"

"And what are they to retract? The picture of us in obvious afterglow, or the speculation that Tahira and my stars did not cross because we both had different destinies?"

"Um, well…how furious are your parents about this?"

"Father is surprisingly prosaic and Mother is thrilled all her plans for a royal wedding won't be wasted."

Liyah jumped up like there was a spring under her behind. "Married?" she screeched.

Sayed winced, but then he smiled. "Under that buttoned-down exterior, you're an emotional firecracker, aren't you?"

"Don't tease me. This is too serious."

An arrested expression came over his face. "Yes, you're right. It is."

"What do you mean?" Had he changed his mind already?

He pulled her to him and leaned down to kiss her softly. "Think about it, will you do that for me?"

"Marriage?" she asked, afraid to believe.

"Yes." He kissed her again, as if he couldn't help himself. "Until tonight."

"What's happening tonight?"

"We're having dinner."

"Don't we have dinner every night?" He smiled indulgently like she'd said something sweetly funny. "Tonight's dinner will be special."

"Why?"

"I'm going to ask you a question and if you give me the right answer I'll show you the secret passage and the hidden room my great-great-grandfather built for trysts with his wife."

"Don't you mean his mistress?"

"No. He was a romantic and wanted to give her a very special wedding gift."

"So, he built a hidden room."

"Yes."

"No wonder."

"What?" Sayed asked.

"You're so incredible." She smiled up at him. "It's in the genes."

"I tried to tell you."

"So, you're going to ask me a question tonight?"

"Yes."

"Even though I'm not a princess?"

"I have told you many times, I esteem *you* highly. If I mistook what was required of me and that hurt you, I am truly sorry, but I have not wanted you out of my sight since the first time my gaze fell on you."

"You don't mean that."

"I do."

Man, he really wanted her. Like, a lot.

"You promise?"

"You have my word as emir of Zeena Sahra and *your man*."

"Sayed…" She reached up and kissed him with every bit of pent-up emotion inside her.

He picked her up with an arm under her bottom and another against her back for stability, carrying her into the bedroom without breaking their locked lips.

He loomed over her on the bed. "We are not supposed to do this here."

"You're better at breaking rules than you give yourself credit for." His mother had been right. Sayed did have a wide streak of impetuousness.

He gave her that smile again. "It's you, you're very good at tempting me to break them, *habibti*."

"Well, I may have gone to a little extra trouble with my appearance today."

He laughed, the sound so free and happy it filled her own heart with joy. "No need, you are always gorgeous to me. But I do like this dress on you."

"It's a *dishdasha*," she teased.

"Oh, is it? Pardon me."

She grinned. "It might be just as pretty off."

"Doubtful. You, on the other hand, will be infinitely more accessible naked and nothing is more beautiful to me than your body."

"Don't say things like that."

"Why not?"

"I'll believe them."

He cupped her face in his big hands. "I will never lie to you, on my honor."

Too choked to speak, she nodded.

They spent the next minutes undressing between drugging kisses.

She made a sound of victory when he was down to his sexy black silk knit boxers.

He laughed, his hands already busy on her skin.

"You wear more layers than me," she told him. "I think there's something wrong with that."

"The challenge will prevent you from becoming bored."

"Right, because you aren't challenging enough."

He proved just how challenging he could be…to her self-control, drawing forth the response her body would only ever give to this man. For the first time, there was no bitter in the sweet of that knowledge, either.

He made love to her with passion that felt as driven by the sense of reprieve as her own. Could that be possible?

He certainly hadn't seemed to be upset about the idea of marriage. Though they'd barely talked about it.

Rational thought fled as he drove her arousal higher. Unwilling to be outdone, she did her best to touch him in all the ways she knew drove him crazy.

Their coupling was powerful and intensely intimate, their bodies so in tune for the moments leading up to and during her climax, she felt like they were sharing the same soul.

CHAPTER THIRTEEN

HAVING LEARNED OF Sayed's intention to take Liyah out to dinner, Queen Durrah showed up with an ornate crimson *dishdasha* for Liyah to wear.

"But this is the color of the royal family."

"Yes, my dear, it is. It is also the gown I wore for the formal announcement of my own upcoming nuptials."

Liyah put her hands up as if warding off an attack from the dress. "I can't wear it, what if I tear it or spill something on it?"

"Don't be silly, Aaliyah," the queen said with amusement. "If I had had a daughter, she would have worn this gown to her first formal function when she came of age. It pleases me for you to wear it now."

Tears burned in Liyah's eyes.

The queen tsked and patted Liyah's cheek softly. "None of that now. I'm going to be very happy to welcome you into our family, *ya 'eni*."

"Mom used to call me that," Liyah admitted emotionally.

"Then it will be an honor for you to allow me to do so now. Just as you were the precious in your mother's eyes, you will always be in mine, as well."

The endearment literally meant *my eye,* but it carried more the connotation the queen gave it. And it touched Liyah deeply.

"You should be angry at me."

"No, Aaliyah," Queen Durrah said with certainty. "I have seen more life in my son in the past week than for two decades. You are so good for him. How could I be anything but happy at the idea of you becoming my daughter?"

"He hasn't asked me yet."

"He will."

"It's really special, you know?"

"What?"

"That he insists on asking. For all intents and purposes he's been trapped into this, but he's not treating it like a business proposal."

"All of the men of this family have a romantic streak. They always have had. I should have realized there was a problem when Sayed's showed no sign of coming out with Tahira," the queen mused.

"He told me about the hidden room."

"I always loved that story. I wanted Falah to build me a room, but he told me it had already been done."

"Not so romantic, then." But then a king had to have a practical streak, just like a prince.

"Well...actually..."

"Oh, tell me."

The melecha smiled with obviously fond reminiscence. "He took me to a European castle for our honeymoon."

"You live in a palace."

"He bought me the castle and a title to go with it."

"Being queen wasn't enough?" Liyah teased.

"It was something that was just for me, not Zeena Sahra." Queen Durrah smiled softly. "That castle became our refuge after Umar's death, a place we could take Sayed and simply be a family."

"A place he could still be a boy and play freely," Liyah said softly.

The queen nodded. "And in safety."

* * *

Liyah was still thinking about her visit with Queen Durrah when Hasiba arrived to tell her the driver was waiting with the car.

"Where is Sayed?" Liyah asked Hasiba with some trepi-
dation, worried the older woman would have decided Liyah
took advantage again.

"I believe it is supposed to come as a surprise," Hasiba
said with a conspiratorial smile.

"Okay."

Hasiba reached for Liyah before she left the suite. "I am
truly sorry about before. My emir has never been so happy
as since meeting you. Even back in London, though none of
us understood his dreamy preoccupation was not with his
coming nuptials but the woman that would steal his heart."

If only that were true. "Thank you, Hasiba. Your support means so much."

The older woman pulled Liyah into a tight hug. "You
will be a wonderful emira."

Liyah would do her best.

The limo ride into the city only took about twenty minutes, but it was the longest twenty minutes of her life. It
ended when they pulled up in front of an elegant hotel.

A man dressed in a dark *kameez* rushed forward to lead
Liyah inside and to an old-fashioned cage elevator.

Sayed was waiting beside a table set on a dais in the
center of the large and very full dining room of the hotel's
rooftop restaurant.

He wore a men's *dishdasha* in the same crimson shade
as Liyah's. Though with the elaborate gold embroidery on
her chiffon outer dress, Liyah's was a lot fancier.

His black *abayah* had more moderate masculine embroidery in the same crimson shade. His *egal* was the cer-
emonial black shot with gold and his *keffiyeh* the color of
the royal house, as well.

"You look like the emir," she said in a near-whisper as she took his hand to step up on the dais.

"But you remember always the man underneath the robes," he said with pure satisfaction.

"Yes."

His smile was blinding as he helped her into her chair.

Dinner was amazing, Sayed in top form, practically oozing charm.

Though they consumed no alcohol, she felt tipsy on hope by the time dessert arrived. Several photographs had already been taken throughout the evening, everyone at the tables around them smiling and nodding as if they were as much a part of what was to come as Liyah and Sayed.

Maybe they were.

Sayed would always serve his people with his whole heart.

Sayed waited until the dessert dishes had been taken away before he rose from his chair only to drop to one knee beside hers.

Even knowing he was prompted by the need to prevent more scandal, and maybe save some face in the wake of Tahira's defection, Liyah was overwhelmed with emotion.

"Aaliyah Amari, will you do me the very great honor of agreeing to become my emira and lead the people of Zeena Sahra by my side?"

His words put the weight of reality on this fantasy moment. Sayed was putting more trust in her than she could imagine. He wasn't just asking because it was expedient.

He had to believe in Liyah as a person to trust her with the position of his emira, much less his wife.

"Liyah?" he prompted softly, typically not sounding worried, but patient.

She smiled, feeling the hot track of tears on her cheeks. She hadn't even known she was crying. "Yes, oh, yes, Sayed. I want that more than anything."

"I am so pleased." Then showing the influence of many years spent living in the States, he leaned forward and sealed the deal with a kiss.

The restaurant erupted into applause, camera flashes going from phones as well as reporters strategically waiting in the wings.

Liyah didn't care. If sharing her life with Sayed meant sharing it with the rest of the world, too, then so be it.

As he leaned back, she whispered quietly for his ears alone, "I love you. I just thought you should know."

His dark eyes heated and filled with definite pleasure. "Thank you. I will always treasure that gift."

She hadn't expected him to return the words. Liyah knew Sayed didn't love her, but his genuine appreciation of her feelings gave her hope for the future and certainty that even if he never fell in love with her, she would always have his regard and consideration.

This man would always be faithful—his "three-year drought" proved that—but just as importantly, he valued her affection. He would not take Liyah's love for granted, even if he never returned it.

Sayed waited for the video call to connect. He'd sent Yusuf to London the day before with an envelope to deliver to Gene Chatsfield.

The call connected and Gene's distinguished features filled Sayed's screen. "Sheikh Sayed, to what do I owe this pleasure?"

"Yusuf has delivered my package."

"If you mean this…" The older man lifted the heavy-duty envelope sealed with Sayed's royal family symbol set in crimson wax. "Yes."

"Inside you will find several papers."

Gene's confusion was apparent, but he seemed too preoccupied to be nervous. "Shall I open it, then?"

"Yes."

Gene's face paled as he read the documents in front of him. "You know where she is? My daughter?"

"So now you are claiming her?"

"Denial was a knee-jerk reaction caused by similar situations in the past, none of which ended up being what they claimed."

"You decided Aaliyah's was?"

"She left the locket. I'd given it to her mother. Nothing more than a trinket to me, but she kept it all those years and passed it on to her daughter." Gene swallowed, as if emotion was getting the best of him. "She'd left my picture behind hers. I looked when I remembered."

"If you need further proof, Aaliyah's DNA report is there, as well. Running your own will provide an undeniable match."

"You know I will, because in my position I cannot afford to take anything on word alone."

"Yes."

"But I'm confident of what the test will tell us."

"As am I."

"I would like to see my daughter," Gene said with hope. "Is she working for you now?"

"We are getting married next month."

"What? How is that possible? Is she pregnant?"

"No, she does not yet carry my child. As to how and why, you do not have a place in her life that affords you personal answers of that nature."

A practical man of the world, Gene didn't flinch at the reminder. "I would like to."

"You will have to apologize," Sayed warned.

"Of course."

Sayed wasn't prepared to let it go at that. "Well enough that she believes you are sincere."

"Whatever you may think of me, my children matter to me."

"You will get one opportunity to prove that."

"And if I don't to your satisfaction, I never see my daughter again?"

"You are a man of discernment."

"And you have a reputation for ruthlessness. Does Aaliyah know that, I wonder?"

"She loves me despite my flaws." The satisfaction he felt saying those words was immense.

"I'm very glad to hear that."

"Really?"

"I would not like to think my daughter was marrying for anything but honest emotion and hope for a future."

"Come to Zeena Sahra and tell her that."

"When?"

"Yusuf is waiting to take you to our jet."

"You expect me to drop everything and come now?" Gene asked, showing dismay for the first time.

"Yes. You may bring your fiancé."

The older man waved that off. "She is busy with wedding preparations."

"Then it is the ideal time for you to make this trip."

"You don't lack arrogance, do you?"

"Aaliyah will tell you I do not."

Gene smiled. "Give me a couple of days and I will fly out commercial."

"No. Your visit must be kept under wraps. Your place in Aaliyah's life will not be announced until if and when she is prepared to recognize you as her father."

"I cannot come on a moment's notice."

"With Giatrakos at the helm? I think you can."

Gene frowned. "Fine. She deserves a little sacrifice on my part."

"More than a little, I think, but luckily for you she has me now and no *major* sacrifices on your part will be necessary."

"You called my father?" Aaliyah jumped up and paced across his mother's receiving room. "And he's going to be here within the hour?"

"Give or take, yes."

"But why?"

"Because you deserve an apology for his idiocy."

"What did you threaten him with to force the apology?" she asked suspiciously.

"No threats were required. He was already trying to find you."

"Is that what he told you?"

"Yes."

"I doubt it."

"I'd already hired a private detective and have the retainer receipt and first reports to prove it," Gene Chatsfield said, having entered the room with Yusuf through the side entrance, indicating the bodyguard had brought him into the palace discreetly. "How he missed your location when your engagement is all over the media, I don't know."

Aaliyah spun around to face her father, her face blanching before her expression turned wooden.

Sayed crossed the room and put his arm around her waist. "All will be well. You are not alone."

Gene smiled at them. "You look very good together."

"Why are you here?" Aaliyah asked baldly.

"I owe you an apology. I should have heard you out to begin with, but I'm a suspicious man. I made mistakes in the past and they made me vulnerable to a certain type of people. You were not like them, but I was blinded to that at first."

Sayed was impressed with the older man's openness and sincerity.

Aaliyah didn't look quite as taken with her father's words. "So, you acknowledge I'm your daughter now?" she asked suspiciously.

"Oh, yes."

"Don't you want a DNA test, or something?"

Gene glanced at Sayed and then back to Aaliyah. "Already done. Your fiancé provided your results."

"From the blood test?" Aaliyah asked quietly.

"Yes."

She scanned his face, as if looking for something. "You planned this."

"I did."

"What if he'd kept acting like a bastard about it?" she asked, her vulnerability to that eventuality in her tone.

Though Sayed doubted anyone else would have heard it.

He let her see how serious he was before he promised, "I would have ruined him and destroyed the Chatsfield from London to Sydney."

"Wow."

Sayed guided her to a seat on one of the small sofas and indicated a chair for her father to take.

Once they were all seated, Gene said, "I realize I have a lot of making up to do to build a relationship, but I want to try."

Aaliyah looked up at Sayed. "Is he sincere or is this because I'm going to marry a prince, a pretty ruthless one at that?"

"He is sincere. Believe it."

She nodded. "Okay." Then turned her head to face Gene. "We can work on it."

"You are very forgiving. I am not sure I deserve it."

"I'm pretty sure you don't," Aaliyah said with her usual honesty.

Gene winced. "Touché."

"But Mom wanted me to try, and if you're willing, I am, too. For her sake."

"Thank you."

"I'm not calling you Dad, though."

"No, I imagine we will suffice with Gene and Aaliyah."

"Liyah. My friends call me Liyah."

"I thought Sheikh Sayed called you Aaliyah."

"Only my family calls me that."

Like his parents and him. Sayed smiled.

"And I'm not that." Gene sounded sad.

"Not yet."

"It is something you will work on," Sayed added.

The older man nodded. "Yes, I will. Liyah, I appreciate your willingness to try to forgive me—however, this news will come as a great shock to the children. I want to introduce you to them with the respect you deserve. But at the moment they are scattered throughout the world. They have lessons to learn," he said ruefully, "hard lessons to learn before I would like you to meet them. Myself and Giatrakos are working on it, and they'll all be back together soon. But for now, I would hope that you understand my request to wait."

He was only able to stay one night, but in the time he was at the palace, Gene Chatsfield had shown nothing but genuine desire to build a relationship with the daughter he hadn't known about.

Sayed was glad when both his parents confirmed his instincts that said bringing Gene Chatsfield into Aaliyah's life was the right thing to do.

He returned Aaliyah's locket to her before he left for the airport.

"That was kind of incredible," she said after waving her father off.

"I am glad you enjoyed your time with him."

"He's not nearly the jerk I thought he was."

Sayed agreed. "Just a man with fears and worries like anyone else."

"You know he offered me an equal trust fund to what my half siblings have been given," Aaliyah informed him.

Sayed had expected something like that and would have been disappointed if Gene had not done so. "What did you say?"

"No."

"Good." He'd expected that, as well.

Aaliyah smiled. "I don't need his money. I never did."

"You just wanted family and now you have mine."

"It's a pretty wonderful family."

"My mother and father will be pleased to hear you say so."

She frowned up at him as they walked back into the palace. "You're not going to try some kind of intervention with the Amaris, are you?"

Sayed shook his head. "Absolutely not. If you were not good enough to recognize before becoming emira, they will not be allowed to claim you now."

She nodded decisively. "Good."

"Besides, if we had any of the Amaris in hitting distance, I'm not sure my mother could control herself."

Aaliyah laughed. "Now, that would make an interesting picture for the front page."

"No doubt. Let's avoid it, shall we?"

"Your mom calls me her daughter. I like it."

"So does she."

His father was extremely fond of Aaliyah, as well, but then so was Sayed. More than he'd ever thought he could feel for someone not born into his family.

He wasn't sure he was in love with her, though he thought he might be. Until he knew for certain, he wasn't saying anything. She deserved truth, not confusion.

* * *

Aaliyah's wedding was a royal *event,* attended by dignitaries, heads of state, sheikhs, other royals and European nobility.

But she was most pleased by her father and his fiancée's presence. Aaliyah's only other personal guest was Stephanie Carter, the head housekeeper from the Chatsfield San Francisco, a woman Hena Amari had called friend.

Aaliyah wore white, her dress a traditional Middle Eastern ensemble designed by a prominent Italian designer who had designed several gowns for Queen Durrah. Sayed wore a more ornate version of the outfit he'd proposed to her in.

His coronation took place directly after their wedding, though it wasn't the one everyone had been expecting. Sayed was given the distinction of crown prince, but his father had decided he wasn't ready to retire.

In fact, Sayed had shared with Liyah that King Falah had liked the idea of training his nephew to take Sayed's place as emir before he was crowned melech. She hadn't been surprised, though she didn't tell Sayed so.

She'd had her own little talk with her soon-to-be father-in-law about the timetable for Liyah becoming melecha. She'd let him know in no uncertain terms she wasn't ready yet.

He'd taken it in good humor, and though he'd blustered a bit, he'd given in pretty easily with her idea of training Bilal to follow in Sayed's place.

The entire country celebrated the wedding and crown prince coronation into the early hours of the morning.

Following the pattern he'd established with her, Sayed lifted Liyah into his arms at the reception in the main ballroom and proceeded to carry her up the stairs and down unfamiliar corridors, ending up in his room.

"Our room now," he said as he lowered her to stand beside the bed.

"Yes, our room."

"Tonight, I make love to my emira." The expression in his dark eyes took her breath away.

She reached up and touched his face, loving the fact she was the only woman besides his mother in the entire country allowed such familiarity. "Whatever we are outside that door, when we are together intimately, you are always my *man, ya habibi,* and I will always be first and foremost your woman."

His expression turned nearly beatific. "Yes. I do. I am certain of it."

"What?" she asked, feeling like she'd missed something.

"I love you, *habibti.* I was not certain because I've never experienced anything like what you make me feel, but my heart is yours, from the moment our eyes met unto eternity."

She stopped, her heart going so fast she heard the rush in her ears. "You love me?"

"Yes. It happened so quickly, but you are perfect for me. Everything about you matches something in me."

"I'll never have a pedigree."

"And I thank God for it. You help me to see with my heart, not my position."

"I wasn't born to be a princess."

"But you were, born to be *my* emira."

She was out of arguments. "I love you, too, Sayed, so much."

"One day, you *will* carry my child."

"Yes. You'll be such a wonderful father."

"I had a very good example, just as you did for being mother to our children."

"We went from single to plural pretty fast."

"I've got a dream."

"Of lots of babies?" she asked a little worried.

"Not lots, just maybe four?"

"Four? Wow, you do realize I was an only child, right?"

"But you have so much love to give."

That was one truth she could no longer deny. Gone were the days when Liyah denied her emotions. "You're being persuasive again."

He turned and grabbed something off the bed and handed it to her. "Thank you for marrying me."

She smiled and stepped back from the box. "Just a second."

She'd asked Hasiba to make sure Liyah's gift for Sayed had been dropped off in the suite. She found it on the desk, wrapped in burgundy paper, the royal crest holding the gold ribbon together instead of a bow.

She rushed back into the room and offered it to him. "Thank *you* for marrying me."

"Your love is all the gift I need," he said fervently.

"Ditto."

He smiled and opened the gift, his expression going very solemn as he opened the jeweler's box. It was a traditional wedding bracelet, of the type brides gave their husband in Zeena Sahra. Though it was not leather, or hand woven from her hair.

It had something to do with their Bedouin roots, but all Liyah knew was that she approved the symbolism of it.

"The eternal circle of love and commitment," Sayed said with satisfaction.

"Yes, because I will always love you and am in this thing for life."

"As am I." He slipped the heavy platinum masculine bracelet on, a single ruby for his royal house offset left of center on the top.

She'd used the last of her savings to buy it and couldn't think of a better use of her mother's final gift to Liyah.

"Now it is your turn."

"Is it?" she asked, so full of love and happiness she didn't think any gift could add to it.

"Yes. I remember you once told me, we are supposed to keep things even."

She laughed, remembering. "That was about getting naked."

"We will get to that."

"Promise?" she teased.

"Oh, yes. Now, open your gift."

Liyah tore the paper off the flat box and pulled off its lid, but was a little confused when she saw it was filled with legal documents. "What are these?"

"You know the hotel where I proposed?"

"Yes." She'd loved the rooftop restaurant.

"I bought it for you."

"You bought me a hotel?"

"It's in your blood, but you'll have to keep a general manager as your duties as emira will not allow for a full-time occupation outside of the palace."

"Your mother explained." Queen Durrah had been giving Liyah "princess lessons" daily since she agreed to marry Sayed.

"And you do not mind?"

"No, Sayed. When I say I love you, I mean the you that is emir, too."

"You are amazing, *habibti. Intee albi.*"

"And you are my heart. We'll beat for each other. I love you so much, Sayed."

"As I love you. With everything that I am or ever will be."

"I know it."

"You do?"

"The proof is in the pudding, as they say." Her heart was so full it was hard to get the words out, but she did. "First you gave me the gift of family, both my father and your own parents, cousins and aunt. Then there's the hotel—the grand romantic gesture the men in your family are known for."

"I should have realized I loved you when I started negotiations for the hotel."

"Maybe."

"Perhaps you need a little more proof." Sayed's meaning was clear in the hunger glowing in his espresso eyes.

"I'll never say no to that type of proof."

Nor would she ever balk at giving it. Love had turned her from repressed into passionately expressive.

And Sayed adored her that way. He said so.

They made love throughout the night, taking turns expressing their spiritual affection in carnal ways no less beautiful than the emotion that flowed between them.

Ultimately, Hena Amari had gifted Liyah with Sayed, her final request leading her daughter to London where fate ordained she connect with the other half of her soul.

Liyah whispered a prayer of gratitude as she slipped into sleep, wrapped in the arms of her one true love, and hoped her mother could hear it, as well.

* * * * *

*If you enjoyed this book, look out for
the next instalment of* THE CHATSFIELD:
*PLAYBOY'S LESSON by Melanie Milburne,
coming next month.*

Available May 20, 2014

#3241 PLAYBOY'S LESSON
The Chatsfield
by Melanie Milburne

Lucca Chatsfield lives life by one simple motto: no rings, no strings. Adored everywhere, he's yet to meet a woman who can resist his charm. Until he's sent to the principality of Preitalle and finds his greatest challenge ever...Princess Charlotte.

#3242 RAVELLI'S DEFIANT BRIDE
The Legacies of Powerful Men
by Lynne Graham

Belle will do anything to give her siblings the security she never had. So when gorgeous Cristo Ravelli offers marriage, she won't say no. But with the ring on her finger Belle quickly discovers there's more to a marriage than saying "I do"!

#3243 WHEN DA SILVA BREAKS THE RULES
Blood Brothers
by Abby Green

Not only are Cesar Da Silva's family secrets about to be exposed... he's been caught kissing Lexie Anderson! The reclusive billionaire has smashed his own rules by romancing the high-profile actress. And judging by their chemistry this match is bound to be explosive!

#3244 THE MAN SHE CAN'T FORGET
by Maggie Cox

Gabriel knows he should walk away from Lara Bradley, and *must* show her that a happy-ever-after with him is futile. But proving just how wrong he is for her only makes him realize how just *right* she makes him feel....

HPCNM0514RA

#3245 THE HEARTBREAKER PRINCE
Royal & Ruthless
by Kim Lawrence
Forced to take a bride to avoid war with a neighboring kingdom, Prince Kamel has little patience with pampered princess Hannah, but it's his duty, and it can't be ignored. There's no love between them, but there must be heirs. And there *will* be passion....

#3246 WHAT THE GREEK CAN'T RESIST
The Untamable Greeks
by Maya Blake
CEO Arion Pantelides is always in control—but gives in to oblivion for one night with a stunning stranger...only to discover her shocking secret. Perla Lowell will show Arion she has *nothing* to hide. Until she discovers she's pregnant with his child!

#3247 A QUESTION OF HONOR
by Kate Walker
Crown prince Karim had one task: retrieve rebellious princess Clementina and return her home—pure and untouched—to her unwanted bridegroom. His honor requires him to fulfill his role, but can he resist all temptation to keep her for himself?

#3248 AN HEIR TO BIND THEM
by Dani Collins
Jaya Powers couldn't refuse gorgeous millionaire Theo Makricosta when she worked for him, and she can't refuse him now! Only this time she has a secret. Their night together had consequences that will change Theo's perfectly ordered existence forever....

REQUEST YOUR
FREE BOOKS!

HARLEQUIN *Presents*

PASSION GUARANTEED SEDUCTION

2 FREE NOVELS PLUS
2 FREE GIFTS!

YES! Please send me 2 FREE Harlequin Presents® novels and my 2 FREE gifts (gifts are worth about $10). After receiving them, if I don't wish to receive any more books, I can return the shipping statement marked "cancel." If I don't cancel, I will receive 6 brand-new novels every month and be billed just $4.30 per book in the U.S. or $4.99 per book in Canada. That's a saving of at least 14% off the cover price! It's quite a bargain! Shipping and handling is just 50¢ per book in the U.S. and 75¢ per book in Canada.* I understand that accepting the 2 free books and gifts places me under no obligation to buy anything. I can always return a shipment and cancel at any time. Even if I never buy another book, the two free books and gifts are mine to keep forever.

106/306 HDN FVRK

Name _____ (PLEASE PRINT) _____

Address _____ Apt. # _____

City _____ State/Prov. _____ Zip/Postal Code _____

Signature (if under 18, a parent or guardian must sign)

Mail to the **Harlequin® Reader Service:**
IN U.S.A.: P.O. Box 1867, Buffalo, NY 14240-1867
IN CANADA: P.O. Box 609, Fort Erie, Ontario L2A 5X3

**Are you a current subscriber to Harlequin Presents books
and want to receive the larger-print edition?
Call 1-800-873-8635 or visit www.ReaderService.com.**

* Terms and prices subject to change without notice. Prices do not include applicable taxes. Sales tax applicable in N.Y. Canadian residents will be charged applicable taxes. Offer not valid in Quebec. This offer is limited to one order per household. Not valid for current subscribers to Harlequin Presents books. All orders subject to credit approval. Credit or debit balances in a customer's account(s) may be offset by any other outstanding balance owed by or to the customer. Please allow 4 to 6 weeks for delivery. Offer available while quantities last.

Your Privacy—The Harlequin® Reader Service is committed to protecting your privacy. Our Privacy Policy is available online at www.ReaderService.com or upon request from the Harlequin Reader Service.

We make a portion of our mailing list available to reputable third parties that offer products we believe may interest you. If you prefer that we not exchange your name with third parties, or if you wish to clarify or modify your communication preferences, please visit us at www.ReaderService.com/consumerschoice or write to us at Harlequin Reader Service Preference Service, P.O. Box 9062, Buffalo, NY 14269. Include your complete name and address.

CHARLOTTE'S hand fluttered like a little bird inside the cage
of his, sending a shock wave of heat through his pelvis like
the back draft of a fire. Lucca released her hand and had
to physically stop himself from wriggling his fingers to rid
himself of the electric tingling her touch had evoked.

"Thank you, Your Royal Highness," he said with
exaggerated politeness. He might be an irascible rake, but he
knew how to behave when the occasion called for it, even if
he privately thought it was all complete and utter nonsense.
In his opinion people were people. Rich or poor. Royal or
common.

She pressed her lips together so tightly as if she were
trying to hold an invisible piece of paper between them
steady. He wasn't sure if it was out of annoyance or a gesture
of nervousness or shyness, but it drew his gaze like starving
eyes to a feast. She had a bee-stung mouth, full lipped and
rosy-pink without the adornment of lipstick or even a layer of

clear lip gloss. It was a mouth that looked capable of intense passion, but it seemed somewhat at odds with the rest of her downplayed and rather starchily set features.

A feather of intrigue tickled Lucca's interest. Did she have a wild side behind those frumpy clothes and that frosty facade?

Maybe his exile here wouldn't be a complete waste of time after all....

* * *

Step into the gilded world of **THE CHATSFIELD!**
Where secrets and scandal lurk behind every door...

Reserve your room!

June 2014

HPEXP0514-1

Revenge and seduction intertwine...

Harlequin Presents welcomes you to the
world of The Chatsfield:
Synonymous with style, spectacle...and scandal!

SHEIKH'S SCANDAL by *Lucy Monroe* May 2014

PLAYBOY'S LESSON by *Melanie Milburne* June 2014

SOCIALITE'S GAMBLE by *Michelle Conder* July 2014

BILLIONAIRE'S SECRET by *Chantelle Shaw* August 2014

TYCOON'S TEMPTATION by *Trish Morey* September 2014

RIVAL'S CHALLENGE by *Abby Green* October 2014

REBEL'S BARGAIN by *Annie West* November 2014

HEIRESS'S DEFIANCE by *Lynn Raye Harris* December 2014

Step into the gilded world of The Chatsfield!
Where secrets and scandal lurk behind
every door...

Reserve your room!

HARLEQUIN®
Presents®

Revenge and seduction intertwine...

Is gorgeous billionaire Cesar Da Silva finally off the market? Read the final book in Abby Green's gripping Blood Brothers trilogy!

Cesar Da Silva hits the headlines!

Not only are his family secrets about to be exposed, but he's been caught kissing Lexie Anderson!

The reclusive billionaire has certainly smashed his own rules by romancing the high-profile actress, and if their chemistry is anything to go by, this is one match that's bound to be explosive....

WHEN DA SILVA BREAKS THE RULES

by

Abby Green

Available June 2014,
wherever books and ebooks are sold!